EX LIBRIS
VINTAGE CLASSICS

THE COMPLETE NOVELS

Franz Kafka was born in Prague in 1883, the son of a rich Jewish Czech merchant. After studying law he worked for a Prague insurance company. In later years he settled down in a Berlin suburb to concentrate on writing. In 1912 he met a young woman from Berlin, Felicie (Felice) Bauer, and was twice briefly engaged to her. His unhappy love affairs, his difficult relationship with his father, and his own inflexible intellectual honesty and intense sensitivity combined to weaken his health and in 1917 he discovered he was suffering from tuberculosis. In 1920 he met Milena Jesenska-Pollak, with whom he later corresponded. In 1923 he met Dora Dymant and lived with her for a time in Prague before he entered a sanitorium near Vienna. He died in 1924. Kafka published only seven works in his lifetime and left directions that his unpublished writings should be destroyed. These instructions were disregarded by his friend and executor Max Brod. *The Trial* appeared in 1925, followed by *The Castle* in 1926, *America* in 1927 and *The Great Wall of China*, a selection of his shorter fiction, in 1931.

ALSO BY FRANZ KAFKA

Fiction

Metamorphosis and Other Stories
Complete Short Stories
America
The Trial
The Castle

Non-fiction

The Diaries of Franz Kafka
Letters to Felice
Letters to Milena

FRANZ KAFKA

The Complete Novels

The Trial
America
The Castle

TRANSLATED FROM THE GERMAN BY
Willa and Edwin Muir

VINTAGE BOOKS
London

Published by Vintage 2008

8 10 9

The Trial first published in Great Britain by
Victor Gollancz in 1935
Translated from the German *(Der Prozess)* by
Willa and Edwin Muir

America first published in Great Britain by
George Routledge in 1938
Definitive edition published by
Martin Secker & Warburg Ltd in 1949
Translated from the German (*Amerika*)
by Willa and Edwin Muir

The Castle first published in Great Britain by
Martin Secker & Warburg Ltd in 1930
Translated from the German *(Das Schloss)* by
Willa and Edwin Muir

First published together as
The Penguin Complete Novels of Franz Kafka
by Penguin Books Ltd in 1983

Vintage
Random House, 20 Vauxhall Bridge Road, London SW1V 2SA

www.vintage-classics.info

Addresses for companies within The Random House Group Limited
can be found at: www.randomhouse.co.uk
The Random House Group Limited Reg. No. 954009

A CIP catalogue record for this book is available from British Library

ISBN 9780099518440

The Random House Group Limited supports The Forest Stewardship Council (FSC®), the leading international forest certification organisation. Our books carrying the FSC label are printed on FSC® certified paper. FSC is the only forest certification scheme endorsed by the leading environmental organisations, including Greenpeace. Our paper procurement policy can be found at
www.randomhouse.co.uk/environment

Printed and bound in Great Britain by Clays Ltd, St Ives PLC

CONTENTS

The Trial

Translated from the German
by Willa and Edwin Muir

1

THE ARREST – CONVERSATION WITH FRAU GRUBACH THEN FRÄULEIN BÜRSTNER

Someone must have been telling lies about Joseph K., for without having done anything wrong he was arrested one fine morning. His landlady's cook, who always brought him breakfast at eight o'clock, failed to appear on this occasion. That had never happened before. K. waited for a little while longer, watching from his pillow the old lady opposite, who seemed to be peering at him with a curiosity unusual even for her, but then, feeling both put out and hungry, he rang the bell. At once there was a knock at the door and a man entered whom he had never seen before in the house. He was slim and yet well knit, he wore a closely fitting black suit, which was furnished with all sorts of pleats, pockets, buckles, and buttons, as well as a belt, like a tourist's outfit, and in consequence looked eminently practical, though one could not quite tell what actual purpose it served. 'Who are you?' asked K., half raising himself in bed. But the man ignored the question, as though his appearance needed no explanation, and merely said: 'Did you ring?' 'Anna is to bring me my breakfast,' said K., and then with silent intensity studied the fellow, trying to make out who he could be. The man did not submit to this scrutiny for very long, but turned to the door and opened it slightly so as to report to someone who was evidently standing just behind it: 'He says Anna is to bring him his breakfast.' A short guffaw from the next room came in answer; one could not tell from the sound whether it was produced by several individuals or merely by one. Although the strange man could not have learned anything from it that he did not know already, he now said to K., as if passing on a statement: 'It can't be done.' 'This is news indeed,' cried K., springing out of bed and quickly pulling on his trousers. 'I must see what people these are next door, and how Frau Grubach can account to me for such behaviour.' Yet it occurred to him at once that he should not have said this aloud and that by doing so he had in a way admitted the stranger's right to an interest in his actions; still, that did not seem important to him at the moment. The stranger, however, took his words in some such sense, for he asked: 'Hadn't you better stay here?' 'I shall neither stay here nor let you address me until you have introduced yourself.' 'I meant well enough,' said the stranger, and then of his own accord threw the door open. In the next room, which K. entered more slowly than he had intended, everything looked at first glance almost as it had done the evening before. It was Frau Grubach's living-room; perhaps among all the furniture, rugs, china, and photographs with which it was crammed there was a little more free space than usual, yet one did not perceive that at first, especially as the main change consisted in the presence of a man who was sitting at the open window reading a book, from which he now glanced up. 'You should have stayed in your room! Didn't Franz tell you that?' 'Yes, yes, but what are you doing here?' asked K., looking from his new acquaintance to the man called Franz, who was still standing by the door, and then back again. Through the open window he had another glimpse of the old woman, who with truly senile inquisitiveness had moved along to the window exactly opposite, in order to see all that could be seen. 'I'd better get Frau Grubach –' said K., as if wrenching himself away from the two men (though they were standing at quite a distance from him) and making as if to go out. 'No,' said the man at the window, flinging the book down on the table and getting up. 'You can't go out, you are arrested.' 'So it seems,' said K. 'But what for?' he added. 'We are not authorized to tell you that. Go to your room and wait there. Proceedings have been instituted against you, and you will be informed of everything in due course. I am exceeding my instructions in speaking freely to you like this. But I hope nobody hears me except Franz, and he himself has been too free with you, against his express instructions. If you continue to have as good luck as you have had in the choice of your warders, then you can be confident of the final result.' K. felt he must sit down, but now he saw that there was no seat in the whole room except the chair beside the window. 'You'll soon discover that we're telling you the truth,' said Franz, advancing towards him simultaneously with the other man. The latter overtopped K. enormously and kept clapping him on the shoulder. They both examined his nightshirt and said that he would have to wear a less fancy shirt now, but that they would take charge of this one and the rest of his underwear and, if his case turned out well, restore them to him later. 'Much better give these things to us than hand them over to the depot,' they said, 'for in the depot there's lots of thieving, and besides they sell everything there after a certain length of time, no matter whether your case is settled or not. And you never know how long these cases will last, especially these days. Of course you would get the money out of the depot in the long run, but in the first place the prices they pay you are always wretched, for they sell your things to the best briber, not the best bidder, and anyhow it's well known that money dwindles a lot if it passes from hand to hand from one year to another.' K. paid hardly any attention to this advice, any right to dispose of his own things which he might possess he did not prize very highly; far more important to him was the necessity to understand his situation clearly; but with these people beside him he could not even think, the belly of the second warder – for they could only be warders – kept butting against him in an almost friendly way, yet if he looked up he caught sight of a face which did not in the least suit that fat body, a dry, bony face with a great nose, twisted to one side, which seemed to be consulting over his head with the other warder. Who could these men be? What were they talking about? What authority could they represent? K. lived in a country with a legal constitution, there was universal peace, all the laws were in force; who dared seize him in his own dwelling? He had always been inclined to take things easily, to believe in the worst only when the worst happened, to take no care for the morrow even when the outlook was threatening. But that struck him as not being the right policy here, one could certainly regard the whole thing as a joke, a rude joke which his colleagues in the Bank had concocted for some unknown reason, perhaps because this was his thirtieth birthday, that was of course possible, perhaps he had only to laugh knowingly in these men's faces and they would laugh with him, perhaps they were merely porters from the street corner – they looked very like it – nevertheless his very first glance at the man Franz had decided him for the time being not to give away any advantage that he might possess over these people. There was a slight risk that later on his friends might possibly say he could not take a joke, but he had in mind – though it was not usual with him to learn from experience – several occasions, of no importance in themselves, when against all his friends' advice he had behaved with deliberate recklessness and without the slightest regard for possible consequences, and had had in the end to pay dearly for it. That must not happen again, at least not this time; if this was a comedy he would insist on playing it to the end.

But he was still free. 'Allow me,' he said, passing quickly between the warders to his room. 'He seems to have some sense,' he heard one of them saying behind him. When he reached his room he at once pulled out the drawer of his desk, everything lay there in perfect order, but in his agitation he could not find at first the identification papers for which he was looking. At last he found his bicycle licence and was about to start off with it to the warders, but then it seemed too trivial a thing, and he searched again until he found his birth certificate. As he was re-entering the next room the opposite door opened and Frau Grubach showed herself. He saw her only for an instant, for no sooner did she recognize him than she was obviously overcome by embarrassment, apologized for intruding, vanished, and shut the door again with the utmost care. 'Come in, do,' he would just have had time to say. But he merely stood holding his papers in the middle of the room, looking at the door, which did not open again, and was only recalled to attention by a shout from the warders, who were sitting at a table by the open window and, as he now saw, devouring his breakfast. 'Why didn't she come in?' he asked. 'She isn't allowed to,' said the tall warder, 'since you're under arrest.' 'But how can I be under arrest? And particularly in such a ridiculous fashion?' 'So now you're beginning it all over again?' said the warder, dipping a slice of bread and butter into the honey-pot. 'We don't answer such questions.' 'You'll have to answer them,' said K. 'Here are my papers, now show me yours, and first of all your warrant for arresting me.' 'Oh, good Lord,' said the warder. 'If you would only realize your position, and if you wouldn't insist on uselessly annoying us two, who probably mean better by you and stand closer to you than any other people in the world.' 'That's so, you can believe that,' said Franz, not raising to his lips the coffee-cup he held in his hand, but instead giving K. a long, apparently significant, yet incomprehensible look. Without wishing it K. found himself decoyed into an exchange of speaking looks with Franz, none the less he tapped his papers and repeated: 'Here are my identification papers.' 'What are your papers to us?' cried the tall warder. 'You're behaving worse than a child. What are you after? Do you think you'll bring this fine case of yours to a speedier end by wrangling with us, your warders, over papers and warrants? We are humble subordinates who can scarcely find our way through a legal document and have nothing to do with your case except to stand guard over you for ten hours a day and draw our pay for it. That's all we are, but we're quite capable of grasping the fact that the high authorities we serve, before they would order such an arrest as this must be quite well informed about the reasons for the arrest and the person of the prisoner. There can be no mistake about that. Our officials, so far as I know them, and I know only the lowest grades among them, never go hunting for crime in the populace, but, as the Law decrees, are drawn towards the guilty and must then send out us warders. That is the Law. How could there be a mistake in that?' 'I don't know this Law,' said K. 'All the worse for you,' replied the warder. 'And it probably exists nowhere but in your own head,' said K.; he wanted in some way to enter into the thoughts of the warders and twist them to his own advantage or else try to acclimatize himself to them. But the warder merely said in a discouraging voice: 'You'll come up against it yet.' Franz interrupted: 'See, Willem, he admits that he doesn't know the Law and yet he claims he's innocent.' 'You're quite right, but you'll never make a man like that see reason,' replied the other. K. gave no further answer; 'Must I,' he thought, 'let myself be confused still worse by the gabble of those wretched hirelings? – they admit themselves that's all they are. They're talking of things, in any case, which they don't understand. Plain stupidity is the only thing that can give them such assurance. A few words with a man on my own level of intelligence would make everything far clearer than hours of talk with these two.' He walked up and down a few times in the free part of the room; at the other side of the street he could still see the old woman, who had now dragged to the window an even older man, whom she was holding round the waist. K. felt he must put an end to this farce. 'Take me to your superior officer,' he said. 'When he orders me, not before,' retorted the warder called Willem. 'And now I advise you,' he went on, 'to go to your room, stay quietly there, and wait for what may be decided about you. Our advice to you is not to let yourself be distracted by vain thoughts, but to collect yourself, for great demands will be made upon you. You haven't treated us as our kind advances to you deserved, you have forgotten that we, no matter who we may be, are at least free men compared to you; that is no small advantage. All the same, we are prepared, if you have any money, to bring you a little breakfast from the coffeehouse across the street.'

Without replying to this offer K. remained standing where he was for a moment. If he were to open the door of the next room or even the door leading to the hall, perhaps the two of them would not dare to hinder him, perhaps that would be the simplest solution of the whole business, to bring it to a head. But perhaps they might seize him after all, and if he were once down, all the superiority would be lost which in a certain sense he still retained. Accordingly, instead of a quick solution he chose that certainty which the natural course of things would be bound to bring, and went back to his room without another word having been said by him or by the warders.

He flung himself on his bed and took from the washstand a fine apple which he had laid out the night before for his breakfast. Now it was all the breakfast he would have, but in any case, as the first few bites assured him, much better than the breakfast from the filthy night café would have been, which the grace of his warders might have secured him. He felt fit and confident, he would miss his work in the Bank that morning, it was true, but that would be easily overlooked, considering the comparatively high post he held there. Should he give the real reason for his absence? He considered doing so. If they did not believe him, which in the circumstances would be understandable, he could produce Frau Grubach as a witness, or even the two odd creatures over the way, who were now probably meandering back again to the window opposite his room. K. was surprised, at least he was surprised considering the warders' point of view, that they had sent him to his room and left him alone there, where he had abundant opportunities to take his life. Though at the same time he also asked himself, looking at it from his own point of view, what possible ground he could have to do so. Because two warders were sitting next door and had intercepted his breakfast? To take his life would be such a senseless act that, even if he wished, he could not bring himself to do it because of its very senselessness. If the intellectual poverty of the warders were not so manifest, he might almost assume that they too saw no danger in leaving him alone, for the very same reason. They were quite at liberty to watch him now while he went to a wall-cupboard where he kept a bottle of good brandy, while he filled a glass and drank it down to make up for his breakfast, and then drank a second to give him courage, the last one only as a precaution, for the improbable contingency that it might be needed.

Then a shout came from the next room which made him start so violently that his teeth rattled against the glass. 'The Inspector wants you,' was its tenor. It was merely the tone of it that startled him, a curt, military bark with which he would never have credited the warder Franz. The command itself was actually welcome to him. 'At last,' he shouted back, closing the cupboard and hurrying at once into the next room. There the two warders were standing, and, as if that were a matter of course, immediately drove him back into his room again. 'What are you thinking of?' they cried. 'Do you imagine you can appear before the Inspector in your shirt? He'll have you well thrashed, and us too.' 'Let me alone, damn you,' cried K., who by now had been forced back to his wardrobe. 'If you grab me out of bed, you can't expect to find me all dressed up in my best suit.' 'This doesn't help you any,' said the warders, who as soon as K. raised his voice always grew quite calm, indeed almost rueful, and thus contrive either to confuse him or to some extent bring him to his senses. 'Silly formalities!' he growled, but immediately lifted a coat from a chair and held it up for a little while in both hands, as if displaying it to the warders for their approval. They shook their heads. 'It must be a black coat,' they said. Thereupon K. flung the coat on the floor and said – he did not himself know in what sense he meant the words – 'But this isn't the capital charge yet.' The warders smiled, but stuck to their: 'It must be a black coat.' 'If it's to dispatch my case any quicker, I don't mind,' replied K., opening the wardrobe where he searched for a long time among his many suits, chose his best black one, a lounge suit which had caused almost a sensation among his acquaintances because of its elegance, then selected another shirt and began to dress with great care. In his secret heart he thought he had managed after all to speed up the proceedings, for the warders had forgotten to make him take a bath. He kept an eye on them to see if they would remember the ducking, but of course it never occurred to them, yet on the other hand Willem did not forget to send Franz to the Inspector with the information that K. was dressing.

When he was fully dressed he had to walk, with Willem treading on his heels, through the next room, which was now empty, into the adjoining one, whose double doors were flung open. This room, as K. knew quite well, had recently been taken by a Fräulein Bürstner, a typist, who went very early to work, came home late, and with whom he had exchanged little more than a few words in passing. Now the night-table beside her bed had been pushed into the middle of the floor to serve as a desk, and the Inspector was sitting behind it. He had crossed his legs, and one arm was resting on the back of the chair.

In a corner of the room three young men were standing looking at Fräulein Bürstner's photographs, which were stuck into a mat hanging on the wall. A white blouse dangled from the latch of the open window. In the window over the way the two old creatures were again stationed, but they had enlarged their party, for behind them, towering head and shoulders above them, stood a man with a shirt open at the neck and a reddish, pointed beard, which he kept pinching and twisting with his fingers. 'Joseph K.?' asked the Inspector, perhaps merely to draw K.'s distracted glance upon himself. K. nodded. 'You are presumably very surprised at the events of this morning?' asked the Inspector, with both hands rearranging the few things that lay on the night-table, a candle and a matchbox, a book and a pin-cushion, as if they were objects which he required for his interrogation. 'Certainly,' said K., and he was filled with pleasure at having encountered a sensible man at last, with whom he could discuss the matter. 'Certainly, I am surprised, but I am by no means very surprised.' 'Not very surprised?' asked the Inspector, setting the candle in the middle of the table and then grouping the other things round it. 'Perhaps you misunderstand me,' K. hastened to add. 'I mean' – here K. stopped and looked round him for a chair. 'I suppose I may sit down?' he asked. 'It's not usual,' answered the Inspector. 'I mean,' said K. without further parley, 'that I am very surprised, of course, but when one has lived for thirty years in this world and had to fight one's way through it, as I have had to do, one becomes hardened to surprises and doesn't take them too seriously. Particularly the one this morning.' 'Why particularly the one this morning?' 'I won't say that I regard the whole thing as a joke, for the preparations that have been made seem too elaborate for that. The whole staff of the boarding-house would have to be involved, as well as all your people, and that would be past a joke. So I don't say that it's a joke.' 'Quite right,' said the Inspector, looking to see how many matches there were in the matchbox. 'But on the other hand,' K. went on, turning to everybody there, he wanted to bring in the three young men standing beside the photographs as well, 'on the other hand, it can't be an affair of any great importance either. I argue this from the fact that though I am accused of something, I cannot recall the slightest offence that might be charged against me. But that even is of minor importance, the real question is, who accuses me? What authority is conducting these proceedings? Are you officers of the Law? None of you has a uniform, unless your suit' – here he turned to Franz – 'is to be considered a uniform, but it's more like a tourist's outfit. I demand a clear answer to these questions, and I feel sure that after an explanation we shall be able to part from each other on the best of terms.' The Inspector flung the matchbox down on the table. 'You are labouring under a great delusion,' he said. 'These gentlemen here and myself have no standing whatever in this affair of yours, indeed we know hardly anything about it. We might wear the most official uniforms and your case would not be a penny the worse. I can't even confirm that you are charged with an offence, or rather I don't know whether you are. You are under arrest, certainly, more than that I do not know. Perhaps the warders have given you a different impression, but they are only irresponsible gossips. However, if I can't answer your questions, I can at least give you a piece of advice; think less about us and of what is going to happen to you, think more about yourself instead. And don't make such an outcry about your feeling innocent, it spoils the not unfavourable impression you make in other respects. Also you should be far more reticent, nearly everything you have just said could have been implied in your behaviour with the help of a word here and there, and in any case does not redound particularly to your credit.'

K. stared at the Inspector. Was he to be taught lessons in manners by a man probably younger than himself? To be punished for his frankness by a rebuke? And about the cause of his arrest and about its instigator was he to learn nothing?

He was thrown into a certain agitation, and began to walk up and down – nobody hindered him – pushed back his cuffs, fingered his shirt-front, ruffled his hair, and as he passed the three young men said: 'This is sheer nonsense!' Whereupon they turned towards him and regarded him sympathetically but gravely; at last he came to a stand before the Inspector's table. 'The advocate Hasterer is a personal friend of mine,' he said. 'May I telephone to him?' 'Certainly,' replied the Inspector, 'but I don't see what sense there would be in that, unless you have some private business of your own to consult him about.' 'What sense would there be in that?' cried K., more in amazement than exasperation. 'What kind of man are you, then? You ask me to be sensible and you carry on in the most senseless way imaginable yourself! It's enough to drive me mad. People first fall upon me in my own house and then lounge about the room and leave me to rack my brains in vain for the reason. What sense would there be in telephoning to an advocate when I'm supposed to be under arrest? All right, I won't telephone.' 'But do telephone if you want to,' replied the Inspector, waving an arm towards the entrance hall, where the telephone was, 'please do telephone.' 'No, I don't want to now,' said K., going over to the window. Across the street the party of three were still on the watch, and their enjoyment of the spectacle received its first slight check when K. appeared at the window. The two old people moved as if to get up, but the man at the back blandly reassured them. 'Here's a fine crowd of spectators!' cried K. in a loud voice to the Inspector, pointing at them with his finger. 'Go away,' he shouted across. The three of them immediately retreated a few steps, the two ancients actually took cover behind the younger man, who shielded them with his massive body and to judge from the movements of his lips was saying something which, owing to the distance, could not be distinguished. Yet they did not remove themselves altogether, but seemed to be waiting for the chance to return to the window again unobserved. 'Officious, inconsiderate wretches!' said K. as he turned back to the room again. The Inspector was possibly of the same mind, K. fancied, as far as he could tell from a hasty side-glance. But it was equally possible that the Inspector had not even been listening, for he had pressed one hand firmly on the table and seemed to be comparing the length of his fingers. The two warders sat on a chest draped with an embroidered cloth, rubbing their knees. The three young men were looking aimlessly round them with their hands on their hips. It was as quiet as in some deserted office. 'Come, gentlemen,' cried K., it seemed to him for the moment as if he were responsible for all of them, 'from the look of you this affair of mine seems to be settled. In my opinion the best thing now would be to bother no more about the justice or injustice of your behaviour and settle the matter amicably by shaking hands on it. If you are of the same opinion, why, then –' and he stepped over to the Inspector's table and held out his hand. The Inspector raised his eyes, bit his lips, and looked at K.'s hand stretched out to him; K. still believed he was going to close with the offer. But instead he got up, seized a hard round hat lying on Fräulein Bürstner's bed, and with both hands put it carefully on his head, as if he were trying it on for the first time. 'How simple it all seems to you!' he said to K. as he did so. 'You think we should settle the matter amicably, do you? No, no, that really can't be done. On the other hand I don't mean to suggest that you should give up hope. Why should you? You are only under arrest, nothing more. I was requested to inform you of this. I have done so, and I have also observed your reactions. That's enough for today, and we can say good-bye, though only for the time being, naturally. You'll be going to the Bank now, I suppose?' 'To the Bank?' asked K. 'I thought I was under arrest?' K. asked the question with a certain defiance, for though his offer to shake hands had been ignored, he felt more and more independent of all these people, especially now that the Inspector had risen to his feet. He was playing with them. He considered the idea of running after them to the front door as they left and challenging them to take him prisoner. So he said again: 'How can I go to the Bank, if I am under arrest?' 'Ah, I see,' said the Inspector, who had already reached the door. 'You have misunderstood me. You are under arrest, certainly, but that need not hinder you from going about your business. You won't be hampered in carrying on in the ordinary course of your life.' 'Then being arrested isn't so very bad,' said K., going up to the Inspector. 'I never suggested that it was,' said the Inspector. 'But in that case it would seem there was no particular necessity to tell me about it,' said K., moving still closer. The others had drawn near too. They were all gathered now in a little space beside the door. 'It was my duty,' said the Inspector. 'A stupid duty,' said K. inflexibly. 'That may be,' replied the Inspector, 'but we needn't waste our time with such arguments. I was assuming that you would want to go to the Bank. As you are such a quibbler over words, let me add that I am not forcing you to go to the Bank, I was merely assuming that you would want to go. And to facilitate that, and render your arrival at the Bank as unobtrusive as possible, I have detained these three gentlemen here, who are colleagues of yours, to be at your disposal.' 'What?' cried K., gaping at the three of them. These insignificant anaemic young men, whom he had observed only as a group standing beside the photographs, were actually clerks in the Bank, not colleagues of his, that was putting it too strongly and indicated a gap in the omniscience of the Inspector, but they were subordinate employees of the Bank all the same. How could he have failed to notice that? He must have been very taken up with the Inspector and the warders not to recognize these three young men. The stiff Rabensteiner swinging his arms, the fair Kullich with the deep-set eyes, and Kaminer with his insupportable smile, caused by a chronic muscular twitch. 'Good morning!' said K. after a pause, holding out his hand to the three politely bowing figures. 'I didn't recognize you. Well, shall we go to our work now, eh?' The young men nodded, smiling and eagerly, as if they had been waiting all the time merely for this, but when K. turned to get his hat, which he had left in his room, they all fled one after the other to fetch it, which seemed to indicate a certain embarrassment. K. stood still and watched them through the two open doors; the languid Rabensteiner, naturally, brought up the rear, for he merely minced along at an elegant trot. Kaminer handed over the hat and K. had to tell himself expressly, as indeed he had often to do in the Bank, that Kaminer's smile was not intentional, that the man could not smile intentionally if he tried. Then Frau Grubach, who did not appear to be particularly conscious of any guilt, opened the front door to let the whole company out, and K. glanced down, as so often before, at her apron-string, which made such an unreasonably deep cut in her massive body. Down below he decided, his watch in his hand, to take a taxi so as to save any further delay in reaching the Bank, for he was already half an hour late. Kaminer ran to the corner to get a taxi, the other two were obviously doing their best to distract K., when suddenly Kullich pointed to the opposite house door, where the tall man with the reddish, pointed beard was emerging into sight, and immediately, a little embarrassed at showing himself in his full height, retreated against the wall and leaned there. The old couple must be still coming down the stairs. K. was annoyed at Kullich for drawing his attention to the man, whom he had already identified, indeed whom he had actually expected to see. 'Don't look across,' he said hurriedly, without noticing how strange it must seem to speak in that fashion to grown-up men. But no explanation proved necessary, for at that moment the taxi arrived, they took their seats, and drove off. Then K. rememembered that he had not noticed the Inspector and the warders leaving, the Inspector had usurped his attention so that he did not recognize the three clerks, and the clerks in turn had made him oblivious of the Inspector. That did not show much presence of mind, and K. resolved to be more careful in this respect. Yet in spite of himself he turned round and craned from the back of the car to see if he could perhaps catch sight of the Inspector and the warders. But he immediately turned away again and leaned back comfortably in the corner without even having attempted to distinguish one of them. Unlikely as it might seem, this was just the moment when he would have welcomed a few words from his companions, but the others seemed to be suddenly tired. Rabensteiner gazed out to the right, Kullich to the left, and only Kaminer faced him with his nervous grin, which, unfortunately, on grounds of humanity could not be made a subject of conversation.

That spring K. had been accustomed to pass his evenings in this way: after work whenever possible – he was usually in his office until nine – he would take a short walk, alone or with some of his colleagues, and then go to a beer hall, where until eleven he sat at a table patronized mostly by elderly men. But there were exceptions to this routine, when, for instance, the Manager of the Bank, who highly valued his diligence and reliability, invited him for a drive or for dinner at his villa. And once a week K. visited a girl called Elsa, who was on duty all night till early morning as a waitress in a cabaret and during the day received her visitors in bed.

But on this evening – the day had passed quickly, filled with pressing work and many flattering and friendly birthday wishes – K. resolved to go straight home. During every brief pause in the day's work he had kept this resolve in mind; without his quite knowing why, it seemed to him that the whole household of Frau Grubach had been thrown into great disorder by the events of the morning and that it was his task alone to put it right again. Once order was restored, every trace of these events would be obliterated and things would resume their old course. From the three clerks themselves nothing was to be feared, they had been absorbed once more in the great hierarchy of the Bank, no change was to be remarked in them. K. had several times called them singly and collectively to his room, with no other purpose than to observe them: each time he had dismissed them again with a quiet mind.

When at half-past nine he arrived at the house where he lived he found a young lad in the street doorway, standing with his legs wide apart and smoking a pipe. 'Who are you?' K. asked at once, bringing his face close to the lad's; one could not see very well in the darkness of the entrance. 'I'm the house-porter's son, sir,' said the lad, taking the pipe from his mouth and stepping aside. 'The house-porter's son?' asked K., tapping his stick impatiently on the ground. 'Do you want anything, sir? Shall I fetch my father?' 'No, no,' said K., and his voice had a reassuring note, as if the lad had done something wrong but was to be forgiven. 'It's all right,' he said and went on, yet before he climbed the stair he turned round for another look.

He had intended to go straight to his room, but as he wanted to speak to Frau Grubach he stopped instead to knock at her door. She was sitting darning at a table, on which lay a heap of old stockings. K. excused himself awkwardly for knocking so late, but Frau Grubach was most cordial and would hear of no apology, she was always glad to have a talk with him, he knew very well that he was her best and most valued boarder. K. looked round the room, it had reverted completely to its old state, the breakfast dishes which had stood that morning on the table by the window had apparently been cleared away. Women's hands are quietly effective, he thought. He himself might have smashed the dishes on the spot, but he certainly could never have quietly carried them away. He gazed at Frau Grubach with a certain gratitude. 'Why are you still working at this late hour?' he asked. They were both sitting at the table now, and from time to time K. buried one hand in the pile of stockings. 'There's a lot to do,' she said; 'during the day my time belongs to my boarders; for keeping my own things in order I have only the evenings.' 'I'm afraid I've been responsible for giving you extra work today.' 'How is that?' she asked, becoming more intent, the work resting in her lap. 'I mean the men who were here this morning.' 'Oh, that,' she said, resuming her composure, 'that didn't give me much to do.' K. looked on in silence while she took up her darning again. ('She seems surprised that I mentioned it,' he thought, 'she seems to think it not quite right that I should mention it. All the more need for me to do so. I couldn't mention it to anyone but this old woman.') 'It must certainly have made more work,' he said at last, 'but it won't happen again.' 'No, that can't happen again,' she said reassuringly, with an almost sorrowful smile. 'Do you really mean it?' asked K. 'Yes,' she said softly, 'and above all you mustn't take it too much to heart. Lots of things happen in this world! As you've spoken so frankly to me, Herr K., I may as well admit to you that

I listened for a little behind the door and that the two warders told me a few things too. It's a matter of your happiness, and I really have that at heart, more perhaps than I should, for I am only your landlady. Well, then, I heard a few things, but I can't say that they were particularly bad. No. You are under arrest, certainly, but not as a thief is under arrest. If one's arrested as a thief, that's a bad business, but as for this arrest – It gives me the feeling of something very learned, forgive me if what I say is stupid, it gives me the feeling of something abstract which I don't understand, but which I don't need to understand either.'

'What you've just said is by no means stupid, Frau Grubach, at least I'm partly of the same opinion, except that I judge the whole thing still more severely and consider this assignation of guilt to be not only abstract but a pure figment. I was taken by surprise, that was all. If immediately on wakening I had got up without troubling my head about Anna's absence and had come to you without regarding anyone who tried to bar my way, I could have breakfasted in the kitchen for a change and could have got you to bring me my clothes from my room; in short, if I had behaved sensibly, nothing further would have happened, all this would have been nipped in the bud. But one is so unprepared. In the Bank, for instance, I am always prepared, nothing of that kind could possibly happen to me there, I have my own attendant, the general telephone and the office telephone stand before me on my desk, people keep coming in to see me, clients and clerks, and above all, my mind is always on my work and so kept on the alert; it would be an actual pleasure to me if a situation like that cropped up in the Bank. Well, it's past history now and I didn't really intend to speak about it again, only I wanted to hear your judgement, the judgement of a sensible woman, and I am very glad we are in agreement. But now you must give me your hand on it, an agreement such as this must be confirmed with a handshake.'

'Will she take my hand? The Inspector wouldn't do it,' he thought, gazing at the woman with a different, a critical eye. She stood up because he had stood up, she was a little embarrassed, for she had not understood all that he had said. And because of her embarrassment she said something which she had not intended to say and which was, moreover, rather out of place. 'Don't take it so much to heart, Herr K.,' she said with tears in her voice, forgetting, naturally, to shake his hand. 'I had no idea that I was taking it to heart,' said K., suddenly tired and seeing how little it mattered whether she agreed with him or not.

At the door he asked; 'Is Fräulein Bürstner in?' 'No,' replied Frau Grubach, and in giving this dry piece of information she smiled with honest if belated sympathy. 'She's at the theatre. Do you want to ask her something? Shall I give her a message?' 'Oh, I just wanted a word or two with her.' 'I'm afraid I don't know when she will be back; when she goes to the theatre she's usually late.' 'It's of no consequence,' said K., turning to the door, his head sunk on his breast. 'I only wanted to apologize to her for having borrowed her room today.' 'That's quite unnecessary, Herr K., you are too scrupulous, the Fräulein knows nothing about it, she hasn't been back since early this morning, everything has been put back in its place again too, see for yourself.' And she opened the door of Fräulein Bürstner's room. 'Thanks, I believe you,' said K., but went in through the open door all the same. The moon shone softly into the dark chamber. As far as one could see everything was really in its proper place, and the blouse was no longer dangling from the latch of the window. The pillows on the bed looked strangely high, they were lying partly in the moonlight. 'The Fräulein often comes home late,' said K., looking at Frau Grubach as if she were to blame for it: 'Young people are like that,' said Frau Grubach apologetically. 'Certainly, certainly,' said K., 'but it can go too far.' 'That it can,' said Frau Grubach, 'how right you are, Herr K.! In this case especially, perhaps. I have no wish to speak ill of Fräulein Bürstner, she is a dear, good girl, kind, decent, punctual, industrious, I admire all these qualities in her, but one thing is undeniable, she should have more pride, should keep herself more to herself. This very month I have met her twice already on outlying streets, and each time with a different gentleman. It worries me, and as sure as I stand here, Herr K., I haven't told anybody but you, but I'm afraid there's no help for it, I shall have to talk to the Fräulein herself about it. Besides, it isn't the only thing that has made me suspicious of her.' 'You're quite on the wrong track,' said K., with a sudden fury which he was scarcely able to hide, 'and you have obviously misunderstood my remark about the Fräulein, it wasn't meant in that way. In fact I frankly warn you against saying anything to the Fräulein, you're quite mistaken, I know the Fräulein very well, there isn't a word of truth in what you say. But perhaps I'm going too far myself. I don't want to interfere, you can say what you like to her. Good night.' 'Good night, Herr K.,' said Frau Grubach imploringly, hurrying after him to his door, which he had already opened, 'I don't really mean to say anything to the Fräulein yet, of course I'll wait to see what happens before I do anything, you're the only one I've spoken to, in confidence. After all it must be to the interest of all my boarders that I try to keep my house respectable, and that is all I'm anxious about in this case.' 'Respectable!' cried K., through the chink of the door; 'if you want to keep your house respectable you'll have to begin by giving me notice.' Then he shut the door and paid no attention to the faint knocking that ensued.

On the other hand, as he felt no desire to sleep, he resolved to stay awake and take the opportunity of noting at what hour Fräulein Bürstner returned. Perhaps when she did so it might still be possible, unsuitable though the hour was, to have a few words with her. As he lounged by the window and shut his tired eyes, he actually considered for a moment paying Frau Grubach out by persuading Fräulein Bürstner to give notice along with him. Yet he saw at once that this was an excessive reaction, and he began to suspect himself of wishing to change his lodgings because of that morning's events. Nothing could be more senseless, not to say useless and equivocal.

When he became weary of gazing out into the empty street he lay down on the sofa, after having slightly opened the door to the entrance hall, so that from where he was lying he might see at once anyone who came in. Until about eleven he lay quietly on the sofa smoking a cigar. But then he could not endure lying there any longer and took a step or two into the entrance hall, as if that would make Fräulein Bürstner come all the sooner. He felt no special desire to see her, he could not even remember exactly how she looked, but he wanted to talk to her now, and he was exasperated that her being so late should further disturb and derange the end of such a day. She was to blame, too, for the fact that he had not eaten any supper and that he had put off the visit to Elsa he had proposed making that evening. He could remedy both omissions still, it was true, by going straight to the wine restaurant where Elsa worked. He would do that later, he decided, after his talk with Fräulein Bürstner.

It was a little after half-past eleven when he heard somebody on the stairs. Absorbed in his thoughts, he had been marching up and down the entrance hall for some time as if it were his own room, and now he fled behind his bedroom door. It was Fräulein Bürstner coming in. As she locked the front door she shivered and drew her silk shawl round her slim shoulders. In a minute she would be going into her room, where K. certainly could not intrude at such an hour; he would therefore have to speak to her now, but unfortunately he had forgotten to switch on the light in his room, so that if he were to emerge out of the darkness it would look as if he were waylaying her and at least must be somewhat alarming. No time was to be lost, so in his confusion he whispered through the chink of the door: 'Fräulein Bürstner.' It sounded like a prayer, not like a summons. 'Is anyone there?' asked Fräulein Bürstner, looking round with wide-open eyes. 'It's I,' said K., stepping forward. 'Oh, Herr K.!' said Fräulein Bürstner, smiling. 'Good evening,' and she held out her hand to him. 'I should like to have a word or two with you, will you allow me to do so now?' 'Now?' asked Fräulein Bürstner. 'Must it be now? A little unusual, isn't it?' 'I've been waiting for you ever since nine.' 'Well, I was at the theatre, you know, I had no idea you were waiting.' 'What I want to talk to you about didn't happen till today.' 'Oh, well, I have no serious objection, except that I am so tired I can scarcely stand on my feet. So come for a few minutes to my room. We can't possibly talk here, we should waken somebody, and I should loathe that for our own sakes even more than for theirs. Wait here till I have turned on the light in my room, and then you can switch off the light here.' K. did so, but waited until Fräulein Bürstner from her room again invited him, in a whisper, to come in. 'Take a seat,' she said, pointing to the sofa; she herself stood leaning against the foot of the bed in spite of her confessed weariness; she did not even take off her small but lavishly flower-bedecked hat. 'Well, what is it? I am really curious.' She crossed her ankles. 'Perhaps you will say,' began K., 'that there was no urgent need to speak about it now, but –' 'I never listen to preambles,' said Fräulein Bürstner. 'That makes it easier for me,' said K. 'This morning your room was thrown into some slight confusion and the fault was mine in a certain sense, it was done by strange people against my will, and yet as I have said the fault was mine; I want to beg your pardon for this.' 'My room?' asked Fräulein Bürstner, and she cast a critical eye round the room instead of looking at him. 'That is so,' said K., and now they gazed into each other's eyes for the first time. 'The actual manner in which it happened isn't worth mentioning.' 'But surely that's the really interesting part,' said Fräulein Bürstner. 'No,' said K. 'Well,' said Fräulein Bürstner, 'I don't want to pry into secrets; if you insist that it is uninteresting, I shall not argue the point. You have begged my pardon and I herewith freely grant it, particularly as I can find no trace of disturbance.' With her open palms pressed to her hips, she made a tour of the room. Beside the mat where the photographs were stuck she stopped. 'Look here,' she cried, 'my photographs are all mixed up! That is really horrid. So someone has actually been in my room who had no right to come in.' K. nodded and silently cursed the clerk Kaminer, who could never control his stupid, meaningless fidgeting. 'It is curious,' said Fräulein Bürstner, 'that I should be compelled now to forbid you to do something which you ought to forbid yourself to do, that is to enter my room in my absence.' 'But I have explained to you, Fräulein,' said K., going over to the photographs, 'that it was not I who interfered with these photographs; still, as you won't believe me, I have to confess that the

Interrogation Commission brought three Bank clerks here, one of whom, and I shall have him dismissed at the first opportunity, must have meddled with your photographs.' In answer to the Fräulein's inquiring look he added: 'Yes, there was an Interrogation Commission here today.' 'On your account?' asked the Fräulein. 'Yes,' replied K. 'No!' cried the girl, laughing. 'Yes, it was,' said K. 'Why, do you think I must be innocent?' 'Well, innocent,' said the Fräulein, 'I don't want to commit myself, at a moment's notice, to a verdict with so many possible implications, besides, I don't really know you; all the same, it must be a serious crime that would bring an Interrogation Commission down on a man. Yet as you are still at large – at least I gather from the look of you that you haven't just escaped from prison – you couldn't really have committed a serious crime.' 'Yes,' said K., 'but the Interrogation Commission might have discovered, not that I was innocent, but that I was not so guilty as they had assumed.' 'Certainly, that is possible,' said Fräulein Bürstner, very much on the alert. 'You see,' said K., 'you haven't much experience in legal matters.' 'No, I haven't,' said Fräulein Bürstner, 'and I have often regretted it, for I would like to know everything there is to know, and law courts interest me particularly. A court of law has a curious attraction, hasn't it? But I'll soon remedy my ignorance in that respect, for next month I am joining the clerical staff of a lawyer's office.' 'That's excellent,' said K. 'Then you'll be able to help me a little with my case.' 'That may well be,' said Fräulein Bürstner; 'why not? I like to make good use of my knowledge.' 'But I mean it seriously,' said K., 'or at least half-seriously, as you yourself mean it. The case is too trifling to need a lawyer, but I could do very well with an adviser.' 'Yes, but if I am to be an adviser I must know what it's all about,' said Fräulein Bürstner. 'That's just the snag,' said K. 'I don't know that myself.' 'Then you've simply been making fun of me,' said Fräulein Bürstner, extravagantly disappointed, 'it was surely unnecessary to choose this late hour for doing so.' And she walked away from the photographs, where they had been standing together for a long time. 'But, Fräulein,' said K., 'I'm not making fun of you. Why won't you believe me? I have already told you all I know. In fact more than I know, for it was not a real Interrogation Commission. I called it that because I didn't know what else to call it. There was no interrogation at all, I was merely arrested, but it was a Commission.' Fräulein Bürstner sat down on the sofa and laughed again. 'What was it like, then?' she asked. 'Horrible,' said K., but he was no longer thinking of what he was saying, for he was completely taken up in staring at Fräulein Bürstner, who was leaning her head on one hand – her elbow was resting on the sofa cushions – while with the other she slowly caressed her hip. 'That's too general,' she said. 'What's too general?' asked K. Then he came to himself and asked: 'Shall I let you see how it happened?' He wanted to move about and yet he did not want to leave. 'I'm tired,' said Fräulein Bürstner. 'You came home so late,' said K. 'So you've gone the length of reproaching me, and I deserve it too, for I should never have let you in. And there was no need for it, either, that's evident.' 'There was a need for it. I'll make you see that in a minute,' said K. 'May I shift this night-table from beside your bed?' 'What an idea!' cried Fräulein Bürstner. 'Of course not!' 'Then I can't show you how it happened,' said K. in agitation, as if some immeasurable wrong had been inflicted upon him. 'Oh, if you need it for your performance, shift the table by all means,' said Fräulein Bürstner, and after a pause added in a smaller voice: 'I'm so tired that I'm letting you take too many liberties.' K. stationed the table in the middle of the room and sat down behind it. 'You must picture to yourself exactly where the various people are, it's very interesting. I am the Inspector, over there on the chest two warders are sitting, beside the photographs three young men are standing. At the latch of the window – just to mention it in passing – a white blouse is dangling. And now we can begin. Oh, I've forgotten about myself, the most important person; well, I'm standing here in front of the table. The Inspector is lounging at his ease with his legs crossed, his arm hanging over the back of the chair like this, an absolute boor. And now we can really begin. The Inspector shouts as if he had to waken me out of my sleep, he actually bawls; I'm afraid, if I am to make you understand, I'll have to bawl too, but it's only my name that he bawls.' Fräulein Bürstner, who was listening with amusement, put her finger to her lips to keep K. from shouting, but it was too late, K. was too absorbed in his role, he gave a long-drawn shout: 'Joseph K.,' less loud indeed than he had threatened, but with such explosive force that it hung in the air a moment before gradually spreading through the room.

Then there was a knocking at the door of the adjoining room, a loud, sharp, regular tattoo. Fräulein Bürstner turned pale but put her hand to her heart. K. was violently startled, it took him a moment or so to withdraw his thoughts from the events of the morning and the girl before whom he was acting them. No sooner had he come to himself than he rushed over to Fräulein Bürstner and seized her hand. 'Don't be afraid,' he whispered, 'I'll put everything right. But who can it be? There's only the living-room next door, nobody sleeps there.' 'No,' Fräulein Bürstner whispered in his ear, 'since yesterday a nephew of Frau Grubach has been sleeping there, a Captain. There was no other room he could have. I forgot all about it. Why did you have to shout like that? I'm all upset.' 'There's no need for that,' said K., and as she sank back on the cushions he kissed her on the brow. 'Away with you, away with you,' she said, hastily sitting up again, 'do go away, do go now, what are you thinking about, he's listening at the door, he hears everything. How you torment me!' 'I won't go,' said K., 'until you are a little calmer. Come to the far corner of the room, he can't hear us there.' She let herself be led there. 'You forget,' he said, 'that though this may mean unpleasantness for you, it is not at all dangerous. You know how Frau Grubach, who has the decisive voice in this matter, particularly as the Captain is her nephew, you know how she almost venerates me and absolutely believes everything I say. She is also dependent on me, I may say, for she has borrowed a fair sum of money from me. I shall confirm any explanation of our being together here that you like to invent, if it is in the least plausible, and I pledge myself to make Frau Grubach not only publicly accept it but also really and honestly believe it. You needn't consider me at all. If you want to have it announced that I assaulted you, then Frau Grubach will be informed accordingly and she will believe it without losing her confidence in me, she's so devoted to me.' Fräulein Bürstner, silent and somewhat limp, stared at the floor. 'Why shouldn't Frau Grubach believe that I assaulted you?' K. added. He was gazing at her hair, evenly parted, looped low, firmly restrained reddish hair. He expected her to look up at him, but she said without changing her posture: 'Forgive me, I was terrified at the sudden knocking rather than at any consequence of the Captain's being there. It was so still after you shouted and then there came these knocks, that was why I was so terrified, I was sitting quite near the door, too, the knocking seemed to be just beside me. I thank you for your offer, but I'm not going to accept it. I can bear the responsibility for anything that happens in my room, no matter who questions it. I'm surprised you don't see the insult to me that is implied in your suggestion, over and above your good intentions, of course, which I do appreciate. But now go, leave me to myself, I need more than ever to be left in peace. The few minutes you begged for have stretched to half an hour and more.' K. clasped her hand and then her wrist. 'But you aren't angry with me?' he asked. She shook his hand off and answered: 'No, no, I'm never angry with anybody.' He felt for her wrist again, she let him take it this time and so led him to the door. He was firmly resolved to leave. But at the door he stopped as if he had not expected to find a door there; Fräulein Bürstner seized this moment to free herself, open the door, and slip into the entrance hall, where she whispered: 'Now, please do come! Look' – she pointed to the Captain's door, underneath which showed a strip of light – 'he has turned on his light and is amusing himself at our expense.' 'I'm just coming,' K. said, rushed out, seized her, and kissed her first on the lips, then all over the face, like some thirsty animal lapping greedily at a spring of long-sought fresh water. Finally he kissed her on the neck, right on the throat, and kept his lips there for a long time. A slight noise from the Captain's room made him look up. 'I'm going now,' he said; he wanted to call Fräulein Bürstner by her first name, but he did not know what it was. She nodded wearily, resigned her hand for him to kiss, half turning away as if she were unaware of what she did, and went into her room with down-bent head. Shortly afterwards K. was in his bed. He fell asleep almost at once, but before doing so he thought for a little about his behaviour, he was pleased with it, yet surprised that he was not still more pleased; he was seriously concerned for Fräulein Bürstner because of the Captain.

2

FIRST INTERROGATION

K. was informed by telephone that next Sunday a short inquiry into his case would take place. His attention was drawn to the fact that these inquiries would not follow each other regularly, perhaps not every week, but at more frequent intervals as time went on. It was in the general interest, on the one hand, that the case should be quickly concluded, but on the other hand the interrogations must be thorough in every respect, although, because of the strain involved, they must never last too long. For this reason the expedient of these rapidly succeeding but short interrogations had been chosen. Sunday had been selected as the day of inquiry so that K. might not be disturbed in his professional work. It was assumed that he would agree to this arrangement, but if he preferred some other day they would meet his wishes to the best of their ability. For instance, it would be possible to hold the inquiries during the night, although then K. would probably not be fresh enough. At any rate they would expect him on Sunday, if K. had no objection. It was, of course, understood that he must appear without fail, he did not need to be reminded of that. He was given the number of the house where he had to go, it was a house in an outlying suburban street where he had never been before.

On receiving this message K. replaced the receiver without

answering; his mind was made up to keep the appointment on Sunday, it was absolutely essential, the case was getting under way and he must fight it; this first interrogation must also be the last. He was still standing thoughtfully beside the telephone, when he heard behind him the voice of the Deputy Manager, who wanted to telephone and found K. barring his way. 'Bad news?' asked the Deputy Manager casually, not really wanting to know but merely eager to get K. away from the telephone. 'No, no,' said K., stepping aside but without going away. The Deputy Manager lifted the receiver and said, speaking round it while he waited to be connected: 'Oh, a word with you, Herr K. Would you do me the favour of joining a party on my yacht on Sunday morning? There will be quite a large party, doubtless some of your friends will be among them. Herr Hasterer, the advocate, among others. Will you come? Do come!' K. made an effort to attend to what the Deputy Manager was saying. It was of no slight importance to him, for this invitation from a man with whom he had never got on very well was a sort of friendly overture and showed how important K. had become to the Bank and how valuable his friendship or at least his neutrality had become to its second highest official. The Deputy Manager had definitely humbled himself in giving this invitation, even though he had merely dropped it casually while waiting at the telephone to get a connexion. Yet K. had to humble the man a second time, for he said: 'Thanks very much. But I'm sorry I have no time on Sunday, I have a previous engagement.' 'A pity,' said the Deputy Manager, turning to speak into the telephone, which had just been connected. It was not a short conversation, but in his confusion K. remained standing the whole time beside the instrument. Not till the Deputy Manager had rung off did he start out of his reverie in some alarm and say, to excuse his aimless loitering: 'I have just been rung up and asked to go somewhere, but they forgot to tell me at what time.' 'Well, you can ring up and ask,' said the Deputy Manager. 'It isn't so important as all that,' said K., though in saying so he crippled still further his first lame excuse. The Deputy Manager, turning to go, went on making remarks about other topics. K. forced himself to answer, but what he was really thinking was that it would be best to go to the address at nine o'clock on Sunday morning, since that was the hour at which all the law courts started their business on week-days.

Sunday was dull. K. was tired, for he had stayed late at his restaurant the night before because of a celebration; he had nearly overslept. In a great hurry, without taking time to think or co-ordinate the plans which he had drawn up during the week, he dressed and rushed off, without his breakfast, to the suburb which had been mentioned to him. Strangely enough, though he had little time to study passers-by, he caught sight of the three clerks already involved in his case: Rabensteiner, Kullich, and Kaminer. The first two were journeying in a street-car which crossed in front of him, but Kaminer was sitting on the terrace of a café and bent inquisitively over the railing just as K. passed. All three were probably staring after him and wondering where their chief was rushing off to; a sort of defiance had kept K. from taking a vehicle to his destination, he loathed the thought of chartering anyone, even the most casual stranger, to help him along in this case of his, also he did not want to be beholden to anyone or to initiate anyone even remotely in his affairs, and last of all he had no desire to belittle himself before the Interrogation Commission by a too scrupulous punctuality. Nevertheless he was hurrying fast, so as if possible to arrive by nine o'clock, although he had not even been required to appear at any specified time.

He had thought that the house would be recognizable even at a distance by some sign which his imagination left unspecified, or by some unusual commotion before the door. But Juliusstrasse, where the house was said to be and at whose end he stopped for a moment, displayed on both sides houses almost exactly alike, high grey tenements inhabited by poor people. This being Sunday morning, most of the windows were occupied, men in shirt-sleeves were leaning there smoking or holding small children cautiously and tenderly on the window-ledges. Other windows were piled high with bedding, above which the dishevelled head of a woman would appear for a moment. People were shouting to one another across the street; one shout just above K.'s head caused great laughter. Down the whole length of the street at regular intervals, below the level of the pavement, were planted little general grocery shops, to which short flights of steps led down. Women were thronging into and out of these shops or gossiping on the steps outside. A fruit hawker who was crying his wares to the people in the windows above, progressing almost as inattentively as K. himself, almost knocked K. down with his push-cart. A phonograph which had seen long service in a better quarter of the town began stridently to murder a tune.

K. penetrated deeper into the street, slowly, as if he had now abundant time, or as if the Examining Magistrate might be leaning from one of the windows with every opportunity of observing that he was on the way. It was a little after nine o'clock. The house was quite far along the street, it was of unusual extent, the main entrance was particularly high and wide. It was clearly a service entrance for trucks, the locked doors of various warehouses surrounded the courtyard and displayed the names of firms some of which were known to K. from the Bank ledgers. Against his usual habit, he studied these external appearances with close attention and remained standing for a little while in the entrance to the courtyard. Near him a barefooted man was sitting on a crate reading a newspaper. Two lads were seesawing on a hand-barrow. A sickly young girl was standing at a pump in her night-jacket and gazing at K. while the water poured into her bucket. In one corner of the courtyard a line was stretched between two windows, where washing was already being hung up to dry. A man stood below superintending the work with an occasional shout.

K. turned towards the stairs to make his way up to the Interrogation Chamber, but then came to a standstill again, for in addition to this staircase he could see in the courtyard three other separate flights of stairs and besides these a little passage at the other end which seemed to lead into a second courtyard. He was annoyed that he had not been given more definite information about the room, these people showed a strange negligence or indifference in their treatment of him, he intended to tell them so very positively and clearly. Finally, however, he climbed the first stairs and his mind played in retrospect with the saying of the warder Willem that an attraction existed between the Law and guilt, from which it should really follow that the Interrogation Chamber must lie in the particular flight of stairs which K. happened to choose.

On his way up he disturbed many children who were playing on the stairs and looked at him angrily as he strode through their ranks. 'If I ever come here again,' he told himself, 'I must either bring sweets to cajole them with or else a stick to beat them.' Just before he reached the first floor he had actually to wait for a moment until a marble came to rest, two children with the lined, pinched face of adult rogues holding him meanwhile by his trousers; if he had shaken them off he must have hurt them, and he feared their outcries.

His real search began on the first floor. As he could not inquire for the Interrogation Commission he invented a joiner called Lanz – the name came into his mind because Frau Grubach's nephew, the Captain, was called Lanz – and so he began to inquire at all the doors if a joiner called Lanz lived there, so as to get a chance to look into the rooms. It turned out, however, that that was quite possible without further ado, for almost all the doors stood open, with children running out and in. Most of the flats, too, consisted of one small single-windowed room in which cooking was going on. Many of the women were holding babies in one arm and working over the stove with the arm that was left free. Half-grown girls who seemed to be dressed in nothing but an apron kept busily rushing about. In all the rooms the beds were still occupied, sick people were lying in them, or men who had not wakened yet, or others who were resting there in their clothes. At the doors which were shut K. knocked and asked if a joiner called Lanz lived there. Generally a woman opened, listened to his question, and then turned to someone in the room, who thereupon rose from the bed. 'The gentleman's asking if a joiner called Lanz lives here.' 'A joiner called Lanz?'

asked the man from the bed. 'Yes,' said K., though it was beyond question that the Interrogation Commission did not sit here and his inquiry was therefore superfluous. Many seemed convinced that it was highly important for K. to find the joiner Lanz, they took a long time to think it over, suggested some joiner who, however, was not called Lanz, or a name which had some quite distant resemblance to Lanz, or inquired of their neighbours, or escorted K. to a door some considerable distance away, where they fancied such a man might be living as a lodger, or where there was someone who could give better information than they could. In the end K. scarcely needed to ask at all, for in this way he was conducted over the whole floor. He now regretted his plan, which at first had seemed so practical. As he was approaching the fifth floor he decided to give up the search, said good-bye to a friendly young workman who wanted to conduct him farther, and descended again. But then the uselessness of the whole expedition filled him with exasperation, he went up the stairs once more and knocked at the first door he came to on the fifth storey. The first thing he saw in the little room was a great pendulum clock which already pointed to ten. 'Does a joiner called Lanz live here?' he asked. 'Please go through,' said a young woman with sparkling black eyes, who was washing children's clothes in a tub, and she pointed with her damp hand to the open door of the next room.

K. felt as though he were entering a meeting-hall. A crowd of the most variegated people – nobody troubled about the newcomer – filled a medium-sized two-windowed room, which just below the roof was surrounded by a gallery, also quite packed, where the people were able to stand only in a bent posture with their heads and backs knocking against the ceiling. K., feeling the air too thick for him, stepped out again and said to the young woman, who seemed to have taken him up wrongly: 'I asked for a joiner, a man called Lanz.' 'I know,' said the woman, 'just go right in.' K. might not have obeyed if she had not come up to him, grasped the handle of the door, and said: 'I must shut this door after you, nobody else must come in.'

'Very sensible,' said K., 'but the room is surely too full already.' However, he went in again.

Between the two men who were talking together just inside the door – the one was making with both outstretched hands a gesture as if paying out money while the other was looking him sharply in the eye – a hand reached out and seized K. It belonged to a little red-cheeked lad. 'Come along, come along,' he said. K. let himself be led off, it seemed that in the confused, swarming crowd a slender path was kept free after all, possibly separating two different factions; in favour of this supposition was the fact that immediately to right and left of him K. saw scarcely one face looking his way, but only the backs of people who were addressing their words and gestures to the members of their own party. Most of them were dressed in black, in old, long, and loosely hanging Sunday coats. These clothes were the only thing that baffled K., otherwise he would have taken the meeting for a local political gathering.

At the other end of the hall, towards which K. was being led, there stood on a low and somewhat crowded platform a little table, set at a slant, and behind it, near the very edge of the platform, sat a fat little wheezing man who was talking with such merriment to a man sprawling just behind him with his elbow on the back of the chair and his legs crossed. That fat little man now and then flung his arms into the air, as if he were caricaturing someone. The lad who was escorting K. found it difficult to announce his presence. Twice he stood on tiptoe and tried to say something, without being noticed by the man up above. Not till one of the people on the platform pointed out the lad did the man turn to him and bend down to hear his faltered words. Then he drew out his watch and with a quick glance at K., 'You should have been here an hour and five minutes ago,' he said. K. was about to answer, but had no time to do so, for scarcely had the man spoken when a general growl of disapproval followed in the right half of the hall. 'You should have been here an hour and five minutes ago,' repeated the man in a raised voice, casting another quick glance into the body of the hall.

Immediately the muttering grew stronger and took some time to subside, even though the man said nothing more. Then it became much quieter in the hall than at K.'s entrance. Only the people in the gallery still kept up their comments. As far as one could make out in the dimness, dust, and reek, they seemed to be worse dressed than the people below. Some had brought cushions with them, which they put between their heads and the ceiling, to keep their heads from getting bruised.

K. made up his mind to observe rather than speak, consequently he offered no defence of his alleged lateness in arriving and merely said: 'Whether I am late or not, I am here now.' A burst of applause followed, once more from the right side of the hall. 'These people are easy to win over,' thought K., disturbed only by the silence in the left half of the room, which lay just behind him and from which only one or two isolated hand-claps had come. He considered what he should say to win over the whole of the audience once and for all, or if that were not possible, at least to win over most of them for the time being.

'Yes,' said the man, 'but I am no longer obliged to hear you now' – once more the muttering arose, this time unmistakable in its import, for, silencing the audience with a wave of the hand, the man went on: 'yet I shall make an exception for once on this occasion. But such a delay must not occur again. And now step forward.' Someone jumped down from the platform to make room for K., who climbed on to it. He stood crushed against the table, the crowd behind him was so great that he had to brace himself to keep from knocking the Examining Magistrate's table and perhaps the Examining Magistrate himself off the platform.

But the Examining Magistrate did not seem to worry, he sat quite comfortably in his chair and after a few final words to the man behind him took up a small note-book, the only object lying on the table. It was like an ancient school exercise-book, grown dog's-eared from much thumbing. 'Well, then,' said the Examining Magistrate, turning over the leaves and addressing K. with an air of authority, 'you are a house-painter?' 'No,' said K., 'I'm the junior manager of a large Bank.' This answer evoked such a hearty outburst of laughter from the Right party that K. had to laugh too. People doubled up with their hands on their knees and shook as if in spasms of coughing. There were even a few guffaws from the gallery. The Examining Magistrate, now indignant, and having apparently no authority to control the people in the body of the hall, proceeded to vent his displeasure on those in the gallery, springing up and scowling at them till his eyebrows, hitherto inconspicuous, contracted in great black bushes above his eyes.

The Left half of the hall, however, was still as quiet as ever, the people there stood in rows facing the platform and listened unmoved to what was going on up there as well as to the noise in the rest of the hall, indeed they actually suffered some of their members to initiate conversations with the other faction. These people of the Left party, who were not so numerous as the others, might in reality be just as unimportant, but the composure of their bearing made them appear of more consequence. As K. began his speech he was convinced that he was actually representing their point of view.

'This question of yours, Herr Examining Magistrate, about my being a house-painter – or rather, not a question, you simply made a statement – is typical of the whole character of this trial that is being foisted on me. You may object that it is not a trial at all; you are quite right, for it is only a trial if I recognize it as such. But for the moment I do recognize it, on grounds of compassion, as it were. One can't regard it except with compassion, if one is to regard it at all. I do not say that your procedure is contemptible, but I should like to present that epithet to you for your private consideration.' K. stopped and looked down into the hall. He had spoken sharply, more sharply than he had intended, but with every justification. His words should have merited applause of some kind, yet all was still, the audience were clearly waiting intently for what was to follow; perhaps in that silence an outbreak was preparing which would put an end to the whole thing. K. was annoyed when the door at the end of the hall opened at that moment, admitting the young washerwoman, who seemed to have finished her work; she distracted some of the audience in spite of all the caution with which she entered. But the Examining Magistrate himself rejoiced K.'s heart, for he seemed to be quite dismayed by the speech. Until now he had been on his feet, for he had been surprised by K.'s speech as he got up to rebuke the gallery. In this pause he resumed his seat, very slowly, as if he wished his action to escape remark. Presumably to calm his spirit, he turned over the note-book again.

'That won't help you much,' K. continued; 'your very note-book, Herr Examining Magistrate, confirms what I say.' Emboldened by the mere sound of his own cool words in that strange assembly, K. simply snatched the note-book from the Examining Magistrate and held it up with the tips of his fingers, as if it might soil his hands, by one of the middle pages, so that the closely written, blotted, yellow-edged leaves hung down on either side. 'These are the Examining Magistrate's records,' he said, letting it fall on the table again. 'You can continue reading it at your ease, Herr Examining Magistrate, I really don't fear this ledger of yours though it is a closed book to me, for I would not touch it except with my finger-tips and cannot even take it in my hand.' It could only be a sign of deep humiliation, or must at least be interpreted as such, that the Examining Magistrate now took up the note-book where it had fallen on the table, tried to put it to rights again, and once more began to read it.

The eyes of the people in the first row were so tensely fixed upon K. that for a while he stood silently looking down at them. They were without exception elderly men, some of them with white beards. Could they possibly be the influential men, the men who would carry the whole assembly with them, and did they refuse to be shocked out of the impassivity into which they had sunk ever since he began his speech, even although he had publicly humiliated the Examining Magistrate?

'What has happened to me,' K. went on, rather more quietly than before, trying at the same time to read the faces in the first row, which gave his speech a somewhat distracted effect, 'what has happened to me is only a single instance and as such of no great importance, especially as I do not take it very seriously, but it is representative of a misguided policy which is being directed against many other people as well. It is for these that I take up my stand here, not for myself.'

He had involuntarily raised his voice. Someone in the audience clapped his hands high in the air and shouted: 'Bravo! Why not? Bravo! And bravo again!' A few men in the first row pulled at their beards, but none turned round at this interruption. K., too, did not attach any importance to it, yet felt cheered nevertheless; he no longer considered it necessary to get applause from everyone, he would be quite pleased if he could make the audience start thinking about the question and win a man here and there through conviction.

'I have no wish to shine as an orator,' said K., having come to this conclusion, 'nor could I if I wished. The Herr Examining Magistrate, no doubt, is much the better speaker, it is part of his vocation. All I desire is the public ventilation of a public grievance. Listen to me. Some ten days ago I was arrested, in a manner that seems ridiculous even to myself, though that is immaterial at the moment. I was seized in bed before I could get up, perhaps – it is not unlikely, considering the Examining Magistrate's statement – perhaps they had orders to arrest some house-painter who is just as innocent as I am, only they hit on me. The room next to mine was requisitioned by two coarse warders. If I had been a dangerous bandit they could not have taken more careful precautions. These warders, moreover, were degenerate ruffians, they deafened my ears with their gabble, they tried to induce me to bribe them, they attempted to get my clothes and underclothes from me under dishonest pretexts, they asked me to give them money ostensibly to bring me some breakfast after they had brazenly eaten my own breakfast under my eyes. But that was not all. I was led into a third room to confront the Inspector. It was the room of a lady whom I deeply respect, and I had to look on while this room was polluted, yes polluted, on my account but not by any fault of mine, through the presence of these warders and this Inspector. It was not easy for me to remain calm. I succeeded, however, and I asked the Inspector with the utmost calm – if he were here, he would have to substantiate that – why I had been arrested. And what was the answer of this Inspector, whom I can see before me now as he lounged in a chair belonging to the lady I have mentioned, like an embodiment of crass arrogance? Gentlemen, he answered in effect nothing at all, perhaps he really knew nothing; he had arrested me and that was enough. But that is not all, he had brought three minor employees of my Bank into the lady's room, who amused themselves by fingering and disarranging certain photographs, the property of the lady. The presence of these employees had another object as well, of course, they were expected, like my landlady and her maid, to spread the news of my arrest, damage my public reputation, and in particular shake my position in the Bank. Well, this expectation has entirely failed of its success, even my landlady, a quite simple person – I pronounce her name in all honour, she is called Frau Grubach – even Frau Grubach has been intelligent enough to recognize that an arrest such as this is no more worth taking seriously than some wild prank committed by stray urchins at the street corners. I repeat, the whole matter has caused me nothing but some unpleasantness and passing annoyance, but might it not have had worse consequences?'

When K. stopped at this point and glanced at the silent Examining Magistrate, he thought he could see him catching someone's eye in the audience, as if giving a sign. K. smiled and said: 'The Herr Examining Magistrate sitting here beside me has just given one of you a secret sign. So there are some among you who take your instructions from up here. I do not know whether the sign was meant to evoke applause or hissing, and now that I have divulged the matter prematurely I deliberately give up all hope of ever learning its real significance. It is a matter of complete indifference to me, and I publicly empower the Herr Examining Magistrate to address his hired agents in so many words, instead of making secret signs to them, to say at the proper moment: Hiss now, or alternatively: Clap now.'

The Examining Magistrate kept fidgeting on his chair with

embarrassment or impatience. The man behind him to whom he had been talking bent over him again, either to encourage him or to give him some particular counsel. Down below, the people in the audience were talking in low voices but with animation. The two factions who had seemed previously to be irreconcilable were now drifting together, some individuals were pointing their fingers at K., others at the Examining Magistrate. The fuggy atmosphere in the room was unbearable, it actually prevented one from seeing the people at the other end. It must have been particularly inconvenient for the spectators in the gallery, who were forced to question the members of the audience in a low voice, with fearful side-glances at the Examining Magistrate, to find out what was happening. The answers were given as furtively, the informant generally putting his hand to his mouth to muffle his words.

'I have nearly finished,' said K., striking the table with his fist, since there was no bell. At the shock of the impact the heads of the Examining Magistrate and his adviser started away from each other for a moment. 'I am quite detached from this affair, I can therefore judge it calmly, and you, that is to say if you take this alleged court of justice at all seriously, will find it to your great advantage to listen to me. But I beg you to postpone until later any comments you may wish to exchange on what I have to say, for I am pressed for time and must leave very soon.'

At once there was silence, so completely did K. already dominate the meeting. The audience no longer shouted confusedly as at the beginning, they did not even applaud, they seemed already convinced or on the verge of being convinced.

'There can be no doubt –' said K., quite softly, for he was elated by the breathless attention of the meeting; in that stillness a subdued hum was audible which was more exciting than the wildest applause – 'there can be no doubt that behind all the actions of this court of justice, that is to say in my case, behind my arrest and today's interrogation, there is a great organization at work. An organization which not only employs corrupt warders, stupid Inspectors, and Examining Magistrates of whom the best that can be said is that they recognize their own limitations, but also has at its disposal a judicial hierarchy of high, indeed of the highest rank, with an indispensable and numerous retinue of servants, clerks, police, and other assistants, perhaps even hangmen, I do not shrink from that word. And the significance of this great organization, gentlemen? It consists in this, that innocent persons are accused of guilt, and senseless proceedings are put in motion against them, mostly without effect, it is true, as in my own case. But considering the senselessness of the whole, how is it possible for the higher ranks to prevent gross corruption in their agents? It is impossible. Even the highest Judge in this organization will have to admit corruption in his court. So the warders try to steal the clothes off the bodies of the people they arrest, the Inspectors break into strange houses, and innocent men, instead of being fairly examined, are humiliated in the presence of public assemblies. The warders mentioned certain depots where the property of prisoners is kept; I should like to see these depots where the hard-earned property of arrested men is left to rot, or at least what remains of it after thieving officials have helped themselves.'

Here K. was interrupted by a shriek from the end of the hall; he peered from beneath his hand to see what was happening, for the reek of the room and the dim light together made a whitish dazzle of fog. It was the washerwoman, whom K. had recognized as a potential cause of disturbance from the moment of her entrance. Whether she was at fault now or not, one could not tell. All K. could see was that a man had drawn her into a corner by the door and was clasping her in his arms. Yet it was not she who had uttered the shriek but the man; his mouth was wide open and he was gazing up at the ceiling. A little circle had formed round them, the gallery spectators nearby seemed to be delighted that the seriousness which K. had introduced into the proceedings should be dispelled in this manner. K.'s first impulse was to rush across the room, he naturally imagined that everybody would be anxious to have order restored and the offending couple at least ejected from the meeting, but the first rows of the audience remained quite impassive, no one stirred and no one would let him through. On the contrary they actually obstructed him, someone's hand – he had no time to turn round – seized him from behind by the collar, old men stretched out their arms to bar his way, and by this time K. was no longer thinking about the couple, it seemed to him as if his freedom were being threatened, as if he were being arrested in earnest, and he sprang recklessly down from the platform. Now he stood eye to eye with the crowd. Had he been mistaken in these people? Had he overestimated the effectiveness of his speech? Had they been disguising their real opinions while he spoke, and now that he had come to the conclusion of his speech were they weary at last of pretence? What faces these were around him! Their little black eyes darted furtively from side to side, their beards were stiff and brittle, and to take hold of them would be like clutching bunches of claws rather than beards. But under the beards – and this was K.'s real discovery – badges of various sizes and colours gleamed on their coat-collars. They all wore these badges, so far as he could see. They were all colleagues, these ostensible parties of the Right and the Left, and as he turned round suddenly he saw the same badges on the coat-collar of the Examining Magistrate, who was sitting quietly watching the scene with his hands on his knees. 'So!' cried K., flinging his arms in the air, his sudden enlightenment had to break out, 'every man jack of you is an official, I see, you are yourselves the corrupt agents of whom I have been speaking, you've all come rushing here to listen and nose out what you can about me, making a pretence of party divisions, and half of you applauded merely to lead me on, you wanted some practice in fooling an innocent man. Well, much good I hope it's done you, for either you have merely gathered some amusement from the fact that I expected you to defend the innocent or else – keep off or I'll strike you,' cried K. to a trembling old man who had pushed quite close to him – 'or else you have really learned a thing or two. And I wish you joy of your trade.' He hastily seized his hat, which lay near the edge of the table, and amid universal silence, the silence of complete stupefaction, if nothing else, pushed his way to the door. But the Examining Magistrate seemed to have been still quicker than K., for he was waiting at the door. 'A moment,' he said. K. paused but kept his eyes on the door, not on the Examining Magistrate; his hand was already on the latch. 'I merely wanted to point out,' said the Examining Magistrate, 'that today – you may not yet have become aware of the fact – today you have flung away with your own hand all the advantages which an interrogation invariably confers on an accused man.' K. laughed, still looking at the door. 'You scoundrels, I'll give you all an interrogation yet,' he shouted, opened the door, and hurried down the stairs. Behind him rose the buzz of animated discussion, the audience had apparently come to life again and were analysing the situation like expert students.

3

IN THE EMPTY INTERROGATION CHAMBER – THE STUDENT – THE OFFICES

During the next week K. waited day after day for a new summons, he would not believe that his refusal to be interrogated had been taken literally, and when no appointment was made by Saturday evening, he assumed that he was tacitly expected to report himself again at the same address and at the same time. So he betook himself there on Sunday morning, and this time went straight up through the passages and stairways; a few people who remembered him greeted him from their doors, but he no longer needed to inquire of anybody and soon came to the right door. It opened at once to his knock, and without even turning his head to look at the woman, who remained standing beside the door, he made straight for the adjoining room. 'There's no sitting today,' said the woman. 'Why is there no sitting?' he asked; he could not believe it. But the woman convinced him by herself opening the door of the next room. It was really empty and in its emptiness looked even more sordid than on the previous Sunday. On the table, which still stood on the platform as before, several books were lying. 'May I glance at the books?' asked K., not out of any particular curiosity, but merely that his visit here might not be quite pointless. 'No,' said the woman, shutting the door again, 'that isn't allowed. The books belong to the Examining Magistrate.' 'I see,' said K., nodding, 'these books are probably law books, and it is an essential part of the justice dispensed here that you should be condemned not only in innocence but also in ignorance.' 'That must be it,' said the woman, who had not quite understood him. 'Well, in that case I had better go again,' said K. 'Shall I give the Examining Magistrate a message?' asked the woman. 'Do you know him?' asked K. 'Of course,' replied the woman, 'my husband is the Law-Court Attendant, you see.' Only then did K. notice that the ante-room, which had contained nothing but a washtub last Sunday, now formed a fully furnished living-room. The woman remarked his surprise and said: 'Yes, we have free house-room here, but we must clear the room on the days when the Court is sitting. My husband's post has many disadvantages.' 'I'm not so much surprised at the room,' said K., looking at her severely, 'as at the fact that you're married.' 'Perhaps you're hinting at what happened during the last sitting, when I caused a disturbance while you were speaking,' said the woman. 'Of course I am,' said K. 'It's an old story by this time, and almost forgotten, but at the moment it made me quite furious. And now you say yourself that you're a married woman.' 'It didn't do you any harm to have your speech interrupted; what you said made a bad enough impression, to judge from the discussion afterwards.' 'That may be,' said K., refusing to be deflected, 'but it does not excuse you.' 'I stand excused in the eyes of everyone who knows me,' said the woman. 'The man you saw embracing me has been persecuting me for a long time. I may not be a temptation to most men, but I am to him. There's no way of keeping him off, even my husband has grown reconciled to it now; if he isn't to lose his job he must put up with it, for that man you saw is one of the students and will probably rise to great power yet. He's always after me, he was here today, just before you came.'

'It all hangs together,' said K., 'it doesn't surprise me.' 'You are anxious to improve things here, I think,' said the woman slowly and watchfully, as if she were saying something which was risky both to her and to K. 'I guessed that from your speech, which personally I liked very much. Though, of course, I only heard part of it, I missed the beginning and I was down on the floor with the student while you were finishing. It's so horrible here,' she said after a pause, taking K.'s hand. 'Do you think you'll manage to improve things?' K. smiled and twisted his hand round within her soft fingers. 'Actually,' he said, 'it isn't my place to improve things here, as you put it, and if you were to tell the Examining Magistrate so, let us say, he would either laugh at you or have you punished. As a matter of fact, I should never have dreamed of interfering of my own free will, and shouldn't have lost an hour's sleep over the need for reforming the machinery of justice here. But the fact that I am supposed to be under arrest forces me to intervene – I am under arrest, you know – to protect my own interests. But if I can help you in any way at the same time, I shall be very glad, of course. And not out of pure altruism, either, for you in turn might be able to help me.' 'How could I do that?' asked the woman. 'By letting me look at the books on the table there, for instance.' 'But of course!' cried the woman, dragging him hastily after her. They were old dog-eared volumes, the cover of one was almost completely split down the middle, the two halves were held together by mere threads. 'How dirty everything is here!' said K., shaking his head, and the woman had to wipe away the worst of the dust with her apron before K. would put out his hand to touch the books. He opened the first of them and found an indecent picture. A man and a woman were sitting naked on a sofa, the obscene intention of the draughtsman was evident enough, yet his skill was so small that nothing emerged from the picture save the all-too-solid figures of a man and a woman sitting rigidly upright, and because of the bad perspective, apparently finding the utmost difficulty even in turning towards each other. K. did not look at any of the other pages, but merely glanced at the title-page of the second book, it was a novel entitled: *How Grete was Plagued by her Husband Hans*. 'These are the law books that are studied here,' said K. 'These are the men who are supposed to sit in judgement on me.' 'I'll help you,' said the woman. 'Would you like me to?' 'Could you really do that without getting yourself into trouble? You told me a moment ago that your husband is quite at the mercy of the higher officials.' 'I want to help you, all the same,' said the woman. 'Come, let us talk it over. Don't bother about the danger to me. I only fear danger when I want to fear it. Come.' She settled herself on the edge of the platform and made room for him beside her. 'You have lovely dark eyes,' she said, after they had sat down, looking up into K.'s face. 'I've been told that I have lovely eyes too, but yours are far lovelier. I was greatly struck by you as soon as I saw you, the first time you came here. And it was because of you that I slipped later into the meeting-hall, a thing I never usually do and which, in a manner of speaking, I am actually forbidden to do.' 'So this is all it amounts to,' thought K., 'she's offering herself to me, she's corrupt like the rest of them, she's tired of the officials here, which is understandable enough, and accosts any stranger who takes her fancy with compliments about his eyes.' And K. rose to his feet as if he had uttered his thoughts aloud and sufficiently explained his position. 'I don't think that could help me,' he said; 'to help me effectively one would need connexions with the higher officials. But I'm sure you know only the petty subordinates that swarm round here. You must know them quite well and could get them to do a lot, I don't doubt, but the utmost that they could do would have no effect whatever on the final result of the case. And you would simply have alienated some of your friends. I don't want that. Keep your friendship with these people, for it seems to me that you need it. I say this with regret, since to make some return for your compliment I must confess that I like you too, especially when you gaze at me with such sorrowful eyes, as you are doing now, though I assure you there's no reason whatever for it. Your place is among the people I have to fight, but you're quite at home there, you love this student, no doubt, or if you don't love him at least you prefer him to your husband. It's easy to tell that from what you say.' 'No,' she cried without getting up but merely catching hold of K.'s hand, which he did not withdraw quickly enough. 'You mustn't go away yet, you mustn't go with mistaken ideas about me. Could you really bring yourself to go away like that? Am I really of so little account in your eyes that you won't even do me the kindness of staying for a little longer?' 'You misunderstand me,' said K., sitting down, 'if you really want me to stay I'll stay with pleasure, I have time enough; I came here expecting to find the Court in session. All that I meant was merely to beg you not to do anything for me in this case of mine. But that needn't offend you when you consider that I don't care at all what the outcome of the case is, and that I would only laugh at it if I were sentenced. Assuming, that is, that the case will ever come to a proper conclusion, which I very much doubt. Indeed, I fancy that it has probably been dropped already or will soon be dropped, through the laziness or the forgetfulness or it may be even through the fears of those who are responsible for it. Of course it's possible that they will make a show of carrying it on, in the hope of getting money out of me, but they needn't bother, I can tell you now, for I shall never bribe anyone. That's something you could really do for me, however; you could inform the Examining Magistrate, or anyone who could be depended on to spread the news, that nothing will induce me to bribe these officials, not even any of the artifices in which they are doubtless so ingenious. The attempt would be quite hopeless, you can tell them that frankly. But perhaps they have come to that conclusion already, and even if they haven't, I don't much mind whether they get the information or not. It would merely save them some trouble and me, of course, some unpleasantness, but I should gladly endure any unpleasantness that meant a set-back for them. And I shall take good care to see that it does. By the way, do you really know the Examining Magistrate?' 'Of course,' said the woman. 'He was the first one I thought of when I offered you my help. I didn't know that he was only a petty official, but as you say so it must naturally be true. All the same. I fancy that the reports he sends up to the higher officials have some influence. And he writes out so many reports. You say that the officials are lazy, but that certainly doesn't apply to all of them, particularly to the Examining Magistrate, he's always writing. Last Sunday, for instance, the session lasted till late in the evening. All the others left, but the Examining Magistrate stayed on in the court-room, I had to bring a lamp for him, I only had a small kitchen lamp, but that was all he needed and he began to write straight away. In the meantime my husband came home, he was off duty on that particular Sunday, we carried back our furniture, set our room to rights again, then some neighbours arrived, we talked on by candlelight, to tell the truth we simply forgot the Examining Magistrate and went to bed. Suddenly, in the middle of the night, it must have been far into the night by then, I woke up, the Examining Magistrate was standing beside our bed shielding the lamp with his hand to keep the light from falling on my husband, a needless precaution, for my husband sleeps so soundly that not even the light would have wakened him. I was so startled that I almost cried out, but the Examining Magistrate was very kind, warned me to be careful, whispered to me that he had been writing till then, that he had come to return the lamp, and that he would never forget the picture I had made lying asleep in my bed. I only tell you this to show that the Examining Magistrate is kept really busy writing reports, especially about you, for your interrogation was certainly one of the main items in the two days' session. Such long reports as that surely can't be quite unimportant. But besides that you can guess from what happened that the Examining Magistrate is beginning to take an interest in me, and that at this early stage – for he must have noticed me then for the first time – I could have great influence with him. And by this time I have other proofs that he is anxious to win my favour. Yesterday he sent me a pair of silk stockings through the student, who works with him and whom he is very friendly with, making out that it was a reward for cleaning the court-room, but that was only an excuse, for to do that is only my duty and my husband is supposed to be paid for it. They're beautiful stockings, look' – she stretched out her legs, pulled her skirts above her knees, and herself contemplated the stockings – 'they're beautiful stockings, but too fine, all the same, and not suitable for a woman like me.'

Suddenly she broke off, laid her hand on K.'s hand as if to reassure him, and said: 'Hush, Bertold is watching us.' K. slowly raised his eyes. In the door of the court-room a young man was standing, he was small, his legs were slightly bowed, and he strove to add dignity to his appearance by wearing a short, straggling reddish beard, which he was always fingering. K. stared at him with interest, this was the first student of the mysterious judicature whom he had encountered, as it were, on human terms, a man, too, who would presumably attain to one of the higher official positions some day. The student, however, seemed to take not the slightest notice of K., he merely made a sign to the woman with one finger, which he withdrew for a moment from his beard, and went over to the window. The woman bent over K., and whispered: 'Don't be angry with me, please don't think badly of me, I must go to him now, and he's a dreadful-looking creature, just see what bandy legs he has. But I'll come back in a minute and then I'll go with you if you'll take me with you, I'll go with you wherever you like, you can do with me what you please. I'll be glad if I can only get out of here for a long time, and I wish it could be for ever.' She gave K.'s hand a last caress, jumped up, and ran to the window. Despite himself K.'s hand reached out after hers in the empty air. The woman really attracted him, and after mature reflection he could find no valid reason why he should not yield to that attraction. He dismissed without difficulty the fleeting suspicion that she might be trying to lay a trap for him on the instructions of the Court. In what way could she entrap him? Wasn't he still free enough to flout the authority of this Court once and for all, at least as far as it concerned him? Could he not trust himself to this trifling extent? And her offer of help had sounded sincere and was probably not altogether worthless. And probably there could be no more fitting revenge on the Examining Magistrate and his henchman than to wrest this woman from them and take her himself. Then some night the Examining Magistrate, after long and arduous labour on his lying reports about K., might come to the woman's bed and find it empty. Empty because she had gone off with K., because the woman now standing in the window, that supple, voluptuous warm body under the dark dress of rough material, belonged to K. and to K. alone.

After arguing himself in this way out of his suspicions, he began to feel that the whispered conversation in the window was going on too long, and started knocking on the table with his knuckles and then with his fist. The student glanced briefly at K. across the woman's shoulder, but did not let himself be put out, indeed moved closer to her and put his arms around her. She drooped her head as if attentively listening to him, and as she did so he kissed her loudly on the throat without at all interrupting his remarks. In this action K. saw confirmed the tyranny which the student exercised over the woman, as she had complained, and he sprang to his feet and began to pace up and down the room. With occasional side-glances at the student he meditated how to get rid of him as quickly as possible, and so it was not unwelcome to him when the fellow, obviously annoyed by his walking up and down, which had turned by now to an angry trampling, said: 'If you're so impatient, you can go away. There was nothing to hinder your going long ago, nobody would have missed you. In fact, it was your duty to go away, and as soon as I came in too, and as fast as your legs would carry you.' There was intense rage in these words, but there was also the insolence of a future official of the Court addressing an abhorrent prisoner. K. stepped up quite close to the student and said with a smile: 'I am impatient, that is true, but the easiest way to relieve my impatience would be for you to leave us. Yet if by any chance you have come here to study – I hear that you're a student – I'll gladly vacate the room and go away with this woman. I fancy you've a long way to go yet in your studies before you can become a Judge. I admit I'm not very well versed in the niceties of your legal training, but I assume that it doesn't consist exclusively in learning to make rude remarks, at which you seem to have attained a shameless proficiency.' 'He shouldn't have been allowed to run around at large,' said the student, as if seeking to explain K.'s insulting words to the woman. 'It was a mistake, I told the Examining Magistrate that. He should at least have been confined to his room between the interrogations. There are times when I simply don't understand the Examining Magistrate.' 'What's the use of talking?' said K., stretching out his hand to the woman. 'Come along.' 'Ah, that's it,' said the student, 'no, no, you don't get her,' and with a strength which one would not have believed him capable of he lifted her in one arm and, gazing up at her tenderly, ran, stooping a little beneath his burden, to the door. A certain fear of K. was unmistakable in this action, and yet he risked infuriating K. further by caressing and clasping the woman's arm with his free hand. K. ran a few steps after him, ready to seize and if necessary to throttle him, when the woman said: 'It's no use, the Examining Magistrate has sent for me, I daren't go with you; this little monster,' she patted the student's face, 'this little monster won't let me go.' 'And you don't want to be set free,' cried K., laying his hand on the shoulder of the student, who snapped at it with his teeth. 'No,' cried the woman, pushing K. away with both hands. 'No, no, you mustn't do that, what are you thinking of? It would be the ruin of me. Let him go, oh, please let him go! He's only obeying the orders of the Examining Magistrate and carrying me to him.' 'Then let him go, and as for you, I never want to see you again,' said K., furious with disappointment, and he gave the student a punch in the back that made him stumble for a moment, only to spring off more nimbly than ever out of relief that he had not fallen. K. slowly walked after them, he recognized that this was the first unequivocal defeat that he had received from these people. There was no reason, of course, for him to worry about that, he had received the defeat only because he had insisted on giving battle. While he stayed quietly at home and went about his ordinary vocations he remained superior to all these people and could clear any of them out of his path with a hearty kick. And he pictured to himself the highly comic situation which would arise if, for instance, this wretched student, this puffed-up hobble-dehoy, this bandy-legged twiddle-beard, had to kneel by Elsa's bed some day wringing his hands and begging for favours. This picture pleased K. so much that he decided, if ever the opportunity came, to take the student along to visit Elsa.

Out of curiosity K. hurried to the door, he wanted to see where the woman was being carried off to, for the student could scarcely bear her in his arms across the street. But the journey was much shorter than that. Immediately opposite the door a flight of narrow wooden stairs led, as it seemed, to a garret, it had a turning so that one could not see the other end. The student was now carrying the woman up this stairway, very slowly, puffing and groaning, for he was beginning to be exhausted. The woman waved her hand to K. as he stood below, and shrugged her shoulders to suggest that she was not to blame for this abduction, but very little reluctance could be read into that dumb show. K. looked at her expressionlessly, as if she were a stranger, he was resolved not to betray to her either that he was disappointed or even that he could not easily get over any disappointment he might feel.

The two had already vanished, yet K. still stood in the doorway. He was forced to the conclusion that the woman not only had betrayed him, but had also lied in saying that she was being carried to the Examining Magistrate. The Examining Magistrate surely could not be sitting waiting in a garret. The little wooden stairway did not reveal anything, no matter how long one regarded it. But K. noticed a small card pinned up beside it, and crossing over he read in childish, unpractised handwriting: 'Law-Court Offices upstairs.' So the Law-Court offices were up in the attics of this tenement? That was not an arrangement likely to inspire much respect, and for an accused man it was reassuring to reckon how little money this Court could have at its disposal when it housed its offices in a part of the building where the tenants, who themselves belonged to the poorest of the poor, flung their useless lumber. Though, of course, the possibility was not to be ignored that the money was abundant enough, but that the officials pocketed it before it could be used for the purposes of justice. To judge from K.'s experience hitherto, that was indeed extremely probable, yet if it were so, such disreputable practices, while certainly humiliating to an accused man, suggested more hope for him than a merely pauperized condition of the Law Courts. Now K. could understand too why in the beginning they had been ashamed to summon him into their attics and had chosen instead to molest him in his lodgings. And how well-off K. was compared with the Magistrate, who had to sit in a garret, while K. had a large room in the Bank with a waiting-room attached to it and could watch the busy life of the city through his enormous plate-glass window. True, he drew no secondary income from bribes or peculation and could not order his attendant to pick up a woman and carry her to his room. But K. was perfectly willing to renounce these advantages, at least in this life.

K. was still standing beside the card when a man came up from below, looked into the room through the open door, from which he could also see the court-room, and then asked K. if he had seen a woman about anywhere. 'You are the Law-Court Attendant, aren't you?' asked K. 'Yes,' said the man. 'Oh, you're the defendant K., now I recognize you, you're welcome.' And he held out his hand to K., who had not expected that. 'But no sitting was announced for today,' the Law-Court Attendant went on, as K. remained silent. 'I know,' said K., gazing at the Attendant's civilian clothes, which displayed on the jacket, as the sole emblem of his office, two gilt buttons in addition to the ordinary ones, gilt buttons that looked as if they had been stripped from an old army coat. 'I was speaking to your wife a moment ago. She's not here now. The student has carried her up to the Examining Magistrate.' 'There you are,' said the Attendant, 'they're always carrying her away from me. Today is Sunday too, I'm not supposed to do any work, but simply to get me away from the place they sent me out on a useless errand. And they took care not to send me too far away, so that I had some hopes of being able to get back in time if I hurried. And there was I running as fast as I could, shouting the message through the half-open door of the office I was sent to, nearly breathless so that they could hardly make me out, and back again at top speed, and yet the student was here before me, he hadn't so far to come, of course, he had only to cut down that short wooden staircase from the attics. If my job didn't depend on it, I would have squashed that student flat against the wall long ago. Just beside this card. It's a daily dream of mine. I see him squashed flat here, just a little above the floor, his arms wide, his fingers spread, his bandy legs writhing in a circle, and splashes of blood all round. But so far it's only been a dream.' 'Is there no other remedy?' asked K., smiling. 'Not that I know of,' said the Law-Court Attendant. 'And now it's getting worse than ever, up till now he has been carrying her off for his own pleasure, but now, as I've been expecting for a long time, I may say, he's carrying her to the Examining Magistrate as well.' 'But isn't your wife to blame too?' asked K., he had to keep a grip of himself while asking this, he still felt so jealous. 'But of course,' said the Law-Court Attendant, 'she's actually most to blame of all. She simply flung herself at him. As for him, he runs after every woman he sees. In this building alone he's already been thrown out of five flats he managed to insinuate himself into. And my wife is the best-looking woman in the whole tenement, and I'm in a position where I can't defend myself.' 'If that's how things stand, then there's no help, it seems,' said K. 'And why not?' asked the Law-Court Attendant. 'If he only got a good thrashing some time when he was after my wife – he's a coward, anyway – he would never dare to do it again. But I can't thrash him, and nobody else will oblige me by doing it, for they're all afraid of him, he's too influential. Only a man like you could do it.' 'But why a man like me?' asked K. in astonishment. 'You're under arrest, aren't you?' said the Law-Court Attendant. 'Yes,' said K., 'and that means I have all the more reason to fear him, for though he may not be able to influence the outcome of the case, he can probably influence the preliminary interrogations.' 'Yes, that's so,' said the Law-Court Attendant, as if K.'s view of the matter were as self-evident as his own. 'Yet as a rule none of our cases can be looked on as prejudiced.' 'I am not of that opinion,' said K., 'but that needn't prevent me from taking the student in hand.' 'I should be very thankful to you,' said the Law-Court Attendant rather formally; he did not appear really to believe that his heart's desire could be fulfilled. 'It may be,' K. went on, 'that some more of your officials, probably all of them, deserve the same treatment.' 'Oh yes,' said the Law-Court Attendant, as if he were assenting to a commonplace. Then he gave K. a confidential look, such as he had not yet ventured in spite of all his friendliness, and added: 'A man can't help being rebellious.' But the conversation seemed to have made him uneasy, all the same, for he broke it off by saying: 'I must report upstairs now. Would you like to come too?' 'I have no business there,' said K. 'You can have a look at the offices. Nobody will pay any attention to you.' 'Why, are they worth seeing?' asked K. hesitatingly, but suddenly feeling a great desire to go. 'Well,' said the Law-Court Attendant, 'I thought it might interest you.' 'Good,' said K. at last, 'I'll come with you.' And he ran up the stairs even more quickly than the Attendant.

On entering he almost stumbled, for behind the door there was an extra step. 'They don't show much consideration for the public,' he said. 'They show no consideration of any kind,' replied the Law-Court Attendant. 'Just look at this waiting-room.' It was a long passage, a lobby communicating by roughly hewn doors with the different offices on the floor. Although there was no window to admit light, it was not entirely dark, for some of the offices were not properly boarded off from the passage but had an open frontage of wooden rails, reaching, however, to the roof, through which a little light penetrated and through which one could see a few clerks as well, some writing at their desks, and some standing close to the rails peering through the interstices at the people in the lobby. There were only a few people in the lobby, probably because it was Sunday. They made a very modest showing. At almost regular intervals they were sitting singly along a row of wooden benches fixed to either side of the passage. All of them were shabbily dressed, though to judge from the expression of their faces, their bearing, the cut of their beards, and many almost imperceptible little details, they obviously belonged to the upper classes. As there was no hat-rack in the passage, they had placed their hats under the benches, in this probably following each other's example. When those who were sitting nearest the door caught sight of K. and the Law-Court Attendant, they rose in acknowledgement, followed in turn by their neighbours, who also seemed to think it necessary to rise, so that everyone stood as the two men passed. They did not stand quite erect, their backs remained bowed, their knees bent, they stood like street beggars. K. waited for the Law-Court Attendant, who kept slightly behind him, and said: 'How humbled they must be!' 'Yes,' said the Law-Court Attendant, 'these are the accused men, all of them are accused of guilt.' 'Indeed!' said K. 'Then they're colleagues of mine.' And he turned to the nearest, a tall, slender, almost grey-haired man. 'What are you waiting here for?' asked K. courteously. But this unexpected question confused the man, which was the more deeply embarrassing as he was obviously a man of the world who would have known how to comport himself anywhere else and would not lightly have renounced his natural superiority. Yet in this place he did not know even how to reply to a simple question and gazed at the other clients as if it were their duty to help him, as if no one could expect him to answer should help not be forthcoming. Then the Law-Court Attendant stepped up and said, to reassure the man and encourage him: 'This gentleman merely asked what you are waiting for. Come, give him an answer.' The familiar voice of the Law-Court Attendant had its effect: 'I'm waiting –' the man started to say, but could get out no more. He had previously begun by intending to make an exact reply to the question but did not know how to go on. Some of the other clients had drifted up and now clustered round, and the Law-Court Attendant said to them: 'Off with you, keep the passage clear.' They drew back a little, but not to their former places. Meanwhile the man had collected himself and actually replied with a faint smile: 'A month ago I handed in several affidavits concerning my case and I am waiting for the result.' 'You seem to put yourself to a great deal of trouble,' said K. 'Yes,' said the man, 'for it is my case.' 'Everyone doesn't think as you do,' said K. 'For example, I am under arrest too, but as sure as I stand here I have neither put in any affidavit nor attempted anything whatever of the kind. Do you consider such things necessary, then?' 'I can't exactly say,' replied the man, once more deprived of all assurance; he evidently thought that K. was making fun of him, and appeared to be on the point of repeating his first answer all over again for fear of making a new mistake, but under K.'s impatient eye he merely said: 'Anyhow, I have handed in my affidavits.' 'Perhaps you don't believe that I am under arrest?' asked K. 'Oh yes, certainly,' said the man, stepping somewhat aside, but there was no belief in his answer, merely apprehension. 'So you don't really believe me?' asked K. and, provoked without knowing it by the man's humility, he seized him by the arm as if to compel him to believe. He had no wish to hurt him, and besides had grasped him quite loosely, yet the man cried out as if K. had gripped him with glowing pincers instead of with two fingers. That ridiculous outcry was too much for K.; if the man would not believe that he was under arrest, so much the better; perhaps he actually took him for a Judge. As a parting gesture he gripped the man with real force, flung him back on the bench, and went on his way. 'Most of these accused men are so sensitive,' said the Law-Court Attendant. Behind them almost all the clients were now gathered round the man, whose cries had already ceased, and they seemed to be eagerly asking him about the incident. A warder came up to K., he was mainly recognizable by his sword, whose sheath, at least to judge from its colour, was of aluminium. K. gaped at it and actually put out his hand to feel it. The warder, who had come to inquire into the commotion, asked what had happened. The Law-Court Attendant tried to put him off with a few words, but the warder declared that he must look into this matter himself, saluted, and strutted on with hasty but very short steps, probably resulting from gout.

K. did not trouble his head for long over him and the people in the lobby, particularly as, when he had walked half-way down the lobby, he saw a turning leading to the right through an opening which had no door. He inquired of the Law-Court Attendant if this was the right way, the Law-Court Attendant nodded, and K. then turned into it. It troubled him that he had always to walk one or two paces ahead of the Law-Court Attendant, in a place like this it might look as if he were a prisoner under escort. Accordingly he paused several times to wait for the Law-Court Attendant, but the man always dropped behind again. At last K. said, to put an end to his discomfort: 'I've seen the place now, and I think I'll go.' 'You haven't seen everything yet,' said the Law-Court Attendant innocently. 'I don't want to see everything,' said K., who by now felt really tired. 'I want to get away, how does one reach the outside door?' 'You surely haven't lost your way already?' asked the Law-Court Attendant in surprise. 'You just go along here to the corner and then turn to the right along the lobby straight to the door.' 'You come too,' said K. 'Show me the way, there are so many lobbies here, I'll never find the way.' 'There's only the one way,' said the Law-Court Attendant reproachfully. 'I can't go back with you, I must deliver my message and I've lost a great deal of time through you already.' 'Come with me,' said K. still more sharply, as if he had at last caught the Law-Court Attendant in a falsehood. 'Don't shout like that,' whispered the Law-Court Attendant, 'there are offices everywhere hereabouts. If you don't want to go back by yourself, then come a little farther with me, or wait here until I've delivered my message, then I'll be glad to take you back.' 'No, no,' said K., 'I won't wait and you must come with me now.' K. had not yet even glanced round the place where he was, and only when one of the many wooden doors opened did he turn his head. A girl whose attention must have been caught by K.'s raised voice appeared and asked: 'What does the gentleman want?' A good way behind her he could also see a male figure approaching in the half-light. K. looked at the Law-Court Attendant. The man had said that nobody would pay any attention to him, and now two people were already after him, it wouldn't take much to bring all the officials down on him, demanding an explanation of his presence. The only comprehensible and acceptable one was that he was an accused man and wished to know the date of his next interrogation, but that explanation he did not wish to give, especially as it was not even in accordance with the truth, for he had come only out of curiosity or, what was still more impossible as an explanation of his presence, out of a desire to assure himself that the inside of this legal system was just as loathsome as its external aspect. And it seemed, indeed, that he had been right in that assumption, he did not want to make any further investigation, he was dejected enough by what he had already seen, he was not at that moment in a fit state to confront any higher official such as might appear from behind one of these doors, he wanted to quit the place with the Attendant, or, if need be, alone.

But his dumb immobility must make him conspicuous, and the girl and the Law-Court Attendant were actually gazing at him as if they expected some immense transformation to happen to him the next moment, a transformation which they did not want to miss. And at the end of the passage now stood the man whom K. had noticed before in the distance; he was holding on to the lintel of the low doorway and rocking lightly on his toes, like an eager spectator. But the girl was the first to see that K.'s behaviour was really caused by a slight feeling of faintness; she produced a chair and asked: 'Won't you sit down?' K. sat down at once and leaned his elbows on the arms of the chair so as to support himself still more securely. 'You feel a little dizzy, don't you?' she asked. Her face was close to him now, it had that severe look which the faces of many women have in the first flower of their youth. 'Don't worry,' she said. 'That's nothing out of the common here, almost everybody has an attack of that kind the first time they come here. This is your first visit? Well, then, it's nothing to be surprised at. The sun beats on the roof here and the hot roof-beams make the air dull and heavy. That makes this place not particularly suitable for offices, in spite of the other great advantages it has. But the air, well, on days when there's a great number of clients to be attended to, and that's almost every day, it's hardly breathable. When you consider, too, that all sorts of washing are hung up here to dry – you can't wholly prohibit the tenants from washing their dirty linen – you won't find it surprising that you should feel a little faint. But in the end one gets quite used to it. By the time you've come twice or thrice you'll hardly notice how oppressive it is here. Do you really feel better now?' K. did not answer, he realized too painfully the shame of being delivered into the hands of these people by his sudden weakness; besides, even now that he knew the cause of the faintness, it did not get any better but grew somewhat worse instead. The girl noticed this at once, and to help K. seized a bar with a hook at the end that leaned against the wall and opened with it a little skylight just above K. to let in the fresh air. Yet so much soot fell in that she had to close the skylight again at once and wipe K.'s hands clean with her handkerchief, since K. was too far gone to attend to himself. He would have preferred to sit quietly there until he recovered enough strength to walk away, yet the less he was bothered by these people the sooner he would recover. But now the girl said: 'You can't stay here, we're causing an obstruction here' – K. glanced round inquiringly to see what he could be obstructing – 'if you like, I'll take you to the sick-room. Please give me a hand,' she said to the man standing in the door, who at once came over. But K. had no wish to go to the sick-room, he particularly wanted to avoid being taken any farther, the farther he went the worse it must be for him. 'I'm quite able to go away now,' he said and got up from his comfortable seat, which had relaxed him so that he trembled as he stood. But he could not hold himself upright. 'I can't manage it after all,' he said, shaking his head, and with a sigh sat down again. He thought of the Law-Court Attendant, who could easily get him out of the place in spite of his weakness, but he seemed to have vanished long ago. K. peered between the girl and the man standing before him, but could see no sign of the Law-Court Attendant.

'I fancy,' said the man, who was stylishly dressed and was wearing a conspicuously smart grey waistcoat ending in two long sharp points, 'that the gentleman's faintness is due to the atmosphere here, and the best thing to do – and what he would like best – is not to take him to the sick-room at all, but out of these offices altogether.' 'That's it!' cried K., in his excessive joy almost breaking into the man's words, 'I should feel better at once, I'm sure of it, I'm not so terribly weak either, I only need a little support under my arms, I won't give you much trouble, it isn't very far after all, just take me to the door, then I'll sit for a little on the stairs and recover in no time, for I don't usually suffer from these attacks, I was surprised myself by this one. I am an official too and accustomed to office air, but this is really more than one can bear, you said so yourselves. Will you have the goodness, then, to let me lean upon you a little, for I feel dizzy and my head goes round when I try to stand up by myself.' And he lifted his shoulders to make it easier for the two of them to take him under the arms.

Yet the man did not respond to his request but kept his hands quietly in his pockets and laughed. 'You see,' he said to the girl. 'I hit the nail on the head. It's only here that this gentleman feels upset, not in other places.' The girl smiled too, but tapped the man lightly on the arm with her finger-tips, as if he had gone too far in jesting like that with K. 'But dear me,' said the man, still laughing, 'I'll show the gentleman to the door, of course I will!' 'Then that's all right,' said the girl, drooping her pretty head for a moment. 'Don't take his laughter too much to heart,' she said to K., who had sunk again into vacant melancholy and apparently expected no explanation. 'This gentleman – may I introduce you?' (the gentleman waved his hand to indicate permission) – 'this gentleman, then, represents our Inquiries Department. He gives clients all the information they need, and as our procedure is not very well known among the populace, a great deal of information is asked for. He has an answer to every question, if you ever feel like it you can try him out. But that isn't his only claim to distinction, he has another, the smartness of his clothes. We – that's to say the staff – made up our minds that the Clerk of Inquiries, since he's always dealing with clients and is the first to see them, must be smartly dressed so as to create a good first impression. The rest of us, as you must have noticed at once from myself, are very badly and old-fashionedly dressed, I'm sorry to say; there isn't much sense anyhow in spending money on clothes, for we're hardly ever out of these offices, we even sleep here. But, as I say, we considered that in his case good clothes were needed. And as the management, which in this respect is somewhat peculiar, refused to provide these clothes, we took up a collection – some of the clients contributed too – and we bought him this fine suit and some others as well. Nothing more would be needed now to produce a good impression, but he spoils it all again by his laughter which puts people off.' 'That's how it is,' said the gentleman ironically, 'yet I don't understand, Fräulein, why you should tell this gentleman all our intimate secrets, or rather thrust them on him, for he doesn't want to hear them at all. Just look at him, he's obviously much too busy with his own thoughts.' K. felt no inclination even to make a retort, the girl's intentions were no doubt good, probably she merely wanted to distract him or give him a chance to pull himself together, but she had not gone the right way about it. 'Well, I needed to explain your laughter to him,' the girl said. 'It sounded insulting,' 'I fancy he would overlook much worse insults if I would only take him out of here.' K. said nothing, he did not even look up, he suffered the two of them to discuss him as if he were an inanimate object, indeed he actually preferred that. Then suddenly he felt the man's hand under one arm and the girl's hand under the other. 'Up you get, you feeble fellow,' said the man. 'Many thanks to both of you,' said K., joyfully surprised, and he got up slowly and himself moved these strangers' hands to the places where he felt most in need of support. 'It must seem to you,' said the girl softly in K.'s ear as they neared the passage, 'as if I were greatly concerned to show the Clerk of Inquiries in a good light, but you can believe me, I only wanted to speak the truth about him. He isn't a hard-hearted man. He isn't obliged so help sick people out of here, and yet he does so, as you can see. Perhaps none of us are hard-hearted, we should be glad to help everybody, yet as Law-Court officials we easily take on the appearance of being hard-hearted and of not wishing to help. That really worries me.' 'Wouldn't you like to sit down here for a little?' asked the Clerk of Inquiries; they were out in the main lobby now and just opposite the client to whom K. had first spoken. K. felt almost ashamed before the man, he had stood so erect before him the first time; now it took a couple of people to hold him up, the Clerk of Inquiries was balancing his hat on the tips of his fingers, his hair was in disorder and hung down over his sweat-drenched forehead. But the client seemed to see nothing of all this, he stood up humbly before the Clerk of Inquiries (who stared through him) and merely sought to excuse his presence. 'I know,' he said, 'that the decision of my affidavits cannot be expected today. But I came all the same, I thought that I might as well wait here, it is Sunday, I have lots of time and here I disturb nobody.' 'You needn't be so apologetic,' replied the Clerk of Inquiries. 'Your solicitude is entirely to be commended; you're taking up extra room here, I admit, but so long as you don't inconvenience me, I shan't hinder you at all from following the progress of your case as closely as you please. When one sees so many people who scandalously neglect their duty, one learns to have patience with men like you. You may sit down.' 'How well he knows how to talk to clients!' whispered the girl. K. nodded but immediately gave a violent start when the Clerk of Inquiries asked again: 'Wouldn't you like to sit down here?' 'No,' said K. 'I don't want a rest.' He said this with the utmost possible decision, though in reality he would have been very glad to sit down. He felt as if he were seasick. He felt he was on a ship rolling in heavy seas. It was as if the waters were dashing against the wooden walls, as if the roaring of breaking waves came from the end of the passage, as if the passage itself pitched and rolled and the waiting clients on either side rose and fell with it. All the more incomprehensible, therefore, was the composure of the girl and the man who were escorting him. He was delivered into their hands, if they let him go he must fall like a block of wood. They kept glancing around with their sharp little eyes. K. was aware of their regular advance without himself taking part in it, for he was now being almost carried from step to step. At last he noticed that they were talking to him, but he could not make out what they were saying, he heard nothing but the din that filled the whole place, through which a shrill unchanging note like that of a siren seemed to ring. 'Louder,' he whispered with bowed head, and he was ashamed, for he knew that they were speaking loudly enough, though he could not make out what they said. Then, as if the wall in front of him had been split in two, a current of fresh air was at last wafted towards him, and he heard a voice near him saying: 'First he wants to go, then you tell him a hundred times that the door is in front of him and he makes no move to go.' K. saw that he was standing before the outside door, which the girl had opened. It was as if all his energies returned at one bound; to get a foretaste of freedom he set his feet at once on a step of the staircase and from there said good-bye to his conductors, who bent their heads down to hear him. 'Many thanks,' he said several times, then shook hands with them again and again and only left off when he thought he saw that they, accustomed as they were to the office air, felt ill in the relatively fresh air that came up the stairway. They could scarcely answer him and the girl might have fallen if K. had not shut the door with the utmost haste. K. stood still for a moment, put his hair to rights with the help of his pocket mirror, lifted up his hat, which lay on the step below him – the Clerk of Inquiries must have thrown it there – and then leapt down the stairs so buoyantly and with such long strides that he became almost afraid of his own reaction. His usually sound constitution had never provided him with such surprises before. Could his body possibly be meditating a revolution and preparing to spring something new on him, since he had borne with the old state of affairs so effortlessly? He did not entirely reject the idea of going to consult a doctor at the first opportunity, in any case he had made up his mind – and there he could consult himself – to spend all his Sunday mornings in future to better purpose.

4

FRÄULEIN BÜRSTNER'S FRIEND

In the next few days K. found it impossible to exchange even a word with Fräulein Bürstner. He tried to get hold of her by every means he could think of, but she always managed to elude him. He went straight home from his office and sat on the sofa in his room, with the light out and the door open, concentrating his attention on the entrance hall. If the maid on her way past shut the door of his apparently empty room, he would get up after a while and open it again. He rose every morning an hour earlier than usual on the chance of catching Fräulein Bürstner alone, before she went to her work. But none of these stratagems succeeded. Then he wrote a letter to her, sending it both to her office and to her house address, in which he once more tried to justify his behaviour, offered to make any reparation required, promised never to overstep the bounds that she should prescribe for him, and begged her to give him an opportunity of merely speaking to her, more especially as he could arrange nothing with Frau Grubach until he had first consulted with her, concluding with the information that next Sunday he would wait in his room all day for some sign that she was prepared either to grant his request or at least to explain why, even although he was pledging his word to defer to her in everything, she would not grant it. His letters were not returned, but neither were they answered. On Sunday, however, he was given a sign whose meaning was sufficiently clear. In the early morning K. observed through the keyhole of his door an unusual commotion in the entrance hall, which soon explained itself. A teacher of French, she was a German girl called Montag, a sickly, pale girl with a slight limp who till now had occupied a room of her own, was apparently moving into Fräulein Bürstner's room. For hours she kept on trailing through the entrance hall. She seemed to be always forgetting some article of underwear or a scrap of drapery or a book that necessitated a special journey to carry it into the new apartment.

When Frau Grubach brought in his breakfast – since K. had flown out at her she had devoted herself to performing even the most trifling services for him – K. could not help breaking the silence between them for the first time. 'Why is there such a row in the entrance hall today?' he asked as he poured out his coffee. 'Couldn't it be put off to some other time? Must the place be spring-cleaned on a Sunday?' Although K. did not glance up at Frau Grubach, he could observe that she heaved a sigh of relief. These questions, though harsh, she construed as forgiveness or as an approach towards forgiveness. 'The place is not being spring-cleaned, Herr K.,' she said. 'Fräulein Montag is moving in with Fräulein Bürstner and shifting her things across.' She said no more, waiting first to see how K. would take it and if he would allow her to go on. But K. kept her on the rack, reflectively stirring his coffee and remaining silent. Then he looked up at her and said: 'Have you given up your previous suspicions of Fräulein Bürstner?' 'Herr K.,' cried Frau Grubach, who had been merely waiting for this question and now stretched out her clasped hands towards him, 'you took a casual remark of mine far too seriously. It never entered my head to offend you or anyone else. You have surely known me long enough, Herr K., to be certain of that. You have no idea how I have suffered during these last few days! I to speak ill of my boarders! And you, Herr K., believed it! And said I should give you notice! Give you notice!' The last ejaculation was already stifled in her sobs, she raised her apron to her face and wept aloud.

'Please don't cry, Frau Grubach,' said K., looking out through the window, he was really thinking of Fräulein Bürstner and of the fact that she had taken a strange girl into her room. 'Please don't cry,' he said again as he turned back to the room and found Frau Grubach still weeping. 'I didn't mean what I said so terribly seriously either. We misunderstood each other. That can happen occasionally even between old friends.' Frau Grubach took her apron from her eyes to see whether K. was really appeased. 'Come now, that's all there was to it,' said K., and then ventured to add, since to judge from Frau Grubach's expression her nephew the Captain would not have divulged anything: 'Do you really believe that I would turn against you because of a strange girl?' 'That's just it, Herr K.,' said Frau Grubach, it was her misfortune that as soon as she felt relieved in her mind she immediately said something tactless, 'I kept asking myself: Why should Herr K. bother himself so much about Fräulein Bürstner? Why should he quarrel with me because of her, though he knows that every cross word from him makes me lose my sleep? And I said nothing about the girl that I hadn't seen with my own eyes.' K. made no reply to this, he should have driven her from the room at the very first word, and he did not want to do that. He contented himself with drinking his coffee and leaving Frau Grubach to feel that her presence was burdensome. Outside he could hear again the trailing step of Fräulein Montag as she limped from end to end of the entrance hall. 'Do you hear that?' asked K., indicating the door. 'Yes,' said Frau Grubach, sighing, 'I offered to help her and to order the maid to help too, but she's self-willed, she insists on moving everything herself. I'm surprised at Fräulein Bürstner. I often regret having Fräulein Montag as a boarder, but now Fräulein Bürstner is actually taking her into her own room.' 'You mustn't worry about that,' said K., crushing with the spoon the sugar left at the bottom of his cup. 'Does it mean any loss to you?' 'No,' said Frau Grubach, 'in itself it's quite welcome to me, I am left with an extra room, and I can put my nephew, the Captain, there. I've been bothered in case he might have disturbed you these last few days, for I had to let him occupy the living-room next door. He's not very careful.' 'What an idea!' said K., getting up. 'There's no question of that. You really seem to think I'm hypersensitive because I can't stand Fräulein Montag's trailings to and fro – there she goes again, coming back this time.' Frau Grubach felt quite helpless. 'Shall I tell her, Herr K., to put off moving the rest of her things until later? If you like I'll do so at once.' 'But she's got to move into Fräulein Bürstner's room!' cried K. 'Yes,' said Frau Grubach, she could not quite make out what K. meant. 'Well then,' said K., 'she must surely be allowed to shift her things there.' Frau Grubach simply nodded. Her dumb helplessness, which outwardly had the look of simple obstinacy, exasperated K. still more. He began to walk up and down from the window to the door and back again, and by doing that he hindered Frau Grubach from being able to slip out of the room, which she would probably have done.

K. had just reached the door again when there was a knock. It was the maid, who announced that Fräulein Montag would like a word or two with Herr K. and that she accordingly begged him to come to the dining-room, where she was waiting for him. K. listened grimly to the message, then he turned an almost sarcastic eye on the horrified Frau Grubach. His look seemed to say that he had long foreseen this invitation of Fräulein Montag's, and that it accorded very well with all the persecution he had had to endure that Sunday morning from Frau Grubach's boarders. He sent the maid back with the information that he would come at once, then went to his wardrobe to change his coat, and in answer to Frau Grubach, who was softly lamenting over the behaviour of the importunate Fräulein Montag, had nothing to say but to request her to remove his breakfast tray. 'Why, you've scarcely touched anything,' said Frau Grubach. 'Oh, take it away, all the same,' cried K. It seemed to him as if Fräulein Montag were mixed up with everything, it was too sickening.

As he crossed the entrance hall he glanced at the closed door of Fräulein Bürstner's room. Still, he had not been invited there, but to the dining-room, where he flung open the door without knocking.

It was a very long narrow room with one large window. There was only enough space in it to wedge two cupboards at an angle on either side of the door, the rest of the room was completely taken up by the long dining-table, which began near the door and reached to the very window, making it almost inaccessible. The table was already laid, and for many people too, since on Sunday almost all the boarders had their midday dinner in the house.

When K. entered, Fräulein Montag advanced from the window along one side of the table to meet him. They greeted each other in silence. Then Fräulein Montag said, holding her head very erect as usual: 'I don't know if you know who I am.' K. stared at her with contracted brows. 'Of course I do,' he said, 'you've been staying quite a long time with Frau Grubach, haven't you?' 'But you don't take much interest in the boarders, I fancy,' said Fräulein Montag. 'No,' said K. 'Won't you take a seat?' asked Fräulein Montag. In silence they pulled out two chairs at the very end of the table and sat down opposite each other. But Fräulein Montag immediately stood up again, for she had left her little handbag lying on the window-sill and now went to fetch it; she trailed for it along the whole length of the room. As she came back, swinging her bag lightly in her hand, she said: 'I've been asked by my friend to say something to you, that's all. She wanted to come herself, but she is feeling a little unwell today. She asks you to excuse her and listen to me instead. She would not have said anything more to you, in any case, than I am going to say. On the contrary, I fancy that I can actually tell you more, as I am relatively impartial. Don't you think so too?'

'Well, what is there to say?' replied K., who was weary of seeing Fräulein Montag staring so fixedly at his lips. Her stare was already trying to dominate any words he might utter. 'Fräulein Bürstner evidently refuses to grant me the personal interview I asked for.' 'That is so,' said Fräulein Montag, 'or rather that isn't it at all, you put it much too harshly. Surely, in general, interviews are neither deliberately accepted nor refused. But it may happen that one sees no point in an interview, and that is the case here. After that last remark of yours I can speak frankly, I take it. You have begged my friend to communicate with you by letter or by word of mouth. Now, my friend, at least that is what I must assume, knows what this conversation would be about, and is therefore convinced, for reasons of which I am ignorant, that it would be to nobody's benefit if it actually took place. To tell the truth, she did not mention the matter to me until yesterday and only in passing, she said among other things that you could not attach very much importance to this interview either, for it could only have been by accident that you hit on the idea, and that even without a specific explanation you would soon come to see how silly the whole affair was, if indeed you didn't see that already. I told her that that might be quite true, but that I considered it advisable, if the matter were to be completely cleared up, that you should receive an explicit answer. I offered myself as an intermediary, and after some hesitation my friend yielded to my persuasions. But I hope that I have served your interests, too, for the slightest uncertainty even in the most trifling matter is always a worry, and when, as in this case, it can be easily dispelled, it is better that that should be done at once.' Thank you,' said K., and he slowly rose to his feet, glanced at Fräulein Montag, then at the table, then out through the window – the sun was shining on the house opposite – and walked to the door. Fräulein Montag followed him for a few steps, as if she did not quite trust him. But at the door they had both to draw back, for it opened and Captain Lanz entered. This was the first time that K. had seen him close at hand. He was a tall man in the early forties with a tanned, fleshy face. He made a slight bow which included K. as well as Fräulein Montag, then went up to her and respectfully kissed her hand. His movements were easy. His politeness towards Fräulein Montag was in striking contrast to the treatment which she had received from K. All the same, Fräulein Montag did not seem to be offended with K., for she actually purposed, K. fancied, to introduce him to the Captain. But K. did not wish to be introduced, he was not in the mind to be polite either to the Captain or to Fräulein Montag, the hand-kissing had in his eyes turned the pair of them into accomplices who, under a cloak of the utmost amiability and altruism, were seeking to bar his way to Fräulein Bürstner. Yet he fancied that he could see even more than that, he recognized that Fräulein Montag had chosen a very good if somewhat two-edged weapon.

She had exaggerated the importance of the connexion between Fräulein Bürstner and K., she had exaggerated above all the importance of the interview he had asked for, and she had tried at the same time so to manipulate things as to make it appear that it was K. who was exaggerating. She would find that she was deceived. K. wished to exaggerate nothing, he knew that Fräulein Bürstner was an ordinary little typist who could not resist him for long. In coming to this conclusion he deliberately left out of account what Frau Grubach had told him about Fräulein Bürstner. He was thinking all this as he quitted the room with a curt word of leave-taking. He made straight for his own room, but a slight titter from Fräulein Montag, coming from the dining-room behind him, put it into his head that perhaps he could provide a surprise for the pair of them, the Captain as well as Fräulein Montag. He glanced round and listened to make sure that no interruption was likely from any of the adjacent rooms, all was still, nothing was to be heard but a murmur of voices in the dining-room and the voice of Frau Grubach coming from the passage leading to the kitchen. The opportunity seemed excellent, and K. went over to Fräulein Bürstner's door and knocked softly. When nothing happened he knocked again, but again no answer came. Was she sleeping? Or was she really unwell? Or was she pretending she wasn't there, knowing that it could only be K. who was knocking so softly? K. assumed that she was pretending and knocked more loudly, and at last, as his knocking had no result, cautiously opened the door, not without a feeling that he was doing something wrong and even more useless than wrong. There was nobody in the room. Moreover it had scarcely any resemblance now to the room which K. had seen. Against the wall two beds stood next to each other, three chairs near the door were heaped with dresses and underclothes, a wardrobe was standing open. Fräulein Bürstner had apparently gone out while Fräulein Montag was saying her piece in the dining-room. K. was not very much taken aback, he had hardly expected at this stage to get hold of Fräulein Bürstner so easily, he had made this attempt, indeed, mainly to annoy Fräulein Montag. Yet the shock was all the greater when, as he was shutting the door again, he saw Fräulein Montag and the Captain standing talking together in the open door of the dining-room. They had perhaps been standing there all the time, they scrupulously avoided all appearance of having been observing him, they talked in low voices, following K.'s movements only with the abstracted gaze one has for people passing when one is deep in conversation. All the same, their glances weighed heavily upon K., and he made what haste he could to his room, keeping close against the wall.

5

THE WHIPPER

A few evenings later K. was passing along the Bank corridor from his office to the main staircase – he was almost the last to leave, only two clerks in the dispatch department were still at work by the dim light of a glow lamp – when he heard convulsive sighs behind a door, which he had always taken to be the door of a lumber-room, although he had never opened it. He stopped in astonishment and listened to make sure that he had not been mistaken – all was still, yet in a little while the sighing began again. At first he thought of fetching one of the dispatch clerks, he might need a witness, but then he was seized by such uncontrollable curiosity that he literally tore the door open. It was, as he had correctly assumed, a lumber-room. Bundles of useless old papers and empty earthenware ink-bottles lay in a tumbled heap behind the threshold. But in the room itself stood three men, stooping because of the low ceiling, by the light of a candle stuck on a bookcase. 'What are you doing here?' asked K., in a voice broken with agitation but not loud. One of the men, who was clearly in authority over the other two and took the eye first, was sheathed in a sort of dark leather garment which left his throat and a good deal of chest and the whole of his arms bare. He made no answer. But the other two cried: 'Sir! We're to be flogged because you complained about us to the Examining Magistrate.' And only then did K. realize that it was actually the warders Franz and Willem, and that the third man was holding a rod in his hand with which to beat them. 'Why,' said K., staring at them, 'I never complained, I only told what happened in my rooms. And, anyhow, your behaviour there was not exactly blameless.' 'Sir,' said Willem, while Franz openly tried to take cover behind him from the third man, 'if you only knew how badly we are paid, you wouldn't be so hard on us. I have a family to feed and Franz here wants to get married, a man tries to make whatever he can, and you don't get rich on hard work, not even if you work day and night. Your fine shirts were a temptation, of course that kind of thing is forbidden to warders, it was wrong, but it's a tradition that body-linen is the warders' perquisite, it has always been the case, believe me; and it's understandable too, for what importance can such things have for a man who is unlucky enough to be arrested? Yet if he insists on telling, punishment is bound to follow.' 'I had no idea of all this, nor did I ever demand that you should be punished, I was only defending a principle.' 'Franz,' Willem turned to the other warder, 'didn't I tell you that the gentleman never asked for us to be punished? Now you see that he didn't even know we should be punished.' 'Don't be taken in by what they say,' remarked the third man to K., 'the punishment is as just as it is inevitable.' 'Don't listen to him,' said Willem, interrupting himself to clap his hand to his mouth, over which he had got a stinging blow with the rod. 'We are only being punished because you accused us; if you hadn't, nothing would have happened, not even if they had discovered what we did. Do you call that justice? Both of us, and especially myself, have a long record of trustworthy service as warders – you must yourself admit that, officially speaking, we guarded you quite well – we had every prospect of advancement and would certainly have been promoted to be Whippers pretty soon, like this man here, who simply had the luck never to be complained of, for a complaint of that kind really happens very seldom indeed. And all is lost now, sir, our careers are done for, we'll be set to do much more menial work than a warder's, and, besides that, we're in for a whipping, and that's horribly painful.' 'Can that birch-rod cause such terrible pain?' asked K., studying the switch, which the man waved to and fro in front of him. 'We'll have to take off all our clothes first,' said Willem. 'Ah, I see,' said K., and he looked more attentively at the Whipper, who was tanned like a sailor and had a brutal, healthy face. 'Is there no way of getting these two off their whipping?' K. asked him. 'No,' said the man, smilingly shaking his head. 'Strip,' he ordered the warders. And he said to K.: 'You mustn't believe all they say, they're so terrified of the whipping that they've already lost what wits they had. For instance, all that this one here' – he pointed to Willem – 'says about his possible career is simply absurd. See how fat he is – the first cuts of the birch will be quite lost in fat. Do you know what made him so fat? He stuffs himself with the breakfasts of all the people he arrests. Didn't he eat up your breakfast too? There, you see, I told you so. But a man with a belly like that couldn't ever become a Whipper, it's quite out of the question.' 'There are Whippers just like me,' maintained Willem, loosening his trouser belt. 'No,' said the Whipper, drawing the switch across his back so that he winced, 'you aren't supposed to be listening, you're to take off your clothes.' 'I'll reward you well if you'll let them go,' said K., and without glancing at the Whipper again – such things should be done with averted eyes on both sides – he drew out his pocket-book. 'So you want to lay a complaint against me too,' said the Whipper, 'and get me a whipping as well? No, no!' 'Do be reasonable,' said K. 'If I had wanted these two men to be punished, I shouldn't be trying to buy them off now. I could simply leave, shut this door after me, close my eyes and ears, and go home; but I don't want to do that, I really want to see them set free; if I had known that they would be punished or even that they could be punished, I should never have mentioned their names. For I don't in the least blame them, it is the organization that is to blame, the high officials who are to blame.' 'That's so,' cried the warders and at once got a cut of the switch over their backs, which were bare now. 'If it was one of the high Judges you were flogging,' said K., and as he spoke he thrust down the rod which the Whipper was raising again, 'I certainly wouldn't try to keep you from laying on with a will, on the contrary I would pay you extra to encourage you in the good work.' 'What you say sounds reasonable enough,' said the man, 'but I refuse to be bribed. I am here to whip people, and whip them I shall.' The warder Franz, who, perhaps hoping that K.'s intervention might succeed, had thus far kept as much as possible in the background, now came forward to the door clad only in his trousers, fell on his knees, and clinging to K.'s arm whispered: 'If you can't get him to spare both of us, try to get me off at least. Willem is older than I am, and far less sensitive too; besides he's had a small whipping already, some years ago, but I've never been in disgrace yet, and I was only following Willem's lead in what I did, he's my teacher, for better or worse. My poor sweetheart is waiting for me at the door of the Bank. I'm so ashamed and miserable.' He dried his tear-wet face on K.'s jacket. 'I can't wait any longer,' said the Whipper, grasping the rod with both hands and making a cut at Franz, while Willem cowered in a corner and secretly watched without daring to turn his head. Then the shriek rose from Franz's throat, single and irrevocable, it did not seem to come from a human being but from some tortured instrument, the whole corridor rang with it, the whole building must hear it. 'Don't,' cried K.; he was beside himself, he stood staring in the direction from which the clerks must presently come running, but he gave Franz a push, not a violent one but violent enough nevertheless to make the half-senseless man fall and convulsively claw at the floor with his hands; but even then Franz did not escape his punishment, the birch-rod found him where he was lying, its point swished up and down regularly as he writhed on the floor. And now a clerk was already visible in the distance and a few paces behind him another. K. quickly slammed the door, stepped over to a window close by, which looked out on the courtyard, and opened it. The shrieks had completely stopped. To keep the clerks from approaching any nearer, K. cried; 'It's me.' 'Good evening, Herr Assessor,' they cried back. 'Has anything happened?' 'No, no,' replied K. 'It was only a dog howling in the courtyard.' As the clerks still did not budge, he added; 'You can go back to your work.' And to keep himself from being involved in any conversation he leaned out of the window. When after a while he glanced into the corridor again, they were gone. But he stayed beside the window, he did not dare to go back into the lumber-room, and he had no wish to go home either. It was a little square courtyard into which he was looking down, surrounded by offices, all the windows were dark now, but the topmost panes cast back a faint reflection of the moon. K. intently strove to pierce the darkness of one corner of the courtyard, where several hand-barrows were jumbled close together. He was deeply disappointed that he had not been able to prevent the whipping, but it was not his fault that he had not succeeded; if Franz had not shrieked – it must have been very painful certainly, but in a crisis one must control oneself – if he had not shrieked, then K., in all probability at least, would have found some other means of persuading the Whipper. If the whole lower grade of this organization were scoundrels, why should the Whipper, who had the most inhuman office of all, turn out to be an exception? Besides, K. had noticed his eyes glittering at the sight of the banknote, obviously he had set about his job in earnest simply to raise his price a little higher. And K, would not have been stingy, he was really very anxious to get the warders off; since he had set himself to fight the whole corrupt administration of this Court, it was obviously his duty to intervene on this occasion. But at the moment when Franz began to shriek, any intervention became impossible. K. could not afford to let the dispatch clerks and possibly all sorts of other people arrive and surprise him in a scene with these creatures in the lumber-room. No one could really demand that sacrifice from him. If a sacrifice had been needed, it would almost have been simpler to take off his own clothes and offer himself to the Whipper as a substitute for the warders. In any case the Whipper certainly would not have accepted such a substitution, since without gaining any advantage he would have been involved in a grave dereliction of duty, for as long as this trial continued, K. must surely be immune from molestation by the servants of the Court. Though of course ordinary standards might not apply here either. At all events, he could have done nothing but slam the door, though even that action had not shut off all danger. It was a pity that he had given Franz a push at the last moment, the state of agitation he was in was his only excuse.

He still heard the steps of the clerks in the distance; so as not to attract their attention he shut the window and began to walk away in the direction of the main staircase. At the door of the lumber-room he stopped for a little and listened. All was as silent as the grave. The man might have beaten the warders till they had given up the ghost, they were entirely delivered into his power. K.'s hand was already stretched out to grasp the door-handle when he withdrew it again. They were past help by this time, and the clerks might appear at any moment; but he made a vow to hush up the incident and to deal trenchantly, so far as lay in his power, with the real culprits, the high officials, none of whom had yet dared show his face. As he descended the outside steps of the Bank he carefully observed everyone he passed, but even in the surrounding streets he could perceive no sign of a girl waiting for anybody. So Franz's tale of a sweetheart waiting for him was simply a lie, venial enough, designed merely to procure more sympathy for him.

All the next day K. could not get the warders out of his head; he was absent-minded and to catch up on his work had to stay in his office even later than the day before. As he passed the lumber-room again on his way out he could not resist opening the door. And what confronted him, instead of the darkness he had expected, bewildered him completely. Everything was still the same, exactly as he had found it on opening the door the previous evening. The files of old papers and the ink-bottles were still tumbled behind the threshold, the Whipper with his rod and the warders with all their clothes on were still standing there, the candle was burning on the bookcase, and the warders immediately began to cry out: 'Sir!' At once K. slammed the door shut and then beat on it with his fists, as if that would shut it more securely. He ran almost weeping to the clerks, who were quietly working at the copying-presses and looked up at him in surprise. 'Clear that lumber-room out, can't you?' he shouted. 'We're being smothered in dirt!' The clerks promised to do so next day. K. nodded, he could hardly insist on their doing it now, so late in the evening, as he had originally intended. He sat down for a few moments, for the sake of their company, shuffled through some duplicates, hoping to give the impression that he was inspecting them, and then, seeing that the men would scarcely venture to leave the building along with him, went home, tired, his mind quite blank.

6

K.'S UNCLE – LENI

One afternoon – it was just before the day's letters went out and K. was very busy – two clerks bringing him some papers to sign were violently thrust aside and his Uncle Karl, a petty squire from the country, came striding into the room. K. was the less alarmed by the arrival of his uncle since for a long time he had been shrinking from it in anticipation. His uncle was bound to turn up, he had been convinced of that for about a month past. He had often pictured him just as he appeared now, his back slightly bent, his panama hat crushed in his left hand, stretching out his right hand from the very doorway, and then thrusting it recklessly across the desk, knocking over everything that came in its way. His uncle was always in a hurry, for he was harassed by the disastrous idea that whenever he came to town for the day he must get through all the programme he had drawn up for himself, besides missing not a single chance of a conversation or a piece of business or an entertainment. In all this K., who as his former ward was peculiarly obliged to him, had to help him as best he could and also sometimes put him up for the night. 'The family skeleton,' he was in the habit of calling him.

Immediately after his first greetings – he had no time to sit down in the chair which K. offered him – he begged K. to have a short talk with him in strict privacy. 'It is necessary,' he said, painfully gulping, 'it is necessary for my peace of mind.' K. at once sent his clerks out of the room with instructions to admit no one. 'What is this I hear, Joseph?' cried his uncle when they were alone, sitting down on the desk and making himself comfortable by stuffing several papers under him without looking at them. K. said nothing, he knew what was coming, but being suddenly released from the strain of exacting work, he resigned himself for the moment to a pleasant sense of indolence and gazed out through the window at the opposite side of the street, of which only a small triangular section could be seen from where he was sitting, a slice of empty house-wall between two shop-windows. 'You sit there staring out of the window!' cried his uncle, flinging up his arms. 'For God's sake, Joseph, answer me. Is it true? Can it be true?' 'Dear Uncle,' said K., tearing himself out of his reverie. 'I don't know in the least what you mean.' 'Joseph,' said his uncle warningly, 'you've always told the truth, as far as I know. Am I to take these words of yours as a bad sign?' 'I can guess, certainly, what you're after,' said K. accommodatingly. 'You've probably heard something about my trial.' 'That is so,' replied his uncle, nodding gravely. 'I have heard about your trial.' 'But from whom?' asked K. 'Erna wrote to me about it,' said his uncle. 'She doesn't see much of you, I know, you don't pay much attention to her, I regret to say, and yet she heard about it. I got the letter this morning and of course took the first train here. I had no other reason for coming, but it seems to be a sufficient one. I shall read you the bit from her letter that mentions you.' He took the letter from his pocket-book. 'Here it is. She writes: "I haven't seen Joseph for a long time, last week I called at the Bank, but Joseph was so busy that

I couldn't see him; I waited for almost an hour, but I had to leave then, for I had a piano lesson. I should have liked very much to speak to him, perhaps I shall soon have the chance. He sent me a great big box of chocolates for my birthday, it was very nice and thoughtful of him. I forgot to write and mention it at the time, and it was only your asking that reminded me. For I may tell you that chocolate vanishes on the spot in this boarding-house, hardly do you realize that you've been presented with a box when it's gone. But about Joseph, there is something else that I feel I should tell you. As I said, I was not able to see him at the Bank because he was engaged with a gentleman. After I had waited meekly for a while I asked an attendant if the interview was likely to last much longer. He said that that might very well be, for it had probably something to do with the case which was being brought against the Herr Assessor. I asked what case, and was he not mistaken, but he said he was not mistaken, there was a case and a very serious one too, but more than that he did not know. He himself would like to help the Herr Assessor, for the Herr Assessor was a good and just man, but he did not know how he was to do it, and he only wished that some influential gentleman would take the Herr Assessor's part. To be sure, that was certain to happen and everything would be all right in the end, but for the time being, as he could see from the Herr Assessor's state of mind, things looked far from well. Naturally I did not take all this too seriously, I tried to reassure the simple fellow and forbade him to talk about it to anyone else, and I'm sure it's just idle gossip. All the same it might be as well, if you, dearest Father, were to inquire into it on your next visit to town, it will be easy for you to find out the real state of things, and if necessary to get some of your influential friends to intervene. Even if it shouldn't be necessary, and that is most likely, at least it will give your daughter an early chance of welcoming you with a kiss, which is a joyful thought." A good child,' said K.'s uncle when he had finished reading, wiping a tear from his eye. K. nodded, he had completely forgotten Erna among the various troubles he had had lately, and the story about the chocolates she had obviously invented simply to save his face before his uncle and aunt. It was really touching, and the theatre tickets which he now resolved to send her regularly would be a very inadequate return, but he did not feel equal at present to calling at her boarding-house and chattering to an eighteen-year-old schoolgirl. 'And what have you got to say now?' asked his uncle, who had temporarily forgotten all his haste and agitation over the letter, which he seemed to be re-reading. 'Yes, Uncle,' said K., 'it's quite true.' 'True?' cried his uncle. 'What is true? How on earth can it be true? What case is this? Not a criminal case, surely?' 'A criminal case,' answered K. 'And you sit there coolly with a criminal case hanging round your neck?' cried his uncle, his voice growing louder and louder. 'The cooler I am, the better in the end,' said K. wearily. 'Don't worry.' 'That's a fine thing to ask of me,' cried his uncle. 'Joseph, my dear Joseph, think of yourself, think of your relatives, think of your good name. You have been a credit to us until now, you can't become a family disgrace. Your attitude,' he looked at K. with his head slightly cocked, 'doesn't please me at all, that isn't how an innocent man behaves if he's still in his senses. Just tell me quickly what it is all about, so that I can help you. It's something to do with the Bank, of course?' 'No,' said K., getting up. 'But you're talking too loudly, Uncle. I feel pretty certain the attendant is standing behind the door listening, and I dislike the idea. We had better go out somewhere. I'll answer all your questions then as far as I can. I know quite well that I owe the family an explanation.' 'Right,' cried his uncle, 'quite right, but hurry, Joseph, hurry!' 'I have only to leave some instructions,' said K., and he summoned his chief assistant by telephone, who appeared in a few minutes. In his agitation K.'s uncle indicated to the clerk by a sweep of the hand that K. had sent for him, which, of course, was already obvious enough. K., standing beside his desk, pointed to various papers and in a low voice explained to the young man, who listened coolly but attentively, what remained to be done in his absence. His uncle disturbed him by standing beside him round-eyed and biting his lips nervously; he was not actually listening, but the mere suggestion was disturbing enough in itself. He next began to pace up and down the room, pausing every now and then by the window or before a picture, with sudden ejaculations, such as: 'It's completely incomprehensible to me' or 'Goodness knows what's to come of this.' The young man behaved as if he noticed nothing, quietly heard K.'s instructions to the end, took a few notes, and went, after having bowed both to K., and to his uncle, who, however, turned his back abruptly, gazed out of the window, flung out his arms, and clutched at the curtains. The door had scarcely closed when K.'s uncle cried: 'At last the creature's gone; now we can go too. At last!' Unluckily K. could find no means to make his uncle stop inquiring about the case in the main vestibule, where several clerks and attendants were standing about, while the Deputy Manager himself was crossing the floor. 'Come now, Joseph,' began his uncle, returning a brief nod to the bows of the waiting clerks, 'tell me frankly now what this case is all about.' K. made a few non-committal remarks, laughing a little, and only on the staircase explained to his uncle that he had not wanted to speak openly before the clerks. 'Right,' said his uncle, 'but get it off your chest now.' He listened with bent head, puffing hastily at a cigar. 'The first thing to grasp, Uncle,' said K., 'is that this is not a case before an ordinary court.' 'That's bad,' said his uncle. 'How?' asked K., looking at his uncle. 'I mean that it's bad,' repeated his uncle. They were standing on the outside steps of the Bank; as the doorkeeper seemed to be listening, K. dragged his uncle away; they were swallowed up in the street traffic. The uncle, who had taken K.'s arm, now no longer inquired so urgently about the case, and for a while they actually walked on in silence. 'But how did this happen?' his uncle asked at last, stopping so suddenly that the people walking behind him shied off in alarm. 'Things like this don't come on one suddenly, they roll up for a long time beforehand, there must have been indications. Why did you never write to me? You know I would do anything for you, I'm still your guardian in a sense and till now I have been proud of it. Of course I'll do what I can to help you, only it's rather difficult so late in the day, when the case is already in full swing. The best thing, at any rate, would be for you to take a short holiday and come to stay with us in the country. You've got a bit thinner, I notice that now. You'd get back your strength in the country, that would be all to the good, for this trial will certainly be a severe strain on you. But besides that, in a sense you'd be getting away from the clutches of the Court. Here they have all sorts of machinery which they can set automatically in motion against you if they like, but if you were in the country they would have to appoint agents or get at you by letter or telegram or telephone. That would naturally weaken the effect, not that you would escape them altogether, but you'd have a breathing-space.' 'Still, they might forbid me to go away,' said K., who was beginning to follow his uncle's line of thought. 'I don't think they would do that,' said his uncle reflectively, 'after all, they wouldn't lose so much by your going away.' 'I thought,' said K., taking his uncle's arm to keep him from standing still, 'that you would attach even less importance to this business than I do, and now you are taking it so seriously.' 'Joseph!' cried his uncle, trying to get his arm free so as to hold up the traffic again, only K. would not let him, 'you're quite changed, you always used to have such a clear brain, and is it going to fail you now? Do you want to lose this case? And do you know what that would mean? It would mean that you would be simply ruined. And that all your relatives would be ruined too or at least dragged in the dust. Joseph, pull yourself together. Your indifference drives me mad. Looking at you, one would almost believe the old saying: "A litigant always loses."' 'Dear Uncle,' said K., 'it's no use getting excited, it's as useless on your part as it would be on mine. No case is won by getting excited, you might let my practical experience count for something, look how I respect yours, as I have always done, even when you astonish me. Since you tell me that the family would be involved in any scandal arising from the case – I don't see myself how that could be so, but it doesn't really matter – I'll submit willingly to your judgement. Only I think going to the country would be inadvisable even from your point of view, for it would look like flight and therefore guilt. Besides, though I'm more closely pressed here, I can push the case on my own more energetically.' 'Quite right,' said his uncle in a tone of relief, as if he saw their minds converging at last, 'I only made the suggestion because I thought your indifference would endanger the case while you stayed here, and that it might be better if I took it up for you instead. But if you intend to push it energetically yourself, that of course would be far better.' 'We're agreed on that, then,' said K. 'And now can you suggest what the first step should be?' 'I'll have to do a bit of thinking about it, naturally,' said his uncle, 'you must consider that I have lived in the country for twenty years almost without a break, and my flair for such matters can't be so good as it was. Various connexions of mine with influential persons who would probably know how to tackle this affair have slackened in the course of time. I'm a bit isolated in the country, but you know that yourself. Actually it's only in emergencies like this that one becomes aware of it. Besides, this affair of yours has come on me more or less unexpectedly, though strangely enough, after Erna's letter, I guessed at something of the kind, and as soon as I saw you today I was almost sure of it. Still that doesn't matter, the important thing now is to lose no time.' Before he had finished speaking he was already on tiptoe waiting for a taxi, and now, shouting an address to the driver, he dragged K. into the car after him. 'We'll drive straight to Huld, the Advocate,' he said. 'He was at school with me. You know his name, of course? You don't? That is really extraordinary. He has quite a considerable reputation as a defending counsel and a poor man's lawyer. But it's as a human being that I'm prepared to pin my faith to him.' 'I'm willing to try anything you suggest,' said K., though the hasty headlong way in which his uncle was dealing with the matter caused him some perturbation. It was not very flattering to be driven to a poor man's lawyer as a petitioner. 'I don't know,' he said, 'that in a case like this one can employ an advocate.' 'But of course,' said his uncle. 'That's obvious. Why not? And now tell me everything that has happened up to now, so that I have some idea where we stand.' K. at once began his story and left out no single detail, for absolute frankness was the only protest he could make against his uncle's assumption that the case was a terrible disgrace. Fräulein Bürstner's name he mentioned only once and in passing, but that did not detract from his frankness, since Fräulein Bürstner had no connexion with the case. As he told his story he gazed out through the window and noted that they were approaching the very suburb where the Law Court had its attic offices; he drew his uncle's attention to this fact, but his uncle did not seem to be particularly struck by the coincidence. The taxi stopped before a dark house. His uncle rang the bell of the first door on the ground floor; while they were waiting he bared his great teeth in a smile and whispered: 'Eight o'clock, an unusual time for clients to call. But Huld won't take it ill of me.' Behind a grille in the door two great dark eyes appeared, gazed at the two visitors for a moment, and then vanished again; yet the door did not open. K. and his uncle assured each other that they had really seen a pair of eyes. 'A new maid, probably afraid of strangers,' said K.'s uncle and knocked again. Once more the eyes appeared and now they seemed almost sombre, yet that might have been an illusion created by the naked gas-jet which burned just over their heads and kept hissing shrilly but gave little light. 'Open the door!' shouted K.'s uncle, banging upon it with his fists, 'we're friends of the Herr Advocate's.' 'The Herr Advocate is ill,' came a whisper from behind them. A door had opened at the other end of the little passage and a man in a dressing-gown was standing there imparting this information in a hushed voice. K.'s uncle, already furious at having had to wait so long, whirled round shouting: 'Ill? You say he's ill?' and bore down almost threateningly on the man as if he were the alleged illness in person. 'The door has been opened,' said the man, indicated the Advocate's door, caught his dressing-gown about him, and disappeared. The door was really open, a young girl – K. recognized the dark, somewhat protuberant eyes – was standing in the entrance hall in a long white apron, holding a candle in her hand.

'Next time be a little smarter in opening the door,' K.'s uncle threw at her instead of a greeting, while she sketched a curtsy. 'Come on, Joseph,' he cried to K., who was slowly insinuating himself past the girl. 'The Herr Advocate is ill,' said the girl, as K.'s uncle, without any hesitation, made towards an inner door. K. was still gaping at the girl, who turned her back on him to bolt the house door; she had a doll-like rounded face; not only were her pale cheeks and her chin quite round in their modelling, but her temples and the line of her forehead as well. 'Joseph!' K.'s uncle shouted again, and he asked the girl: 'Is it his heart?' 'I think so,' said the girl; she had now found time to precede him with the candle and open the door of a room. In one corner, which the candlelight had not yet reached, a face with a long beard attached rose from a pillow. 'Leni, who is it?' asked the Advocate, blinded by the candlelight; he could not recognize his visitors. 'It's your old friend Albert,' said K.'s uncle. 'Oh, Albert,' said the Advocate, sinking back on his pillow again, as if there were no need to keep up appearances before this visitor. 'Are you really in a bad way?' asked K.'s uncle, sitting down on the edge of the bed. 'I can't believe it. It's one of your heart attacks and it'll pass over like all the others.' 'Maybe,' said the Advocate in a faint voice, 'but it's worse than it's ever been before. I find it difficult to breathe, can't sleep at all, and am losing strength daily.' 'I see,' said K.'s uncle, pressing his panama hat firmly against his knee with his huge hand. 'That's bad news. But are you being properly looked after? And it's so gloomy in here, so dark. It's a long time since I was here last, but it looked more cheerful then. And this little maid of yours doesn't seem to be very bright, or else she's concealing the fact.' The girl was still standing near the door with her candle; as far as one could make out from the vague flicker of her eyes, she seemed to be looking at K. rather than at his uncle, even while the latter was speaking about her. K. was leaning against a chair which he had pushed near her. 'When a man is as ill as I am,' said the Advocate, 'he must have quiet. I don't find it uncheerful.' After a slight pause he added: 'And Leni looks after me well, she's a good girl.' But this could not convince K.'s uncle, who was visibly prejudiced against the nurse, and though he made no reply to the sick man he followed her with a stern eye as she went over to the bed, set down the candle on the bedside table, bent far over her patient, and whispered to him while she rearranged the pillows. K.'s uncle, almost forgetting that he was in a sick-room, jumped to his feet and prowled up and down behind the girl; K. would not have been surprised if he had seized her by the skirts and dragged her away from the bed. K. himself looked on with detachment, the illness of the Advocate was not entirely unwelcome to him, he had not been able to stem his uncle's growing ardour for his cause, and he thankfully accepted the situation, which had deflected that ardour without any connivance from him. Then his uncle, perhaps only with the intention of annoying the nurse, cried out: 'Fräulein, please be so good as to leave us alone for a while; I must consult my friend on some personal business.' The girl, who was still bending far over the sick man smoothing the sheet beside the wall, merely turned her head and said quite calmly, in striking contrast to the furious stuttering and frothing of K.'s uncle: 'You see my master is ill; you cannot consult him on any business.' Probably she reiterated the phrase out of simple good nature; all the same it could have been construed as ironical even by an unprejudiced observer, and K.'s uncle naturally flared up as if he had been stung. 'You damned –' he spluttered, but he was so furious that it was difficult to make out the language he used. K. started up in alarm, though he had expected some such outburst, and rushed over to his uncle with the firm intention of clapping both hands over his mouth and so silencing him. Fortunately the patient raised himself up in bed behind the girl. K.'s uncle made a wry grimace as if he were swallowing some nauseous draught and he said in a smoother voice: 'I assure you we aren't altogether out of our senses; if what I ask were impossible I should not ask it. Please go away now.' The girl straightened herself beside the bed, turning full towards K.'s uncle, but with one hand, at least so K. surmised, she was patting the hand of the Advocate. 'You can discuss anything before Leni,' said the Advocate in a voice of sheer entreaty. 'This does not concern myself,' said K.'s uncle, 'it is not my private affair.' And he turned away as if washing his hands of the matter, although willing to give the Advocate a moment for reconsideration. 'Then whom does it concern?' asked the Advocate in an exhausted voice, lying down again. 'My nephew,' said K.'s uncle, 'I have brought him here with me.' And he presented his nephew: Joseph K., Assessor. 'Oh,' said the sick man with much more animation, stretching out his hand to K., 'forgive me, I didn't notice you. Go now, Leni,' he said to the nurse, clasping her by the hand as if saying good-bye to her for a long time, and she went submissively enough. 'So you haven't come,' he said at last to K.'s uncle, who was now appeased and had gone up to the bed again, 'to pay me a sick visit; you've come on business.' It was as if the thought of a sick visit had paralysed him until now, so rejuvenated did he look as he supported himself on his elbow, which must itself have been something of a strain; and he kept combing with his fingers a strand of hair in the middle of his beard. 'You look much better already,' said K.'s uncle, 'since that witch went away.' He broke off, whispered: 'I bet she's listening,' and sprang to the door. But there was no one behind the door and he returned again, not so much disappointed, since her failure to listen seemed to him an act of sheer malice, as disgusted. 'You are unjust to her,' said the Advocate, without adding anything more in defence of his nurse; perhaps by this reticence he meant to convey that she stood in no need of defence. Then in a much more friendly tone he went on: 'As for this case of your nephew's, I should certainly consider myself very fortunate if my strength proved equal to such an arduous task; I'm very much afraid that it will not do so, but at any rate I shall make every effort; if I fail, you can always call in someone else to help me. To be quite honest, the case interests me too deeply for me to resist the opportunity of taking some part in it. If my heart does not hold out, here at least it will find a worthy obstacle to fail against.' K. could not fathom a single word of all this, he glanced at his uncle, hoping for some explanation, but with the candle in his hand his uncle was sitting on the bedside table, from which a medicine-bottle had already rolled on to the carpet, nodding assent to everything that the Advocate said, apparently agreeing with everything and now and then casting a glance at K. which demanded from him a like agreement. Could his uncle have told the Advocate all about the case already? But that was impossible, the course of events ruled it out. 'I don't understand –' he therefore began. 'Oh, perhaps I have misunderstood you?' asked the Advocate, just as surprised and embarrassed as K. 'Perhaps I have been too hasty. Then what do you want to consult me about? I thought it concerned your case?' 'Of course it does,' said K.'s uncle, turning to K. with the question: 'What's bothering you?' 'Well, but how do you come to know about me and my case?' asked K. 'Oh, that's it,' said the Advocate, smiling. 'I'm an Advocate, you see, I move in circles where all the various cases are discussed, and the more striking ones are bound to stick in my mind, especially one that concerns the nephew of an old friend of mine. Surely that's not so extraordinary.' 'What's bothering you?' K.'s uncle repeated. 'You're all nerves.' 'So you move in these circles?' asked K. 'Yes,' replied the Advocate. 'You ask questions like a child,' said K.'s uncle. 'Whom should I associate with if not with men of my own profession?' added the Advocate. It sounded incontrovertible and K. made no answer. 'But you're attached to the Court in the Palace of Justice, not to the one with the skylight,' he wanted to say, yet could not bring himself actually to say it. 'You must consider,' the Advocate continued in the tone of one perfunctorily explaining something that should be self-evident, 'you must consider that this intercourse enables me to benefit my clients in all sorts of ways, some of which won't even bear mentioning. Of course I'm somewhat handicapped now because of my illness, but in spite of that, good friends of mine from the Law Courts visit me now and then and I learn lots of things from them. Perhaps more than many a man in the best of health who spends all his days in the Courts. For example, there's a dear friend of mine visiting me at this very moment,' and he waved a hand towards a dark corner of the room. 'Where?' asked K., almost roughly, in his first shock of astonishment. He looked round uncertainly; the light of the small candle did not nearly reach the opposite wall. And then some form or other in the dark corner actually began to stir. By the light of the candle, which his uncle now held high above his head, K. could see an elderly gentleman sitting there at a little table. He must have been sitting without even drawing a breath, to have remained for so long unnoticed. Now he got up ceremoniously, obviously displeased to have his presence made known. With his hands, which he flapped like short wings, he seemed to be deprecating all introductions or greetings, trying to show that the last thing he desired was to disturb the other gentlemen, and that he only wanted to be translated again to the darkness where his presence might be forgotten. But that privilege could no longer be his. 'I may say you took us by surprise,' said the Advocate in explanation, and he waved his hand to encourage the gentleman to approach, which he did very slowly and hesitatingly, glancing around him all the time, but with a certain dignity. 'The Chief Clerk of the Court – oh, I beg your pardon, I have not introduced you – this is my friend Albert K., this is his nephew the Assessor Joseph K., and this is the Chief Clerk of the Court – the Herr Clerk of the Court, to return to what I was saying, has been so good as to pay me a visit. The value of such a visit can really be appreciated only by the initiated who know how dreadfully our dear Clerk of the Court is overwhelmed with work. Yet he came to see me all the same, we were talking here peacefully, as far as my ill health permitted; we didn't actually forbid Leni to admit visitors, it was true, for we expected none, but we naturally thought that we should be left in peace, and then came your furious tattoo, Albert, and the Herr Clerk of the Court withdrew into the corner with his chair and his table, but now it seems we have the chance, that is, if you care to take it, of making the discussion general, since this case concerns us all, and we can reassemble our forces again. – Please, Herr Clerk of the Court,' he said with a bow and an obsequious smile, indicating an arm-chair near the bed. 'Unfortunately I can only stay for a few minutes longer,' said the Chief Clerk of the Court affably, seating himself in the chair and looking at his watch, 'my duties call me. But I don't want to miss this opportunity of becoming acquainted with a friend of my friend here.' He bowed slightly to K.'s uncle, who appeared very flattered to make this new acquaintance, yet, being by nature incapable of expressing obligation, requited the Clerk of the Court's words with a burst of embarrassed but raucous laughter. A hateful moment! K. could observe everything calmly, for nobody paid any attention to him. The Chief Clerk of the Court, now that he had been brought into prominence, seized the lead, as seemed to be his usual habit. The Advocate, whose first pretence of weakness had probably been intended simply to drive away his visitors, listened attentively, cupping his hand to his ear. K.'s uncle as candle-bearer – he was balancing the candle on his knee, the Advocate often glanced at it in apprehension – had soon rid himself of his embarrassment and was now delightedly absorbed in the Clerk of the Court's eloquence and the delicate wave-like gestures of the hand with which he accompanied it. K., leaning against the bedpost, was completely overlooked by the Clerk of the Court, perhaps by deliberate intention, and served merely as an audience to the other old gentleman. Besides, he could hardly follow the conversation and spent one minute thinking of the nurse and the rude treatment she had received from his uncle, and next wondering if he had not seen the Clerk of the Court before, perhaps actually among the audience during his first interrogation. He might be mistaken, yet the Clerk of the Court would have fitted excellently into the first row of the audience, the elderly gentlemen with the brittle beards.

Then a sound from the entrance hall as of breaking crockery made them all prick up their ears. 'I'll go and see what has happened,' said K., and he went out, rather slowly, to give the others a last chance to call him back. Hardly had he reached the entrance hall and begun to think of groping his way in the darkness, when a hand much smaller than his own covered the hand with which he was still holding the door and gently drew the door shut. It was the nurse who had been waiting there. 'Nothing has happened,' she whispered. 'I simply flung a plate against the wall to bring you out.' K. said in his embarrassment: 'I was thinking of you too.' 'That's all the better,' said the nurse. 'Come this way.' A step or two brought them to a door panelled with thick glass, which opened. 'In here,' she said. It was evidently the Advocate's office; as far as one could see in the moonlight, which brilliantly lit up a small square section of the floor in front of each of the two large windows, it was fitted out with antique solid furniture. 'Here,' said the nurse, pointing to a dark chest with a high carved back. After he had sat down K. still kept looking round the room, it was a lofty, spacious room, the clients of this 'poor man's' lawyer must feel lost in it. K. pictured to himself the timid, short steps with which they would advance to the huge table. But then he forgot all this and had eyes only for the nurse, who was sitting very close to him, almost squeezing him against the opposite arm of the bench. 'I thought,' she said, 'you would come out of your own accord, without waiting till I had to call you out. A queer way to behave. You couldn't keep your eyes off me from the very moment you came in, and yet you leave me to wait. And you'd better just call me Leni,' she added quickly and abruptly, as if there were not a moment to waste. 'I'll be glad to,' said K. 'But as for my queer behaviour, Leni, that's easy to explain. In the first place I had to listen to these old men jabbering. I couldn't simply walk out and leave them without any excuse, and in the second place I'm not in the least a bold young man, but rather shy, to tell the truth, and you too, Leni, really didn't look as if you were to be had for the asking.' 'It isn't that,' said Leni, laying her arm along the back of the seat and looking at K. 'But you didn't like me at first and you probably don't like me even now.' 'Liking is a feeble word,' said K. evasively. 'Oh!' she said, with a smile, and K.'s remark and that little exclamation gave her a certain advantage over him. So K. said nothing more for a while. As he had grown used to the darkness in the room, he could not distinguish certain details of the furnishings. He was particularly struck by a large picture which hung to the right of the door, and bent forward to see it more clearly. It represented a man in a Judge's robe; he was sitting on a high throne-like seat, and the gilding of the seat stood out strongly in the picture. The strange thing was that the Judge did not seem to be sitting in dignified composure, for his left arm was braced along the back and the side-arm of his throne, while his right arm rested on nothing, except for the hand, which clutched the other arm of the chair; it was as if in a moment he must spring up with a violent and probably wrathful gesture to make some fateful observation or even to pronounce sentence. The accused might be imagined as standing on the lowest step leading up to the chair of justice; the top step, which was covered with a yellowish carpet, was shown in the picture. 'Perhaps that is my Judge,' said K., pointing with his finger at the picture. 'I know him,' said Leni, and she looked at the picture too. 'He often comes here. That picture was painted when he was young, but it could never have been in the least like him, for he's a small man, almost a dwarf. Yet in spite of that he had himself drawn out to that length in the portrait, for he's madly vain like everybody else here. But I'm a vain person, too, and it upsets me that you don't like me in the least.' To this last statement K. replied merely by putting his arm round her and drawing her to him; she leaned her head against his shoulder in silence. But to the rest of her remarks he answered: 'What's the man's rank?' 'He is an Examining Magistrate,' she said, seizing the hand with which K. held her and beginning to play with his fingers. 'Only an Examining Magistrate again,' said K. in disappointment. 'The higher officials keep themselves well hidden. But he's sitting on a high seat.' 'That's all invention,' said Leni, with her face bent over his hand. 'Actually he sits on a kitchen chair, with an old horse-rug doubled under him. But must you eternally be brooding over your case?' she queried slowly. 'No, not at all,' said K. 'Probably I brood far too little over it.' 'That isn't the mistake you make,' said Leni. 'You're too unyielding, that's what I've heard.' 'Who told you that?' asked K.; he could feel her body against his breast and gazed down at her rich, dark, firmly knotted hair. 'I should give away too much if I told you that,' replied Leni. 'Please don't ask me for names, take my warning to heart instead, and don't be so unyielding in future, you can't put up a resistance against this Court, you must admit your fault. Make your confession at the first chance you get. Until you do that, there's no possibility of getting out of their clutches, none at all. Yet even then you won't manage it without help from outside, but you needn't trouble your head about that, I'll see to it myself.' 'You know a great deal about this Court and the intrigues that prevail in it!' said K., lifting her on to his knee, for she was leaning too heavily against him. 'That's better,' she said, making herself at home on his knee by smoothing her skirt and pulling her blouse straight. Then she clasped both her hands round his neck, leaned back, and looked at him for a long time. 'And if I don't make a confession of guilt, then you can't help me?' K. asked experimentally. 'I seem to recruit women helpers,' he thought almost in surprise; 'first Fräulein Bürstner, then the wife of the Law-Court Attendant, and now this cherishing little creature who appears to have some incomprehensible passion for me. She sits there on my knee as if it were the only right place for her!' 'No,' said Leni, shaking her head slowly, 'then I can't help you. But you don't in the least want my help, it doesn't matter to you, you're stiff-necked and never will be convinced.' After a while she asked: 'Do you have a sweetheart?' 'No,' said K. 'Oh, yes, you do,' she said. 'Well, yes I have,' said K. 'Just imagine it, I have told you she didn't exist and yet I am carrying her photograph in my pocket.' At her entreaty he showed her Elsa's photograph; she studied it, curled up on his knee. It was a snapshot taken of Elsa as she was finishing a skirt dance such as she often gave at the cabaret, her skirt was still flying round her like a fan, her hands were planted on her firm hips, and with her chin thrown up she was laughing over her shoulder at someone who did not appear in the photograph. 'She's very tightly laced,' said Leni, indicating the place where in her opinion the tight-lacing was evident. 'I don't like her, she's rough and clumsy. But perhaps she's soft and kind to you, one might guess that from the photograph. Big strong girls like that often can't help being soft and kind. But would she be capable of sacrificing herself for you?' 'No,' said K. 'She is neither soft nor kind, nor would she be capable of sacrificing herself for me. And up till now I have demanded neither the one thing nor the other from her. In fact I've never even examined this photograph as carefully as you have.' 'So she doesn't mean so very much to you,' said Leni. 'She isn't your sweetheart after all.' 'Oh, yes,' replied K. 'I refuse to take back my words.' 'Well, granted that she's your sweetheart,' said Leni, 'you wouldn't miss her very much, all the same, if you were to lose her or exchange her for someone else – me, for instance?' 'Certainly,' said K., smiling, 'that's conceivable, but she has one great advantage over you, she knows nothing about my case, and even if she knew she wouldn't bother her head about it. She wouldn't try to get me to be less unyielding.' 'That's no advantage,' said Leni. 'If that's all the advantage she has over me I shan't lose courage. Has she any physical defect?' 'Any physical defect?' asked K. 'Yes,' said Leni. 'For I have a slight one. Look.' She held up her right hand and stretched out the two middle fingers, between which the connecting web of skin reached almost to the top joint, short as the fingers were. In the darkness K. could not make out at once what she wanted to show him, so she took his hand and made him feel it. 'What a freak of nature!' said K. and he added, when he had examined the whole hand: 'What a pretty little paw!' Leni looked on with a kind of pride while K. in astonishment kept pulling the two fingers apart and then putting them side by side again, until at last he kissed them lightly and let them go. 'Oh!' she cried at once. 'You have kissed me!' She hastily scrambled up until she was kneeling open-mouthed on his knees. K. looked up at her almost in dumbfounderment; now that she was so close to him she gave out a bitter exciting odour as of pepper; she clasped his head to her, bent over him, and bit and kissed him on the neck, biting into the very hairs of his head. 'You have exchanged her for me,' she cried over and over again. 'Look, you have exchanged her for me after all!' Then her knees slipped, with a faint cry she almost fell on the carpet, K. put his arms round her to hold her up and was pulled down with her. 'You belong to me now,' she said.

'Here's the key of the door, come whenever you like,' were her last words, and as he took his leave a final aimless kiss landed on his shoulder. When he stepped out on to the pavement a light rain was falling; he was making for the middle of the street so as perhaps to catch a last glimpse of Leni at her window, but a car which was waiting before the house and which in his distraction he had never noticed suddenly emitted his uncle, who seized him by the arms and banged him against the house door as if he wanted to nail him there. 'Boy!' he cried, 'how could you do it! You have terribly damaged your case, which was beginning to go quite well. You hide yourself away with a filthy little trollop, who is obviously the Advocate's mistress into the bargain, and stay away for hours. You don't even seek any pretext, you conceal nothing, no, you're quite open, you simply run off to her and stay beside her. And all this time we three sit there, your uncle, who is doing his best for you, the Advocate, who has to be won over to your side, above all the Chief Clerk of the Court, a man of importance, who is actually in charge of your case at its present stage. There we sit, consulting how to help you, I have to handle the Advocate circumspectly, and the Advocate in turn the Clerk of the Court, and one might think you had every reason to give me at least some support. Instead of which you absent yourself. You were away so long that there was no concealing it; of course the two gentlemen, being men of the world, didn't talk about it, they spared my feelings, but finally even they couldn't get over it, and as they couldn't mention it they said nothing at all. We sat there for several minutes in complete silence, listening for you to come back. And all in vain. At last the Chief Clerk of the Court, who had stayed much longer than he intended, got up and said good night, evidently very sorry for me without being able to help me, his kindness was really extraordinary, he stood waiting for a while longer at the door before he left. And I was glad when he went, let me tell you; by that time I felt hardly able to breathe. And the poor Advocate felt it even worse, the good man couldn't utter a word as I took leave of him. In all probability you have helped to bring him to the verge of collapse and so hastened the death of a man on whose good offices you are dependent. And you leave me, your uncle, to wait here in the rain for hours; just feel, I'm wet through and through!'

7

ADVOCATE – MANUFACTURER – PAINTER

One winter morning – snow was falling outside the window in a foggy dimness – K. was sitting in his office, already exhausted in spite of the early hour. To save his face before his subordinates at least, he had given his clerk instructions to admit no one, on the plea that he was occupied with an important piece of work. But instead of working he twisted in his chair, idly rearranged the things lying on his writing-table, and then, without being aware of it, let his outstretched arm rest on the table and sat on with bowed head, immobile.

The thought of his case never left him now. He had often considered whether it would not be better to draw up a written defence and hand it in to the Court. In this defence he would give a short account of his life, and when he came to an event of any importance explain for what reasons he had acted as he did, intimate whether he approved or condemned his way of action in retrospect, and adduce grounds for the condemnation or approval. The advantages of such a written defence, as compared with the mere advocacy of an expert in the Law who himself was not impeccable, were undoubted. K. had no idea what the Advocate was doing about the case; at any rate it did not amount to much, it was more than a month since Huld had sent for him, and even during the first few consultations K. had formed the impression that the man could not do much for him. To begin with, he had hardly cross-questioned him at all. And there were so many questions to put. To ask questions was surely the main thing. Indeed K. felt that he himself could draw up all the necessary questions. But the Advocate, instead of asking questions, either did all the talking or sat quite dumb opposite him, bent slightly forward over his writing-table, probably because of his hardness of hearing, stroking a strand of hair in the middle of his beard and gazing at the carpet, perhaps at the very spot where K. had lain with Leni. Now and then he would give K. some empty admonitions such as people hand out to children. Admonitions as useless as they were wearisome, for which K. did not intend to pay a penny at the final reckoning. After the Advocate thought he had humbled him sufficiently, he usually set himself to encourage him again. He had already, so he would relate, won many similar cases either outright or partially. Cases which, though at bottom not quite so difficult, perhaps, as this one, had been outwardly still more hopeless. He had a summary of these cases in a drawer of his desk – at this he tapped one of them – but he regretted he couldn't show it, as it dealt with official secrets. Nevertheless the vast experience he had gained through all these cases would now redound to K.'s benefit. He had started on K.'s case at once, of course, and the first plea was almost ready for presentation. That was very important, for the first impression made by the defence often determined the whole course of subsequent proceedings. Though, unfortunately, it was his duty to warn K., it sometimes happened that the first plea was not read by the Court at all. They simply filed it among the other papers and pointed out that for the time being the observation and interrogation of the accused were more important than any formal petition. If the petitioner pressed them, they generally added that before the verdict was pronounced all the material accumulated, including, of course, every document relating to the case, the first plea as well, would be carefully examined. But unluckily even that was not quite true in most cases, the first plea was often mislaid or lost altogether and, even if it were kept intact till the end, was hardly ever read; that was of course, the Advocate admitted, merely a rumour. It was all very regrettable, but not wholly without justification. K. must remember that the proceedings were not public; they could certainly, if the Court considered it necessary, become public, but the Law did not prescribe that they must be made public. Naturally, therefore, the legal records of the case, and above all the actual charge-sheets, were inaccessible to the accused and his counsel, consequently one did not know in general, or at least did not know with any precision, what charges to meet in the first plea; accordingly it could be only by pure chance that it contained really relevant matter. One could draw up genuinely effective and convincing pleas only later on, when the separate charges and the evidence on which they were based emerged more definitely or could be guessed at from the interrogations. In such circumstances the Defence was naturally in a very ticklish and difficult position. Yet that, too, was intentional. For the Defence was not actually countenanced by the Law, but only tolerated, and there were differences of opinion even on that point, whether the Law could be interpreted to admit such tolerance at all. Strictly speaking, therefore, none of the Advocates was recognized by the Court, all who appeared before the Court as Advocates being in reality merely in the position of hole-and-corner Advocates. That naturally had a very humiliating effect on the whole profession, and the next time K. visited the Law-Court offices he should take a look at the Advocates' room, just for the sake of having seen it once in his life. He would probably be horrified by the kind of people he found assembled there. The very room, itself small and cramped, showed the contempt in which the Court held them. It was lit only by a small skylight, which was so high up that if you wanted to look out, you had to get some colleague to hoist you on his back, and even then the smoke from the chimney close by choked you and blackened your face. To give only one example of the state the place was in – there had been for more than a year now a hole in the floor, not so big that you could fall through the floor, but big enough to let a man's leg slip through. The Advocates' room was in the very top attic, so that if you stumbled through the hole your leg hung down into the lower attic, into the very corridor where the clients had to wait. It wasn't saying too much if the Advocates called these conditions scandalous. Complaints to the authorities had not the slightest effect, and it was also strictly forbidden for the Advocates to make any structural repairs or alterations at their own expense. Still, there was some justification for this attitude on the part of the authorities. They wanted to discourage defending counsel as much as possible, the whole onus of the Defence must be laid on the accused himself. A reasonable enough point of view, yet nothing could be more erroneous than to deduce from this that accused persons had no need of Advocates when appearing before this Court. On the contrary, in no other Court was legal assistance so necessary. For the proceedings were not only kept secret from the general public, but from the accused as well. Of course only within possible limits, but it proved possible to a very great extent. For even the accused had no access to the Court records, and to guess from the course of an interrogation what documents the Court had up its sleeve was very difficult, particularly for an accused person, who was himself implicated and had all sorts of worries to distract him. Now here was where defending counsel stepped in. Generally speaking, an Advocate was not allowed to be present during the examination, consequently he had to cross-question the accused immediately after an interrogation, if possible at the very door of the Court of Inquiry, and piece together from the usually confused reports he got anything that might be of use for the Defence. But even that was not the most important thing, for one could not elicit very much in that way, though of course here as elsewhere a capable man could elicit more than others. The most important thing was the Advocate's personal connexion with officials of the Court; in that lay the chief value of the Defence. Now K. must have discovered from experience that the very lowest grade of the Court organization was by no means perfect and contained venal and corrupt elements, whereby to some extent a breach was made in the watertight system of justice. This was where most of the petty Advocates tried to push their way in, by bribing and listening to gossip, in fact there had actually been cases of purloining documents, at least in former times. It was not to be gainsaid that these methods could achieve for the moment surprisingly favourable results, on which the freelance Advocates prided themselves, spreading them out as a lure for new clients, but they had no effect on the further progress of the case, or only a bad effect. Nothing was of any real value but respectable personal connexions with the higher officials, that was to say higher officials of subordinate rank, naturally. Only through these could the course of the proceedings be influenced, imperceptibly at first, perhaps, but more and more strongly as the case went on. Of course very few Advocates had such connexions, and here K.'s choice had been a very fortunate one. Perhaps only one or two other Advocates could boast of the same connexions as Dr Huld. These did not worry their heads about the mob in the Advocates' room and had nothing whatever to do with them. But their relations with the Court officials were all the more intimate. It was not even necessary that Dr Huld should always attend the Court, wait in the anteroom of the Examining Magistrates till they chose to appear, and be dependent on their moods for earning perhaps a delusive success or a definite snub. No, as K. had himself seen, the officials, and very high ones among them, visited Dr Huld of their own accord, voluntarily providing information with great frankness or at least in broad enough hints, discussing the next turn of the various cases; more, even sometimes letting themselves be persuaded to a new point of view. Certainly one should not rely too much on their readiness to be persuaded, for definitely as they might declare themselves for a new standpoint favourable to the Defence, they might well go straight to their offices and issue a statement in the directly contrary sense, a verdict far more severe on the accused than the original intention which they claimed to have renounced. Against that, of course, there was no remedy, for what they said to you in private was simply said to you in private and could not be followed up in public, even if the Defence were not obliged for other reasons to do its utmost to retain the favour of these gentlemen. On the other hand it had also to be considered that these gentlemen were not moved by mere human benevolence or friendly feeling in paying visits to defending counsel – only to experienced counsel, of course; they were in a certain sense actually dependent on the Defence. They could not help feeling the disadvantages of a judiciary system which insisted on secrecy from the start. Their remoteness kept the officials from being in touch with contemporary life; for the average case they were excellently equipped, such a case proceeded almost mechanically and only needed a push now and then; yet confronted with quite simple cases, or particularly difficult cases, they were often utterly at a loss, they did not have any right understanding of human relations, since they were confined day and night to the workings of their judicial system, while in such cases a knowledge of human nature itself was indispensable. Then it was that they came to the Advocates for advice, with a servant behind them carrying the papers that were usually kept so secret. In that window over there many a gentleman one would never have expected to encounter had sat gazing out hopelessly into the street, while the Advocate at his desk examined his papers in order to give him good counsel. And it was on such occasions as these that one could perceive how seriously these gentlemen took their vocation and how deeply they were plunged into despair when they came upon obstacles which the nature of things kept them from overcoming. Their position was not easy, and one must not do them an injustice by regarding it as easy. The ranks of officials in this judiciary system mounted endlessly, so that not even adepts could survey the hierarchy as a whole. And the proceedings of the Courts were generally kept secret from subordinate officials, consequently they could hardly ever quite follow in their further progress the cases on which they had worked; any particular case thus appeared in their circle of jurisdiction often without their knowing whence it came, and passed from it they knew not whither. Thus the knowledge was only to be derived from a study of the various single stages of the case: the final verdict and the reasons for that verdict lay beyond the reach of these officials. They were forced to restrict themselves to that stage of the case which was prescribed for them by their Law, and as for what followed, in other words the results of their own work, they generally knew less about it than the Defence, which as a rule remained in touch with the accused almost to the end of the case. So in that respect, too, they could learn much that was worth knowing from the Defence. Would it surprise K., then, keeping all this in mind, to find that the officials lived in a state of irritability which sometimes expressed itself in offensive ways when they dealt with their clients? That was the universal experience. All the officials were in a constant state of touchiness, even when they appeared calm. Naturally the petty hedge-lawyers were most liable to suffer from it. The following story, for example, was current, and it had all the appearance of truth. An old official, a well-meaning, quiet man, had a difficult case in hand which had been greatly complicated by the Advocate's petitions, and he had studied it continuously for a whole day and night – the officials were really more conscientious than one would believe. Well, towards morning, after twenty-four hours of work with probably very little result, he went to the entrance door, hid himself behind it, and flung down the stairs every Advocate who tried to enter. The Advocates gathered down below on the stair-head and took counsel what they should do; on the one hand they had no real claim to be admitted and consequently could hardly take any legal action against the official, and also, as already mentioned, they had to guard against antagonizing the body of officials. But on the other hand every day they spent away from the Court was a day lost to them, and so a great deal depended on their getting in. At last they all agreed that the best thing to do was to tire out the old gentleman. One Advocate after another was sent rushing upstairs to offer the greatest possible show of passive resistance and let himself be thrown down again into the arms of his colleagues. That lasted for about an hour, then the old gentleman – who was exhausted in any case by his work overnight – really grew tired and went back to his office. The Advocates down below would not believe it at first and sent one of their number up to peep behind the door and assure himself that the room was actually vacant. Only then were they able to enter, and from all accounts they did not dare even to grumble. For although the pettiest Advocate might be to some extent capable of analysing the state of things in the Court, it never occurred to the Advocates that they should suggest or insist on any improvements in the system, while – and this was very characteristic – almost every accused man, even quite ordinary people among them, discovered from the earliest stages a passion for suggesting reforms which often wasted time and energy that could have been better employed in other directions. The only sensible thing was to adapt oneself to existing conditions. Even if it were possible to alter a detail for the better here or there – but it was simple madness to think of it – any benefit arising from that would profit clients in the future only, while one's own interests would be immeasurably injured by attracting the attention of the ever-vengeful officials. Anything but draw attention to oneself from above! One must lie low, no matter how much it went against the grain. Must try to understand that this great organization remained, so to speak, in a state of delicate balance, and that if someone took it upon himself to alter the disposition of things around him, he ran the risk of losing his footing and falling to destruction, while the organization would simply right itself by some compensating reaction in another part of its machinery – since everything interlocked – and remain unchanged, unless, indeed, which was very probable, it became still more rigid, more vigilant, more severe, and more ruthless. One must really leave the Advocates to do their work, instead of interfering with them. Reproaches were not of much use, particularly when the offender was unable to perceive the full scope of the grounds for them; all the same, he must say that K. had very greatly damaged his case by his discourtesy to the Chief Clerk of the Court. That influential man could already almost be eliminated from the list of those who might be got to do something for K. He now ignored with unmistakable coldness even the slightest reference to the case. In many ways the functionaries were like children. Often they could be so deeply offended by the merest trifle – unfortunately, K.'s behaviour could not be classed as a trifle – that they would stop speaking even to old friends, give them the cold shoulder, and work against them in all imaginable ways. But then, suddenly, in the most surprising fashion and without any particular reason, they would be moved to laughter by some small jest which you only dared to make because you felt you had nothing to lose, and then they were your friends again. It was both easy and difficult to handle them, you could hardly lay down any fixed principles for dealing with them. Sometimes you felt astonished to think that one single ordinary lifetime sufficed to gather all the knowledge needed for a fair degree of success in such a profession. There were dark hours, of course, such as came to everybody, in which you thought you had achieved nothing at all, in which it seemed to you that only the cases predestined from the start to succeed came to a good end, which they would have reached in any event without an Advocate's help, while every one of the others was doomed to fail in spite of all your running about, all your exertions, all the illusory little victories on which you plumed yourself. That was a frame of mind, of course, in which nothing at all seemed certain, and so you could not positively deny the suggestion that your intervention might have side-tracked some cases which would have run quite well on the right lines had they been left alone. A desperate kind of self-assurance, to be sure, yet it was the only kind available at such times. These moods – for of course they were only moods, nothing more – afflicted Advocates more especially when a case which they had conducted with all satisfaction to the desired point was suddenly taken out of their hands. That was beyond all doubt the worst thing that could happen to an Advocate. Not that a client ever dismissed his Advocate from a case, such a thing was not done, an accused man, once having briefed an Advocate, must stick to him whatever happened. For how could he keep going by himself, once he had called in someone to help him? So that never happened, but it did sometimes happen that the case took a turn where the Advocate could no longer follow it. The case and the accused and everything were simply withdrawn from the Advocate; then even the best connexions with officials could no longer achieve any result, for even they knew nothing. The case had simply reached the stage where further assistance was ruled out, it had vanished into remote, inaccessible Courts, where even the accused was beyond the reach of an Advocate. Then you might come home some day and find on your table all the countless pleas relating to the case, which you had drawn up with such pains and such flattering hopes; they had been returned to you because in the new stage of the process they were not admitted as relevant; they were mere waste paper. It did not follow that the case was lost, by no means, at least there was no evidence for such an assumption; you simply knew nothing more about the case and would never know anything more about it. Now, very luckily, such occurrences were exceptional, and even if K.'s case were a case of that nature, it still had a long way to go before reaching that stage. For the time being, there were abundant opportunities for an Advocate's labour, and K. might rest assured that they would be exploited to the uttermost. The first plea, as before mentioned, was not yet handed in, but there was no hurry; far more important were the preliminary consultations with the relevant officials, and they had already taken place. With only partial success, as must be frankly admitted. It would be better for the time being not to divulge details which might have a bad influence on K. by elating or depressing him unduly, yet this much could be asserted, that certain officials had expressed themselves very graciously and had also shown great readiness to help, while others had expressed themselves less favourably, but in spite of that had by no means refused their collaboration. The result on the whole was therefore very gratifying, though one must not seek to draw any definite conclusion from that, since all preliminary negotiations began in the same way and only in the course of further developments did it appear whether they had real value or not. At any rate nothing was yet lost, and if they could manage to win over the Chief Clerk of the Court in spite of all that had happened – various moves had already been initiated towards that end – then, to use a surgeon's expression, this could be regarded as a clean wound and one could wait further developments with an easy mind.

In such and similar harangues the Advocate was inexhaustible. He reiterated them every time K. called on him. Progress had always been made, but the nature of the progress could never be divulged. The Advocate was always working away at the first plea, but it had never reached a conclusion, which at the next visit turned out to be an advantage, since the last few days would have been very inauspicious for handing it in, a fact which no one could have foreseen. If K., as sometimes happened, wearied out by the Advocate's volubility, remarked that, even taking into account all the difficulties, the plea seemed to be getting on very slowly, he was greeted with the retort that it was not getting on slowly at all, although they would have been much further on by now had K. come to the Advocate in time. Unfortunately he had neglected to do so and that omission was likely to keep him at a disadvantage, and not merely a temporal disadvantage, either.

The one welcome interruption to these visits was Leni, who always so arranged things that she brought in the Advocate's tea while K. was present. She would stand behind K.'s chair, apparently looking on, while the Advocate stooped with a kind of miserly greed over his cup and poured out and sipped his tea, but all the time she was letting K. surreptitiously hold her hand. There was total silence. The Advocate sipped, K. squeezed Leni's hand, and sometimes Leni ventured to caress his hair. 'Are you here still?' the Advocate would ask, after he had finished. 'I wanted to take the tea-tray away again,' Leni would answer, there would follow a last hand-clasp, the Advocate would wipe his mouth and begin again with new energy to harangue K.

Was the Advocate seeking to comfort him or to drive him to despair? K. could not tell, but he soon held it for an established fact that his defence was not in good hands. It might be all true, of course, what the Advocate said, though his attempts to magnify his own importance were transparent enough and it was likely that he had never till now conducted such an important case as he made K.'s out to be. But his continual bragging of his personal connexions with the officials was suspicious. Was it so certain that he was exploiting these connexions for K.'s benefit? The Advocate never forgot to mention that these officials were subordinate officials, therefore officials in a dependent position, for whose advancement certain turns in the various cases might in all probability be of some importance. Could they possibly employ the Advocate to bring about such turns in the case, turns which were bound, of course, to be unfavourable to the accused? Perhaps they did not always do that, it was hardly likely, there must be occasions on which they arranged that the Advocate should score a point or two as a reward for his services, since it was to their own interest for him to keep up his professional reputation. But if that were really the position, into which category were they likely to put K.'s case, which, as the Advocate maintained, was a very difficult, therefore important case, and had roused great interest in the Court from the very beginning? There could not be very much doubt what they would do. A clue was already provided in the fact that the first plea had not yet been handed in, though the case had lasted for months, and that according to the Advocate all the proceedings were still in their early stages, words which were obviously well calculated to lull the accused and keep him in a helpless state, in order suddenly to overpower him with the verdict or at least with the announcement that the preliminary examination had been concluded in his disfavour and the case handed over to higher authorities.

It was absolutely necessary for K. to intervene personally. In states of intense exhaustion, such as he experienced this winter morning, when all these thoughts kept running at random through his head, he was particularly incapable of resisting this conviction.

The contempt which he had once felt for the case was no longer justified. Had he stood alone in the world he could easily have ridiculed the whole affair, though it was also certain that in that event it could never have arisen at all. But now his uncle had dragged him to this Advocate, family considerations had come in; his position was no longer quite independent of the course the case took, he himself, with a certain inexplicable satisfaction, had imprudently mentioned it to some of his acquaintances, others had come to learn of it in ways unknown to him, his relations with Fräulein Bürstner seemed to fluctuate with the case itself – in short, he hardly had the choice now to keep up the case or let it drop, he was in the middle of it and must look to himself. For him to be so tired was a bad look-out.

Yet there was no need for exaggerated anxiety at the moment. In a relatively short time he had managed to work himself up to his present high position in the Bank and to maintain himself in that position and win recognition from everybody; surely if the abilities which had made this possible were to be applied in unravelling his own case, there was no doubt that it would go well. Above all, if he were to achieve anything, it was essential that he should eliminate from his mind the idea of possible guilt. There was no such guilt. This legal action was nothing more than a business deal such as he had often concluded to the advantage of the Bank, a deal within which, as always happened, lurked various dangers which were simply to be obviated. The right tactics were to avoid letting one's thoughts stray to one's own possible shortcomings, and to cling as firmly as one could to the thought of one's advantage. From this standpoint the conclusion was inevitable that the case must be withdrawn from the Advocate as soon as possible, preferably that very evening. According to the Advocate that was something unheard of, it was true, and very likely an insult, but K. could not endure that his efforts in the case should be thwarted by moves probably originating in the office of his own representative. Once the Advocate was shaken off, the plea must be sent in at once and the officials be urged daily, if possible, to give their attention to it. This would never be achieved by sitting meekly in the attic lobby like the others with one's hat under the seat. K. himself, or one of the women, or some other messenger must keep at the officials day after day and force them to sit down at their desks and study K.'s papers instead of gaping out into the lobby through the wooden rails. These tactics must be pursued unremittingly, everything must be organized and supervised; the Court would encounter for once an accused man who knew how to stick up for his rights.

Yet even though K. believed he could manage all this, the difficulty of drawing up the plea seemed overwhelming. At one time, not more than a week ago, he had regarded the possibility of having to draw up his own plea with merely a slight feeling of shame, it never even occurred to him that there might be difficulties in the way. He could remember that one of those mornings, when he was up to his ears in work, he had suddenly pushed everything aside and seized his jotting-pad with the idea of drafting the plan of such a plea and handing it to the Advocate by way of egging him on, but just at that moment the door of the Manager's room opened and the Deputy Manager came in guffawing uproariously. That had been a very painful moment for K., though, of course, the Deputy Manager had not been laughing at the plea, of which he knew nothing, but at a funny story from the Stock Exchange which he had just heard, a story which needed illustrating for the proper appreciation of the point, so that the Deputy Manager, bending over the desk, took K.'s pencil from his hand and drew the required picture on the page of the jotting-pad which had been intended for the plea.

Today K. was no longer hampered by feelings of shame; the plea simply had to be drawn up. If he could find no time for it in his office, which seemed very probable, then he must draft it in his lodgings by night. And if his nights were not enough, then he must ask for furlough. Anything but stop half-way, that was the stupidest thing one could do in any affair, not only in business. No doubt it was a task that meant almost interminable labour. One did not need to have a timid and fearful nature to be easily persuaded that the completion of this plea was a sheer impossibility. Not because of laziness or obstructive malice, which could only affect the Advocate, but because to meet an unknown accusation, not to mention other possible charges arising out of it, the whole of one's life would have to be passed in review, down to the smallest actions and accidents, clearly formulated and examined from every angle. And how dreary such a task would be! It would do well enough, perhaps, as an occupation for one's second childhood in years of retirement, when the long days needed filling up. But at this time when K. should be devoting his mind entirely to work, when every hour was hurried and crowded – for he was still in full career and rapidly becoming a rival even to the Deputy Manager – when his evenings and nights were all too short for the pleasures of a bachelor life this was the time when he must sit down to such a task! Once more his train of thought had led him into self-pity. Almost involuntarily, simply to make an end of it, he put his finger on the button which rang the bell in the waiting-room. While he pressed it he glanced at the clock. It was eleven o'clock, he had wasted two hours in dreaming, a long stretch of precious time, and he was, of course, still wearier than he had been before. Yet the time had not been quite lost, he had come to decisions which might prove valuable. The attendants brought in several letters and two cards from gentlemen who had been waiting for a considerable time. They were, in fact, extremely important clients of the Bank who should on no account have been kept waiting at all. Why had they come at such an unsuitable hour? – and why, they might well be asking in their turn behind the door, did the assiduous K. allow his private affairs to usurp the best time of day? Weary of what had gone before and wearily awaiting what was to come, K. got up to receive the first of his clients.

This was a jovial little man, a manufacturer whom K. knew well. He regretted having disturbed K. in the middle of important work and K. on his side regretted that he had kept the manufacturer waiting for so long. But his very regret he expressed in such a mechanical way, with such a lack of sincerity in his assurances, that the manufacturer could not have helped noticing it, had he not been so engrossed by the business in hand. As it was, he tugged papers covered with statistics out of every pocket, spread them before K., explained various entries, corrected a trifling error which his eye had caught even in this hasty survey, reminded K. of a similar transaction which he had concluded with him about a year before, mentioned casually that this time another bank was offering better terms to secure the deal, and finally sat in eager silence waiting for K.'s comments. K. had actually followed the man's argument quite closely in its early stages, the thought of such an important piece of business had its attractions for him too, but unfortunately not for long, he had soon ceased to listen and merely nodded now and then as the manufacturer's claims waxed in enthusiasm, until in the end he lost even that interest and confined himself to staring at the other's bald head bent over the papers and asking himself when the fellow would begin to realize that all his eloquence was being wasted. When the manufacturer stopped speaking, K. actually thought for a moment that the pause was intended to give him the chance of confessing that he was not in a fit state to attend to business. And it was merely with regret that he perceived the intent look on the manufacturer's face, the alertness, as if prepared for every objection, which indicated that the interview was supposed to continue. So he bowed his head as at a word of command and began slowly to move his pencil point over the papers, pausing here and there to stare at some figure. The manufacturer suspected K. of looking for flaws in the scheme, perhaps the figures were not quite reliable after all, perhaps they were not the decisive factors in the deal, or at any rate he laid his hand over them and shifting closer to K. began to expound the general policy behind the transaction. 'It's difficult,' said K., pursing his lips, and now that the papers, the only things he had to hold on to, were covered up, he sank weakly against the arm of his chair. He glanced up slightly, but only slightly, when the door of the Manager's room opened, disclosed the Deputy Manager, a blurred figure who looked as if veiled in some kind of gauze. K. did not bother about this apparition, but merely registered its immediate effect, which was very gratifying for him. For the manufacturer at once bounded from his chair and rushed over to the Deputy Manager, though K. could have wished him to be ten times quicker, since he was afraid the apparition might vanish again. His fear was superfluous, the two gentlemen met each other, shook hands, and advanced together towards K.'s desk. The manufacturer lamented that his proposals were being cold-shouldered by the Assessor, indicating K., who under the Deputy Manager's eye had once more bent over the papers. Then as the two of them leaned against his desk, and the manufacturer set himself to win the newcomer's approval for his scheme, it seemed to K. as though two giants of enormous size were bargaining above his head for himself. Slowly, lifting his eyes as far as he dared, he peered up to see what they were about, then picked one of the documents from the desk at random, laid it flat on his open palm, and gradually raised it, rising himself with it, to their level. In doing so he had no definite purpose, but merely acted with the feeling that this was how he would have to act when he had finished the great task of drawing up the plea which was completely to acquit him. The Deputy Manager, who was giving his full attention to the conversation, merely glanced at the paper without even reading what was on it, for anything that seemed important to the Assessor was unimportant to him, took it from K.'s hand, said: 'Thanks, I know all that already,' and quietly laid it back on the desk again. K. darted an angry look at him, but the Deputy Manager did not notice that, or, if he did, was only amused, he laughed loudly several times, visibly disconcerted the manufacturer by a quick thrust, at once saved him by countering himself, and finally invited the man into his private office, where they could decide the transaction together. 'It is a very important proposal,' he said to the manufacturer, 'I entirely agree. And the Herr Assessor,' – even in saying this he went on addressing himself only to the manufacturer – 'will I am sure be relieved if we take it off his shoulders. This business needs thinking over. And he seems to be overworked today; besides, there are some people who have been waiting for him in the ante-room for hours.' K. had still enough self-command to turn away from the Deputy Manager and address his friendly but somewhat fixed smile solely to the manufacturer; except for this he made no response, supporting himself with both hands on the desk, bending forward a little like an obsequious clerk, and looked on while the two men, still talking away, gathered up the papers and disappeared into the Manager's room. In the very doorway, the manufacturer turned round to remark that he would not say good-bye yet, for of course he would report the result of the interview to the Herr Assessor; besides, there was another little matter he had to mention.

At last K. was alone. He had not the slightest intention of interviewing any more clients and vaguely realized how pleasant it was that the people waiting outside believed him to be still occupied with the manufacturer, so that nobody, not even the attendant, would disturb him. He went over to the window, perched on the sill, holding on to the latch with one hand, and looked down on the square below. The snow was still falling, the sky had not yet cleared.

For a long time he sat like this, without knowing what really troubled him, only turning his head from time to time with an alarmed glance towards the ante-room, where he fancied, mistakenly, that he heard a noise. But as no one came in he recovered his composure, went over to the wash-basin, washed his face in cold water, and returned to his place at the window with a clearer mind. The decision to take his defence into his own hands seemed now more grave to him than he had originally fancied. So long as the Advocate was responsible for the case it had not come really home to him, he had viewed it with a certain detachment and kept beyond reach of immediate contact with it, he had been able to intervene whenever he liked but could also withdraw whenever he liked. Now, on the other hand, if he were to conduct his own defence he would be putting himself completely at the defence of the Court, at least for the time being, a policy which would eventually bring about his absolute and definite acquittal, but would meanwhile, provisionally at least, involve him in far greater dangers than before. If he had ever doubted that, his state of mind today in his encounter with the Deputy Manager and the manufacturer would have been more than enough to convince him. What a stupor had overcome him, merely because he had decided to conduct his own defence! And what would develop later on? What days were lying in wait for him? Would he ever find the right path through all these difficulties? If he were to put up a thoroughgoing defence – and any other kind would be a waste of time – to put up a thoroughgoing defence, did that not involve cutting himself off from every other activity? Would he be able to survive that? And how was he to conduct his case from a Bank office? It was not merely the drawing up of a plea; that might be managed on a few weeks' furlough, though to ask for leave of absence just now would be decidedly risky; it was a matter of substantial action, whose duration it was impossible to foresee. What an obstacle had suddenly arisen to block K.'s career!

And this was the moment when he was supposed to do Bank work? He looked down at his desk. This the time to interview clients and bargain with them? While his case was unfolding itself, while up in the attics the Court clerks were poring over the charge papers, was he to devote his attention to the affairs of the Bank? It looked like a kind of torture sanctioned by the Court, arising from his case and concomitant with it. And would allowances be made for his peculiar position when his work in the Bank came to be judged? Never, and by nobody. The existence of his case was not exactly unknown in the Bank, though it was not quite clear who knew of it and how much they knew. But apparently the rumour had not yet reached the Deputy Manager, otherwise K. could hardly have failed to perceive it, since the man could have exploited his knowledge without any scruples as a colleague or as a human being. And the Manager himself? He was certainly well disposed to K. and as soon as he heard of the case would probably be willing enough to lighten K.'s duties as far as lay in his power, but his good intentions would be checkmated, for K.'s waning prestige was no longer sufficient to counterbalance the influence of the Deputy Manager, who was gaining a stronger hold on the Manager and exploiting the latter's invalid condition to his own advantage. So what had K. to hope? It might be that he was only sapping his powers of resistance by harbouring these thoughts; still, it was necessary to have no illusions and to view the position as clearly as the moment allowed.

Without any particular motive, merely to put off returning to his desk, he opened the window. It was difficult to open, he had to push the latch with both hands. Then there came into the room through the great window a blend of fog and smoke, filling it with a faint smell of burning soot. Some snowflakes fluttered in too. 'An awful autumn,' came the voice of the manufacturer from behind K.; returning from his colloquy with the Deputy Manager he had entered the room unobserved. K. nodded and shot an apprehensive glance at the man's attaché-case, from which doubtless he would now extract all his papers in order to inform K. how the negotiations had gone. But the manufacturer, catching K.'s, eye, merely tapped his attaché-case without opening it and said: 'You would like to know how it has turned out? The final settlement is as good as in my pocket. A charming fellow, your Deputy Manager, but dangerous to reckon with.' He laughed and shook K. by the hand, trying to make him laugh too. But now K.'s suspicions seized on the fact that the manufacturer had not offered to show him the papers, and he found nothing to laugh at. 'Herr Assessor,' said the manufacturer, 'you're under the weather today. You look so depressed.' 'Yes,' said K., putting his hand to his brow, 'a headache, family troubles.' 'Ah, yes,' said the manufacturer, who was a hasty man and could never listen quietly to anybody, 'we all have our troubles.' K. had involuntarily taken a step towards the door, as if to show the manufacturer out, but the latter said: 'Herr Assessor, there's another little matter I should mention to you. I'm afraid this isn't exactly the moment to bother you with it, but the last two times I've been here I forgot to mention it. And if I put off mentioning it any longer it will probably lose its point altogether. And that would be a pity, since my information may have some real value for you.' Before K. had time to make any reply the man stepped up close to him, tapped him with one finger on the chest, and said in a low voice: 'You're involved in a case, aren't you?' K. started back, crying out: 'The Deputy Manager told you that.' 'Not at all,' said the manufacturer. 'How should the Deputy Manager know anything about it?' 'How do you know about it?' asked K., pulling himself together. 'I pick up scraps of information about the Court now and then,' said the manufacturer, 'and that accounts for what I have to mention.' 'So many people seem to be connected with the Court!' said K. with a bowed head, as he led the manufacturer back to the desk. They sat down as before and the manufacturer began: 'Unfortunately it isn't much that I can tell you. But in these affairs one shouldn't leave the smallest stone unturned. Besides, I feel a strong desire to help you, no matter how modest the help. We have always been good business friends till now, haven't we? Well, then.' K. wanted to excuse himself for his behaviour that morning, but the manufacturer would not hear of it, pushed his attaché-case firmly under his arm to show that he was in a hurry to go, and continued: 'I heard of your case from a man called Titorelli. He's a painter, Titorelli is only his pseudonym, I don't know at all what his real name is. For years he has been in the habit of calling at my office from time to time, bringing little paintings for which I give him a sort of alms – he's almost a beggar. And they're not bad pictures, moors and heaths and so on. These deals – we have got into the way of them – pass off quite smoothly. But there was a time when he turned up too frequently for my taste, I told him so, we fell into conversation, I was curious to know how he could keep himself going entirely by his painting, and I discovered to my astonishment that he really earned his living as a portrait-painter. He worked for the Court, he said. For what Court, I asked. And then he told me about this Court. With your experience you can well imagine how amazed I was at the tales he told me. Since then he brings me the latest news from the Court every time he arrives, and in this way I have gradually acquired a considerable insight into its workings. Of course Titorelli wags his tongue too freely, and I often have to put a stopper on him, not just because he's naturally a liar, but chiefly because a business man like myself has so many troubles of his own that he can't afford to bother much about other people's. That's only by the way. Perhaps – I thought to myself – Titorelli might be of some use to you, he knows many of the Judges, and even if he can hardly have much influence himself, he can at least advise you how to get in touch with influential men. And even if you can't take him as an oracle, still it seems to me that in your hands his information might become important. For you are as good as a lawyer yourself. I'm always saying: Assessor K. is almost a lawyer. Oh, I have no anxiety about your case. Well, would you care to go and see Titorelli? On my recommendation he will certainly do all he can for you, I really think you should go. It needn't be today, of course, some time, any time will do. Let me add that you needn't feel bound to go just because I advise you to, not in the least. No, if you think you can dispense with Titorelli, it's certainly better to leave him entirely out of it. Perhaps you've a detailed plan of your own already drawn up and Titorelli might spoil it. Well, in that case you'd much better not go to see him. It certainly means swallowing one's pride to go to such a fellow for advice. Anyhow, do just as you like. Here is my letter of recommendation and here is the address.'

K. took the letter, feeling dashed, and stuck it in his pocket. Even in the most favourable circumstances the advantages which his recommendation could bring him must be outweighed by the damage implied in the fact that the manufacturer knew about his case and that the painter was spreading news of it. He could hardly bring himself to utter the few obligatory words of thanks to the manufacturer, who was already on his way out. 'I'll go to see the man,' he said as he shook hands at the door, 'or write to him to call here, since I'm so busy.' 'I knew,' said the manufacturer, 'that you could be depended on to find the best solution.

Though I must say I should have thought you would rather avoid receiving people like this Titorelli at the Bank, if you mean to discuss your case with him. Besides, it's not always advisable to let such people get their hands on letters of yours. But I'm sure you've thought it all over and know what you are doing.' K. nodded and accompanied the manufacturer a stage farther, through the waiting-room. In spite of his outward composure he was horrified at his own lack of sense. His suggestion of writing to Titorelli had been made merely to show the manufacturer that he appreciated the recommendation and meant to lose no time in making contact with the painter, but, left to himself, he would not have hesitated to write to Titorelli had he regarded the man's assistance as important. Yet it needed the manufacturer to point out the dangers lurking in such an action. Had he really lost his powers of judgement to that extent already? If it was possible for him to think of explicitly inviting a questionable character to the Bank in order to stage a discussion of his case with only a door between him and the Deputy Manager, was it not also possible and even extremely probable that he was overlooking other dangers as well, or blindly running into them? There wasn't always someone at his side to warn him. And this was the moment, just when he intended to concentrate all his energies on the case, this was the moment for him to start doubting the alertness of his faculties! Must the difficulties he was faced with in carrying out his office work begin to affect the case as well? At all events he simply could not understand how he could ever have thought of writing to Titorelli and inviting him to come to the Bank.

He was still shaking his head over this when the attendant came up to him and indicated three gentlemen sitting on a bench in the waiting-room. They had already waited for a long time to see K. Now that the attendant accosted K. they sprang to their feet, each one of them eager to seize the first chance of monopolizing K.'s attention. If the Bank officials were inconsiderate enough to make them waste their time in the waiting-room, they felt entitled in their turn to behave with the same lack of consideration. 'Herr Assessor,' one of them began. But K. sent for his overcoat and said to all three of them while the attendant helped him into it: 'Forgive me, gentlemen, I'm sorry to tell you that I have no time to see you at present. I can't say how desolated I am, but I have to go out on urgent business and must leave the building at once. You have seen for yourselves how long I have been held up by my last caller. Would you be so good as to come back tomorrow or at some other time? Or could we talk the matter over on the telephone, perhaps? Or perhaps you could inform me now, briefly, what your business is, and I shall give you an explicit answer in writing. Though it would certainly be much better if you made an appointment for some other time.' These suggestions threw the three men, whose time had thus been wasted to no purpose at all, into such astonishment that they gazed at each other dumbly. 'That's settled, then?' asked K., turning to the attendant, who was bringing him his hat. Through the open door of his room he could see that the snow was now falling more thickly. Consequently he put up his coat-collar and buttoned it high round his neck.

At that very moment the Deputy Manager stepped out of the next room, glanced smilingly at K. in his overcoat talking to the clients, and asked: 'Are you going out, Herr Assessor?' 'Yes,' said K., straightening himself, 'I have to go out on business.' But the Deputy Manager had already turned to the three clients. 'And these gentlemen?' he asked. 'I believe they have already been waiting a long time.' 'We have settled what we are to do,' said K. But now the clients could no longer be held in check, they clustered round K. protesting that they would not have waited for hours unless their business had been important, not to say urgent, necessitating immediate discussion at length, and in private at that. The Deputy Manager listened to them for a moment or two, meanwhile observing K., who stood holding his hat and dusting it spasmodically, then he remarked: 'Gentlemen, there is a very simple solution. If you will be content with me, I put myself gladly at your disposal instead of the Herr Assessor. Your business must, of course, be attended to at once. We are business men like yourselves and know how valuable time is to a business man. Will you be so good as to come with me?' And he opened the door which led to the waiting-room of his own office.

How clever the Deputy Manager was at poaching on the preserves which K. was forced to abandon! But was not K. abandoning more than was absolutely needful? While with the vaguest and – he could not but admit it – the faintest of hopes, he was rushing away to see an unknown painter, his prestige in the Bank would suffer irreparable injury. It would probably be much better for him to take off his overcoat again and conciliate at least the two clients waiting next door for their turn to receive the Deputy Manager's attention. K. might actually have attempted this if he had not at that moment caught sight of the Deputy Manager himself in K.'s own room, searching through his files as if they belonged to him. In great agitation K. appeared in the doorway of the room and the Deputy Manager exclaimed: 'Oh, you're not away yet.' He turned his face towards K. – the deep lines scored upon it seemed to speak of power rather than old age – and immediately resumed his search. 'I'm looking for a copy of an agreement,' he said, 'which the firm's representative thinks should be among your papers. Won't you help me to look?' K. took a step forward, but the Deputy Manager said: 'Thanks, now I've found it,' and carrying a huge package of documents, which obviously contained not only the copy of the agreement but many other papers as well, he returned to his office.

'I'm not equal to him just now,' K. told himself, 'but once my personal difficulties are settled he'll be the first to feel it, and I'll make him suffer for it, too.' Somewhat soothed by this thought, K. instructed the attendant, who had been holding open the corridor door for a long time, to inform the Manager at any convenient time that he had gone out on a business call, and then, almost elated at the thought of being able to devote himself entirely to his case for a while, he left the Bank.

He drove at once to the address where the painter lived, in a suburb which was almost at the diametrically opposite end of the town from where the Court held its meetings. This was an even poorer neighbourhood, the houses were still darker, the streets filled with sludge oozing about slowly on top of the melting snow. In the tenement where the painter lived only one wing of the great double door stood open, and beneath the other wing, in the masonry near the ground, there was a gaping hole out of which, just as K. approached, issued a disgusting yellow fluid, steaming hot, from which a rat fled into the adjoining canal. At the foot of the stairs an infant lay belly down on the ground bawling, but one could scarcely hear its shrieks because of the deafening din that came from a tinsmith's workshop at the other side of the entry. The door of the workshop was open; three apprentices were standing in a half-circle round some object on which they were beating with their hammers. A great sheet of tin hanging on the wall cast a pallid light, which fell between two of the apprentices and lit up their faces and aprons. K. flung only a fleeting glance at all this, he wanted to get out of the neighbourhood as quickly as possible, he would merely ask the painter a few searching questions and return at once to the Bank. His work at the Bank for the rest of the day would benefit should he have any luck at all on this visit. When he reached the third floor he had to moderate his pace, he was quite out of breath, both the stairs and the storeys were disproportionately high, and the painter was supposed to live quite at the top, in an attic. The air was stifling; there was no well for these narrow stairs, which were enclosed on either side by blank walls, showing only at rare intervals a tiny window very high up. Just as K. paused to take breath, several young girls rushed out of one of the flats and laughingly raced past him up the stairs. K. slowly followed them, catching up with one who had apparently stumbled and been left behind, and as they ascended together he asked her: 'Does a painter called Titorelli live here?' The girl, who had a slight spinal deformity and seemed scarcely thirteen years old, nudged him with her elbow and peered up at him knowingly. Neither her youth nor her deformity had saved her from being prematurely debauched. She did not even smile, but stared unwinkingly at K. with shrewd, bold eyes. K. pretended not to have noticed her behaviour and asked: 'Do you know the painter Titorelli?' She nodded and asked in her turn: 'What do you want him for?' K. thought it a good chance to find out a little more about Titorelli while he still had time: 'I want him to paint my portrait,' he said. 'To paint your portrait?' she repeated, letting her jaw fall open, then she gave K. a little slap as if he had said something extraordinarily unexpected or stupid, lifted her abbreviated skirts with both hands, and raced as fast as she could after the other girls, whose shrieks were already dying away in the distance. Yet at the very next turn of the stair K. ran into all of them. Obviously the hunch-back had reported K.'s intention, and they were waiting there for him. They stood lined up on either side of the stairway, squeezing against the walls to leave room for K. to pass, and smoothing their skirts down with their hands. All their faces betrayed the same mixture of childishness and sophistication which had prompted this idea of making him run the gauntlet between them. At the top end of the row of girls, who now closed in behind K. with spurts of laughter, stood the hunch-back ready to lead the way. Thanks to her, he was able to make straight for the right door. He had intended to go on up the main stairs, but she indicated a side-stair that branched off towards Titorelli's dwelling. This stairway was extremely narrow, very long, without any turning, could thus be surveyed in all its length, and was abruptly terminated by nothing but Titorelli's door. In contrast to the rest of the stairway this door was relatively brightly lit by a little fanlight set at an angle above it, and was made of unpainted planks on which sprawled the name Titorelli in red, traced in sweeping brush-strokes. K. with his escort was hardly more than half-way up the stairs when someone above, obviously disturbed by the clatter of so many feet, opened the door a little way, and a man who seemed to be wearing nothing but a nightshirt appeared in the opening. 'Oh!' he cried when he saw the approaching mob, and promptly vanished. The hunch-back clapped her hands in joy, and the other girls crowded K. from behind to urge him on faster.

Yet they were still mounting towards the top when the painter flung the door wide open and with a deep bow invited K. to enter. As for the girls, he turned them off, he would not admit one of them, eagerly as they implored and hard as they tried to enter by force if not by permission. The hunch-back alone managed to slip under his outstretched arm, but he rushed after her, seized her by the skirts, whirled her once round his head, and then set her down before the door among the other girls, who had not dared meanwhile, although he had quitted his post, to cross the threshold. K. did not know what to make of all this, for they seemed to be on the friendliest terms together. The girls outside the door, craning their necks behind one another, shouted various jocular remarks at the painter which K. did not understand, and the painter was laughing too as he almost hurled the hunch-back through the air. Then he shut the door, bowed once more to K., held out his hand, and said in introduction: 'I'm the painter Titorelli.' K. pointed at the door, behind which the girls were whispering, and said: 'You seem to be a great favourite here.' 'Oh, these brats!' said the painter, trying unsuccessfully to button his nightshirt at the neck. He was barefooted and besides the nightshirt had on only a pair of wide-legged yellow linen trousers girt by a belt with a long end flapping to and fro. 'These brats are a real nuisance,' he went on, while he desisted from fiddling with his nightshirt, since the top button had just come off, fetched a chair and urged K. to sit down. 'I painted one of them once – not any of those you saw – and since then they've all persecuted me. When I'm here myself they can only get in if I let them, but whenever I go away there's always at least one of them here. They've had a key made for my door, and they lend it round. You can hardly imagine what a nuisance that is. For instance, if I bring a lady here whom I want to paint, I unlock the door with my own key and find, say, the hunch-back over there at the table, reddening her lips with my paint brushes, while her little sisters, who she's supposed to keep an eye on, are sprawling over the whole place and messing up every corner of the room. Or, and this actually happened last night, I come home very late – by the way, that's why I'm in this state of disrepair, and the room too, please excuse it – I come home late, then, and start climbing into bed and something catches me by the leg; I look under the bed and haul out another of these pests. Why they should make such a set at me I don't know, you must have noticed yourself that I don't exactly encourage them. And, of course, all this disturbs me in my work. If it hadn't been that I have free quarters in this studio I should have cleared out long ago.' Just then a small voice piped behind the door with anxious cajolery: 'Titorelli, can we come in now?' 'No,' replied the painter. 'Not even me?' the voice asked again. 'Not even you,' said the painter, and he went to the door and locked it.

Meanwhile K. had been looking round the room; it would never have occurred to him that anyone could call this wretched little hole a studio. You could scarcely take two strides in any direction. The whole room, floor, walls, and ceiling, was a box of bare wooden planks with cracks showing between them. Opposite K., against a wall, stood a bed with a variegated assortment of coverings. In the middle of the room an easel supported a canvas covered by a shirt whose sleeves dangled on the floor. Behind K. was the window, through which in the fog one could not see farther than the snow-covered roof of the next house.

The turning of the key in the lock reminded K. that he had not meant to stay long. Accordingly he fished the manufacturer's letter from his pocket, handed it to the painter, and said: 'I heard of you from this gentleman, a friend of yours, and have come here at his suggestion.' The painter hastily read the letter through and pitched it on to the bed. If the manufacturer had not so explicitly claimed acquaintance with Titorelli as a poor man dependent on his charity, one might actually have thought that Titorelli did not know the manufacturer or at least could not remember him. On top of this he now asked: 'Have you come to buy pictures or to have your portrait painted?' K. stared at him in amazement. What could have been in the letter? He had assumed as a matter of course that the manufacturer would tell Titorelli that he had come for no other purpose than to inquire about his case. He had been altogether too rash and reckless in rushing to this man. But he must make a relevant reply of some kind, and so he said with a glance at the easel: 'You're working on a painting just now?' 'Yes,' said Titorelli, stripping the shirt from the easel and throwing it on the bed after the letter. 'It's a portrait. A good piece of work, but not quite finished yet.' K. was apparently in luck, the opportunity to mention the Court was being literally thrown at his head, for this was obviously the portrait of a Judge. Also it strikingly resembled the portrait hanging in the Advocate's office. True, this was quite a different Judge, a stout man with a black bushy beard which reached far up on his cheeks on either side; moreover the other portrait was in oils, while this was lightly and as yet indistinctly sketched in pastel. Yet everything else showed a close resemblance, for here too the Judge seemed to be on the point of starting menacingly from his high seat, bracing himself firmly on the arms of it. 'That must be a Judge,' K. felt like saying at once, but he checked himself for the time being and approached the picture as if he wished to study the detail. A large figure rising in the middle of the picture from the high back of the chair he could not identify, and he asked the painter whom it was intended to represent. It still needed a few more touches, the painter replied, and fetched a crayon from a table, armed with which he worked a little at the outline of the figure but without making it any more recognizable to K. 'It is Justice,' said the painter at last. 'Now I can recognize it,' said K. 'There's the bandage over the eyes, and here are the scales. But aren't there wings on the figure's heels, and isn't it flying?' 'Yes,' said the painter, 'my instructions were to paint it like that; actually it is Justice and the goddess of Victory in one.' 'Not a very good combination, surely,' said K., smiling. 'Justice must stand quite still, or else the scales will waver and a just verdict will become impossible.' 'I had to follow my client's instructions,' said the painter. 'Of course,' said K., who had not wished to give any offence by his remark. 'You have painted the figure as it actually stands above the high seat.' 'No,' said the painter, 'I have neither seen the figure nor the high seat, that is all invention, but I am told what to paint and I paint it.' 'How do you mean?' asked K., deliberately pretending that he did not understand. 'It's surely a Judge sitting on his seat of justice?' 'Yes,' said the painter, 'but it is by no means a high Judge and he has never sat on such a seat in his life.' 'And yet he has himself painted in that solemn posture? Why, he sits there as if he were the actual President of the Court.' 'Yes, they're very vain, these gentlemen,' said the painter. 'But their superiors give them permission to get themselves painted like that. Each one of them gets precise instructions how he may have his portrait painted. Only you can't judge the detail of the costume and the seat itself from this picture, unfortunately, pastel is really unsuited for this kind of thing.' 'Yes,' said K. 'it's curious that you should have used pastel.' 'My client wished it,' said the painter, 'he intends the picture for a lady.' The sight of the picture seemed to have aroused his ardour, he rolled up his shirt-sleeves, took several crayons in his hand, and as K. watched the delicate crayon-strokes a reddish shadow began to grow round the head of the Judge, a shadow which tapered off in long rays as it approached the edge of the picture. This play of shadow bit by bit surrounded the head like a halo or a high mark of distinction. But the figure of Justice was left bright except for an almost imperceptible touch of shadow; that brightness brought the figure sweeping right into the foreground and it no longer suggested the goddess of Justice, or even the goddess of Victory, but looked exactly like a goddess of the Hunt in full cry. The painter's activities absorbed K. against his will, and in the end he began to reproach himself for having stayed so long without even touching on the business that brought him. 'What is the name of this Judge?' he asked suddenly. 'I'm not allowed to tell,' replied the painter, stooping over the picture and ostentatiously ignoring the guest whom at first he had greeted with such consideration. K. put this down to caprice and was annoyed that his time should be wasted in such a manner. 'You're in the confidence of the Court, I take it?' he asked. The painter laid down his crayons at once, straightened himself, rubbed his hands, and looked at K. with a smile. 'So the truth has come out at last,' he said. 'You want to find out something about the Court, as your letter of recommendation told me, I may say, and you started talking about my paintings only to win me over. But I don't take that ill, you could hardly know that that wasn't the right way to tackle me. Oh, please don't apologize!' he said sharply, as K. tried to make some excuse. And then he continued: 'Besides, you were quite right in what you said; I am in the confidence of the Court.' He paused, as if he wanted to give K. time to digest this fact. Now they could hear the girls behind the door again. They seemed to be crowding round the keyhole, perhaps they could see into the room through the cracks in the door as well. K. abandoned any attempt at apology, for he did not want to deflect the conversation, nor did he want the painter to feel too important, and so become in a sense inaccessible, accordingly he asked: 'Is your position an official appointment?' 'No,' said the painter curtly, as if the question had cut him short. K., being anxious to keep him going, said: 'Well, such unrecognized posts often carry more influence with them than the official ones.' 'That is just how it is with me.' said the painter, knitting his brow and nodding. 'The manufacturer mentioned your case to me yesterday, he asked me if I wouldn't help you, I said to him: "Let the man come and see me some time," and I'm delighted to see you here so soon. The case seems to lie very near your heart, which, of course, is not in the least surprising. Won't you take off your coat for a moment?' Although K. had it in mind to stay only for a short time, this request was very welcome to him. He had begun to feel the air in the room stifling, several times already he had eyed with amazement a little iron stove in the corner which did not seem even to be working, the sultry heat in the place was inexplicable. He took off his overcoat, unbuttoning his jacket as well, and the painter said apologetically: 'I must have warmth. It's very cosy in here, isn't it? I'm well enough off in that respect.' K. said nothing to this, for it was not the warmth that made him so uncomfortable, it was rather the stuffy, oppressive atmosphere; the room could not have been aired for a long time. His discomfort was still more intensified when the painter begged him to sit down on the bed, while he himself took the only chair in the room, which stood beside the easel. Titorelli also seemed to misunderstand K.'s reasons for sitting on the extreme edge of the bed, he urged him to make himself comfortable and actually pushed the reluctant K. deep down among the bedclothes and pillows. Then he returned to his chair again and at last put his first serious question, which made K. forget everything else. 'Are you innocent?' he asked. 'Yes,' said K. The answering of this question gave him a feeling of real happiness, particularly as he was addressing a private individual and therefore need fear no consequences. Nobody else had yet asked him such a frank question. To savour to the full his elation he added: 'I am completely innocent,' 'I see,' said the painter, bending his head as if in thought. Suddenly he raised it again and said: 'If you are innocent, then the matter is quite simple.' K.'s eyes darkened, this man who said he was in the confidence of the Court was talking like an ignorant child. 'My innocence doesn't make the matter any simpler,' said K. But after all he could not help smiling, and then he slowly shook his head. 'I have to fight against countless subtleties in which the Court is likely to lose itself. And in the end, out of nothing at all, an enormous fabric of guilt will be conjured up.' 'Yes, yes, of course,' said the painter, as if K. were needlessly interrupting the thread of his ideas. 'But you're innocent all the same?' 'Why, yes,' said K. 'That's the main thing,' said the painter. He was not to be moved by argument, yet in spite of his decisiveness it was not clear whether he spoke out of conviction or out of mere indifference. K. wanted first to be sure of this, so he said: 'You know the Court much better than I do, I feel certain, I don't know much more about it than what I've heard from all sorts and conditions of people. But they all agree on one thing, that charges are never made frivolously, and that the Court, once it has brought a charge against someone, is firmly convinced of the guilt of the accused and can be dislodged from that conviction only with the greatest difficulty.' 'The greatest difficulty?' cried the painter, flinging one hand in the air. 'Never in any case can the Court be dislodged from that conviction. If I were to paint all the Judges in a row on one canvas and you were to plead your case before it, you would have more hope of success than before the actual Court.' 'I see,' said K. to himself, forgetting that he merely wished to probe the painter.

Again a girl's voice piped from behind the door: 'Titorelli, won't he be going away soon?' 'Quiet there!' cried the painter over his shoulder. 'Can't you see that I'm engaged with this gentleman?' But the girl, not to be put off, asked: 'Are you going to paint him?' And when the painter did not reply she went on: 'Please don't paint him, such an ugly man as that.' The others yelled agreement in a confused jabbering. The painter made a leap for the door, opened it a little – K. could see the imploring, outstretched, clasped hands of the girls – and said: 'If you don't stop that noise I'll fling you all down the stairs. Sit down here on the steps and see that you keep quiet.' Apparently they did not obey him at once, for he had to shout in an imperious voice: 'Down with you on the steps!' After that all was still.

'Excuse me,' said the painter, returning to K. again. K. had scarcely glanced towards the door, he had left it to the painter to decide whether and in what manner he was to be protected. Even now he scarcely made a movement when the painter bent down to him and whispered in his ear, so that the girls outside might not hear: 'These girls belong to the Court too.' 'What?' cried K., screwing his head round to stare at the painter. But Titorelli sat down again on his chair and said half in jest, half in explanation: 'You see, everything belongs to the Court.' 'That's something I hadn't noticed,' said K. shortly; the painter's general statement stripped his remark about the girls of all its disturbing significance. Yet K. sat gazing for some time at the door, behind which the girls were now sitting quietly on the stairs. One of them had thrust a blade of straw through a crack between the planks and was moving it slowly up and down.

'You don't seem to have any general idea of the Court yet,' said the painter, stretching his legs wide in front of him and tapping with his shoes on the floor. 'But since you're innocent you won't need it anyhow. I shall get you off all by myself.' 'How can you do that?' asked K. 'For you told me yourself a few minutes ago that the Court was quite impervious to proof.' 'Impervious only to proof which one brings before the Court,' said the painter, raising one finger as if K. had failed to perceive a fine distinction. 'But it is quite a different matter with one's efforts behind the scenes; that is, in the consulting-rooms, in the lobbies or, for example, in this very studio.' What the painter now said no longer seemed incredible to K., indeed it agreed in the main with what he had heard from other people. More, it was actually hopeful in a high degree. If a Judge could really be so easily influenced by personal connexions as the Advocate insisted, then the painter's connexions with these vain functionaries were especially important and in any case not to be undervalued. That made the painter an excellent recruit to the ring of helpers which K. was gradually gathering round him. His talent for organization had once been the pride of the Bank, and now that he had to act entirely on his own responsibility this was his chance to prove it to the uttermost. Titorelli observed the effect his words had produced upon K. and then said with a slight uneasiness: 'Perhaps it strikes you that I talk almost like a jurist? It's my long association with the gentlemen of the Court that has made me grow like that. I have many advantages from it, of course, but I'm losing a great deal of my *élan* as an artist.' 'How did you come in contact with the Judges to begin with?' asked K.; he wanted to win the painter's confidence first, before actually enlisting him in his service. 'That was quite simple,' said the painter. 'I inherited the connexion. My father was the Court painter before me. It's the only post that is always hereditary. New people are of no use for it. There are so many complicated and various and above all secret rules laid down for the painting of the different grades of functionaries that a knowledge of them must be confined to certain families. Over there in that chest, for instance, I keep all my father's drawings, which I never show to anyone. And only a man who has studied them can possibly paint the Judges. Yet even if I were to lose them, I have enough private knowledge tucked away in my head to make my post secure against all comers. For every Judge insists on being painted as the great old Judges were painted, and nobody can do that but me.' 'Yours is an enviable situation,' said K., who was thinking of his own post in the Bank. 'So your position is unassailable?' 'Yes, unassailable,' replied the painter, proudly bracing his shoulders. 'And for that reason, too, I can venture to help a poor man with his case now and then.' 'And how do you do it?' asked K., as if it were not himself who had just been described as a poor man. But Titorelli refused to be drawn in and went on: 'In your case, for instance, as you are completely innocent, this is the line I shall take.' The repeated mention of his innocence was already making K. impatient. At moments it seemed to him as if these repetitions were based on a naïve assumption that his case was bound to turn out well, and on these terms the painter's help would be worth having. But in spite of his doubts K. held his tongue and did not interrupt the man. He was not prepared to renounce Titorelli's assistance, on that point he was decided; the painter was no more questionable as an ally than the Advocate, Indeed he very much preferred the painter's offer of assistance, since it was made so much more ingenuously and frankly.

Titorelli drew his chair closer to the bed and continued in a low voice: 'I forgot to ask you first what sort of acquittal you want. There are three possibilities, that is, definite acquittal, ostensible acquittal, and indefinite postponement. Definite acquittal is of course the best, but I haven't the slighest influence on that kind of verdict. As far as I know, there is no single person who could influence the verdict of definite acquittal. The only deciding factor seems to be the innocence of the accused. Since you're innocent, of course it would be possible for you to ground your case on your innocence alone. But then you would require neither my help nor help from anyone.'

This lucid explanation took K. aback at first, but he replied in the same subdued voice as the painter: 'It seems to me that you're contradicting yourself.' 'In what way?' asked the painter patiently, leaning back with a smile. The smile awoke in K. a suspicion that he was now about to expose contradictions not so much in the painter's statements as in the Court procedure itself. However, he was not abashed but went on: 'You made the assertion earlier that the Court is impervious to proof, later you qualified that assertion by confining it to the public sessions of the Court, and now you actually say that an innocent man requires no help before the Court. That alone implies a contradiction. But, in addition, you said at first that the Judges can be moved by personal intervention, and now you deny that definite acquittal, as you call it, can ever be achieved by personal intervention. In that lies the second contradiction.' 'These contradictions are easy to explain,' said the painter. 'We must distinguish between two things: what is established by the Law, and what I have discovered through personal experience; you must not confuse the two. In the code of the Law, which I may say I have not read, it is of course laid down on the one hand that the innocent shall be acquitted, but it is not stated on the other hand that the Judges are open to influence. Now, my experience is diametrically opposed to that. I have not met one case of definite acquittal, and I have met many cases of influential intervention. It is possible, of course, that in all the cases known to me there was none in which the accused was really innocent. But is not that probable? Among so many cases no single case of innocence? Even as a child I used to listen carefully to my father when he spoke of cases he had heard about; the Judges, too, who came to his studio were always telling stories about the Court, in our circle it is still the sole topic of discussion; no sooner did I get the chance to attend the Court myself than I took full advantage of it, I have listened to countless cases in their most crucial stages, and followed them as far as they could be followed, and yet – I must admit it – I have never encountered one case of definite acquittal.' 'Not one case of definite acquittal, then,' said K. as if he were speaking to himself and his hopes, 'but that merely confirms the opinion that I have already formed of this Court. It is an aimless institution from any point of view. A single executioner could do all that is needed.' 'You mustn't generalize,' said the painter in displeasure. 'I have only quoted my own experience.' 'That's quite enough,' said K. 'Or have you ever heard of acquittals in earlier times?' 'Such acquittals,' replied the painter, 'there must certainly have been. Only it is very difficult to prove the fact. The final decisions of the Court are never recorded, even the Judges can't get hold of them, consequently we have only legendary accounts of ancient cases. These legends certainly provide instances of acquittal; actually the majority of them are about acquittals, they can be believed, but they cannot be proved. All the same, they shouldn't be entirely left out of account, they must have an element of truth in them, and besides they are very beautiful. I myself have painted several pictures founded on such legends.' 'Mere legends cannot alter my opinion,' said K. 'and I fancy that one cannot appeal to such legends before the Court?' The painter laughed. 'No, one can't do that,' he said. 'Then there's no use talking about them,' said K., willing for the time being to fall in with the painter's views, even where they seemed improbable or contradicted other reports he had heard. He had no time now to inquire into the truth of all the painter said, much less disprove it, the utmost he could hope to do was to get the man to help him in some way, even should the help prove inconclusive. Accordingly he said; 'Let us leave definite acquittal out of account, then; you mentioned two other possibilities as well.' 'Ostensible acquittal and postponement. These are the only possibilities,' said the painter. 'But won't you take off your jacket before we go on to speak of them? You look very hot.' 'Yes,' said K., who had been paying no attention to anything but the painter's expositions, but now that he was reminded of the heat found his forehead drenched in sweat. 'It's almost unbearable.' The painter nodded as if he comprehended K.'s discomfort quite well. 'Couldn't we open the window?' asked K. 'No,' replied the painter. 'It's only a sheet of glass let into the roof, it can't be opened.' Now K. realized that he had been hoping all the time that either the painter or himself would suddenly go over to the window and fling it open. He was prepared to gulp down even mouthfuls of fog if he could only get air. The feeling of being desperately cut off from the fresh air made his head swim. He brought the flat of his hand down on the feather bed and said in a feeble voice: 'That's both uncomfortable and unhealthy.' 'Oh no,' said the painter in defence of his window. 'Because it's sealed down it keeps the warmth in much better than a double window, though it's only a simple pane of glass. And if I want to air the place, which isn't really necessary, for the air comes in everywhere through the chinks, I can always open one of the doors or even both of them.' Somewhat reassured by this explanation, K. glanced round to discover the second door. The painter saw what he was doing and said: 'It's behind you, I had to block it up by putting the bed in front of it.' Only now did K. see the little door in the wall. 'This is really too small for a studio,' said the painter, as if to forestall K.'s criticisms. 'I simply had to put my things where I could. Of course it's a bad place for a bed, just in front of that door. The Judge whom I'm painting just now, for instance, always comes in by that door, and I've had to give him a key for it so that he can wait for me in the studio if I happen to be out. Well, he usually arrives early in the morning, while I'm still asleep. And of course however fast asleep I am, it wakens me with a start when the door behind my bed suddenly opens. You would lose any respect you have for the Judges if you could hear the curses that welcome him when he climbs over my bed in the early morning. I could certainly take the key away from him again, but that would only make things worse. It would be easy enough to burst open any of the doors here.' All during these exchanges K. kept considering whether he should take off his jacket, but at last he realized that if he did not he would be incapable of staying any longer in the room, so he took it off, laying it, however, across his knee, to save time in putting it on again whenever the interview was finished. Scarcely had he taken off his jacket when one of the girls cried: 'He's taken off his jacket now,' and he could hear them all crowding to peer through the cracks and view the spectacle for themselves. 'The girls think,' said the painter, 'that I'm going to paint your portrait and that's why you are taking off your jacket.' 'I see,' said K., very little amused, for he did not feel much better than before, although he was now sitting in his shirt-sleeves. Almost morosely he asked: 'What did you say the other two possibilities were?' He had already forgotten even the names of them. 'Ostensible acquittal and indefinite postponement,' said the painter. 'It lies with you to choose between them. I can help you to either of them, though not without taking some trouble, and, as far as that is concerned, the difference between them is that ostensible acquittal demands intense concentration at long intervals, while postponement taxes your strength less but means a steady strain. First, then, let us take ostensible acquittal. If you decide on that, I shall write down on a sheet of paper an affidavit of your innocence. The text for such affidavits has been handed down to me by my father and allows of no quibbling. Then with this affidavit I shall make a round of the Judges I know, beginning, let us say, with the Judge I am painting now, when he comes for his sitting tonight. I shall lay the affidavit before him, explain to him that you are innocent, and myself guarantee your innocence. And that is not merely a formal guarantee but a real and binding one.' In the eyes of the painter there was a faint suggestion of reproach that K. should lay upon him the burden of such a responsibility. 'That would be very kind of you,' said K. 'And the Judge would believe you and yet not give me a definite acquittal?' 'As I have already explained,' replied the painter. 'Besides, it is not in the least certain that every Judge will believe me; some Judges, for instance, will ask to see you in person. And then I should have to take you with me to call on them. Though when that happens the battle is already half won, particularly as I should tell you beforehand, of course, exactly what line to take with the Judge. The real difficulty comes with the Judges who turn you down at the start – and that's sure to happen too. I should go on hammering at them, of course, but we might have to do without them, though one cannot afford to do that, since dissent by individual Judges cannot affect the result. Well then, if I get a sufficient number of Judges to subscribe to the affidavit, I shall then deliver it to the Judge who is actually conducting your trial. Possibly I may have secured his signature too, then everything will be settled fairly soon, a little sooner than usual. Generally speaking, there should be no difficulties worth mentioning after that, the accused at this stage can feel supremely confident. Indeed it's remarkable, but true, that people's confidence mounts higher at this stage than after their acquittal. There's no need for them to do much more. The Judge is covered by the guarantees of the other Judges subscribing to the affidavit, and so he can grant an acquittal with an easy mind, and though some formalities may remain to be settled, he will undoubtedly grant the acquittal to please me and his other friends. Then you can walk out of the Court a free man.' 'So then I'm free,' said K. doubtfully. 'Yes,' said the painter, 'but only ostensibly free, or more exactly, provisionally free. For the Judges of the lowest grade, to whom my acquaintances belong, haven't the power to grant a final acquittal, that power is reserved for the highest Court of all, which is quite inaccessible to you, to me, and to all of us. What the prospects are up there we do not know and, I may say in passing, do not even want to know. The great privilege, then, of absolving from guilt our Judges do not possess, but they do have the right to take the burden of the charge off your shoulders. That is to say, when you are acquitted in this fashion the charge is lifted from your shoulders for the time being, but it continues to hover above you and can, as soon as an order comes from on high, be laid upon you again. As my connexion with the Court is such a close one, I can also tell you how in the routine of the Law-Court offices the distinction between definite and ostensible acquittal takes formal effect. In definite acquittal the documents relating to the case are completely annulled, they simply vanish from sight, not only the charge but also the records of the case and even the acquittal are destroyed, everything is destroyed. That's not the case with ostensible acquittal. The documents remain as they were, except that the affidavit is added to them and a record of the acquittal and the grounds for granting it. The whole dossier continues to circulate, as the regular official routine demands, passing on to the higher Courts, being referred to the lower ones again, and thus swinging backwards and forwards with greater or smaller oscillations, longer or shorter delays. These peregrinations are incalculable. A detached observer might sometimes fancy that the whole case had been forgotten, the documents lost, and the acquittal made absolute. No one really acquainted with the Court could think such a thing. No document is ever lost, the Court never forgets anything. One day – quite unexpectedly – some Judge will take up the documents and look at them attentively, recognize that in this case the charge is still valid, and order an immediate arrest. I have been speaking on the assumption that a long time elapses between the ostensible acquittal and the new arrest; that is possible and I have known of such cases, but it is just as possible for the acquitted man to go straight home from the Court and find officers already waiting to arrest him again. Then, of course, all his freedom is at an end.' 'And the case begins all over again?' asked K. almost incredulously. 'Certainly,' said the painter. 'The case begins all over again, but again it is possible, just as before, to secure an ostensible acquittal. One must again apply all one's energies to the case and never give in.' These last words were probably uttered because he noticed that K. was looking somewhat faint. 'But,' said K., as if he wanted to forestall any more revelations, 'isn't the engineering of a second acquittal more difficult than the first?' 'On that point,' said the painter, 'one can say nothing with certainty. You mean, I take it, that the second arrest might influence the Judges against signing a new affidavit? That is not so. Even while they are pronouncing the first acquittal the Judges foresee the possibility of the new arrest. Such a consideration, therefore, hardly comes into question. But it may happen, for hundreds of reasons, that the Judges are in a different frame of mind about the case, even from a legal view-point, and one's efforts to obtain a second acquittal must consequently be adapted to the changed circumstances, and in general must be every whit as energetic as those that secured the first one.' 'But this second acquittal isn't final either,' said K., turning away his head in repudiation. 'Of course not,' said the painter. 'The second acquittal is followed by the third arrest, the third acquittal by the fourth arrest, and so on. That is implied in the very idea of ostensible acquittal.' K. said nothing. 'Ostensible acquittal doesn't seem to appeal to you,' said the painter. 'Perhaps postponement would suit you better. Shall I explain to you how postponement works?' K. nodded. The painter was lolling back in his chair, his night-shirt gaped open, he had thrust one hand inside it and was lightly fingering his breast. 'Postponement,' he said, gazing in front of him for a moment as if seeking a completely convincing explanation, 'postponement consists in preventing the case from ever getting any further than its first stages. To achieve that it is necessary for the accused and his agent, but more particularly his agent, to remain continuously in personal touch with the Court. Let me point out again that this does not demand such intense concentration of one's energies as an ostensible acquittal, yet on the other hand it does require far greater vigilance. You daren't let the case out of your sight, you visit the Judge at regular intervals as well as in emergencies and must do all that is in your power to keep him friendly; if you don't know the Judge personally, then you must try to influence him through other Judges whom you do know, but without giving up your efforts to secure a personal interview. If you neglect none of these things, then you can assume with fair certainty that the case will never pass beyond its first stages. Not that the proceedings are quashed, but the accused is almost as likely to escape sentence as if he were free. As against ostensible acquittal postponement has this advantage, that the future of the accused is less uncertain, he is secured from the terrors of sudden arrest and doesn't need to fear having to undergo – perhaps at a most inconvenient moment – the strain and agitation which are inevitable in the achievement of ostensible acquittal. Though postponement, too, has certain drawbacks for the accused, and these must not be minimized. In saying this I am not thinking of the fact that the accused is never free; he isn't free either, in any real sense, after the ostensible acquittal. There are other drawbacks. The case can't be held up indefinitely without at least some plausible grounds being provided. So as a matter of form a certain activity must be shown from time to time, various measures have to be taken, the accused is questioned, evidence is collected, and so on. For the case must be kept going all the time, although only in the small circle to which it has been artificially restricted. This naturally involves the accused in occasional unpleasantness, but you must not think of it as being very unpleasant. For it's all a formality, the interrogations, for instance, are only short ones; if you have neither the time nor the inclination to go, you can excuse yourself on occasion, with some Judges you can even plan your interviews a long time ahead, all that it amounts to is a formal recognition of your status as an accused man by regular appearances before your Judge.' Already while these last words were being spoken K. had taken his jacket across his arm and got up. 'He's getting up now,' came the cry at once from behind the door. 'Are you going already?' asked the painter, who had also got up. 'I'm sure it's the air here that is driving you away. I'm sorry about it. I had a great deal more to tell you. I have had to express myself very briefly. But I hope my statements were lucid enough.' 'Oh yes,' said K., whose head was aching with the strain of forcing himself to listen. In spite of K.'s confirmation, the painter went on to sum up the matter again, as if to give him a last word of comfort: 'Both methods have this in common, that they save the accused from coming up for sentence.' 'But they also prevent an actual acquittal,' said K. in a low voice, as if embarrassed by his own perspicacity. 'You have grasped the kernel of the matter,' said the painter quickly. K. laid his hand on his overcoat, but could not even summon the resolution to put on his jacket. He would have liked best of all to bundle them both together and rush out with them into the fresh air. Even the thought of the girls could not move him to put on his garments, although their voices were already piping, in anticipation, the news that he was doing so. The painter was anxious to guess K.'s intentions, so he said: 'I take it that you haven't come to any decision yet on my suggestions. That's right. In fact, I should have advised you against it had you attempted an immediate decision. It's like splitting hairs to distinguish the advantages and disadvantages. You must weigh everything very carefully. On the other hand you mustn't lose too much time either.' 'I'll come back again soon,' said K., in a sudden fit of resolution putting on his jacket, flinging his overcoat across his shoulders and hastening to the door, behind which the girls at once began shrieking. K. felt he could almost see them through the door. 'But you must keep your word,' said the painter, who had not followed him, 'or else I'll have to come to the Bank myself to make inquiries.' 'Unlock this door, will you?' said K., tugging at the handle, which the girls, as he could tell from the resistance, were hanging on to from outside. 'You don't want to be bothered by the girls, do you?' asked the painter. 'You had better take this way out,' and he indicated the door behind the bed. K. was perfectly willing and rushed back to the bed. But instead of opening the bedside door the painter crawled right under the bed and said from down there: 'Wait just a minute. Wouldn't you like to see a picture or two that you might care to buy?' K. did not want to be discourteous, the painter had really taken an interest in him and promised to help him further, also it was entirely owing to K.'s distractedness that the matter of a fee for the painter's services had not been mentioned, consequently he could not turn aside his offer now, and so he consented to look at the pictures, though he was trembling with impatience to be out of the place. Titorelli dragged a pile of unframed canvases from under the bed, they were so thickly covered with dust that when he blew some of it from the topmost, K. was almost blinded and choked by the cloud that flew up. 'Wild Nature, a heathscape,' said the painter, handing K. the picture. It showed two stunted trees standing far apart from each other in darkish grass. In the background was a many-hued sunset. 'Fine,' said K., 'I'll buy it.' K.'s curtness had been unthinking and so he was glad when the painter, instead of being offended, lifted another canvas from the floor. 'Here's the companion picture,' he said. It might be intended as a companion picture, but there was not the slightest difference that one could see between it and the other, here were the two trees, here the grass, and there the sunset. But K. did not bother about that. 'They're fine prospects,' he said. 'I'll buy both of them and hang them up in my office.' 'You seem to like the subject,' said the painter, fishing out a third canvas. 'By a lucky chance I have another of these studies here.' But it was not merely a similar study, it was simply the same wild heathscape again. The painter was apparently exploiting to the full this opportunity to sell off his old pictures. 'I'll take that one as well,' said K. 'How much for the three pictures?' 'We'll settle that next time,' said the painter. 'You're in a hurry today and we're going to keep in touch with each other, anyhow. I may say I'm very glad you like these pictures and I'll throw in all the others under the bed as well. They're heathscapes every one of them, I've painted dozens of them in my time. Some people won't have anything to do with these subjects because they're too depressing, but there are always people like yourself who prefer depressing pictures.' But by now K. had no mind to listen to the professional pronouncements of the peddling painter. 'Wrap the pictures up,' he cried, interrupting Titorelli's garrulity, 'my attendant will call tomorrow and fetch them.' 'That isn't necessary,' said the painter. 'I think I can manage to get you a porter to take them along with you now.' And at last he reached over the bed and unlocked the door. 'Don't be afraid to step on the bed,' he said. 'Everybody who comes here does that.' K. would not have hesitated to do it even without his invitation, he had actually set one foot plump on the middle of the feather bed, but when he looked out through the open door he drew his foot back again. 'What's this?' he asked the painter. 'What are you surprised at?' returned the painter, surprised in his turn. 'These are the Law-Court offices. Didn't you know that there were Law-Court offices here? There are Law-Court offices in almost every attic, why should this be an exception? My studio really belongs to the Law-Court offices, but the Court has put it at my disposal.' It was not so much the discovery of the Law-Court offices that startled K.; he was much more startled at himself, at his complete ignorance of all things concerning the Court. He accepted it as a fundamental principle for an accused man to be always forearmed, never to let himself be caught napping, never to let his eyes stray unthinkingly to the right when his judge was looming up on the left – and against that very principle he kept offending again and again. Before him stretched a long passage, from which was wafted an air compared to which the air in the studio was refreshing. Benches stood on either side of the passage, just as in the lobby of the offices that were handling K.'s case. There seemed, then, to be exact regulations for the interior disposition of these offices. At the moment there was no great coming and going of clients. A man was half sitting, half reclining on a bench, his face was buried in his arms and he seemed to be asleep; another man was standing in the dusk at the end of the passage. K. now stepped over the bed, the painter followed him with the pictures. They soon found a Law-Court Attendant – by this time K. recognized these men from the gold buttons added to there ordinary civilian clothing – and the painter gave him instructions to accompany K. with the pictures. K. tottered rather than walked, keeping his handkerchief pressed to his mouth. They had almost reached the exit when the girls came rushing to meet them, so K. had not been spared even that encounter. The girls had obviously seen the second floor of the studio opening and had made a detour at full speed, coming round by another stairway. 'I can't escort you any farther,' cried the painter laughingly, as the girls surrounded him. 'Till our next meeting. And don't take too long to think it over!' K. did not even look back. When he reached the street he hailed the first cab that came along. He must get rid of the Attendant, whose gold buttons offended his eyes, even though, likely enough, they escaped everyone else's attention. The Attendant, zealously dutiful, got up beside the coachman on the box, but K. made him get down again. Midday was long past when K. reached the Bank. He would have liked to leave the pictures in the cab, but was afraid that some day he might be required to give an account of them to the painter. So he had them carried into his office and locked them in the bottom drawer of his desk, to save them for the next few days at least from the eyes of the Deputy Manager.

8

THE COMMERCIAL TRAVELLER – DISMISSAL OF THE ADVOCATE

At long last K. had made up his mind to take his case out of the Advocate's hands. He could not quite rid himself of doubts about the wisdom of this step, but his conviction of its necessity prevailed. To screw himself to the decision cost him a lot of energy, on the day when he resolved to visit the Advocate his work lagged behind, he had to stay very late in the office, and so he did not reach the Advocate's door until well past ten o'clock. Before actually ringing the bell he thought it over once again, it might be better to dismiss the Advocate by telephone or by letter, a personal interview was bound to prove painful. Still, he did not want to lose the advantage of a personal interview, any other mode of dismissal would be accepted in silence or with a few formal words of acknowledgement, and unless he were to extract information from Leni he would never learn how the Advocate had reacted to the dismissal and what consequences for himself were likely to ensue according to the Advocate's opinion, which was not without its importance. Face to face with the Advocate, one could spring the dismissal on him as a surprise, and however guarded the man might be, K. would be easily able to learn from his demeanour all that he wanted to know. It was even possible that he might perceive the wisdom of leaving the case in the Advocate's hands after all and might withdraw his ultimatum.

The first ring at the Advocate's door produced, as usual, no result. 'Leni could be a little quicker,' thought K. But it was enough to be thankful for that no third party had come nosing in, as usually happened, the man in the dressing-gown, for instance, or some other interfering creature. K. glanced at the farther door as he pressed the button a second time, but on this occasion both doors remained firmly shut. At last a pair of eyes appeared at the grille in the Advocate's door, but they were not Leni's eyes. Someone shot back the bolt, but still blocked the way, calling down the lobby: 'It's him,' and only then flinging the door open. K. had been pushing against the door, for he could already hear a key being hastily turned in the neighbouring lock, and when it suddenly opened he was literally precipitated into the hall and caught a glimpse of Leni, for whom the warning cry must have been intended, rushing down the lobby in her nightgown. He peered after her for a moment and then turned to see who had opened the door. It was a dried-up little man with a long beard, he was holding a candle in one hand. 'Are you employed here?' asked K. 'No,' said the man, 'I don't belong to the house, I'm only a client, I've come here on business.' 'In your shirt-sleeves?' asked K., indicating the man's unceremonious attire. 'Oh, excuse me,' said the man, peering at himself by the light of the candle as if he had been unaware of his condition. 'Is Leni your mistress?' inquired K. curtly. He was straddling his legs slightly, his hands, in which he was holding his hat, clasped behind his back. The mere possession of a thick greatcoat gave him a feeling of superiority over the meagre little fellow. 'Oh God,' said the other, raising one hand before his face in horrified repudiation, 'no, no, what are you thinking of?' 'You look an honest man,' said K., smiling, 'but all the same – come along.' He waved him on with his hat, urging him to go first. 'What's your name?' K. asked as they were proceeding. 'Block, a commercial traveller,' said the little man, turning round to introduce himself, but K. would not suffer him to remain standing. 'Is that your real name?' went on K. 'Of course,' came the answer, 'why should you doubt it?' 'I thought you might have some reason for concealing your name,' said K. He was feeling at ease now, at ease as one is when speaking to an inferior in some foreign country, keeping one's own affairs to oneself and discussing with equanimity the other man's interests, which gain consequence for the attention one bestows on them yet can be dismissed at will. As they came to the Advocate's study K. halted, opened the door, and called to the fellow, who was meekly advancing along the lobby: 'Not so fast, show a light here.' K. fancied that Leni might have hidden herself in the study, he made the commercial traveller shine the candle into all the corners, but the room was empty. In front of the Judge's portrait K. caught the fellow from behind by the braces and pulled him back. 'Do you know who that is?' he asked, pointing upward at the picture. The man raised the candle, blinked up at the picture, and said: 'It's a Judge.' 'A high Judge?' asked K., stationing himself beside the other to observe what impression the portrait made on him. The man gazed up with reverence. 'It is a high Judge,' he said. 'You haven't much insight,' said K., 'that's the lowest of the low among the Judges.' 'Now, I remember,' said the man, letting the candle sink. 'I've been told that before.' 'But of course,' cried K., 'how could I forget, of course you must have heard it before.' 'But why, why must I?' asked the man, moving towards the door, for K. was propelling him from behind. When they were out in the lobby K. said: 'I suppose you know where Leni's hiding?' 'Hiding?' said he. 'No, she should be in the kitchen making soup for the Advocate.' 'Why didn't you tell me that at first?' asked K. 'I was going to take you there but you called me back,' answered the man, as if bewildered by these contradictory demands. 'You fancy you're being very sly,' said K., 'lead the way then!' K. had never yet been in the kitchen, and it was surprisingly large and well furnished. The cooking-stove alone was three times the size of an ordinary stove; the rest of the fittings could not be seen in detail since the sole light came from a small lamp hanging near the door. Leni was standing by the stove in a white apron, as usual, emptying eggs into a pan that simmered on an alcohol flame. 'Good evening, Joseph,' she said, glancing over her shoulder. 'Good evening,' said K., waving the commercial traveller to a chair some distance away, on which the man obediently sat down. Then K. went quite close up behind Leni, leaned over her shoulder, and asked: 'Who's this man?' Leni put her disengaged arm round K., stirring the soup with the other, and pulled him forward. 'He's a miserable creature,' she said, 'a poor commercial traveller called Block. Just look at him.' They both glanced round. The commercial traveller was sitting in the chair K. had indicated for him; having blown out the candle, which was no longer needed, he was snuffing the wick with his fingers. 'You were in your nightgown,' said K., turning Leni's head forcibly to the stove. She made no answer. 'Is he your lover?' asked K. She reached for a soup-bowl but K. imprisoned both her hands and said: 'Give me an answer?' She said: 'Come into the study and I'll tell you all about it.' 'No,' said K., 'I want you to tell me here.' She slipped her arm into his and tried to give him a kiss but K. fended her off, saying: 'I don't want you to kiss me now.' 'Joseph,' said Leni, gazing at him imploringly and yet frankly, 'surely you're not jealous of Herr Block?' Then she turned to the commercial traveller and said: 'Rudi, come to the rescue, you can see that I'm under suspicion, put that candle down.' One might have thought that he had been paying no attention, but he knew at once what she meant. 'I can't think what you have to be jealous about either,' he said, with no great acumen. 'Nor can I, really,' replied K., regarding him with a smile. Leni laughed outright and profited by K.'s momentary distraction to hook herself on to his arm, whispering: 'Leave him alone now, you can see the kind of creature he is. I've paid him a little attention because he's one of the Advocate's best clients, but that was the only reason. What about yourself? Do you want to see the Advocate tonight? He's far from well today; all the same, if you like I'll tell him you're here. But you're certainly going to spend the night with me. It's such a long time since you were here last, even the Advocate has been asking after you. It won't do to neglect your case! And I've got some information for you, too, things I've found out. But the first thing is to get your coat off.' She helped him out of his coat, took his hat from him, ran into the hall to hang them up, and then ran back to keep an eye on the soup. 'Shall I announce you first or give him his soup first?' 'Announce me first,' said K. He felt irritated, for he had originally intended to discuss the whole case thoroughly with Leni, especially the question of dismissing the Advocate, and the commercial traveller's being there spoiled the situation. But again it struck him that his affairs were too important to allow a decisive interference by a petty commercial traveller, and so he called back Leni, who was already out in the lobby. 'No, let him have his soup first,' he said, 'it'll strengthen him for his interview with me, and he'll need it.' 'So you're one of the Advocate's clients too,' said the commercial traveller quietly from his corner, as if confirming a statement. His comment was but ill received. 'What's that got to do with you?' said K., and Leni put in: 'You be quiet.' To K. Leni said: 'Well, then, I'll take him his soup first,' and she poured the soup into a bowl. 'Only there's a risk that he might go to sleep immediately, he always falls asleep after food.' 'What I have to say to him will keep him awake all right,' said K., who took every chance of letting it be known that his interview with the Advocate promised to be momentous; he wanted Leni to question him about it and only then would he ask her advice. But Leni merely followed out to the letter the orders he gave her. As she passed him with the bowl of soup she deliberately nudged him and whispered: 'I'll announce you the minute he's finished his soup, so that I can have you back as soon as possible.' 'Get along,' said K., 'get along with you.' 'Don't be so rude,' she said, turning right round in the doorway, soup-bowl and all.

K. stood gazing after her; now it was definitely settled that he would dismiss the Advocate, and it was just as well that he should have no chance of discussing it beforehand with Leni; the whole affair was rather beyond her scope and she would certainly have tried to dissuade him, possibly she might even have prevailed on him to put it off this time, and he would have continued to be a prey to doubts and fears until in the long run he carried out his resolve, since it was too imperative a resolve to be dropped. But the sooner it was carried out the less he would suffer. Perhaps, after all, the commercial traveller might be able to throw some light on the subject.

K. turned towards the man, who immediately gave a start as if to jump to his feet. 'Keep your seat,' said K., drawing a chair up beside him. 'You're an old client of the Advocate's, aren't you?' 'Yes,' said the traveller, 'a very old client.' 'How long has he been in charge of your affairs?' asked K. 'I don't quite know what affairs you mean,' said the traveller; 'in my business affairs – I'm a corndealer – the Advocate has been my representative since the very beginning, that must be for the past twenty years, and in my private case, which is probably what you are thinking of, he has been my Advocate also from the beginning, which is more than five years ago. Yes, well over five years now,' he confirmed, drawing out an old pocket-book. 'I have it all written down here. I can give you the exact dates if you like. It's difficult to keep them in one's head. My case probably goes back further than I said, it began just after my wife's death, certainly more than five and a half years ago.' K. moved his chair closer to the man. 'So the Advocate has an ordinary practice as well?' he asked. This alliance between business and equity seemed to him uncommonly touching. 'Of course,' said the traveller, adding in a whisper: 'They even say that he's a better Advocate for business rights than for the other kind.' Then apparently he regretted having ventured so far, for he laid a hand on K.'s shoulder and said: 'Don't give me away, I implore you.' K. patted him soothingly on the knee and said: 'No, I'm not an informer.' 'He's a revengeful man, you see,' said the traveller. 'Surely he wouldn't harm a faithful client like you?' said K. 'Oh, yes,' said the traveller, 'once he's roused he draws no distinctions; besides, I'm not really faithful to him.' 'How is that?' asked K. 'Perhaps I oughtn't to tell you,' said the traveller doubtfully. 'I think you can risk it,' said K. 'Well,' said the traveller, 'I'll tell you a certain amount, but in your turn you must tell me one of your secrets, so that we stand surety for each other with the Advocate.' 'You're very cautious,' said K., 'but I'll entrust you with a secret that will allay all your suspicions. In what way, then, are you unfaithful to the Advocate?' 'Well,' said the traveller hesitatingly, as if confessing something dishonourable, 'I have other Advocates as well as him.' 'That's nothing very dreadful,' said K., somewhat disappointed. 'It's supposed to be,' said the traveller, who had not breathed freely since making his confession but now gained a little confidence from K.'s rejoinder. 'It's not allowed. And least of all is it allowed to consult hedge-advocates when one is a client of an official Advocate. And that's exactly what I've been doing, I have five hedge-advocates besides this one?' 'Five!' cried K., amazed at the mere number, 'five Advocates besides this one?' The traveller nodded: 'I'm even trying out a sixth one.' 'But what do you need so many for?' asked K. 'I need every one of them,' said the traveller. 'Tell me why, will you?' asked K. 'With pleasure,' said the traveller. 'To begin with I don't want to lose my case, as you can well understand. And so I daren't ignore anything that might help me! If there's even the faintest hope of an advantage for myself I daren't reject it. That's how I've spent every penny I possess on this case of mine. For instance, I've drawn all the money out of my business; my business offices once filled nearly a whole floor of the building where now I need only a small back room and an assistant clerk. Of course it's not only the withdrawal of my money that has brought the business down, but the withdrawal of my energies. When you're trying to do anything you can to help your case along you haven't much energy to spare for other things.' 'So you've been working on your own behalf as well,' interrupted K., 'that's precisely what I wanted to ask you about.' 'There's not much to tell you,' said the traveller. 'I did try my hand at it in the beginning, but I soon had to give it up. It's too exhausting, and the results are disappointing. Merely attending the Court to keep an eye on things proved too much, for me, at least. It makes you feel limp even to sit about and wait your turn. But you know yourself what the air's like.' 'How do you know I was ever up there?' asked K. 'I happened to be in the lobby when you were passing through.' 'What a coincidence!' cried K., quite carried away and completely forgetting the ridiculous figure the traveller had cut in his estimation. 'So you saw me! You were in the lobby when I passed through. Yes, I did pass through the lobby once.' 'It's not such a coincidence as all that,' said the traveller, 'I'm up there nearly every day.' 'I'm likely to be up there, too, often enough after this,' said K., 'only I can hardly expect to be received with such honour as on that occasion. Everyone stood up. I suppose they took me for a Judge.' 'No,' said the traveller, 'it was the Attendant we stood up for. We knew you were an accused man. News of that kind spreads rapidly.' 'So you knew that already,' commented K., 'then perhaps you thought me somewhat high and mighty. Did no one say anything?' 'No,' said the traveller, 'people got quite a different impression. But it's a lot of nonsense.' 'What's a lot of nonsense?' asked K. 'Why do you insist on asking?' said the traveller, irritably. 'Apparently you don't know the people there and you might take it up wrongly. You must remember that in these Courts things are always coming up for discussion that are simply beyond reason, people are too tired and distracted to think and so they take refuge in superstition. I'm as bad as anyone myself. And one of the superstitions is that you're supposed to tell from a man's face, especially the line of his lips, how his case is going to turn out. Well, people declared that judging from the expression of your lips you would be found guilty, and in the near future too. I tell you, it's a silly superstition and in most cases completely at variance with the facts, but if you live among these people it's difficult to escape the prevailing opinion. You can't imagine what a strong effect such superstitions have. You spoke to a man up there, didn't you? And he could hardly utter a word in answer. Of course there's many a reason for being bewildered up there, but one of the reasons why he couldn't bring out an answer was the shock he got from looking at your lips. He said afterwards that he saw on your lips the sign of his own condemnation.' 'On my lips?' asked K., taking out a pocket-mirror and studying them. 'I can't see anything peculiar about my lips. Do you?' 'I don't either,' said the traveller, 'not in the least.' 'How superstitious these people are!' cried K. 'Didn't I tell you so?' asked the traveller. 'Do they meet each other so frequently, then, and exchange all these ideas?' queried K., 'I've never had anything to do with them myself.'

'As a rule they don't meet much,' said the traveller, 'it would be hardly possible, there are too many of them. Besides, they have few interests in common. Occasionally a group believes it has found a common interest, but it soon finds out its mistake. Combined action against the Court is impossible. Each case is judged on its own merits, the Court is very conscientious about that, and so common action is out of the question. An individual here and there may score a point in secret, but no one hears it until afterwards, no one knows how it has been done. So there's no real community, people drift in and out of the lobbies together, but there's not much conversation. The superstitious beliefs are an old tradition and simply hand themselves down.' 'I saw all the people in the lobby,' remarked K., 'and thought how pointless it was for them to be hanging about.' 'It's not pointless at all,' said the traveller, 'the only pointless thing is to try taking independent action. As I told you, I have five Advocates besides this one. You might think – as I did once – that I could safely wash my hands of the case. But you would be wrong. I have to watch it more carefully than if I had only one Advocate. I suppose you don't understand that?' 'No,' said K., laying his hand appealingly on the other's to keep him from talking so fast, 'I would only like to beg you to speak more slowly, all these things are extremely important to me and I can't follow so quickly.' 'I'm glad you reminded me,' said the traveller; 'of course you're a newcomer, you're young in the matter. Your case is six months old, isn't it? Yes, that's what I heard. An infant of a case! But I've had to think these things out I don't know how many times, they've become a second nature to me.' 'I suppose you're thankful to think that your case is so far advanced,' asked K., not liking to make a direct inquiry how the traveller's case stood. But he received no direct answer either. 'Yes, I've carried my burden for five long years,' said the traveller, drooping his head, 'it's no small achievement, that.' Then he sat silent for a little. K. listened to hear if Leni was coming back. On the one hand he did not want her to come in just then, for he had many questions still to ask, nor did he want her to find him so deep in intimate conversation with the traveller, but on the other hand he was annoyed because she was spending so much time with the Advocate while he was in the house, much more time than was needed for handing over a bowl of soup. 'I can still remember exactly,' began the traveller again, and K. was at once all attention, 'the days when my case was at much the same stage as yours is now. I had only this Advocate then, and I wasn't particularly satisfied with him.' 'Now I'm going to find out things,' thought K., nodding his head eagerly, as if that would encourage the traveller to bring out all the right information. 'My case,' went on the traveller, 'wasn't making any progress; there were of course interrogations, and I attended every one of them, I collected evidence, I even laid all my account-books before the Court, which wasn't necessary at all, as I discovered later. I kept running to the Advocate, he presented various petitions –' 'Various petitions?' asked K. 'Yes, certainly,' said the traveller. 'That's an important point for me,' said K., 'for in my case he's still boggling over the first petition. He's done nothing at all yet. Now I see how scandalously he's neglecting me.' 'There might be several excellent reasons why the petition isn't ready yet,' said the traveller. 'Let me tell you that my petitions turned out later to be quite worthless. I even had a look at one of them, thanks to the kindness of a Court official. It was very learned but it said nothing of any consequence. Crammed with Latin in the first place, which I don't understand, and then whole pages of general appeals to the Court, then flattering references to particular officials, who weren't actually named but were easy enough for anyone versed in these matters to recognize, then some self-praise of the Advocate himself, in the course of which he addressed the Court with a crawling humility, ending up with an analysis of various cases from ancient times that were supposed to resemble mine. I must say that this analysis, in so far as I could follow it, was very careful and thorough. You're not to think that I'm passing judgement on the Advocate's work; that petition, after all, was only one of many; but at any rate, and this is what I'm coming to, I couldn't see that my case was making any progress.' 'What kind of progress did you expect to see?' asked K. 'A good question,' said the traveller with a smile, 'it's very rarely that progress in these cases is visible at all. But I didn't know that then. I'm a business man, I wanted to see palpable results, the whole negotiation should be either on the up-grade, I thought, or on the down-grade and coming to a finish. Instead of that there were only ceremonial interviews, one after another, mostly of the same tenor, where I could reel off the responses like a litany; several times a week messengers came to my place of business or to my house or wherever I was to be found, and that, of course, was a nuisance (today I'm much better off in that respect, for telephone calls bother me less); and besides all that, rumours about my case began to spread among my business friends, but especially among my relatives, so that I was being harassed on all sides without the slightest sign of any intention on the part of the Court to bring my case up for judgement in the near future. So I went to the Advocate and made my complaint. He treated me to a lengthy explanation but refused utterly to take action in my sense of the word, saying that nobody could influence the Court to appoint a day for hearing a case, and that to urge anything of the kind in a petition – as I wanted him to do – was simply unheard of and would only ruin myself and him. I thought: what this Advocate won't or can't do, another will and can. So I looked round for other Advocates. I may as well tell you now that not one of them ever prayed the Court to fix a day for the settlement of my case, or managed to obtain such a settlement; it is really an impossibility – with one qualification that I shall explain later – and the Advocate had not misled me there, although I found no cause for regretting having called in the other Advocates. I suppose Dr Huld has told you plenty of things about the hedge-advocates, he has probably described them as contemptible creatures, and so they are, in a sense. All the same, in speaking of them and contrasting himself and his colleagues with them he always makes a small mistake, which I may as well call your attention to in passing. He always refers to the Advocates of his own circle as the "great Advocates", by way of contrast. Now that's untrue; any man can call himself "great", of course, if he pleases, but in this matter the Court tradition must decide. And according to the Court tradition, which recognizes both small and great Advocates outside the hole-and-corner Advocates, our Advocate and his colleagues rank only among the small Advocates, while the really great Advocates, whom I have merely heard of and never seen, stand as high above the small Advocates as these above the despised hedge-advocates.' 'The really great Advocates?' asked K. 'Who are they, then? How does one get at them?' 'So you've never heard of them,' said the traveller. 'There's hardly an accused man who doesn't spend some time dreaming of them after hearing about them. Don't you give way to that temptation. I have no idea who the great Advocates are and I don't believe they can be got at. I know of no single instance in which it could be definitely asserted that they had intervened. They do defend certain cases, but only when they want to, and they never take action, I should think, until the case is already beyond the province of the lower Court. Generally speaking, it's better to put them out of one's mind altogether, or else one finds interviews with ordinary Advocates so stale and stupid, with their niggling counsels and proposals – I have experienced it myself – that one feels like throwing the whole thing up and taking to bed with one's face to the wall. And of course that would be stupider still, for even in bed one wouldn't find peace.' 'So you didn't entertain the thought of going to the great Advocates?' asked K. 'Not for long,' said the traveller, smiling again; 'unfortunately one can never quite forget about them, especially during the night. But at that time I was looking for immediate results, and so I went to the hedge-advocates.'

'How you're putting your heads together!' cried Leni, who had come back with the soup-bowl and was standing in the doorway. They were indeed sitting so close to each other that they must have bumped their heads together at the slightest movement; the traveller, who was not only a small man but stooped forward as he sat, spoke so low that K. was forced to bend down to hear every word he said. 'Give us a moment or two,' cried K., warning Leni off, the hand which he still kept on the traveller's hand twitched with irritation. 'He wanted me to tell him about my case,' said the traveller to Leni. 'Well, go on telling him,' said she. Her tone in speaking to the traveller was kindly but a little contemptuous. That annoyed K.; the man, after all, as he had discovered, possessed a certain value, he had had experiences and knew how to communicate them. Leni apparently misjudged him. To K.'s further annoyance Leni removed the traveller's candle, which he had been grasping all this time, wiped his hand with her apron, and knelt down to scratch off some tallow which had dripped on his trousers. 'You were going to tell me about your hedge-advocates,' said K., pushing Leni's hand away without comment. 'What do you think you're doing?' she asked, giving K. a small slap and resuming her task. 'Yes, the hedge-advocates,' said the traveller, passing his hand over his brow as if in reflection. K. wanted to help him out and added: 'You were looking for immediate results and so you went to the hedge-advocates.' 'That's right,' said the traveller, but he did not continue. 'Perhaps he doesn't want to talk of it before Leni,' thought K., suppressing his impatience to hear the rest of the story and not urging the man any more.

'Did you announce me?' he asked Leni instead. 'Of course,' she said, 'and the Advocate's waiting for you. Leave Block alone now, you can talk to him later, for he's staying here.' K. still hesitated. 'Are you staying here?' he asked the traveller; he wanted the man to speak for himself, he disliked the way Leni discussed him as if he were absent, he was filled with obscure irritation today against Leni. And again it was Leni who did the speaking: 'He often sleeps here.' 'Sleeps here?' cried K., he had thought that the traveller would wait only till the interview with the Advocate was brought to a speedy conclusion, and that then they would go off together to discuss the whole business thoroughly in private. 'Yes,' said Leni, 'everyone isn't like you, Joseph, getting an interview with the Advocate at any hour they choose. It doesn't even seem to strike you as surprising that a sick man like the Advocate should agree to see you at eleven o'clock at night. You take all that your friends do for you far too much as a matter of course. Well, your friends, or I at least, like doing things for you. I don't ask for thanks and I don't need any thanks, except that I want you to be fond of me.' 'Fond of you?' thought K., and only after framing the words did it occur to him: 'But I am fond of her.' Yet he said, ignoring the rest of her remarks: 'He agrees to see me because I'm his client. If I needed others' help even to get an interview with my lawyer, I'd have to be bowing and scraping at every turn.' 'How difficult he is today, isn't he?' said Leni to the traveller. 'Now it's my turn to be treated as if I were absent,' thought K., and his irritation extended to the traveller too when the latter, copying Leni's discourtesy, remarked: 'But the Advocate has other reasons for agreeing to see him. His is a much more interesting case than mine. Besides, it's only beginning, probably still at a hopeful stage, and so the Advocate likes handling it. You'll see a difference later on.' 'Yes, yes,' said Leni, regarding the traveller laughingly, 'what a tongue-wagger!' Here she turned to K. and went on: 'You mustn't believe a word he says. He's a nice fellow but his tongue wags far too much. Perhaps that's why the Advocate can't bear him. Anyhow, he never consents to see him unless he's in the mood. I've tried my best to change that, but it can't be done. Only fancy, sometimes I tell the Advocate Block is here and he puts off seeing him for three days together. And then if Block isn't on the spot when he's called for, his chance is gone and I have to announce him all over again. That's why I let Block sleep here, for it has happened before now that the Advocate has rung for him in the middle of the night. So Block has to be ready night and day. It sometimes happens, too, that the Advocate changes his mind, once he has discovered that Block actually is on the spot, and refuses the interview.' K. threw a questioning glance at the traveller, who nodded and said, with the same frankness as before, or perhaps merely discomposed by a feeling of shame: 'Yes, one becomes very dependent on one's Advocate in the course of time.' 'He's just pretending to complain,' said Leni, 'for he likes sleeping here, as he has often told me.'

She went over to a small door and pushed it open. 'Would you like to see his bedroom?' she asked. K. followed her and gazed from the threshold into a low-roofed chamber which had room only for a narrow bed. One had to climb over the bedposts to get into the bed. At the head of it, in a recess in the wall, stood a candle, an ink-well, and a pen, carefully arranged beside a bundle of papers, probably documents concerning the traveller's case. 'So you sleep in the maid's room?' asked K., turning to the traveller. 'Leni lets me have it,' said he, 'it's very convenient.' K. gave him a long look; the first impression he had had of the man was perhaps, after all, the right one; the traveller was a man of experience, certainly, since his case had lasted for years, yet he had paid dearly for his experience. Suddenly K. could no longer bear the sight of him. 'Put him to bed,' he cried to Leni, who seemed not to comprehend what he meant. Yet what he wanted was to get away to the Advocate and dismiss from his life not only him but Leni and the commercial traveller too. Before he could reach the room, however, the traveller spoke to him in a low voice: 'Herr Assessor.' K. turned round angrily. 'You've forgotten your promise,' said the traveller, reaching out imploringly towards K. 'You were going to tell me one of your secrets.' 'True,' said K., casting a glance also at Leni, who was regarding him attentively, 'well, listen then, though it's almost an open secret by this time. I'm going to the Advocate now to dismiss him from my case.' 'Dismiss him!' exclaimed the traveller; he sprang from his seat and rushed round the kitchen with upraised arms, crying as he ran: 'He's dismissing the Advocate!' Leni made a grab for K. but the traveller got in her way, an awkwardness which she requited with her fists. Still clenching her fists she chased after K., who was well ahead of her. He got inside the Advocate's room before she caught up with him; he tried to close the door behind him, but Leni put one foot in the crack and reached through it to grab his arm and haul him back. K. caught her wrist and squeezed it so hard that she had to loose her hold with a whimper. She would not dare to force her way right in, but K. made certain by turning the key in the lock.

'I've been waiting a long time for you,' said the Advocate from his bed, laying on the table a document which he had been reading by the light of a candle, and putting on a pair of spectacles through which he scrutinized K. sharply. Instead of apologizing K. said: 'I shan't detain you long.' This remark, as it was no apology, the Advocate ignored, saying: 'I shall not see you again at such a late hour.' 'That agrees with my intentions,' retorted K. The Advocate gave him a questioning look and said: 'Sit down.' 'Since you ask me to,' said K., pulling up a chair to the night-table and seating himself. 'I fancied I heard you locking the door,' said the Advocate. 'Yes,' said K., 'that was because of Leni.' He was not thinking of shielding anyone, but the Advocate went on: 'Has she been pestering you again?' 'Pestering me?' asked K. 'Yes,' said the Advocate, chuckling until he took a fit of coughing, after which he began to chuckle once more. 'I suppose you can't have helped noticing that she pesters you?' he asked, patting K.'s hand, which in his nervous distraction he had laid on the night-table and now hastily withdrew. 'You don't attach much importance to it,' went on the Advocate as K. remained silent. 'So much the better. Or else I might have had to apologize for her. It's a peculiarity of hers, which I have long forgiven her and which I wouldn't mention now had it not been for your locking the door. This peculiarity of hers, well, you're the last person I should explain it to, but you're looking so bewildered that I feel I must, this peculiarity of hers consists in her finding nearly all accused men attractive. She makes up to all of them, loves them all, and is loved in return; she often tells me about these affairs to amuse me, when I allow her. It doesn't surprise me so much as it seems to surprise you. If you have the right eye for these things, you can see that accused men are often attractive. It's a remarkable phenomenon, almost a natural law. For of course the fact of being accused make no alteration in a man's appearance that is immediately obvious and recognizable. These cases are not like ordinary criminal cases, most of the defendants continue in their usual vocations, and if they are in the hands of a good Advocate their interests don't suffer much. And yet those who are experienced in such matters can pick out one after another all the accused men in the largest of crowds. How do they know them? you will ask. I'm afraid my answers won't seem satisfactory. They know them because accused men are always the most attractive. It can't be a sense of guilt that makes them attractive, for – it behoves me to say this as an Advocate, at least – they aren't all guilty, and it can't be the justice of the penance laid on them that makes them attractive in anticipation, for they aren't all going to be punished, so it must be the mere charge preferred against them that in some way enhances their attraction. Of course some are much more attractive than others. But they are all attractive, even that wretched creature Block.'

By the time the Advocate finished this harangue K. had completely regained his composure, he had even frankly nodded as if in agreement with the last words, whereas he was really confirming his own long-cherished opinion that the Advocate invariably attempted, as now, to bring in irrelevant generalizations in order to distract his attention from the main question, which was: how much actual work had been achieved in furthering the case? Presumably the Advocate felt that K. was more hostile than usual, for now he paused to give him the chance of putting in a word, and then asked, since K. remained silent: 'Did you come here this evening for some specific reason?' 'Yes,' said K., shading the light of the candle a little with one hand so as to see the Advocate better. 'I came to tell you that I dispense with your services as from today.' 'Do I understand you rightly?' asked the Advocate, half propping himself up in bed with one hand on the pillows. 'I expect so,' said K., sitting bolt upright as if on guard. 'Well, that's a plan we can at least discuss,' said the Advocate after a pause. 'It's no plan, it's a fact,' said K. 'Maybe,' said the Advocate, 'but we mustn't be in too much of a hurry.' He used the word 'we' as if he had no intention of letting K. detach himself, as if he meant to remain at least K.'s adviser if not his official agent. 'It's not a hurried decision,' said K., slowly getting up and retreating behind his chair. 'I have thought it well over, perhaps even for too long. It is my final decision.' 'Then you might allow me a few comments,' said the Advocate, throwing off his coverings and sitting on the edge of the bed. His bare legs, sprinkled with white hairs, trembled with cold. He asked K. to hand him a rug from the sofa. K. fetched the rug and said: 'It's quite unnecessary for you to expose yourself to a chill.' 'I have grave enough reasons for it,' said the Advocate, wrapping the bed-quilt round his shoulders and tucking the rug round his legs. 'Your uncle is a friend of mine, and I've grown fond of you, too, in the course of time. I admit it freely. It's nothing to be ashamed of.' This outburst of sentiment from the old man was most unwelcome to K., for it compelled him to be more explicit in his statements, which he would have liked to avoid, and disconcerted him too, as he admitted to himself, although without in the least affecting his decision. 'I am grateful for your friendly attitude,' he said, 'and I appreciate that you have done all you could do for what you thought to be my advantage. But for some time now I have been growing convinced that your efforts are not enough. I shall not, of course, attempt to thrust my opinions on a man so much older and more experienced than myself; if I have unwittingly seemed to do so, please forgive me, but I have grave enough reasons for it, to use your own phrase, and I am convinced that it is necessary to take much more energetic steps in this case of mine than have been taken so far.' 'I understand you,' said the Advocate, 'you are feeling impatient.' 'I'm not impatient,' said K., a little irritated and therefore less careful in his choice of words, 'you must have noticed on my very first visit here, when I came with my uncle, that I did not take my case very seriously; if I wasn't forcibly reminded of it, so to speak, I forgot it completely. Still my uncle insisted on my engaging you as my representative, and I did so to please him. One would naturally have expected the case to weigh even less on my conscience after that, since one engages an Advocate to shift the burden a little on to his shoulders. But the very opposite of that resulted. I was never so plagued by my case in earlier days as since engaging you to be my Advocate. When I stood alone I did nothing at all, yet it hardly bothered me; after acquiring an Advocate, on the other hand, I felt that the stage was set for something to happen, I waited with unceasing and growing expectancy for something to happen, and you did nothing whatever. I admit that you gave me information about the Court which I probably could not have obtained elsewhere. But that is hardly adequate assistance for a man who feels this thing secretly encroaching upon him and literally touching him to the quick.' K. had pushed the chair away and now stood upright, his hands in his jacket pockets. 'After a certain stage in one's practice,' said the Advocate quietly in a low voice, 'nothing really new ever happens. How many of my clients have reached the same point in their cases and stood before me in exactly the same frame of mind as you and said the same things!' 'Well,' said K., 'then they were all as much in the right as I am. That doesn't counter my arguments.' 'I wasn't trying to counter them,' said the Advocate, 'but I should like to add that I expected you to show more judgement than the others, especially as I have given you far more insight into the workings of the Court and my own procedure than I usually give my clients. And now I cannot help seeing that in spite of everything you haven't enough confidence in me. You don't make things very easy for me.' How the Advocate was humbling himself before K.! And without any regard for his professional dignity, which was surely most sensitive on this very point. Why was he doing it? If appearances spoke true he was in great demand as an Advocate and wealthy as well, the loss of K.'s business or the loss of his fees could not mean much to such a man. Besides, he was an invalid and should himself have contemplated the possibility of losing clients. Yet he was clinging to K. with insistence! Why? Was it personal affection for K.'s uncle, or did he really regard the case as so extraordinary that he hoped to win prestige either from defending K. or – a possibility not to be excluded – from pandering to his friends in the Court? His face provided no clue, searchingly as K. scrutinized it. One could almost suppose that he was deliberately assuming a blank expression, while waiting for the effect of his words.

But he was obviously putting too favourable an interpretation on K.'s silence when he went on to say: 'You will have noticed that although my office is large enough I don't employ any assistants. That wasn't so in former years, there was a time when several young students of the Law worked for me, but today I work alone. This change corresponds in part to the change in my practice, for I have been confining myself more and more to cases like yours, and in part to a growing conviction that has been borne in upon me. I found that I could not delegate the responsibility for these cases to anyone else without wronging my clients and imperilling the tasks I have undertaken. But the decision to cover all the work myself entailed the natural consequences: I had to refuse most of the cases brought to me and apply myself only to those which touched me nearly – and I can tell you there's no lack of wretched creatures, even in this very neighbourhood, ready to fling themselves on any crumb I choose to throw them. And then I broke down under stress of overwork. All the same, I don't regret my decision, perhaps I ought to have taken a firmer stand and refused more cases, but the policy of devoting myself single-mindedly to the cases I did accept has proved both necessary and successful judging from the results. I once read a very finely worded description of the difference between an Advocate for ordinary legal rights and an Advocate for cases like these. It ran like this: the one Advocate leads his client by a slender thread until the verdict is reached, but the other lifts his client on his shoulders from the start and carries him bodily without once letting him down until the verdict is reached, and even beyond it. That is true. But it is not quite true to say that I do not at all regret devoting myself to this great task. When, as in your case, my labours are as completely misunderstood, then, yes, then and only then, I come near to regretting it.' This speech, instead of convincing K., only made him impatient. He fancied that the very tone of the Advocate's voice suggested what was in store for him should he prove complaisant; the same old exhortations would begin again, the same references to the progress of the petition, to the more gracious mood of this or that official, while not forgetting the enormous difficulties that stood in the way – in short, the same stale platitudes would be brought out again either to delude him with vague menaces. That must be stopped once and for all, so he said: 'What steps do you propose to take in my case if I retain you as my representative?' The Advocate meekly accepted even this insulting question and replied: 'I should continue with those measures that I have already begun.' 'I knew it,' said K., 'well, it's a waste of time to go on talking.' 'I'll make one more attempt,' said the Advocate, as if it were K. who was at fault and not himself. 'I have an idea that what makes you so wrong-headed not only in your judgement of my capacities but also in your general behaviour is the fact that you have been treated too well, although you are an accused man, or rather, more precisely, that you have been treated with negligence, with apparent negligence. There's a reason for the negligence, of course; it's often safer to be in chains than to be free. But I'd like to show you how other accused men are treated, and perhaps you may learn a thing or two. I shall now send for Block; you'd better unlock the door and sit here beside the bed-table.' 'With pleasure,' said K., fulfilling these injunctions; he was always ready to learn. As a precaution, however, he asked once more: 'You realize that I am dispensing with your services?' 'Yes,' said the Advocate, 'but you may change your mind about it yet.' He lay back in bed again, drew the quilt over his knees, and turned his face to the wall. Then he rang the bell.

Almost at the same moment Leni was on the spot, darting quick glances to learn what was happening; she seemed to find it reassuring that K. was sitting so quietly beside the Advocate's bed. She nodded to him with a smile, but he gazed at her blankly. 'Fetch Block,' said the Advocate. Instead of fetching Block, however, she merely went to the door, called out: 'Block! The Advocate wants you!' and then, probably because the Advocate had his face turned to the wall and was paying no attention to her, insinuated herself behind K., where she distracted him during all the rest of the proceedings by leaning over the back of his chair or running her fingers, gently and tenderly enough, through his hair over his temples. In the end K. sought to prevent her by holding on to her hand, which after a little resistance she surrendered to him.

Block had answered the summons by coming immediately, yet he hesitated outside the door, apparently wondering whether he was to come in or not. He raised his eyebrows and cocked his head as if listening for the summons to be repeated. K. could have encouraged the man to come in, but he was determined to make a final break not only with the Advocate but with all the persons in the house, and so he remained immobile. Leni too was silent. Block noticed that at least no one was turning him away, and he tiptoed into the room with anxious face and hands clutched behind him, leaving the door open to secure his retreat. He did not once look at K., but kept his eyes fixed on the humped-up quilt beneath which the Advocate was not even visible, since he had shifted close up to the wall. A voice, however, came from the bed, saying: 'Is that Block?' This question acted like a blow upon Block, who had advanced a goodish way; he staggered, as if he had been hit on the chest and then beaten on the back, and, submissively drooping, stood still, answering: 'At your service.' 'What do you want?' asked the Advocate. 'You've come at the wrong time.' 'Wasn't I called for?' said Block, more to himself than to the Advocate, thrusting out his hands as if to guard himself, and preparing to back out. 'You were called for,' said the Advocate, 'and yet you've come at the wrong time.' After a pause he added: 'You always come at the wrong time.' From the moment when the Advocate's voice was heard Block averted his eyes from the bed and stood merely listening, gazing into the far corner, as if to meet a shaft from the Advocate's eyes were more than he could bear. But it was difficult for him even to listen, since the Advocate was speaking close to the wall and in a voice both low and quick. 'Do you want me to go away?' asked Block. 'Well, since you're here,' said the Advocate, 'stay!' One might have fancied that instead of granting Block his desire the Advocate had threatened to have him beaten, for the fellow now began to tremble in earnest. 'Yesterday,' said the Advocate, 'I saw my friend the Third Judge and gradually worked the conversation round to your case. Would you like to know what he said?' 'Oh, please,' said Block. Since the Advocate made no immediate reply, Block implored him again and seemed on the point of getting down on his knees. But K. intervened with a shout: 'What's that you're doing?' Leni had tried to stifle his shout and so he gripped her other hand as well. It was no loving clasp in which he held her; she sighed now and then and struggled to free herself. But it was Block who paid the penalty for K.'s outburst; the Advocate shot the question at him: 'Who is your Advocate?' 'You are,' said Block. 'And besides me?' asked the Advocate. 'No one besides you,' said Block. 'Then pay no heed to anyone else,' said the Advocate. Block took the full force of these words, he gave K. an angry glare and shook his head violently at him. If these gestures had been translated into speech they would have made a tirade of abuse. And this was the man with whom K. had wished to discuss his own case in all friendliness! 'I shan't interfere again,' said K., leaning back in his chair. 'Kneel on the floor or creep on all fours if you like, I shan't bother.' Yet Block had some self-respect left, at least where K. was concerned, for he advanced upon him flourishing his fists and shouting as loudly as he dared in the Advocate's presence: 'You're not to talk to me in that tone, it isn't allowed. What do you mean by insulting me? Before the Herr Advocate, too, who admits us here, both of us, you and me, only out of charity? You're no better than I am, you're an accused man too and have the same charges on your conscience. If you think you're a gentleman as well, let me tell you I'm as great a gentleman as you, if not a greater. And I'll have you address me as such, yes, you especially. For if you think you have the advantage of me because you're allowed to sit there at your ease and watch me creeping on all fours, as you put it, let me remind you of the old maxim: people under suspicion are better moving than at rest, since at rest they may be sitting in the balance without knowing it, being weighed together with their sins.' K. said not a word, he merely stared in unwinking astonishment at this madman. What a change had come over the fellow in the last hour! Was it his case that agitated him to such an extent that he could not distinguish friend from foe? Did he not see that the Advocate was deliberately humiliating him, for no other purpose on this occasion than to make a display of his power before K. and so perhaps cow K. into acquiescence as well? Yet if Block were incapable of perceiving this, or if he were so afraid of the Advocate that he could not allow himself to perceive it, how did it come about that he was sly enough or brave enough to deceive the Advocate and deny that he was having recourse to other Advocates? And how could he be so foolhardy as to attack K., knowing that K. might betray his secret? His foolhardiness went even further, he now approached the Advocate's bed and laid a complaint against K. 'Herr Advocate,' he said, 'did you hear what this man said to me? His case is only a few hours old compared with mine, and yet, though I have been five years involved in my case, he takes it on himself to give me advice. He even abuses me. Knows nothing at all and abuses me, me, who have studied as closely as my poor wits allow every precept of duty, piety, and tradition.' 'Pay no heed to anyone,' said the Advocate, 'and do what seems right to yourself.' 'Certainly,' said Block, as if to give himself confidence, and then with a hasty side-glance knelt down close beside the bed. 'I'm on my knees, my Advocate,' he said. But the Advocate made no reply. Block cautiously caressed the quilt with one hand. In the silence that now reigned Leni said, freeing herself from K.: 'You're hurting me. Let go. I want to be with Block.' She went over and sat on the edge of the bed. Block was greatly pleased by her arrival; he made impressive gestures, though in dumb show, imploring her to plead his cause with the Advocate. Obviously he was urgently in need of any information which the Advocate might give, but perhaps he only wanted to hand it on to his other Advocates for exploitation. Leni apparently knew exactly the right way to coax the Advocate; she pointed to his hand and pouted her lips as if giving a kiss. Block immediately kissed the hand, repeating the performance twice at Leni's instigation. But the Advocate remained persistently unresponsive. Then Leni, displaying the fine lines of her taut figure, bent over close to the old man's face and caressed his long white hair. That finally evoked an answer. 'I hesitate to tell him,' said the Advocate, and one could see him shaking his head, perhaps only the better to enjoy the pleasure of Leni's hand. Block listened with downcast eyes, as if it were a duty laid upon him. 'Why do you hesitate, then?' asked Leni. K. had the feeling that he was listening to a well-rehearsed dialogue which had been often repeated and would be often repeated and only for Block would never lose its novelty. 'How has he been behaving today?' inquired the Advocate instead of answering. Before providing this information Leni looked down at Block and watched him for a moment as he raised his hands towards her and clasped them appealingly together. At length she nodded gravely, turned to the Advocate, and said: 'He has been quiet and industrious.' An elderly business man, a man with a long beard, begging a young girl to say a word in his favour! Let him make what private reservations he would, in the eyes of his fellow-men he could find no justification. It was humiliating even to an onlooker. So the Advocate's methods, to which K. fortunately had not been long enough exposed, amounted to this: that the client finally forgot the whole world and lived only in hope of toiling along this false path until the end of his case should come in sight. The client ceased to be a client and became the Advocate's dog. If the Advocate were to order this man to crawl under the bed as if into a kennel and bark there, he would obey the order. K. listened to everything with critical detachment, as if he had been commissioned to observe the proceedings closely, to report them to a higher authority, and to put down a record of them in writing. 'What has he been doing all day?' went on the Advocate. 'I locked him into the maid's room,' said Leni, 'to keep him from disturbing me at my work, that's where he usually stays, anyhow. And I could peep at him now and then through the ventilator to see what he was doing. He was kneeling all the time on the bed, reading the book you lent him, which was spread out on the window-sill. That made a good impression on me, since the window looks out on an air-shaft and doesn't give much light. So the way Block stuck to his reading showed me how faithfully he does what he is told.' 'I'm glad to hear that,' said the Advocate. 'But did he understand what he was reading?' All this time Block's lips were moving unceasingly, he was obviously formulating the answers he hoped Leni would make. 'Well, of course,' said Leni, 'that's something I don't know with certainty. At any rate, I could tell that he was thorough in his reading. He never got past the same page all day and he was following the lines with his fingers. Whenever I looked at him he was sighing to himself as if the reading cost him a great effort. Apparently the book you gave him to read is difficult to understand.' 'Yes,' said the Advocate, 'these scriptures are difficult enough. I don't believe he really understands them. They're meant only to give him an inkling how hard the struggle is that I have to carry on in his defence. And for whom do I carry on this hard struggle? It's almost ridiculous to put it into words – I do it for Block. He must learn to understand what that means. Did he read without stopping?' 'Almost without a stop,' answered Leni, 'he asked me only once for a drink of water, and I handed it to him through the ventilator. Then about eight o'clock I let him out and gave him something to eat.' Block gave a fleeting glance at K. as if expecting to see him impressed by this virtuous record. His hopes seemed to be mounting, his movements were less constrained, and he kept shifting his knees a little. It was all the more noticeable that the Advocate's next words struck him rigid. 'You are praising him up,' said the Advocate. 'But that only makes it more difficult for me to tell him. For the Judge's remarks were by no means favourable either to Block or to his case.' 'Not favourable?' asked Leni. 'How can that be possible?' Block was gazing at her as intently as if he believed her capable of giving a new and favourable turn to the words long pronounced by the Judge. 'Not favourable,' said the Advocate. 'He was even annoyed when I mentioned Block. "Don't speak about Block," he said. "But he's my client," I said.

"You are wasting yourself on the man," he said. "I don't think his case is hopeless," said I. "Well, you're wasting yourself on him," he repeated. "I don't believe it," said I, "Block is sincerely concerned about his case and devotes himself to it. He almost lives in my house to keep in touch with the proceedings. One doesn't often find such zeal. Of course, he's personally rather repulsive, his manners are bad, and he is dirty, but as a client he is beyond reproach" – I said "beyond reproach", and it was a deliberate exaggeration. To that he replied: "Block is merely cunning. He has acquired a lot of experience and knows how to keep on manipulating the situation. But his ignorance is even greater than his cunning. What do you think he would say if he discovered that his case had actually not begun yet, if he were to be told that the bell marking the start of the proceedings hadn't even been rung?" – Quiet there, Block,' said the Advocate, for Block was just rising up on trembling legs, obviously to implore an explanation. This was the first time the Advocate had addressed a direct word to Block. With lack-lustre eyes he looked down, his glance was partly vague and partly turned upon Block, who slowly shrank back under it on his knees again. 'That remark of the Judge's has no possible significance for you,' said the Advocate. 'Don't get into a panic at every word. If you do it again I'll never tell you anything. I can't begin a statement without your gazing at me as if your final sentence had come. You should be ashamed to behave like that before my client. And you're destroying his confidence in me. What's the matter with you? You're still alive, you're still under my protection. Your panic is senseless. You've read somewhere or other that a man's condemnation often comes by a chance word from some chance person at some odd time. With many reservations that is certainly true, but it is equally true that your panic disgusts me and appears to betray a lack of the necessary confidence in me. All that I said was to report a remark made by a Judge. You know quite well that in these matters opinions differ so much that the confusion is impenetrable. This Judge, for instance, assumes that the proceedings begin at one point, and I assume that they begin at another point. A difference of opinion, nothing more. At a certain stage of the proceedings there is an old tradition that a bell must be rung. According to the Judge, that marks the beginning of the case, I can't tell you now all the arguments against him, you wouldn't understand them, let it be sufficient for you that there are many arguments against his view.' In embarrassment Block sat plucking at the hair of the skin rug lying before the bed, his terror of the Judge's utterance was so great that it ousted for a while his respectful fear of the Advocate and he was thinking only of himself, turning the Judge's words round and surveying them from all sides. 'Block,' said Leni in a tone of warning, catching him by the collar and jerking him upwards a little. 'Leave the rug alone and listen to the Advocate.'

K. did not understand how the Advocate could ever have imagined that this performance would win him over. If the Advocate had not already succeeded in alienating him, this scene would have finished him once and for all.

9

IN THE CATHEDRAL

An Italian colleague who was on his first visit to the town and had influential connexions that made him important to the Bank was to be taken in charge by K. and shown some of the town's art treasures and monuments. It was a commission that K. would once have felt to be an honour, but at the present juncture, now that all his energies were needed even to retain his prestige in the Bank, he was reluctant in his acceptance of it. Every hour that he spent away from the Bank was a trial to him; true, he was by no means able to make the best use of his office hours as once he had done, he wasted much time in the merest pretence of doing real work, but that only made him worry the more when he was not at his desk. In his mind he saw the Deputy Manager, who had always spied upon him, prowling every now and then into his office, sitting down at his desk, running through his papers, receiving clients who had become almost old friends of K.'s in the course of many years, and turning them against him, perhaps even discovering mistakes that he had made, for K. now saw himself continually threatened by mistakes intruding into his work from all sides and was no longer able to circumvent them. Consequently if he were charged with a mission, however honourable, which involved his leaving the office on business or even taking a short journey – and missions of that kind by some chance had recently come his way fairly often – then he could not help suspecting that there was a plot to get him out of the way while his work was investigated, or at least that he was considered far from indispensable in the office. Most of these missions he could easily have refused. Yet he did not dare do so, since, if there were even the smallest ground for his suspicions, a refusal to go would only have been taken as an admission of anxiety. For that reason he accepted every one of them with apparent coolness, and on one occasion when he was expected to take an exhausting two days' journey said nothing even about a severe chill he had, to avoid the risk of having the prevailing wet autumnal weather advanced as an excuse for his not going. When he came back from his journey with a racking headache, he discovered that he had been selected to act as escort next day for the Italian visitor. The temptation simply to refuse, for once, was very great, especially since the charge laid upon him was not strictly a matter of business; still, it was a social duty towards a colleague and doubtless important enough, only it was of no importance to himself, knowing, as he did, that nothing could save him except work well done, in default of which it would not be of the slightest use to him were the Italian to find him the most enchanting companion; he shrank from being exiled from his work even for a single day, since he had too great a fear of not being allowed to return, a fear which he well knew to be exaggerated but which hampered him all the same. The difficulty on this occasion was to find a plausible excuse; his knowledge of Italian was certainly not very great but it was at least adequate, and there was a decisive argument in the fact that he had some knowledge of art, acquired in earlier days, which was absurdly overestimated in the Bank owing to his having been for some time, purely as a matter of business, a member of the Society for the Preservation of Ancient Monuments. Rumour had it that the Italian was also a connoisseur, and if so, the choice of K. to be his escort seemed inevitable.

It was a very wet and windy morning when K. arrived in his office at the early hour of seven o'clock, full of irritation at the programme before him, but determined to accomplish at least some work before being distracted from it by the visitor. He was very tired, for he had spent half the night studying an Italian grammar as some slight preparation; he was more tempted by the window, where he had recently been in the habit of spending much time, than by his desk, but he resisted the temptation and sat down to work. Unfortunately at that very moment the attendant appeared, reporting that he had been sent by the Manager to see if the Herr Assessor was in his office yet, and, if he was, to beg him to be so good as to come to the reception-room; the gentleman from Italy had already arrived. 'All right,' said K., stuffed a small dictionary into his pocket, tucked under his arm an album for sightseers, which he had procured in readiness for the stranger, and went through the Deputy Manager's office into the Manager's room. He was glad that he had turned up early enough to be on the spot immediately when required, probably no one had really expected him to do so. The Deputy Manager's office, of course, was as empty as in the dead of night, very likely the attendant had been told to summon the Deputy Manager too, and without result. When K. entered the reception-room the two gentlemen rose from their deep arm-chairs. The Manager smiled kindly on K., he was obviously delighted to see him, he performed the introduction at once, the Italian shook K. heartily by the hand and said laughingly that someone was an early riser from the bed. K. did not quite catch what he meant, for it was an odd phrase the sense of which did not dawn on him at once. He answered with a few polite formalities which the Italian received with another laugh, meanwhile nervously stroking his bushy iron-grey moustache. This moustache was obviously perfumed; one was almost tempted to go close up and have a sniff at it. When they all sat down again and a preliminary conversation began, K. was greatly disconcerted to find that he only partly understood what the Italian was saying. He could understand him almost completely when he spoke slowly and quietly, but that happened very seldom, the words mostly came pouring out in a flood, and he made lively gestures with his head as if enjoying the rush of talk. Besides, when this happened, he invariably relapsed into a dialect which K. did not recognize as Italian but which the Manager could both speak and understand, as indeed K. might have expected, considering that this Italian came from the very south of Italy, where the Manager had spent several years. At any rate, it became clear to K. that little chance remained of his coming to an understanding with the Italian, for the man's French was just as difficult to follow and it was no use watching his lips for clues, since their movements were covered by the bushy moustache. K. began to foresee vexations and for the moment gave up trying to follow the talk – while the Manager was present to understand all that was said it was an unnecessary effort to make – confining himself to peevish observation of the Italian lounging so comfortably and yet lightly in his armchair, tugging every now and then at the sharply peaked corners of his short little jacket, and once raising his arms with loosely fluttering hands to explain something which K. found it impossible to understand, although he was leaning foward to watch every gesture. In the end, as K. sat there taking no part in the conversation, only mechanically following with his eyes the see-saw of the dialogue, his earlier weariness made itself felt again, and to his horror, although fortunately just in time, he caught himself absent-mindedly rising to turn his back on the others and walk away. At long last the Italian looked at his watch and sprang to his feet. After taking leave of the Manager he pressed up to K. so close that K. had to push his chair back in order to have any freedom of movement. The Manager, doubtless seeing in K.'s eye that he was in desperate straits with this unintelligible Italian, intervened so cleverly and delicately that it appeared as if he were merely contributing little scraps of advice, while in reality he was briefly conveying to K. the sense of all the remarks with which the Italian unweariedly interrupted him. In this way K. learned that the Italian had some immediate business to attend to, that unfortunately he was likely to be pressed for time, that he had no intention of rushing round to see all the sights in a hurry, that he would much rather – of course only if K. were agreed, the decision lay with K. alone – confine himself to inspecting the Cathedral, but thoroughly. He was extremely delighted to have the chance of doing so in the company of such a learned and amiable gentleman – this was how he referred to K. who was trying hard to turn a deaf ear to his words and grasp as quickly as possible what the Manager was saying – and he begged him, if it were convenient, to meet him there in a couple of hours, say at about ten o'clock. He had certain hopes of being able to arrive there about that time. K. made a suitable rejoinder, the Italian pressed the Manager's hand, then K.'s hand, then the Manager's hand again, and, followed by both of them, turning only half towards them by this time but still maintaining a flow of words, departed towards the door. K. stayed a moment or two with the Manager, who was looking particularly unwell that day. He felt that he owed K. an apology and said – they were standing intimately together – that he had at first intended to escort the Italian himself, but on second thoughts – he gave no definite reason – he had decided that K. had better go. If K. found that he could not understand the man to begin with he mustn't let that upset him, for he wouldn't take long to catch the sense of what was said, and even if he didn't understand very much it hardly mattered, since the Italian cared little whether he was understand or not. Besides, K.'s knowledge of Italian was surprisingly good and he would certainly acquit himself well. With that K. was dismissed to his room. The time still at his disposal he devoted to copying from the dictionary various unfamiliar words which he would need in his tour of the Cathedral. It was an unusually exasperating task; attendants came in with letters, clerks arrived with inquiries, standing awkwardly in the doorway when they saw that K. was busy, yet not removing themselves until he answered, the Deputy Manager did not miss the chance of making himself a nuisance and appeared several times, taking the dictionary out of K.'s hand and with obvious indifference turning the pages over; even clients were dimly visible in the antechamber whenever the door opened, making deprecating bows to call attention to themselves but uncertain whether they had been remarked or not – all this activity rotated around K. as if he were the centre of it, while he himself was occupied in collecting the words he might need, looking them up in the dictionary, copying them out, practising their pronunciation, and finally trying to learn them by heart. His once excellent memory seemed to have deserted him, and every now and then he grew so furious with the Italian who was causing him all this trouble that he stuffed the dictionary beneath a pile of papers with the firm intention of preparing himself no further, yet he could not help seeing that it would not do to march the Italian round the art treasures of the Cathedral in dumb silence, and so with even greater rage he took the dictionary out again.

Just at half-past nine, as he was rising to go, the telephone rang; Leni bade him good morning and asked how he was; K. thanked her hastily and said he had no time to talk to her, since he must go to the Cathedral. 'To the Cathedral?' asked Leni. 'Yes, to the Cathedral.' 'But why the Cathedral?' cried Leni. K. tried to explain briefly to her, but hardly had he begun when Leni suddenly said: 'They're driving you hard.' Pity which he had not asked for and did not expect was more than K. could bear, he said two words of farewell, but even as he hung up the receiver he murmured half to himself and half to the faraway girl who could no longer hear him: 'Yes, they're driving me hard.'

By now it was growing late, he was already in danger of not being in time for the appointment. He drove off in a taxi-cab;

at the last moment he remembered the album which he had found no opportunity of handing over earlier, and so took it with him now. He laid it on his knees and drummed on it impatiently with his fingers during the whole of the journey. The rain had slackened, but it was a raw, wet, murky day, one would not be able to see much in the Cathedral, and there was no doubt that standing about on the cold stone flags would make K.'s chill considerably worse.

The Cathedral Square was quite deserted, and K. recollected how even as a child he had been struck by the fact that in the houses of this narrow square nearly all the window-blinds were invariably drawn down. On a day like this, of course, it was more understandable. The Cathedral seemed deserted too, there was naturally no reason why anyone should visit it as such a time. K. went through both of the side aisles and saw no one but an old woman muffled in a shawl who was kneeling before a Madonna with adoring eyes. Then in the distance he caught sight of a limping verger vanishing through a door in the wall. K. had been punctual, ten o'clock was striking just as he entered, but the Italian had not yet arrived. He went back to the main entrance, stood there undecidedly for a while, and then circled round the building in the rain, to make sure that the Italian was perhaps not waiting at some side door. He was nowhere to be seen. Could the Manager have made some mistake about the hour? How could anyone be quite sure of understanding such a man? Whatever the circumstances, K. would at any rate have to wait half an hour for him. Since he was tired he felt like sitting down, went into the Cathedral again, found on a step a remnant of carpet-like stuff, twitched it with his toe towards a near-by bench, wrapped himself more closely in his greatcoat, turned up his collar, and settled himself. By way of filling in time he opened the album and ran idly through it, but he soon had to stop, for it was growing so dark that when he looked up he could distinguish scarcely a single detail in the neighbouring aisle.

Away in the distance a large triangle of candle-flames flickered on the high altar; K. could not have told with any certainty whether he had noticed them before or not. Perhaps they had been newly kindled. Vergers are by profession stealthy-footed, one never remarks them. K. happened to turn round and saw not far behind him the gleam of another candle, a tall thick candle fixed to a pillar. It was lovely to look at, but quite inadequate for illuminating the altar-pieces, which mostly hung in the darkness of the side chapels; it rather heightened the darkness. So the Italian was as sensible as he was discourteous in not coming, for he would have seen nothing, he would have had to content himself with scrutinizing a few pictures inch-meal by the light of K.'s pocket-torch. Curious to see what effect it would have, K. went up to a small side chapel near by, mounted a few steps to a low balustrade, and bending over it shone his torch on the altar-piece. The errant light hovered over it like an intruder. The first thing K. perceived, partly by guess, was a huge armoured knight on the outermost verge of the picture. He was leaning on his sword, which was stuck into the bare ground, bare except for a stray blade of grass or two. He seemed to be watching attentively some event unfolding itself before his eyes. It was surprising that he should stand so still without approaching nearer to it. Perhaps he had been set there to stand guard. K., who had not seen any pictures for a long time, studied this knight for a good while, although the greenish light of the torch made his eyes blink. When he played the torch over the rest of the altar-piece he discovered that it was a portrayal of Christ being laid in the tomb, quite conventional in style although a fairly recent painting. He pocketed the torch and returned again to his seat.

In all likelihood it was now needless to wait any longer for the Italian, but the rain was probably pouring down outside, and since it was not so cold in the Cathedral as K. had expected, he decided to linger there for the present. Quite near him rose the great pulpit, on its small vaulted canopy two plain golden crucifixes were slanted so that their shafts crossed at the tip. The outer balustrade and the stonework connecting it with the supporting columns were wrought all over with foliage in which little angels were entangled, now vivacious and now serene. K. went up to the pulpit and examined it from all sides, the carving of the stonework was delicate and thorough, the deep caverns of darkness among and behind the foliage looked as if caught and imprisoned there; K. put his hand into one of them and lightly felt the contour of the stone, he had never known that this pulpit existed. By pure chance he noticed a verger standing behind the nearest row of benches, a man in a loose-hanging black garment with a snuff-box in his left hand; he was gazing at K. 'What's the man after?' thought K. 'Do I look a suspicious character? Does he want a tip?' But when he saw that K. had become aware of him, the verger started pointing with his right hand, still holding a pinch of snuff in his fingers, in some vaguely indicated direction. His antics seemed to have little meaning. K. hesitated for a while, but the verger did not cease pointing at something or other and emphasizing the gesture with nods of his head. 'What does the man want?' said K. in a low tone, he did not dare to raise his voice in this place; then he pulled out his purse and made his way along the benches towards him. But the verger at once made a gesture of refusal, shrugged his shoulders, and limped away. With something of the same gait, a quick, limping motion, K. had often as a child imitated a man riding on horseback. 'A childish ancient,' thought K., 'with only wits enough to be a verger. How he stops when I stop and peers to see if I am following him!' Smiling to himself, K. went on following him through the side aisle almost as far as the high altar; the old man kept pointing in another direction, but K. deliberately refrained from looking round to see what he was pointing at, the gesture could have no other purpose than to shake K. off. At last he desisted from the pursuit, he did not want to alarm the old man too much; besides, in case the Italian were to turn up after all, it might be better not to scare away the only verger.

As he returned to the nave to find the seat on which he had left the album lying, K. caught sight of a small side pulpit attached to a pillar almost immediately adjoining the choir, a simple pulpit of plain, bleak stone. It was so small that from a distance it looked like an empty niche intended for a statue.

There was certainly no room for the preacher to take a full step backwards from the balustrade. The vaulting of the stone canopy, too, began very low down and curved forward, although without ornamentation, in such a way that a medium-sized man could not stand upright beneath it but would have to keep leaning over the balustrade. The whole structure was designed to harass the preacher; there seemed no comprehensible reason why it should be there at all while the other pulpit, so large and finely decorated, was available.

And K. certainly would not have noticed it had not a lighted lamp been fixed above it, the usual sign that a sermon was going to be preached. Was a service going to be held now? In the empty church? K. peered down at the small flight of steps which led upwards to the pulpit, hugging the pillar as it went, so narrow that it looked like an ornamental addition to the pillar rather than a stairway for human beings. But at the foot of it, K. smiled in astonishment, there actually stood a clerical figure ready to ascend, with his hand on the balustrade and his eyes fixed on K. The priest gave a little nod and K. crossed himself and bowed, as he ought to have done earlier. The priest swung himself lightly on to the stairway and mounted into the pulpit with short, quick steps. Was he really going to preach a sermon? Perhaps the verger was not such an imbecile after all and had been trying to urge K. towards the preacher, a highly necessary action in that deserted building. But somewhere or other there was an old woman before an image of the Madonna; she ought to attend the service too. And if it were going to be a service, why was it not introduced by the organ? But the organ remained silent, its tall pipes looming faintly in the darkness.

K. wondered whether this was not the time to remove himself quickly; if he did not go now he would have no chance of doing so during the service, he would have to stay as long as that lasted, he was already behindhand in the office and was no longer obliged to wait for the Italian; he looked at his watch, it was eleven o'clock. But could it really be a sermon? Could K. represent the congregation all by himself? What if he had been a stranger merely visiting the church? That was more or less his position. It was absurd to think that a sermon was going to be preached at eleven in the morning on a week-day, in such dreadful weather. The priest – he was beyond doubt a priest, a young man with a smooth, dark face – was obviously mounting the pulpit simply to turn out the lamp, which had been lit by mistake.

It was not so, however, the priest after examining the lamp screwed it higher instead, then turned slowly towards the balustrade and gripped the angular edge of it with both hands. He stood like that for a while, looking around him without moving his head. K. had retreated a good distance and was leaning his elbows on the foremost pew. Without knowing exactly where the verger was stationed, he was vaguely aware of the old man's bent back, peacefully at rest as if his task had been fulfilled. What stillness there was now in the Cathedral! Yet K. had to violate it, for he was not minded to stay; if it were this priest's duty to preach a sermon at such and such an hour regardless of circumstances, let him do it, he could manage it without K.'s support, just as K.'s presence would certainly not contribute to its effectiveness. So he began slowly to move off, feeling his way along the pew on tiptoe until he was in the broad centre aisle, where he advanced undisturbed except for the ringing noise that his lightest footstep made on the stone flags and the echoes that sounded from the vaulted roof faintly but continuously, in manifold and regular progression. K. felt a little forlorn as he advanced, a solitary figure between the rows of empty seats, perhaps with the priest's eyes following him; and the size of the Cathedral struck him as bordering on the limit of what human beings could bear. When he came to the seat where he had left the album he simply snatched the book up without stopping and took it with him. He had almost passed the last of the pews and was emerging into the open space between himself and the doorway when he heard the priest lifting up his voice. A resonant, well-trained voice. How it rolled through the expectant Cathedral! But it was no congregation the priest was addressing, the words were unambiguous and inescapable, he was calling out: 'Joseph K.!'

K. started and stared at the ground before him. For the moment he was still free, he could continue on his way and vanish through one of the small, dark, wooden doors that faced him at no great distance. It would simply indicate that he had not understood the call, or that he had understood it and did not care. But if he were to turn round he would be caught, for that would amount to an admission that he had understood it very well, that he was really the person addressed, and that he was ready to obey. Had the priest called his name a second time K. would certainly have gone on, but since there was a persistent silence, though he stood waiting a long time, he could not help turning his head a little just to see what the priest was doing. The priest was standing calmly in the pulpit as before, yet it was obvious that he had observed K.'s turn of the head. It would have been like a childish game of hide-and-seek if K. had not turned right round to face him. He did so, and the priest beckoned him to come nearer. Since there was now no need for evasion, K. hurried back – he was both curious and eager to shorten the interview – with long flying strides towards the pulpit. At the first rows of seats he halted, but the priest seemed to think the distance still too great, he stretched out an arm and pointed with sharply bent forefinger to a spot immediately before the pulpit. K. followed this direction too; when he stood on the spot indicated he had to bend his head far back to see the priest at all. 'You are Joseph K.?' said the priest, lifting one hand from the balustrade in a vague gesture. 'Yes,' said K., thinking how frankly he used to give his name and what a burden it had recently become to him; nowadays people he had never seen before seemed to know his name. How pleasant it was to have to introduce oneself before being recognized! 'You are an accused man,' said the priest in a very low voice. 'Yes,' said K., 'so I have been informed.' 'Then you are the man I seek,' said the priest. 'I am the prison chaplain.' 'Indeed,' said K. 'I had you summoned here,' said the priest, 'to have a talk with you.' 'I didn't know that,' said K. 'I came here to show an Italian round the Cathedral.' 'A mere detail,' said the priest. 'What is that in your hand? Is it a prayer-book?' 'No,' replied K., 'it is an album of sights worth seeing in the town.' 'Lay it down,' said the priest. K. pitched it away so violently that it flew open and slid some way along the floor with dishevelled leaves. 'Do you know that your case is going badly?' asked the priest. 'I have that idea myself,' said K. 'I've done what I could, but without any success so far. Of course, my first petition hasn't been presented yet.' 'How do you think it will end?' asked the priest. 'At first I thought it must turn out well,' said K., 'but now I frequently have my doubts. I don't know how it will end. Do you?' 'No,' said the priest, 'but I fear it will end badly. You are held to be guilty. Your case will perhaps never get beyond a lower Court. Your guilt is supposed, for the present, at least, to have been proved.' 'But I am not guilty,' said K.; 'it's a misunderstanding. And if it comes to that, how can any man be called guilty? We are all simply men here, one as much as the other.' 'That is true,' said the priest, 'but that's how all guilty men talk.' 'Are you prejudiced against me too?' asked K. 'I have no prejudices against you,' said the priest. 'I thank you,' said K.; 'but all the others who are concerned in these proceedings are prejudiced against me. They are influencing even outsiders. My position is becoming more and more difficult.' 'You are misinterpreting the facts of the case,' said the priest. 'The verdict is not so suddenly arrived at, the proceedings only gradually merge into the verdict.' 'So that's how it is,' said K., letting his head sink. 'What is the next step you propose to take in the matter?' asked the priest. 'I'm going to get more help,' said K., looking up again to see how the priest took his statement. 'There are several possibilities I haven't explored yet.' 'You cast about too much for outside help,' said the priest disapprovingly, 'especially from women. Don't you see that it isn't the right kind of help?' 'In some cases, even in many I could agree with you,' said K., 'but not always. Women have great influence. If I could move some women I know to join forces in working for me, I couldn't help winning through. Especially before this Court, which consists almost entirely of petticoat-hunters. Let the Examining Magistrate see a woman in the distance and he almost knocks down his desk and the defendant in his eagerness to get at her.' The priest drooped over the balustrade, apparently feeling for the first time the oppressiveness of the canopy above his head. What could have happened to the weather outside? There was no longer even a murky daylight; black night had set in. All the stained glass in the great window could not illumine the darkness of the wall with one solitary glimmer of light. And at this very moment the verger began to put out the candles on the high altar, one after another. 'Are you angry with me?' asked K. of the priest. 'It may be that you don't know the nature of the Court you are serving.' He got no answer. 'These are only personal experiences,' said K. There was still no answer from above. 'I wasn't trying to insult you,' said K. And at that the priest shrieked from the pulpit: 'Can't you see anything at all?' It was an angry cry, but at the same time sounded like the involuntary shriek of one who sees another fall and is startled out of himself.

Both were now silent for a long time. In the prevailing darkness the priest certainly could not make out K.'s features, while K. saw him distinctly by the light of the small lamp. Why did he not come down from the pulpit? He had not preached a sermon, he had only given K. some information which would be likely to harm him rather than help him when he came to consider it. Yet the priest's good intentions seemed to K. beyond question, it was not impossible that they could come to some agreement if the man would only quit his pulpit, it was not impossible that K. could obtain decisive and acceptable counsel from him which might, for instance, point the way, not towards some influential manipulation of the case, but towards a circumvention of it, a getting rid of it altogether, a mode of living completely outside the jurisdiction of the Court. This possibility must exist, K. had of late given much thought to it. And should the priest know of such a possibility, he might perhaps impart his knowledge if he were appealed to, although he himself belonged to the Court and as soon as he heard the Court impugned had forgotten his own gentle nature so far as to shout K. down.

'Won't you come down here?' said K. 'You haven't got to preach a sermon. Come down beside me.' 'I can come down now,' said the priest, perhaps repenting of his outburst. While he detached the lamp from its hook he said: 'I had to speak to you first from a distance. Otherwise I am too easily influenced and tend to forget my duty.'

K. waited for him at the foot of the steps. The priest stretched out his hand to K. while he was still on the way down from a higher level. 'Have you a little time for me?' asked K. 'As much time as you need,' said the priest, giving K. the small lamp to carry. Even close at hand he still wore a certain air of solemnity. 'You are very good to me,' said K. They paced side by side up and down the dusky aisle. 'But you are an exception among those who belong to the Court. I have more trust in you than in any of the others, though I know many of them. With you I can speak openly.' 'Don't be deluded,' said the priest. 'How am I being deluded?' asked K. 'You are deluding yourself about the Court,' said the priest. 'In the writings which preface the Law that particular delusion is described thus: before the Law stands a door-keeper on guard. To this door-keeper there comes a man from the country who begs for admittance to the Law. But the door-keeper says that he cannot admit the man at the moment. The man, on reflection, asks if he will be allowed, then, to enter later. "It is possible," answers the door-keeper, "but not at this moment." Since the door leading into the Law stands open as usual and the door-keeper steps to one side, the man bends down to peer through the entrance. When the door-keeper sees that, he laughs and says: "If you are so strongly tempted, try to get in without my permission. But note that I am powerful. And I am only the lowest door-keeper. From hall to hall, keepers stand at every door, one more powerful than the other. Even the third of these has an aspect that even I cannot bear to look at." These are difficulties which the man from the country has not expected to meet, the Law, he thinks, should be accessible to every man and at all times, and when he looks more closely at the door-keeper in his furred robe, with his huge pointed nose and long thin, Tartar beard, he decides that he had better wait until he gets permission to enter. The door-keeper gives him a stool and lets him sit down at the side of the door. There he sits waiting for days and years. He makes many attempts to be allowed in and wearies the door-keeper with his importunity. The door-keeper often engages him in brief conversation, asking him about his home and about other matters, but the questions are put quite impersonally, as great men put questions, and always conclude with the statement that the man cannot be allowed to enter yet. The man, who has equipped himself with many things for his journey, parts with all he has, however valuable, in the hope of bribing the door-keeper. The door-keeper accepts it all, saying, however, as he takes each gift: "I take this only to keep you from feeling that you have left something undone." During all these long years the man watches the door-keeper almost incessantly. He forgets about the other door-keepers, and this one seems to him the only barrier between himself and the Law. In the first years he curses his evil fate aloud; later, as he grows old, he only mutters to himself. He grows childish, and since in his prolonged watch he has learned to know even the fleas in the door-keeper's fur collar, he begs the very fleas to help him and to persuade the door-keeper to change his mind. Finally his eyes grow dim and he does not know whether the world is really darkening around him or whether his eyes are only deceiving him. But in the darkness he can now perceive a radiance that streams immortally from the door of the Law. Now his life is drawing to a close. Before he dies, all that he has experienced during the whole time of his sojourn condenses in his mind into one question, which he has never yet put to the door-keeper. He beckons the door-keeper, since he can no longer raise his stiffening body. The door-keeper has to bend far down to hear him, for the difference in size between them has increased very much to the man's disadvantage. "What do you want to know now?" asks the door-keeper, "you are insatiable." "Everyone strives to attain the Law," answers the man, "how does it come about, then, that in all these years no one has come seeking admittance but me?" The door-keeper perceives that the man is at the end of his strength and his hearing is failing, so he bellows in his ear: "No one but you could gain admittance through this door, since this door was intended only for you. I am now going to shut it."'

'So the door-keeper deluded the man,' said K. immediately, strongly attracted by the story. 'Don't be too hasty,' said the priest, 'don't take over an opinion without testing it. I have told you the story in the very words of the scriptures. There's no mention of delusion in it.' 'But it's clear enough,' said K., 'and your first interpretation of it was quite right. The door-keeper gave the message of salvation to the man only when it could no longer help him.' 'He was not asked the question any earlier,' said the priest, 'and you must consider, too, that he was only a door-keeper, and as such fulfilled his duty.' 'What makes you think he fulfilled his duty?' asked K. 'He didn't fulfil it. His duty might have been to keep all strangers away, but this man, for whom the door was intended, should have been let in.' 'You have not enough respect for the written word and you are altering the story,' said the priest. 'The story contains two important statements made by the door-keeper about admission to the Law, one at the beginning, the other at the end. The first statement is: that he cannot admit the man at the moment, and the other is: that this door was intended only for the man. If there were a contradiction between the two, you would be right and the door-keeper would have deluded the man. But there is no contradiction. The first statement, on the contrary, even implies the second. One could almost say that in suggesting to the man the possibility of future admittance the door-keeper is exceeding his duty. At that moment his apparent duty is to refuse admittance and indeed many commentators are surprised that the suggestion should be made at all, since the door-keeper appears to be a precisian with a stern regard for duty. He does not once leave his post during these many years, and he does not shut the door until the very last minute; he is conscious of the importance to his office, for he says: "I am powerful"; he is respectful to his superiors, for he says: "I am only the lowest door-keeper"; he is not garrulous, for during all these years he puts only what are called "impersonal questions"; he is not to be bribed, for he says in accepting a gift: "I take this only to keep you from feeling that you have left something undone"; where his duty is concerned he is to be moved neither by pity nor rage, for we are told that the man "wearied the door-keeper with his importunity"; and finally even his external appearance hints at a pedantic character, the large, pointed nose and the long, thin, black, Tartar beard. Could one imagine a more faithful door-keeper? Yet the door-keeper has other elements in his character which are likely to advantage anyone seeking admittance and which make it comprehensible enough that he should somewhat exceed his duty in suggesting the possibility of future admittance. For it cannot be denied that he is a little simple-minded and consequently a little conceited. Take the statements he makes about his power and the power of the other door-keepers and their dreadful aspect which even he cannot bear to see – I hold that these statements may be true enough, but that the way in which he brings them out shows that his perceptions are confused by simpleness of mind and conceit. The commentators note in this connexion: "That right perception of any matter and a misunderstanding of the same matter do not wholly exclude each other." One must at any rate assume that such simpleness and conceit, however sparingly indicated, are likely to weaken his defence of the door; they are breaches in the character of the door-keeper. To this must be added the fact that the door-keeper seems to be a friendly creature by nature, he is by no means always on his official dignity. In the very first moments he allows himself the jest of inviting the man to enter in spite of the strictly maintained veto against entry; then he does not, for instance, send the man away, but gives him, as we are told, a stool and lets him sit down beside the door. The patience with which he endures the man's appeals during so many years, the brief conversations, the acceptance of the gifts, the politeness with which he allows the man to curse loudly in his presence the fate for which he himself is responsible – all this lets us deduce certain motions of sympathy. Not every door-keeper would have acted thus. And finally, in answer to a gesture of the man's he stoops low down to give him the chance of putting a last question. Nothing but mild impatience – the door-keeper knows that this is the end of it all – is discernible in the words: "You are insatiable." Some push this mode of interpretation even farther and hold that these words express a kind of friendly admiration, though not without a hint of condescension. At any rate the figure of the door-keeper can be said to come out very differently from what you fancied.' 'You have studied the story more exactly and for a longer time than I have,' said K. They were both silent for a little while. Then K. said: 'So you think the man was not deluded?' 'Don't misunderstand me,' said the priest, 'I am only showing you the various opinions concerning that point. You must not pay too much attention to them. The scriptures are unalterable and the comments often enough merely express the commentator's bewilderment. In this case there even exists an interpretation which claims that the deluded person is really the door-keeper.' 'That's a far-fetched interpretation,' said K. 'On what is it based?' 'It is based,' answered the priest, 'on the simple-mindedness of the door-keeper. The argument is that he does not know the Law from inside, he knows only the way that leads to it, where he patrols up and down. His ideas of the interior are assumed to be childish, and it is supposed that he himself is afraid of the other guardians whom he holds up as bogies before the man. Indeed, he fears them more than the man does, since the man is determined to enter after hearing about the dreadful guardians of the interior, while the door-keeper has no desire to enter, at least not so far as we are told. Others again say that he must have been in the interior already, since he is after all engaged in the service of the Law and can only have been appointed from inside. This is countered by arguing that he may have been appointed by a voice calling from the interior, and that anyhow he cannot have been far inside, since the aspect of the third door-keeper is more than he can endure. Moreover, no indication is given that during all these years he ever made any remarks showing a knowledge of the interior, except for the one remark about the door-keepers. He may have been forbidden to do so, but there is no mention of that either. On these grounds the conclusion is reached that he knows nothing about the aspect and significance of the interior, so that he is in a state of delusion. But he is deceived also about his relation to the man from the country, for he is subject to the man and does not know it. He treats the man instead as his own subordinate, as can be recognized from many details that must be still fresh in your mind. But, according to his view of the story, it is just as clearly indicated that he is really subordinated to the man. In the first place, a bondman is always subject to a free man. Now the man from the country is really free, he can go where he likes, it is only the Law that is closed to him, and access to the Law is forbidden him only by one individual, the door-keeper. When he sits down on the stool by the side of the door and stays there for the rest of his life, he does it of his own free will; in the story there is no mention of any compulsion. But the door-keeper is bound to his post by his very office, he does not dare strike out into the country, nor apparently may he go into the interior of the Law, even should he wish to. Besides, although he is in the service of the Law, his service is confined to this one entrance; that is to say, he serves only this man for whom alone the entrance is intended. On that ground too he is subject to the man. One must assume that for many years, for as long as it takes a man to grow up to the prime of life, his service was in a sense an empty formality, since he had to wait for a man to come, that is to say someone in the prime of life, and so had to wait a long time before the purpose of his service could be fulfilled, and, moreover, had to wait on the man's pleasure, for the man came of his own free will. But the termination of his service also depends on the man's term of life, so that to the very end he is subject to the man. And it is emphasized throughout that the door-keeper apparently realizes nothing of all this. That is not in itself remarkable, since according to this interpretation the door-keeper is deceived in a much more important issue, affecting his very office. At the end, for example, he says regarding the entrance to the Law: "I am now going to shut it," but at the beginning of the story we are told that the door leading into the Law stands always open, and if it stands open always, that is to say at all times, without reference to the life or death of the man, then the door-keeper is incapable of closing it. There is some difference of opinion about the motive behind the door-keeper's statement, whether he said he was going to close the door merely for the sake of giving an answer, or to emphasize his devotion to duty, or to bring the man into a state of grief and regret in his last moments. But there is no lack of agreement that the door-keeper will not be able to shut the door. Many indeed profess to find that he is subordinate to the man even in wisdom, towards the end, at least, for the man sees the radiance that issues from the door of the Law while the door-keeper in his official position must stand with his back to the door, nor does he say anything to show that he has perceived the change.' 'That is well argued,' said K., after repeating to himself in a low voice several passages from the priest's exposition. 'It is well argued, and I am inclined to agree that the door-keeper is deluded. But that has not made me abandon my former opinion, since both conclusions are to some extent compatible. Whether the door-keeper is clear-sighted or deluded does not dispose of the matter. I said the man is deluded. If the door-keeper is clear-sighted, one might have doubts about that, but if the door-keeper himself is deluded, then his delusion must of necessity be communicated to the man. That makes the door-keeper not, indeed, a swindler, but a creature so simple-minded that he ought to be dismissed at once from his office. You mustn't forget that the door-keeper's delusions do himself no harm but do infinite harm to the man.' 'There are objections to that,' said the priest. 'Many aver that the story confers no right on anyone to pass judgement on the door-keeper. Whatever he may seem to us, he is yet a servant of the Law; that is, he belongs to the Law and as such is set beyond human judgement. In that case one dare not believe that the door-keeper is subordinate to the man. Bound as he is by his service, even at the door of the Law, he is incomparably freer than anyone at large in the world. The man is only seeking the Law, the door-keeper is already attached to it. It is the Law that has placed him at his post; to doubt his integrity is to doubt the Law itself.' 'I don't agree with that point of view,' said K. shaking his head, 'for if one accepts it, one must accept as true everything the door-keeper says. But you yourself have sufficiently proved how impossible it is to do that.' 'No,' said the priest, 'it is not necessary to accept everything as true, one must only accept it as necessary.' 'A melancholy conclusion,' said K. 'It turns lying into a universal principle.'

K. said that with finality, but it was not his final judgement. He was too tired to survey all the conclusions arising from the story, and the trains of thought into which it was leading him were unfamiliar, dealing with impalpabilities better suited to a theme for discussion among Court officials than for him. The simple story had lost its clear outline, he wanted to put it out of his mind, and the priest, who now showed great delicacy of feeling, suffered him to do so and accepted his comment in silence, although undoubtedly he did not agree with it.

They paced up and down for a while in silence, K. walking close beside the priest without being able to orient himself in the darkness. The lamp in his hand had long since gone out. The silver image of some saint once glimmered into sight immediately before him, by the sheen of its own silver, and was instantaneously lost in the darkness again. To keep himself from being utterly dependent on the priest, K. asked: 'Aren't we near the main doorway now?' 'No,' said the priest, 'we're a long way from it. Do you want to leave already?' Although at that moment K. had not been thinking of leaving, he answered at once: 'Of course, I must go. I'm the assistant manager of a Bank, they're waiting for me, I only came here to show a business friend from abroad round the Cathedral.' 'Well,' said the priest, reaching out his hand to K., 'then go.' 'But I can't find my way out alone in this darkness,' said K. 'Turn left to the wall,' said the priest, 'then follow the wall without leaving it and you'll come to a door.' The priest had already taken a step or two away from him, but K. cried out in a loud voice. 'Please wait a moment.' 'I am waiting,' said the priest. 'Don't you want anything more to do with me?' asked K. 'No,' said the priest. 'You were so friendly to me for a time,' said K., 'and explained so much to me, and now you let me go as if you cared nothing about me.' 'But you have to leave now,' said the priest. 'Well, yes,' said K., 'you must see that I can't help it.' 'You must first see that I can't help being what I am,' said the priest. 'You are the prison chaplain,' said K., groping his way nearer to the priest again; his immediate return to the Bank was not so necessary as he had made out, he could quite well stay longer. 'That means I belong to the Court,' said the priest. 'So why should I make any claims upon you? The Court makes no claims upon you. It receives you when you come and it relinquishes you when you go.'

10

THE END

On the evening before K.'s thirty-first birthday – it was about nine o'clock, the time when a hush falls on the streets – two men came to his lodging. In frock-coats, pallid and plump, with top-hats that were apparently uncollapsible. After some exchange of formalities regarding precedence at the front door, they repeated the same ceremony more exhaustively before K.'s door. Without having been informed of their visit, K. was sitting also dressed in black in an arm-chair near the door, slowly pulling on a pair of new gloves that fitted tightly over the fingers, looking as if he were expecting guests. He stood up at once and scrutinized the gentlemen with curiosity. 'So you are appointed for me?' he asked. The gentlemen bowed, each indicating the other with the hand that held the top-hat. K. admitted to himself that he had been expecting different visitors. He went to the window and took another look at the dark street. Nearly all the windows at the other side of the street were also in darkness; in many of them the curtains were drawn. At one lighted tenement window some babies were playing behind bars, reaching with their little hands towards each other although not able to move themselves from the spot. 'Tenth-rate old actors they send for me,' said K. to himself, glancing round again to confirm the impression. 'They want to finish me off cheaply.' He turned abruptly towards the men and asked: 'What theatre are you playing at?' 'Theatre?' said one, the corners of his mouth twitching as he looked for advice to the other, who acted as if he were a dumb man struggling to overcome an unnatural disability. 'They're not prepared to answer questions,' said K. to himself and went to fetch his hat.

While still on the stairs the two of them tried to take K. by the arms, and he said: 'Wait till we're in the street, I'm not an invalid.' But just outside the street door they fastened on him in a fashion he had never before seen or experienced. They kept their shoulders close behind his and instead of crooking their elbows, wound their arms round his at full length, holding his hands in a methodical, practised, irresistible grip. K. walked rigidly between them, the three of them were interlocked in a unity which would have brought all three down together had one of them been knocked over. It was a unity such as can be formed almost by lifeless elements alone.

Under the street lamps K. attempted time and time again, difficult though it was at such very close quarters, to see his companions more clearly than had been possible in the dusk of his room. 'Perhaps they are tenors,' he thought, as he studied their fat double chins. He was repelled by the painful cleanliness of their faces. One could literally see that the cleansing hand had been at work in the corners of the eyes, rubbing the upper lip, scrubbing out the furrows at the chin.

When that occurred to K. he halted, and in consequence the others halted too; they stood on the verge of an open, deserted square adorned with flower-beds. 'Why did they send you, of all people!' he said; it was more a cry than a question. The gentlemen obviously had no answer to make, they stood waiting with their free arms hanging, like sick-room attendants waiting while their patient takes a rest. 'I won't go any farther,' said K. experimentally. No answer was needed to that, it was sufficient that the two men did not loosen their grip and tried to propel K. from the spot; but he resisted them. 'I shan't need my strength much longer, I'll expend all the strength I have,' he thought. Into his mind came a recollection of flies struggling away from the fly-paper till their little legs were torn off. 'The gentlemen won't find it easy.'

And then before them Fräulein Bürstner appeared, mounting a small flight of steps leading into the square from a low-lying side-street. It was not quite certain that it was she, but the resemblance was close enough. Whether it was really Fräulein Bürstner or not, however, did not matter to K.; the important thing was that he suddenly realized the futility of resistance. There would be nothing heroic in it were he to resist, to make difficulties for his companions, to snatch at the last appearance of life in the exertion of struggle. He set himself in motion, and the relief his warders felt was transmitted to some extent even to himself. They suffered him now to lead the way, and he followed the direction taken by the Fräulein ahead of him, not that he wanted to overtake her or to keep her in sight as long as possible, but only that he might not forget the lesson she had brought into his mind. 'The only thing I can do now,' he told himself, and the regular correspondence between his steps and the steps of the other two confirmed his thought, 'the only thing for me to go on doing is to keep my intelligence calm and discriminating to the end. I always wanted to snatch at the world with twenty hands, and not for a very laudable motive, either. That was wrong, and am I to show now that not even a whole year's struggling with my case has taught me anything? Am I to leave this world as a man who shies away from all conclusions? Are people to say of me after I am gone that at the beginning of my case I wanted it to finish, and at the end of it wanted it to begin again? I don't want that to be said. I am grateful for the fact that these half-dumb, stupid creatures have been sent to accompany me on this journey, and that I have been left to say to myself all that is needed.'

The Fräulein meanwhile had bent into a side-street, but by this time K. could do without her and submitted himself to the guidance of his escort. In complete harmony all three now made their way across a bridge in the moonlight, the two men readily yielded to K.'s slightest movement, and when he turned slightly towards the parapet they turned, too, in a solid front. The water, glittering and trembling in the moonlight, divided on either side of a small island, on which the foliage of trees and bushes rose in thick masses, as if bunched together. Beneath the trees ran gravel paths, now invisible, with convenient benches on which K. had stretched himself at ease many a summer. 'I didn't mean to stop altogether,' he said to his companions, shamed by their obliging compliance. Behind K.'s back the one seemed to reproach the other gently for the mistaken stop they had made, and then all three went on again.

They passed through several steeply-rising streets, in which policemen stood or patrolled at intervals; sometimes a good way off, sometimes quite near. One with a bushy moustache, his hand on the hilt of his sabre, came up as of set purpose close to the not quite harmless-looking group. The two gentlemen halted, the policeman seemed to be already opening his mouth, but K. forcibly pulled his companions forward. He kept looking round cautiously to see if the policeman was following; as soon as he had put a corner between himself and the policeman he started to run, and his two companions, scant of breath as they were, had to run beside him.

So they came quickly out of the town, which at this point merged almost without transition into the open fields. A small stone quarry, deserted and bleak, lay quite near to a still completely urban house. Here the two men came to a standstill, whether because this place had been their goal from the very beginning or because they were too exhausted to go farther. Now they loosened their hold of K., who stood waiting dumbly, took off the top-hats and wiped the sweat from their brows with pocket handkerchiefs, meanwhile surveying the quarry. The moon shone down on everything with that simplicity and serenity which no other light possesses.

After an exchange of courteous formalities regarding which of them was to take preference in the next task – these emissaries seemed to have been given no specific assignments in the charge laid jointly upon them – one of them came up to K. and removed his coat, his waistcoat, and finally his shirt. K. shivered involuntarily, whereupon the man gave him a light, reassuring pat on the back. Then he folded the clothes carefully together, as if they were likely to be used again at some time, although perhaps not immediately. Not to leave K. standing motionless, exposed to the night breeze, which was chilly enough, he took him by the arm and walked him up and down a little, while his partner investigated the quarry to find a suitable spot. When he found it he beckoned, and K.'s companion led him over there. It was a spot near the cliff-side where a loose boulder was lying. The two of them laid K. down on the ground, propped him against the boulder, and settled his head upon it. But in spite of the pains they took and all the willingness K. showed, his posture remained contorted and unnatural-looking. So one of the men begged the other to let him dispose K. all by himself, yet even that did not improve matters. Finally they left K. in a position which was not even the best of the positions they had already rehearsed. Then one of them opened his frock-coat and out of a sheath that hung from a belt girt round his waistcoat drew a long, thin, double-edged butcher's knife, held it up, and tested the cutting edges in the moonlight. Once more the odious ceremonial of courtesy began, the first handed the knife across K. to the second, who handed it across K. back again to the first. K. now perceived clearly that he was supposed to seize the knife himself, as it travelled from hand to hand above him, and plunge it into his own breast. But he did not do so, he merely turned his head, which was still free to move, and gazed around him. He could not completely rise to the occasion, he could not relieve the officials of all their tasks; the responsibility for this last failure of his lay with him who had not left him the remnant of strength necessary for the deed. His glance fell on the top storey of the house adjoining the quarry. With a flicker as of a light going up, the casements of a window there suddenly flew open; a human figure, faint and insubstantial at that distance and that height, leaned abruptly far forward and stretched both arms still farther. Who was it? A friend? A good man? Someone who sympathized? Someone who wanted to help? Was it one person only? Or were they all there? Was help at hand? Were there some arguments in his favour that had been overlooked? Of course there must be. Logic is doubtless unshakeable, but it cannot withstand a man who wants to go on living. Where was the Judge whom he had never seen? Where was the High Court, to which he had never penetrated? He raised his hands and spread out all his fingers.

But the hands of one of the partners were already at K.'s throat, while the other thrust the knife into his heart and turned it there twice. With failing eyes K. could still see the two of them, cheek leaning against cheek, immediately before his face, watching the final act. 'Like a dog!' he said: it was as if he meant the shame of it to outlive him.

America

Translated from the German
by Willa and Edwin Muir

1

THE STOKER

As Karl Rossmann, a poor boy of sixteen who had been packed off to America by his parents because a servant girl had seduced him and got herself with child by him, stood on the liner slowly entering the harbour of New York, a sudden burst of sunshine seemed to illumine the Statue of Liberty, so that he saw it in a new light, although he had sighted it long before. The arm with the sword rose up as if it newly stretched aloft, and round the figure blew the free winds of heaven.

'So high!' he said to himself, and was gradually edged to the very rail by the swelling throng of porters pushing past him, since he was not thinking at all of getting off the ship.

A young man with whom he had struck up a slight acquaintance on the voyage called out in passing: 'Not very anxious to go ashore, are you?' 'Oh, I'm quite ready,' said Karl with a laugh, and being both strong and in high spirits he heaved his box on to his shoulder. But as his eye followed his acquaintance, who was already moving on among the others, lightly swinging a walking-stick, he realized with dismay that he had forgotten his umbrella down below. He hastily begged his acquaintance, who did not seem particularly gratified, to oblige him by waiting beside the box for a minute, took another survey of the situation to get his bearings for the return journey, and hurried away. Below decks he found to his disappointment that a gangway which made a handy short-cut had been barred for the first time in his experience, probably in connexion with the disembarkation of so many passengers, and he had painfully to find his way down endless recurring stairs, through corridors with countless turnings, through an empty room with a deserted writing-table, until in the end, since he had taken this route no more than once or twice and always among a crowd of other people, he lost himself completely. In his bewilderment, meeting no one and hearing nothing but the ceaseless shuffling of thousands of feet above him, and in the distance, like faint breathing, the last throbbings of the engines, which had already been shut off, he began unthinkingly to hammer on a little door by which he had chanced to stop his wanderings.

'It isn't locked,' a voice shouted from inside, and Karl opened the door with genuine relief. 'What are you hammering at the door for, like a madman?' asked a huge man, scarcely even glancing at Karl. Through an opening of some kind a feeble glimmer of daylight, all that was left after the top decks had used it up, fell into the wretched cubby-hole in which a bunk, a cupboard, a chair and the man were packed together, as if they had been stored there. 'I've lost my way,' said Karl. 'I never noticed it during the voyage, but this is a terribly big ship.' 'Yes, you're right there,' said the man with a certain pride, fiddling all the time with the lock of a little sea-chest, which he kept pressing with both hands in the hope of hearing the wards snap home. 'But come inside,' he went on, 'you don't want to stand out there!' 'I'm not disturbing you?' asked Karl. 'Why, how should you disturb me?' 'Are you a German?' Karl asked to reassure himself further, for he had heard a great deal about the perils which threatened newcomers to America, particularly from the Irish. 'That's what I am, yes,' said the man. Karl still hesitated. Then the man suddenly seized the door handle and pulling the door shut with a hasty movement swept Karl into the cabin.

'I can't stand being stared at from the passage,' he said, beginning to fiddle with his chest again, 'people keep passing and staring in, it's more than a man can bear.' 'But the passage is quite empty,' said Karl, who was standing squeezed uncomfortably against the end of the bunk. 'Yes, now,' said the man. 'But it's now we were speaking about,' thought Karl, 'it's hard work talking to this man.' 'Lie down on the bunk, you'll have more room there,' said the man. Karl scrambled in as well as he could, and laughed aloud at his first unsuccessful attempt to swing himself over. But scarcely was he in the bunk when he cried: 'Good Lord, I've quite forgotten my box!' 'Why, where is it?' 'Up on deck, a man I know is looking after it. What's his name again?' And he fished a visiting-card from a pocket which his mother had made in the lining of his coat for the voyage. 'Butterbaum, Franz Butterbaum.' 'Can't you do without your box?' 'Of course not.' 'Well, then, why did you leave it in a stranger's hands?' 'I forgot my umbrella down below and rushed off to get it; I didn't want to drag my box with me. Then on top of that I got lost.' 'You're all alone? Without anyone to look after you?' 'Yes, all alone.' 'Perhaps I should join up with this man,' the thought came into Karl's head, 'where am I likely to find a better friend?' 'And now you've lost the box as well. Not to mention the umbrella.' And the man sat down on the chair as if Karl's business had at last acquired some interest for him. 'But I think my box can't be lost yet.' 'You can think what you like,' said the man, vigorously scratching his dark, short, thick hair. 'But morals change every time you come to a new port. In Hamburg your Butterbaum might maybe have looked after your box; while here it's most likely that they've both disappeared.' 'But then I must go up and see about it at once,' said Karl, looking round for the way out. 'You just stay where you are,' said the man, giving him a push with one hand on the chest, quite roughly, so that he fell back on the bunk again. 'But why?' asked Karl in exasperation. 'Because there's no point in it,' said the man, 'I'm leaving too very soon, and we can go together. Either the box is stolen and then there's no help for it, or the man has left it standing where it was, and then we'll find it all the more easily when the ship is empty. And the same with your umbrella.' 'Do you know your way about the ship?' asked Karl suspiciously, and it seemed to him that the idea, otherwise plausible, that his things would be easier to find when the ship was empty must have a catch in it somewhere. 'Why, I'm a stoker,' said the man. 'You're a stoker!' cried Karl delightedly, as if this surpassed all his expectations, and he rose up on his elbows to look at the man more closely. 'Just outside the room where I slept with the Slovaks there was a little window through which we could see into the engine-room.' 'Yes, that's where I've been working,' said the stoker. 'I have always had a passion for machinery,' said Karl, following his own train of thought, 'and I would have become an engineer in time, that's certain, if I hadn't had to go to America.' 'Why did you have to go?' 'Oh, that!' said Karl, dismissing the whole business with a wave of the hand. He looked with a smile at the stoker, as if begging his indulgence for not telling. 'There was some reason for it, I suppose,' said the stoker, and it was hard to tell whether in saying that he wanted to encourage or discourage Karl to tell. 'I could be a stoker now too,' said Karl, 'it's all one to my father and mother what becomes of me.' 'My job's going to be free,' said the stoker, and to point his full consciousness of it, he stuck his hands into his trouser pockets and flung his legs in their baggy, leather-like trousers on the bunk to stretch them. Karl had to shift nearer to the wall. 'Are you leaving the ship?' 'Yes, we're paid off today.' 'But why? Don't you like it?' 'Oh, that's the way things are run; it doesn't always depend on whether a man likes it or not. But you're quite right, I don't like it. I don't suppose you're thinking seriously of being a stoker, but that's just the time when you're most likely to turn into one. So I advise you strongly against it. If you wanted to study engineering in Europe, why shouldn't you study it here? The American universities are ever so much better than the European ones.' 'That's possible,' said Karl, 'but I have hardly any money to study on. I've read of someone who worked all day in a shop and studied at night until he became a doctor, and a mayor, too, I think, but that needs a lot of perseverence, doesn't it? I'm afraid I haven't got that. Besides, I wasn't a particularly good scholar; it was no great wrench for me to leave school. And maybe the schools here are more difficult. I can hardly speak any English at all. Anyhow, people here have a prejudice against foreigners, I think.' 'So you've come up against that kind of thing too, have you? Well, that's all to the good. You're the man for me. See here, this is a German ship we're on, it belongs to the Hamburg-American line; so why aren't the crew all Germans, I ask you? Why is the Chief Engineer a Roumanian? A man called Schubal. It's hard to believe it. A measly hound like that slave-driving us Germans on a German ship! You mustn't think' – here his voice failed him and he gesticulated with his hands – 'that I'm complaining for the sake of complaining. I know you have no influence and that you're a poor lad yourself. But it's too much!' And he brought his fist several times down on the table, never taking his eyes from it while he flourished it. 'I've signed on in ever so many ships' – and he reeled off twenty names one after the other as if they were one word, which quite confused Karl – 'and I've done good work in all of them, been praised, pleased every captain I ever had, actually stuck to the same cargo boat for several years, I did' – he rose to his feet as if that had been the greatest achievement of his life – 'and here on this tub, where everything's done by rule and you don't need any wits at all, here I'm no good, here I'm just in Schubal's way, here I'm a slacker who should be kicked out and doesn't begin to earn his pay. Can you understand that? I can't.' 'Don't you put up with it!' said Karl excitedly. He had almost lost the feeling that he was on the uncertain boards of a ship, beside the coast of an unknown continent, so much at home did he feel here in the stoker's bunk. 'Have you seen the Captain about it? Have you asked him to give you your rights?' 'Oh, get away with you, out you get, I don't want you here. You don't listen to what I say, and then you give me advice. How could I go to the Captain?' Wearily the stoker sat down again and hid his face in his hands.

'I can't give him any better advice,' Karl told himself. And it occurred to him that he would have done better to go and get his box instead of handing out advice that was merely regarded as stupid. When his father had given him the box for good he had said in jest: 'How long will you keep it?' and now the faithful box had perhaps been lost in earnest. His sole remaining consolation was that his father could hardly learn of his present situation, even if he were to inquire. All that the shipping company could say was that he had safely reached New York. But Karl felt sorry to think that he had hardly used the things in the box yet, although, to take an instance, he should long since have changed his shirt. So his economies had started at the wrong point, it seemed; now, at the very beginning of his career, when it was essential to show himself in clean clothes, he would have to appear in a dirty shirt. Otherwise the loss of the box would not have been so serious, for the suit which he was wearing was actually better than the one in the box, which in reality was merely an emergency suit that his mother had hastily mended just before he left. Then he remembered that in the box there was a piece of Veronese Salami which his mother had packed as an extra tit-bit, only he had not been able to eat more than a scrap of it, for during the voyage he had been quite without any appetite, and the soup which was served in the steerage had been more than sufficient for him. But now he would have liked to have the salami at hand, so as to present it to the stoker. For such people were easily won over by the gift of some trifle or other; Karl had learned that from his father, who deposited cigars in the pockets of the subordinate officials with whom he did business, and so won them over. Yet all that Karl now possessed in the way of gifts was his money, and he did not want to touch that for the time being, in case he should have lost his box. Again his thoughts turned back to the box, and he simply could not understand why he should have watched it during the voyage so vigilantly that he had almost lost his sleep over it, only to let that same box be filched from him so easily now. He remembered the five nights during which he had kept a suspicious eye on a little Slovak whose bunk was two places away from him on the left, and who had designs, he was sure, on the box. This Slovak was merely waiting for Karl to be overcome by sleep and doze off for a minute, so that he might manoeuvre the box away with a long, pointed stick which he was always playing or practising with during the day. By day the Slovak looked innocent enough, but hardly did night come on than he kept rising up from his bunk to cast melancholy glances at Karl's box. Karl had seen this quite clearly, for every now and then someone would light a little candle, although it was forbidden by the ship's regulations, and with the anxiety of the emigrant would peer into some incomprehensible prospectus of an emigration agency. If one of these candles was burning near him, Karl could doze off for a little, but if it was further away or if the place was quite dark, he had to keep his eyes open. The strain of this task had quite exhausted him, and now perhaps it had all been in vain. Oh, that Butterbaum, if ever he met him again!

At that moment, in the distance, the unbroken silence was disturbed by a series of small, short taps, like the tapping of children's feet; they came nearer, growing louder, until they sounded like the tread of quietly marching men. Men in single file, as was neutral in the narrow passage, and a clashing as of arms could be heard. Karl, who had been on the point of relaxing himself in a sleep free of all worries about boxes and Slovaks, started up and nudged the stoker to draw his attention, for the head of the procession seemed just to have reached the door. 'That's the ship's band,' said the stoker, 'They've been playing up above and have come back to pack up. All's clear now, and we can go. Come!' He took Karl by the hand, snatched at the last moment a framed picture of the Madonna from the wall above the bed, stuck it into his breast pocket, seized his chest, and with Karl hastily left the cubby-hole.

'I'm going to the office now to give them a piece of my mind. All the passengers are gone; I don't need to care what I do.' The stoker kept repeating this theme with variations, and as he walked on kicked out his foot sideways at a rat which crossed his way, but merely drove it more quickly into its hole, which it reached just in time. He was slow in all his movements, for though his legs were long they were massive as well.

They went through part of the kitchen, where some girls in dirty white aprons – which they splashed deliberately – were washing dishes in great tubs. The stoker hailed a girl called Lina, put his arm round her waist, and since she coquettishly resisted the embrace dragged her a part of the way with him. 'It's pay-day; aren't you coming along?' he asked. 'Why take the trouble; you can bring me the money here,' she replied, squirming under his arm and running away. 'Where did you pick up that good-looking boy?' she cried after him, but without waiting for an answer. They could hear the laughter of the other girls, who had all stopped their work.

But they went on and came to a door above which there was a little pediment, supported by tiny, gilded caryatides. For a ship's fitting it looked extravagantly sumptuous. Karl realized that he had never been in this part of the ship, which during the voyage had probably been reserved for passengers of the first and second class; but the doors that cut it off had now been thrown open to prepare for the cleaning down of the ship. Indeed, they had already met some men with brooms on their shoulders, who had greeted the stoker. Karl was amazed at the extent of the ship's organization; as a steerage passenger he had seen very little of it. Along the corridors ran wires of electric installations, and a little bell kept sounding every now and then.

The stoker knocked respectfully at the door, and when someone cried 'Come in!' urged Karl with a wave of the hand to enter boldly. Karl stepped in, but remained standing beside the door. The three windows of this room framed a view of the sea, and gazing at the cheerful motion of the waves his heart beat faster, as if he had not been looking at the sea without interruption for five long days. Great ships crossed each other's courses in either direction, yielding to the assault of the waves only as far as their ponderous weight permitted them. If one almost shut one's eyes, these ships seemed to be staggering under their own weight. From their masts flew long, narrow pennants which, though kept taut by the speed of their going, at the same time fluttered a little. Probably from some battleship there could be heard salvoes, fired in salute, and a warship of some kind passed at no great distance; the muzzles of its guns, gleaming with the reflections of sunlight on steel, seemed to be nursed along by the sure, smooth motion, although not on an even keel.

Only a distant view of the smaller ships and boats could be had, at least from the door, as they darted about in swarms through the gaps between the great ships. And behind them all rose New York, and its skyscrapers stared at Karl with their hundred thousand eyes. Yes, in this room one realized where one was.

At a round table three gentlemen were sitting, one a ship's officer in the blue ship's uniform, the two others harbour officials in black American uniforms. On the table lay piles of various papers, which the officer first glanced over, pen in hand, and then handed to the two others, who read them, made excerpts, and filed them away in portfolios, except when they were not actually engaged in taking down some kind of protocol which one of them dictated to his colleagues, making clicking noises with his teeth all the time.

By the first window a little man was sitting at a desk with his back to the door; he was busy with some huge ledgers ranked on a stout book-shelf on a level with his head. Beside him stood an open safe which, at first glance at least, seemed empty.

The second window was vacant and gave the better view. But near the third two gentleman were standing conversing in low tones. One of them was leaning against the window; he was wearing the ship's uniform and playing with the hilt of his sword. The man to whom he was speaking faced the window, and now and then a movement of his disclosed part of a row of decorations on the breast of his interlocutor. He was in civilian clothes and carried a thin bamboo cane which, as both hands were resting on his hips, also stood out like a sword.

Karl did not have much time to see all this, for almost at once an attendant came up to them and asked the stoker, with a glance which seemed to indicate that he had no business here, what he wanted. The stoker replied as softly as he had been asked that he wished to speak to the Head Purser. The attendant made a gesture of refusal with his hand, but all the same tiptoed toward the man with the ledgers, avoiding the round table by a wide detour. The ledger official – this could clearly be seen – stiffened all over at the words of the attendant, but at last turned round towards this man who wished to speak to him and waved him away violently, repudiating the attendant too, to make quite certain. The attendant then sidled back to the stoker and said in the voice of one imparting a confidence: 'Clear out of here at once!'

At this reply the stoker turned his eyes on Karl, as if Karl were his heart, to whom he was silently bewailing his grief. Without stopping to think, Karl launched himself straight across the room, actually brushing against one of the officers' chairs, while the attendant chased after him, swooping with widespread arms as if to catch an insect; but Karl was the first to reach the Head Purser's desk, which he gripped firmly in case the attendant should try to drag him away.

The whole room naturally sprang to life at once. The ship's officer at the table leapt to his feet; the harbour officials looked on calmly but attentively; the two gentlemen by the window moved closer to each other; the attendant, who thought it was no longer his place to interfere, since his masters were now involved, stepped back. The stoker waited tensely by the door for the moment when his intervention should be required. And the Head Purser at last made a complete rightabout turn in his chair.

From his secret pocket, which he did not mind showing to these people, Karl hauled out his passport, which he opened and laid on the desk in lieu of further introduction. The Head Purser seemed to consider the passport irrevelant, for he flicked it aside with two fingers, whereupon Karl, as if that formality were satisfactorily settled, put it back in his pocket again.

'May I be allowed to say,' he then began, 'that in my opinion an injustice has been done to my friend the stoker? There's a certain man Schubal aboard who bullies him. He has a long record of satisfactory service on many ships, whose names he can give you, he is diligent, takes an interest in his work, and it's really hard to see why on this particular ship, where the work isn't so heavy as on cargo boats, for instance, he should get so little credit. It must be sheer slander that keeps him back and robs him of the recognition that should certainly be his. I have confined myself, as you can see, to generalities; he can lay his specific complaints before you himself.' In saying this Karl had addressed all the gentlemen present, because in fact they were all listening to him, and because it seemed much more likely that among so many at least one just man might be found, than that the one just man should be the Head Purser. Karl also guilefully concealed the fact that he had known the stoker for such a short time. But he would have made a much better speech had he not been distracted by the red face of the man with the bamboo cane, which was now in his line of vision for the first time.

'It's all true, every word of it,' said the stoker before anyone even asked him, indeed before anyone so much as looked at him. This over-eagerness on his part might have proved a great mistake if the man with the decorations who, it now dawned on Karl, was of course the Captain, had not clearly made up his mind to hear the case. For he stretched out his hand and called to the stoker: 'Come here!' in a voice as firm as a rock. Everything now depended on the stoker's behaviour, for about the justice of his case Karl had no doubt whatever.

Luckily it appeared at this point that the stoker was a man of some worldly experience. With exemplary composure he drew out of his sea-chest, at the first attempt, a little bundle of papers and a notebook, walked over with them to the Captain as if that were a matter of course, entirely ignoring the Head Purser, and spread out his evidence on the window-ledge. There was nothing for the Head Purser to do but also to come forward. 'The man is a notorious grumbler,' he said in explanation, 'he spends more time in the pay-room than in the engine-room. He has driven Schubal, who's a quiet fellow, to absolute desperation. Listen to me!' here he turned to the stoker. 'You're a great deal too persistent in pushing yourself forward. How often have you been flung out of the pay-room already, and serve you right too, for your impudence in demanding things to which you have no right whatever? How often have you gone running from the pay-room to the Purser's office? How often has it been patiently explained to you that Schubal is your immediate superior, and that it's him you have to deal with, and him alone? And now you actually come here, when the Captain himself is present, to pester him with your impudence, and as if that weren't enough you bring a mouth-piece with you to reel off the absurd grievances you've drilled into him, a boy I've never even seen on the ship before!'

Karl forcibly restrained himself from springing forward. But the Captain had already intervened with the remark: 'Better hear what the man has to say for himself. Schubal's getting a good deal too big for his boots these days, but that doesn't mean I think you're right.' The last words were addressed to the stoker; it was only natural that the Captain should not take his part at once, yet everything seemed to be going the right way. The stoker began to state his case and controlled himself so far at the very beginning as to call Schubal 'Mr Schubal'. Standing beside the Head Purser's vacant desk, Karl felt so pleased that in his delight he kept pressing the letter-scales down with his finger. Mr Schubal was unfair! Mr Schubal gave the preference to foreigners! Mr Schubal ordered the stoker out of the engine-room and made him clean water-closets, which was not a stoker's job at all! At one point even the capability of Mr Schubal was called in question, as being more apparent than real. At this point Karl fixed his eyes on the Captain and stared at him with earnest deference, as if they had been colleagues, to keep him from being influenced against the stoker by the man's awkward way of expressing himself. All the same, nothing definite emerged from the stoker's outpourings, and although the Captain still listened thoughtfully, his eyes expressing a resolution to hear the stoker this time to the end, the other gentlemen were growing impatient and the stoker's voice no longer dominated the room, which was a bad sign. The gentleman in civilian clothes was the first to show his impatience by bringing his bamboo stick into play and tapping, though only softly, on the floor. The others still looked up now and then; but the two harbour officials, who were clearly pressed for time, snatched up their papers again and began, though somewhat absently, to glance over them; the ship's officer turned to his desk, and the Head Purser, who now thought he had won the day, heaved a loud ironical sigh. From the general dispersion of interest the only one who seemed to be exempt was the attendant, who sympathized to some extent with this poor man confronting the great, and gravely nodded to Karl as though trying to explain something.

Meanwhile, outside the windows, the life of the harbour went on; a flat barge laden with a mountain of barrels, which must have been wonderfully well packed, since they did not roll off, went past, almost completely obscuring the daylight; little motor-boats, which Karl would have liked to examine thoroughly if he had had time, shot straight past in obedience to the slightest touch of the man standing erect at the wheel. Here and there curious objects bobbed independently out of the restless water, were immediately submerged again and sank before his astonished eyes; boats belonging to the ocean liners were rowed past by sweating sailors; they were filled with passengers sitting silent and expectant as if they had been stowed there, except that some of them could not refrain from turning their heads to gaze at the changing scene. A movement without end, a restlessness transmitted from the restless element to helpless human beings and their works!

But everything demanded haste, clarity, exact statement; and what was the stoker doing? Certainly he was talking himself into a sweat; his hands were trembling so much that he could no longer hold the papers he had laid on the window-ledge; from all points of the compass complaints about Schubal streamed into his head, each of which, it seemed to him, should have been sufficient to dispose of Schubal for good; but all he could produce for the Captain was a wretched farrago in which everything was lumped together. For a long time the man with the bamboo cane had been staring at the ceiling and whistling to himself; the harbour officials now detained the ship's officer at their table and showed no sign of ever letting him go again; the Head Purser was clearly restrained from letting fly only by the Captain's composure; the attendant stood at attention, waiting every moment for the Captain to give an order concerning the stoker.

At that Karl could no longer remain inactive. So he advanced slowly towards the group, running over in his mind the more rapidly all the ways in which he could most adroitly handle the affair. It was certainly high time; a little longer, and they might quite well both of them be kicked out of the office. The Captain might be a good man and might also, or so it seemed to Karl, have some particular reason at the moment to show that he was a just master; but after all he wasn't a mere instrument to be recklessly played on, and that was exactly how the stoker was treating him in the boundless indignation of his heart.

Accordingly Karl said to the stoker: 'You must put things more simply, more clearly; the Captain can't do justice to what you are telling him. How can he know all the mechanics and ship's boys by name, far less by their first names, so that when you mention So-and-so he can tell at once who is meant? Take your grievances in order, tell the most important ones first and the lesser ones afterwards; perhaps you'll find that it won't be necessary even to mention most of them. You always explained them clearly enough to me!' If boxes could be stolen in America, one could surely tell a lie now and then as well, he thought in self-excuse.

But was his advice of any use? Might it not already be too late? The stoker certainly stopped speaking at once when he heard the familiar voice, but his eyes were so blinded with tears of wounded dignity, of dreadful memory, of extreme present grief, that he could hardly even recognize Karl. How could he at this stage – Karl silently realized this, facing the now silent stoker – how could he at this stage suddenly change his style of argument, when it seemed plain to him that he had already said all there was to say without evoking the slightest sympathy, and at the same time that he had said nothing at all, and could not expect these gentlemen to listen to the whole rigmarole over again? And at such a moment Karl, his sole supporter, had to break in with so-called good advice which merely made it clear that everything was lost, everything.

'If I had only spoken sooner, instead of looking out of the window,' Karl told himself, dropping his eyes before the stoker and letting his hands fall to his sides as a sign that all hope was ended.

But the stoker mistook the action, feeling, no doubt, that Karl was nursing some secret reproach against him, and, in the honest desire to disabuse him, crowned all his other offences by starting to wrangle at this moment with Karl. At this very moment, when the men at the round table were completely exasperated by the senseless babble that disturbed their important labours, when the Head Purser was gradually beginning to find the Captain's patience incomprehensible and was just on the point of exploding, when the attendant, once more entirely translated to his masters' sphere, was measuring the stoker with savage eyes, and when, finally, the gentleman with the bamboo cane, whom even the Captain eyed now and then in a friendly manner, already quite bored by the stoker, indeed disgusted at him, had pulled out a little notebook and was obviously preoccupied with quite different thoughts, glancing first at the notebook and then at Karl.

'I know,' said Karl, who had difficulty in turning aside the torrent which the stoker now directed at him, but yet could summon up a friendly smile for him in spite of all dissension, 'that you're right, you're right, I have never doubted it.' In his fear of being struck by the stoker's gesticulating hands he would have liked to catch hold of them, and still better to force the man into a corner so as to whisper a few soothing, reassuring words to him which no one else could hear. But the stoker was past all bounds. Karl now began actually to take a sort of comfort in the thought that in case of need the stoker could overwhelm the seven men in the room with the very strength of his desperation. But on the desk, as he could see at a glance, there was a bell-arrangement with far too many buttons; the mere pressure of one hand on them would raise the whole ship and call up all the hostile men that filled its passage-ways.

But here, in spite of his air of bored detachment, the gentleman with the bamboo cane came over to Karl and asked, not very loudly yet clearly enough to be heard above the stoker's ravings: 'By the way, what's your name?' At that moment, as if someone behind the door had been waiting to hear this remark, there was a knock. The attendant looked across at the Captain; the Captain nodded. Thereupon the attendant went to the door and opened it. Outside was standing a middle-sized man in an old military coat, not looking at all like the kind of person who would attend to machinery – and yet he was Schubal. If Karl had not guessed this from the expression of satisfaction which lit up all eyes, even the Captain's, he must have recognized it with horror from the demeanour of the stoker, who clenched his fists at the end of his outstretched arms with a vehemence that made the clenching of them seem the most important thing about him, to which he was prepared to sacrifice everything else in life. All his strength was concentrated in his fists, including the very strength that held him upright.

And so here was the enemy, fresh and gay in his shore-going clothes, a ledger under his arm, probably containing a statement of the hours worked and the wages due to the stoker, and he was openly scanning the faces of everyone present, a frank admission that his first concern was to discover on which side they stood. All seven of them were already his friends, for even though the Captain had raised some objections to him earlier, or had pretended to do so because he felt sorry for the stoker, it was now apparent that he had not the slightest fault to find with Schubal. A man like the stoker could not be too severely repressed, and if Schubal were to be reproached for anything, it was for not having subdued the stoker's recalcitrance sufficiently, since the fellow had dared to face the Captain after all.

Yet it might still be assumed that the confrontation of Schubal and the stoker would achieve, even before a human tribunal, the result which would have been awarded by divine justice, since Schubal, even if he were good at making a show of virtue, might easily give himself away in the long run. A brief flare-up of his evil nature would suffice to reveal it to those gentlemen, and Karl would arrange for that. He already had a rough and ready knowledge of the shrewdness, the weaknesses, the temper of the various individuals in the room, and in this respect the time he had spent there had not been wasted. It was a pity that the stoker was not more competent; he seemed quite incapable of decisive action. If one were to thrust Schubal at him, he would probably split the man's hated skull with his fists. But it was beyond his power to take the couple of steps needed to bring Schubal within reach. Why had Karl not foreseen what so easily could have been foreseen: that Schubal would inevitably put in an appearance, if not of his own accord, then by order of the Captain? Why had he not outlined an exact plan of campaign with the stoker when they were on their way here, instead of simply walking in, hopelessly unprepared, as soon as they found a door, which was what they had done? Was the stoker even capable of saying a word by this time, of answering yes and no, as he must do if he were now to be cross-examined, although, to be sure, a cross-examination was almost too much to hope for? There he stood, his legs a-sprawl, his knees uncertain, his head thrown back, and the air flowed in and out of his open mouth as if the man had no lungs to control its motion.

But Karl himself felt more strong and clear-headed than perhaps he had ever been at home. If only his father and mother could see him now, fighting for justice in a strange land before men of authority, and, though not yet triumphant, dauntlessly resolved to win the final victory! Would they revise their opinion of him? Set him between them and praise him? Look into his eyes at last, at last, those eyes so filled with devotion to them? Ambiguous questions, and this the most unsuitable moment to ask them!

'I have come here because I believe this stoker is accusing me of dishonesty or something. A maid in the kitchen told me she saw him making in this direction. Captain, and all you other gentlemen, I am prepared to show papers to disprove any such accusation, and, if you like, to adduce the evidence of unprejudiced and incorruptible witnesses, who are waiting outside the door now.' Thus spake Schubal. It was, to be sure, a clear and manly statement, and from the altered expression of the listeners one might have thought they were hearing a human voice for the first time after a long interval. They certainly did not notice the holes that could be picked in that fine speech. Why, for instance, had the first relevant word that occurred to him been 'dishonesty'? Should he have been accused of that, perhaps instead of nationalistic prejudice? A maid in the kitchen had seen the stoker on his way to the office, and Schubal had immediately divined what that meant? Wasn't it his consciousness of guilt that had sharpened his apprehension? And he had immediately collected witnesses, had he, and then called them unprejudiced and incorruptible to boot? Imposture, nothing but imposture! And these gentlemen were not only taken in by it, but regarded it with approval? Why had he allowed so much time to elapse between the kitchen-maid's report and his arrival here? Simply in order to let the stoker weary the gentlemen, until they began to lose their powers of clear judgement, which Schubal feared most of all. Standing for a long time behind the door, as he must have done, had he deliberately refrained from knocking until he heard the casual question of the gentleman with the bamboo cane, which gave him grounds to hope that the stoker was already despatched?

Everything was clear enough now and Schubal's very behaviour involuntarily corroborated it, but it would have to be proved to those gentlemen by other and still more palpable means. They must be shaken up. Now then, Karl, quick, make the best of every minute you have, before the witnesses come in and confuse everything!

At that very moment, however, the Captain waved Schubal away, and at once – seeing that his case seemed to be provisionally postponed – he stepped aside and was joined by the attendant, with whom he began a whispered conversation involving many side glances at the stoker and Karl, as well as the most impressive gestures. It was as if Schubal were rehearsing his next fine speech.

'Didn't you want to ask this youngster something, Mr Jacob?' the Captain said in the general silence to the gentleman with the bamboo cane.

'Why, yes,' replied the other, with a slight bow in acknowledgement of the Captain's courtesy. And he asked Karl again: 'What is your name?'

Karl, who thought that his main business would be best served by satisfying his stubborn questioner as quickly as possible, replied briefly, without, as was his custom, introducing himself by means of his passport, which he would have had to tug out of his pocket: 'Karl Rossmann.'

'But really!' said the gentleman who had been addressed as Jacob, recoiling with an almost incredulous smile. The Captain too, the Head Purser, the ship's officer, even the attendant, all showed an excessive astonishment on hearing Karl's name. Only the Harbour Officials and Schubal remained indifferent.

'But really!' repeated Mr Jacob, walking a little stiffly up to Karl, 'then I'm your Uncle Jacob and you're my own dear nephew. I suspected it all the time!' he said to the Captain before embracing and kissing Karl, who dumbly submitted to everything.

'And what may your name be?' asked Karl when he felt himself released again, very courteously, but quite coolly, trying hard to estimate the consequences which this new development might have for the stoker. At the moment, there was nothing to indicate that Schubal could extract any advantage out of it.

'But don't you understand your good fortune, young man?' said the Captain, who thought that Mr Jacob was wounded in his dignity by Karl's question, for he had retired to the window, obviously to conceal from the others the agitation on his face, which he also kept dabbing with a handkerchief. 'It is Senator Edward Jacob who has just declared himself to be your uncle. You have now a brilliant career in front of you, against all your previous expectations, I dare say. Try to realize this, as far as you can in the first shock of the moment, and pull yourself together!'

'I certainly have an Uncle Jacob in America,' said Karl, turning to the Captain, 'but if I understand rightly, Jacob is only the surname of this gentleman.'

'That is so,' said the Captain, encouragingly.

'Well, my Uncle Jacob, who is my mother's brother, had Jacob for a Christian name, but his surname must of course be the same as my mother's, whose maiden name was Bendelmayer.'

'Gentlemen!' cried the Senator, coming forward in response to Karl's explanation, quite cheerful now after his recuperative retreat to the window. Everyone except the Harbour Officials laughed a little, some as if really touched, others for no visible reason.

'Yet what I said wasn't so ridiculous as all that,' thought Karl.

'Gentlemen,' repeated the Senator, 'you are involved against my will and your own in a little family scene, and so I can't but give you an explanation, since, I fancy, no one but the Captain here' – this reference was followed by a reciprocal bow – 'is fully informed of the circumstances.'

'Now I must really attend to every word,' Karl told himself, and glancing over his shoulder he was delighted to see that life was beginning to return to the figure of the stoker.

'For the many years of my sojourn in America – though sojourn is hardly the right word to use of an American citizen, and I am an American citizen from my very heart – for all these many years, then, I have lived completely cut off from my relatives in Europe, for reasons which, in the first place, do not concern us here, and in the second, would really give me too much pain to relate. I actually dread the moment when I may be forced to explain them to my dear nephew, for some frank criticisms of his parents and their friends will be unavoidable, I'm afraid.'

'It is my uncle, no doubt about it,' Karl told himself, listening eagerly, 'he must have had his name changed.'

'Now, my dear nephew has simply been turned out – we may as well call a spade a spade – has simply been turned out by his parents, just as you turn a cat out of the house when it annoys you. I have no intention of extenuating what my nephew did to merit that punishment, yet his transgression was of a kind that merely needs to be named to find indulgence.'

'That's not too bad,' thought Karl, 'but I hope he won't tell the whole story. Anyhow, he can't know much about it. Who would tell him?'

'For he was,' Uncle Jacob went on, rocking himself a little on the bamboo cane which was braced in front of him, a gesture that actually succeeded in deprecating any unnecessary solemnity which otherwise must have characterized his statement, 'for he was seduced by a maidservant, Johanna Brummer, a person of round about thirty-five. It is far from my wishes to offend my nephew by using the world "seduced", but it is difficult to find another and equally suitable word.'

Karl, who had moved up quite close to his uncle, turned round to read from the gentlemen's faces, the impression the story had made. None of them laughed, all were listening patiently and seriously. After all, one did not laugh at the nephew of a Senator on the first possible opportunity. It was rather the stoker who now smiled at Karl, though very faintly, but that was satisfactory in the first place, as a sign of reviving life, and excusable in the second place, since in the stoker's bunk Karl had tried to make an impenetrable mystery of this very story which was now being made so public.

'Now this Brummer,' Uncle Jacob went on, 'had a child by my nephew, a healthy boy, who was given the baptismal name of Jacob, evidently in memory of my unworthy self, since my nephew's doubtless quite casual references to me had managed to make a deep impression on the woman. Fortunately, let me add. For the boys parents, to avoid alimony or being personally involved in any scandal – I must insist that I know neither how the law stands in their district nor their general circumstances – to avoid the scandal, then, and the payment of alimony, they packed off their son, my dear nephew, to America, shamefully unprovided-for, as you can see, and the poor lad, but for the signs and wonders which still happen in America if nowhere else, would have come to a wretched end in New York, being thrown entirely on his own resources, if this servant girl hadn't written a letter to me, which after long delays reached me the day before yesterday, giving me the whole story, along with a description of my nephew and, very wisely, the name of the ship as well. If I were setting out to entertain you, gentlemen, I could read a few passages to you from this letter' – he pulled out and flourished before them two huge, closely written sheets of letter-paper. 'You would certainly be interested, for the letter is written with somewhat simple but well-meant cunning and with much loving care for the father of the child. But I have no intention either of entertaining you for longer than my explanation needs, or of wounding at the very start the perhaps still sensitive feelings of my nephew, who if he likes can read the letter for his own instruction in the seclusion of the room already waiting for him.'

But Karl had no feelings for Johanna Brummer. Hemmed in by a vanishing past, she sat in her kitchen beside the kitchen dresser, resting her elbows on top of it. She looked at him whenever he came to the kitchen to fetch a glass of water for his father or do some errand for his mother. Sometimes, awkwardly sitting sideways at the dresser, she would write a letter, drawing her inspiration from Karl's face. Sometimes she would sit with her hand over her eyes, heeding nothing that was said to her. Sometimes she would kneel in her tiny room next to the kitchen and pray to a wooden crucifix; then Karl would feel shy if he passed by and caught a glimpse of her through the crack of the slightly open door. Sometimes she would bustle about her kitchen and recoil, laughing like a witch, if Karl came near her. Sometimes she would shut the kitchen door after Karl entered, and keep hold of the door-handle until he had to beg to be let out. Sometimes she would bring him things which he did not want and press them silently into his hand. And once she called him 'Karl' and, while he was still dumbfounded at this unusual familiarity, led him into her room, sighing and grimacing, and locked the door. Then she flung her arms round his neck, almost choking him, and while urging him to take off her clothes, she really took off his and laid him on her bed, as if she would never give him up to anyone and would tend and cherish him to the end of time. 'Oh Karl, my Karl!' she cried; it was as if her eyes were devouring him, while his eyes saw nothing at all and he felt uncomfortable in all the warm bedclothes which she seemed to have piled up for him alone. Then she lay down by him and wanted some secret from him, but he could tell her none, and she showed anger, either in jest or in earnest, shook him, listened to his heart, offered her breast that he might listen to hers in turn, but could not bring him to do it, pressed her naked belly against his body, felt with her hand between his legs, so disgustingly that his head and neck started up from the pillows, then thrust her body several times against him – it was as if she were part of himself, and for that reason, perhaps, he was seized with a terrible feeling of yearning. With the tears running down his cheeks he reached his own bed at last, after many entreaties from her to come again. That was all that had happened, and yet his uncle had managed to make a great song out of it. And it seemed the cook had also been thinking about him and had informed his uncle of his arrival. That had been very good of her and he would make some return for it later, if he could.

'And now,' cried the Senator, 'I want you to tell me candidly whether I am your uncle or not?'

'You are my uncle,' said Karl, kissing his hand and receiving a kiss on the brow. 'I'm very glad to have found you, but you're mistaken if you think my father and mother never speak kindly of you. In any case, you've got some points quite wrong in your story; I mean that it didn't all happen like that in reality. But you can't really be expected to understand things at such a distance, and I fancy it won't do any great harm if these gentlemen are somewhat incorrectly informed about the details of an affair which can't have much interest for them.'

'Well spoken,' said the Senator, leading Karl up to the Captain, who was visibly sympathetic, and asking: 'Haven't I a splendid nephew?'

'I am delighted,' said the Captain, making a bow which showed his military training, 'to have met your nephew, Mr Senator. My ship is highly honoured in providing the scene for such a reunion. But the voyage in the steerage must have been very unpleasant, for we have, of course, all kinds of people travelling steerage. We do everything possible to make conditions tolerable, far more, for instance, than the American lines do, but to turn such a passage into pleasure is more than we've been able to manage yet.'

'It did me no harm,' said Karl.

'It did him no harm!' repeated the Senator, laughing loudly.

'Except that I'm afraid I've lost my box –' and with that he remembered all that had happened and all that remained to be done, and he looked round him and saw the others still in the same places, silent with respect and surprise, their eyes fixed upon him. Only the Harbour Officials, in so far as their severe, self-satisfied faces were legible, betrayed some regret at having come at such an unpropitious time, and the watch which they had laid on the table before them was probably more important to them than everything that had happened in the room or might still happen there.

The first to express his sympathy, after the Captain, was curiously enough the stoker. 'I congratulate you heartily,' he said, and shook Karl's hand, making the gesture a token of something like gratitude. Yet when he turned to the Senator with the same words the Senator drew back, as if the stoker were exceeding his rights; and the stoker immediately retreated.

But the others now saw what should be done and at once pressed in a confused throng round Karl and the Senator. So it happened that Karl actually received Schubal's congratulations, accepted them and thanked him for them. The last to advance in the ensuing lull were the Harbour Officials, who said two words in English, which made a ludicrous impression.

The Senator now felt moved to extract the last ounce of enjoyment from the situation by refreshing his own and the other's minds with the less important details, and this was not merely tolerated but of course welcomed with interest by everyone. So he told them that he had entered in his notebook, for consultation in a possible emergency, his nephew's most distinctive characteristics as enumerated by the cook in her letter. Bored by the stoker's ravings, he had pulled out the notebook simply to distract himself, and had begun for his own amusement to compare the cook's descriptions, which were not so exact as a detective might wish, with Karl's appearance. 'And that's how to find a nephew!' he concluded proudly, as if he wanted to be congratulated all over again.

'What will happen to the stoker now?' asked Karl, ignoring his uncle's last remarks. In his new circumstances he thought he was entitled to say whatever came into his mind.

'The stoker will get what he deserves,' said the Senator, 'and what the Captain considers to be right. I think we have had enough and more than enough of the stoker, a view in which every gentleman here will certainly concur.'

'But that's not the point in a question of justice,' said Karl. He was standing between his uncle and the Captain, and, perhaps influenced by his position, thought that he was holding the balance between them.

And yet the stoker seemed to have abandoned hope. His hands were half stuck into the belt of his trousers, which together with a strip of checked shirt had come prominently into view during his excited tirade. That did not worry him in the least; he had displayed the misery of his heart, now they might as well see the rags that covered his body, and then they could thrust him out. He had decided that the attendant and Schubal, as the two least important men in the room, should do him that last kindness. Schubal would have peace then and no longer be driven to desperation, as the Head Purser had put it. The Captain could take on crowds of Roumanians; Roumanian would be spoken all over the ship; and then perhaps things would really be all right. There would be no stoker pestering the head office any more with his ravings, yet his last effort would be held in almost friendly memory, since, as the Senator expressly declared, it had been the direct cause of his recognizing his nephew. The nephew himself had several times tried to help him already and so had more than repaid him beforehand for his services in the recognition scene; it did not even occur to the stoker to ask anything else from him now. Besides, even if he were the nephew of a senator, he was far more from being a captain yet, and it was from the mouth of the Captain that the stern verdict would fall. And thinking all this, the stoker did his best not to look at Karl, though unfortunately in that roomful of enemies there was no other resting-place for his eyes.

'Don't mistake the situation,' said the Senator to Karl, 'this may be a question of justice, but at the same time it's a question of discipline. On this ship both of these, and most especially the latter, are entirely within the discretion of the Captain.'

'That's right,' muttered the stoker. Those who heard him and understood smiled uneasily.

'But we have already obstructed the Captain far too long in his official duties, which must be piling up considerably now that he has reached New York, and it's high time we left the ship, instead of adding to our sins by interfering quite unnecessarily in this petty quarrel between two mechanics and so making it a matter of importance. I understand your attitude perfectly, my dear nephew, but that very fact justifies me in hurrying you away from here immediately.'

'I shall have a boat lowered for you at once,' said the Captain, without deprecating in the least the Senator's words, to Karl's great surprise, since his uncle could be said to have humbled himself. The Head Purser rushed hastily to his desk and telephoned the Captain's order to the bos'un. 'There's hardly any time left,' Karl told himself, 'but I can't do anything without offending everybody. I really can't desert my uncle now, just when he's found me. The Captain is certainly polite, but that's all. In matters of discipline his politeness fades out. And my uncle certainly meant what he said. I don't want to speak to Schubal; I'm sorry that I even shook hands with him. And the other people here are of no consequence.'

Thinking these things he slowly went over to the stoker, pulled the man's right hand out of his belt and held it gently in his.

'Why don't you say something?' he asked. 'Why do you put up with everything?'

The stoker merely knitted his brows, as if he were seeking

some formula for what he had to say. While doing this he looked down at his own hand in Karl's.

'You've been unjustly treated, more than anyone else on this ship; I know that well enough.' And Karl drew his fingers backwards and forwards between the stoker's, while the stoker gazed round him with shining eyes, as if blessed by a great happiness that no one could grudge him.

'Now you must get ready to defend yourself, answer yes and no, or else these people won't have any idea of the truth. You must promise me to do what I tell you, for I'm afraid, and I've good reason for it, that I won't be able to help you any more.' And then Karl burst out crying and kissed the stoker's hand, taking that seamed, almost nerveless hand and pressing it to his cheek like a treasure which he would soon have to give up. But now his uncle the Senator was at his side and very gently yet firmly led him away.

'The stoker seems to have bewitched you,' he said, exchanging an understanding look with the Captain over Karl's head. 'You felt lonely, then you found the stoker, and you're grateful to him now; that's all to your credit, I'm sure. But if only for my sake, don't push things too far, learn to understand your position.'

Outside the door a hubbub had arisen, shouts could be heard; it sounded even as if someone were being brutally banged against the door. A sailor entered in a somewhat dishevelled state with a girl's apron tied round his waist. 'There's a mob outside,' he cried, thrusting out his elbows as if he were still pushing his way through a crowd. He came to himself with a start and made to salute the Captain, but at that moment he noticed the apron, tore if off, threw it on the floor and shouted: 'This is a bit much; they've tied a girl's apron on me.' Then he clicked his heels together and saluted. Someone began to laugh, but the Captain said severely: 'This is a fine state of things. Who is outside?'

'It's my witnesses,' said Schubal, stepping forward. 'I humbly beg your pardon, sir, for their bad behaviour. The men sometimes go a bit wild when they've finished a voyage.'

'Bring them in here at once!' the Captain ordered, then

immediately turning to the Senator said, politely but hastily: 'Have the goodness now, Mr Senator, to take your nephew and follow this man, who will conduct you to your boat. I need hardly say what a pleasure and an honour it has been to me to make your personal acquaintance. I only wish, Mr Senator, that I may have an early opportunity to resume our interrupted talk about the state of the American fleet, and that it may be again interrupted in as pleasant a manner.'

'One nephew is quite enough for me, I assure you,' said Karl's uncle, laughing. 'And now accept my best thanks for your kindness and good-bye. Besides it isn't altogether impossible that we' – he put his arm warmly round Karl – 'might see quite a lot of you on our next voyage to Europe.'

'That would give me great pleasure,' said the Captain. The two gentlemen shook hands with each other, Karl barely touched the Captain's hand in silent haste, for the latter's attention was already engrossed by the fifteen men who were now being shepherded into the room by Schubal, somewhat chastened but still noisy enough. The sailor begged the Senator to let him lead the way and opened a path through the crowd for him and Karl, so that they passed with ease through ranks of bowing men. It seemed that these good-natured fellows regarded the quarrel between Schubal and the stoker as a joke, and not even the Captain's presence could make them take it seriously. Karl noticed among them the kitchen-maid Lina, who with a sly wink at him was now tying round her waist the apron which the sailor had flung away, for it was hers.

Still following the sailor, they left the office and turned into a small passage which brought them in a couple of steps to a little door, from which a short ladder led down to the boat that was waiting for them. Their conductor leapt down into the boat with a single bound, and the sailors in the boat rose and saluted. The Senator was just warning Karl to be careful how he came down, when Karl, as he stood on the top rung, burst into violent sobs. The Senator put his right hand under Karl's chin, drew him close to him and caressed him with his left hand. In this posture they slowly descended step by step and, still clinging together, entered the boat, where the Senator found a comfortable place for Karl, immediately facing him. At a sign from the Senator the sailors pushed off from the ship and at once began rowing at full speed. They were scarcely a few yards from the ship when Karl made the unexpected discovery that they were on the side of the ship towards which the windows of the office looked out. All three windows were filled with Schubal's witnesses, who saluted and waved in the most friendly way; Uncle Jacob actually waved back and one of the sailors showed his skill by flinging a kiss towards the ship without interrupting the regular rhythm of his rowing. It was now as if there were really no stoker at all. Karl took a more careful look at his uncle, whose knees were almost touching his own, and doubts came into his mind whether this man would ever be able to take the stoker's place. And his uncle evaded his eye and stared at the waves on which their boat was tossing.

2

UNCLE JACOB

In his uncle's house Karl soon became used to his new circumstances. But, indeed, his uncle indulged his slightest wishes and Karl had never to learn by hard experience, which so much embitters one's first acquaintance with foreign countries.

Karl's room was on the sixth floor of a house whose five other floors, along with three more in the basement, were taken up by his uncle's business. It was so light, what with its two windows and a door opening on a balcony, that Karl was filled with fresh astonishment every morning on coming into it out of his tiny bedroom. Where might he not have had to stay, if he had landed in this country as a destitute little emigrant? Indeed, as his uncle, with his knowledge of the emigration laws, thought highly probable, Karl might not have been admitted into the United States at all and might have been sent home again without regard to the fact that he no longer had a home. In this country sympathy was something you could not hope for; in that respect America resembled what Karl had read about it; except that those who were fortunate seemed really to enjoy their good fortune here, sunning themselves among their carefree friends.

A narrow outside balcony ran along the whole length of Karl's room. But what would have been at home the highest vantage point in the town allowed him here little more than a view of one street, which ran perfectly straight between two rows of squarely chopped buildings and therefore seemed to be fleeing into the distance, where the outlines of a cathedral loomed enormous in a dense haze. From morning to evening and far into the dreaming night that street was the channel for a constant stream of traffic which, seen from above, looked like an inextricable confusion, for ever newly improvised, of foreshortened human figures and the roofs of all kinds of vehicles, sending into the upper air another confusion, more riotous and complicated, of noises, dust, and smells, all of it enveloped and penetrated by a flood of light which the multitudinous objects in the street scattered, carried off and again busily brought back, with an effect as palpable to the dazzled eye as if a glass roof stretched over the street were being violently smashed into fragments at every moment.

Cautious in all things, Uncle Jacob advised Karl for the time being to take up nothing seriously. He should certainly examine and consider everything, but without committing himself. The first days of a European in America might be likened to a rebirth, and though Karl was not to worry about it unduly, since one got used to things here more quickly than an infant coming into the world from the other side, yet he must keep in mind that first judgements were always unreliable and that one should not let them prejudice the future judgements which would eventually shape one's life in America. He himself had known newcomers, for example, who, instead of following these wise precepts had stood all day on their balconies gaping down at the street like lost sheep. That was bound to lead to bewilderment! The solitary indulgence of idly gazing at the busy life of New York was permissible in anyone travelling for pleasure, perhaps even advisable within limits; but for the one who intended to remain in the States it was sheer ruination, a term by no means too emphatic, although it might be exaggerated. And, indeed, Uncle Jacob frowned with annoyance if ever he found Karl out on the balcony when he paid one of his visits, which always occurred once daily and at the most diverse hours. Karl soon noticed this and in consequence denied himself as much as possible the pleasure of lingering on the balcony.

However, it was by no means the sole pleasure that he had. In his room stood an American writing-desk of superior construction, such as his father had coveted for years and tried to pick up cheaply at all kinds of auction sales without ever succeeding, his resources being much too small. This desk, of course, was beyond all comparison with the so-called American writing-desk which turned up at auction sales in Europe. For example, it had a hundred compartments of different sizes, in which the President of the Union himself could have found a fitting place for each of his state documents; there was also a regulator at one side and by turning a handle you could produce the most complicated combination and permutations of the compartments to please yourself and suit your requirements. Thin panels sank slowly and formed the bottom of a new series or the top of existing drawers promoted from below; even after one turn of the handle the disposition of the whole was quite changed and the transformation took place slowly or at delirious speed according to the rate at which you wound the thing round. It was a very modern invention, yet it reminded Karl vividly of the traditional Christmas panorama which was shown to gaping children in the market-place at home, where he too, well wrapped in his winter clothes, had often stood enthralled, closely comparing the movement of the handle, which was turned by an old man, with the changes in the scene, the jerky advance of the Three Holy Kings, the shining out of the Star and the humble life of the Holy Manger. And it had always seemed to him that his mother, as she stood behind him, did not follow every detail with sufficient attention. He would draw her close to him, until he could feel her pressing against his back, and shouting at the top of his voice would keep pointing out to her the less noticeable occurrences, perhaps a little hare among the grass in the foreground, sitting up on its hind legs and then crouching as if to dart off again, until his mother would cover his mouth with her hand and very likely relapse into her former inattention. The desk was certainly not made merely to remind him of such things, yet in the history of its invention there probably existed some vague connexion similar to that in Karl's memory. Unlike Karl, Uncle Jacob by no means approved of this particular desk; he had merely wanted to buy a well-appointed writing-desk for Karl, but nowadays these were all furnished with this new apparatus, which had also the advantage that it could be fitted to more old-fashioned desks without great expense. At any rate, Karl's uncle never omitted to advise him against using the regulator at all, if possible, and reinforced his advice by pointing out that the mechanism was very sensitive, could easily be put out of order and was very expensive to repair again. It was not hard to guess that these remarks were merely pretexts, though on the other hand it would have been quite easy to lock the regulator and yet Uncle Jacob refrained from doing so.

In the first few days, during which Karl and his uncle naturally had a good number of talks together, Karl mentioned that at home he had been fond of playing the piano, though he had not played it much, having had no teaching except his mother's rudimentary instructions. Karl was quite well aware that to volunteer this information was virtually to ask for a piano, but he had already used his eyes sufficiently to know that his uncle could afford to be lavish. Yet this suggestion was not acted upon at once; but some eight days later his uncle said, almost as if making a reluctant admission, that the piano had just arrived and Karl, if he liked, could supervise its transport. That was an easy enough task, yet not much easier than the transport itself, for the building had a furniture lift in which, without any difficulty, a whole furniture van could have been accommodated, and in this lift the piano soared up to Karl's room. Karl could have gone up himself in the same lift as the piano and the workmen, but just beside it there was an ordinary lift free, so he went up in that instead, keeping himself at the same elevation as the other by means of a lever and staring fixedly through the glass panels at the beautiful instrument which was now his property. When he had it safely in his room and struck the first notes on it, he was filled with such foolish joy that instead of going on playing he jumped up and with his hands on his hips gazed rapturously at the piano from a little distance. The acoustics of the room were excellent and they had the effect of quite dispelling his first slight discomfort at living in a steel house. True, in the room itself, despite the external appearance of the building, one could see not the slightest sign of steel, nor could one have discovered in the furnishings even the smallest detail which did not harmonize with the comfort of the whole. At first Karl set great hopes on his piano-playing and sometimes unashamedly dreamed, at least before falling asleep, of the possibility that it might exert a direct influence upon his life in America. When he opened his windows and the street noises came in, it certainly sounded strange to hear on the piano an old army song of his native country which soldiers, sprawling of an evening at barrack windows and gazing into the darkness of some square outside, sang to each other from window to window – but the street, if he looked down it afterwards, remained unchanged, only one small section of a great wheel which afforded no hand-hold unless one knew all the forces controlling its full orbit. Uncle Jacob tolerated the piano-playing and said not a word against it, especially as Karl indulged very seldom in it; indeed, he actually brought Karl the scores of some American marches, among them the national anthem, but pure love of music could hardly explain the fact that he asked Karl one day, quite seriously, whether he would not like to learn the violin or the French horn as well.

The learning of English was naturally Karl's first and most important task. A young teacher from a neighbouring commercial college appeared in his room every morning at seven and found him already over his exercise books at the desk, or walking up and down the room committing words to memory. Karl saw clearly that if he were to acquire English there was no time to be lost and that this was also his best chance of giving his uncle especial pleasure by making rapid progress. And indeed, though he had to confine himself at first to the simplest greetings, he was soon able to carry on in English an increasingly large part of his conversation with his uncle, whereupon more intimate topics simultaneously came up for discussion. The first American poem – a description of a fire – which Karl managed to recite to his uncle one evening, made that gentleman quite solemn with satisfaction. They were both standing at the window in Karl's room, Uncle Jacob was looking out at the sky, from which all brightness had already faded, bringing his hands together slowly and regularly in time with the verses, while Karl stood erect beside him and with eyes fixed on vacancy delivered himself of the difficult lines.

The better Karl's English became, the greater inclination his uncle showed to introduce him to his friends, arranging only that on such occasions the English teacher should always be at his elbow. The first person to whom Karl was introduced one morning was a slender, incredibly supple young man, whom Uncle Jacob brought into the room with a string of fulsome compliments. He was obviously one of these many millionaires' sons who are regarded as failures by their parents' standards and who lead strenuous lives which an ordinary man could scarcely endure for a single average day without breaking down. And as if he knew or divined this and faced it as best he could, there was always about his lips and eyes an unchanging smile of happiness, which seemed to embrace himself, anyone he was speaking to and the whole world.

With the unconditional approval of Uncle Jacob, it was arranged that this young man, whose name was Mr Mack, should take Karl out riding every morning at half-past five, either in the riding-school or in the open air. Karl hesitated at first before consenting, since he had never sat on a horse and wished first to learn a little about riding, but as his uncle and Mack insisted so much, arguing that riding was simply a pleasure and a healthy exercise and not at all an art, he finally agreed. Of course, that meant that he had now to leave his bed at half-past four every morning, which was often a great hardship to him, since he suffered from an actual longing for sleep, probably in consequence of the unremitting attention which he had to exercise all day long; but as soon as he came into his bathroom he ceased to be sorry for himself. Over the full length and breadth of the bath stretched the spray – which of his schoolmates at home, no matter how rich, had anything equal to it and for his own use alone? – and there Karl could lie outstretched – this bath was wide enough to let him spread out his arms – and let the stream of lukewarm, hot, and again lukewarm and finally ice-cold water pour over any part of him at pleasure, or over his whole body at once. He lay there as if in a still faintly surviving enjoyment of sleep and loved to catch with his closed eyelids the last separately falling drops which, as they broke, flowed down over his face.

At this riding-school, where his uncle's towering motor car deposited him, the English teacher would be already waiting, while Mack invariably arrived later. But Mack could be late with an easy mind, for the actual life of the riding-school did not begin until he came. The horses started out of their semi-slumber when he entered, the whips cracked more loudly through the room, and on the gallery running round it single figures suddenly appeared, spectators, grooms, riding-pupils, or whatever they were. Karl employed the time before Mack's arrival in practising riding a little, though only the most rudimentary first exercises. There was a tall man who could reach the backs of the biggest horses almost without raising his arm, and he invariably gave Karl his scanty quarter-of-an-hour's instruction. The results which Karl achieved were not impressive and he learned by heart many exclamations of pain in English, gasping them out to his English teacher, who always leant against the door, usually in a very sleepy condition. But almost all his disatisfaction with riding ceased once Mack appeared. The tall man was sent away and soon nothing could be heard in the hall, which was still half in darkness, but the hoofs of galloping horses and hardly anything seen but Mack's uplifted arm, as he signalled his orders to Karl. After half an hour of this pleasure, fleeting as a dream, a halt was called. Mack was then always in a great hurry, said goodbye to Karl, patted him a few times on the cheek if he was particularly pleased with his riding and vanished, too pressed for time even to accompany Karl through the door. Then Karl and the English teacher climbed into the car and drove to their lesson, generally round byways, for if they had plunged into the traffic of the great street which led directly from the riding-school to his uncle's house it would have meant too great a loss of time. In any case, the English teacher soon ceased to act as escort, since Karl, who blamed himself for needlessly forcing the tired man to go with him to the riding-school, especially since the English required in his intercourse with Mack was very simple, begged his uncle to absolve the man from that duty. And after some reflection his uncle acceded to his wish.

It took a relatively long time before Uncle Jacob would consent to allow Karl even the slightest insight into his business, although Karl often begged him to do so. It was a sort of commission and despatch agency such as, to the best of Karl's knowledge, was probably not to be found in Europe. For the business did not consist in the transference of wares from the producer to the consumer or to the dealer, but in the handling of all the necessary goods and raw materials going to and between the great manufacturing trusts. It was consequently a business which embraced simultaneously the purchasing, storing, transport and sale of immense quantities of goods and had to maintain the most exact, unintermittent telephonic and telegraphic communication with its various clients. The telegraphists' hall was not smaller but larger than the telegraphic office of Karl's native town, through which he had once been shown by one of his schoolmates, who was known there. In the telephone hall, wherever one looked, the doors of the telephone boxes could be seen opening and shutting, and the noise was maddening. His uncle opened the first of these doors and in the glaring electric light Karl saw an operator, quite oblivious to any sound from the door, his head bound in a steel band which pressed the receivers against his ears. His right arm was lying on a little table as if it were strangely heavy and only the fingers holding the pencil kept twitching with inhuman regularity and speed. In the words which he spoke into the mouthpiece he was very sparing and often one noticed that though he had some objection to raise or wished to obtain more exact information, the next phrase that he heard compelled him to lower his eyes and go on writing before he could carry out his intention. Besides he did not need to say anything, as Uncle Jacob explained to Karl in a subdued voice, for the same conversation which this man was taking down was being taken down at the same time by two other operators and would then be compared with the other versions, so that errors might as far as possible be eliminated. At the moment when Uncle Jacob and Karl emerged from the box a messenger slipped into it and came out with the notes which the operator had just written. Through the hall there was a perpetual tumult of people rushing hither and thither. Nobody said good-day, greetings were omitted, each man fell into step behind anyone who was going the same way, keeping his eyes on the floor, over which he was set on advancing as quickly as he could, or giving a hurried glance at a word or figure here and there on the papers he held in his hand, which fluttered with the wind of his progress.

'You have really gone far,' Karl once said on one of these journeys through the building, which took several days to traverse in its entirety, even if one did nothing more than have a look at each department.

'And let me tell you I started it all myself thirty years ago. I had a little business at that time near the docks and if five crates came up for unloading in one day I thought it a great day and went home swelling with pride. Today my warehouses cover the third largest area in the port and my old store is the restaurant and storeroom for my sixty-fifth group of porters.'

'It's really wonderful,' said Karl.

'Developments in this country are always rapid,' said his uncle, breaking off the conversation.

One day his uncle appeared just before dinner, which Karl had expected to take alone as usual, and asked him to put on his black suit at once and join him for dinner, together with two of his business friends. While Karl was changing in the next room, his uncle sat down at the desk and looked through the English exercise which Karl had just finished, then brought down his hand on the desk and exclaimed aloud: 'Really first rate!'

Doubtless Karl's changing went all the more smoothly on hearing these words of praise, but in any case he was now pretty certain of his English.

In his uncle's dining-room, which he could still remember from the evening of his arrival, two tall, stout gentlemen rose to their feet, one of them called Green, the other Pollunder, as appeared during the subsequent conversation. For Uncle Jacob hardly ever dropped a word about any of his acquaintances and always left it to Karl to discover by his own observation whatever was important or interesting about them. During the dinner itself only intimate business matters were discussed, which meant for Karl an excellent lesson in commercial English, and Karl was left silently to occupy himself with his food, as if he were a child who had merely to sit up straight and empty his plate; but Mr Green leaned across to him and asked him in English, unmistakably exerting himself to pronounce every word with the utmost distinctness, what in general were his first impressions of America? With a few side glances at his uncle, Karl replied fairly fully in the dead silence that followed and in his gratitude and his desire to please used several characteristic New York expressions. At one of his phrases all three gentlemen burst out laughing together and Karl was afraid that he had made a gross mistake;

but no, Mr Pollunder explained to him that he had actually said something very smart. Mr Pollunder, indeed, seemed to have taken a particular fancy to Karl, and while Uncle Jacob and Mr Green returned once more to their business consultations Mr Pollunder asked Karl to bring his chair nearer, asked him countless questions about his name, his family and his voyage and at last, to give him a reprieve, began hastily, laughing and coughing, to tell about himself and his daughter, with whom he lived in a little country house in the neighbourhood of New York, where, however, he was only able to pass the evenings, for he was a banker and his profession kept him in New York the whole day. Karl was warmly invited to come out to the country house; an American so new and untried as Karl must be in need of occasional recuperation from New York. Karl at once asked his uncle's leave to accept the invitation and his uncle gave it with apparent pleasure, yet without naming any stated time or even letting it come into consideration, as Karl and Mr Pollunder had expected.

But the very next day Karl was summoned to one of his uncle's offices, (his uncle had ten different offices in that building alone), where he found his uncle and Mr Pollunder reclining somewhat monosyllabically in two easy-chairs.

'Mr Pollunder,' said Uncle Jacob, who could scarcely be distinguished in the evening dusk of the room, 'Mr Pollunder has come to take you with him to his country house, as was mentioned yesterday.'

'I didn't know it was to be today,' replied Karl, 'or else I'd have got ready.'

'If you're not ready, then perhaps we'd better postpone the visit to some other time,' remarked his uncle.

'What do you need to get ready?' cried Mr Pollunder. 'A young man is always ready for anything.'

'It isn't on his account,' said Uncle Jacob, turning to his guest, 'but he would have to go up to his room again, and that would delay you.'

'There's plenty of time for that,' said Mr Pollunder. 'I allowed for a delay and left my office earlier.'

'You see,' said Uncle Jacob, 'what a lot of trouble this visit of yours has caused already.'

'I'm very sorry,' said Karl, 'but I'll be back again in a minute,' and he made to rush away.

'Don't hurry yourself,' said Mr Pollunder, 'you aren't causing me the slightest trouble; on the contrary, it's a pleasure to have you visiting me.'

'You'll miss your riding lesson tomorrow. Have you called it off?'

'No,' said Karl; this visit to which he had been looking forward so much was beginning to be burdensome. 'I didn't know –'

'And you mean to go in spite of that?' asked his uncle.

Mr Pollunder, that kind man, came to Karl's help.

'We'll stop at the riding-school on the way and put everything right.'

'There's something in that,' said Uncle Jacob. 'But Mack will be expecting you.'

'He won't be expecting me,' said Karl, 'but he'll turn up anyhow.'

'Well then?' said Uncle Jacob, as if Karl's answer had not been the slightest excuse.

Once more Mr Pollunder solved the problem: 'But Clara' – she was Mr Pollunder's daughter – 'expects him too, and this very evening, and surely she has the preference over Mack?'

'Certainly,' said Uncle Jacob. 'Well then, run away to your room,' and as if involuntarily, he drummed on the arm of his chair several times. Karl was already at the door when his uncle detained him once more with the question: 'Of course you'll be back here again tomorrow morning for your English lesson?'

'But my dear sir!' cried Mr Pollunder, turning round in his chair with astonishment, as far as his stoutness would permit him. 'Can't he stay with us at least over tomorrow? Couldn't I bring him back early in the morning the day after?'

'That's quite out of the question,' retorted Uncle Jacob. 'I can't have his studies broken up like this. Later on, when he has taken up a regular profession of some kind, I'll be very glad to let him accept a kind and flattering invitation even for a long time.'

'What a contradiction!' thought Karl.

Mr Pollunder looked quite melancholy. 'But for one evening and one night it's hardly worth while.'

'That's what I think too,' said Uncle Jacob.

'One must take what one can get,' said Mr Pollunder, and now he was laughing again. 'All right, I'll wait for you,' he shouted to Karl, who, since his uncle said nothing more, was hurrying away.

When he returned in a little while, ready for the journey, he found only Mr Pollunder in the office; his uncle had gone. Mr Pollunder shook Karl quite gaily by both hands, as if he wished to assure himself as strongly as possible that Karl was coming after all. Karl, still flushed with haste, for his part wrung Mr Pollander's hands in return; he was elated at the thought of the visit.

'My uncle wasn't annoyed at my going?'

'Not at all! He didn't mean all that very seriously. He has your education so much at heart.'

'Did he tell you himself that he didn't mean it seriously?'

'Oh yes,' said Mr Pollunder, drawling the words, and thus proving that he could not tell a lie.

'It's strange how unwilling he was to give me leave to visit you, although you are a friend of his.'

Mr Pollunder too, although he did not admit it, could find no explanation for the problem, and both of them, as they drove through the warm evening in Mr Pollunder's car, kept turning it over in their minds for a long time, although they spoke of other things.

They sat close together and Mr Pollunder held Karl's hand in his while he talked. Karl was eager to hear as much as he could about Miss Clara, as if his impatience with the long journey could be assuaged by listening to stories that made the time appear shorter. He had never driven through the streets of

New York in the evening, but though the pavements and roadways were thronged with traffic changing its direction every minute, as if caught up in a whirlwind and roaring like some strange element quite unconnected with humanity, Karl, as he strained his attention to catch Mr Pollunder's words, had no eye for anything but Mr Pollunder's dark waistcoat, which was peacefully spanned by a gold chain. Out of the central streets where the theatre-goers, urged by extreme and unconcealed fear of being late, hurried along with flying steps or drove in vehicles at the utmost possible speed, they came by intermediate stages to the suburbs, where their car was repeatedly diverted by mounted police into side alleys, as the main roadway was occupied by a demonstration of metal-workers on strike and only the most necessary traffic could be permitted to use the crossroads. When the car, emerging out of dark, dully echoing narrow lanes, crossed one of these great thoroughfares which were as wide as squares, there opened out on both sides an endless perspective of pavements filled with a moving mass of people, slowly shuffling forward, whose singing was more homogeneous than any single human voice. But in the roadway, which was kept free, mounted policemen could be seen here and there sitting on motionless horses, or banner-bearers, or inscribed streamers stretching across the street, or a labour leader surrounded by colleagues and stewards, or an electric tram which had not escaped quickly enough and now stood dark and empty while the driver and the conductor lounged on the platform. Small groups of curious spectators stood at a distance watching the actual demonstrators, rooted to their places although they had no clear idea of what was really happening. But Karl merely leaned back happily on the arm which Mr Pollunder had put round him; the knowledge that he would soon be a welcome guest in a well-lighted country house surrounded by high walls and guarded by watch-dogs filled him with extravagant well-being, and although he was now beginning to feel sleepy and could no longer catch perfectly all that Mr Pollunder was saying, or at least only intermittently, he pulled himself together from time to time and rubbed his eyes to discover whether Mr Pollunder had noticed his drowsiness, for that was something he wished to avoid at any price.

3

A COUNTRY HOUSE NEAR NEW YORK

'Well, here we are,' said Mr Pollunder in one of Karl's most absent moments. The car was standing before a house which, like the country houses of most rich people in the neighbourhood of New York, was larger and taller than a country house designed for only one family has any need to be. Since there were no lights except in the lower part of the house, it was quite impossible to estimate how high the building was. In front of it rustled chestnut trees and between them – the gate was already open – a short path led to the front-door steps. Karl felt so tired on getting out that he began to suspect the journey must have been fairly long after all. In the darkness of the chestnut avenue he heard a girl's voice saying beside him: 'So this is Mr Jacob at last.'

'My name is Rossmann,' said Karl, taking the hand held out to him by a girl whose silhouette he could now perceive.

'He is only Jacob's nephew,' said Mr Pollunder in explanation, 'his own name is Karl Rossmann.'

'That doesn't make us any the less glad to see him,' said the girl, who did not bother much about names.

All the same Karl insisted on asking, while he walked towards the house between Mr Pollunder and the girl: 'Are you Miss Clara?'

'Yes,' she said, and now a little light from the house picked out her face, which was inclined towards him, 'but I didn't want to introduce myself here in the darkness.'

'Why, has she been waiting for us at the gate?' thought Karl, gradually wakening up as he walked along.

'By the way, we have another guest this evening,' said Clara.

'Impossible!' cried Mr Pollunder irritably.

'Mr Green,' said Clara.

'When did he come?' asked Karl, as if seized by a premonition.

'Just a minute ago. Didn't you hear his car in front of yours?'

Karl looked up at Mr Pollunder to discover what he thought of the situation, but his hands were thrust into his trouser pockets and he merely stamped his feet a little on the path.

'It's no good living just outside New York; it doesn't save you from being disturbed. We'll simply have to get a house farther away; even if I have to spend half the night driving before I get home.'

They remained standing by the steps.

'But it's a long time since Mr Green was here last,' said Clara, who obviously agreed with her father yet wanted to soothe him and take him out of himself.

'Why should he come just this evening?' said Pollunder, and the words rolled furiously over his sagging lower lip, which like all loose, heavy flesh was easily agitated.

'Why indeed!' said Clara.

'Perhaps he'll soon go away again,' remarked Karl himself astonished at the sympathy uniting him to these people who had been complete strangers to him a day ago.

'Oh no,' said Clara, 'he has some great business or other with Papa which will probably take a long time to settle, for he has already threatened me in fun that I'll have to sit up till morning if I'm going to play the polite hostess.'

'That's the last straw. So he's going to stay all night!' cried Pollunder, as if nothing could be worse. 'I really feel half inclined,' he said, and the idea restored some of his good humour, 'I really feel half inclined Mr Rossmann, to put you in the car again and drive you straight back to your uncle. This evening's spoilt beforehand, and who knows when your uncle will trust you here again. But if I bring you back tonight he won't be able to refuse us your company next time.'

And he took hold of Karl's hand, to carry out his plan on the instant. But Karl made no move and Clara begged her father to let him stay, since she and Karl at least need not let Mr Green disturb them at all, and finally Pollunder himself grew aware that his resolution was not of the firmest. Besides – and that was perhaps the decisive thing – they suddenly heard Mr Green shouting from the top of the steps down into the garden: 'Where on earth are you?'

'Coming,' said Pollunder and he began to climb the steps. Behind him came Karl and Clara, who now studied each other in the light.

'What red lips she has,' Karl said to himself, and he thought of Mr Pollunder's lips and how beautifully they had been metamorphosed in his daughter.

'After dinner,' she said, 'we'll go straight to my room, if you would like that, so that we at least can be rid of Mr Green, even if Papa has to put up with him. And then perhaps you'll be so kind as to play the piano for me, for Papa has told me how well you can play; I'm sorry to say I'm quite incapable of practising and never touch my piano, much as I really love music.'

Karl was quite prepared to fall in with Clara's suggestion, though he would have liked to have Mr Pollunder join them as well. But the sight of Green's gigantic figure – he had already got used to Pollunder's bulk – which gradually loomed above them as they climbed the steps, dispelled all Karl's hopes of luring Mr Pollunder away from the man that evening.

Mr Green hailed them in a great hurry, as if much time had already been lost, took Mr Pollunder's arm, and pushed Karl and Clara before him into the dining-room which, chiefly because of the flowers on the table rising from sprays of green foliage, looked very festive and so made the presence of the importunate Mr Green doubly regrettable. Karl was just consoling himself, as he waited beside the table until the others were seated, with the thought that the great glass doors leading to the garden would remain open, for a strong fragrance was wafted in as if one sat in an arbour, when Mr Green snorted and rushed to close these very glass doors, bending down to the bolts at the bottom, stretching up to the ones at the top, and all with such youthful agility that the servant, when he hurried across, found nothing left to do. Mr Green's first words when he returned to the table expressed his astonishment that Karl had obtained his uncle's permission to make this visit. He raised one spoonful of soup after another to his mouth and explained to Clara on his right and to Mr Pollunder on his left why he was so astonished, and how solicitously Uncle Jacob watched over Karl, so that his affection for Karl was too great to be called the mere affection of an uncle.

'Not content with his uncalled-for interference here, he insists on interfering between me and my uncle, too,' thought Karl, and he could not swallow a drop of the golden-coloured soup. But then, not wishing to show how upset he felt, he began silently to pour the soup down his throat. The meal went on with torturing slowness. Mr Green alone, assisted by Clara, showed any liveliness and found occasion for a short burst of laughter now and then. Mr Pollunder let himself be drawn into the conversation once or twice, when Mr Green started to talk about business. But he soon withdrew even from such discussions and Mr Green had to surprise him into speech by bringing them up again unexpectedly. Moreover, Mr Green kept insisting on the fact (and at this point Karl, who was listening as intently as if something were threatening him, had to be told by Clara that the roast was at his elbow and that he was at a dinner party) that he had had no intention beforehand of paying this unexpected visit. For though the business he came to discuss was of special urgency, yet the most important part of it at least could have been settled in town that day, leaving the minor details to be tackled next day or later. And so, long before closing hours, he had actually called at Mr Pollunder's office, but had not found him there, and so he had had to telephone home that he would not be back that night and to drive out here.

'Then I must ask your pardon,' said Karl loudly, before anyone else had time to answer, 'for I am to blame that Mr Pollunder left his office early today, and I am very sorry.'

Mr Pollunder tried to cover his face with his table napkin, while Clara, though she smiled at Karl, smiled less out of sympathy than out of a desire to influence him in some way.

'No apology is required,' said Mr Green, carving a pigeon with incisive strokes of the knife, 'quite the contrary, I am delighted to pass the evening in such pleasant company instead of dining alone at home, where I have only an old housekeeper to wait on me, and she's so old that it's as much as she can do to get from the door to the table, and I can lean right back in my chair for minutes at a time to watch her making the journey. It wasn't until recently that I managed to persuade her to let my man carry the dishes as far as the door of the dining-room; but the journey from the door to the table is her perquisite, so far as I can make out.'

'Heavens,' cried Clara, 'what fidelity!'

'Yes, there's still fidelity in the world,' said Mr Green, putting a slice of pigeon into his mouth, where his tongue, as Karl chanced to notice, took it in charge with a flourish. Karl felt nearly sick and got up. Almost simultaneously Mr Pollunder and Clara caught up with him: 'We'll escape together in a little while. Have patience.'

Meanwhile, Mr Green had calmly gone on eating, as if it were Mr Pollunder's and Clara's natural duty to comfort Karl after he had made him sick.

The dinner was lingered out particularly by the exhaustiveness with which Mr Green dissected each course, which did not keep him however from attacking each new course with fresh energy; it really looked as if he were resolved radically to recuperate from the offices of his old housekeeper. Now and again he bestowed praise on Miss Clara's expertness in housekeeping, which visibly flattered her, while Karl on the contrary felt tempted to ward it off, as if it were an assault. Mr Green, however, was not content with attacking Clara, but deplored frequently, without looking up from his plate, Karl's extraordinary lack of appetite. Mr Pollunder defended Karl's lack of appetite, although as the host he should have encouraged him to eat. And because of the constraint under which he had suffered during the whole dinner, Karl grew so touchy that against his better knowledge he actually construed Mr Pollunder's words as an unkindness. And it was another symptom of his condition that all at once he would eat far too much with indecorous speed, only to sit drooping for a long time afterwards, letting his knife and fork rest on the table, quite silent and motionless, so that the man who served the dishes often did not know what to do with them.

'I'll have to tell your uncle the Senator tomorrow how you offended Miss Clara by not eating your dinner,' said Mr Green, and he betrayed the facetious intention of his words only by the way in which he plied his knife and fork.

'Just look at the girl, how downcast she is,' he went on, chucking Clara under the chin. She let him do it and closed her eyes.

'Poor little thing!' he cried, leaning back, purple in the face, and laughing with the vigour of a full-fed man. Karl vainly sought to account for Mr Pollunder's behaviour. He was sitting looking at his plate, as if the really important event were happening there. He did not pull Karl's chair closer to him and, when he did speak, he spoke to the whole table, while to Karl he had nothing particular to say. On the other hand he suffered Green, that disreputable old New York roué deliberately to fondle Clara, to insult himself, Karl, Pollunder's guest, or at least to treat him like a child, and to go on from strength to strength, working himself up to who knew what dreadful deeds.

After rising from the table – when Green noticed the general intention he was the first to get up and as it were drew all the others with him – Karl turned aside to one of the great windows set in narrow white sashes which opened on to the terrace, and which in fact, as he saw on going nearer, were really doors. What had become of the dislike which Mr Pollunder and his daughter had felt in the beginning for Green, and which had seemed at that time somewhat incomprehensible to Karl? Now they were standing side by side with the man and nodding at him. The smoke from Mr Green's cigar, a present from Pollunder – a cigar of a thickness which Karl's father in Austria had sometimes mentioned as an actual fact but had probably never seen with his own eyes – spread through the room and bore Green's influence even into nooks and corners where he would never set foot in person. Far off as he was, Karl could feel his nose prickling with the smoke, and Mr Green's demeanour, which he merely glanced at from the window with a hasty turn of the head, seemed infamous to him. He began to think it not at all inconceivable that his uncle had demurred for so long against giving permission for this visit simply because he knew Mr Pollunder's weak character and accordingly envisaged as a possibility, even if he did not exactly foresee, that Karl might be exposed to insult. As for the American girl, Karl did not like her either, although she was very nearly as beautiful as he had pictured her. Ever since Mr Green's gallantries began he had been actually surprised by the beauty of which her face was capable, and especially by the brilliance of her lively eyes. A dress which fitted so closely to its wearer's body he had never seen before; small wrinkles in the soft, closely-woven, yellowish material, betrayed the force of the tension. And yet Karl cared nothing for her and would gladly have given up all thought of going to her room, if instead he could only open the door beside him – and he had laid his hands on the latch just in case – and climb into the car or, if the chauffeur were already asleep, walk by himself back to New York. The clear night with its benevolent full moon was free to everyone and to be afraid of anything out there, in the open, seemed senseless to Karl. He pictured to himself – and for the first time he began to feel happy in that room – how in the morning – he could hardly get back on foot sooner than that – he would surprise his uncle. True, he had never yet been in his uncle's bedroom, nor did he even know where it was, but he would soon find out. Then he would knock at the door and at the formal 'come in' rush into the room and surprise his dear uncle, whom until now he had known only fully dressed and buttoned to the chin, sitting up in bed in his nightshirt, his astonished eyes fixed on the door. In itself that might not perhaps be very much, but one had only to consider what consequences it might lead to. Perhaps he might breakfast with his uncle for the first time, his uncle in bed, he himself sitting on a chair, the breakfast on a little table between them; perhaps that breakfast together would become a standing arrangement; perhaps as a result of such informal breakfasting, as was almost inevitable, they would meet oftener than simply once a day and so of course be able to speak more frankly to each other. After all, it was merely the lack of a frank interchange of confidences that had made him a little refractory, or better still, mulish, towards his uncle today. And even if he had to spend the night here on this occasion – and unfortunately it looked very like that, although they left him to stand by the window and amuse himself – perhaps this unlucky visit would become the turning-point in his relations with his uncle; perhaps his uncle was lying in bed and thinking the very same things at that moment.

A little comforted, he turned round. Clara was standing beside him saying: 'Don't you like being with us at all? Won't you try to make yourself a little more at home here? Come on, I'll make a last attempt.'

She led him across the room towards the door. At a side table the two gentlemen were sitting, drinking out of tall glasses a light effervescent liquid which was unknown to Karl and which he would have liked to taste. Mr Green had his elbows on the table and his face was pushed as close to Mr Pollunder as he could get it; if one had not known Mr Pollunder, one might quite easily have suspected that some criminal plan was being discussed here and no legitimate business. While Mr Pollunder's eyes followed Karl to the door with a friendly look, Mr Green, though as a rule one's eyes involuntarily follow those of the man one is talking to, did not once glance round at Karl; and it seemed to Karl that in behaving like this Mr Green was pointing his conviction that each of them, Karl on his part and

Green on his, must fight for his own hand and that any obligatory social connexion between them would be determined in time by the victory or destruction of one of them.

'If that's what he thinks,' Karl told himself, 'he's a fool. I really don't want anything from him and he should leave me in peace.'

Hardly had he set foot in the corridor when it occurred to him that he had probably been discourteous, for his eyes had been so firmly fixed on Green that Clara had had almost to drag him from the room. He went all the more willingly with her now. As they passed along the corridors he could scarcely credit his eyes at first, when at every twenty paces he saw a servant in rich livery holding a huge candelabrum with a shaft so thick that both the man's hands were required to grasp it.

'The new electric wiring has been laid on only in the dining-room so far,' explained Clara. 'We've just newly bought this house and we're having it completely reconstructed, that is so far as an old house with all its odd perculiarities can be reconstructed.'

'So you have actually old houses in America too,' said Karl.

'Of course,' said Clara with a laugh, pulling him along. 'You have some queer ideas about America.'

'You shouldn't laugh at me,' he said in vexation. After all he knew both Europe and America, while she knew only America.

In passing, Clara flung a door open with a light push of her hand and said without stopping. 'That's where you're going to sleep.'

Karl of course wanted to look at the room straight away, but Clara exclaimed with impatience, raising her voice almost to shouting pitch, that there was plenty of time for that later and that he must come with her first. They had a kind of tug-of-war in the corridor until it came into Karl's mind that he need not do everything Clara told him, and he wrested himself free and stepped into the room. The surprising darkness outside the window was explained by the spreading branches of a large tree swaying there. He could hear the twitter of birds. To be sure, in the room itself, which the moonlight had not yet reached, one could distinguish hardly anything. Karl felt sorry that he had not brought the electric torch which his uncle had given him. In this house an electric torch was absolutely indispensable; given a couple of torches, the servants could have been sent to their beds. He sat down on the window-ledge and stared out into the darkness, listening. A bird which he had disturbed seemed to be fluttering through the leafage of the old tree. The whistle of a suburban train sounded somewhere across the fields. Otherwise all was still.

But not for long, for Clara came rushing in. Visibly furious, she cried: 'What's the meaning of this?' and beat her hand against her skirt. Karl decided not to answer her until she should show more politeness. But she advanced upon him with long strides, exclaiming: 'Well, are you coming with me or are you not?' and either intentionally or in sheer agitation struck him so hard on the chest that he would have fallen out of the window if at the very last minute he had not launched himself from the window-ledge so that his feet touched the floor.

'I might have fallen out of the window,' he said reproachfully.

'It's a pity you didn't. Why are you so uncivil? I'll push you right out the next time.'

And she actually seized him and carried him in her athletic arms almost as far as the window, since he was too surprised to remember to brace himself. But then he came to his senses, freed himself with a twist of the hips and caught hold of her instead.

'Oh, you're hurting me!' she said at once.

But now Karl felt that it was not safe to let her go. He gave her freedom to take any steps she liked, but followed her close, keeping hold of her. It was easy enough to grip her in her tight dress.

'Let me go,' she whispered, her flushed face so close to his that he had to strain to see her. 'Let me go; I'll give you something you don't expect.' – 'Why is she sighing like that?' thought Karl. 'It can't hurt her, I'm not squeezing her,' and he still did not let her go. But suddenly, after a moment of unguarded, silent immobility, he again felt her strength straining against his body and she had broken away from him, locked him in a well-applied wrestling hold, knocked his legs from under him by some footwork in a technique strange to him and thrust him before her with amazing control, panting a little, to the wall. But there was a sofa by the wall on which she laid him down, keeping at a safe distance from him, and said: 'Now move if you can.'

'Cat, wild cat!' was all that Karl could shout in the confusion of rage and shame which he felt within him. 'You must be crazy, you wild cat!'

'Take care what you say,' she said and she slipped one hand to his throat, on which she began to press so strongly that Karl could only gasp for breath, while she swung the other fist against his cheek, touching it as if experimentally, and then again and again drew it back, farther and farther, ready to give him a buffet at any moment.

'What would you say,' she asked, 'if I punished you for your rudeness to a lady by sending you home with your ears well boxed? It might do you good for the rest of your life, although you wouldn't care to remember it. I'm really sorry about you, you're a passably good-looking boy, and if you'd learned jujutsu you'd probably have beaten me. All the same, all the same – I feel enormously tempted to box your ears for you now that you're lying there. I'd probably regret it; but if I should do it, let me tell you that it'll be because I can't help it. And of course it won't be only one box on the ear I'll give you, but I'll let fly right and left till you're black and blue. And perhaps you're one of these men of honour – I could easily believe it – and couldn't survive the disgrace of having your ears boxed, and would have to do away with yourself. But why were you so horrid to me? Don't you like me? Isn't it worth while to come to my room? Ah, look out! I very nearly let fly at you by accident just now. And if I let you off tonight, see that you behave better next time. I'm not your uncle to put up with your tantrums. Anyhow, let me point out that if I let you off now, you needn't think that the disgrace is all the same whether your ears are boxed or not. I'd rather box your ears soundly for you than have you thinking that. I wonder what Mack will say when I tell him about all this?'

At the thought of Mack she loosened her grip; in his muzzy confusion Karl saw Mack as a deliverer. For a little while he could still feel Clara's hand on his throat, and so he squirmed for a few minutes before lying still.

She urged him to get up; he neither answered nor stirred. She lit a candle somewhere, the room grew light, a blue ziz-zag pattern appeared on the ceiling, but Karl lay with his head on the sofa cushion exactly as Clara had placed it and did not move a finger's breadth. Clara walked round the room, her skirt rustling about her legs; she seemed to pause for a long time by the window.

'Got over your tantrums?' he heard her asking at last. Karl thought it hard that in his room which Mr Pollunder had assigned him for the night he could find no peace. The girl kept wandering about, stopping and talking now and then, and he was heartily sick of her. All he wanted to do was to fall asleep at once and get out of the place later. He did not even want to go to bed, he merely wanted to stay where he was on the sofa. He was only waiting for the girl to leave, so that he could spring to the door after her, bolt it, and then fling himself back on the sofa again. He felt an intense need to stretch and yawn, but he did not want to do that before Clara. And so he lay staring at the ceiling, feeling his face becoming more and more rigid, and a fly which was hovering about flitted before his eyes without his quite knowing what it was.

Clara stepped over to him again and leaned across his line of vision; and if he had not made an effort he would have had to look at her.

'I'm going now,' she said. 'Perhaps later on you'll feel like coming to see me. The door is the fourth from this one on the same side of the corridor. You pass the three next doors, that's to say, and the one after that is the right one. I'm not going downstairs again; I shall just stay in my room. You've made me thoroughly tired too. I shan't exactly expect you, but if you want to come, then come. Remember that you promised to play the piano for me. But perhaps you're feeling quite prostrate and can't move; well then, stay here and have a good sleep. I shan't tell my father anything about our little scuffle, not for the present; I mention that merely in case you start worrying about it.' And in spite of her ostensible tiredness she ran lightly out of the room.

Karl at once sat up; this lying down had already become unendurable. For the sake of using his limbs he went to the door and looked out into the corridor. But how dark it was! He felt glad when he had shut the door and bolted it and stood again by his table in the light of the candle. He made up his mind to stay no longer in this house, but to go down to Mr Pollunder, tell him frankly how Clara had treated him – admitting his defeat did not matter a straw to him – and with that abundant justification ask leave to drive or to walk home. If Mr Pollunder had any objection to his immediate return, then Karl would at least ask him to instruct a servant to conduct him to the nearest hotel. As a rule, hosts were not treated in the way which Karl planned, but still more seldom were guests treated as Clara had treated him. She had actually regarded as a kindness her promise to say nothing to Mr Pollunder about their scuffle, and that was really too outrageous. Had he been invited to a wrestling match, then, that he should be ashamed of being thrown by a girl who had apparently spent the greater part of her life in learning wrestling holds? After all, she had probably been taking lessons from Mack. She could tell him everything if she liked; he was certainly intelligent, Karl felt sure of that, although he had never had occasion to prove it in any single instance. But Karl knew also that if he were to have lessons from Mack he would make much greater progress than Clara had done; then he could come here again one day, most likely without any invitation, would begin by studying the scene of action, an exact knowledge of which had been a great advantage to Clara, and then he would seize that same Clara and fling her down on the very sofa where she had flung him tonight.

Now he had merely to find his way back to the dining-room, where in his first embarrassment he had probably laid down his hat in some unsuitable place. Of course he would take the candle with him, but even with a light it was not easy to find one's bearings. For instance, he did not even know whether his room was on the same floor as the dining-room. On the way here Clara had kept pulling him, so that he had no chance to look around him. Mr Green and the servants with the great candlesticks had also given him something to think about; in short, he actually could not remember whether they had climbed one or two flights of stairs or none at all. To judge from the view, the room was fairly high up, and so he tried to convince himself that they must have climbed stairs; yet at the front door there had been steps to climb, so why should not this side of the house be raised above ground-level too? If only there were a ray of light to be seen from some door in the corridor or a voice to be heard in the distance, no matter how faintly!

His watch, a present from his uncle, pointed to eleven; he took the candle and went out into the corridor. The door he left open, so that if his search should prove unsuccessful he might at least find his room again and in case of dire need the door of Clara's room. For safety he fixed the door open with a chair, so that it might not shut of itself. In the corridor he made the unwelcome discovery – naturally he turned to the left, away from Clara's room – that there was a draught blowing against his face, which though quite feeble might nevertheless easily blow out the candle, so that he had to guard the flame with his hand and often stop altogether to let the dying flame recover. It was a slow method of progress and it made the way seem doubly long. Karl had already passed great stretches of blank wall completely devoid of doors; one could not imagine what lay behind them. And then he came to one door after another; he tried to open several of them; they were locked and the rooms obviously unoccupied. It was an incredible squandering of space and Karl thought of the east end of New York which his uncle had promised to show him, where it was said that several families lived in one little room and the home of a whole family consisted of one corner where the children clustered round their parents. And here so many rooms stood empty and seemed to exist merely to make a hollow sound when you knocked on the door. Mr Pollunder seemed to Karl to be misled by false friends and infatuated with his daughter, which was his ruin. Uncle Jacob had certainly judged him rightly, and only his axiom that it was not his business to influence Karl's judgement of other people was responsible for this visit and all this wandering through corridors. Tomorrow Karl would tell his uncle that quite frankly, for if he followed his own axiom his uncle should be glad to hear a nephew's judgement even on himself. Besides, that axiom was probably the only thing in his uncle which displeased Karl, and even that displeasure was not unqualified.

Suddenly the wall on one side of the corridor came to an end and an ice-cold, marble balustrade appeared in its place. Karl set the candle beside him and cautiously leaned over. A breath of dark emptiness met him. If this was the main hall of the house – in the glimmer of the candle a piece of vault-like ceiling could be seen – why had they not come through it? What purpose could be served by this great, deep chamber? One stood here as if in the gallery of a church. Karl almost regretted that he could not stay in the house till morning; he would have liked Mr Pollunder to show him all round it by daylight and explain everything to him.

The balustrade was quite short and soon Karl was once more groping along a closed corridor. At a sudden turning he ran full tilt into the wall, and only the unanswering care with which he convulsively held the candle saved it from falling and going out. As the corridor seemed to have no end – no window appeared through which he could see where he was, nothing stirred either above him or below him – Karl began to think that he was going round in a circle and had a faint hope that he would come to the door of his room again; but neither it nor the balustrade reappeared. Until now he had refrained from shouting, for he did not want to raise a noise in a strange house at such a late hour; but now he realized that it would not matter in this unlighted house, and he was just preparing to send a loud 'haloo' echoing along the corridor in both directions when he noticed a little light approaching from behind him, the way that he had come. Now at last he could realize the length of that straight corridor. The house was a fortress, not a mansion. His joy on seeing that saving light was so great that he forgot all caution and ran towards it. At the first few steps he took, his candle blew out. But he paid no attention, for he did not need it any longer; here was an old servant with a lantern coming towards him and he would soon show him the right way.

'Who are you?' asked the servant, holding the lantern up to Karl's face and illumining his own as well. His face had a somewhat formal look because of a great white beard which ended on his breast in silken ringlets. 'He must be a faithful servant if they let him wear a beard like that,' though Karl, gazing fixedly at the beard in all its length and breadth, without feeling any constraint because he himself was being observed in turn. He replied at once that he was a guest of Mr Pollunder's, that he had left his room to go to the dining-room, but could not find it.

'Oh yes,' said the servant, 'we haven't had the electric light laid on yet.'

'I know,' said Karl.

'Won't you light your candle at my lantern?' asked the servant.

'If you please,' said Karl, doing so.

'There's such a draught here in the corridors,' said the servant. 'Candles easily get blown out; that's why I have a lantern.'

'Yes, a lantern is much more practical,' said Karl.

'Why, you're all covered with candle-drippings,' said the servant, holding up the candle to Karl's suit.

'I never even noticed it!' cried Karl, feeling distressed, for it was his black suit, which his uncle said looked best of all upon him. His wrestling match with Clara could not have been very good for the suit either, it now occurred to him. The servant was obliging enough to clean the suit as well as could be done on the spot: Karl kept turning round and showing him another mark here and there, which the man obediently removed.

'But why should there be such a draught here?' asked Karl, as they went on again.

'Well, there's a great deal of building still to be done,' said the servant. 'The reconstruction work has been started, of course, but it's getting on very slowly. And now the builders' workmen have gone on strike, as perhaps you know. Building up a house like this gives lots of trouble. Several large breaches have been made in the walls, which nobody has filled in, and the draught blows through the whole house. If I didn't stuff my ears with cotton-wool I wouldn't stand it.'

'Then shouldn't I speak louder?' asked Karl.

'No, you have a clear voice,' said the servant. 'But to come back to this building; especially in this part, near the chapel, which will certainly have to be shut off from the rest of the house later, the draught is simply unendurable.'

'So the balustrade along this corridor gives on to a chapel?'

'Yes.'

'I thought that at the time,' said Karl.

'It is well worth seeing,' said the servant. 'If it hadn't been for that, Mr Mack probably wouldn't have bought the house.'

'Mr Mack?' asked Karl. 'I thought the house belonged to Mr Pollunder.'

'Yes, certainly,' said the servant, 'but it was Mr Mack who decided the purchase. Don't you know Mr Mack?'

'Oh yes,' said Karl. 'But what connexion does he have with Mr Pollunder?'

'He is the young lady's fiancé,' said the servant.

'I certainly didn't know that,' said Karl, stopping short.

'Do you find that so surprising?' asked the servant.

'I'm only thinking it over. If you don't know about such connexions, you can easily make the worst kind of mistakes,' replied Karl.

'I'm only surprised that they haven't told you about it,' said the servant.

'Yes, that's true,' said Karl, feeling abashed.

'Probably they thought you knew,' said the servant, 'it's old news by this time. But here we are,' and he opened a door behind which appeared a stair that led straight down to the back door of the dining-room which was still as brightly illumined as at Karl's arrival.

Before Karl went down to the dining-room, from which the voices of Mr Pollunder and Mr Green could be heard still talking as they had talked two hours before, the servant said: 'If you like, I'll wait for you here and take you back to your room. It's always difficult to find one's way about here on the first evening.'

'My room will never see me again,' said Karl, without knowing why he felt sad as he gave this information.

'It won't be so bad as all that,' said the servant, smiling in a slightly superior way and patting him on the arm. Probably he construed Karl's words as meaning that Karl intended to stay up all night in the dining-room, talking and drinking with the two gentlemen. Karl did not want to make any confessions just then, also he reflected that this servant, whom he liked better than the other servants in the house, would be able to direct him on his way to New York, and so he said: 'If you would wait here, it would certainly be a great kindness and I gratefully accept it. I'll come up in a little while, in any case, and tell you what I'm going to do. I think that I may need your help yet.' 'Good,' said the servant, setting his lantern on the floor and seating himself on a low pedestal, which was probably vacant on account of the reconstruction work. 'I'll wait here, then. You can leave the candle with me too,' he added, as Karl made to go downstairs with the lighted candle in his hand.

'I'm not noticing what I'm doing,' said Karl, and he handed the candle to the servant, who merely nodded to him, though it was impossible to say whether the nod was deliberate or whether it was caused by his stroking his beard with his hand.

Karl opened the door, which through no fault of his rattled noisily, for it consisted of a single glass panel that almost jumped from the frame if the door were opened quickly and held fast only by the handle. Karl let the door swing back again in alarm, for he had wanted to enter the room as quietly as possible.

Without turning round he was aware that behind him the servant, who had apparently descended from his pedestal, was now shutting the door carefully and without the slightest sound.

'Forgive me for disturbing you,' he said to the two gentlemen, who stared at him with round, astonished faces. At the same time he flung a hasty glance round the room, to see if he could discover his hat somewhere. But it was nowhere to be seen; the dishes on the dining-table had all been cleared away; perhaps, he thought uncomfortably, the hat had been carried off to the kitchen along with them.

'But where have you left Clara?' asked Mr Pollunder, to whom the intrusion, however, did not seem to be unwelcome, for he at once changed his position in the chair and turned his face full upon Karl. Mr Green put on an air of indifference, pulled out a pocket-book, in size and thickness a giant of its kind, seemed to be searching in its many compartments for some particular paper, but during the search kept reading other papers which chanced to come his way.

'I have a request to make which you must not misunderstand,' said Karl, walking up hastily to Mr Pollunder and putting his hand on the arm of his chair, to get as near to him as he could.

'And what request can that be?' asked Mr Pollunder, giving Karl a frank open look. 'It is granted already.' And he put his arm round Karl and drew him between his knees. Karl submitted willingly, though as a rule he felt much too grown up for such treatment. But of course it made the utterance of his request all the more difficult.

'And how do you really like being here?' asked Mr Pollunder. 'Don't you find that one gets a kind of free feeling on coming out of the town into the country? Usually' – and he looked askance at Mr Green, a glance of unmistakable meaning, which was partly screened by Karl – 'usually I get that feeling every evening.'

'He talks,' thought Karl, 'as if he knew nothing about this huge house, the endless corridors, the chapel, the empty rooms, the darkness everywhere.'

'Well,' said Mr Pollunder, 'out with your request!' And he gave Karl, who stood silent, a friendly shake.

'Please,' said Karl, and much as he lowered his voice he could not keep Green, sitting there, from hearing everything, though he would gladly have concealed from him this request, which might easily be construed as an insult to Pollunder – 'Please let me go home now, late as it is.'

And once he had put the worst into words, all the rest came pouring out after it, and he said without the slightest insincerity things of which he had never even thought before. 'I want above all to get home. I'll be glad to come again, for wherever you are, Mr Pollunder, I'll always be glad to stay. Only tonight I can't stay here. You know that my uncle was unwilling to give me permission for this visit. He must have had good reasons for that, as for everything that he does, and I had the presumption literally to force permission from him against his better judgement. I simply exploited his affection for me. It doesn't matter at all what his objections were; all that I know with absolute certainty is that there was nothing in these objections which could offend you, Mr Pollunder, for you're the best, the very best friend that my uncle has. Nobody else can even remotely be compared with you among my uncle's friends. And that is the only excuse for my disobedience, though an insufficient one. You probably have no first-hand knowledge of the relations between my uncle and me, so I'll mention only the main points. Until my English studies are finished and while I am still insufficiently versed in practical things, I am entirely dependent on my uncle's kindness, which I can accept, of course, being a relation. You mustn't think that I'm in a position yet to earn my living decently – and God forbid that I should do it in any other way. I'm afraid my education has been too impractical for that. I managed to scrape through four classes of a European High School with moderate success, and for earning a livelihood that means less than nothing, for our schools are very much behind the times in their teaching methods. You would laugh if I were to tell you the kind of things I learned. If a boy can go on studying, finish his school course and enter the University, then, probably, it all straightens out in the long run and he finishes up with a proper education that lets him do something and gives him the confidence to set about earning a living. But unluckily I was torn right out of that systematic course of study. Sometimes I think I know nothing, and in any case the best of my knowledge wouldn't be adequate for America. Some of the high schools in my country have been reformed recently, teaching modern languages and perhaps even commercial subjects, but when I left my primary school there were none of these. My father certainly wanted me to learn English, but in the first place I couldn't foresee then that I would have such bad luck and that I would actually need English, and in the second place I had to learn a great deal of other things at school, so that I didn't have much time to spare – I mention all this to show you how dependent I am on my uncle, and how deeply I am bound to him in consequence. You must admit that in these circumstances I am not in a position to offend in the slightest against even his unexpressed wishes. And so if I am to make good even half of the offence which I have committed against him, I must go home at once.'

During this long speech of Karl's, Mr Pollunder had listened attentively, now and then tightening his arm round Karl, though imperceptibly, particularly when Uncle Jacob was mentioned, and several times gazing seriously and as if expectantly at Green, who was still occupied with his pocket-book. But Karl had felt more and more restless the more clearly he became aware of his relation to his uncle during his speech, and involuntarily he struggled to free himself from Pollunder's arm. Everything cramped him here; the road leading to his uncle through that glass door, down the steps, through the avenue, along the country roads, through the suburbs to the great main street where his uncle's house was, seemed to him a strictly ordered whole, which lay there empty, smooth, and prepared for him, and called to him with a strong voice. Mr Pollunder's kindness and Mr Green's loathsomeness ran into a blur together, and all that he asked from that smoky room was permission to leave.

He felt cut off from Mr Pollunder, prepared to do battle against Mr Green, and yet all round him was a vague fear, whose impact troubled his sight.

He took a step back and now stood equally distant from Mr Pollunder and Mr Green.

'Hadn't you something to say to him?' asked Mr Pollunder, turning to Mr Green and seizing the man's hand imploringly.

'I don't know what I could have to say to him,' said Mr Green, who had taken a letter from his pocket-book at last and laid it before him on the table. 'It is to his credit that he wants to go back to his uncle, and one might naturally assume that that would give his uncle great pleasure. Unless he has angered his uncle already too deeply by his disobedience, which is only too possible. In that case it would certainly be better for him to stay here. It's difficult to say anything definite; we're both friends of his uncle and it would be hard to say whether Mr Pollunder's or my friendship ranks highest; but we can't see into his uncle's mind, especially at so many miles' distance from New York.'

'Please, Mr Green,' said Karl, overcoming his distaste and approaching Mr Green, 'I can tell from what you say that you too think it would be best for me to go back at once.'

'I said nothing of the kind,' replied Mr Green, and he once more returned to his contemplation of the letter, running his fingers over the edges of it. Apparently he wished to indicate that he had been asked a question by Mr Pollunder and had answered it, while Karl was no concern of his at all.

Meanwhile Mr Pollunder stepped over to Karl and gently led him away from Mr Green to the big window.

'Dear Mr Rossmann,' he said, bending down to Karl's ear and as a preparation for what he had to say passing his handkerchief over his face until it encountered his nose, which he blew, 'you must not think that I wish to keep you here against your will. There is no question of that. I can't put the car at your disposal, I admit, for it's parked in a public garage a good distance from here, since I haven't had the time yet to build a garage for myself here, where everything is still under construction. The chauffeur again doesn't sleep here but somewhere near the garage; I really don't know where, myself. Besides, he isn't supposed to be on duty just now; he's merely expected to appear at the right time in the morning. But all this would be no obstacle to your returning at once, for if you insist upon it I'll accompany you at once to the nearest railway station, though it's so far away that you wouldn't get home much sooner than if you came with me in my car tomorrow morning – we start at seven.'

'Then, Mr Pollunder, I would rather go by train all the same,' said Karl. 'I never thought of the train. You say yourself that I would arrive sooner by train than if I left tomorrow in your car.'

'But it would make only a very little difference.'

'All the same, all the same, Mr Pollunder,' said Karl, 'I'll always be glad to come here again, remembering your kindness, that is, of course, if after my behaviour tonight you ever invite me again; and perhaps next time I'll be able to explain more clearly why every minute that keeps me away from my uncle now is so important to me.' And as if he had already received permission to go away, he added: 'But you mustn't come with me on any account. It's really quite unnecessary. There's a servant outside who'll be glad to show me the way to the station. Now, I have only to find my hat.' And with these words he walked across the room to take a last hasty look, in case his hat were lying somewhere.

'Perhaps I could help you out with a cap?' said Mr Green, drawing a cap from his pocket. 'Maybe it will service you for the time being?'

Karl stopped in amazement and said: 'But I can't deprive you of your cap. I can go quite well with my head bare. I don't need anything.'

'It isn't my cap. You just take it!'

'In that case, thanks,' said Karl, so as not to delay any longer, taking the cap. He put it on and could not help laughing, for it fitted him perfectly; then he took it off again and examined it, but could not find the particular thing that he was looking for; it seemed a perfectly new cap. 'It fits so well!' he said.

'So the cap fits!' cried Mr Green, thumping the table.

Karl was already on his way to the door to fetch the servant, when Mr Green got up, stretched himself after his ample meal and his long rest, struck himself resoundingly on the chest, and said in a voice between advice and command: 'Before you go, you must say good-bye to Miss Clara.'

'Yes, you must do that,' agreed Mr Pollunder, who had also got up. From the way in which he spoke one could tell that the words did not come from his heart; he kept flapping his hands feebly against the side of his trousers and buttoning and re-buttoning his jacket, which after the fashion of the moment was quite short and scarcely reached his hips, an unbecoming garment for such a stout man as Mr Pollunder. One also had the definite feeling as he stood there beside Mr Green that Mr Pollunder's fatness was not a healthy fatness. His massive back was somewhat bent, his paunch looked soft and flabby, an actual burden, and his face was pallid and worried. Mr Green, on the other hand, was perhaps even fatter than Mr Pollunder, but it was a homogeneous, balanced fatness; he stood with his heels together like a soldier, he bore his head with a jaunty erectness. He looked like a great athlete, a captain of athletes.

'You are to go first then,' Mr Green continued, 'to Miss Clara. That is bound to be pleasant for you and it suits my time-table excellently as well. For before you leave here I have as a matter of fact something of interest to tell you, which will probably also decide whether you are to go back or not. But I am unfortunately bound by my orders to divulge nothing to you before midnight. You can imagine that I'm sorry for that myself, since it upsets my night's rest, but I shall stick to my instructions. It is a quarter-past eleven now, so that I can finish discussing my business with Mr Pollunder, which you would only interrupt; besides, you can have a very pleasant time with Miss Clara. Then at twelve punctually you will report here, where you will learn what is necessary.'

Could Karl reject this request, which demanded from him only the minimum of politeness and gratitude towards Mr

Pollunder and which, moreover, had been put by a man customarily rude and indifferent, while Mr Pollunder, whom it really concerned, intervened neither by word nor glance? And what was the interesting news which he was not to learn until midnight? If it did not hasten his return by at least the forty-five minutes that it now made him waste, it would have little interest for him. But his greatest scruple was whether he dared visit Clara at all, seeing that she was his enemy. If only he had the stone-chisel with him which his uncle had given him as a letter weight! Clara's room might prove a really dangerous den. Yet it was quite impossible to say anything against Clara here, for she was Pollunder's daughter and, as he had just heard, Mack's fiancée as well. If she had only behaved a very little differently towards him, he would have frankly admired her for her connexions. He was still considering all this when he perceived that no reflection was expected from him, for Green opened the door and said to the servant, who jumped up from his pedestal: 'Conduct this young man to Miss Clara.'

'This is how commands are executed,' thought Karl, as the servant, almost running, groaning with infirmity, led him by a remarkably short cut to Clara's room. As Karl was passing his own room, whose door was still open, he asked leave to go in for a minute, hoping to compose himself. But the servant would not allow it.

'No,' he said, 'you must come along to Miss Clara. You heard that yourself.'

'I only want to stay there a minute,' said Karl, thinking what a relief it would be to lie on the sofa for a little, to quicken up the time between now and midnight.

'Don't obstruct me in the execution of my duty,' said the servant.

'He seems to imagine it's a punishment to be taken to Miss Clara,' thought Karl, and he went on a few steps, but then defiantly stopped again.

'Do come, young sir,' said the servant, 'since you're still here. I know that you wanted to leave this very night, but we don't always get what we want, and I told you already that it would hardly be possible.'

'I do want to leave and I will leave too,' said Karl, 'and I'm merely going to say good-bye to Miss Clara.'

'Is that so?' said the servant, and Karl could see that he did not believe a word of it. 'Why are you so unwilling to say good-bye then? Do come along.'

'Who is that in the corridor?' said Clara's voice, and they saw her leaning out of a door near by, a big red-shaded table-lamp in her hand. The servant hurried up to her and gave his message; Karl slowly followed him, 'You're late in coming,' said Clara.

Without answering her for the moment, Karl said to the servant softly, but in a tone of stern command, for he already knew the man's character: 'You'll wait for me just outside this door!'

'I was just going to bed,' said Clara, setting the lamp on the table. As he had done in the dining-room, the servant carefully shut this door too from the outside. 'It's after half-past eleven already.'

'After half-past eleven?' said Karl interrogatively, as if alarmed at these figures. 'But in that case I must say good-bye at once,' he went on, 'for at twelve punctually I must be down in the dining-room.'

'What urgent business you seem to have!' said Clara, absently smoothing the folds of her loose nightdress. Her face was glowing and she kept on smiling. Karl decided that there was no danger of getting into another quarrel with Clara. 'Couldn't you play the piano for a little after all, as Papa promised yesterday and you yourself promised tonight?'

'But isn't it too late now?' asked Karl. He would have liked to oblige her, for she was quite different now from what she had been before; it was as if she had somehow ascended into the Pollunder circle and into Mack's as well.

'Yes, it is late,' she said, and her desire for music seemed already to have passed. 'And every sound here echoes through the whole house; I'm afraid that if you play now it will waken up the very servants in the attics.'

'Then I won't bother to play; you see, I hope to come back again another day; besides, if it isn't too great a bother, you might visit my uncle and have a look at my room while you are there. I have a marvellous piano. My uncle gave it to me. Then, if you like, I'll play all my pieces to you; there aren't many of them, unfortunately, and they don't suit such a fine instrument either, which needs a really great player to use it. But you may have the pleasure of hearing a good player if you tell me beforehand when you are coming, for my uncle means to engage a famous teacher for me – you can imagine how I look forward to it – and his playing would certainly make it worth your while to pay me a visit during one of my lessons. To be quite frank, I'm glad that it's too late to play, for I can't really play yet, you would be surprised how badly I play. And now allow me to take my leave; after all it must be your bedtime.' And as Clara was looking at him with a kindly expression and seemed to bear him no ill-will because of the quarrel, he added with a smile, while he held out his hand: 'In my country people say "Sleep well and sweet dreams".'

'Wait,' she said, without taking his hand, 'perhaps you might play after all.' And she disappeared through a little side door, beside which the piano stood.

'What next?' thought Karl. 'I can't wait long, even if she is nice to me.' There was a knock at the corridor door and the servant, without daring quite to open it, whispered through a little chink: 'Excuse me; I've just been called away and can't wait any longer.'

'Then you can go,' said Karl, who now felt confident that he could find his way alone to the dining-room. 'But leave the lantern for me at the door. How late is it?'

'Almost a quarter to twelve,' said the servant.

'How slowly the time passes,' said Karl to himself. The servant was shutting the door when Karl remembered that he had not given him a tip, took a shilling from his trouser pocket

– in the American fashion he now always carried his loose coins jingling in his trouser pocket, his bank-notes, on the other hand, in his waistcoat pocket – and handed it to the servant with the words: 'For your kindness.'

Clara had already come back, patting her trim hair with her fingers, when it occurred to Karl that he should not have let the servant go after all, for who would now show him the way to the railway station? Well, Mr Pollunder would surely manage to hunt up a servant somewhere, and perhaps the old servant had been summoned to the dining-room and so would be again at his disposal.

'Won't you really play a little for me? One hears music so seldom here that it's a pity to miss any opportunity of hearing it.'

'It's high time I began then,' said Karl without further consideration, sitting down at once at the piano.

'Do you want any special music?' asked Clara.

'No, thanks, I can't even read music correctly,' replied Karl, and he began to play. It was a little air which, as he knew perfectly well, had to be played somewhat slowly to make it even comprehensible, especially to strangers; but he strummed it out in blatant march time. When he ended it the shattered silence of the house closed round them again, almost distressfully. They sat there as if frozen with embarrassment and did not move.

'Quite good,' said Clara, but there was no formula of politeness which could have flattered Karl after that performance.

'How late is it?' he asked.

'A quarter to twelve.'

'Then I still have a little time,' he said and thought to himself: 'Which is it to be? I needn't play through all the ten tunes I know, but I might play one at least as well as I can.' And he began to play his beloved soldier's song. So slowly that the roused longing of his listener yearned for the next note, which Karl held back and yielded reluctantly. He had actually to pick out the keys first with his eyes as in playing all of his tunes, but he also felt rising within him a song which reached past the end of this song, seeking another end which it could not find. 'I'm no good,' said Karl after he had finished, gazing at Clara with tears in his eyes.

Then from the next room came a sound of handclapping, 'Someone has been listening!' cried Karl, taken aback. 'Mack,' said Clara softly. And already he heard Mack shouting: 'Karl Rossmann, Karl Rossmann!'

Karl swung both feet over the piano stool and opened the door. He saw Mack half sitting and half reclining in a huge double bed with the blankets loosely flung over his legs. A canopy of blue silk was the sole and somewhat school-girlish ornament of the bed, which was otherwise quite plain and roughly fashioned out of heavy wood. On the bedside table only a candle was burning, but the sheets and Mack's nightshirt were so white that the candle-light falling upon them was thrown off in an almost dazzling reflection; even the canopy shone, at least at the edges, with its slightly billowing silk tent which was not stretched quite taut. But immediately behind Mack the bed and everything else sank into complete darkness. Clara leaned against the bed-post and had eyes now only for Mack.

'Hallo,' said Mack, reaching his hand to Karl. 'You play very well; up to now I've only known your talent for riding.'

'I'm as bad at the one as at the other,' said Karl. 'If I'd known you were listening, I certainly wouldn't have played. But your young lady –' He stopped, he hesitated to say 'fiancée', since Mack and Clara obviously shared the same bed already.

'But I guessed it,' said Mack, 'and so Clara had to lure you out here from New York, or else I would never have heard your playing. It's certainly amateurish enough, and even in these two airs, which have been set very simply and which you have practised a good deal, you made one or two mistakes; but all the same it pleased me greatly, quite apart from the fact that I never despise players of any kind. But won't you sit down and stay for a little while with us? Clara, give him a chair.'

'Thanks,' said Karl awkwardly. 'I can't stay, glad as I would be to stay here. It's taken me too long to discover that there are such comfortable rooms in this house,'

'I'm having everything reconstructed in this style,' said Mack.

At that moment twelve strokes of a bell rang out in rapid succession, each breaking into the one before. Karl could feel on his cheeks the wind made by the swinging of that great bell. What sort of village could it be which had such bells!

'It's high time I was gone,' said Karl, stretching out his hand to Mack and Clara without shaking theirs and rushing off into the corridor.

He found no lantern there and regretted having tipped the servant so soon.

He began to feel his way along the wall to his own room, but had hardly covered half the way when he saw Mr Green hurriedly bobbing towards him with an upraised candle. In the hand holding the candle he was also clutching a letter.

'Rossmann why didn't you come? Why have you kept me waiting? What on earth has kept you so long with Miss Clara?'

'How many questions!' thought Karl, 'and now he's pushing me to the wall,' for indeed Green was standing quite close to Karl, who had to lean his back against the wall. In this corridor Green took on an almost absurd size, and Karl wondered in jest if he could have eaten up good Mr Pollunder.

'You certainly aren't a man of your word. You promised to come down at twelve and instead of that here you are prowling round Miss Clara's door. But I promised you some interesting news at midnight, and here it is.' And with that he handed Karl the letter. On the envelope was written: 'To Karl Rossmann, to be delivered personally at midnight, wherever he may be found.'

'After all,' said Mr Green, while Karl opened the letter, 'I think I am due some thanks for driving out here from New York on your account, so that you shouldn't expect me to chase after you through these corridors as well.'

'From my uncle,' said Karl, almost as soon as he glanced at the letter. 'I have been expecting it,' he said, turning to Mr Green.

'Whether you were expecting it or not doesn't matter to me in the least. You just read it,' said Green, holding up the candle to Karl.

Karl read by its light:

DEAR NEPHEW,

As you will already have realized during our much too brief companionship, I am essentially a man of principle. That is unpleasant and depressing not only to those who come in contact with me, but also to myself as well. Yet it is my principles that have made me what I am, and no one can ask me to deny my fundamental self. Not even you, my dear nephew. Though you would be my first choice, if it ever occurred to me to permit such a general assault upon me. Then I would pick you up, of all people, with these two arms that are now holding this paper and set you above my head. But as for the moment nothing indicates that this could ever happen, I must, after the incident of today, expressly send you away from me, and I urgently beg you neither to visit me in person, nor to try to get in touch with me either by writing or through intermediaries. Against my wishes you decided this evening to leave me; stick, then, to that decision all your life. Only then will it be a manly decision. As the bringer of this news I have chosen Mr Green, my best friend, who no doubt will find indulgent words for you which at the moment are certainly not at my disposal. He is an influential man and, if only for my sake, will give you his advice and help in the first independent steps which you take. To explain our separation, which now as I end this letter once more seems incomprehensible to me, I have to keep telling myself again and again, Karl, that nothing good comes out of your family. If Mr Green should forget to hand you your box and umbrella, remind him of them.

With best wishes for your future welfare,
Your faithful
UNCLE JACOB

'Are you finished?' asked Green.

'Yes,' said Karl. 'Have you brought the box and the umbrella with you?' he asked.

'Here it is,' said Green, setting Karl's old travelling box, which until now he had held in his left hand concealed behind his back, beside Karl on the floor.

'And the umbrella?' Karl asked again.

'Everything here,' said Green, bringing out the umbrella too, which had been hanging from one of his trouser pockets. 'A man called Schubal, an engineer in the Hamburg-American Line, brought the things; he maintained that he found them on the ship. You can find an opportunity to thank him sometime.'

'Now I have my old things back again at least,' said Karl, laying the umbrella on the box.

'But you should take better care of them in future, the Senator asked me to tell you,' said Mr Green, and then asked, obviously out of private curiosity: 'What queer kind of box is that?'

'It's the kind of box that soldiers in my country take with them when they join the army,' replied Karl. 'It's my father's old army chest. It's very useful too,' he added with a smile, 'provided you don't leave it behind you somewhere.'

'After all, you've been taught your lesson,' said Mr Green, 'and I bet you haven't a second uncle in America. Here is something else for you, a third-class ticket to San Francisco. I've decided on sending you there because in the first place your chances of earning a living are much better in the West, and in the second your uncle has got a finger in everything here that might suit you and a meeting between you must be strictly avoided. In 'Frisco you can tackle anything you like; just begin at the bottom and try gradually to work your way up.'

Karl could not detect any malice in these words; the bad news which had lain sheathed in Green the whole evening was delivered, and now he seemed a harmless man with whom one could speak more frankly perhaps, than with anybody else. The best of men, chosen through no fault of his own to be the bearer of such a secret and painful message, must appear a suspicious character so long as he had to keep it to himself. 'I shall leave this house at once,' said Karl, hoping that his resolution would be approved by Green's experience, 'for I was invited as my uncle's nephew, while as a stranger I have no business here. Would you be so good as to show me the way out and tell me how I can get to the nearest inn?'

'As quick as you like,' said Green, 'you're not afraid of giving me trouble, are you?'

On seeing the huge strides which Green was taking, Karl at once came to a stop; so much haste seemed highly suspicious, and he seized Green by the coat-tail, suddenly realizing the true situation, and said: 'There's one thing more you must explain: on the envelope you gave me it was merely stated that I was to receive it at midnight, wherever I might be found. Why, then, on the strength of that letter, did you keep me here when I wanted to leave at a quarter past eleven? In doing that you exceeded your instructions.'

Green accompanied his reply with a wave of the hand which indicated with melodramatic exaggeration the silliness of Karl's question, saying: 'Was it stated on the envelope that I should run myself to death chasing about after you, and did the contents of the letter give any hint that the inscription was to be construed in such a way? If I had not kept you here, I should have had to hand you the letter precisely at midnight on the open road.'

'No,' said Karl, quite unmoved, 'it isn't quite so. It says on the envelope: "To be delivered at midnight," You might have been too tired, perhaps, to follow me at all, or I might have reached my uncle's by midnight, though I grant you, Mr Pollunder thought not, or as a last resort it might have been your duty to take me back to my uncle in your own car, which you so conveniently forgot to mention, since I was insisting on going back. Does not the inscription quite plainly convey that midnight was to be the final term for me? And it is you who are to blame that I missed it.'

Karl looked at Green with shrewd eyes and clearly saw the shame over this exposure was conflicting in the man with joy at the success of his designs. At last he pulled himself together and said sharply, as if breaking into Karl's accusations, although Karl had been silent for a long time: 'Not a word more!' And pushed Karl, who had once more picked up his box and his umbrella, out through a little door which he flung open before him.

To his astonishment Karl found himself in the open air. An outside stair without railings led downwards before him. He had simply to descend it and then turn to the right to reach the avenue which led to the road. In the bright moonlight he could not miss his way. Below him in the garden he could hear the manifold barking of dogs who had been let loose and were rushing about in the shadow of the trees. In the stillness he could distinctly hear them thudding on the grass as they landed after making their great bounds.

Without being molested by the dogs Karl safely got out of the garden. He could not tell with certainty in which direction New York lay. In coming here he had paid too little attention to details which might have been useful to him now. Finally he told himself that he need not of necessity go to New York, where nobody expected him and one man certainly did not expect him. So he chose a chance direction and set out on his way.

4

THE ROAD TO RAMESES

In the small inn which Karl reached after a short walk and which was merely a last little eating-house for New York car and lorry drivers and so very seldom used as a night lodging, he asked for the cheapest bed that could be had, since he thought he had better begin to save at once. In keeping with his request, the landlord waved him up a stair as if he were a menial, and at the top of the stair a dishevelled old hag, peevish at being roused from her sleep, received him almost without listening to him, warning him all the time to tread softly, and conducted him into a room whose door she shut on him, but not before giving him a whispered: 'Hst!'

Karl could not make out at first whether the window curtains had merely been drawn or whether there was no window in the room at all, it was so dark; but in the end he noticed a skylight, whose covering he drew aside, whereupon a little light came in. There were two beds in the room, both of them already occupied. He saw two young men lying there in a heavy sleep; they did not look very trustworthy, chiefly because without any understandable reason they were sleeping in their clothes; one of them actually had his boots on.

At the moment when Karl uncovered the skylight one of the sleepers raised his arms and legs a little way in the air, which was such a curious sight that in spite of his cares Karl laughed to himself.

He soon realized that, quite apart from the absence of anything to sleep on, there being neither a couch nor a sofa, he would not be able to get any sleep here, since he could not risk losing his newly recovered box and the money he was carrying on him. But he did not want to go away either, for he did not know how he was to get past the old woman and the landlord if he left the house so soon. After all, he was perhaps just as safe here as on the open road. It was certainly strange that no sign of luggage was to be seen in the whole room, so far as he could make out in the half light. But perhaps, indeed very probably, the two young men were servants who had to get up early because of the boarders and for that reason slept with their clothes on. In that case it was no great honour, certainly, to sleep in their room, but it was all the less risky. Yet he must not fall asleep on any account until he was certain of this beyond all doubt.

Under the bed a candle was standing, along with matches. Karl softly crept over and fetched them. He had no scruples about lighting the candle, for on the landlord's authority the room belonged as much to him as to the other two men, who besides had already enjoyed half a night's sleep and being in possession of the beds held an immeasurable advantage over him. However, by moving about as quietly as possible, he naturally took every care not to waken them.

First of all he wanted to examine his box, so as to survey his things, of which by this time he had only a vague memory, and the most precious of which might well have disappeared. For once Schubal got his hands on anything there was little hope that you would get it back unscathed. Of course, he might have been counting on a big tip from Uncle Jacob, but on the other hand if anything were missing he could easily shift the blame on to the original guardian of the box, Mr Butterbaum.

Karl's first glance inside the box horrified him. How many hours had he spent during the voyage in arranging and rearranging the things in this box, and now everything was in such wild confusion that as soon as he turned the key the lid sprang up of itself.

But soon he realized to his delight that the sole cause of the disorder was that someone had added the suit he had worn during the voyage, which the box, of course, was not intended to hold. Not the slightest thing was missing. In the secret pocket of his jacket he found not only his passport but also the money which his parents had given him, so that, including what he had upon him, he was amply furnished with money for the time being. Even the underclothes which he had worn on arriving were there, freshly washed and ironed. He at once put his watch and his money in the trusty secret pocket. The only regrettable thing was that the Veronese salami, which was still there too, had bestowed its smell upon everything else. If he could not find some way of eliminating that smell, he had every prospect of walking about for months enveloped in it.

As he was searching for some things at the very bottom – a pocket Bible, some letter paper and some photographs of his parents – the cap fell from his head into the box. In its old surroundings he recognized it at once; it was his own cap, the cap which his mother had given him to wear during the voyage. All the same, out of prudence he had not worn the cap on the boat, for he knew that in America everybody wore caps instead of hats, so that he did not want to wear his cap out before arriving. And Mr Green had used it simply to make a fool of him. Could Uncle Jacob have instructed him to do that as well? And with an involuntary wrathful movement he gripped the lid of the box, which shut with a bang.

Now there was no help for it; the two sleepers were aroused. First one of them stretched and yawned, and then the other immediately followed suit. Almost all the contents of the box were lying in a heap on the table; if these men were thieves, they merely had to walk across the room and take what they fancied. Both to forestall this possibility and to know where he stood, Karl went over with the candle in his hand to the beds and explained how he happened to be there. They did not seem to have expected any explanation, for, still far too sleepy to talk, they merely gazed at him without any sign of surprise. They were both young men, but heavy work or poverty had prematurely sharpened the bones of their faces; unkempt beards hung from their chins; their hair, which had not been cut for a long time, lay matted on their heads; and they rubbed and knuckled their deep-set eyes, still heavy with sleep.

Karl resolved to take every advantage of their momentary weakness and so he said: 'My name is Karl Rossmann and I am a German. Please tell me, as we are occupying the same room, what your names are and what country you come from. I may as well say that I don't expect a share of your beds, for I was late in arriving and in any case I have no intention of sleeping. And you mustn't draw the wrong conclusions from the good suit I have on; I am quite poor and without any prospects.'

The smaller of the two men – the one with his boots on – indicating by his arms, legs and general demeanour that he was not interested in all this and had no time for such remarks, lay down again and immediately went to sleep; the other, a dark-skinned man, also lay down again, but before falling asleep said with a languid wave of the hand: 'That chap there is called Robinson, and he's an Irishman, I'm called Delamarche and I'm a Frenchman, and now please be quiet.' Scarcely had he said this when with a great puff he blew out Karl's candle and fell back on the pillow.

'Well, that danger is averted for the moment,' Karl told himself, turning back to the table. If their sleepiness was not a pretext, everything was all right. The only disagreeable thing was that one of them was an Irishman. Karl could no longer remember in what book he had once read at home that if you went to America you must be on your guard against the Irish. While he was staying with his uncle he certainly had had an excellent opportunity to go thoroughly into the question of the Irish danger, but because he believed he was now well provided for to the end of his life he had completely neglected it. So he resolved that he would at least have a good look at this Irishman by the help of the candle, which he lit again, and found that the man really looked more bearable than the Frenchman. His cheeks had still a trace of roundness and he smiled in his sleep in quite a friendly way, so far as Karl could make out, standing at a distance on tiptoe.

Firmly resolved in spite of everything not to go to sleep, Karl sat down on the only chair in the room, postponed packing his box for the time being, since the whole night still lay before him in which to do it, and turned the leaves of his Bible for a little while, without reading anything. Then he took up a photograph of his parents, in which his small father stood very erect behind his mother, who sat in an easy-chair slightly sunk into herself. One of his father's hands lay on the back of the chair, the other, which was clenched to a fist, rested on a picture-book lying open on a fragile table beside him. There was another photograph in which Karl had been included together with his parents. In it his father and mother were eyeing him sharply, while he was staring at the camera, as the photographer bade him. But he had not taken this photograph with him on the voyage.

He gazed all the more attentively now at the one lying before him and tried to catch his father's eye from various angles. But his father refused to come to life, no matter how much his expression was modified by shifting the candle into different positions; nor did his thick, horizontal moustache look in the least real; it was not a good photograph. His mother, however, had come out better; her mouth was twisted as if she had been hurt and were forcing herself to smile. It seemed to Karl that anyone who saw the photograph must be so forcibly struck with this that he would begin immediately to think it an exaggerated, not to say foolish, interpretation. How could a photograph convey with such complete certainty the secret feelings of the person shown in it? And he looked away from the photograph for a little while. When he glanced at it again he noticed his mother's hand, which dropped from the arm of the chair in the foreground, near enough to kiss. He wondered if it might not be better to write to his parents, as both of them (and his father very strictly on leaving him at Hamburg) had enjoined him. On that terrible evening when his mother, standing by the window, had told him he was to go to America, he had made a fixed resolution never to write; but what did resolve of an inexperienced boy matter here, in these new surroundings? He might as well have vowed then that two months in America would see him commanding the American Militia, instead of which here he was in a garret beside two vagrants, in an eating-house outside New York, the right place for him, too, as he could not but admit. And with a smile he scrutinized his parents' faces, as if to read in them whether they still wanted to hear news of their son.

Thus preoccupied, he soon became aware that he was very tired after all and would scarcely manage to keep awake all night. The photograph fell from his hands, and he laid his face on it, finding the coolness pleasant to his cheek; and with a comfortable feeling he fell asleep.

He was awakened early in the morning by someone tickling him under the armpit. It was the Frenchman who had taken that liberty. But the Irishman too was standing beside Karl's table, and both were staring at him with no less interest that he had shown in them during the night. Karl was not surprised that in getting up they had not wakened him; there was no need to impute evil intentions to their stealthy movements, for he had been sleeping heavily, and they had not had much to do in the way of dressing, or, from all appearances of washing either.

Now they introduced themselves properly, with a certain formality, and Karl learned that they were both mechanics who had been out of work for a long time in New York and so had come down in the world considerably. In proof of this Robinson unbuttoned his jacket to show that he had no shirt on, but one might have guessed that from the loose fit of the collar which was merely fastened to the neck of his jacket. They were making their way to the little town of Butterford, two days on foot from New York, where it was rumoured that work was to be had. They had no objection to Karl's accompanying them, and promised to take turns at carrying his box, and also, if they got work themselves, to find him a job as an apprentice, an easy matter when work was to be had at all. Karl had scarcely agreed to this when they advised him in a friendly manner to get out of his good suit, which would only be a hindrance to him looking for a job. In that very house there was an excellent chance to dispose of the suit, for the old woman dealt in old clothes. They helped Karl, who had not yet quite decided what do do about the suit, to take if off, and then they carried it away. Left to himself Karl, still heavy with sleep, slowly put on his old travelling suit, reproaching himself meanwhile for having sold the good one, which might perhaps hinder him from getting an apprentice's job but would be a good recommendation in looking for a better situation, and he had just opened the door to call the two men back when he met them face to face, furnished with half a dollar which they laid on the table as the proceeds of the sale, looking at the same time so gleeful that it was difficult to believe that had not raked off a profit for themselves – and a disgustingly big profit, too.

But there was not time to tell them off about that, for the old woman came in, just as sleepy as she had been the night before, and drove all three of them out into the passage with the explanation that the room had to be got ready for new occupants. There was no question of that, needless to say; she did it out of mere malice. Karl, who had started to pack his box had to look on while she grabbed his things with both hands and flung them into the box with such violence that they might have been wild animals she was determined to master. The two mechanics kept dodging round her, tugging at her skirt, clapping her on the back, but if they fancied they were helping Karl at all they were quite mistaken. When the old woman had shut the box, she thrust the handle into Karl's fingers, shook off the mechanics, and drove all three from the room with the threat that if they did not get out there would be no coffee for them. Obviously she had quite forgotten that Karl had not been with the mechanics from the start, for she lumped the three of them together. After all, the mechanics had sold her Karl's suit, which argued a certain solidarity.

They had to walk up and down the passage for a long time, and the Frenchman, who had taken Karl by the arm, swore with great fluency, threatening to knock down the landlord if he dared to show himself and furiously beating his clenched fists together as if in preparation for the encounter. At last an innocent little boy appeared, who was so small that he had to stand on tiptoe to hand the coffee-can to the Frenchman. Unluckily there was nothing but a can, and they could not make the boy understand that glasses were also needed. So only one of them could drink at a time, while the other two stood by and waited. Karl could not bring himself to drink coffee in this way, but he did not want to offend the other two, and so, when his turn came, though he raised the can to his lips he drank nothing.

As a parting gesture the Irishman flung the can on the stone flags. Observed by no one, they left the house and stepped out into the thick, yellowish morning mist. They walked on in silence side by side at the edge of the road; Karl had to carry his box, since the others were not likely to relieve him unless he asked them. Now and then an automobile shot out of the mist and all three turned their heads to gaze after the large monsters, which were so remarkable to look at and passed so quickly that they never even noticed whether anyone was sitting inside. Later they began to meet columns of vehicles bringing provisions to New York, which streamed past in five rows taking up the whole breadth of the road and so continuously that no one could have got across to the other side. At intervals the road widened into a kind of a square, in the middle of which rose a structure like a tower, where a policeman was stationed to supervise everything, directing with a little staff the traffic of the main road and of the adjoining side roads, the only supervision the traffic received until it reached the next square and the next policeman, although meanwhile it was adequately and gratuitously controlled by the silent vigilance of the lorrymen and chauffeurs. Karl was surprised most of all by the general quiet. Had it not been for the bellowing of the careless cattle bound for the slaughter-house, you would probably have heard nothing but the clatter of hoofs and the whirring of motor vehicles. Of course the speed at which they went was not always the same. At some of the squares, because of a great rush of traffic from the side roads, large-scale adjustments had to be made and then whole rows of vehicles came to a standstill, jerking forward by inches, but after that for a little while everything would fly past at lightning speed again until, as if governed by a single brake, the traffic slowed down once more. And yet no trace of dust rose from the road; all this speeding went on in perfectly limpid air. There were no pedestrians, no market women straggling singly along the road towards the town, as in Karl's country, but every now and then appeared great, flat motor-trucks, on which stood some twenty women with baskets on their backs, perhaps market women after all, craning their necks to oversee the traffic in their impatience for a quicker journey. There were also similar trucks on which a few men lounged about with their hands in their trousers pockets. These trucks all bore different inscriptions, and on one of them Karl read with an ejaculation of surprise: 'Dock labourers wanted by the Jacob Despatch Agency.' The truck happened to be going rather slowly and a lively little stoop-shouldered man standing on the step invited the three wanderers to hop in. Karl dodged behind the mechanics, as if his uncle were on the truck and might catch sight of him. He was glad that his two companions refused the invitation, though he found some grounds for offence in the scornful way they did so. They had no business to think they were too good to work for his uncle. He immediately let them know it, though not of course in so many words. Delamarche turned on him and told him not to interfere in things which he did not understand; this way of taking on men was a scandalous fraud and the firm of Jacob was notorious throughout the whole United States. Karl made no reply, but from that moment kept close to the Irishman and begged him to carry the box for a little while, which he actually did, after Karl had asked him several times. But he kept grumbling about the weight of the box, until it turned out that all he wanted was to relieve it of the Veronese salami, to which it seemed he had taken a fancy before he left the inn. Karl had to unpack it, but the Frenchman grabbed it and, with a knife somewhat like a dagger, sliced it up and ate almost the whole of it himself. Robinson got only a piece now and then and Karl, who had been forced to carry the box again, seeing that he did not want to leave it standing on the road, got nothing at all, as if he had had his share beforehand. It seemed too silly to beg for a piece, but he began to feel bitter.

The mist had already vanished; in the distance gleamed a high mountain, which receded in wave-like ridges towards a still more distant summit, veiled in a sunlit haze. By the side of the road were badly tilled fields clustered round big factories which rose up blackened with smoke in the open country. Isolated blocks of tenements were set down at random, and their countless windows quivered with manifold movement and light, while on all the flimsy little balconies women and children were busy in numberless ways, half concealed and half revealed by washing of all kinds, hung up or spread out to dry, which fluttered around them in the morning wind and billowed mightily. If one's eyes strayed from the houses one saw larks high in the heavens and lower down the swallows, darting not very far above the heads of the wayfarers.

There was much that reminded Karl of his home, and he could not decide whether he was doing well in leaving New York and going into the interior. New York had the sea, which meant the opportunity to return at any moment to his own country. And so he came to a standstill and said to his two companions that he felt like going back to New York after all. And when Delamarche simply made as if to drive him on, he refused to be driven and protested that it was his business to decide for himself. The Irishman had to intervene and explain that Butterford was a much finer place than New York, and both had to coax him insistently for a while before he would go on again. And even then he would not have consented had he not told himself that it would probably be better for him to reach a place where it would not be so easy to think of returning home. He would certainly work and push his fortune all the better there, if he were not hindered by idle thoughts of home.

And now it was he who led the two others, and they were so delighted by his enthusiasm that, without even being asked, they carried the box in turns and Karl simply could not make out in what way he had caused them such happiness. They now came to rising country, and when they stopped here and there they could see on looking back the panorama of New York and its harbour, extending more and more spaciously below them. The bridge connecting New York with Brooklyn hung delicately over the East River, and if one half-shut one's eyes it seemed to tremble. It appeared to be quite bare of traffic, and beneath it stretched a smooth empty tongue of water. Both the huge cities seemed to stand there empty and purposeless. As for the houses, it was scarcely possible to distinguish the large ones from the small. In the invisible depths of the streets life probably went on after its own fashion, but above them nothing was discernible save a light fume, which though it never moved seemed the easiest thing in the world to dispel. Even to the harbour, the greatest in the world, peace had returned, and only now and then, probably influenced by some memory of an earlier view close at hand, did one fancy that one saw a ship cutting the water for a little distance. But one could not follow it for long; it escaped one's eyes and was no more to be found.

Delamarche and Robinson clearly saw much more; they pointed to right and left and their outstretched hands gestured over squares and gardens which they named by their names. They could not understand how Karl could stay for two months in New York and yet see hardly anything of the city but one street. And they promised, when they had made enough money in Butterford, to take him to New York with them and show him all the sights worth seeing, above all, of course, the places where you could enjoy yourself to your heart's content. Thinking that, Robinson began to sing at the top of his voice a song which Delamarche accompanied by clapping his hands; Karl recognized it as an operatic melody of his own country, which pleased him more in the English version than it had ever pleased him at home. So there followed a little open-air concert, in which all took part; though the city at their feet, which was supposed to enjoy that melody so much, remained apparently indifferent.

Once Karl asked where Jacob's Despatch Agency lay, and Delamarche and Robinson at once stabbed the air with their forefingers, indicating perhaps the same point and perhaps points miles asunder. When they went on again, Karl asked how soon they would be able to return to New York if they got good jobs? Delamarche said they could easily do it in a month, for there was a scarcity of labour in Butterford and wages were high. Of course they would put their money into a common fund, so that chance differences in their earnings might be equalized as among friends. The common fund did not appeal to Karl, although as an apprentice he would naturally earn less than a skilled worker. In any case, Robinson went on, if there was no work in Butterford they would of course have to wander farther and either get jobs as workers on the land, or perhaps try panning for gold in California, which, to judge from Robinson's circumstantial tales, was the plan that appealed to him most.

'But why did you turn mechanic if you want to go looking

for gold?' asked Karl, who was reluctant to admit the necessity for more distant and uncertain journeys.

'Why a mechanic?' said Robinson. 'Certainly not to let my mother's son die of hunger. There's big money in the gold-fields.'

'Was at one time,' said Delamarche.

'Still is,' said Robinson, and he told of countless people he knew who had grown rich there, who were still there, but of course did not need to lift a finger now, yet for old friendship's sake would help him to wealth and any friends of his too, naturally.

'We'll squeeze jobs out of Butterford all right,' said Delamarche, and in saying this he uttered Karl's dearest wish; yet it could hardly be called a confident statement.

During the day they stopped only once at an eating-house, and in front of it in the open air, at a table which to Karl's eyes seemed to be made of iron, ate almost raw flesh which could not be cut but only hacked with their knives and forks. The bread was baked in a cylindrical shape and in each of the loaves was stuck a long knife. With this meal a black liquor was supplied, which burnt one's throat. But Delamarche and Robinson liked it; they kept raising their glasses to the fulfilment of various toasts, clinking them together high in the air for a minute at a time. At a neighbouring table workmen in lime-stained blouses were sitting, all drinking the same liquor. Cars passing in great numbers flung swathes of dust over the table. Enormous newspapers were being handed round and there was excited talk of a strike among the building workers: the name Mack was often mentioned. Karl inquired regarding him and learned that he was the father of the Mack he knew, and the greatest building contractor in New York. The strike was supposed to be costing him millions and possibly endangering his financial position. Karl did not believe a word of what was said by these badly informed and spiteful people.

The meal was spoiled even more for Karl by the doubt in his mind how it was going to be paid for. The natural thing would have been for each to pay his shot, but both Delamarche and

Robinson casually remarked that the price of their last night's lodging had emptied their pockets. Watch, ring or anything else that could be sold, was to be seen on neither of them. And Karl could hardly point out that they had lined their pockets over the sale of his suit; that would be an insult, and good-bye for ever. But the astonishing thing was that neither Delamarche nor Robinson bothered themselves about the payment; on the contrary they were in such good spirits that they kept trying to make up to the waitress, who moved with heavy stateliness from table to table. Her hair was loosened at the sides and tumbled over her brow and cheeks; she kept putting it back by pushing it up with her hand. At last, just when they thought they were going to get a friendly word from her, she came up to their table, planted both hands on it and asked: 'Who is paying?' Never did hands shoot out more quickly than those of Delamarche and Robinson as they pointed at Karl. Karl was not taken aback, for he had foreseen this, and he saw no harm in paying a trifling bill for his comrades, from whom he expected assistance in turn, although it would certainly have been more decent of them to discuss the matter frankly before the crucial moment. All that troubled him was that he would first have to fish the money out of the secret pocket. His original intention had been to save up his money in case of extreme need and for the time being to put himself, as it were, on a level with his friends. The advantage which he held over them through possessing that money and above all through concealing it was easily outweighed by the fact that they had lived in America since their childhood, that they had ample skill and experience for wage-earning, and finally that they were not accustomed to anything better than their present circumstances. Karl's original intention to save his money, then, need not be affected by his paying the bill now, since after all he could spare a quarter of a dollar; he could simply lay a quarter on the table and tell them that that was all he had, and that he was willing to part with it to get them all to Butterford. For a journey on foot a quarter should be ample. But he did not know whether he had enough small change, and anyhow his change was beside the wad of banknotes in the recesses of his secret pocket, where it was difficult to get hold of anything without emptying the whole lot on to the table. Besides, it was quite unnecessary for his companions to know anything about the secret pocket at all. By good luck, however, his friends seemed to be much more interested in the waitress than in how Karl was to produce the money for the bill. Delamarche, under cover of asking her to make out the bill, had lured her in between himself and Robinson, and the only way in which she could repel their familiarities was by pushing their faces away with the flat of her hand. Meantime, sweating with the effort, Karl gathered in one hand under the table the money he felt for and extracted, coin by coin, from the secret pocket with the other. At long last, although he was not yet familiar with American money, he judged that he had enough small coins to make up the sum and laid them all on the table. The clink of money at once put an end to all by-play. To Karl's annoyance and to the general surprise it turned out that almost a whole dollar was lying there. No one asked why Karl had said nothing about this money, which would have been sufficient for a comfortable railway journey to Butterford; yet Karl felt deeply embarrassed all the same. After paying the bill, he slowly pocketed the coins again, but from his very fingers Delamarche snatched one of them, as a special tip for the waitress, whom he embraced ardently with one hand while giving her the coin with the other.

Karl felt grateful to them for not saying anything about his money as they walked away together, and for a while he actually considered confessing his whole wealth to them, but then refrained, as he could not find a suitable opportunity. Towards evening they came to a more rustic, fertile neighbourhood. All around they could see endless fields stretching across gentle hills in their first green; rich country villas bordered the road on either side, and for hours they walked between gilded garden railings; several times they crossed the same slow stream, and often they heard above them trains thundering over the lofty viaducts.

The sun was just setting behind the level edge of distant

woods when they mounted a gentle rise crowned with a clump of trees and flung themselves on the grass so as to rest from their travels. Delamarche and Robinson lay flat and stretched themselves mightily. Karl sat up and gazed at the road a few yards below, on which motor-cars flew lightly past one another as they had done the whole day, as if a certain number of them were always being despatched from some distant place and the same number were being awaited in another place equally distant. During the whole day since early morning Karl had seen not a single car stopping, not a single passenger getting out.

Robinson proposed that they should spend the night here, since they were all very tired and would be able to start all the earlier in the morning; besides, they would scarcely find a cheaper and more suitable place to spend the night before complete darkness fell. Delamarche was of the same mind, but Karl felt obliged to remark that he had enough money to pay for a night's lodgings for them all in some hotel. Delamarche replied that they might still need the money; better to save it for the present. He made no concealment of the fact that they were counting on Karl's money. As his first proposal had been accepted, Robinson went on to suggest that before going to sleep they should have a good meal to strengthen them up for the morning, and that one of them should fetch food for all three from the hotel close by on the main road, which bore the lighted sign: 'Hotel Occidental'. As he was the youngest and nobody else offered to go, Karl had no hesitation in volunteering for the job, and after the others had announced that they wanted bacon, bread and beer, he went across to the hotel.

It seemed that they must be near a big town, for the very first room of the hotel that Karl entered was filled with a noisy crowd, and at the buffet, which ran along the whole length and two sides of the room, a host of waiters with white aprons kept rushing about yet could not satisfy their impatient customers, for loud cursing and the pounding of fists on tables sounded unceasingly from all quarters. No one paid any attention to Karl; in the body of the saloon itself there was no service; the customers, crowded at tiny tables scarcely big enough for three people, had to fetch everything they wanted from the buffet. On each table stood a big bottle of oil, vinegar or something of the kind, and all the food that was brought from the buffet was liberally dosed from the bottle before being eaten. If Karl was to reach the buffet at all, where his real difficulties would probably begin because of the huge crowd standing at it, he would have to squeeze his way between the countless tables, and this of course, in spite of every care, could not be done without rudely disturbing the customers, who, however, accepted every inconvenience apathetically, even when Karl cannoned violently into a table – through no fault of his own, certainly – and almost knocked it over. He apologized, but obviously without being understood; nor could he for his part make out any of the remarks that were shouted at him.

At the buffet he found with difficulty a few inches of free space, where his view was obscured for a long time by the elbows of the men standing on either side of him. It seemed a universal custom here to plant your elbow on the counter and rest your head on your hand. Karl could not help remembering how his Latin teacher Doctor Krumpal had hated that posture, and how he would steal up silently and unexpectedly and knock your elbow off the desk with a playful rap of a ruler which suddenly appeared from nowhere.

Karl was squeezed close against the counter, for scarcely had he reached it when a table was set up behind him, and a wide hat kept brushing against his back whenever the customer sitting there leaned backwards a little in talking. Also there seemed to be little hope of his getting anything out of the waiters, even after his two unmannerly neighbours had gone away satisfied. Once or twice Karl snatched at a waiter's apron across the counter, but the waiter always tore himself away with a grimace. Not one of them would stop; they did nothing but rush to and fro. If there had even been anything suitable to eat near at hand Karl would have grabbed it, inquired what the price was, laid down the money and taken himself off with relief. But in front of him there were only dishes of fish which looked like herring, with dark scales gleaming golden at the edges. They might be very dear and would probably sate nobody's hunger. There were also small casks of rum within reach, but he did not want to bring his friends rum; as it was, whenever they had the chance they seemed to drink only concentrated alcohol, and he had no wish to encourage them in that.

So nothing remained for Karl but to find another point of vantage and start all over again. But by now the hour had considerably advanced. The clock at the other end of the room, whose hands could still just be discerned through the smoke if one looked very intently, showed that it was after nine. Yet the rest of the counter was even more crowded than the first place he had found, which was in a retired corner. Also the room was filling up more and more, as the evening went on. New customers kept pushing through the main door with loud halloos. At several places customers had autocratically cleared the counter and seated themselves upon it and were drinking to one another; that was the best position of all, you could overlook the whole room.

Karl still pressed forward, but any real hope of achieving anything had vanished. He blamed himself for having volunteered to run this errand without knowing anything of the local conditions. His friends would swear at him, with perfect right, and might perhaps even think that he had brought nothing back simply in order to save his money. He had now reached a part of the room where hot meat-dishes and fine yellow potatoes were being devoured at all the tables; it was incomprehensible to him how the customers had got hold of them.

Then a few steps in front of him he saw an elderly woman who clearly belonged to the hotel staff and was talking and laughing with a customer. As she talked she kept poking at her hair with a hair-pin. Karl at once decided to confide his wants to this woman, mainly because as the only woman in the room she stood out as an exception in the general hubbub, and also for the simple reason that she was the only hotel employee he could get hold of, that is to say, if she did not rush away on her own business at the first word he addressed to her. But quite the opposite happened. Karl had not even spoken to her, he had only dodged round her for a little while, when, as often happens in the middle of a conversation, she looked aside and caught sight of him and, interrupting what she was saying, asked him kindly and in English as clear as the grammar-book if he wanted anything.

'Yes, indeed,' said Karl, 'I can't get a single thing anywhere in this place.'

'Then come with me, my boy,' she said, and she said goodbye to her acquaintance, who raised his hat, which in this room seemed an incredible mark of politeness; then taking Karl by the hand she went up to the counter, pushed a customer aside, lifted a flap-door, went along a passage behind the counter, where they had to side-step the tirelessly rushing waiters, and opened a double door concealed in the wall, which led straight into a large, cool store-room. 'You have to know the workings of these places,' Karl said to himself.

'Well now, what do you want?' she asked, bending down to him kindly. She was very fat, so that her body quivered, but by comparison her face was almost delicately modelled. Karl felt almost tempted, gazing at the great variety of eatables neatly set out on shelves and tables, to invent a more elegant supper on the spur of the moment in order that instead, especially as he might get it more cheaply from this influential lady; but in the end he mentioned nothing but bacon, bread and beer after all, as he could not think of anything more suitable.

'Nothing more?' asked the woman.

'No, thanks,' said Karl, 'but enough for three people.'

When the woman inquired who the two others were, Karl told her in a few brief words about his companions; he felt glad to be asked some questions.

'But that's prison fare,' said the woman, obviously expecting Karl to order something else. But Karl was now afraid that she might bestow the food on him as a gift and refuse to accept any money and so he kept silent. 'That won't take long to get ready,' said the woman, and she walked over to a table with an agility wonderful in one so fat, cut with a long, thin, saw-edged knife a great piece of bacon richly streaked with lean, took a loaf from a shelf, lifted three bottles of beer from the floor, and put them in a light straw basket, which she handed to Karl. As she was doing this she explained to him that she had brought him here because the food in the buffet, though it was quickly replenished, always lost its freshness in the smoke and all the steam. Still, for the people out there anything was good enough. This struck Karl quite dumb, for he could not see how he had earned such special treatment. He thought of his companions who, in spite of all their American experience, would probably never have reached this store-room, but would have had to be content with the stale food in the buffet. No sound from the saloon could be heard here; the walls must be very thick to keep this vaulted chamber so cool. Karl had already been holding the straw basket in his hand for some time, yet he thought neither of paying nor of going away. Not until the woman made to put in the basket, as an extra, a bottle similar to those standing on the table outside, did he make a move, refusing it with a shiver.

'Have you much farther to go?' asked the woman.

'To Butterford,' replied Karl.

'That's a long way still,' said the woman.

'Another day's journey,' said Karl.

'Isn't it more than that?' asked the woman.

'Oh no,' said Karl.

The woman rearranged some things on the tables; a waiter came in, looked round interrogatively, and was directed by her to a huge platter, on which lay a large heap of sardines lightly strewn with parsley, which he then bore in his raised hands into the saloon.

'Why should you spend the night in the open air?' asked the woman. 'We have room enough here. Come and sleep here with us in the hotel.'

The thought was very tempting to Karl, particularly as he had slept so badly the previous night.

'I have my luggage out there,' he said hesitatingly and not without a certain pride.

'Then just bring it here,' said the woman, 'that's no hindrance.'

'But what about my friends?' said Karl, realizing at once that they were certainly a hindrance.

'They can spend the night here too, of course,' said the woman. 'Do come! Don't be so difficult.'

'My friends are first-rate comrades,' said Karl, 'but they're not exactly clean.'

'Haven't you seen the dirt in the saloon?' asked the woman with a grimace. 'We can well take in the hardest cases. All right, I'll have three beds got ready at once. Only in an attic, I'm afraid, for the hotel is full; I've had to move into an attic myself, but at any rate it's better than sleeping out.'

'I can't bring my friends here,' said Karl. He pictured to himself the row the two of them would make in the passages of this fine hotel; Robinson would dirty everything and Delamarche would not fail to molest the woman herself.

'I don't see why that should be impossible,' she said, 'but if you insist on it, then leave your friends behind and come without them.'

'That wouldn't do,' said Karl. 'They're my friends and I must stick to them.'

'You're very obstinate,' said the woman, turning her eyes away, 'when people mean well by you and try to do you a good turn, you do your best to hinder them.' Karl realized all this, but he saw no way out, so he merely said: 'My best thanks to you for your kindness.' Then he remembered that he had not paid her yet, and he asked what he owed.

'You can pay me when you bring the basket back,' said the woman. 'I must have it tomorrow morning at the latest.'

'Thank you,' said Karl. She opened a door which led straight into the open air and said, as he stepped out with a bow: 'Good night. But you're not doing the right thing.' He was already a few yards away when she cried after him again: 'Till tomorrow morning!'

Hardly was he outside when he heard again the undiminished roar of the saloon, with which was now mingled the blare of wind instruments. He was glad that he had not to go out through the saloon. All five doors of the hotel were now illuminated and made the road in front of it bright from one side to the other. Automobiles were still careering along the road, although more intermittently, looming into sight more rapidly than by day, feeling for the road before them with the white beams of their headlights, which paled as they crossed the lighted zone of the hotel only to blaze out again as they rushed into the farther darkness.

Karl found his friends sleeping soundly; but then he had been far too long away. He was just preparing to set out temptingly on paper the food he had brought, making all ready before waking his companions, when to his horror he saw his box, which he had left securely locked and whose key he had in his pocket, standing wide open and half its contents scattered about on the grass.

'Get up!' he cried. 'There have been thieves here, and you lying sleeping!'

'Why, is anything missing?' asked Delamarche. Robinson was not quite awake, yet his hand was already reaching towards the beer.

'I don't know,' cried Karl, 'but the box is open. It was very careless of you to go to sleep and leave the box here at anybody's mercy.'

Delamarche and Robinson laughed, and Delamarche said: 'Then you'd better not stay away so long next time. It's only a step or two to the hotel and yet you take three hours to go there and come back. We were hungry, we thought that you might have something to eat in your box, so we just tickled the lock until it opened. But there was nothing in it after all and your stuff can easily go back again.'

'I see,' said Karl, staring at the quickly emptying basket and listening to the curious noise which Robinson made in drinking, for the beer seemed first to plunge right down into his throat and gurgle up again with a sort of whistle before finally pouring its flood into the deep.

'Have you had enough now?' he asked, when the two of them paused to take a breath for a moment.

'Why, didn't you have your supper in the hotel?' asked Delamarche, who thought that Karl was putting in a claim for his share.

'If you want any more, then hurry up,' said Karl, going over to his box.

'He seems to be in a huff,' said Delamarche to Robinson.

'I'm not in a huff,' said Karl, 'but do you think it's right to break open my box and fling out my things while I'm away? I know that one must put up with a lot from friends and I've been prepared to do that; but this is too much. I'm going to spend the night in the hotel, and I'm not going with you to Butterford. Finish your supper quickly; I've got to take back the basket.'

'Just listen to him, Robinson,' said Delamarche. 'That's a fine way of talking. He's a German all right. You did warn me against him at the beginning, but I'm a kind-hearted fool and so I let him come with us all the same. We've given him our confidence, we've dragged him with us all day and lost half a day at least on his account, and now – just because he's chummed up with somebody at the hotel – he gives us the go-by, simply gives us the go-by. But because he's a lying German he doesn't do it frankly but makes his box a pretext, and being an ill-mannered German he can't leave us without insulting our honour and calling us thieves, just because we had a little fun with his box.'

Karl, who was packing his things, said without turning round: 'The more you say, the easier you make it for me to leave you. I know quite well what friendship is. I have had friends in Europe too and none of them can accuse me of ever behaving falsely or meanly to him. I'm not in touch with them now, naturally, but if I ever go back to Europe again they'll all be glad to see me, and they'll welcome me at once as a friend. As for you, Delamarche and Robinson, I'm supposed to have betrayed you, am I, after you were so kind – and I'll never forget that – as to let me join up with you and have a chance of an apprentice's job in Butterford? But that isn't how it is at all. I think none the less of you because you own nothing, but you grudge me my few possessions and try to humiliate me because of them, and that I cannot endure. And you break open my box and offer no word of excuse, but abuse me instead and my people as well – and that simply makes it impossible for me to stay with you. All the same, this doesn't really apply to you, Robinson. I have nothing against you except that you are far too dependent on Delamarche.'

'So now we see,' said Delamarche, stepping over to Karl and giving him a slight push, as if to insist on his attention, 'so now we see you at last in your true colours. All day you've trotted behind me, hanging on to my coat-tails and doing whatever I did and keeping as quiet as a mouse. But now that somebody in the hotel's backing you up, you begin to throw your weight about. You're a little twister, and I'm not so sure that we're going to put up with that kind of thing. I'm not sure that we aren't going to make you pay for what you've learned by watching us today. We envy him, Robinson – envy him, says he – because of his possessions. One day's work in Butterford – not to mention California – and we'll have ten times as much as anything you've shown us yet, or anything you've got hidden in the lining of that coat. So keep your tongue quiet!'

Karl had risen from his box and saw Robinson also advancing upon him, still sleepy but a little enlivened by the beer. 'If I stay here longer,' he said, 'I'll maybe get some more surprises. It seems to me you want to beat me up.'

'Nobody's patience lasts for ever,' said Robinson.

'You'd better keep out of it, Robinson,' said Karl, without taking his eyes from Delamarche, 'in your heart you know that I'm right, but you've got to make a show of agreeing with Delamarche!'

'Are you maybe thinking of bribing him?' asked Delamarche.

'Never occurred to me,' said Karl. 'I'm glad to be going and

I want to have nothing more to do with either of you. There's only one thing more I want to say: you have reproached me for having money and concealing it from you. Granted that's true, wasn't it the right thing to do with people that I had known only for a few hours, and isn't the way you're carrying on now a proof of how right I was?'

'Keep quiet,' said Delamarche to Robinson, though Robinson had not moved. Then he said to Karl: 'Seeing that you're making such a parade of honesty, why not stretch your honesty a little farther, now that we're having a friendly heart-to-heart, and tell us why you really want to go to the hotel?' Karl had to take a step back over the box, Delamarche had pushed up so close to him. But Delamarche was not to be deflected, he kicked the box aside, took another step forward, planting his foot on a white dickey that had been left lying on the grass and repeated his question.

As if in answer a man with a powerful flash-lamp climbed up from the road towards the group. It was one of the waiters from the hotel. As soon as he caught sight of Karl he said: 'I've been looking for you for nearly half an hour. I've been hunting through all the bushes on both sides of the road. The Manageress sent me to tell you that she needs that straw basket she lent you.'

'Here it is,' said Karl in a voice trembling with agitation. Delamarche and Robinson had drawn aside in pretended humility, as they always did when decent-looking strangers appeared. The waiter picked up the basket and said: 'The Manageress also told me to ask you whether you haven't changed your mind and would like to sleep in the hotel after all. The other two gentlemen would be welcome too, if you care to bring them with you. The beds are all ready for you. It's warm enough tonight, but it's far from safe to sleep in this place; you often come across snakes.'

'Since the Manageress is so kind, I'll accept her invitation after all,' said Karl, and waited for his companions to say something. But Robinson stood there quite dumb and Delamarche was looking up at the stars with his hands in his trousers pockets. Both were obviously expecting Karl to take them with him without further ado.

'In that case,' said the waiter, 'I have orders to take you to the hotel and carry your luggage there.'

'Then please just wait a moment,' said Karl, bending down to put in his box a few things which were still lying about.

Suddenly he straightened himself. The photograph, which had been lying on the very top, was missing and nowhere to be found. Everything else was there, except the photograph. 'I can't find the photograph,' he said to Delamarche imploringly.

'What photograph?' asked Delamarche.

'The photograph of my parents,' said Karl.

'We haven't seen any photograph in the box, Mr Rossmann,' said Robinson.

'But that's quite impossible,' said Karl, and his beseeching glances brought the waiter nearer. 'It was lying on the top and now it's gone. I do wish you hadn't played about with my box.'

'We're not making any mistake,' said Delamarche, 'there was no photograph in the box.'

'It was more important to me than all the other things in the box,' said Karl to the waiter, who was walking about looking in the grass. 'For it's irreplaceable; I can't get another one.' And when the waiter gave up the hopeless search, Karl added: 'It was the only photograph of my parents that I possessed.'

Then the waiter said aloud, without any attempt to mitigate the words: 'Maybe we could run through these gentlemen's pockets.'

'Yes,' said Karl at once, 'I must find the photograph. But before searching their pockets, let me say this, that whoever gives me the photograph of his own accord can have my box and everything in it.' After a moment of general silence Karl said to the waiter: 'It seems my friends prefer to have their pockets searched. But even now I promise the box and everything in it to anyone in whose pocket the photograph is found. More I can't do.'

The waiter immediately set about searching Delamarche, who seemed to him more difficult to handle than Robinson, whom he left to Karl. He impressed upon Karl they they must both be searched simultaneously, otherwise one of them might get rid of the photograph unobserved. As soon as he put his hand into Robinson's pocket, Karl found a scarf belonging to himself, but he refrained from taking it and called to the waiter: 'Whatever you find on Delamarche, let him keep it. I want nothing but the photograph, only the photograph.'

In searching the breast pocket of Robinson's coat Karl's hand came in contact with the man's hot, flabby chest and he became aware that he might be doing his companion a great injustice. That made him hurry as fast as he could. But all was in vain; no photograph was to be found either on Robinson or on Delamarche.

'It's no good,' said the waiter.

'They've probably torn up the photograph and flung the pieces away,' said Karl. 'I thought they were friends, but in their hearts they only wished me ill. Not so much Robinson; it would never have occurred to him that I set such store on the photograph; that's more like Delamarche.' Karl could now see only the waiter, whose flash-lamp lit up a tiny circle, while everything else, including Delamarche and Robinson, lay in deep darkness.

There was naturally no question now of the two men going to the hotel with Karl. The waiter swung the box on to his shoulder, Karl picked up the straw basket, and they set off. Karl had already reached the road when, starting out of his thoughts, he stopped and shouted up into the darkness: 'Listen to me. If either of you has the photograph and will bring it to me at the hotel, he can still have the box, and I swear that I won't make any charge against him.' No actual answer came, only a stifled word could be heard, the beginning of a shout from Robinson, whose mouth was obviously stopped at once by Delamarche. Karl waited for a long time, in case the men above him might change their minds. He shouted twice, at intervals: 'I'm still here!'

But no sound came in reply, except that a stone rolled down the slope, perhaps a chance stone, perhaps a badly aimed throw.

5

THE HOTEL OCCIDENTAL

On reaching the hotel Karl was at once conducted to a sort of office, in which the Manageress, with a notebook in her hand, was dictating a letter to a young stenographer sitting at a typewriter. The consummately precise dictation, the controlled and buoyant tapping of the keys raced on to the ticking, noticeable only now and then, of a clock standing against the wall, whose hands pointed to almost half-past eleven. 'There!' said the Manageress, shutting the notebook; the stenographer jumped up and put the lid on the typewriter without taking her eyes from Karl during these mechanical actions. She looked like a schoolgirl still, her overall was neatly ironed, even pleated at the shoulders; her hair was piled up high; and it was a little surprising, after noting these details, to see the gravity of her face. After making a bow, first to the Manageress, then to Karl, she left the room and Karl involuntarily flung a questioning glance at the Manageress.

'It's splendid that you've come after all,' said the Manageress. 'And what about your friends?'

'I haven't brought them with me,' said Karl.

'They'll be moving on very early in the morning, I suppose,' said the Manageress, as if to explain the matter to herself.

'But mustn't she think in that case that I'll have to start early too?' Karl asked himself, and so he said to put an end to all misunderstanding: 'We parted on bad terms.'

The Manageress seemed to construe this as excellent news. 'So then you're free?' she said.

'Yes, I'm free,' said Karl, and nothing seemed more worthless than his freedom.

'Listen, wouldn't you like to take a job here in the hotel?' asked the Manageress.

'Very much,' said Karl, 'but I have terribly little experience. For instance, I can't even use a typewriter.'

'That's not very important,' said the Manageress. 'You'd be given only a small job to begin with, and it would be your business to work your way up by diligence and attentiveness. But in any case I think it would be better and wiser for you to settle down somewhere, instead of wandering about like this. I don't think you're made for that kind of thing.'

'My uncle would subscribe to that too,' Karl told himself, nodding in agreement. At the same time he reminded himself that though the Manageress had shown such concern for him, he had not yet introduced himself. 'Please forgive me,' he said, 'for not having introduced myself before. My name is Karl Rossmann.'

'You're a German, aren't you?'

'Yes,' said Karl, 'I haven't been long in America.'

'Where do you come from?'

'From Prague, in Bohemia,' said Karl.

'Just think of that!' cried the Manageress in English with a strong German inflection, almost flinging her hands in the air. 'Then we're compatriots, for my name is Grete Mitzelbach and I come from Vienna. And I know Prague quite well; I worked for half a year in the "Golden Goose" in Wenceslaus Square. Only think of that!'

'When was that?' asked Karl.

'Many, many years ago now.'

'The old "Golden Goose",' said Karl, 'was pulled down two years ago.'

'Well, well,' said the Manageress, quite absorbed in her thoughts of past days.

But all at once, becoming animated again, she seized both Karl's hands and cried: 'Now that you turn out to be a countryman of mine, you mustn't go away on any account. You mustn't offend me by doing that. How would you like, for instance, to be a lift-boy? Just say the word and it's done. If you've seen something of this country, you'll realize that it isn't very easy to get such posts, for they're the best start in life that you can think of. You come in contact with all the hotel guests, people are always seeing you and giving you little errands to do; in short, every day you have the chance to better yourself. I'll fix everything up for you; leave it to me.'

'I should like quite well to be a lift-boy,' said Karl after a slight pause. It would be very foolish to have any scruples about accepting a post as lift-boy because of his High School education. Here in America he had much more cause to be ashamed of his High School. Besides, Karl had always admired lift-boys; he thought them very ornamental.

'Isn't a knowledge of languages required?' he asked next.

'You speak German and perfectly good English; that's quite enough.'

'I've learned English only in the last two and a half months in America,' said Karl, for he thought he had better not conceal his one merit. 'That's a sufficient recommendation in itself,' said the Manageress. 'When I think of the difficulties I had with my English! Of course, that's thirty years ago now. I was talking about it only yesterday. For yesterday was my fiftieth birthday.' And she smilingly tried to read in Karl's face the impression which such a dignified age made upon him.

'Then I wish you much happiness,' said Karl.

'Well, it always comes in useful,' said she, shaking Karl's hand and looking a little melancholy over the old German phrase which had come quite naturally to the tip of her tongue.

'But I am keeping you here,' she cried all at once. 'And you must be tired, and we can talk over everything much better tomorrow. My pleasure in meeting a countryman has made me forget everything else. Come, I'll show you your room.'

'I have one more favour to beg,' said Karl, glancing at the telephone which stood on the table. 'It's possible that tomorrow morning these one-time friends of mine may bring me a photograph which I urgently need. Would you be so kind as to telephone to the porter to send the men up to me, or else call me down?'

'Certainly,' said the Manageress, 'but wouldn't it do if they gave him the photograph? What photograph is it, if I may ask?'

'It's a photograph of my parents,' said Karl. 'No, I must speak to the men myself.' The Manageress said nothing further and telephoned the order to the porter's office, giving 536 as the number of Karl's room.

They went through a door facing the entrance door and along a short passage, where a small lift-boy was leaning against the railing of a lift, fast asleep. 'We can work it ourselves,' said the Manageress softly, ushering Karl into the lift. 'A working day of from ten to twelve hours is really rather much for a boy like that,' she added, while they ascended. 'But America's a strange country. Take this boy, for instance; he came here only half a year ago with his parents; he's an Italian. At the moment it looks as if he simply wouldn't be able to stand the work, his face has fallen away to nothing and he goes to sleep on the job, although he's naturally a very willing lad – but let him only go on working here or anywhere else in America for another six months and he'll be able to take it all in his stride, and in another five years he'll be a strong man. I could spend hours telling you about such cases. You're not one of them, for you're a strong lad already; you're seventeen, aren't you?'

'I'll be sixteen next month,' replied Karl.

'Not even sixteen!' said the Manageress. 'Then you don't need to worry!'

At the top of the building she led Karl to a room which, being a garret, had a sloping wall, but was lit by two electric lamps and looked most inviting. 'Don't be surprised at the furnishings,' said the Manageress, 'for this isn't a hotel room, but one of my rooms; I have three of them, so that you won't disturb me in the least. I'll lock the connecting doors and you'll be quite private. Tomorrow, as a new hotel employee, you will of course be given your own room. If your friends had come with you, I would have put you all in the large attic where the hotel servants sleep; but as you are alone I think you would be better here, though you'll have nothing but a sofa to lie on. And now sleep well and gather strength for your work. Tomorrow it won't be so very hard.'

'Thank you very much indeed for your kindness.'

'Wait,' she said, stopping by the door, 'I'll have to keep you from being wakened up too early.' And she went to a side door opening out of the room, knocked on it and cried: 'Therese!'

'Yes, madam,' replied the voice of the typist.

'When you waken me in the morning go round by the passage; there's a guest sleeping in this room. He's dead tired.' She smiled at Karl while saying this. 'Do you understand?'

'Yes, madam.'

'Well then, good night.'

'Good night.'

'I have slept,' said the Manageress in explanation, 'very badly for several years. I have every right to be satisfied with my present position and don't really need to worry. But all my earlier worries must be taking it out of me now and keeping me from sleeping. If I fall asleep by three in the morning, I can count myself lucky. But as I have to be at my post by five, or half-past five at the latest, I have to be wakened and very gently wakened, to prevent me from turning more nervous than I am already. And so Therese wakens me. But now I've really told you everything there is to tell and I'm not away yet. Good night.' And in spite of her bulk she almost flitted out of the room.

Karl was looking forward to his sleep, for the day had taken a great deal out of him. And more comfortable quarters for a long, unbroken sleep he could not wish for. The room was certainly not intended for a bedroom, it was rather the Manageress's living-room, or more exactly reception-room, and a wash-stand had been specially put in it for his use that night; yet he did not feel like an intruder, but only that he was being well looked after. His box was there all right, waiting for him, and certainly had not been so safe for a long time. On a low chest of drawers, over which a large-meshed woollen cover had been flung, several framed photographs were standing; in making his round of the room Karl stopped to look at them. They were nearly all old photographs, mostly of girls in old-fashioned, uncomfortable clothes, a small, high-crowned hat insecurely perched on each head and the right hand resting on the handle of a sun-shade; girls who stood facing the spectator and yet refused to meet his eyes. Among the photographs of the men Karl was particularly struck by a young soldier who had laid his cap on a table and was standing erect with a thatch of wild, black hair and a look of suppressed but arrogant amusement. Someone had retouched the buttons of his uniform with dots of gold paint. All these photographs probably came from Europe, and by turning them over it would be possible to make sure, yet Karl did not want to lay a finger upon them. He would have liked to set up the photograph of his parents in the room he was going to have, just like these photographs here.

He was just stretching himself on the sofa and looking forward to his sleep after washing himself thoroughly from head to foot, which he had taken care to do as quietly as possible on account of the girl next door, when he thought he heard a low knock at a door. He could not make out at once which door it was; it might well have been only some random noise. Nor was it repeated at once, and he was half asleep by the time it came again. But now it was unmistakably a knock and it came from the door of the typist's room. Karl tiptoed to the door and asked so softly that, even if the girl in the next room were sleeping after all, it could not waken her: 'Do you want anything?'

At once the reply came in an equally soft voice: 'Won't you open the door? The key is on your side.'

'Certainly,' said Karl, 'only I must put on some clothes first.'

There was a slight pause, then the girl said: 'You don't need to do that. Unlock the door and go back to bed again; I'll wait for a little.'

'Good,' said Karl and did as she had suggested, except that

he switched on the electric light as well. 'I'm in bed now,' he said then, somewhat more loudly. Then the typist emerged from her dark room fully dressed as she had left the office; apparently she had not even thought of going to bed.

'Please excuse me,' she said, drooping a little before Karl's sofa, 'and please don't tell on me. And I won't disturb you for long; I know you're dead tired.'

'I'm not so tired as all that,' said Karl, 'but maybe it might have been better if I had put on some clothes.' He had to lie quite flat to keep himself covered to the neck, for he had no nightshirt.

'I'll only stay a minute,' she said, looking about for a chair. 'May I sit beside the sofa?' Karl nodded. She set her chair so close to the sofa that Karl had to squeeze against the wall to look up at her. She had a round, regularly formed face, except that the brow looked unusually high, but that might have been an effect of the way her hair was done, which did not quite suit her. Her dress was very clean and neat. In her left hand she was crushing a handkerchief.

'Are you going to stay here long?' she asked.

'It isn't quite settled yet,' replied Karl, 'but I think I'm going to stay.'

'That would be splendid,' she said, passing the handkerchief over her face, 'for I feel so lonely here.'

'I'm surprised at that,' said Karl. 'The Manageress is very kind to you, isn't she? She doesn't treat you like an employee at all. I actually thought you were a relation of hers.'

'Oh no,' she said, 'my name is Therese Berchtold; I come from Pomerania.'

Karl also introduced himself. At that, she looked him full in the face for the first time, as if he had become a little more strange to her by mentioning his name. They were both silent for a while. Then she said: 'You mustn't think that I'm ungrateful. If it weren't for the Manageress I'd be in a much worse state. I used to be a kitchen-maid here in the hotel and in great danger of being dismissed too, for I wasn't equal to the heavy work. They expect a lot from you here. A month ago a kitchen-maid simply fainted under the strain and had to lie up in hospital for fourteen days. And I'm not very strong, I was often ill as a child, and so I've been slow in catching up; you would never think, would you, that I'm eighteen? But I'm getting stronger now.'

'The work here must really be very tiring,' said Karl. 'I saw a lift-boy downstairs standing sleeping on his feet.'

'The lift-boys have the best of it, all the same,' she said. 'They make quite a lot in tips and in spite of that they don't have to work nearly so hard as the girls in the kitchen. But for once in my life I really was lucky, for one day the Manageress needed a girl to arrange the table-napkins for a banquet and she went down for a kitchen-maid; now there are about fifty kitchen-maids here and I just happened to be handy; well, I gave her great satisfaction, for I have always been very good at arranging table-napkins. And so from that day she kept me with her and trained me by stages till I became her secretary. And I've learned a great deal.'

'Is there so much writing to be done here, then?' asked Karl.

'Oh, a great deal,' she replied, 'more than you would imagine. You saw yourself that I was working up to half-past eleven tonight, and that's quite usual. Of course, I don't type all the time, for I do lots of errands in the town as well.'

'What's the name of this town?' asked Karl.

'Don't you know?' she said. 'Rameses.'

'Is it a big town?' asked Karl.

'Very big,' she replied. 'I don't enjoy visiting it. But wouldn't you really like to go to sleep now?'

'No, no,' said Karl, 'you haven't told me yet why you came to see me.'

'Because I have no one to talk to. I'm not complaining, but there's really no one, and it makes me happy to find someone at last who will let me talk. I saw you below in the saloon, I was just coming to fetch the Manageress when she took you off to the store-room.'

'That saloon is a terrible place,' said Karl.

'I don't even notice it these days,' she replied. 'But I only wanted to say that the Manageress is as kind to me as if she were my mother. Yet there's too great a difference between our positions for me to speak freely to her. I used to have good friends among the kitchen-maids, but they've all left here long ago and I scarcely know the new girls. And besides, it often seems to me that the work I'm doing now is a greater strain than what I did before, that I don't even do it so well as the other, and that the Manageress keeps me on merely out of charity. After all, it really needs a better education than I have had to be a secretary. It's a sin to say it, but often and often I feel it's driving me out of my mind. For God's sake,' she burst out, speaking much more rapidly and hastily touching Karl's shoulder, since he kept his hands below the blankets, 'don't tell the Manageress a word of this, or else I'm really done for. If besides worrying her by my work, I were to cause her actual pain as well, that would really be too much.'

'Of course I won't tell her anything,' replied Karl.

'Then that's all right,' she said, 'and you must go on staying here. I'd be glad if you would, and if you like we could be friends. As soon as I saw you, I felt I could trust you. And yet – you see how wicked I am – I was afraid too that the Manageress might make you her secretary in my place and dismiss me. It took me a long time, sitting by myself next door, while you were below in the office, to straighten it all out in my mind until I saw that it might actually be a very good thing if you were to take over my work, for you certainly would understand it better. If you didn't want to do the errands in the town, I could keep that job for myself. But apart from that, I would certainly be of much more use in the kitchen, especially as I'm stronger now than I used to be.'

'It's all settled already,' said Karl, 'I'm to be a lift-boy and you're to go on being secretary. But if you even hint at these plans of yours to the Manageress, I'll tell her all you've told me tonight, sorry as I would be to do it.'

Karl's tone alarmed Therese so greatly that she flung herself down beside the sofa, weeping and hiding her face in the bed-clothes.

'Oh, I shan't tell,' said Karl, 'but you mustn't say anything either.'

Now he could not help coming a little out from under his coverings, and stroked her arm softly, but he did not find the right words to say and could only reflect that this girl's life was a bitter one. Finally he comforted her so far that she grew ashamed of her weeping, looked at him gratefully, advised him to sleep long next morning, and promised, if she could find time, to come up at eight o'clock and waken him.

'You are so clever at wakening people,' said Karl.

'Yes, some things I can do,' she said, ran her hand softly over the bed-clothes in farewell, and rushed off to her room.

Next day Karl insisted on beginning work at once, although the Manageress wanted him to take the day off and have a look round the town. He told her frankly that he would have plenty of opportunities for sightseeing later, but that for the moment the most important thing for him was to make a start with his job, for he had already broken off one career in Europe to no purpose and was now beginning again as a lift-boy at an age when his contemporaries, if they were ambitious, had every expectation of being promoted to more responsible work. It was right and needful for him to begin as a lift-boy, but equally needful for him to advance with extra rapidity. In these circumstances he would take no pleasure at all in strolling idly through Rameses. He would not even consent to go for a short walk with Therese, when she suggested it. He could not rid his mind of the idea that if he did not work hard he might sink as low as Delamarche and Robinson.

The hotel tailor fitted him for a lift-boy's uniform, which was resplendent enough with gold buttons and gold braid, but made him shudder a little when he put it on, for under the arms particularly the short jacket was cold, stiff and incurably damp with the sweat of the many boys who had worn it before him. The jacket had to be altered for Karl, especially over the chest, since not one of the ten spare jackets would even meet upon him. Yet in spite of the stitching that needed to be done, and although the master-tailor seemed to be exacting in his standards – twice he pitched the uniform back into the workshop after it was apparently finished – the fitting was completed in barely five minutes, and Karl left the tailor's room already clad in closely fitting trousers and a jacket which, in spite of the master-tailor's categorical assurances to the contrary, was very tight indeed and tempted Karl to indulge in breathing exercises, for he wanted to see if it was still possible to breathe at all.

Then he reported to the Head Waiter, under whose direction he was to be, a slender, handsome man with a big nose, who might well have been in the forties. The Head Waiter had no time to exchange even a word with him and simply rang for a lift-boy, who chanced to be the very one that Karl had seen yesterday. The Head Waiter called him only by his first name, Giacomo, but it took Karl some time to identify the name, for in the English pronunciation it was unrecognizable. The boy was instructed to show Karl all the duties of a lift-boy, but he was so shy and hasty that, little as there was actually to be shown, Karl could scarcely make out that little from him. No doubt Giacomo was annoyed too because he had been removed from the lift service, apparently on Karl's account, and had been assigned to help the chamber-maids, which seemed degrading in his eyes because of certain experiences, which, however, he did not divulge. Karl's deepest disappointment was the discovery that a lift-boy had nothing to do with the machinery of the lift but to set it in motion by simply pressing a button, while all repairs were done exclusively by the mechanics belonging to the hotel; for example, in spite of half a year's service on the lift, Giacomo had never seen with his own eyes either the dynamo in the cellar or the inner mechanism of the lift, although, as he said himself, that would have delighted him. Indeed the work was monotonous, and the twelve-hours' shifts, alternately by day and night, were so exhausting that according to Giacomo one simply could not bear it if one did not sleep on one's feet for a few minutes now and then. Karl made no comment, but he was perfectly aware that that very trick had cost Giacomo his post.

Karl was very pleased that the lift he had to attend to was reserved for the upper floors, since he would not have to deal with the wealthy guests, who were the most exacting. Still, he would not learn so much as at the other lifts, and it was good only for a beginning.

After the very first week he realized that he was quite equal to the job. The brasswork in his lift was the most brightly polished of all; none of the thirty other lifts had anything to compare with it, and it might have been still brighter if the other boy who partnered him had come anywhere near him in thoroughness and had not felt confirmed in his negligence by Karl's strict attention to duty. He was a native American of the name of Rennell, a conceited youth with dark eyes and smooth, somewhat hollow cheeks. He had an elegant suit of his own which he wore on his free evenings, when he hurried off to the town faintly smelling of perfume; now and then he would even ask Karl to take his duty of an evening, saying that he had been called away on family business and paying little heed to the contradiction between such pretexts and his festive appearance. All the same, Karl liked him quite well and was pleased to see Rennell stopping beside the lift in his fine suit before going out on one of these evenings, making his excuses again while he pulled on his gloves, and then stalking off along the corridor. Besides, Karl thought it only natural that he should oblige an older colleague in this way at the start; he had no intention of making it a permanent arrangement. For running the lift up and down was tiring enough in itself, and especially during the evening; there was almost no respite from it.

So Karl also learned how to make the quick, low bow which was expected of lift-boys, and to accept tips with lightning speed. They vanished into his waistcoat pocket, and no one could have told from his expression whether they were big or small. For ladies he opened the door with a little air of gallantry and swung himself into the lift slowly after them, since in their anxiety about their hats, dresses and fal-lals they took a longer time than men to get inside. While working the lift he stood close beside the door, since that seemed the most unobtrusive place, with his back to his passengers, holding the door-lever in his hand so that he was ready the instant they arrived to slide the door sideways without delaying or startling them. Only seldom did anyone tap him on the shoulder during a journey to ask some little piece of information; then he would turn round smartly as if he had been expecting the request and give the answer in a loud voice. Often, particularly after the theatres or the arrival of certain express trains, there was such a rush, in spite of the numerous lifts, that as soon as he had deposited one set of passengers on the top floor he had to fly back again for those who were waiting below. It was possible, by pulling on a wire cable which passed through the lift, to increase its ordinary speed, though this was forbidden by the regulations and was also supposed to be dangerous. So Karl never did it while he was carrying passengers, but as soon as he had unloaded them upstairs and was returning for more, he had no scruples at all and hauled on the cable with strong, rhythmical heaves like a sailor. Besides, he knew that the other lift-boys did it as well, and he did not want to lose his passengers to them. Individual guests who had been staying in the hotel for quite some time – a common habit here – showed occasionally by a smile that they recognized Karl as their lift-boy. These marks of kindness Karl accepted gravely but with gratitude. Sometimes, if he were not so rushed as usual, he could take on little errands as well, fetching some trifle or other which a guest had forgotten in his room and did not want the trouble of going up for; then Karl would soar aloft all by himself in the lift, which seemed peculiarly his own at such times, enter the strange room, where curious things which he had never seen before were lying about or hanging on clothes-pegs, smell the characteristic odour of some unfamiliar soap or perfume or toothpaste and hurry back, not lingering even a moment, with the required object, though he usually got the vaguest instructions for finding it. He often regretted that he could not go on longer errands, which were reserved for special attendants and message-boys equipped with bicycles, even with motor-bicycles. The utmost he could do was to undertake commissions to the dining-room or the gambling-rooms.

After twelve-hours' shift, coming off duty at six o'clock in the evening for three days and for the next three at six o'clock in the morning, he was so weary that he went straight to bed without heeding anyone. His bed was in the lift-boys' dormitory; the Manageress, who turned out to be not quite so influential as he had thought on the first evening, had indeed tried to get him a room for himself, and might even have succeeded in doing so, but when Karl saw what difficulties it caused and that she had to keep ringing up his immediate superior, the busy Head Waiter, on his account, he refused it and convinced her of the sincerity of his refusal by telling her that he did not want to make the other boys jealous through receiving a privilege which he had not really earned.

As a quiet place to sleep in, the dormitory certainly left much to be desired. For each boy had his own time-table for eating, sleeping, recreation and incidental services during his free twelve hours; so that the place was always in a turmoil. Some would be lying asleep with blankets pulled over their ears to deaden noises, and if one of them were roused he would yell with such fury about the din made by the rest that all the other sleepers, no matter how soundly they slept, were bound to waken up. Almost every boy had a pipe, which was indulged in as a sort of luxury, and Karl got himself one too and soon acquired a taste for it. Now smoking was of course forbidden on duty, and the consequence was that in the dormitory everyone smoked if he was not actually asleep. As a result, each bed stood in its own smoke cloud and the whole room was enveloped in a general haze. Although the majority agreed in principle that lights should be kept burning only at one end of the room during the night, it was impossible to enforce this. Had the suggestion been carried out, those who wanted to sleep could have done so in peace in the half of the room which lay in darkness – it was a huge room with forty beds – while the others in the lighted part could have played at dice or cards and done all the other things for which light was needed. A boy whose bed was in the lighted half of the room and who wanted to sleep could have lain down on one of the vacant beds in the dark half; for there were always enough beds vacant, and no boy objected to another's making a temporary use of his bed. But it was impossible to stick to this arrangement for even a single night. There would always be a couple of boys, for instance, who had taken advantage of the darkness to snatch some sleep and then felt inclined for a game of cards on a board stretched between their beds: naturally enough they switched on the nearest electric light, which wakened up those who were sleeping with their faces turned towards its glare. Of course, one could squirm away from the light for a while, but in the end the only thing to do was to start a game of cards with one's own wakeful neighbour and switch on another light. And that meant pipes going too, all round. Here and there, to be sure, some determined sleepers – among whom Karl was usually to be counted – burrowed their heads under the pillows instead of lying on top of them; but how was one to go on sleeping if the boy in the next bed got up in the very middle of the night for a few hours' roistering in the town before going on duty and washed his face with a clatter and much scattering of water at the wash-basin fixed at the head of one's own bed, if he not only put on his boots noisily but even stamped them on the floor to get his feet thoroughly into them – most of the boys' boots were too narrow, in spite of the shape of American footwear – and if he finally, not being able to find some trifle or other to complete his toilet, simply lifted one's pillow off one's face, the pillow beneath which one had of course long given up trying to sleep and was waiting merely to let fly at him? Now the boys were also great lovers of sport, and most of them young, strong lads who wanted to miss no chance of training their bodies. So if you were startled out of your sleep in the night by an uproar, you were sure to find a boxing-match in full career on the floor beside your bed, while expert spectators in their shirts and drawers stood on all the beds round about, with every light turned on. It happened once that in such a midnight boxing-match one of the combatants fell over Karl as he was sleeping, and the first thing he saw on opening his eyes was a stream of blood from the boy's nose which, before anything could could be done about it, bespattered all the bed-clothes. Karl often spent nearly the whole of his twelve hours in trying to get a few hours' sleep. He was strongly enough tempted to take part in the general fun; but then it always came into his mind that the others had gained a better start in life and that he must catch up on them by harder work and a little renunciation. So, although he was eager to get sufficient sleep, chiefly on account of his work, he complained neither to the Manageress nor to Therese about the conditions in the dormitory; for all the other boys suffered in the same way without really grumbling about it, and besides, the tribulations of the dormitory were a necessary part of the job which he had gratefully accepted from the hands of the Manageress.

Once a week, on changing from day to night duty, he had a free period of twenty-four hours, part of which he devoted to seeing the Manageress once or twice and exchanging a few words with Therese, usually in some corner or other, or in a corridor, very rarely indeed in her room, whenever he caught her off duty for a moment or two. Sometimes too he escorted her on her errands to the town, which had all to be executed at top speed. They would rush to the nearest underground station almost at a run, Karl carrying the basket; the journey flashed past in a second, as if the train were being pulled through a vacuum, and they were already getting out and clattering up the stairs at the other end without waiting for the lift, which was too slow for them; then the great squares appeared, from which the streets rayed out star-fashion, bringing a tumult of steadily streaming traffic from every side; but Karl and Therese stuck close together and hurried to the different offices, laundries, warehouses and shops to do the errands which could not easily be attended to by telephone, mostly purchases of a minor nature or trifling complaints. Therese soon noticed that Karl's assistance was not to be despised; indeed, that in many cases it greatly expedited matters. In his company she had never to stand waiting, as at other times, for the overdriven shopkeepers to attend to her. He marched up to the counter and rapped on it with his knuckles until someone came; in his newly acquired and still somewhat pedantic English, easy to distinguish from a hundred other accents, he shouted across high walls of human beings; he went up to people without hesitation, even if they were haughtily withdrawn in the recesses of the longest shops. He did all this not out of arrogance, nor from any lack of respect for difficulties, but because he felt himself in a secure position which gave him certain rights; the Hotel Occidental was not to be despised as a customer, and after all, Therese sorely needed help in spite of her business experience.

'You should always come with me,' she often said, laughing happily, when they returned from a particularly successful expedition.

During the month and a half that Karl stayed at Rameses, he was only thrice in Therese's room for long visits of a few hours at a time. It was naturally smaller than the Manageress's rooms; the few things in it were crowded round the window; but after his experiences in the dormitory Karl could appreciate the value of a private, relatively quiet room, and though he never expressly said so, Therese could see how much he liked being there. She had no secrets from him, and indeed it would not have been very easy to keep secrets from him after that visit of hers on the first night. She was an illegitimate child; her father was a foreman mason who had sent for her and her mother from Pomerania; but as if that had been his whole duty, or as if the work-worn woman and the sickly child whom he met at the landing-stage had disappointed his expectations, he had gone off to Canada without much explanation shortly after their arrival, and they had received neither a letter not any other word from him, which indeed was not wholly surprising, for they were lost beyond discovery among the tenements in the east end of New York.

On one occasion Therese told Karl – he was standing beside her at the window looking down at the street – of her mother's death. How her mother and she one winter evening – she must have been about five then – were hurrying through the streets, each carrying a bundle, to find some shelter for the night. How her mother had first taken her hand – there was a snowstorm and it was not very easy to make headway – until her own hand grew numb and she let Therese go without even looking to see what had become of her, so that the child had to make shift to hang on by herself to her mother's skirts. Often Therese stumbled and even fell, but her mother seemed to be beyond herself and went on without stopping. And what snowstorms you got in the long, straight streets of New York! Karl had no experience of what winter in New York was like. If you walked against the wind, which kept whirling round and round, you could not open your eyes even for a minute, the wind lashed the snow into your face all the time, you walked and walked but got no farther forward; it was enough to make you desperate. A child naturally was at an advantage compared with a grown-up; it could duck under the wind and get through and even find a little pleasure in the struggle. So that night Therese was hardly able to understand her mother's situation, and she was now firmly convinced that if she had only acted then more wisely towards her mother – of course, she was such a very little girl – her mother might not have had to die such a wretched death. Her mother had had no work at all for two days; her last coin was gone; they had passed the day in the open without a bite, and the bundles they carried contained nothing but useless odds and ends which, perhaps out of superstition, they did not dare throw away. There was a prospect of work the very next morning at a new building, but Therese's mother was afraid, as she had tried to explain the whole day, that she might not be able to take advantage of the chance, for she felt dead tired and that very morning had coughed up a great deal of blood in the street to the alarm of passers-by; her only wish was to get into some place where she could be warm and rest. And just that evening it was impossible to find even a corner. Sometimes a janitor would not let them inside the doorway of a building, where they might at least have sheltered a little from the cold; but if they did get past the janitor they scurried through oppressive, icy corridors, climbed countless stairs, circled narrow balconies overlooking courtyards, beating upon doors at random, at one moment not daring to speak to anyone and at another imploring everyone they met; and once or twice her mother sat down breathlessly on a step in some quiet doorway, drew Therese, who was almost reluctant, to her breast and kissed her with painful insistence on the lips. When Therese realized afterwards that these were her mother's last kisses, she could not understand how she could have been so blind as not to know it, small creature though she was. Some of the doors they passed by stood open to let out a stifling fug; in the smoky reek which filled these rooms, as if they were on fire, nothing could be discerned but some figure looming in the doorway who discouraged them, either by stolid silence or by a curt word, from expecting accommodation within. On looking back, Therese thought it was only in the first few hours that her mother was really seeking for a place of shelter, for after about midnight she spoke to no one at all, although she was on her feet, with brief interruptions, until dawn, and although these tenements never locked their doors all night and there was a constant traffic of people whom she could not help meeting. Of course, they were not actually running about from place to place, but they were moving as fast as their strength would permit, perhaps in reality at a kind of crawling shuffle. And Therese could not tell whether between midnight and five o'clock in the morning they had been in twenty buildings, or in two, or only in one. The corridors of these tenements were cunningly contrived to save space, but not to make it easy to find one's way about; likely enough they had trailed again and again through the same corridor. Therese had a dim recollection of emerging from the door of a house which they had been traversing endlessly, only to turn back, or so it seemed to her, when they had reached the street, and plunge again into it. For a child like her it was of course an incomprehensible torture to be dragged along, sometimes holding her mother's hand, sometimes clinging to her skirts, without a single word of comfort, and in her bewilderment the only explanation she could find was that her mother wanted to run away from her. So for safety's sake Therese clutched all the more firmly at her mother's skirts with one hand even when her mother was holding her by the other hand, and sobbed at intervals. She did not want to be left behind among these people who went stamping up the stairs before them or came behind them, invisibly, round the next turn of the stairway below, people who stood quarrelling in the corridors before a door and pushed each other into it by turns. Drunk men wandered about the place dolefully singing, and Therese's mother was lucky to slip with her through their hands, which almost barred the way. At such a late hour of night, when no one was paying much attention to anything and rights were no longer insisted on, she could certainly have cadged a place in one of the common doss-houses run by private owners, several of which they passed, but Therese was unaware of this and her mother was past all thought of resting. Morning found them, at the dawn of a fine Winter day, both leaning against a house wall; perhaps they had slept for a little while there, perhaps only stared about them with open eyes. It appeared that Therese had lost her bundle, and her mother made to beat her as a punishment for her negligence; but Therese neither heard nor felt any blow. Then they went on again through the wakening streets, Therese's mother next to the wall; they crossed a bridge, where her mother's hand brushed rime from the railing, and at length – Therese accepted it as a matter of course at the time but now she could not understand it – they fetched up at the very building where her mother had been asked to report that morning. She did not tell Therese whether to wait or go away, and Therese took this as a command to wait, since that was what she preferred to do. So she sat down on a heap of bricks and looked on while her mother undid her bundle, took out a gay scrap of material, and bound it round the head-cloth which she had been wearing all night. Therese was too tired even to think of helping her mother. Without giving in her name at the foreman's office, as was customary, and without inquiring of anyone, her mother began to climb a ladder, as if she already knew the task that was allotted to her. Therese was surprised at this, since the hod-women usually worked on ground level, mixing the lime, carrying the bricks and performing other simple duties. So she thought that her mother was going to do some better-paid kind of work today, and sleepily smiled up to her. The building was not very high yet, it had hardly reached the first storey, though the tall scaffolding for the rest of the structure, still without its connecting boards, rose up into the blue sky. Reaching the top of the wall, her mother skilfully skirted round the bricklayers, who went on stolidly setting brick on brick and for some incomprehensible reason paid no attention to her; with gentle fingers she felt her way cautiously along a wooden partition which served as a railing, and Therese, dozing below, was amazed at such skill and fancied that her mother glanced at her kindly. But in her course her mother now came to a little heap of bricks, beyond which the railing and obviously also the wall came to an end; yet she did not stop for that but walked straight on to the heap of bricks, and there her skill seemed to desert her, for she knocked down the bricks and fell sheer over them to the ground. A shower of bricks came after her and then, a good few minutes later, a heavy plank detached itself from somewhere and crashed down upon her. Therese's last memory of her mother was seeing her lying there in her checked skirt, which had come all the way from Pomerania, her legs thrown wide, almost covered by the rough plank atop of her, while people came running up from every side and a man shouted down angrily from the top of the wall.

It was late when Therese finished her story. She had told it with a wealth of detail unusual for her, and notably at quite unimportant passages, such as when she described the scaffolding poles each rising to heaven by itself, she had been compelled to stop now and then with tears in her eyes. The most trifling circumstance of that morning was still stamped exactly on her memory after more than ten years, and because the sight of her mother on the half-finished house-wall was the last living memory of her mother, and she wanted to bring it still more vividly before her friend, she tried to return to it again after she had ended her story, but then she faltered, put her face in her hands and said not another word.

Still, they had merry hours too in Therese's room. On his first visit Karl had seen a text-book of commercial correspondence lying there and had asked leave to borrow it. They arranged at the same time that Karl should write out the exercises in the book and bring them to Therese, who had already studied them as far as her own work required, for correction. Now Karl lay for whole nights in his bed in the dormitory with cotton-wool in his ears, shifting into every conceivable posture to relax himself, and read the book and scribbled the exercises in a little notebook with a fountain pen which the Manageress had given him in reward for drawing up methodically and writing out neatly a long inventory of hers. He managed to turn to his advantage most of the distracting interruptions of the other boys by perpetually asking them for advice on small points of the English language, so that they grew tired of it and left him in peace. Often he was amazed that the others were so reconciled to their present lot, that they did not feel its provisional character, nor even realize the need to come to a decision about their future occupations, and in spite of Karl's example read nothing at all except tattered and filthy copies of detective stories which were passed from bed to bed.

At their conferences Therese now corrected Karl's exercises, perhaps rather too painstakingly. Differences of opinion arose. Karl adduced his great New York professor in his support, but that gentleman counted for as little with Therese as the grammatical theories of the lift-boys. She would take the fountain pen from Karl's hand and score out the passages which she was convinced were erroneous. But in such dubious cases, although the matter could hardly be brought before a higher authority than Therese, Karl would score out, for the sake of accuracy, the strokes which Therese had made against him. Sometimes the Manageress would turn up and give the decision in Therese's favour, yet that was not definite, as Therese was her secretary. At the same time, however, she would establish a general amnesty, for tea would be made, cakes sent for and Karl urged to tell stories about Europe, with many interruptions from the Manageress, who kept inquiring and exclaiming, so that he realized how many things had been radically changed in a relatively short time, and how much had probably changed since his own departure and would always go on changing.

Karl might have been about a month in Rameses when one evening Rennell said to him in passing that a man called Delamarche had stopped him in front of the hotel and questioned him about Karl. Having no cause to make a secret of it, Rennell had replied truthfully that Karl was a lift-boy but had prospects of getting a much better post because of the interest the Manageress took in him. Karl noted how carefully Delamarche had handled Rennell, for he had actually invited him to a meal that evening.

'I want nothing more to do with Delamarche,' said Karl, 'and you'd better be on your guard against him too!'

'Me?' said Rennell, stretching himself and hurrying off. He was the best-looking youngster in the hotel, and it was rumoured among the other boys, though no one knew who had started the story, that a fashionable lady who had been staying in the hotel for some time had kissed him, to say the least of it, in the lift. Those who knew this rumour found it very titillating to watch the self-possessed lady passing by with her calm, light step, her filmy veil and tightly laced figure, for her external appearance gave not the slightest indication that such behaviour was possible on her part. She stayed on the first floor, which was not served by Rennell's lift, but one could not of course forbid guests to enter another lift if their own lifts were engaged at the moment. So now and then it happened that she used Karl's and Rennell's lift, yet only when Rennell was on duty. This might have been chance, but nobody believed it, and when the lift started off with the two of them, there was an almost uncontrollable excitement among the lift-boys which actually made it necessary once for the Head Waiter to intervene. Now, whether the lady or the rumour was the cause, the fact remained that Rennell was changing, he had become much more self-confident, he left the polishing of the lift entirely to Karl, who was only waiting for the chance of a radical explanation on this point, and no longer was to be seen in the dormitory. No other boy had so completely deserted the community of the lift-boys, for, at least in questions concerning their work, they generally held strictly together and had an organization of their own which was recognized by the hotel management.

All this flashed through Karl's mind, together with reflections on Delamarche, but he went on with his work as usual. Towards midnight he had a little diversion, for Therese, who often surprised him with small gifts, brought him a big apple and a bar of chocolate. They talked together for a while, scarcely conscious of the interruptions caused by the lift journeys. They came to speak of Delamarche, and Karl realized that he must really have let himself be influenced by Therese in coming to the conclusion that he was a dangerous man, for after what Karl had told her that was Therese's opinion of him. Karl himself believed that he was only a shiftless creature who had let himself be demoralized by ill-luck and would be easy enough to get on with. But Therese contradicted him violently and in a long harangue insisted that he should promise never to speak to Delamarche again. Instead of giving the promise, Karl kept urging her to go to bed, for midnight was long since past, and when she refused, he threatened to leave his post and take her to her room. When at last she was ready to go, he said: 'Why bother yourself so needlessly, Therese? If it will make you sleep any better, I'm ready to promise that I won't speak to Delamarche unless I can't avoid it.' Then came a crowd of passengers, for the boy in the neighbouring lift had been withdrawn for some other duty and Karl had to attend to both lifts.

Some of the guests grumbled at the dislocation, and a gentleman who was escorting a lady actually tapped Karl lightly with his walking cane to make him hurry, an admonition which was quite unnecessary. It would not have been so bad if the guests, when they saw that one lift was unattended, had made directly for Karl's lift; but instead of that they drifted to the next lift and stood there holding the handle of the door or even walked right into the lift, an act which the lift-boys were expressly forbidden by the regulations to permit in any circumstances. So Karl had to rush up and down until he was quite exhausted, without earning the consciousness that he was efficiently fulfilling his duty. On top of this, towards three o'clock in the morning a luggage porter, an old man with whom he was on fairly friendly terms, asked some slight help from him which he could not give, for guests were standing before both his lifts and it required all his presence of mind to decide immediately which group to take first. He was consequently relieved when the other boy came back, and he called out a few words of reproach to him because he had stayed away so long, although it was probably no fault of his.

After four o'clock a lull set in which Karl badly needed. He leant wearily against the balustrade beside his lift slowly eating the apple, which gave out a strong fragrance as soon as he bit into it, and gazed down into a lighted shaft surrounded by the great windows of the store-rooms, behind which hanging masses of bananas gleamed faintly in the darkness.

6

THE CASE OF ROBINSON

Then someone tapped him on the shoulder. Karl, who naturally thought it was a guest, hastily stuck the apple in his pocket and hurried to the lift almost without glancing at the man.

'Good evening, Mr Rossmann,' said the man, 'it's me, Robinson.'

'But you look quite different,' said Karl, shaking his head.

'Yes, I'm doing well,' said Robinson, contemplating his clothes, which consisted of garments that might have been fine enough separately but were so ill-assorted they looked positively shabby. What struck the eye most was a white waistcoat, obviously worn for the first time, with four little black-bordered pockets, to which Robinson tried to draw attention by expanding his chest.

'These things of yours are expensive,' said Karl, and he thought in passing of his good simple suit, in which he could have held his own even with Rennell, but which his two bad friends had sold.

'Yes,' said Robinson, 'I buy myself something nearly every day. How do you like the waistcoat?'

'Quite well,' said Karl.

'But these aren't real pockets, they're just made to look like pockets,' said Robinson, taking Karl's hand so that he might prove it for himself. But Karl recoiled, for an unendurable reek of brandy came from Robinson's mouth.

'You've started drinking again,' said Karl, going back to the balustrade.

'No,' said Robinson, 'not very much,' and he added, contradicting his first complacency: 'What else can a man do in this world?' A lift journey interrupted their talk, and scarcely had Karl reached the bottom again when a telephone message came asking him to fetch the hotel doctor, for a lady on the seventh floor had fainted. During this errand Karl secretly hoped that Robinson would have disappeared before he returned, for he did not want to be seen with him and, thinking of Therese's warning, did not want to hear about Delamarche either. But Robinson was still waiting with the wooden gravity of a very drunk man just as a high hotel official in frock-coat and top-hat went past, fortunately, as it seemed, without paying any attention to the intruder.

'Wouldn't you like to come and see us, Rossmann? We're living in great style now,' said Robinson, leering seductively at Karl.

'Does the invitation come from you or from Delamarche?' asked Karl.

'From me and Delamarche. Both of us together,' said Robinson.

'Then let me tell you, and you can pass it on to Delamarche: that break between us, if it wasn't obvious enough to you at the time, was final. You two have done me more harm than anyone else has ever done. Can you have taken it into your heads not to leave me in peace even now?'

'But we're your friends,' said Robinson disgustingly, maudlin tears rising to his eyes. 'Delamarche asked me to tell you that he'll make it all up to you. We're living now with Brunelda, a lovely singer.' And at the name he started to sing in a high quavering voice, but Karl silenced him in time, hissing at him: 'Shut your mouth this minute; don't you know where you are?'

'Rossmann,' said Robinson, intimidated as far as singing was concerned, 'I'm a friend of yours, I am; say what you like. And now you've got such a fine job here, couldn't you lend me something?'

'You would only drink it,' said Karl. 'Why, I can see a brandy bottle in your pocket, and you must have been drinking out of it while I was away, for you were fairly sober at the start.'

'That's only to strengthen me when I'm out on a journey,' said Robinson apologetically.

'Well, I'm not going to bother about you any more,' said Karl.

'But what about the money?' said Robinson, opening his eyes wide.

'I suppose Delamarche told you to bring money back. All right, I'll give you some money, but only on condition that you go away at once and never come here again. If you want to get in touch with me, you can write me a letter; Karl Rossmann, Lift Boy, Hotel Occidental, will always find me. But I tell you again, you must never come looking for me here. I'm in service here and I have no time for visitors. Well, will you have the money on these conditions?' asked Karl, putting his hand into his waistcoat pocket, for he had made up his mind to sacrifice the tips he had received that night. Robinson merely nodded in answer to the question, breathing heavily. Karl interpreted this wrongly and asked again: 'Yes or no?'

Then Robinson beckoned him nearer and with writhings which told their own story whispered: 'Rossmann, I feel awfully sick.'

'What the devil!' cried Karl, and with both hands he dragged him to the stair railings. And a stream poured from Robinson's mouth into the deep. In the pauses of his sickness he felt helplessly and blindly for Karl.

'You're a good lad,' he would say then, or: 'It's stopped now,' which however was far short of being the case, or: 'The swine, what sort of stuff is this they have poured into me!' In his agitation and loathing Karl could not bear to stay beside him any longer and began to walk up and down. Here, in the corner beside the lift, Robinson was not likely to be seen, but what if someone should notice him, one of these rich and fussy guests who were always waiting to complain to the first hotel official they saw, who would revenge himself for it on the whole staff in his fury; or what if he were seen by one of these hotel detectives, who were always being changed and consequently were known only to the hotel management, so that one suspected a detective in every man who peered at things, though he might be merely short-sighted? And some waiter down below only needed to go to the store-rooms to fetch something – for the restaurant buffet went on all night – to be shocked at the sight of the disgusting mess at the foot of the shaft and telephone to Karl asking in God's name what was wrong up there. Could Karl refuse to acknowledge Robinson in that case? And if he did refuse, was not Robinson stupid and desperate enough simply to cling to Karl instead of apologizing? And would not Karl be dismissed at once, since it was unheard of for a lift-boy, the lowest and most easily replaced member of the stupendous hierarchy of the hotel staff, to allow a friend of his to defile the hotel and perhaps even drive away guests? Could a lift-boy be tolerated who had such friends, and who allowed them actually to visit him during working hours? Did it not look as if such a lift-boy must himself be a drunkard or even worse, for what assumption was more natural than that he stuffed his friends with food from the hotel stores until they could not help defiling, as Robinson had done, any part of this scrupulously clean hotel they happened to be in? And why should such a boy restrict himself to stealing food and drink, since he had literally innumerable opportunities for theft because of the notorious negligence of the guests, the wardrobes standing open everywhere, the valuables lying about on tables, the caskets flung wide open, the keys thrown down at random?

Just then Karl spied in the distance a number of guests coming upstairs from a beer-cellar, in which a variety performance had newly finished. He stationed himself beside his lift and did not dare even to look round at Robinson for fear of what he might see. It gave him a little comfort that no sound, not even a groan, was to be heard from that direction. He attended to his guests and kept going up and down with them, but he could not quite conceal his distraction and on every downward journey was prepared to encounter some catastrophic surprise.

At last he had time to look after Robinson, who was cowering abjectly in his corner with his face pressed against his knees. He had pushed his hard round hat far back off his brow.

'You must really go now,' said Karl softly but firmly. 'Here is the money. If you're quick I can find time to show you the shortest way.'

'I'll never be able to move,' said Robinson, wiping his forehead with a minute handkerchief, 'I'll just die here. You can't imagine how bad I feel. Delamarche takes me into all his expensive drinking-dens; but I can't stand the silly stuff you get here; I tell him that every day.'

'Well, you simply can't stay here,' said Karl. 'Remember

where you are. If you're discovered here you'll get into trouble and I'll lose my job. Do you want that?'

'I can't get up,' said Robinson. 'I'd rather jump down there,' and he pointed between the stair railings down into the air-shaft 'as long as I sit here like this, I can bear it, but I can't get up; I tried it once while you were away.'

'Then I'll fetch a taxi to take you to the hospital,' said Karl, tugging a little at Robinson's legs, for he seemed in danger of subsiding into complete lethargy at any moment. But as soon as he heard the word hospital, which seemed to rouse horrible associations, he began to weep loudly and held out his hands to Karl, as if begging for mercy.

'Be quiet,' said Karl, and he struck down Robinson's hands, ran across to the lift-boy whose work he had taken on that night, begged him to oblige him in return for a little while, hurried back to Robinson, who was still sobbing, jerked him violently to his feet and whispered to him: 'Robinson, if you want me to help you, you must pull yourself together and try to hold yourself straight for a short distance. I'm going to take you to my bed, where you can stay till you feel better again. You'll be surprised how quickly you'll recover. But now you must really behave sensibly, for there are all sorts of people in the passages and my bed is in a big dormitory. If you attract even the slightest attention, I can do nothing more for you. And you must keep your eyes open; I can't cart you about if you look as if you were on the point of death.'

'I'll do everything you tell me,' said Robinson, 'but you won't manage to hold me up by yourself. Can't you get Rennell too?'

'Rennell isn't here,' said Karl.

'Oh, of course,' said Robinson, 'Rennell's with Delamarche. The two of them sent me to see you. I've got all mixed up.' Karl took advantage of these and other incomprehensible monologues of Robinson to push him along, and without accident managed to get him as far as a corner, from which a more dimly lit passage led to the lift-boys' dormitory. A lift-boy came running towards them and passed them at full speed just at that moment. Until now they had had only harmless encounters; between four and five was the quietest time; and Karl was well aware that if he could not get rid of Robinson now, there was no hope of doing so in the early morning, after the day's work had begun.

At the far end of the dormitory a big fight or an entertainment of some kind was going on; he could hear the rhythmical clapping of hands, the agitated stamping of feet, and shouts of encouragement. In the part of the dormitory near the door a very few sound sleepers were to be seen in the beds; the majority lay on their backs staring at the roof, while here and there a boy, clothed or unclothed as he chanced to be, sprang out of bed to see how things were going at the other end of the room. So Karl managed to guide Robinson who had now become somewhat used to walking, as far as Rennell's bed without rousing much attention, for the bed was quite near the door and luckily unoccupied; in his own bed, as he could see from the distance, a strange boy whom he did not know was quietly sleeping. As soon as Robinson felt the bed under him he went to sleep at once, with one leg hanging outside.

Karl drew the blankets quite over Robinson's face and thought there was no need to worry for the time being, as the man was not likely to waken before six at the earliest, and by then he would he here himself and perhaps with Rennell's help would find some means of smuggling him out of the hotel. The dormitory was never inspected by the higher authorities of the hotel, except on extraordinary occasions; several years previously the lift-boys had succeeded in abolishing the routine inspections which had been customary before then; so from that side there was nothing to be feared either.

When Karl got back to his lift again, he saw that both his own lift and its neighbour were vanishing upwards. He waited in some trepidation for this to explain itself. His own lift came down first, and out of it stepped the boy who had run past him in the passage a little while before.

'Here, where have you been, Rossmann?' he asked. 'Why did you go away? why didn't you report your absence?'

'But I asked him to attend to my lift for a minute,' said Karl, indicating the boy in the next lift, which had just arrived. 'I did as much for him for two whole hours when the traffic was at its worst.'

'That's all very well,' said the boy in question, 'but it won't do. Don't you know that you must report even the shortest absence from duty to the Head Waiter's office? That's what the telephone's there for. I'd have been glad to do your work, but you know yourself that it isn't so easy. There was a crowd of new arrivals off the 4.30 express standing at both the lifts. I couldn't take your lift first and leave my own guests waiting could I, so I just went up first in my own lift!'

'Well?' asked Karl tensely, as both boys fell silent.

'Well,' said the boy from the next lift, 'that was the very moment the Head Waiter came along and saw the people waiting for your lift and no one attending to it; he flew into a rage and asked me, for I was on the spot in no time, where you were; of course I had no idea, for you didn't even tell me where you were going; and so he telephoned straight off to the dormitory for another boy to come at once.'

'I met you in the passage, didn't I?' asked the new boy. Karl nodded.

'Of course,' the other boy assured him, 'I told him at once that you had asked me to take your place, but would he listen to excuses? You don't seem to know him yet. And we were to tell you that you're to go to the office at once. So you'd better not wait any longer, but just leg it. Perhaps he'll let you off after all; you weren't away for more than two minutes really. You just stick to it that you asked me to take your place. Better not mention that you took mine though, that's my advice; nothing can happen to me, for I had leave of absence; but there isn't any good in mentioning that and mixing it up with this business, since it has nothing to do with it.'

'It's the first time I have ever left my post,' said Karl.

'It always happens like that, but nobody believes it,' said the boy, running to his lift, for there were people coming.

Karl's deputy, a boy of about fourteen, who obviously felt sorry for Karl, said: 'They've let boys off this kind of thing often enough already. Usually they shift you to a different job. As far as I know, they've only once made it the sack. You must think up a good excuse. But don't try to tell him that you suddenly felt sick; that'll only make him laugh. Much better say that a guest sent you on an urgent errand to another guest, but you can't remember who the first guest was and you weren't able to find the other one.'

'Well,' said Karl, 'it won't be so very bad.' After all he had heard, he could not believe that the affair would end well. Even if this act of negligence were condoned, Robinson was lying there in the dormitory as a living offence, and it was only too probable that the Head Waiter, vindictive as he was, would not be content with a superficial investigation and would light on Robinson at last. It was true that there was no express prohibition against taking strangers into the dormitory, but that prohibition did not exist simply because there was no point in mentioning what was unthinkable.

When Karl entered the office the Head Waiter was sitting over his morning coffee, taking an occasional sip and studying a list which had apparently been brought him by the Head Porter, who was also there. The latter was a tall bulky man, whose splendid and richly-ornamented uniform – even its shoulders and sleeves were heavy with gold chains and braid – made him look still more broad-shouldered than he actually was. His gleaming black moustache drawn out to two points in the Hungarian fashion never stirred even at the most abrupt movement of his head. Also, because of his stiff, heavy clothing, the man could move only with difficulty and always stood with his legs planted wide apart, so that his weight might be evenly distributed.

Karl entered boldly and quickly, as he was used to do in the hotel; for that slowness and circumstance which passes for politeness among private persons is looked upon as laziness in lift-boys. Besides, he must not appear to be conscious of guilt on his very entrance. The Head Waiter glanced up fleetingly when the door opened, but then immediately returned to his coffee and his reading without paying any further attention to Karl. But the porter seemed to be annoyed at Karl's presence; perhaps he had some secret information or request to impart; at any rate he glared angrily at Karl every few minutes with his head stiffly inclined, and whenever his eyes met Karl's, which was clearly what he wanted, he turned away at once to the Head Waiter again. Yet Karl thought he would be ill-advised to quit the office, now that he was here, without an express order to do so from the Head Waiter. But the Head Waiter was still studying his list and meanwhile eating a piece of cake, from which he now and then shook the sugar, without interrupting his reading. Once a sheet of the list fell to the floor; the porter did not even make any attempt to pick it up, for he knew he could not, nor was it at all necessary, since Karl pounced on the paper and reached it to the Head Waiter, who accepted it with a casual movement of his hand, as if it had flown of its own accord from the floor. The little service had availed nothing, for the porter went on darting his angry looks at Karl.

In spite of that, Karl now felt more composed. The very fact that his offence seemed to have so little importance for the Head Waiter might be taken as a good sign. After all, it was perfectly understandable. A lift-boy was of no importance and so could not take any liberties, but just because he was of no importance, any offence he committed could not be taken seriously. After all, the Head Waiter himself had begun as a lift-boy – indeed his career was the boast of the present generation of lift-boys – it was he who had first organized the lift-boys, and certainly he too must have left his post occasionally without permission, though nobody could force him now to remember that, and though it must not be forgotten that his having been a lift-boy made him all the more severe and unrelenting in keeping the lift-boys in order. But Karl also drew hope from the steadily passing minutes. According to the office clock it was now more than a quarter-past five; Rennell might come back at any moment, perhaps he was back already, for he must have noticed that

Robinson did not return, and in any case Delamarche and Rennell could not have been very far from the Hotel Occidental, it occurred to Karl, for otherwise Robinson, in his wretched condition, would never have reached it. Now, if Rennell found Robinson in his bed, which was bound to happen, then everything would be all right. For practical as Rennell was, especially where his own interests were concerned, he would soon get Robinson out of the hotel in some way or other, which would be all the easier as Robinson must have recovered somewhat by now, and Delamarche was probably waiting outside the hotel to take charge of him. But once Robinson was got rid of, Karl could encounter the Head Waiter with a much quieter mind and for this time perhaps escape with a reprimand, though a severe one. Then he would consult with Therese whether he should tell the Manageress the whole truth – for his part he could see nothing against it – and if that could be done, then the matter could be finally disposed of without much harm done.

Karl had just reassured himself somewhat by these reflections and was beginning unobtrusively to count over the tips he had taken that night, since he had a feeling that they were heavier than usual, when the Head Waiter laid the list on the table, saying: 'Just wait a minute longer, will you, Feodor,' sprang at one bound to his feet and yelled so loudly at Karl that the boy could only stare terror-stricken into the black cavern of his mouth.

'You were absent from duty without leave. Do you know what that means? It means dismissal. I'll listen to no excuses, you can keep your lying apologies to yourself; the fact that you were not there is quite enough for me. If I once pass that over and let you off, all my forty lift-boys will soon be taking to their heels during working hours, and I'll be left to carry my five thousand guests up the stairs on my own shoulder.'

Karl said nothing. The porter came nearer and gave a downward tug to Karl's jacket, which was slightly creased, doubtless intending in this way to draw the Head Waiter's special attention to the slight disorder of the uniform.

'Perhaps you were suddenly taken sick?' asked the Head Waiter craftily.

Karl gave him a scrutinizing look and answered: 'No.'

'So you weren't even sick?' shouted the Head Waiter all the more loudly. 'Then you must have hit on some remarkable new lie. What excuse are you going to offer? Out with it.'

'I didn't know that I had to telephone for permission to leave.'

'That's really priceless,' said the Head Waiter, and he seized Karl by the collar and almost slung him across the room till they were both facing the lift regulations, which were pinned to the wall. The porter came on their heels. 'There! Read it!' said the Head Waiter, pointing at one of the paragraphs. Karl thought that he was to read it to himself. But the Head Waiter shouted: 'Aloud!'

Instead of reading the paragraph aloud, Karl said to the Head Waiter, hoping that this would appease him: 'I know the paragraphs, for I got a copy of the regulations and read them carefully. But it's just the regulation one never needs that one forgets about. I have been working for two months now and I've never left my post once.'

'Well, you'll leave it now,' said the Head Waiter, and he went over to the table, took up the list again, as if to go on reading it, but instead smacked it down on the table again as if it were of no account, and with a deep flush on his brow and cheeks began to stride up and down the room. 'All this trouble over a silly fool of a boy! All this disturbance on night duty!' he exclaimed several times. 'Do you know who was left stranded down below when this fellow here ran away from his lift?' he asked, turning to the porter. And he mentioned a name at which the porter, who certainly knew all the hotel clients and their standing, was so horror-stricken that he had to give a fleeting look at Karl to assure himself that the boy did exist who had deserted a lift and left the bearer of that name to wait a while unattended.

'That's awful!' said the porter, slowly shaking his head in stupefaction over Karl, who watched him gloomily and reflected that this man's shocked stupidity was another item for which he would have to pay. 'Besides, I know you already,' said the porter, stretching out his great, thick, rigid first finger. 'You're the only boy who simply refuses to give me a greeting. Who do you think you are? Every boy that passes the porter's office has to give me a greeting. With the other porters you can do as you like, but I insist on manners. Sometimes I pretend not to notice, but you can take it from me that I know perfectly well who says good day to me and who doesn't, you lout!' And he turned away from Karl and stalked grandly up to the Head Waiter, who, however, instead of commenting on this new accusation, sat down to finish his breakfast, glancing over the morning paper which an attendant had just brought him.

'Sir,' said Karl, thinking that at least he had better put himself right with the Head Porter while the Head Waiter was ignoring him, since he realized that though the porter's reproaches could not do him any harm, his enmity could, 'I most certainly do not pass you without a greeting. I haven't been long in America yet and I have just come from Europe, where people are in the habit of greeting each other excessively, as is well known. And, of course, I haven't been quite able to get over the habit yet; why, only two months ago in New York, where I happened to be taken into good society, I was always being told that I was too profuse in my salutations. And now you say that I don't greet you of all people! I have greeted you every day several times a day. But, of course, not every time I saw you, for I pass you hundreds of times daily.'

'You have to greet me every time, every single time, without exception; you have to stand with your cap in your hand all the time you're speaking to me; and you must always say "sir" when you are speaking to me, and not simply "you". And you must do all that every time, every single time.'

'Every time?' repeated Karl softly, in a questioning tone, for he remembered now that during the whole of his stay in the hotel the Head Porter had seemed to regard him with a severe and reproachful expression, from the very first morning when, being still new to his work and somewhat too free and easy, he had gone up to the man without thinking and had inquired of him insistently and in detail whether two men had not asked for him or maybe left a photograph for him.

'Now you see what such behaviour brings you to,' said the porter, again coming quite close to Karl and pointing at the Head Waiter, still deep in his papers, as if that gentleman were the instrument of his vengeance. 'In your next job you'll remember to be polite to the porter, even if it's only in some stinking tavern.'

Karl understood now that he had really lost his post, for the Head Waiter had already told him so and here was the Head Porter repeating it as an accomplished fact, and in the case of a lift-boy there was probably no need for the hotel management to confirm a dismissal. Yet it had happened with a rapidity he had not expected, for after all he had worked here for two months as well as he could, and certainly better than many of the other boys. But obviously such considerations were taken into account at the decisive moment in no part of the world, neither in Europe, nor in America; the verdict was determined by the first words that happened to fall from the judge's lips in an impulse of fury. Perhaps it would be best to take his leave at once and go away; the Manageress and Therese were probably still asleep and he could say good-bye to them by letter, so as to spare them at least the disappointment and sorrow which they would feel if he said good-bye to them in person; he could hastily pack his box and quietly steal away. If he were to stay even a day longer – and he could certainly have done with a little sleep – all he could expect was the magnifying of the incident into a scandal, reproaches from every side, the unendurable sight of Therese and perhaps the Manageress herself in tears, and possibly on top of all that some punishment as well. But it also confused him to be confronted by two enemies, to have every word that he said quibbled at, if not by the one then by the other, and misconstrued. So he remained silent and for the time being enjoyed the quietness of the room, for the Head Waiter was still reading the newspaper and the Head Porter stood at the table arranging the scattered pages of his list according to their numbers, a task which he found very difficult, being obviously short-sighted.

At last the Head Waiter laid the newspaper aside with a yawn, assured himself with a glance that Karl was still there, and turned the indicator of his table telephone. He shouted: 'Hello' several times, but nobody answered. 'There's no answer,' he said to the Head Porter. The Head Porter who, it seemed to Karl, was following the telephoning with great interest, said: 'It's a quarter to six already. She must be awake by now. Ring harder.' But at that moment, without further summons, the telephone rang in answer. 'This is Isbary speaking,' the Head Waiter began. 'Good morning. I hope I haven't wakened you? I'm sorry. Yes, yes, it's a quarter to six. But I'm really very sorry if I gave you a shock. You should take the telephone off the hook while you're asleep. No, no, there's really no excuse for me, especially as it's only a trivial matter I want to discuss with you. But, of course, I have plenty of time, of course; I'll wait and hold on if you want me to.'

'She must have rushed to the telephone in her night-dress,' the Head Waiter said smiling to the Head Porter, who all the time had been bending over the instrument with an intent expression. 'I must have really disturbed her, for she's usually wakened by the girl who does her typewriting, but this morning she must have missed doing it for some reason or other. I'm sorry if I startled her; she's nervous enough as it is.'

'Why has she gone away from the telephone?'

'To see what has happened to the girl,' replied the Head Waiter, lifting the receiver again, for it had started to ring. 'She'll turn up all right,' he went on, speaking into the telephone. 'You musn't be so easily alarmed by everything. You really do need a thorough rest. Well now, to come to my little affair. There's a liftboy here called' – he turned round with a questioning look at Karl who, listening with close attention, at once provided his name – 'called Karl Rossmann. If I remember rightly, you have shown some interest in him; I am sorry to say that he has ill repaid your kindness, he left his work without permission and has brought me into serious difficulties; I can't tell yet what the consequences may be; and so I have just dismissed him. I hope you won't take it too badly. What did you say? Dismissed, yes, dismissed. But I've just told you that he deserted his lift. No, there I really cannot agree with you, my dear lady. It's a matter of authority, there's too much at stake, a boy like this might corrupt the whole lot of them. With lift-boys particularly you must be devilish strict. No, no, in this case I can't oblige you, much as I like to stand in your good graces. And even if I were to let him stay in spite of everything, simply to keep my temper in exercise, it wouldn't be fair for your sake, yes, for your sake, to have him here. You take an interest in him which he doesn't at all deserve, and I know him, and I know you too, and I'm certain that he'll bring you nothing but severe disappointment which you must be saved from at all costs. I say this quite openly in the boy's own hearing for he's standing only a step away, as bold as brass. He is to be dismissed; no, no, he is to be dismissed once and for all; no, no, he's not to be given some other kind of work, I have no use for him at all. Besides there are other people complaining about him. The Head Porter, for instance, yes, Feodor, of course, yes, Feodor has been complaining about his impoliteness and insolence. What, that shouldn't be enough? My dear lady, you go against your own character in supporting this boy. No, you really shouldn't press me like this.'

At that moment the porter bent down and whispered something into the Head Waiter's ear. The Head Waiter first looked at him in astonishment and then spoke so rapidly into the telephone that for a moment Karl could not quite make him out and came a little nearer on tiptoe.

'My dear Manageress,' he said, 'to be quite frank, I wouldn't have believed that you were such a bad judge of character. I've just learned something about your angel boy which will radically alter your opinion of him, and I almost feel sorry that it is from me it has to come to your ears. This fine pet of yours, this pattern of all virtues, rushes off to the town on every single free night he has and never comes back till morning. Yes, yes, I have evidence of it, unimpeachable evidence, yes. Now can you tell me, perhaps, where he gets hold of the money for these nocturnal adventures? Or how he can be expected to attend properly to his work? And do you want me to go the length of telling you what he does in the town? A boy like that is to be got rid of as quickly as possible. And please let this be a warning to you how careful you should be with boys who turn up from nowhere.'

'But sir,' cried Karl, actually relieved by the gross mistake which seemed to have occurred, for it might well bring about an unlooked-for improvement of the whole situation, 'there must certainly be some mistake. I understand the Head Porter has told you that I am out every night. But that simply isn't true; I spend every night in the dormitory; all the other boys can confirm that. When I'm not sleeping I study commercial correspondence; but I have never left the dormitory a single night. That's quite easy to prove. The Head Porter has evidently mistaken me for someone else, and I see now, too, why he thinks I pass him without a greeting.'

'Will you hold your tongue?' shouted the Head Porter, shaking his fist, where anyone else would have shaken his finger. 'So I've mistaken you for someone else, have I? How could I go on being the Head Porter here if I mistook one person for another? I ask you, Mr Isbary, how could I be the Head Porter here if I mistook people? In all my thirty years' service I've never mistaken anyone yet, as hundreds of waiters who have been here in my time could tell you, and is it likely that I would make a beginning with you, you wretched boy? With that smooth face of yours nobody could mistake? What have mistakes got to do with it, anyway; you could sneak off to the town every night behind my back, and it only needs one look at your face to see that you're a good-for-nothing lout.'

'Enough. Feodor,' said the Head Waiter, whose conversation with the Manageress seemed suddenly to have broken off. 'It's quite a simple matter. We're not particularly concerned about how he spends his nights. No doubt he would like us to undertake a full-dress inquiry into his night-life before he leaves us. I can well imagine that that would delight his heart. Every one of our forty lift-boys would have to be trotted out, if he had his will, to give evidence; they would naturally have mistaken him for someone else too, and so bit by bit the whole staff would have to be dragged in as witnesses; the hotel, of course, would stop working altogether for a time; and though he would be flung out in the end he would at least have had his fun. So we'll leave that out of account. He has already made a fool of the Manageress, that kind-hearted woman, and we'll let it stop there. I won't listen to another word; you're dismissed on the spot for neglecting your duties. I'll give you a note to the cashier, and your wages will be paid up till today. And let me tell you that after the way you have behaved, it's sheer charity to give you wages, and I'm only doing it out of consideration for the Manageress.'

Another ring of the telephone interrupted the Head Waiter before he could sign the note. After listening to the first few words he exclaimed: 'There's nothing but trouble from these lift-boys today!' Then after a while he cried: 'This is unheard-of!' And turning from the telephone, he said to the Head Porter: 'Please, Feodor, hold that boy for a while; we'll have more to say to him yet.' Then he shouted into the telephone: 'Come at once!'

Now the Head Porter could at last vent his rage, which he had not succeeded in doing verbally. He grabbed Karl firmly by the upper arm, yet not with a steady grip which could have been borne; every now and then he loosened his hold and then bit by bit tightened it so cruelly, for he was immensely strong and the pressure seemed as if it would never stop, that everything went dark before Karl's eyes. Moreover, he not merely held Karl, but as if he had been ordered to stretch him as well, jerked him now and then almost off his feet and shook him, saying all the time half interrogatively to the Head Waiter: 'Maybe I'm mistaking him for someone else now, maybe I'm mistaking him for someone else now.'

It was a great relief for Karl when the head lift-boy, a fat panting lad called Best, appeared and distracted the Head Porter's attention for a while. Karl was so exhausted that when to his astonishment Therese came slipping in behind the boy, pale as death, her clothes in disorder, her hair loosely put up, he could hardly summon a smile for her. In a moment she was beside him and had whispered: 'Does the Manageress know?'

'The Head Waiter has told her over the telephone,' replied Karl.

'Then it's all right, then it's all right,' she said quickly, her eyes lighting up.

'No,' said Karl. 'You don't know what they have against me. I must go away, the Manageress is already convinced of that herself. Please don't stay here; go upstairs again; I'll come to say good-bye to you later.'

'But, Rossmann, what are you thinking of? You can stay with us as long as you like. The Head Waiter does anything the Manageress asks him; he's in love with her; I found that out a little time ago. So don't worry.'

'Please, Therese, do go away now. I can't defend myself so well if you are here. And I must defend myself thoroughly, for they're telling lies about me. And the better I can pin them down and defend myself, the more chance I have of staying here. So, Therese –' But then unluckily, in a sudden spasm of pain, he added these words, though in a low tone: 'If only the Head Porter would let me go! I had no idea he was my enemy. But he keeps on crushing and twisting me.' – 'Why did I say that?' he thought simultaneously. 'No woman could listen to it unmoved,' and actually, before he could prevent her with his free arm, Therese had turned to the Head Porter and said: 'Please, sir, let Rossmann go at once. You're hurting him. The Manageress will be here herself in a minute, and then you'll see that this is all a mistake. Let him go; what pleasure can it give you to torture him!' And she actually tugged at the Head Porter's arm. 'Orders, little girl, orders,' said the Head Porter, affectionately pulling Therese to him with his free hand, while with the other he squeezed Karl with all his might, as if he not merely wished to hurt him, but had some particular and, so far, unfulfilled design upon the arm he was holding.

It took Therese some time to disengage herself from the Head Porter's embrace, and she was just about to make an appeal to the Head Waiter, who was still listening to the slow and circumstantial Best, when the Manageress hastily entered.

'Thank God!' cried Therese, and for a moment nothing could be heard in the room but that loud exclamation. The Head Waiter jumped up at once and pushed Best aside.

'So you have come yourself, my dear madam? Because of this trifling matter? After our talk on the telephone I half feared it, but I couldn't actually believe it. And since then your protégé's case had grown worse and worse. I'm afraid I won't merely have to dismiss him, but send him to prison as well. Hear for yourself.' And he gave a sign to Best.

'I would like to have a few words with Rossmann first,' said the Manageress, sitting down on a chair which the Head Waiter insisted on setting out for her.

'Please, Karl, come nearer,' she said. Karl obeyed, or rather was dragged nearer by the Head Porter. 'Let him go, can't you?' said the Manageress in exasperation. 'He isn't a murderer!' The Head Porter actually let him go, but before doing so crushed his arm in a final grip so violently that tears came to his own eyes with the effort.

'Karl,' said the Manageress, folding her hands calmly in her lap and looking at Karl with her head bent – it was not in the least like an interrogation – 'first of all I want to tell you that I still have complete confidence in you. Also the Head Waiter is a just man; I can vouch for that. Both of us at bottom would be glad to keep you here' – here she glanced briefly at the Head Waiter, as if begging him not to interrupt. Nor did he do so. 'So forget everything that may have been said to you here till now. Above all, you mustn't take too seriously anything the Head Porter may have said. He's an irritable man, which is no wonder considering his work; but he has a wife and children too, and he knows that a boy who has to fend for himself needs no extra torments, since the rest of the world will see that he gets his fair share of them.'

It was quite still in the room. The Head Porter looked at the Head Waiter as if expecting support, the Head Waiter looked at the Manageress and shook his head. Best, the lift-boy, grinned idiotically behind the Head Waiter's back. Therese was quietly sobbing with grief and joy and doing her best to keep the others from remarking it.

Yet, although it could only be construed as a bad sign, Karl did not look at the Manageress, who certainly wished him to do so, but in front of him at the floor. The pain in his arm was still shooting in all directions, his shirt-sleeve was sticking to the bruises, and he should really have taken off his jacket to attend to them. What the Manageress said was of course very kindly meant, yet it seemed to him that simply because of the way in which she was acting, the others must think that her kindness was foolish, that he had been enjoying her friendship on false pretences for two months, and that he actually deserved nothing better than to fall into the Head Porter's hands. 'I say this,' went on the Manageress, 'so that you can give me a straight answer, which it's likely you would have done in any case, if I know you.'

'Please, may I go for the doctor in the meantime; the man may be bleeding to death,' the lift-boy Best suddenly put in, very politely, but very disconcertingly.

'Go,' the Head Waiter said to Best, who at once rushed off. And then to the Manageress: 'The case is this. The Head Porter wasn't holding the boy as a joke. Down in the lift-boys' dormitory an utter stranger, completely drunk, was discovered carefully tucked up in one of the beds. The boys naturally wakened him and tried to get rid of him. But then the fellow began to make a great row, shouting that this was Karl Rossmann's bedroom and that he was Rossmann's guest, that Rossmann had brought him here, and would thrash anyone who dared to touch him. Besides, he simply had to wait until Karl Rossmann came back, for Rossmann had promised him money and had gone to fetch it. Please note that, my dear madam: had promised him money and gone to fetch it. You note that too, Rossmann,' the

Head Waiter said over his shoulder to Karl, who had just glanced round at Therese, who in turn was staring at the Head Waiter as if spell-bound and continually pushing a strand of hair from her forehead or else mechanically lifting her hand to her brow for the sake of something to do. 'Perhaps you need reminding of your engagements. For the man below also said that on your return you were going to spend the night with some female singer, whose name nobody could make out, I grant you, since the fellow always burst into song whenever he came to it.'

Here the Head Waiter paused, for the Manageress, grown visibly paler, rose from her chair, pushing it back a little.

'I'll spare you the rest,' said the Head Waiter.

'No, please, no,' said the Manageress, seizing his arm. 'Please go on; I must know everything; that's why I'm here.'

The Head Porter, who now stepped forward and struck himself loudly on the chest to advertise that he had seen through everything from the very beginning, was simultaneously appeased and put in his place by the Head Waiter with the words: 'Yes, you were quite right, Feodor.'

'There isn't much more to tell,' went on the Head Waiter. 'The boys, being what they are, laughed at the man first, then got into a fight with him, and as there are plenty of good boxers among them, he was simply knocked out; and I haven't dared to ask even where he is bleeding and in how many places, for these boys are punishing boxers and a drunk man is of course easy game to them.'

'I see,' said the Manageress, laying her hand on the arm of the chair and looking down at the seat which she had just left. 'Please do say something, Rossmann!' she said then. Therese had rushed across the room and was clinging to her mistress, a thing which Karl had never seen her do before. The Head Waiter was standing close behind the Manageress, slowly smoothing her modest little lace collar, which had slipped somewhat awry. The Head Porter standing beside Karl said: 'Speak up!' but merely used the words to cover the punch which he gave him in the back.

'It's true,' said Karl, more uncertainly than he intended, because of the blow, 'that I put the man in the dormitory.'

'That's all we need to know,' said the Head Porter, speaking for everyone present. The Manageress turned dumbly to the Head Waiter and then to Therese.

'I couldn't help myself,' Karl went on. 'The man is someone I used to know; he came here to pay me a visit after not seeing me for two months; but he was so drunk that he couldn't go away again by himself.'

The Head Waiter, standing beside the Manageress, said softly as if to himself: 'So he came to pay you a visit and later got so drunk that he couldn't leave.' The Manageress whispered something over her shoulder to the Head Waiter, who seemed to raise objections but smiled at her in a way that obviously had nothing to do with Karl. Therese – Karl kept his eyes fixed on her – pressed her face in complete despair against the Manageress and refused to look at anything. The only one who was completely satisfied with Karl's explanation was the Head Porter, who repeated several times: 'That's quite right, you must stand by a pal when he's drunk,' and tried to emphasize this explanation by looking at the others and waving his hands.

'I am to blame, therefore,' said Karl, and paused as if waiting for a kind word from his judges to give him courage for continuing his defence, but none came. 'I am to blame, therefore, only for taking the man to the dormitory – he's called Robinson and he's an Irishman. Everything else he said because he was drunk, and it isn't true.'

'So you didn't promise him money?' asked the Head Waiter.

'Yes,' said Karl, and he felt sorry at having forgotten that; in his haste and confusion he had been too peremptory in declaring himself innocent. 'I did promise him money because he begged me for it. But I had no intention of fetching it, but merely of giving him the tips I got tonight.' And in proof he pulled the money out of his pocket and held out his hand with the few small coins.

'You're tying yourself up more and more,' said the Head

Waiter. 'If we're to believe you, we've got to keep forgetting what you said before. First you only took the man to the dormitory – and I don't even believe that his name is Robinson, for no Irishman was ever called that since Ireland was Ireland – first you only took him to the dormitory – and for that alone you could be flung out on your neck, I may tell you – but you didn't promise him money, yet when the question is sprung on you, it seems you did promise him money. This isn't a game of question and answer, let me remind you; you're supposed to be giving an explanation of yourself. And at first you had no intention of fetching the money, you merely meant to give him the tips you got tonight, and now it turns out that you still have this money on you, and so you must have intended to get some more money, a supposition which is strengthened by your long absence. After all, it wouldn't be strange if you wanted to get some money from your box for him; but it certainly is strange that you deny it so violently, and that you keep on hiding the fact that you made the man drunk here in the hotel, of which there can be no possible doubt, for you yourself admit that he came here by himself but could not leave by himself, and he has told everybody in the dormitory that he is your guest. So now only two things remain in doubt, which you can tell us yourself if you wish to save trouble, but which can be perfectly well established without your help: first, how you managed to get into the storerooms, and second, how you got your hands on enough money to give away?'

'It's impossible to defend oneself where there is no goodwill,' Karl told himself, and he made no further answer to the Head Waiter, deeply as that seemed to afflict Therese. He knew that all he could say would appear quite different to the others, and that whether a good or a bad construction was to be put on his actions depended alone on the spirit in which he was judged.

'He makes no answer,' said the Manageress.

'It is the best thing he can do,' said the Head Waiter.

'He'll soon think out something else,' said the Head Porter, caressing his whiskers with a hand now gentle, though lately so terrible.

'Be quiet,' said the Manageress to Therese, who had begun to sob, standing beside her, 'you see that he has no answer to make, so how can I do anything for him? After all, it is I who am put in the wrong in the Head Waiter's eyes. Tell me, Therese, in your opinion have I omitted anything I could have done for him?' How could Therese know that, and what point was there in giving away so much before these two men by this public question and appeal to the girl?

'Madam,' said Karl, once more pulling himself together, for no other purpose than to spare Therese the effort of answering, 'I think that I haven't brought any discredit on you, and if a proper investigation were made, everyone else would have to agree with me.'

'Everyone else,' said the Head Porter, pointing his finger at the Head Waiter, 'that's meant for you, Mr Isbary.'

'Now, madam,' said Mr Isbary, 'it's half-past six, and it's high time this was settled. I think you had better leave me the last word in this matter, which we have handled far too patiently.'

Little Giacomo came in and made to go up to Karl, but, daunted by the general silence, checked himself and waited.

Since the last words he had said, the Manageress had never taken her eyes off Karl, nor was there any indication that she had heard the Head Waiter's remark. Her eyes looked straight at Karl; they were large and blue, but a little dimmed by age and many troubles. As she stood there gently tilting the chair before her, she looked as if she would say next minute: 'Well, Karl, when I think it over, this business isn't at all clear yet and needs, as you rightly say, a thorough investigation, and we'll proceed to make that now, whether anyone agrees or not, for justice must be done.'

But instead of this, the Manageress said after a short pause which no one dared to interrupt – except that the clock struck half-past six in confirmation of the Head Waiter's words and with it, as everyone knew, all the other clocks in the whole hotel; it rang forebodingly in the ear, like the double beat of a universal great impatience: 'No, Karl, no, no! We won't listen to any more of this. When things are right they look right, and I must confess that your actions don't. I am entitled to say so and I am bound to say so; I am bound to admit it, for it was I who came here with every prepossession in your favour. You see that Therese is silent too.' (But she was not silent, she was crying.)

The Manageress stopped as if suddenly coming to a decision and said: 'Karl, come over here,' and when he went over to her – the Head Waiter and the Head Porter immediately began an animated conversation behind his back – she put her left arm round him and led him, followed by the passive Therese, to the other end of the room, where she began to walk up and down with the two of them, and said: 'It's possible, Karl, and you seem to put faith in it, otherwise I really wouldn't know what to make of you, that an investigation might justify you on separate small points. Why shouldn't it? Maybe you did give a greeting to the Head Porter. I feel certain you did, and I have my own opinion of the Head Porter; you see I am still quite frank with you. But such small justifications won't help you in the least. The Head Waiter, whose knowledge of people I have learned to prize in the course of many years, and who is the most trustworthy man I know, has clearly pronounced your guilt, and I must say it seems undeniable to me. Perhaps you merely acted without thinking, but perhaps too you aren't the boy I thought you were. And yet,' with that she interrupted herself and cast a fleeting glance over her shoulder at the two men, 'I can't help still thinking of you as a fundamentally decent lad.'

'Madam! Madam!' said the Head Waiter, warningly, for he had caught her glance.

'We'll be finished in a minute,' said the Manageress, beginning to admonish Karl more hurriedly: 'Listen, Karl, from what I can make out of this business, I am actually glad that the Head Waiter doesn't want to start an inquiry; for if he were to do it, I should have to prevent it in your own interest. No one must know how or where you got drink for that man, who couldn't have been one of your former friends, as you give out, for you quarrelled violently with them when you left them, so that you wouldn't be so friendly with either of them now. Therefore it must have been an acquaintance you just picked up one night in some drinking-den in the town. How could you hide all these things from me, Karl? If you really couldn't bear the dormitory and began to rake about at night for an innocent reason like that, why did you never say a word about it? You know that I wanted to get you a room of your own and only gave up the idea at your own request. It looks now as if you preferred the general dormitory because you felt that you had more liberty there. And you always put by your money in my safe and brought me the tips you got every week; where in heaven's name, boy, did you get the money for these excursions and where did you intend to find the money for your friend? Of course, these are things that I can't mention to the Head Waiter, for the moment at least, or else perhaps an inquiry might be unavoidable. So you must simply leave the hotel, and as soon as possible too. Go straight to the Pension Brenner – you've been there several times with Therese already – they'll take you in for nothing if you show them this –' and she wrote a few lines on a card with a gold pencil which she pulled out of her blouse, but without interrupting what she was saying – 'I'll send your box after you at once. Therese, run up to the lift-boys' cloakroom and pack his box!' (But Therese did not stir, for as she had endured all the grief, she wanted also to share to the full this turn for the better which Karl's fortunes had taken, thanks to the kindness of the Manageress.)

Someone opened the door a little without showing himself and shut it again at once. It must have been a reminder to Giacomo, for he stepped forward and said: 'Rossmann, I must speak to you.'

'In a minute,' said the Manageress, sticking the card in Karl's pocket as he stood listening with drooping head, 'I'll keep your money for the time being; you know that it's safe in my hands. Stay in your room today and consider your position; tomorrow – I have no time today, and I've been kept far too long here – I'll come to the Brenner and we'll see what more can be done for you. I won't forsake you, you must know that quite well already. You needn't worry about your future, but rather about these last few weeks.' She patted him on the shoulder and then went over to the Head Waiter. Karl raised his head and gazed after the tall stately woman, as she walked away from him with her light step and easy bearing.

'Well, aren't you glad,' said Therese, who had stayed beside him, 'that everything has turned out so well?'

'Oh yes,' said Karl, and he smiled at her, yet could not see why he should be glad because he had been dismissed as a thief. Therese's eyes shone with the purest joy, as if it were a matter of complete indifference to her whether Karl had committed a crime or not, whether he had been justly sentenced or not, if he were only permitted to escape, in shame or in honour. And it was Therese who behaved like this, Therese who was so scrupulous in everything relating to herself that she would turn over in her mind and examine for weeks any half-doubtful word of the Manageress. With deliberate design he said: 'Will you pack my box for me and send it off at once?' In spite of himself he had to shake his head in astonishment, so quickly did Therese catch the implications of the question, and in her conviction that there were things in the box which no one must see, she did not take time even to glance at Karl, even to shake his hand, but merely whispered: 'Certainly, Karl, at once, I'll pack the box this minute.' And she was gone.

But now Giacomo could not restrain himself any longer and, agitated by his long wait, cried: 'Rossmann, the man is kicking up a row in the passage and won't go away. They want to take him to hospital, but he's objecting and saying that you'll never let him be taken to a hospital. He says we must call a taxi and drive him home and that you'll pay the fare. Will you?'

'The man seems to rely on you,' said the Head Waiter. Karl shrugged his shoulders and counted his money into Giacomo's hand. 'That's all I have,' he said.

'I was to ask you too if you're going in the taxi with him,' added Giacomo, jingling the money.

'No, he isn't going,' said the Manageress.

'Well, Rossmann,' said the Head Waiter quickly, without even waiting until Giacomo was out of the room, 'you are dismissed here and now.' The Head Porter nodded several times, as if these were his own words and the Head Waiter merely his mouthpiece. 'The reasons for your dismissal I simply can't mention publicly, for in that case I would have to send you to gaol.' The Head Porter looked very severely at the Manageress, for he knew perfectly well that she was the cause of such excessively mild treatment. 'Now go to Best, change your clothes, hand over your uniform to Best and leave the hotel at once, but at once.'

The Manageress closed her eyes, wishing by this to reassure Karl. As he bowed out, he saw the Head Waiter surreptitiously seizing her hand and fondling it. With heavy steps the Head Porter escorted Karl to the door, which he would not let him shut but held open with his own hands so as to shout after him: 'In a quarter of a minute you will pass, my office and leave by the main door. See to that!'

Karl made what haste he could, so as to avoid any molestation on leaving, but everything went much more slowly than he wanted. First of all, Best could not be found immediately, and at this time during the breakfast hour a great many people were about; then it appeared that another boy had borrowed Karl's old trousers, and Karl had to search the clothes-pegs beside almost all the beds before he found them; so that five minutes at least had elapsed before he reached the main door. Just in front of him a lady was walking accompanied by four gentlemen. They all went over to a big car which was waiting for them; a lackey was holding open the door while he stretched out his free arm sideways at shoulder level, very stiffly, which looked highly impressive. But Karl's hope of getting away unobserved behind this fashionable group was a vain one. For the Head Porter caught him by the hand and dragged him back between two of the gentlemen, with a word of excuse to them.

'Do you call this a quarter of a minute?' he asked, looking askance at Karl, as if he were examining a clock that did not keep time. 'Come in here,' he went on, propelling him into the huge porter's office, which Karl had once been eager enough to inspect but now that he was thrust into it viewed with suspicion. Just inside the door he squirmed round and tried to push the Head Porter away and escape.

'No, no, this way in,' said the Head Porter, turning him round again.

'But I've been thrown out,' said Karl, meaning that nobody in the hotel had a right to give him orders now.

'As long as I keep hold of you, you're not thrown out,' said the porter, which was also true enough.

Besides, Karl could see no actual reason for resisting the porter. After all, what more could happen to him now? Also, the walls of the office consisted entirely of enormous panes of glass, through which you could see the incoming and outgoing streams of guests in the vestibule as clearly as if you were among them. Yes, there seemed to be no nook or corner in the whole office where you could be hidden from their eyes. No matter in how great a hurry the people outside seemed to be, as with outstretched arms, bent heads and peering eyes, holding their luggage high, they sought their way, hardly one of them omitted to cast a glance into the porter's office, for behind the panes announcements and news were always hanging which were intended both for the guests and the hotel staff. Moreover, the porter's office and the vestibule were in direct communication with each other, for at two great sliding windows sat two under-porters perpetually occupied in giving information on the most diverse subjects. These men were indeed over-burdened, and Karl had a shrewd guess that the Head Porter, for what he knew of him, had circumvented this stage in the course of his advancement. These two providers of information – from outside you could not really imagine what it looked like – had always at least ten inquiring faces before them in the window opening. Among these ten, who were continually changing, there was often a perfect babel of tongues, as if each were an emissary from a different country. There were always several making inquiries at the same time, while others again carried on a conversation with each other. The majority wanted to deposit something in the porter's office or take something away, so that wildly gesticulating hands could also be seen rising from the crowd. Or a man was impatient to look at a newspaper, which suddenly unfolded in the air for a moment blotting out all the faces. All this the two under-porters had to deal with. Mere talking would not have sufficed for their work; they gabbled, and one in particular, a gloomy man with a dark beard almost hiding his whole face, poured out information without even taking breath. He neither looked at the counter, where he was perpetually handing things out, nor at the face of this or that questioner, but straight in front of him, obviously to economize and conserve his strength. His beard too must have somewhat interfered with the clearness of his enunciation, and in the short time that he was standing there Karl could make out very little of what was said, though possibly, in spite of the English intonation, it was in some foreign language which was required at the moment. Additionally confusing was the fact that one answer came so quickly on the heels of another as to be indistinguishable from it, so that often an inquirer went on listening intently, in the belief that his question was still being answered, without noticing for some time that his turn was past. You had also to get used to the under-porter's habit of never asking a question to be repeated; even if it was vague only in wording and quite sensible on the whole, he merely gave an almost imperceptible shake of the head to indicate that he did not intend to answer that question and it was the questioner's business to recognize his own error and formulate the question more correctly. This in particular kept many people for a long time in front of the counter. To help the under-porters, each of them was allotted a messenger boy, who had to rush to and fro bringing from a bookcase and various cupboards whatever the under-porter might need. These were the best-paid if also the hardest posts that young boys could get in the hotel; in a sense these boys were still harder put to it than the under-porters, who had merely to think and speak, while the boys had to think and run about at the same time. If they ever brought the wrong thing, the under-porter was too pressed, of course, to give them a long lecture; with one flip of the hand he simply knocked to the floor whatever they had laid on the counter. Very interesting was the changing of the under-porters, which took place shortly after Karl came in. These changes had of course to happen frequently, at least during the day, for probably no man alive could have held out for more than an hour at the counter. At the relief hour a bell rang, and simultaneously there emerged from a side door the two under-porters whose turn had now come, each followed by his messenger boy. For the time being they posted themselves idly by the window and contemplated for a while the people outside, so as to discover exactly what questions were being dealt with. When the moment seemed suitable for intervention, the new-comer could tap on the shoulder the under-porter he was to relieve, who, although until now he had paid no attention to what was going on behind his back, at once responded and left his place. It all happened so quickly that it often surprised the people standing outside, and they almost jumped in alarm when a strange face popped up before them. The two men who were relieved stretched themselves and then poured water over their hot heads at two wash-basins standing ready for them. But the messenger boys could not stretch themselves so soon, being kept busy for a little longer picking up and returning to their places the various objects which had been flung on the floor during their shift.

All this Karl had taken in with the closest attention in a few minutes, and then with a slight headache he quietly followed the Head Porter, who led him farther on. The Head Porter had obviously noticed the deep impression which this method of answering inquiries had made on Karl, for he gave his arm a sudden jerk and said: 'You see that's the way we work here.' Karl had certainly not been idle in the hotel, but he had had no conception of such work as this and he looked up, forgetting almost completely that the Head Porter was his mortal enemy, and nodded with silent appreciation. But this again seemed to the Head Porter an over-valuation of the under-porters and perhaps a piece of presumption towards himself, for he exclaimed, without caring that everyone heard him, and quite as if he had just been making a fool of Karl: 'Of course this work here is the stupidest in the whole hotel; you need only to listen for an hour to know pretty well all the questions that will be asked, and the rest you don't have to answer at all. If you weren't so impudent and ill-mannered, if you hadn't lied, lazed, boozed and thieved, perhaps I might have managed to put you at one of these windows, since it's only a job for dunderheads.' Karl ignored the insult to himself, so indignant was he that the hard and honourable work of the under-porters should be jeered at instead of being recognized, and jeered at moreover by a man who, if he ever ventured to sit down at one of these windows, would certainly cover himself with ridicule in a few minutes and have to abandon the job.

'Let me go,' said Karl, his curiosity concerning the porter's office more than satiated, 'I don't want to have anything more to do with you.'

'That's no reason for letting you go,' said the Head Porter, crushing Karl's arm until it was numb and literally dragging him to the other end of the office. Couldn't the people outside see this bullying? Or, if they saw it, what did they think it meant, since none of them objected to it or even tapped on the glass to show the Head Porter that he was being watched and could not deal with Karl just as he liked?

But Karl soon gave up all hope of getting help from the vestibule, for the Head Porter seized a cord, and over the glass panes of one half of the office black curtains reaching from the roof to the floor were drawn in a twinkling. In this part of the office, too, there were people, but all working at top speed and without an ear or an eye for anything unconnected with their work. Also they were completely dependent on the Head Porter, and instead of helping Karl would rather have helped to conceal anything that the Head Porter took it into his head to do. For instance, there were six under-porters attending to six telephones. Their method of working was obvious at a glance; out of each couple one did nothing but note down conversations, passing on these notes to his neighbour, who despatched the messages by another telephone. The instruments were of the new-fashioned kind which do not need a telephone box, for the ringing of the bell was no louder than a twitter, and a mere whisper into the mouthpiece was electrically amplified until it reached its destination in a voice of thunder. For this reason the three men who were speaking into the telephones were scarcely audible, and one might have thought they were muttering to themselves about something happening in the mouthpiece, while the other three, as if deadened by the thunder coming from their ear-pieces, although no one else could hear a sound, drooped their heads over the sheets of paper on which they had to make their notes. Here too a boy assistant stood beside each of the three whisperers; these three boys did nothing but alternately lean their heads towards their masters in a listening posture and then hastily, as if stung, search for telephone numbers in huge, yellow books: the rustling of so many massed pages easily drowned any noise from the telephones.

Karl simply could not keep himself from watching all this, although the Head Porter, who had sat down, clutched him in a sort of hug.

'It is my duty,' said the Head Porter, shaking Karl as if he only wanted to make him turn his face towards him, 'it is my duty, if the Head Waiter has left anything undone, for whatever reason, to repair his omission in the name of the hotel management, as best I can. We always do our best here to help one another out. If it weren't for that, such a great organization would be unthinkable. You may say that I'm not your immediate superior; well, it's all the more to my credit if I attend to things that other people neglect. Besides, as Head Porter I am in a sense placed over everyone, for I'm in charge of all the doors of the hotel, this main door, the three middle and the ten side doors, not to mention innumerable little doors and doorless exits. Naturally all the service staff who come in contact with me have to obey me absolutely. In return for this great honour, of course, I have myself an obligation to the hotel management to let no one out of the hotel who is in the slightest degree suspicious. And you are just the person who strikes my fancy as being a highly suspicious character.' He was so pleased with himself that he lifted his hands and brought them down again with a heavy smack that hurt. 'It is possible,' he added, enjoying himself royally, 'that you could have slipped out of the hotel by some other door; of course I shouldn't trouble to give out special instructions on your account. But since you're here, I'm going to make the most of you. Besides, I never really doubted that you would keep our rendezvous by the front door, for it is a general rule that impudent and disobedient creatures take to being virtuous just when they're likely to suffer from the consequences. You'll certainly be able to notice that often enough from your own experience.'

'Don't imagine,' said Karl, inhaling the curiously depressing odour given out by the Head Porter, which he had not noticed until he had stood so close to him for so long, 'don't imagine,' he said, 'that I am completely in your power, for I can scream.'

'And I can stop your mouth,' said the Head Porter as calmly and quickly as he probably would have done it in case of need. 'And do you really think, if you brought anyone in, that you could find a single person who would take your word against mine, the word of the Head Porter? So you can see how foolish your hopes are. Let me tell you, when you were still in uniform you actually looked a fairly respectable character, but in that suit of yours, which could only have been made in Europe –!' And he tugged at the most diverse parts of the suit, which, now, although it had been almost new five months ago, was certainly shabby, creased, and above all spotty, chiefly because of the heedlessness of the lift-boys, who were supposed to keep the dormitory floor polished and free from dust according to the general regulation, but in their laziness, instead of giving it a real cleaning, sprinkled the floor every day with some oil or other and at the same time spattered all the clothes on the clothes-stands. One could stow one's clothes where one liked, there was always someone who could not lay his hands on his own clothes, but never failed to find his neighbour's hidden garments and promptly borrow them. And almost invariably it was the boy who had to clean the dormitory that day, so that one's clothes were not only spattered with oil but dripping with it from head to foot. Rennell was the only boy who had found a secret place to hide his expensive clothes in; they were hardly ever discovered, since it was not malice or stinginess that prompted the boys to borrow clothes, but sheer haste and carelessness; they simply picked up garments wherever they found them. Yet even Rennell's suit had a round, reddish splash of oil in the middle of the back, and in the town an expert might have detected, from the evidence of that splash, that the stylish young dandy was a lift-boy after all.

Remembering these things, Karl told himself that he had suffered enough as a lift-boy and yet it had all been in vain, for his job had not proved, as he had hoped, a step to something higher, but had rather pushed him farther down, and even brought him very near prison. On top of this, he was still in the clutches of the Head Porter, who was no doubt considering ways and means of putting him to greater shame. And quite forgetting that the Head Porter was the last man to listen to reason, Karl exclaimed, striking his brow several times with the hand that happened to be free: 'Even if I actually did pass you without a greeting, how can a grown man be so vindictive about such an omission!'

'I am not vindictive,' said the Head Porter, 'I only want to search your pockets. I am convinced, to be sure, that I'll find nothing, for you've probably been careful and slipped everything to your friend bit by bit, a little every day. But searched you must be.' And he thrust his hand into one of Karl's coat pockets with such violence that the side-stitches burst. 'So there's nothing here,' he said, turning over in his hand the contents of the pocket, a calendar issued by the hotel, a sheet of paper containing an exercise in commercial correspondence, a few coat and trouser buttons, the Manageress's card, a nail-file which a guest had once tossed to him as he was packing his trunk, an old pocket mirror which Rennell had once given to him as a reward for taking over his work ten times or so, and a few more trifles. 'So there's nothing here,' said the Head Porter again, flinging everything under the bench, as if that were the proper place for any of Karl's possessions which happened not to be stolen property.

'But this is the last straw,' said Karl to himself – his face must have been flaming red – and as the Head Porter, rendered incautious by greed, was rummaging in his second pocket, Karl slipped out of the sleeves with a jerk, cannoned into an under-porter with his first blind spring, knocking the man violently against his telephone, ran through the stuffy room to the door, actually not so fast as he had intended, but fast enough to get outside before the Head Porter in his heavy coat was able to even rise up. The organization of the hotel could not be so perfect after all; some bells were ringing, it was true, but heaven only knew to what purpose! Members of the hotel staff were careering about the entrance this way and that, in such numbers that one might almost have thought they wanted unobtrusively to make it impossible for anyone to get out, since it was hard to find much sense in all the coming and going; however, Karl was soon in the open air, but had still to keep along the front of the hotel, for an unbroken line of cars was slowly moving past the entrance and he could not reach the road. These cars, in their eagerness to get to their owners as quickly as possible, were actually touching each other, nosing each other forward. A pedestrian here and there, in a particular hurry to cross the road, would climb through the nearest car as if it were a public passage, not caring at all whether there was only a chauffeur in it and a couple of servants, or the most fashionable company. But that kind of behaviour seemed rather high-handed to Karl, and he reflected that one must be very sure of oneself to venture on it; he might easily hit upon a car whose occupants resented it, threw him out and raised a row, and as a runaway suspect lift-boy in his shirt-sleeves there was nothing that he could fear more. After all, the line of cars could not go on for ever, and so long as he stuck close to the hotel there was the less reason to suspect him. Actually he reached a point at last where the line of cars was not exactly broken, but curved away towards the street and loosened out a little. He was just on the point of slipping through into the traffic of the street, where far more suspicious-looking people than himself were probably at large, when he heard his name being called near by. He turned round and saw in a small, low doorway, which looked like the entrance to a vault, a couple of lift-boys whom he knew well, straining and tugging at a stretcher on which, as he now perceived, Robinson was actually lying, his head, face and arms swathed in manifold bandages. It was horrible to see him lift his arms to his eyes to wipe away his tears with the bandages, tears of pain or grief or perhaps even of joy at seeing Karl again.

'Rossmann,' he cried reproachfully, 'why have you kept me waiting so long? For a whole hour I've been struggling to keep myself from being carted away before you came. These fellows' – and he gave one of the lift-boys a clout on the head, as if his bandages secured him from retaliation – 'are absolute devils. Ah, Rossmann, I've had to pay dearly for this visit to you.'

'Why, what have they been doing to you?' said Karl, stepping over to the stretcher, which the lift-boys laughingly set down so as to have a rest.

'You ask that,' groaned Robinson, 'and yet you can see what I look like. Just think of it, they've very likely made me a cripple for life. I have frightful pains from here right down to here' – and he pointed first to his head and then to his toes – 'I only wish you had seen how much my nose bled. My waistcoat is completely ruined, and I had to leave it behind me too; my trousers are in tatters, I'm in my drawers' – and he lifted the blanket a little and invited Karl to look under it. 'What on earth is to become of me? I'll have to lie in bed for months at least, and I may tell you at once there's nobody but you to nurse me; Delamarche is far too impatient. Rossmann, don't leave me!' And Robinson stretched out one hand towards the reluctant Karl, seeking to win him over by caresses. 'Why had I to come and call on you!' he repeated several times, to keep Karl from forgetting that he was partly responsible for his misfortunes. Now it did not take Karl a minute to see that Robinson's lamentations were caused not by his wounds but by the colossal hangover he was suffering from, since just after falling asleep dead-drunk he had been wakened up and to his surprise violently assaulted until he had lost all sense of reality. The trivial nature of his wounds could be seen from the old rags of bandages with which the lift-boys, obviously in jest, had swathed him round and round. And the two boys at either end of the stretcher kept going into fits of laughter. But this was hardly the place to bring Robinson to his senses, for people were streaming past without paying any attention to the group beside the stretcher, often enough taking a flying leap clean over Robinson, while the taxi-driver who had been paid with Karl's money kept crying: 'Come on! Come on!' The lift-boys put out all their strength and raised the stretcher, and Robinson seized Karl's hand, saying coaxingly: 'Come along, do come.' Considering the figure he cut, would not Karl be best provided for in the sheltering darkness of the taxi? And so he settled himself besides Robinson, who leaned his head against him. The two lift-boys heartily shook hands with him through the window, taking leave of their one-time colleague, and the taxi made a sharp turn into the thoroughfare. It looked as if an accident were inevitable, but the all-embracing stream of traffic quietly swept into itself even the arrowy thrust of their vehicle.

7

A REFUGE

It seemed to be an outlying suburban street where the taxi stopped, for everything was quiet and children were sitting playing on the edge of the pavement. A man with a pile of old clothes slung over his shoulder kept a watchful eye on the house-windows above him as he cried his wares. Karl was so weary that he felt out of place when he stepped out of the car on to the asphalt, which lay warm and bright in the morning sunshine.

'Is this really where you live?' he called into the taxi.

Robinson, who had slept peacefully during the whole journey, growled an indistinct affirmative and seemed to be waiting for Karl to carry him out.

'Then you don't need me any more. Good-bye,' said Karl, and started to walk away down the slight slope of the street.

'But Karl, what on earth are you thinking of?' cried Robinson, and his anxiety was so great that he stood up in the car fairly straight, except that his knees were somewhat shaky.

'I've got to go now,' said Karl, who had observed Robinson's speedy recovery.

'In your shirt-sleeves?' asked Robinson.

'I'll soon earn myself another jacket,' replied Karl, and he nodded confidently to Robinson, raised his hand in farewell and would have departed in earnest had not the taxi-driver called out: 'Just a moment, sir!'

Unfortunately it appeared that the man laid claim to a supplementary payment, to cover the extra time he had waited in front of the hotel.

'Of course,' cried Robinson from the car, supporting the justice of this demand, 'you kept me waiting such a long time there. You must give him something more.'

'Yes, that's so,' said the taxi-driver.

'Yes, if I only had anything to give,' said Karl, searching in his trouser pockets although he knew that it was useless.

'I have only you to look to,' said the taxi-driver, planting himself squarely before Karl. 'I can't ask anything from a sick man.'

From the door a young lad with a nose half eaten away drew nearer and stood listening a few paces away. A policeman who was just making his round of the street lowered his head, took a good look at the figure in shirt-sleeves and came to a stop.

Robinson, who had noticed the policeman, made the blunder of shouting to him from the other window of the car: 'It's nothing, it's nothing!' as if a policeman could be chased away like a fly. The children, who had been watching the policeman, saw him stop, had their attention drawn to Karl and the taxi-man and came trotting up. In a doorway across the street an old woman stood stolidly at gaze.

'Rossmann!' shouted a voice from above them. It was Delamarche standing on the balcony of the top floor. It was difficult to see him against the pale blue sky, but he was obviously wearing a dressing-gown and observing the street through a pair of opera glasses. Beside him there was a big red sunshade, under which a woman seemed to be sitting. 'Hello!' he shouted at the very top of his voice, to make himself understood, 'is Robinson there too?'

'Yes,' replied Karl, powerfully supported by a second, far louder 'Yes' from Robinson in the car. 'Hello!' Delamarche shouted back, 'I'm coming at once!'

Robinson leaned out of the car. 'That's a man,' he said, and this praise of Delamarche was directed at Karl, at the driver, at the policeman and anyone else who cared to hear it. Up on the balcony, which they still kept watching absently, although Delamarche had already left it, from under the sunshade there rose a large figure which proved to be indeed a woman in a loose red gown; she lifted the opera glasses from the ledge of the balcony and gazed through them down at the people below, who began to turn their eyes away from her, though lingeringly. Karl looked at the house-door where Delamarche was to appear, and then right through it into the courtyard, which was being traversed by an almost unbroken line of workmen, each of whom bore on his shoulder a small but obviously very heavy box. The taxi-driver had stepped across to his car and to employ the time was polishing the lamps with a rag. Robinson felt all his limbs, seeming astonished because in spite of the most intent examination he could discover none but trivial aches, and then bent down and cautiously began to undo one of the thick bandages around his leg. The policeman held his black baton at a slant before him and quietly waited with that deep patience which policemen must have, whether they are on ordinary duty or on the watch. The lad with the eaten nose sat down on a doorstep and stretched his legs before him. The children gradually crept nearer to Karl, for although he paid no attention to them, he seemed the most important of all to them because of his blue shirt-sleeves.

By the length of time that elapsed before Delamarche's arrival one could measure the great height of the house. And Delamarche came in great haste, having stopped merely to tie the cord round his dressing-gown. 'So here you are!' he cried, with both delight and severity in his tone. At each great stride he took his bright-coloured pyjamas could be seen for an instant. Karl could not quite make out how Delamarche could go about in such negligent attire here, in the town, in this huge tenement, on the open street, as if he were in his private villa. There was a big change in Delamarche, as well as in Robinson. His dark, clean-shaven, scrupulously clean face with its rough modelling of muscle looked proud and inspired respect. The hard glitter of his eyes, which he still kept half-shut, was startling; his violet-coloured dressing-gown was certainly old, spotted and too big for him, but from that squalid garment there emerged at the neck the folded swathes of an enormous scarf of heavy dark silk.

'Well?' he asked, addressing everybody. The policeman stepped a little nearer and leaned against the body of the car. Karl gave a brief explanation.

'Robinson's a bit wobbly, but he can easily climb the stairs if he tries; the driver here wants something extra besides the fare I have already paid him. And now I'm going, good day.'

'You're not going,' said Delamarche.

'I've told him that too,' Robinson announced from the taxi.

'I'm going all the same,' said Karl, taking a few steps. But Delamarche was already beside him, forcibly holding him back.

'I say you're staying here!' he cried.

'Let me go,' said Karl, and he made ready to gain his freedom with his fists if necessary, little hope as he had of downing a man like Delamarche. Yet the policeman was standing by, and the taxi-driver, and the street was not so quiet but that occasional groups of workmen passed through it; would they tolerate it if Delamarche were to mishandle him? He would not like to be left alone with him in a room, but why not here? Delamarche was now quietly paying off the taxi-driver, who pocketed the unmerited and substantial addition to his fare with many bows and out of gratitude went up to Robinson and began to consult him with how he was best to be got out of the car. Karl saw that he was unobserved; perhaps Delamarche would mind it less if he just slipped away; it was best to avoid a quarrel if it could be avoided; and so he simply stepped on to the road as the quickest way of getting clear. The children rushed over to Delamarche to let him know that Karl was escaping, but Delamarche had no need to intervene, for the policeman stretched out his baton and said 'Stop!'

'What's your name?' he asked, tucking his baton under his arm and slowly bringing out a notebook. Karl now looked at him carefully for the first time; he was a powerfully built man, but his hair was already almost white.

'Karl Rossmann,' he said.

'Rossmann,' the policeman echoed him, no doubt simply because he was a quiet conscientious man, but Karl, who was now having his first encounter with the American police, saw in this repetition of his words a certain mistrust. And indeed his position was probably precarious, for even Robinson, though he was so occupied with his own troubles, was making dumb imploring gestures from the car to Delamarche, begging him to help Karl. But Delamarche refused him with a hasty shake of the head and looked on without doing anything, his hands in the huge pockets of the dressing-gown. To a woman who had just come out of the house the lad on the doorstep explained the whole situation from the very beginning. The children stood in a half-circle behind Karl and silently looked up at the policeman.

'Show your identification papers,' said the policeman. That

could only be a formal question; for without a jacket one was not likely to have many identification papers in one's pockets. So Karl remained silent, deciding to answer the next question fully and so if possible to gloss over his lack of identification papers.

But the next question was: 'So you have no papers?' And Karl had to answer: 'Not with me.'

'But that's bad,' said the policeman, looking thoughtfully around him and tapping with two fingers on the cover of his notebook. 'Have you an occupation?' he asked at last.

'I was a lift-boy,' said Karl.

'You were a lift-boy, so you aren't one any longer; and in that case what are you living on now?'

'I'm going to look out for another job.'

'I see; have you just been dismissed?'

'Yes, an hour ago.'

'Suddenly?'

'Yes,' said Karl, raising his hand as in apology. He could not tell the whole story here, and even if that had been possible, it seemed quite hopeless to think of averting a threatened injury by the recital of injuries already suffered. And if he had not been able to get his rights when faced by the kindness of the Manageress and the insight of the Head Waiter, he certainly could not expect to get them from the company gathered here in the street.

'And you were dismissed without your jacket?' asked the policeman.

'Why yes,' said Karl; so in America too it was the habit of authorities to ask questions about what they could see for themselves. (How exasperated his father had been over the pointless inquiries of the officials when he was getting Karl's passport!) Karl felt like running and hiding himself somewhere, if only to escape answering any more questions. And now the policeman put the very question which he feared most of all and which he had been so uneasily expecting that very likely he had behaved with less prudence than he might have done.

'In what hotel were you employed?'

Karl sank his head and did not reply; that was the last question he was prepared to answer. It simply must not happen for him to be escorted by a policeman to the Hotel Occidental again, to start investigations there into which his friends and enemies would all be drawn, to have the Manageress's wavering faith in him completely undermined, should the boy whom she thought was in the Pension Brenner turn up in the custody of a policeman, in his shirt-sleeves, without the card she had given him; while the Head Waiter would probably nod comprehendingly and the Head Porter mention the Hand of God which had at last caught the evil-doer.

'He was employed in the Hotel Occidental,' said Delamarche, stepping over the policeman.

'No,' shouted Karl, stamping his foot, 'that isn't true!' Delamarche surveyed him with his lips pursed in mockery, as if there were many things he could divulge. Among the children Karl's unexpected agitation produced great excitement, and they lined up beside Delamarche to get a better look at Karl. Robinson had stuck his head completely out of the car; he was so intent that he did not move except for an occasional flicker of the eyelids. The boy on the doorstep clapped his hands with delight; the woman beside him gave him a nudge with her elbow to keep him quiet. The porters in the courtyard had just stopped for breakfast and appeared in a bunch with great cans of black coffee, which they kept stirring with long rolls of bread. Several sat down on the edge of the pavement, and they all gulped down their coffee very loudly.

'You know this lad?' the policeman asked Delamarche.

'Better than I have a mind to,' said Delamarche. 'I have done him much kindness in my time, and he gave me little thanks for it, as you can probably imagine, even after the short encounter you've had with him.'

'Yes,' said the policeman, 'he seems to be a hardened young rascal.'

'He is all that,' said Delamarche, 'but even that isn't the worst thing about him.'

'Is that so?' said the policeman.

'Oh,' said Delamarche, who was now warming to his theme and swinging his dressing-gown to and fro with his hands in the pockets, 'he's a fine bird, this fellow. I and my friend there in the car once picked him up when he was down and out, he had no idea at the time of American conditions, he had just come from Europe, where they had no use for him either; well, we took him with us, let him live with us, explained things to him and tried to get him a job, thinking in spite of everything that we'd make a decent human being out of him, and in the end he did the disappearing trick one night, simply vanished, and in circumstances I'd rather not mention now. Is that true or not?' asked Delamarche in conclusion, plucking at Karl's shirt-sleeve.

'Back there, you children!' shouted the policeman, for the children had pressed forward so far that Delamarche had almost stumbled over one of them. Meanwhile the porters, discovering that this cross-examination was more interesting than they had suspected, began to pay some heed to it and gathered in a close ring behind Karl, so that he could not retreat even by a step and had to suffer, too, at his very ear the incessant chatter of these same porters, who babbled rather than spoke in a quite incomprehensible jargon which was perhaps broken English interspersed with Slavonic words.

'Thanks for the information,' said the policeman, saluting Delamarche. 'In any case I'll take him with me and hand him back to the Hotel Occidental.'

But Delamarche said: 'May I ask you as a favour to leave the boy with me for the time being; I have some business to settle with him. I promise you that I'll personally take him back to the hotel afterwards.'

'I can't do that,' said the policeman.

Delamarche said: 'Here is my card,' and handed him the card.

The policeman looked at it respectfully, but said with a polite smile: 'No, it can't be done.'

Much as Karl had been on his guard against Delamarche

hitherto, he saw in him now his only possible salvation. The way he was haggling with the policeman was certainly suspicious, but in any case Delamarche would be more easily induced than the policeman not to deliver him to the hotel. And even if he were brought back to the hotel by Delamarche, it would not be nearly so bad as to be escorted there by a policeman. For a moment, of course, he must not let it be seen that he really wanted to stay with Delamarche, or all was lost. And with an uneasy feeling he watched the policeman's hand, which might rise at any moment to seize him.

'I must at least find out why he was suddenly dismissed,' said the policeman at last, while Delamarche looked away with an offended air and twisted the card between his finger-tips.

'But he isn't dismissed at all!' cried Robinson to everyone's surprise, leaning out of the taxi as far as he could reach, with one hand on the driver's shoulder. 'Far from it; he has a very good job there. He's the head boy in the dormitory and can take anyone in there that he likes. Only he's terribly busy, and if you want to ask him for anything you have to wait for a long time. He's always in conference with the Head Waiter and the Manageress; his post is a confidential one. He's certainly not dismissed. I don't know why he said he was. How can he be dismissed? I got badly hurt in the hotel, and he had instructions to take me home, and since he wasn't wearing his jacket at the time he just came without it. I couldn't wait until he fetched his jacket.'

'Well now,' said Delamarche, spreading out his arms, in a tone which reproached the policeman for his lack of discernment; and these two words of his seemed to bring an incontestable clarity into the vagueness of Robinson's statement.

'But is this true?' asked the policeman, already weakening. 'And if it is true, why does the boy give out that he is dismissed?'

'You'd better tell him,' said Delamarche.

Karl looked at the policeman whose task it was to keep order here among strangers thinking only of their own advantage, and he had some intuition of the man's difficulties. That made him unwilling to tell a lie, so he kept his hands tightly clasped behind his back.

In the house-door an overseer appeared and clapped his hands as a signal that the porters should go back to work again. They shook the grounds out of their coffee cans and, falling silent, drifted reluctantly through the doorway.

'We'll never come to a conclusion this way,' said the policeman, and he made to seize Karl by the arm. Karl involuntarily recoiled a little, became conscious of the free space at his back which the porters' departure had left open, turned about and with a few great bounds for a start set off at full speed. The children let out a single yell and with outstretched arms ran a few steps along with him.

'Stop him!' the policeman shouted down the long, almost empty street, and shouting this cry at regular intervals set out after Karl at an easy run which showed both great strength and practice. It was lucky for Karl that the chase took place in a working-class quarter. The workers had no liking for the authorities. Karl stuck to the middle of the road because there were fewer obstacles there, and he saw occasional workers calmly halting on the pavement to watch him while the policeman shouted 'Stop him!' and kept pointing his baton at him as he ran a parallel course, keeping shrewdly to the smooth pavement. Karl had very little hope and almost lost that altogether when the policeman, as they were nearing some cross-streets where there were sure to be police patrols, began to blow really deafening blasts on his whistle. Karl's only advantage was his light attire; he flew, or rather plunged, down the street, which sloped more and more steeply; but confused by his lack of sleep he often made useless bounds, too high in the air and a vain waste of precious time. Besides, the policeman had his objective before his eyes and had no time to think, whereas Karl had to think first and attend to his running only in the intervals between weighing possibilities and making decisions. His plan, a somewhat desperate one, was to avoid the cross-streets for the time being, since he did not know what they concealed, perhaps for instance he might run straight into a police station; he wanted as long as possible to keep to this main thoroughfare which he could survey from end to end, since it did not terminate until far below, in a bridge vanishing suddenly into a haze of mist and sunshine in mid-air. Acting on this decision, he was just putting on a faster spurt so as to pass the first cross-street in a flash, when he saw not very far in front of him a policeman lurking watchfully by the dark wall of a house in shadow, ready to spring out on him at the right moment. There was nothing for it but to turn into the cross-street, and when from that very street someone gently called him by name – he thought it was a delusion at first, for there had been a ringing in his ears all the time – he hesitated no longer and made an abrupt turn, to take the police as much as possible by surprise, swinging round at a right-angle on one foot into the cross-street.

He had taken only two strides – he had already forgotten that someone had called his name, for the second policeman was now blowing his whistle too, obviously fresh and unwinded, and distant pedestrians ahead of him in the cross-street seemed to be quickening their steps – when an arm darted out from a little doorway seized him and he was drawn into a dark entry, while a voice said: 'Don't move!' It was Delamarche, quite out of breath, his face flushed, his hair sticking damply to his head. He was clad only in his shirt and drawers, his dressing-gown tucked under his arm. The door, which was not a main door but only an inconspicuous side door, he shut and locked at once.

'Wait a minute,' he said, leaning against the wall and breathing heavily with his head thrown back. Karl, almost lying in his arms and hardly knowing what he was doing pressed his face against his breast.

'There they go,' said Delamarche, listening intently and pointing with his finger at the door. The two policemen were really running past, their feet ringing in the empty street like the striking of steel against stone.

'You've been fairly put through it,' said Delamarche to Karl, who was still panting for breath and could not bring out a word. Delamarche laid him cautiously on the floor, knelt down beside him, passed a hand several times over his brow and regarded him.

'I'm all right now,' said Karl, painfully getting up.

'Then let's go,' said Delamarche, who had put on his dressing-gown again, and he pushed Karl, whose head still drooped with weariness, before him, giving him an occasional shake to liven him up.

'You say you're tired?' he said. 'You had the whole street to career about in like a horse, but I had to double through these accursed passages and courtyards. It's a good thing that I'm a bit of a runner too.' In his pride he gave Karl a mighty thump on the back. 'A race with the police like this now and then is good practice.'

'I was dog-tired before I began running,' said Karl.

'There's no excuse for bad running,' said Delamarche. 'If it hadn't been for me they would have nabbed you long since.'

'I think so too,' said Karl. 'I'm much obliged to you.'

'No doubt of that,' said Delamarche.

They went through a long narrow ground-floor lobby which was paved with dark, smooth flagstones. Here and there to right and left a staircase opened out, or a passage giving on a more spacious hall-way. Scarcely any grown people were to be seen, but children were playing on the empty stairs. Beside a stair-rail a little girl was standing weeping so hard that her whole face glistened with tears. As soon as she caught sight of Delamarche she rushed up the stairs, gasping for air, her mouth wide open, and was not reassured until she was quite high up, after looking over her shoulder time and again to make certain that no one was chasing her or likely to chase her.

'I ran her down a minute ago,' said Delamarche laughing, and he flourished his fist at her, whereupon she rushed up still farther, screaming.

The courtyards they threaded were also almost completely forsaken. An occasional porter pushed a two-wheeled hand-barrow before him, a woman was filling a bucket with water at a pump, a postman was quietly making his round, an old man with a white moustache sat before a glass door smoking a pipe with his legs crossed, crates were being unloaded before a dispatch agency while the idle horses imperturbably turned their heads from side to side and a man in overalls supervised the proceedings with a paper in his hand; behind the open window of an office a clerk, sitting at his desk, raised his head and looked thoughtfully out just as Karl and Delamarche went past.

'This is as quiet a place as you could wish for,' said Delamarche. 'In the evening it's pretty noisy for an hour or two, but all day long it's ideal.' Karl nodded; it seemed a good deal too quiet for him. 'I couldn't live anywhere else,' said Delamarche, 'for Brunelda simply can't stand any noise. Do you know Brunelda? Well, you'll soon see her. Take my advice anyhow, and keep as quiet as you can.'

When they reached the stairway which led up to Delamarche's flat, the taxi had already gone and the boy with the half-eaten nose announced, without showing any surprise at Karl's reappearance, that he had lugged Robinson upstairs. Delamarche only nodded to him, as if he were a servant who had merely done his duty, and then drew Karl, who hesitated a moment and gazed out at the sunny street, up the stairs with him. 'We'll soon be there,' said Delamarche several times during the ascent, but his prophecy was tardy in fulfilling itself, for there was always another stair ahead of them, with a barely perceptible change in direction. Once Karl actually had to stop, not from weariness but from helplessness in face of such a length of stairs. 'The flat's very high up,' said Delamarche, as they went on, 'but that has its advantages too. We're not tempted to go out much, we lounge about in our dressing-gowns all day, it's very comfortable. Of course, no visitors ever come up so far either.'

'And what visitors could they have?' thought Karl.

At last on a landing they caught sight of Robinson outside a closed door, and now they had arrived; the stairs were not at an end yet, but went farther in the semi-darkness without any indication that an end was even in sight.

'I thought so!' said Robinson in a muted voice as if he were still suffering pain, 'Delamarche has brought him! Rossmann, where would you be without Delamarche!' Robinson was standing in his underclothes, scantily wrapped in the small blanket he had been given at the Hotel Occidental; there was no visible reason why he did not go into the flat instead of standing here as a laughing-stock for any chance passer-by.

'Is she asleep?' asked Delamarche.

'I don't think so,' said Robinson, 'but I thought it better to wait till you came.'

'We must see first whether she's sleeping,' said Delamarche, bending down to the keyhole. After he had peered through it a long time, turning his head this way and that, he got up and said: 'I can't see her clearly; the curtain's drawn. She's sitting on the couch but she may be asleep.'

'Why, is she ill?' asked Karl, for Delamarche was standing there as if at a loss for advice.

But he retorted in a sharp enough voice: 'Ill?'

'He doesn't know her,' said Robinson, in extenuation.

A few doors farther on two women stepped out into the passage; they wiped their hands on their aprons, eyeing Delamarche and Robinson, and seemed to be talking about them. A young girl with gleaming fair hair bounded out of a door and squeezed between the two women, hanging on to their arms.

'These are disgusting women,' said Delamarche, lowering his voice, it was evident, only out of consideration for the slumbering Brunelda, 'sooner or later I'll report them to the police and then I'll be rid of them for years. Don't look their way,' he snapped at Karl. But Karl had not seen any harm in looking at the women, since in any case he had to stand in the passage waiting for Brunelda to waken. And he shook his head angrily, as if he refused to take any admonitions from Delamarche, and he had just begun walking towards the women to make his meaning clearer, when Robinson caught him by the sleeve with the words: 'Rossmann, take care!' while Delamarche, already exasperated, was roused to such fury by a loud burst of laughter from the girl that whirling his arms and legs he made a great spring at the women, who vanished into their doors as if they had been blown away. 'That's how I have often to clear the passages,' remarked Delamarche, strolling back again; then he remembered that Karl had been refractory and said: 'But I expect very different behaviour from you, or else you're likely to come up against me.'

Then from the room a gentle voice in a tired tone: 'Is that Delamarche?'

'Yes,' answered Delamarche, looking tenderly at the door, 'may we come in?'

'Oh yes,' was the answer, and after casting one more glance at the two standing behind him, Delamarche slowly opened the door.

They stepped into complete darkness. The curtain before the balcony door – there was no window – was completely drawn and let very little light through; but the fact that the room was crammed with furniture and clothes hanging everywhere contributed greatly to make it darker. The air was musty and one could literally smell the dust which had gathered here in corners apparently beyond the reach of any hand. The first things that Karl noticed on entering were three trunks, set just behind one another.

On the couch was lying the woman who had been looking down earlier from the balcony. The red gown had got rumpled a little beneath her and hung in a great peak to the floor; her legs could be seen almost as far as the knee; she was wearing thick white woollen stockings; she had no shoes.

'How hot it is, Delamarche,' she said, turning her face from the wall and languidly extending her hand in the direction of Delamarche, who seized it and kissed it. Karl could see only her double chin, which rolled in sympathy with the turning of her head.

'Would you like me to open the curtain?' asked Delamarche.

'Oh, not that,' she said as if in despair, shutting her eyes, 'that would only make it worse.'

Karl had gone up to the foot of the couch so as to see the woman better; he was surprised at her lamentations, for the heat was nothing out of the common.

'Wait, I'll make you a little more comfortable,' said Delamarche anxiously, and he undid a few buttons at her neck and pulled her dress open at the throat so that part of her breast was laid bare and the soft, yellowish lace border of her chemise appeared.

'Who is that,' said the woman suddenly, pointing a finger at Karl, 'why does he stare at me so hard?'

'You're being a great help, aren't you?' said Delamarche, pushing Karl aside, while he reassured the woman with the words: 'It's only the boy I've brought with me to attend on you.'

'But I don't want anyone!' she cried. 'Why do you bring strange people into the house?'

'But you've always been asking for someone to attend to you,' said Delamarche, kneeling down on the floor, for there was no room whatever on the couch beside Brunelda, in spite of its great breadth.

'Ah, Delamarche,' she said, 'you don't understand me, you don't understand me at all.'

'Then, all right, I don't understand you,' said Delamarche, taking her face between his hands. 'But it doesn't really matter; he can go at once, if you like.'

'Since he is here, he can stay,' she said now, and tired as he was, Karl felt so grateful for these words, though they probably were not kindly meant, that still vaguely thinking of those endless stairs which he might have had to descend again, he stepped over Robinson, now peacefully asleep on his blanket, and said, in spite of Delamarche's angry gesticulations:

'I thank you anyway, for letting me stay here a little longer. I've had no sleep for twenty-four hours and I've done a lot of things and been rather upset. I'm terribly tired. I hardly know where I am. But after I have slept an hour or two you can pack me off straight away and I'll go gladly.'

'You can stay here as long as you like,' said the woman,

adding ironically: 'We have more than room enough here, as you see.'

'Then, you'd better go,' said Delamarche, 'we haven't any use for you.'

'No, let him stay,' said the woman, this time in earnest.

And Delamarche said to Karl as if in obedience to her words: 'Well then, go and lie down somewhere.'

'He can lie down on the curtains, but he must take off his shoes, to keep from tearing them.'

Delamarche showed Karl the place she meant. Between the door and the three trunks a great pile of the most multifarious window curtains had been flung. Had they all been methodically folded, with the heavy ones below and the light ones on top, and had the curtain rods and wooden rings scattered through the pile been taken out, they might have made a tolerable couch, but as it was they made merely a tottering, unstable heap on which, however, Karl lay down at once, for he was too tired to make any particular preparations for sleeping and had also to guard against standing on too much ceremony with his host and hostess.

He had almost fallen into a genuine sleep when he heard a loud cry and started up to see Brunelda sitting erect on the couch, opening her arms wide and flinging them round Delamarche, who was kneeling before her. Karl, shocked at the sight, lay back again and curled up among the curtains to continue his sleep. That he would not be able to endure this place for two days seemed clear enough to him; yet it was all the more necessary to have a thorough sleep to begin with, so that he might have his wits about him and be able to decide quickly on the right course of action.

But Brunelda had been aware of Karl's eyes, big with fatigue, which had startled her once already, and she cried: 'Delamarche, I can't bear this heat, I'm burning, I must take off my clothes, I must have a bath; send the two of them out of the room, wherever you like, into the passage, on to the balcony, so long as they are out of my sight! Here I am in my own home and yet I can't get any peace. If I were only alone with you, Delamarche! Oh God, they're still here! Look at that shameless Robinson sprawling about in his underclothes in the presence of a lady. And look at that boy, that stranger, who has just been staring savagely at me, how he is pretending to lie down again to fool me. Turn them out, Delamarche, they're a burden on me, they're a weight on my breast; if I die now it will be their fault.'

'Out you get at once, out of here!' said Delamarche, advancing on Robinson and stirring him up with one foot, which he put on his chest. Then he shouted to Karl: 'Rossmann, get up! Out on the balcony, both of you! And it'll be your funeral if you come in here before you're called! Now look slippy, Robinson' – at this he kicked Robinson more violently – 'and you, Rossmann, look out or I'll come and attend to you too,' and he clapped his hands loudly twice.

'How long you're taking!' cried Brunelda from the sofa; she had spread her legs wide where she sat so as to get more room for her disproportionately fat body; only with the greatest effort gasping and frequently pausing to recover her breath, could she bend far enough forward to catch hold of her stockings at the top and pull them down a little; she could not possible take off her own clothes; Delamarche would have to do that, and she was now impatiently waiting for him.

Quite dazed with weariness, Karl crept down from the heap of curtains and trailed slowly to the balcony door; a piece of curtain material had wrapped itself round his foot and he dragged it indifferently with him. In his distraction he actually said as he passed Brunelda: 'I wish you good night,' and then wandered past Delamarche, who was drawing aside the curtain of the balcony door, and went out on to the balcony. Immediately behind him came Robinson, who seemed to be equally sleep-sodden, for he was muttering to himself: 'Always being ill-treated! If Brunelda doesn't come too I'm not going on to the balcony.' But in spite of this pronouncement he went out meekly enough on the balcony, where, as Karl had already subsided into the easy-chair, he immediately bedded himself on the stone floor.

When Karl awoke it was evening, the stars were already out and behind the tall houses on the other side of the street the moon was rising. Not until he had surveyed the unknown neighbourhood for a little and taken a few breaths of the cool, reviving air did Karl realize where he was. How imprudent he had been; he had neglected all the counsels of the Manageress, all Therese's warnings, all his own fears; here he was sitting calmly on Delamarche's balcony, where he had slept for half a day as if Delamarche, his mortal enemy, were not just on the other side of the curtain. Robinson, that lazy good-for-nothing, was sprawling on the floor and tugging him by the foot; he seemed indeed to have wakened him in this manner, for he was saying: 'How you can sleep, Rossmann! That's what it is to be young and carefree. How long do you want to go on sleeping? I'd have let you go on sleeping, but in the first place I'm bored with lying on the floor, and in the second place I'm terribly hungry. Come on, get up for a minute, I've got something hidden under your chair, something to eat, and I want to get it out, I'll give you some too.' And Karl, getting up, looked on while Robinson, without getting up, rolled over on his belly and reached under the chair to pull out a sort of silver salver such as is used for holding visiting-cards. On the salver lay one half of a quite black sausage, a few thin cigarettes, an open sardine tin still nearly full and dripping with oil, and a number of sweets, most of them squashed into a mass. Then appeared a big hunk of bread and a kind of perfume bottle, which seemed to contain something else than perfume, however, for Robinson displayed it with particular satisfaction, licking his lips and looking up at Karl.

'You see, Rossmann,' said Robinson, while he devoured sardine after sardine and now and then wiped the oil off his hands with a woollen scarf which Brunelda had apparently forgotten on the balcony, 'you see, Rossmann, that's what you need to do if you don't want to starve. I tell you, I'm just kicked out of the way. And if you're always treated like a dog, you begin to think that you're actually one. A good thing you're here, Rossmann; I have at least someone to talk to. Nobody in the building speaks to me. They hate us. And all because of Brunelda. She's a marvellous woman, of course. I say,' – and he gave Karl a sign to bend down, so that he might whisper to him – 'I once saw her naked. Oh' – and in the memory of that pleasure he began to pinch and slap Karl's leg until Karl shouted: 'Robinson, you're mad!' and forcibly pushed his hand away.

'You're still only a child, Rossmann,' said Robinson, and from under his shirt he pulled out a dagger that he wore on a cord round his neck, removed the sheath and began to slice up the hard sausage. 'You've still a lot to learn. But you've come to the right place to learn things. Do sit down. Won't you have something to eat too? Well, maybe you'll get an appetite watching me. You don't want a drink, either? So you don't want anything at all. And you're not much inclined to talk, either. But I don't care who's on the balcony with me, so long as there's somebody. For I'm often out on the balcony. It's great fun for Brunelda. She only has to get an idea in her head that she's too cold, that she's too hot, that she wants to sleep, that she wants to comb her hair, that she wants to loosen her corset, that she wants to put it on, and then she has me sent on the balcony. Sometimes she actually does what she says, but mostly she just lies on the couch the same as before and never moves. I used sometimes to draw the curtain a little and peep through, but once Delamarche – I know quite well that he didn't want to do it and only did it because Brunelda told him to – but once Delamarche on one of these occasions struck me across the face several times with the whip – can you see the marks? – and since then I haven't dared to peep again. And so I just lie here on the balcony and have nothing to do but eat. The night before last, as I lay up here alone all evening, I still had on the fine clothes which I had the bad luck to lose in your hotel – the swine, tearing a man's expensive clothes off his back – well, as I lay alone and looked down through the railings, everything seemed so miserable that I began to blubber. But it just happened, without my noticing it, that Brunelda had come out here in her red gown – that suits her far the best of them all – and she looked at me for a little while and said: "Robinson, what are you crying for?" Then she lifted up her skirt and wiped my eyes with the hem. Who knows what more she might have done if Delamarche hadn't called her and she hadn't had to go back into the room again at once. I thought, of course, that it was my turn next, and I asked through the curtain if I couldn't come in. And what do you think Brunelda said? "No!" she said, and "what are you thinking of!" she said.'

'But why do you stay here if they treat you like that?' asked Karl.

'Excuse me, Rossmann, but that's a stupid question,' replied Robinson. 'You'll stay here too, even if they treat you still worse. Besides, they don't treat me so very badly.'

'No,' said Karl, 'I'm certainly going away, and this very evening if possible. I'm not going to stay with you.'

'And how, for instance, will you manage to get away tonight?' asked Robinson, who was digging out the soft inside of the loaf and carefully dipping it into the oil in the sardine box. 'How are you going to leave when you mustn't even go into the room?'

'And why shouldn't I go into the room?'

'Because, until we're rung for, we can't go in,' said Robinson, opening his mouth to its full extent and devouring the oily bread, while in the hollow of one hand he caught the oil that dripped from it, making a kind of reservoir in which he dipped the rest of the bread from time to time. 'Things are much stricter now. At first there was only a thin curtain; you couldn't actually see through it, but in the evenings you could watch their shadows on it. But Brunelda didn't like that, and so I had to turn one of her evening cloaks into a curtain and hang it up instead of the old one. Now you can see nothing at all. Then at one time I could always ask whether I might go in and they used to say yes or no accordingly; but I suppose I took too much advantage of that and asked once too often. Brunelda couldn't bear it – and although she's so fat she's very delicate, she often has headaches and almost always gout in her legs – and so it was decided that I mustn't ask any more, but that I could go in whenever the table bell was rung. That rings so loudly that it can waken even me out of my sleep – I once had a cat here to cheer me up, but she was so scared at the bell that she ran away and never came back again; it hasn't rung today yet, you see, for when it does ring, I'm not only allowed to go in, I have to go in – and when such a long time goes by without ringing, it can take a good while before the bell rings again.'

'Yes,' said Karl, 'but what applies to you needn't apply to me at all. Besides, that kind of thing only applies to those who put up with it.'

'But,' cried Robinson, 'why shouldn't it apply to you as well? Of course it applies to you, too. You'd better stay quietly here with me until the bell rings. Then of course you can at least try to get away.'

'What is it really that keeps you here? Simply Delamarche is your friend, or rather was your friend. Do you call this a life? Wouldn't it be better for you in Butterford, where you wanted to go first? Or even in California, where you have friends?'

'Well,' said Robinson, 'nobody could have told that this was going to happen.' And before continuing, he said: 'To your good health, my dear Rossmann,' and took a long pull at the perfume bottle. 'We were hard up against it that time when you let us down so meanly. We could get no work at all the first day or two; besides, Delamarche didn't want work, he could easily have got it, but he always sent me to look for it instead, and I never have any luck. He just loafed around, but by the evening all he brought back with him was a lady's handbag. It was fine enough, made of pearls; he gave it to Brunelda later, but there was almost nothing in it. Then he said we'd better try begging at the doors – you can always pick up something or other that way; so we went begging and I sang in front of the houses to make it look better. And it was just like Delamarche's luck, for we had only been a minute or two at the second door, a very grand flat on the ground floor, and sung a couple of songs to the cook and the butler, when the lady the flat belonged to, Brunelda herself, came up the front steps. Maybe she was too tightly laced; anyhow she couldn't get up to the top of these steps. But how lovely she looked, Rossmann! She was wearing a white dress with a red sunshade. You felt you could eat her. You felt you could drink her up. God, God, she was lovely. What a woman! Tell me yourself, how can such a woman be possible? Of course the cook and the butler rushed down to her at once and almost carried her up. We stood on either side of the door and raised our hats, as people do here. She stopped for a little, for she hadn't quite got her breath back, and I don't know how it actually happened, I was so hungry I didn't know quite what I was doing, and close at hand she was even handsomer, so broad and yet so firm everywhere because of the special stays she had on – I can let you see them in the trunk; well, I couldn't help touching her back, but quite lightly, you know, just a touch. Of course it's a shocking thing for a beggar to touch a rich lady. I only just touched her, but after all I did touch her. Who knows where it might have ended if Delamarche hadn't given me a clip on the ear, and such a clip that both my hands flew to my own face.'

'What things to do!' said Karl, quite absorbed in the story, and he sat down on the floor. 'So that was Brunelda?'

'Yes,' said Robinson, 'that was Brunelda.'

'Didn't you say once that she was a singer?' asked Karl.

'Certainly she is a singer, and a great singer,' replied Robinson, who was rolling a sticky mass of sweetmeats on his tongue and now and then pushing back with his finger some piece that had got crowded out of his mouth. 'Of course we didn't know that at the time; we only saw that she was a rich and fine lady. She behaved as if nothing had happened, and perhaps she hadn't felt anything; for I had touched her really only with the tips of my fingers. But she kept looking at Delamarche, who stared back straight into her eyes – he usually hits it off like that. Then she said to him: "Come inside for a little," and pointed with her sunshade into the house, and Delamarche had to go in front of her. Then the two of them went in and the servants shut the door after them. As for me, I was left forgotten outside, and since I thought it wouldn't be for very long, I sat down on the steps to wait for Delamarche. But instead of Delamarche the butler came out bringing me a whole bowl of soup. "A compliment from Delamarche!" I told myself. The man stood beside me for a time while I ate and told me some things about Brunelda, and then I saw how important this visit might be for us. For Brunelda had divorced her husband, was very wealthy and completely independent! Her ex-husband, a cocoa manufacturer, was still in love with her, to be sure, but she refused to have anything whatever to do with him. He often called at the flat, always dressed in great style as if he were going to a wedding – that's true, word for word, I know the man myself – but in spite of the huge tips he got, the butler never dared to ask Brunelda whether she would receive her husband, for he had asked her before once or twice, and she had always picked up anything she had handy and thrown it at his head. Once she even flung her big hot-water bottle at him and knocked out one of his front teeth. Yes, Rossmann, you may well stare!'

'How do you come to know the husband?' asked Karl.

'He often comes up here,' said Robinson.

'Here?' In his astonishment Karl struck the floor lightly with his hand.

'You may well be surprised,' Robinson went on, 'I was surprised myself when the butler stood there telling me all this. Just think, whenever Brunelda was out, the husband always asked the butler to take him to her room, and he always took away some trifle or other as a keepsake and left something rare and expensive for Brunelda in return and strictly forbade the butler to say who had left it. But once – the servant swears and I believe it – when he left an absolutely priceless piece of porcelain, Brunelda must have recognized it somehow, for she flung it on the floor at once, stamped on it, spat on it and did other things to it as well, so that the servant could hardly carry it away for disgust.'

'But what had her husband done to her?' asked Karl.

'I really don't know,' said Robinson. 'But I think it wasn't anything very serious, at least he himself doesn't know. I have often talked to him about it. I have an appointment with him every day at the corner of the street over there; if I can come, I have always to tell him the latest news; if I can't come, he waits for half an hour and then goes away again. It was a nice extra for me at first, for he paid like a gentleman for the news, but after Delamarche came to know of it I had to hand over the money to him, and so I don't go down there so often now.'

'But what's the man after?' asked Karl. 'What on earth is he after? He surely knows that she doesn't want him.'

'Yes,' sighed Robinson, lighting a cigarette and fanning the smoke high in the air with great sweeps of his arm. Then he seemed to change his attitude and said: 'What does that matter to me? All I know is that he would give a lot of money to be able to lie here on the balcony like us.'

Karl got up, leant against the railing and looked down into the street. The moon was already visible, but its light did not yet penetrate into the depths of the street. Though it had been so empty during the day, the street was now crowded with people, particularly before the house-doors; they were all drifting along slowly and heavily, the shirt-sleeves of the men and the light dresses of the women standing out faintly against the darkness; they were all bareheaded. The various balconies round about were now fully occupied; whole families were sitting there by the light of electric lamps, either round small tables, if the balcony were big enough, or in a single row of armchairs or merely sticking their heads out of their living-rooms. The men sat at ease with their legs stretched out, their feet between the bars of the railing, reading newspapers which extended almost to the floor, or playing cards, apparently without speaking but to the accompaniment of loud bangs on the table; the women's laps were full of sewing-work, and they had nothing but a brief glance now and then for their surroundings or the street below. A fair, delicate woman on the next balcony kept on yawning, turning her eyes up and raising to her mouth a piece of underwear which she was mending; even on the smallest balconies the children managed to chase each other round and make themselves a nuisance to their parents. Inside many of the rooms gramophones could be heard grinding out songs or orchestral music; nobody paid any particular attention to this music, except that now and then the father of a family would give a sign and someone would hurry into the room to put on a new record. At some of the windows could be seen loving couples standing quite motionless; one of these couples was standing at a window opposite; the young man had his arm round the girl and was squeezing her waist.

'Do you know any of your neighbours here?' Karl asked Robinson, who had now also got to his feet, and feeling cold had huddled himself into Brunelda's wrap as well as his blanket.

'Hardly one of them, that's the worst of my situation,' said Robinson, and he pulled Karl closer so as to whisper in his ear, 'or else I wouldn't have much to complain about at the moment. Brunelda has sold everything she had for the sake of Delamarche, and has moved with all she possesses into this suburban flat in order to devote herself entirely to him with nobody to disturb her; besides, that was what Delamarche wanted too.'

'And she had dismissed her servants?' asked Karl.

'That's so,' said Robinson. 'Where could you find accommodation for servants here? Servants like that expect the best of everything. In Brunelda's old flat Delamarche once simply kicked one of these pampered creatures out of the room, he just went on kicking him until the man was outside. The other servants of course took the man's side and staged a row before the door; then Delamarche went out (I wasn't a servant then, but a friend of the family, yet I was outside among the servants all the same) and asked: "What do you want?" The oldest servant, a man called Isidor, told him: "You have nothing to do with us; we are engaged by the mistress." I suppose you notice that they had a great respect for Brunelda. But Brunelda paid no attention to them and ran up to Delamarche – she wasn't so heavy then as she is now – and embraced and kissed him before them all and called him "darling Delamarche". And then she said: "Now send these fools away." Fools – that's what she called the servants; you can imagine the expression on their faces. Then Brunelda took Delamarche's hand and drew it down to the purse she wore at her belt; Delamarche put in his hand and began to pay off the servants; Brunelda did nothing but stand there with the open purse at her waist. Delamarche had to put his hand in over and over again, for he paid out the money without counting it and without checking their claims. At last he said: "Since you won't have anything to do with me, I'll only say in Brunelda's name: Get out, this instant." So they were dismissed; there were some legal proceedings afterwards, Delamarche had actually to go once to court, but I don't know much more about it. Except that as soon as the servants had gone Delamarche said to Brunelda: "So now you have no servants." And she said: "But there's still Robinson." So Delamarche clapped me on the shoulder and said: "Very well, then, you'll be our servant." And then Brunelda patted me on the cheek. If you ever get a chance, Rossmann, you should get her to pat you on the cheek some time. You'll be surprised how lovely it feels.'

'So you've turned into Delamarche's servant, have you?' said Karl, summing up.

Robinson heard the pity in his voice and answered: 'I may be a servant, but very few people know about it. You see, you didn't know it yourself, although you've been here quite a while. Why, you saw how I was dressed last night in the hotel. I had on the finest of fine clothes. Are servants dressed like that? The only thing is that I can't leave here very often, I must always be at hand, there's always something to do in the flat. One man isn't really enough for all the work. You may have noticed that we have a lot of things standing about in the room; what we couldn't sell at the removal we took with us here. Of course it could have been given away, but Brunelda gives nothing away. You can imagine what it meant to carry these things up the stairs.'

'Robinson, did you carry all these things up here?' cried Karl.

'Why, who else was there to do it?' said Robinson. 'I had a man to help me, but he was a lazy rascal; I had to do most of the work alone. Brunelda stood down below beside the van, Delamarche decided up here where the things were to be put, and I had to keep rushing up and down. That went on for two days, a long time, wasn't it? But you've no idea whatever how many things are in that room; all the trunks are full and behind the trunks the whole place is crammed to the very roof. If they had hired a few men for the transport, everything would soon have been finished, but Brunelda wouldn't trust it to anyone but me. That was flattering, of course, but I ruined my health for life during those two days, and what else did I have except my health? Whenever I try to do the least thing, I have pains here and here and here. Do you think the boys in the hotel, these young jumping-jacks – for that's all they are – would ever have got the better of me if I had been in good health? But broken down as I may be, I'll never say a word to Delamarche or Brunelda; I'll work on as long as I can and when I can't do it any longer I'll just lie down and die and then they'll find out, too late, that I was really ill and yet went on working and worked myself to death in their service. Oh Rossmann –' he ended, drying his eyes on Karl's shirt-sleeve. After a while he said: 'Aren't you cold, standing there in your shirt?'

'Go on, Robinson,' said Karl, 'you're always blubbering. I don't believe you're so ill as all that. You look healthy enough, but lying about on the balcony all the time you fancy all sorts of things. You may have an occasional pain in the chest; so have I, so has everybody. If everybody blubbered like you about trifles, there would be nothing but blubbering on all these balconies.'

'I know better,' said Robinson, wiping his eyes with the corner of his blanket. 'The student staying next door with the landlady who cooks for us said to me a little time ago when I brought back the dishes: "Look here, Robinson, you're ill, aren't you?" I'm not supposed to talk to these people and so I simply set down the dishes and started to go away. Then he came right up to me and said: "Listen, man, don't push things too far, you're a sick man." "All right then, what am I to do about it?" I asked him. "That's your business," he said and turned away. The others sitting at the table just laughed, they're all our enemies round here, and so I thought I'd better quit.'

'So you believe anyone who makes a fool of you, and you won't believe anyone who means well by you.'

'But I must surely know how I feel,' exclaimed Robinson indignantly, beginning to cry again almost at once.

'You don't know what's really wrong with you; you should only find some decent work for yourself, instead of being Delamarche's servant. So far as I can tell from your account of it and from what I have seen myself, this isn't service here, it's slavery. Nobody could endure it; I believe you there. But because you're Delamarche's friend you think you can't leave him. That's nonsense; if he doesn't see what a wretched life you're leading, you can't have the slightest obligation to him.'

'So you really think, Rossmann, that I would recover my health if I gave up working here?'

'Certainly,' said Karl.

'Certainly?' Robinson asked again.

'Quite certainly,' said Karl smiling.

'Then I can begin recovering straight away,' said Robinson, looking at Karl.

'How's that?' asked Karl.

'Why, because you are to take over my work here,' replied Robinson.

'Who on earth told you that?' asked Karl.

'Oh, it's an old plan. It's been discussed for days. It began with Brunelda scolding me for not keeping the flat clean enough. Of course I promised to put everything right at once. But, well that was very difficult. For instance, in my state of health, I can't creep into all the corners to sweep away the dust; it's hardly possible to move in the middle of the room, far less get behind the furniture and the piles of stuff. And if the place is to be thoroughly cleaned, the furniture would have to be shifted about, and how could I do that by myself? Besides, it has all to be done very quietly so as not to disturb Brunelda, and she scarcely ever leaves the room. So I promised to give everything a clean-up, but I didn't actually clean it up. When Brunelda noticed that, she told Delamarche that this couldn't go on and that he would have to take on an assistant. "I don't want you, Delamarche," she said, "to reproach me at any time for not running the house properly. I can't put any strain upon myself, you know that quite well, and Robinson isn't enough; in the beginning he was fresh and looked after everything, but now he's always tired and sits most of the time in a corner. But a room with so many things in it as ours needs to be kept in order." So Delamarche considered how it was to be managed, for of course it wouldn't do to take anyone and everyone into such a household as ours, even on trial, since we're spied on from all sides. But as I was a good friend of yours and had heard from Rennell how you had to slave in the hotel, I suggested your name. Delamarche agreed at once, although you were so rude to him before, and of course I was very glad to be of some use to you. For this job might have been made for you; you're young, strong and quick, while I'm no good to anyone. But I must tell you that you're not taken on yet; if Brunelda doesn't like you, that's the end of it. So do your best to be pleasant to her; I'll see to the rest.'

'And what are you going to do if I take on the job?' queried Karl. He felt quite free; he had got over the first alarm which Robinson's announcement had caused him. So Delamarche meant no worse by him than to turn him into a servant – if he had had more sinister intentions, the babbling Robinson would certainly have blabbed them – but if that was how things stood, Karl saw his way to get clear of the place that very night. No one could be compelled to take a job. And though at first he had been worried in case his dismissal from the hotel would hinder him from getting a suitable and if possible fairly respectable post quickly enough to keep him from starving, any post at all now seemed good enough compared with this proposal, which repelled him; he would rather be unemployed and destitute than accept it. But he did not even try to make that clear to Robinson, particularly as Robinson's mind was now completely obsessed by the hope of shifting his burdens on to Karl's shoulders.

'To begin with,' said Robinson, accompanying the words with a reassuring wave of the hand – his elbows were planted on the railings – 'I'll explain everything and show you all the things we have. You've had a good education and I'm sure your handwriting's excellent, so you could make an inventory straightaway of all our stuff. Brunelda has been wanting that done for a long time. If the weather's good tomorrow morning we'll ask Brunelda to sit out on the balcony, and we can work quietly in the room without disturbing her. For that must be your first consideration, Rossmann. Brunelda mustn't be disturbed. Her hearing's very keen; it's probably because she's a singer that her ears are so sensitive. For instance, say that you're rolling out a keg of brandy which usually stands behind the trunks, it makes a noise because it's heavy and all sorts of things are lying about on the floor, so that you can't roll it straight out. Brunelda, let us say, is lying quietly on the couch catching flies, which are a great torment to her. You think she's paying no attention to you, and you go on rolling the keg. She's still lying there quite peacefully. But all at once, just when you're least expecting it and when you're making least noise, she suddenly sits up, bangs with both hands on the couch so that you can't see her for dust – since we came here I have never beaten the dust out of the couch; I really couldn't, she's always lying on it – and begins to yell ferociously, like a man, and goes on yelling for hours. The neighbours have forbidden her to sing, but no one can forbid her to yell; she has to yell; though that doesn't happen very often now, for Delamarche and I have grown careful. It was very bad for her, too. Once she fainted – Delamarche was away at the time – and I had to fetch the student from next door, who sprinkled some fluid over her out of a big bottle; it did her good, too, but the fluid had an awful smell; even now you can smell it if you put your nose to the couch. That student is certainly an enemy of ours, like everybody here; you must be on your guard too and have nothing to do with any of them.'

'But I say, Robinson,' remarked Karl, 'this is a heavy programme. A fine job this that you've recommended me for.'

'Don't you worry,' said Robinson, shutting his eyes and shaking his head, as if shaking off all Karl's possible worries. 'This job has advantages that you wouldn't find in any other. You're always in close attendance on a lady like Brunelda; you sometimes sleep in the same room as she does, and, as you can imagine, there's lots of enjoyment to be got out of that. You'll be well paid, there's plenty of money about; I got no wages, being a friend of Delamarche, though every time I went out Brunelda always gave me something, but you of course will be paid like any other servant. That's what you are, after all. But the most important thing is that I'll be able to make your job much easier for you. Of course I won't do anything just at first, to give myself a chance of getting better, but as soon as I'm even a little better you can count on me. In any case, I'll do all the waiting on Brunelda, doing her hair, for example, and helping her to dress, so far as Delamarche doesn't attend to that. You'll only have to concern yourself with cleaning the room, getting in what we need, and doing the heavy housework.'

'No, Robinson,' said Karl, 'all this doesn't tempt me.'

'Don't be a fool, Rossmann,' said Robinson, putting his face quite close to Karl's, 'don't throw away this splendid chance. Where will you get another job so quickly? Who knows you? What people do you know? The two of us, both full-grown men with plenty of practical skill and experience, wandered about for weeks without finding work. It isn't easy; in fact it's damned difficult.'

Karl nodded, marvelling that Robinson could talk so reasonably. Still, all this advice was beside the point so far as he was concerned; he couldn't stay here; there must be some place for him in the great city; the whole night, he knew, all the hotels were filled to bursting and the guests needed service, and he had had some training in that. He would slip quickly and unobtrusively into some job or other. Just across the street there was a small restaurant on the ground floor, from which came a rush of music. The main entrance was covered only with a big yellow curtain, which billowed out into the street now and then, as a draught of air caught it. Otherwise things were much quieter up and down the street. Most of the balconies were dark; only far in the distance a single light was twinkling here and there; but almost as soon as one fixed one's eye upon it the people beside it got up and thronged back into the house, while the last man left outside put his hand to the lamp and switched it off after a brief glance at the street.

'It's nightfall already,' said Karl to himself, 'if I stay here any longer I'll become one of them.' He turned round to pull aside the curtain of the balcony door. 'What are you doing?' said Robinson, planting himself between Karl and the curtain.

'I'm leaving,' said Karl. 'Let me go! Let me go!'

'But surely you're not going to disturb her,' cried Robinson, 'what are you thinking of!' And he threw his arms round Karl's neck, clinging to him with all his weight and twisted his legs round Karl's legs, so that in a trice he had him down on the floor. But among the lift-boys Karl had learned a little fighting, and so he drove his fist against Robinson's chin, not putting out his whole strength, to avoid hurting him. Quickly and without any scruple Robinson punched him in the belly with his knee before beginning to nurse his chin in both hands, and let out such a howl that a man on the next balcony clapped his hands furiously and shouted: 'Silence!' Karl lay still for a little so as to recover from the pain of Robinson's foul blow. He turned only his head to watch the curtain hanging still and heavy before the room, which was obviously in darkness. It looked as if no one were in the room now; perhaps Delamarche had gone out with Brunelda and the way was perfectly free. For Robinson, who was behaving exactly like a watch-dog, had been finally shaken off.

Then from the far end of the street there came in fitful blasts the sound of drums and trumpets. The single shouts of individuals in a crowd soon blended into a general roar. Karl turned his head again and saw that all the balconies were once more coming to life. Slowly he got up; he could not stand quite straight and had to lean heavily against the railing. Down on the pavement young lads were striding along, waving their caps at the full stretch of their arms and looking back over their shoulders. The middle of the road was still vacant. Some were flourishing tall poles with lanterns on the end of them enveloped in a yellowish smoke. The drummers and the trumpeters, arrayed in broad ranks were just emerging into the light in such numbers that Karl was amazed, when he heard voices behind him, he turned round and saw Delamarche lifting the heavy curtain and Brunelda stepping out of the darkness of the room, in the red gown, with a lace scarf round her shoulders and a dark hood over her hair, which was presumably still undressed and only hastily gathered up, for loose ends straggled here and there. In her hand she held a little fan, which she had opened but did not use, keeping it pressed close to her.

Karl moved sideways along the railing, to make space for the two of them. No one, surely, would force him to stay here, and even if Delamarche tried it Brunelda would let him go at once if he were to ask her. After all, she couldn't stand him; his eyes terrified her. Yet as he took a step towards the door she noticed it and asked: 'Where are you going, boy?' Delamarche's severe eye held Karl an instant and Brunelda drew him to her. 'Don't you want to see the procession down there?' she said, pushing him before her to the railing. 'Do you know what it's about?' Karl heard her asking behind him, and he flinched in an involuntary but unsuccessful attempt to escape from the pressure of her body. He gazed down sadly at the street, as if the cause of his sadness lay there.

For a while Delamarche stood with crossed arms behind Brunelda; then he ran into the room and brought her the opera glasses. Down below the main body of the procession had now come into sight behind the band. On the shoulders of a gigantic man sat a gentleman of whom nothing could be seen at this height save the faint gleam of a bald crown, over which he was holding a top-hat upraised in perpetual greeting. Round about him great wooden placards were being carried which, seen from the balcony, looked blankly white; they were obviously intended to make a sloping rampart round the prominent central figure, against which they were literally leaning. But since the bearers were moving on all the time, the wall of placards kept falling into disrepair and seeking to repair itself again. Beyond the ring of placards, so far as one could judge in the darkness, the whole breadth of the street, although only a trifling part of its length, was filled with the gentleman's supporters, who clapped their hands in rhythm and kept proclaiming in a chanting cadence what seemed to be the gentleman's name, a quite short but incomprehensible name. Single supporters adroitly distributed among the crowd were carrying motor-car lamps of enormous power, which they slowly shone up and down the houses on both sides of the street. At the height where Karl was the light was not unbearable, but on the lower balconies he could see people hastily putting their hands over their eyes whenever it flashed in their faces.

At Brunelda's request Delamarche inquired of the people on the next balcony what the meaning of the demonstration was. Karl was somewhat curious to note whether and how they would answer him. And actually Delamarche was forced to repeat his question three times before he received an answer. He was already bending threateningly over the railing and Brunelda had begun to tap with one foot in exasperation at her neighbours, for Karl could feel her knee moving. Finally some sort of answer was given, but simultaneously everyone on the next balcony, which was packed with people, burst out into loud laughter. At that Delamarche yelled a retort so loudly that, if the whole street had not been filled with noise for the moment, all the people round about must have pricked up their ears in astonishment. In any case it had the effect of making the laughter cease with unnatural abruptness.

'A judge is being elected in our district tomorrow, and the man they are chairing down there is one of the candidates,' said Delamarche quite calmly, returning to Brunelda. 'Oh!' he went on, caressing Brunelda's shoulder, 'we've lost all idea of what's happening in the world.'

'Delamarche,' said Brunelda, reverting to the behaviour of her neighbours, 'how thankful I would be to move out of here, if it wasn't such an effort. But unfortunately I can't face it.' And sighing deeply she kept plucking restlessly and distractedly at Karl's shirt; as unobtrusively as he could he kept pushing away her plump little hand again and again, which was an easy matter, for Brunelda was not thinking of him; she was occupied with quite other thoughts.

But Karl soon forgot her and suffered the weight of her arms on his shoulders, for the proceedings in the street took up all his attention. At the command of small groups of gesticulating men, who marched just in front of the candidate and whose consultations must have had a particular importance, for one could see attentive faces turned to them from all sides, a halt was abruptly called before the little restaurant. A member of this authoritative group made a signal with his upraised hand which seemed to apply to the crowd and to the candidate as well. The crowd fell silent and the candidate, who tried several times to stand upright and several times fell back again on the shoulders of his bearer, made a short speech, waving his top-hat to and fro at lightning speed. He could be seen quite clearly, for during his speech all the motor-car lamps were directed upon him, so that he found himself in the centre of a bright star of light.

Now, too, one could realize the interest which the whole street took in the occurrence. On the balconies where supporters of the candidate were packed, the people joined in chanting his name, stretching their hands far over the railings and clapping with machine-like regularity. On the opposition balconies, which were actually in the majority, a howl of retaliation arose which, however, did not achieve a unified effect, as it came from rival supporters of various candidates. However, all the enemies of the present candidate united in a general cat-calling, and even many of the gramophones were set going again. Between the separate balconies political disputes were being fought out with a violence intensified by the late hour. Most of the people were already in their night-clothes, with overcoats flung over them; the women were enveloped in great dark wraps; the children, with nobody to attend to them, climbed dangerously about the railings of the balcony and came swarming more and more out of the dark rooms in which they had been sleeping. Here and there unrecognizable objects were being flung by particularly heated partisans in the direction of their enemies; sometimes they reached their mark, but most of them fell down into the street, where they provoked yells of rage. When the noise became too much for the leading man in the procession, the drummers and trumpeters received orders to intervene, and their blaring, long-drawn-out flourish, executed with all the force of which they were capable, drowned every human voice up to the very house-tops. And then quite suddenly – almost before one realized it – they would stop, whereupon the crowd in the street, obviously trained for this purpose, at once launched their party song into the momentary general silence – one could see all their mouths wide open in the light of the motor-car lamps – until their opponents, coming to their senses again, yelled ten times as loudly as before from all the balconies and windows, and the party below, after their brief victory, were reduced to complete silence, at least for anyone standing at this height.

'How do you like it, boy?' asked Brunelda, who kept turning and twisting close behind Karl, so as to see as much as possible through her glasses. Karl merely answered with a nod of the head. He noticed out of the corner of his eye that Robinson was busily talking away to Delamarche, obviously about Karl's intentions, but that Delamarche seemed to attach no importance to what he said, for with his right arm round Brunelda he kept pushing Robinson aside with his left. 'Wouldn't you like to look through the glasses?' asked Brunelda, tapping Karl on the chest to show that she meant him.

'I can see well enough,' said Karl.

'Do try,' she said, 'you'll see much better.'

'I have good eyes,' replied Karl, 'I can see everything.' He did not feel it as a kindness but as a nuisance when she put the glasses before his eyes, with the mere words, 'Here, you!' uttered melodiously enough but threateningly. And now the glasses were before Karl's eyes and he could see nothing at all.

'I can't see anything,' he said, trying to get away from the glasses, but she held them firmly, and his head, which was pressed against her breast, he could move neither backwards nor sideways.

'But you can see now,' she said, turning the screw.

'No, I still can't see anything,' said Karl, and he thought that in spite of himself he had relieved Robinson of his duties after all, for Brunelda's insupportable whims were now being wreaked on him.

'When on earth are you going to see?' she said, and turned the screw again; Karl's whole face was now exposed to her heavy breath. 'Now?' she asked.

'No, no, no!' cried Karl, although he could actually distinguish everything now, though very vaguely. But at that moment Brunelda thought of something to say to Delamarche; she held the glasses loosely before Karl's face, and without her noticing it he could peep under the glasses at the street. After that she no longer insisted on having her way and used the glasses for her own pleasure.

From the restaurant below a waiter had emerged and dashing in and out of the door took orders from the leaders. One could see him standing on his toes so as to overlook the interior of the establishment and summon as many of the staff as possible. During these preparations for what was obviously a round of free drinks, the candidate never stopped speaking. The man who was carrying him, the giant specially reserved for him, kept turning round a little after every few sentences, so that the address might reach all sections of the crowd. The candidate maintained a crouching posture most of the time, and tried with backward sweeps of his free hand and of the top-hat in the other to give special emphasis to his words. But every now and then, at almost regular intervals, the flow of his eloquence proved too much for him; he rose to his full height with outstretched arms, he was no longer addressing a group but the whole multitude; he spoke to all the people in the houses up to the very top floors, and yet it was perfectly clear that no one could hear him even in the lowest storeys; indeed, even if they could, nobody would have wanted to hear him, for every window and every balcony was occupied by at least one spouting orator. Meanwhile several waiters were carrying out of the restaurant a table covered with brimming, winking glasses, about the size of a billiard-table. The leaders organized the distribution of the drinks, which was achieved in the form of a march past the restaurant. But although the glasses on the table were always filled again, there were not enough for the mob of people, and two relays of barmen had to keep slipping through the crowd on both sides of the table to supply further needs. The candidate had, of course, stopped speaking and was employing the pause in refreshing his energies. His bearer carried him slowly backwards and forwards, somewhat apart from the crowd and the harsh light, and only a few of his closest supporters accompanied him and threw remarks to him.

'Look at the boy,' said Brunelda, 'he's so busy staring that he's quite forgotten where he is.' And she took Karl by surprise, turning his face towards her with both hands, so that she was gazing into his eyes. But it lasted only a minute, for Karl shook her hands off at once and annoyed that they would not leave him in peace and also eager to go down to the street and see everything close at hand, tried with all his might to free himself from Brunelda's grip and said:

'Please, let me go away.'

'You'll stay with us,' said Delamarche, without turning his eyes from the street, merely stretching out his hand to prevent Karl from going.

'Leave him alone,' said Brunelda, pushing away Delamarche's

hand, 'he'll stay all right.' And she squeezed Karl still more firmly against the railing, so that he would have had to struggle with her to get away from her. And even if he were to free himself, what could he gain by that! Delamarche was standing on his left, Robinson had now moved across to his right; he was literally a prisoner.

'Count yourself lucky that you're not thrown out,' said Robinson, tapping Karl with the hand he had hooked through Brunelda's arm.

'Thrown out?' said Delamarche. 'You don't throw out a runaway thief; you hand him over to the police. And that might happen to him the very first thing tomorrow morning if he doesn't keep quiet.'

From that moment Karl had no further pleasure in the spectacle below. Simply because he could not help it, being crushed against Brunelda and unable to straighten himself, he leaned forward a little over the railing. Full of his own trouble, he gazed absently at the people below, who marched up to the table before the restaurant in squads of about twenty men, seized the glasses, turned round and waved them in the direction of the recuperating candidate, shouted a party slogan, emptied the glasses and set them down on the table again with what must have been a great clatter that was, however, inaudible at this height, in order to make room for the next noisy and impatient squad. On the instructions of the party leaders the brass band which had been playing in the restaurant came out into the street; their great wind instruments glittered against the dark crowd, but the music was almost lost in the general din. The street was now, at least on the side where the restaurant stood, packed far and wide with human beings. From up the hill, the direction from which Karl's taxi had arrived that morning, they came streaming down; from as far as the low-lying bridge they came rushing up; and even the people in the adjoining houses could not resist the temptation to take a personal part in this affair; on the balconies and at the windows there was hardly anyone left but women and children, while the men came pouring out of the house-doors down below. By now the music and the free drinks had achieved their aim; the assembly was great enough at last; one of the leaders, flanked on either side by headlamps, signalled the band to stop playing and gave a loud whistle, and at once the man carrying the candidate hastily turned back and could be seen approaching through a path opening for him by supporters.

The candidate had barely reached the restaurant door when he began a new speech in the blaze of the headlamps, which were now concentrated upon him in a narrow ring. But conditions were much less comfortable than before. His gigantic bearer had now no initiative at all in movement, for the crowd was too dense. His chief supporters, who had previously done their best in all kinds of ways to enhance the effect of his words, now had the greatest difficulty in keeping near him, and only about twenty of them managed to retain their footing beside the bearer. Even he, strong giant as he was, could not take a step of his own free will, and it was out of the question to think of influencing the crowd by turning to face this section or that, by making dramatic advances or retreats. The mob was flowing backwards and forwards without plan, each man propelled by his neighbour, not one braced on his own feet; the opposition party seemed to have gained a lot of new recruits; the bearer, after stemming the tide for a while outside the restaurant door, was now letting himself be swept up and down the street, apparently without resistance; the candidate still kept on uttering words, but it was no longer clear whether he was outlining his programme or shouting for help; and unless Karl was mistaken a rival candidate had made his appearance, or rather several rivals, for here and there, when light suddenly flared up, some figure could be seen, high on the shoulders of the crowd orating with white face and clenched fists to an accompaniment of massed cheering.

'What on earth is happening down there?' asked Karl, turning in breathless bewilderment to his warders.

'How it excites the boy,' said Brunelda to Delamarche, taking hold of Karl's chin so as to turn his face towards her. But that was something Karl did not desire, and made quite reckless by the events down in the street he gave himself such a jerk that Brunelda not only let him go but recoiled and left him quite to himself. 'You have seen enough now,' she said, obviously angered by Karl's behaviour, 'go into the room, make the bed and get everything ready for the night.' She pointed towards the room. That was the very direction Karl had wanted to take for hours past, and he made no objection at all. Then from the street came a loud crash of breaking glass. Karl could not restrain himself and took a flying leap to the railing for a last hasty look down. The opposition had brought off a grand coup, perhaps a decisive one; the car head-lamps of the candidate's party, which had thrown a powerful light on at least the central figures and afforded a measure of publicity which controlled the proceedings up to a point, had all been simultaneously smashed and the candidate and his bearer were now received into the embrace of the general uncertain street lighting, which in its sudden diffusion had the effect of complete darkness. No one could have guessed even approximately the candidate's whereabouts, and the illusoriness of the darkness was still more enhanced by a loud swelling chorus in unison which suddenly broke out from the direction of the bridge and was coming nearer.

'Haven't I told you what to do?' said Brunelda. 'Hurry up. I'm tired,' she added, stretching her arms above her so that her bosom arched out even more than before. Delamarche, whose arm was still round her, drew her into a corner of the balcony. Robinson followed them to push out of the way the remains of his supper, which were still lying there.

Such a favourable opportunity was not to be let slip; this was no time for Karl to look down at the street; he would see enough of what was happening there once he was down below, much better than from up here. In two bounds he was through the room with its dim red lighting, but the door was locked and the key taken away. It must be found at once; yet who could expect to find a key in this disorder and above all in the little space of precious time which Karl had at his disposal. Actually he should be on the stairs by now, running and running. Instead of which he was hunting for a key! He looked in all the drawers that would open, rummaged about on the table, where various dishes, table napkins and pieces of half-begun embroidery were lying about, was allured next by an easy-chair on which lay an inextricable heap of old clothes where the key might possibly be hidden but could never be found, and flung himself finally on the couch, which was indeed evil-smelling, so as to feel in all its nooks and corners for the key. Then he stopped looking and came to a halt in the middle of the room. Brunelda was certain to have the key fastened to her belt, he told himself; so many things hung there; all searching was in vain.

And blindly Karl seized two knives and thrust them between the wings of the door, one above and one below, so as to get the greatest purchase on it from two separate points. But scarcely did he brace himself against the knives when the blades of course broke off. He wished for nothing better; the stumps, with which he could now get closer, would hold the more firmly. And now he wrenched at them with all his strength, his arms outstretched, his legs wide apart, panting and yet carefully watching the door at the same time. It could not resist for much longer; he realized that with joy from the audible loosening of the lock; but the more slowly he went the better; the lock mustn't burst open, or else they would hear it on the balcony; it must loosen itself quite gradually; and he worked with great caution to bring this about, putting his face closer and closer to the lock.

'Just look at this,' he heard the voice of Delamarche. All three of them were standing in the room; the curtain was already drawn behind them; Karl could not have heard them entering; and at the sight of them he let go the knives. But he was given no time to utter a word of explanation or excuse, for in a fit of rage far greater than the occasion merited Delamarche leaped at him, the loose cord of his dressing-gown describing a long figure in the air. At the very last moment Karl evaded his attack; he could have pulled the knives from the door and defended himself with them, but he did not do so; instead, ducking down and then springing up, he seized the broad collar of Delamarche's dressing-gown, jerked it upwards, then pulled it still farther over – the dressing-gown was far too big for Delamarche – and now by good luck had a hold on the head of Delamarche, who, taken completely by surprise, pawed wildly with his hands at first and only after a moment or two began to beat Karl on the back with his fists, but with less than his full strength, while Karl, to protect his face, flung himself against Delamarche's chest. Karl endured the blows, though they made him twist with pain and kept increasing in violence, for it was easy to bear them when he thought he saw victory before him. With his hands round Delamarche's head the thumbs just over the eyes, he pushed him towards the part of the room where the furniture stood the thickest and at the same time with the toe of his shoe tried to twist the cord of the dressing-gown round Delamarche's legs to trip him up.

But since he had to bend all his attention on Delamarche, whose resistance he could feel growing more and more and whose sinewy body was bracing itself with greater enmity against him, he actually forgot that he was not alone in the room with Delamarche. Only too soon the reminder came, for suddenly his feet flew from under him, being wrenched apart by Robinson, who was lying shrieking behind him on the floor. Panting, Karl let go his hold of Delamarche, who recoiled a little. Brunelda, her legs straddling, her knees bent, a bulky figure in the middle of the room, was following the fight with glittering eyes. As if she herself were taking part in it she was breathing deeply, screwing up her eyes and slowly advancing her fists. Delamarche flung back the collar of his dressing-gown and now had the use of his eyes; of course, it was no longer a fight but simply a punishment. He seized Karl by the shirt-front, lifted him nearly off the floor and without even looking at him in his contempt flung him so violently against a chest standing a few steps away that at first Karl thought the searing pains in his back and head caused by the collision were the direct result of Delamarche's handling. 'You scoundrel!' he could hear Delamarche shouting in the darkness that rose before his wavering eyes. And as he sank down fainting beside the chest the words, 'You just wait!' still rang dimly in his ears.

When he came to his senses everything was dark around him; it seemed to be late in the night; from the balcony a faint glimmer of moonlight came into the room beneath the curtain. He could hear the regular breathing of the three sleepers; by far the loudest noise came from Brunelda, who snorted in her sleep as she sometimes did in talking; yet it was not easy to make out where the different sleepers were lying, for the whole room was filled with the sound of their breathing. Not until he had examined his surroundings for a little while did Karl think of himself, and then he was struck with alarm, for although he was quite cramped and stiff with pain he had not imagined that he could have been severely wounded to the effusion of blood. Yet now he felt a weight on his head, and his whole face, his neck, and his breast under the shirt were wet as if with blood. He must get into the light to find out exactly what condition he was in; perhaps they had crippled him, in which case Delamarche would be glad enough to let him go; but what could he hope to do if that were so; there would be no prospects for him at all. The lad with the nose half-eaten away occurred to him, and for a moment he buried his face in his hands.

Then involuntarily he turned towards the outside door and groped his way towards it on all fours. Presently he felt a shoe and then a leg under his finger-tips. That must be Robinson; who else would sleep in his shoes? They must have ordered him to lie across the door so as to keep Karl from escaping. But didn't they know, then, the condition that Karl was in? For the moment he was not thinking of escape; he merely wanted to reach the light. So, as he couldn't get out by the door, he must make for the balcony.

He found the dining-table in a quite different place from the evening before; the couch, which he approached very cautiously, was to his surprise vacant; but in the middle of the room he came upon a high though closely compressed pile of clothes, blankets, curtains, cushions and carpets. At first he thought it was only a small pile, like the one he had found at the end of the couch the previous evening, and that it had merely happened to fall on the floor; but to his astonishment he discovered on creeping farther that a whole van-load of such things was lying there, which, presumably for use in the night, must have been taken out of the trunks where they were kept during the day. He crept right round the pile and soon realised that the whole formed a sort of bed, on top of which, as he discovered by feeling cautiously, Delamarche and Brunelda were sleeping.

So now he knew where they all were and made haste to reach the balcony. It was quite a different world on the other side of the curtain, and he quickly rose to his feet. In the fresh night air he walked up and down the balcony a few times in the full radiance of the moon. He looked down at the street; it was quite still; music was still issuing from the restaurant, but more subdued now; a man was sweeping the pavement before the door; in the street where only a few hours ago the tumult had been so great that the shouting of an electoral candidate could not be distinguished among a thousand other voices, the scratching of the broom on the flagstones could be distinctly heard.

The scraping of table-legs on the next balcony made Karl aware that someone was sitting there reading. It was a young man with a little pointed beard, which he kept continually twisting as he read, his lips moving rapidly at the same time. He was facing Karl, sitting at a little table covered with books; he had taken the electric lamp from the parapet and shored it between two big volumes, so that he sat in a flood of garish light.

'Good evening,' said Karl, for he thought he noticed the young man glancing at him.

But that must have been an error, for the young man, apparently quite unaware of him, put his hand to his eyes to shield them from the light and make out who had suddenly spoken to him, and then, still unable to see anything, held up the electric lamp so as to throw some light on the next balcony.

'Good evening,' he said then in return, with a brief, penetrating look, adding: 'And what do you want?'

'Am I disturbing you?' asked Karl.

'Of course, of course,' said the man, returning the lamp again to its former place.

These words certainly discouraged any attempt at intercourse, but all the same Karl did not quit the corner of the balcony nearest to the man. Silently he watched him reading his book, turning the pages, now and then looking up something in another book, which he always snatched up at lightning speed, and frequently making notes in a jotter, which he did with his face surprisingly close to the paper.

Could this man be a student? It certainly looked as if he were. Not very unlike this – a long time ago now – Karl had sat at home at his parents' table writing out his school tasks, while his father read the newspaper or did book-keeping and correspondence for a society to which he belonged, and his mother was busy sewing, drawing the thread high out of the stuff in her hand. To avoid disturbing his father, Karl used to lay only the exercise book and his writing materials on the table, while he arranged his reference books on chairs to right and left of him. How quiet it had been there! How seldom strangers had visited their home! Even as a small child Karl had always been glad to see his mother turning the key in the outside door of an evening. She had no idea that he had come to such a pass as to try breaking open strange doors with knives.

And what had been the point of all his studying? He had forgotten everything; if he had been given the chance of continuing his studies here, he would have found it a very hard task. Once, he remembered, he had been ill for a whole month at home; what an effort it had cost him afterwards to get used to his interrupted studies again. And now, except for the handbook of English commercial correspondence, he had not read a book for ever so long.

'I say, young man,' Karl found himself suddenly addressed, 'couldn't you stand somewhere else? You disturb me frightfully, staring at me like that. After two o'clock in the morning one can surely expect to be allowed to work in peace on a balcony. Do you want anything from me?'

'Are you studying?' asked Karl.

'Yes, yes,' said the man, taking advantage of this wasted moment to bring new order among his books.

'Then I won't disturb you,' said Karl, 'I'm going indoors again, in any case. Good night.'

The man did not even answer; with abrupt resolution he had returned to his book again after dealing with the disturbance, his head leaning heavily on his right hand.

But just before he reached the curtain Karl remembered why he had actually come out; he did not even know how much he had been hurt. What could it be that was lying so heavy on his head? He put his hand up and stared in astonishment. There was no bloodstained wound such as he had feared in the darkness of the room, but only a turban-like bandage which was still rather wet. To judge from little frills of lace hanging from it here and there, it had been torn from an old chemise of Brunelda's, and Robinson must have wrapped it hurriedly round his head. But he had forgotten to wring it out, and so while Karl was unconscious the water had dripped down his face and under his shirt, and that was what had given him such a shock.

'Are you still there?' asked the man, peering across.

'I'm really going now,' said Karl, 'I only wanted to look at something; it's quite dark indoors.'

'But who are you?' said the man, laying his pen on the open book before him and advancing to the railing. 'What's your name? How do you come to be with these people? Have you been long here? What did you want to look at? Turn on the electric light there, won't you, so that I can see you.'

Karl obeyed, but before answering he drew the curtain more

closely to keep those inside from noticing anything. 'Excuse me,' he said in a whisper, 'for not raising my voice more. If they were to hear me there would be another row.'

'Another?' asked the man.

'Yes,' said Karl, 'I had a terrible row with them this very evening. I must still have a pretty bad lump on my head.' And he felt the back of his head.

'What was the trouble?' asked the man, and as Karl did not at once reply, he added: 'You can safely tell me anything you have against these people. For I hate all three of them, and the Madam in particular. Besides, I'd be surprised to find that they hadn't put you against me already. My name is Joseph Mendel and I am a student.'

'Well,' said Karl, 'they've told me about you already, but nothing bad. You doctored Brunelda once, didn't you?'

'That's right,' said the student, laughing. 'Does the couch still stink of it?'

'Oh yes,' said Karl.

'I'm glad of that, anyway,' said the student, passing his fingers through his hair. 'And why do they give you bumps on the head?'

'We had a quarrel,' said Karl, wondering how he was to explain it to the student. Then he checked himself and asked: 'But am I not disturbing you?'

'In the first place,' said the student, 'you have already disturbed me, and I am unluckily so nervous that I need a long time to get into my stride again. Ever since you began to walk about your balcony I haven't been able to get on with my studies. And then in the second place I always have a breather about three o'clock. So you needn't have any scruples about telling me. Besides, I'm interested.'

'It's quite simple,' said Karl, 'Delamarche wants me to be his servant. But I don't want to. I should have liked to leave this very night. He wouldn't let me go, and he locked the door; I tried to break it open and then there was a row. I'm unlucky to be still here.'

'Why, have you got another job?' asked the student.

'No,' said Karl, 'but that doesn't worry me in the least if I could only get away from here.'

'What,' said the student, 'it doesn't worry you in the least, doesn't it?' And both of them were silent for a moment. 'Why don't you want to stay with these people?' the student asked at last.

'Delamarche is a bad man,' said Karl, 'I've encountered him before. I tramped for a whole day with him once and I was glad to be out of his company. And am I to be his servant now?'

'If all servants were as fastidious in their choice of masters as you are!' said the student, and he seemed to be smiling. 'Look here, during the day I'm a salesman, a miserable counter-jumper, not much more than an errand-boy, in Montly's big store. This Montly is certainly a scoundrel, but that leaves me quite cold; what makes me furious is simply that the pay is wretched. Let that be an example to you.'

'What?' said Karl. 'You are a salesman all day and you study all night?'

'Yes,' said the student, 'there's nothing else to be done. I've tried everything possible, but this is the best way. For years I did nothing but study, day and night, and I almost didn't dare attend lectures in the clothes I had to wear. But that's all behind me now.'

'But when do you sleep?' asked Karl, looking at the student in wonder.

'Oh, sleep!' said the student. 'I'll get some sleep when I'm finished with my studies. I keep myself going on black coffee.' And he turned round, drew a big bottle from under the table, poured black coffee from it into a little cup and tossed it down his throat as if it were medicine which he wanted to get quickly over, to avoid the taste.

'A fine thing, black coffee,' said the student. 'It's a pity you're too far away for me to reach you some.'

'I don't like black coffee,' said Karl.

'I don't either,' said the student, laughing. 'But what could I do without it? If it weren't for black coffee Montly wouldn't keep me for a minute. I say Montly although of course he's not even aware of my existence. I simply don't know how I would get on in the shop if I didn't have a big bottle like this under the counter, for I've never dared to risk stopping the coffee-drinking; but you can believe me that if I did I would roll down behind the counter in a dead sleep. Unfortunately the others have tumbled to that, they call me "Black Coffee", a silly witticism which I'm sure has damaged my career already.'

'And when will you be finished with your studies?' asked Karl.

'I'm getting on slowly,' said the student with drooping head. He left the railing and sat down again at the table; planting his elbows on the open book and passing his fingers through his hair, he said then: 'It might take me another year or two.'

'I wanted to study too,' said Karl, as if that gave him a claim to be on a more confidential footing than the student, now fallen silent, had seen fit to grant.

'Indeed?' said the student, and it was not quite clear whether he was reading his book again or merely staring absently at it. 'You can be glad that you've given up studying. I've studied for years now simply for the sake of mere consistency. I get very little satisfaction out of it and even less hope for the future. What prospects could I have? America is full of quack doctors.'

'I wanted to be an engineer,' put in Karl quickly, as the student seemed to be losing all interest.

'And now you're supposed to be a servant to these people,' said the student, glancing up for a moment, 'that annoys you, of course.'

This conclusion sprang from misunderstanding, but Karl felt that he might turn it to his advantage. So he asked: 'Perhaps I could get a job in the store too?'

The question detached the student completely from his book, but the idea that he might be of some help to Karl in applying for such a post did not enter his mind at all. 'You try it,' he said, 'or rather don't you try it. Getting a job at Montly's is the biggest success I've ever scored. If I had to give up either my studies or my job, of course I'd give up my studies; I spend all my energy trying to keep off the horns of that dilemma.'

'So it's as hard as that to get a job in Montly's,' said Karl more to himself than to the student.

'Why, what do you think?' said the student. 'It's easier to be appointed district judge here than a door-opener at Montly's.'

Karl fell silent. This student, who was so much more experienced than he was and who hated Delamarche for some unknown reason and who certainly felt no ill-will towards himself, could not give him a single word of encouragement to leave Delamarche. And yet he didn't know anything about the danger threatening Karl from the police, which only Delamarche could shield him from at the moment.

'You saw the demonstration down there this evening, didn't you? Anyone who didn't know the ropes could easily imagine, couldn't he, that the candidate, Lobster is his name, would have some prospect of getting in or at least of being considered?'

'I know nothing about politics,' said Karl.

'That's a mistake,' said the student. 'But you have eyes and ears in your head, haven't you? The man obviously has friends and opponents; that surely can't have escaped you. Well, in my opinion the fellow hasn't the slightest prospect of being returned. I happen to know all about him; there's a man staying here who's an acquaintance of his. He's not without ability, and as far as his political views and his political past are concerned, he would actually be the most suitable judge for the district. But no one even imagines that he can get in; he'll come as big a cropper as anyone can; he'll have chucked away his dollars on the election campaign and that will be all.'

Karl and the student gazed at each other for a little while in silence. The student nodded smilingly and pressed his hand against his weary eyes.

'Well, aren't you going to bed yet?' he asked. 'I must start on my reading again. Look, how much I have still to do.' And he fluttered over half the pages of the book, to give Karl an idea of the work that still awaited him.

'Well then, good night,' said Karl, with a bow.

'Come over and see us sometime,' said the student, who had sat down at the table again, 'of course, only if you would like to. You'll always find lots of company here. And I can always have time for you from nine till ten in the evening.'

'So you advise me to stay with Delamarche?' asked Karl.

'Absolutely,' said the student, whose head was already bent over his book. It was as if not he but someone else had said the word; it echoed in Karl's ears as if it had been uttered by a voice more hollow than the student's. Slowly he went up to the curtain, glanced once more at the student, who now sat quite motionless in his ring of light, surrounded by the vast darkness, and slipped into the room. The united breathing of the three sleepers received him. He felt his way along the wall to the couch, and when he found it calmly stretched himself out on it as if it were his familiar bed. Since the student, who knew all about Delamarche and the queer circumstances, and who was moreover an educated man, had advised him to stay here, he had no qualms for the time being. He did not have such high aims as the student; perhaps even at home he would never have succeeded in carrying his studies to their conclusion; and if it were difficult to do that at home, no one could expect him to manage it here in a strange land. But his prospects of finding a post in which he could achieve something, and be appreciated for his achievement, would be greater if he accepted the servant's place with Delamarche for the time being and from that secure position watched for a favourable opportunity. In this very street there appeared to be many offices of middling or inferior status, which in case of need might not be too fastidious in picking their staff. He would be glad to take on a porter's job, if necessary, but after all it was not utterly impossible that he might be taken on simply for office work, and in the future might sit at his own desk as a regular clerk, gazing occasionally out of the open window with a light heart, like the clerk whom he had seen that morning on his expedition through the courtyards. As he shut his eyes he was comforted by the reflection that he was still young and that some day or other he was bound to get away from Delamarche; this household certainly did not look as if it were established for all eternity. Once he got such a post in an office, he would concentrate his mind on his office work; he would not disperse his energies like the student. If it should be necessary, he would devote his nights as well as his days to his office work, which at the start might be actually expected of him, considering his meagre knowledge of business matters. He would think only of the interests of the firm he had to serve, and undertake any work that offered, even work which the other clerks rejected as beneath them. Good intentions thronged into his head, as if his future employer were standing before the couch and could read them from his face.

On such thoughts Karl fell asleep, and only in his first light slumber was disturbed by a deep sigh from Brunelda, who was apparently troubled by bad dreams and twisted and turned on her bed.

8

THE NATURE THEATRE OF OKLAHOMA

At a street corner Karl saw a placard with the following announcement: The Oklahoma Theatre will engage members for its company today at Clayton race-course from six o'clock in the morning until midnight. The great Theatre of Oklahoma calls you! Today only and never again! If you miss your chance now you miss it for ever! If you think of your future you are one of us! Everyone is welcome! If you want to be an artist, join our company! Our Theatre can find employment for everyone, a place for everyone! If you decide on an engagement we congratulate you here and now! But hurry, so that you get in before midnight! At twelve o'clock the doors will be shut and never opened again! Down with all those who do not believe in us! Up, and to Clayton!

A great many people were certainly standing before the placard, but it did not seem to find much approval. There were so many placards; nobody believed in them any longer. And this placard was even more improbable than usual. Above all, it failed in an essential particular, it did not mention payment. If the payment were worth mentioning at all, the placard would certainly have mentioned it; that most attractive of all arguments would not have been forgotten. No one wanted to be an artist, but every man wanted to be paid for his labours.

Yet for Karl there was one great attraction in the placard. 'Everyone is welcome,' it said. Everyone, that meant Karl too. All that he had done till now was ignored; it was not going to be made a reproach to him. He was entitled to apply for a job of which he need not be ashamed, which, on the contrary, was a matter of public advertisement. And just as public was the promise that he too would find acceptance. He asked for nothing better; he wanted to find some way of at least beginning a decent life, and perhaps this was his chance. Even if all the extravagant statements in the placard were a lie, even if the great Theatre of Oklahoma were an insignificant travelling circus it wanted to engage people, and that was enough. Karl did not read the whole placard over again, but once more singled out the sentence: 'Everyone is welcome.' At first he thought of going to Clayton on foot; yet that would mean three hours of hard walking, and in all possibility he might arrive just in time to hear that every available vacancy had been filled. The placard certainly suggested that there were no limits to the number of people who could be engaged, but all advertisements of that kind were worded like that. Karl saw that he must either give it up or else go by train. He counted over his money, which would last him for eight days yet if he did not take this railway journey; he slid the little coins backwards and forwards on the palm of his hand. A gentleman who had been watching him clapped him on the shoulder and said: 'All good luck for your journey to Clayton.' Karl nodded silently and reckoned up his money again,. But he soon came to a decision, counted out the money he needed for the fare and rushed to the underground station. When he got out at Clayton he heard at once the noise of many trumpets. It was a confused blaring; the trumpets were not in harmony but were blown regardless of each other. Still, that did not worry Karl; he took it rather as a confirmation of the fact that the Theatre of Oklahoma was a great undertaking. But when he emerged from the station and surveyed the lay-out before him, he realized that it was all on a much larger scale than he could have conceived possible, and he did not understand how any organization could make such extensive preparations merely for the purpose of taking on employees. Before the entrance to the race-course a long low platform had been set up, on which hundreds of women dressed as angels in white robes with great wings on their shoulders were blowing on long trumpets that glittered like gold. They were not actually standing on the platform, but were mounted on separate pedestals, which could not however be seen, since they were completely hidden by the long flowing draperies of the robes. Now, as the pedestals were very high, some of them quite six feet high, these women looked gigantic, except that the smallness of their heads spoiled a little the impression of size and their loose hair looked too short and almost absurd hanging between the great wings and framing their faces. To avoid monotony, the pedestals were of all sizes; there were women quite low down, not much over life-size, but beside them others soared to such a height that one felt the slightest gust of wind would capsize them. And all these women were blowing their trumpets.

There were not many listeners. Dwarfed by comparison with these great figures, some ten boys were walking about before the platform and looking up at the women. They called each other's attention to this one or that, but seemed to have no idea of entering and offering their services. Only one older man was to be seen; he stood a little to one side. He had brought his wife with him and a child in a perambulator. The wife was holding the perambulator with one hand and with the other supporting herself on her husband's shoulder. They were clearly admiring the spectacle but one could see all the same that they were disappointed. They too had apparently expected to find some sign of work, and this blowing of trumpets confused them. Karl was in the same position. He walked over to where the man was standing, listened for a little to the trumpets, and then said: 'Isn't this the place where they are engaging people for the Theatre of Oklahoma?'

'I thought so too,' said the man, 'but we've been waiting here for an hour and heard nothing but these trumpets. There's not a placard to be seen, no announcers, nobody anywhere to tell you what to do.'

Karl said: 'Perhaps they're waiting until more people arrive. There are really very few here.'

'Possibly,' said the man, and they were silent again. Besides, it was difficult to hear anything through the din of the trumpets. But then the woman whispered to her husband; he nodded and she called at once to Karl: 'Couldn't you go into the racecourse and ask where the workers are being taken on?'

'Yes,' said Karl. 'But I would have to cross the platform, among all the angels.'

'Is that so very difficult?' asked the woman.

She seemed to think it an easy path for Karl, but she was unwilling to let her husband go.

'All right,' said Karl, 'I'll go.'

'That's very good of you,' said the woman, and both she and her husband took Karl's hand and pressed it.

The boys all came rushing up to get a near view of Karl climbing the platform. It was as if the women redoubled their efforts on the trumpets as a greeting to the first applicant. Those whose pedestals Karl had to pass actually took their trumpets from their mouths and leaned over to follow him with their eyes. At the other side of the platform Karl discovered a man walking restlessly up and down, obviously only waiting for people so as to give them all the information they might desire. Karl was just about to accost him, when he heard someone calling his name above him.

'Karl!' cried an angel. Karl looked up and in delighted surprise began to laugh. It was Fanny.

'Fanny!' he exclaimed, waving his hand.

'Come up here!' cried Fanny. 'You're surely not going to pass me like that!' And she parted her draperies so that the pedestal and a little ladder leading up to it became visible.

'Is one allowed to go up?' asked Karl.

'Who can forbid us to shake hands?' cried Fanny, and she looked round indignantly, in case anyone might be coming to intervene. But Karl was already running up the ladder.

'Not so fast!' cried Fanny. 'The pedestal and both of us will come to grief!' But nothing happened. Karl reached the top in safety. 'Just look,' said Fanny, after they had greeted each other, 'just look what a job I've got.'

'It's a fine job,' said Karl, looking round him. All the women near by had noticed him and began to giggle. 'You're almost the highest of them all,' said Karl, and he stretched out his hand to measure the height of the others.

'I saw you at once,' said Fanny, 'as soon as you came out of the station, but I'm in the last row here, unfortunately, nobody can see me, and I couldn't shout either. I blew as loudly as I could, but you didn't recognize me.'

'You all play very badly,' said Karl, 'let me have a turn.'

'Why, certainly,' said Fanny, handing him the trumpet, 'but don't spoil the show or else I'll get the sack.'

Karl began to blow the trumpet; he had imagined it was a roughly fashioned trumpet intended merely to make a noise, but now he discovered that it was an instrument capable of almost any refinement of expression. If all the instruments were of the same quality, they were being very ill-used. Paying no attention to the blaring of the others he played with all the power of his lungs an air which he had once heard in some tavern or other. He felt happy at having found an old friend, and at being allowed to play a trumpet as a special privilege, and at the thought that he might likely get a good post very soon. Many of the women stopped playing to listen; when he suddenly broke off scarcely half of the trumpets were in action; and it took a little while for the general din to work up to full power again.

'But you are an artist,' said Fanny, when Karl handed her the trumpet again. 'Ask to be taken on as a trumpeter.'

'Are men taken on for it too?' said Karl.

'Oh yes,' said Fanny. 'We play for two hours; then we're relieved by men who are dressed as devils. Half of them blow, the other half beat on drums. It's very fine, but the whole outfit is just as lavish. Don't you think our robes are beautiful? And the wings?' She looked down at herself.

'Do you think,' asked Karl, 'that I'll get a job here too?'

'Most certainly,' said Fanny, 'why, it's the greatest theatre in the world. What a piece of luck that we're to be together again. All the same it depends on what job you get. For it would be quite possible for us not to see each other at all, even though we were both engaged here.'

'Is the place really so big as that?' asked Karl.

'It's the biggest theatre in the world,' Fanny said again, 'I haven't seen it yet myself, I admit, but some of the other girls here, who have been in Oklahoma already, say that there are almost no limits to it.'

'But there aren't many people here,' said Karl, pointing down at the boys and the little family.

'That's true,' said Fanny. 'But consider that we pick up people in all the towns, that our recruiting outfit here is always on the road, and that there are ever so many of these outfits.'

'Why, has the theatre not opened yet?' asked Karl.

'Oh yes,' said Fanny, 'it's an old theatre, but it is always being enlarged.'

'I'm surprised,' said Karl, 'that more people don't flock to join it.'

'Yes,' said Fanny, 'it's extraordinary.'

'Perhaps,' said Karl, 'this display of angels and devils frightens people off more than it attracts them.'

'What made you think of that?' said Fanny. 'But you may be right. Tell that to our leader; perhaps it might be helpful.'

'Where is he?' asked Karl.

'On the race-course,' said Fanny, 'on the umpire's platform.'

'That surprises me too,' said Karl, 'why a race-course for engaging people?'

'Oh,' said Fanny, 'we always make great preparations in case there should be a great crowd. There's lots of space on a race-course. And in all the stands where the bets are laid on ordinary days, offices are set up to sign on recruits. There must be two hundred different offices there.'

'But,' cried Karl, 'has the Theatre of Oklahoma such a huge income that it can maintain recruiting establishments to that extent?'

'What does it matter to us?' said Fanny. 'But you'd better go now, Karl, so that you don't miss anything; and I must begin to blow my trumpet again. Do your best to get a job in this outfit, and come and tell me at once. Remember that I'll be waiting very impatiently for the news.'

She pressed his hand, warned him to be cautious in climbing down, set the trumpet to her lips again, but did not blow it until she saw Karl safely on the ground. Karl arranged the robe over the ladder again, as it had been before, Fanny nodded her thanks and Karl, still considering from various angles what he had just heard, approached the man, who had already seen him up on Fanny's pedestal and had come close to it to wait for him.

'You want to join us?' asked the man. 'I am the staff manager of this company and I bid you welcome.' He had a slight permanent stoop as if out of politeness, fidgeted with his feet, though without moving from the spot, and played with his watch chain.

'Thank you,' said Karl, 'I read the placard your company put out and I have come here as I was requested.'

'Quite right,' said the man appreciatively. 'Unluckily there aren't many who do the same.' It occurred to Karl that he could now tell the man that perhaps the recruiting company failed because of the very splendour of its attractions. But he did not say so, for this man was not the leader of the company, and besides it would not be much of a recommendation for him if he began to make suggestions for the improvement of the outfit before even being taken on. So he merely said: 'There is another man waiting out there who wants to report here too and simply sent me on ahead. May I fetch him now?'

'Of course,' said the man, 'the more the better.'

'He has a wife with him too and a small child in a perambulator. Are they to come too?'

'Of course,' said the man, and he seemed to smile at Karl's doubts. 'We can use all of them.'

'I'll be back in a minute,' said Karl, and he ran back to the edge of the platform. He waved to the married couple and shouted that everybody could come. He helped the man to lift the perambulator on to the platform, and then they proceeded together. The boys, seeing this, consulted with each other, and then, their hands in their pockets, hesitating to the last instant, slowly climbed on to the platform and followed Karl and the family. Just then some fresh passengers emerged from the underground station and raised their arms in astonishment when they saw the platform and the angels. However, it seemed that the competition for jobs would now become more lively. Karl felt very glad that he was such an early arrival, perhaps the first of them all; the married couple were apprehensive and asked various questions as to whether great demands would be made on them. Karl told them he knew nothing definite yet, but he had received the impression that everyone without exception would be engaged. He thought they could feel easy in their minds. The staff manager advanced towards them, very satisfied that so many were coming; he rubbed his hands, greeted everyone with a little bow and arranged them all in a row. Karl was the first, then came the husband and wife, and after that the others, When they were all ranged up – the boys kept jostling each other at first and it took some time to get them in order

– the staff manager said, while the trumpets fell silent: 'I greet you in the name of the Theatre of Oklahoma. You have come early,' (but it was already midday), 'there is no great rush yet, so that the formalities necessary for engaging you will soon be settled. Of course you have all your identification papers.'

The boys at once pulled papers out of their pockets and flourished them at the staff manager; the husband nudged his wife, who pulled out a whole bundle of papers from under the blankets of the perambulator. But Karl had none. Would that prevent him from being taken on? He knew well enough from experience that with a little resolution it should be easy to get round such regulations. Very likely he would succeed. The staff manager glanced along the row, assured himself that everyone had papers and since Karl also stood with his hand raised, though it was empty, he assumed that in his case too everything was in order.

'Very good,' said the staff manager, with a reassuring wave of the hand to the boys, who wanted to have their papers examined at once, 'the papers will now be scrutinized in the employment bureaus. As you will have seen already from our placard, we can find employment for everyone. But we must know of course what occupations you have followed until now, so that we can put you in the right places to make use of your knowledge.'

'But it's a theatre,' thought Karl dubiously, and he listened very intently.

'We have accordingly,' went on the staff manager, 'set up employment bureaus in the bookmakers' booths, an office for each trade or profession. So each of you will now tell me his occupation; a family is generally registered at the husband's employment bureau. I shall then take you to the offices, where first your papers and then your qualifications will be checked by experts; it will only be a quite short examination; there's nothing to be afraid of. You will then be signed on at once and receive your further instructions. So let us begin. This first office is for engineers, as the inscription tells you. Is there perhaps an engineer here?'

Karl stepped forward. He thought that his lack of papers made it imperative for him to rush through the formalities with all possible speed; he had also a slight justification in putting himself forward, for he had once wanted to be an engineer. But when the boys saw Karl reporting himself they grew envious and put up their hands too, all of them. The staff manager rose to his full height and said to the boys: 'Are you engineers?' Their hands slowly wavered and sank, but Karl stuck to his first decision. The staff manager certainly looked at him with incredulity, for Karl seemed too wretchedly clad and also too young to be an engineer; but he said nothing further, perhaps out of gratitude because Karl, at least in his opinion, had brought the applicants in. He simply pointed courteously towards the office, and Karl went across to it, while the staff manager turned to the others.

In the bureau for engineers two gentlemen were sitting at either side of a rectangular counter comparing two big lists which lay before them. One of them read while the other made a mark against names in his list. When Karl appeared and greeted them, they laid aside the list at once and brought out two great books, which they flung open.

One of them, who was obviously only a clerk, said: 'Please give me your identity papers.'

'I am sorry to say I haven't got them with me,' said Karl.

'He hasn't got them with him,' said the clerk to the other gentleman, at once writing down the answer in his book.

'You are an engineer?' thereupon asked the other man, who seemed to be in charge of the bureau.

'I'm not an engineer yet,' said Karl quickly, 'but–'

'Enough,' said the gentleman still more quickly, 'in that case you don't belong to us. Be so good as to note the inscription.' Karl clenched his teeth, and the gentleman must have observed that, for he said: 'There's no need to worry. We can employ everyone.' And he made a sign to one of the attendants who were lounging about idly between the barriers: 'Lead this gentleman to the bureau for technicians.'

The attendant interpreted the command literally and took Karl by the hand. They passed a number of booths on either side; in one Karl saw one of the boys, who had already been signed on and was gratefully shaking hands with the gentleman in charge. In the bureau to which Karl was now taken the procedure was similar to that in the first office, as he had foreseen. Except that they now despatched him to the bureau for intermediate pupils, when they heard that he had attended an intermediate school. But when Karl confessed there that it was a European school he had attended, the officials refused to accept him and had him conducted to the bureau for European intermediate pupils. It was a booth on the outer verge of the course, not only smaller but also humbler than all the others. The attendant who conducted him there was furious at the long pilgrimage and the repeated rebuffs, for which in his opinion Karl alone bore the blame. He did not wait for the questioning to begin, but went away at once. So this bureau was probably Karl's last chance. When Karl caught sight of the head of the bureau, he was almost startled at his close resemblance to a teacher who was presumably still teaching in the school at home. The resemblance, however, as immediately appeared, was confined to certain details; but the spectacles resting on the man's broad nose, the fair beard as carefully tended as a prize exhibit, the slightly rounded back and the unexpectedly loud abrupt voice held Karl in amazement for some time. Fortunately, he had not to attend very carefully, for the procedure here was much simpler than in the other offices. A note was certainly taken of the fact that his papers were lacking, and the head of the bureau called it an incomprehensible piece of negligence; but the clerk, who seemed to have the upper hand, quickly glossed it over and after a few brief questions by his superior, while that gentleman was just preparing to put some more important ones, he declared that Karl had been engaged. The head of the bureau turned with open mouth upon his clerk, but the clerk made a definite gesture with his hand, said: 'Engaged,' and at once entered the decision in his book. Obviously the clerk considered a European intermediate pupil to be something so ignominious that anyone who admitted being one was not worth disbelieving. Karl for his part had no objection to this; he went up to the clerk intending to thank him. But there was another little delay, while they asked him what his name was. He did not reply at once; he felt shy of mentioning his own name and letting it be written down. As soon as he had a place here, no matter how small, and filled it satisfactorily, they could have his name, but not now; he had concealed it too long to give it away now. So as no other name occurred to him at the moment, he gave the nickname he had had in his last post: 'Negro.'

'Negro?' said the chief, turning his head and making a grimace, as if Karl had now touched the highwater mark of incredibility. Even the clerk looked critically at Karl for a while, but then he said, 'Negro' and wrote the name down.

'But you surely haven't written down Negro?' his chief shouted at him.

'Yes, Negro,' said the clerk calmly, and waved his hand, as if his superior should now continue the proceedings. And the head of the bureau, controlling himself, stood up and said: 'You are engaged, then, for the –' but he could not get any further, he could not go against his own conscience, so he sat down and said: 'He isn't called Negro.'

The clerk raised his eyebrows, got up himself and said: 'Then it is my duty to inform you that you have been engaged for the Theatre of Oklahoma and that you will now be introduced to our leader.'

Another attendant was summoned, who conducted Karl to the umpire's platform.

At the foot of the steps Karl caught sight of the perambulator, and at that moment the father and mother descended, the mother with the baby on her arm.

'Have you been taken on?' asked the man; he was much more lively than before, and his wife smiled at Karl across her shoulder. When Karl answered that he had just been taken on and was going to be introduced, the man said: 'Then I congratulate you. We have been taken on too. It seems to be a good thing, though you can't get used to everything all at once; but it's like that everywhere.'

They said good-bye to each other again, and Karl climbed up to the platform. He took his time, for the small space above seemed to be crammed with people, and he did not want to be importunate. He even paused for a while and gazed at the great race-course, which extended on every side to distant woods. He was filled with longing to see a horse-race; he had found no opportunity to do so since he had come to America. In Europe he had once been taken to a race-meeting as a small child, but all that he could remember was that he had been dragged by his mother through throngs of people who were unwilling to make room and let him pass. So that actually he had never seen a race yet. Behind him a mechanism of some kind began to whir; he turned round and saw on the board, where the names of the winners appeared, the following inscription being hoisted: 'The merchant Kalla with wife and child.' So the names of those who were engaged was communicated to all the offices from here.

At that moment several gentlemen with pencils and note-books in their hands ran down the stairs, busily talking to each other; Karl squeezed against the railing to let them pass, and then went up, as there was now room for him above. In one corner of the platform with its wooden railing – the whole looked like the flat roof of a small tower – a gentleman was sitting with his arms stretched along the railing and a broad white silk sash hanging diagonally across his chest with the inscription: 'Leader of the tenth recruiting squad of the Theatre of Oklahoma.' On the table stood a telephone, doubtless installed for use during the races but now obviously employed in giving the leader all necessary information regarding the various applicants before they were introduced, for he did not begin by putting questions to Karl, but said to a gentleman sitting beside him with crossed legs, his chin in his hands: 'Negro, a European intermediate pupil.' And as if with that he had nothing more to say to Karl, who was bowing low before him, he glanced down the stairs to see whether anyone else was coming. As no one came, he lent an ear to the conversation which the other gentleman was having with Karl, but for the most part kept looking at the race-course and tapping on the railing with his fingers. These delicate and yet powerful, long and nimble fingers attracted Karl's attention from time to time, although he should really have been giving his whole mind to the other gentleman.

'You've been out of work?' this gentleman began by asking. The question, like almost all the other questions he asked, was very simple and direct, nor did he check Karl's replies by cross-examining him at all; yet the way in which he rounded his eyes while he uttered his questions, the way in which he leaned forward to contemplate their effect, the way in which he let his head sink to his chest while he listened to the replies, in some cases repeating them aloud, invested his inquiries with an air of special significance, which one might not understand but which it made one uneasy to suspect. Many times Karl felt impelled to take back the answer he had given and substitute another which might find more approval, but he always managed to refrain, for he knew what a bad impression such shilly-shallying was bound to make, and how little he really understood for the most part the effect of his answers. Besides, his engagement seemed to be already decided upon, and the consciousness of that gave him support.

To the question whether he had been out of work he replied with a simple 'Yes.'

'Where were you engaged last?' the gentleman asked next.

Karl was just about to answer, when the gentleman raised his first finger and repeated again: 'Last!'

As Karl had understood the question perfectly well, he involuntarily shook his head to reject the confusing additional remark and answered: 'In an office.'

This was the truth, but if the gentleman should demand more definite information regarding the kind of office, he would have to tell lies. However, the necessity did not arise, for the gentleman asked a question which it was quite easy to answer with perfect truth: 'Were you satisfied there?'

'No!' exclaimed Karl, almost before the question was finished. Out of the corner of his eye he could see that the leader was smiling faintly. He regretted the impetuosity of his exclamation, but it was too tempting to launch that no, for during all his last term of service his greatest wish had been that some outside employer of labour might come in and ask him that very question. Still, his negative might put him at another disadvantage if the gentleman were to follow it up by asking why he had not been satisfied? But he asked instead: 'For what kind of post do you feel you are best suited?' This question might contain a real trap, for why was it put at all since he had already been engaged as an actor? But although he saw the difficulty, he could not bring himself to say that he felt particularly suited for the acting profession. So he evaded the question and said, at the risk of appearing obstructive: 'I read the placard in the town, and as it said there that you could employ anyone, I came here.'

'We know that,' said the gentleman, showing by his ensuing silence that he insisted on an answer to the question.

'I have been engaged as an actor,' said Karl, hesitantly, to let the gentleman see that he found himself in a dilemma.

'Quite so,' said the gentleman, and fell silent again.

'No,' said Karl, and all his hopes of being settled in a job began to totter. 'I don't know whether I'm capable of being an actor. But I shall do my best and try to carry out all my instructions.'

The gentleman turned to the leader, both of them nodded; Karl seemed to have given the right answer, so he took courage again and standing erect waited for the next question. It ran: 'What did you want to study originally?'

To define the question more exactly – the gentleman seemed to lay great weight on exact definition – he added: 'In Europe, I mean,' at the same time removing his hand from his chin and waving it slightly as if to indicate both how remote Europe was and how unimportant were any plans that might have been made there.

Karl said: 'I wanted to be an engineer.' This answer almost stuck in his throat; it was absurd of him, knowing as he did the kind of career he had had in America, to bring up the old day-dream of having wanted to be an engineer – would he ever have become an engineer even in Europe? – but he simply did not know what other answer to make and so gave this one.

Yet the gentleman took it seriously, as he took everything seriously. 'Well, you can't turn into an engineer all at once,' he said, 'but perhaps it would suit you for the time being to be attached to some minor technical work.'

'Certainly,' said Karl. He was perfectly satisfied; true, if he accepted the offer, he would be transferred from the acting profession to the lower status of technical labourer, but he really believed that he would be able to do more justice to himself at technical work. Besides, he kept on telling himself, it was not so much a matter of the kind of work as of establishing oneself permanently somewhere.

'Are you strong enough for heavy work?' asked the gentleman.

'Oh yes,' said Karl.

At that, the gentleman asked Karl to come nearer and felt his arm.

'He's a strong lad,' he said then, pulling Karl by the arm towards the leader. The leader nodded smilingly, reached Karl his hand without changing his lazy posture, and said: 'Then that's all settled. In Oklahoma we'll look into it again. See that you do honour to our recruiting squad!'

Karl made his bow, and also turned to say good-bye to the other gentleman, but he, as if his functions were now discharged, was walking up and down the platform gazing at the sky. As Karl went down the steps the announcement board beside them was showing the inscription: 'Negro, technical worker.'

As everything here was taking an orderly course, Karl felt that after all he would not have minded seeing his real name on the board. The organization was indeed scrupulously precise, for at the foot of the steps Karl found a waiting attendant who fastened a band round his arm. When Karl lifted his arm to see what was written on the band, there, right enough, were the words 'technical worker.'

But wherever he was to be taken now, he decided that he must first report to Fanny how well everything had gone. To his great sorrow he learned from the attendant that both the angels and the devils had already left for the next town on the recruiting squad's itinerary, to act as advance agents for the arrival of the troop next day. 'What a pity,' said Karl; it was the first disappointment that he had had in this new undertaking, 'I had a friend among the angels.'

'You'll see her again in Oklahoma,' said the attendant, 'but now come along; you're the last.'

He led Karl along the inner side of the platform on which the angels had been posted; there was nothing left but the empty pedestals. Yet Karl's assumption that if the trumpeting were stopped more people would be encouraged to apply was proved wrong, for there were now no grown-up people at all before the platform, only a few children fighting over a long, white feather which had apparently fallen out of an angel's wing. A boy was holding it up in the air, while the other children were trying to push down his head with one hand and reach for the feather with the other.

Karl pointed out the children, but the attendant said without looking: 'Come on, hurry up, it's taken a long time for you to get engaged. I suppose they weren't sure of you?'

'I don't know,' said Karl in astonishment, but he did not believe it. Always, even in the most unambiguous circumstances, someone could be found to take pleasure in suggesting trouble to his fellow-men. But at the friendly aspect of the Grand Stand which they were now approaching, Karl soon forgot the attendant's remark. For on this stand there was a long wide bench covered with a white cloth; all the applicants who had been taken on sat on the bench below it with their backs to the race-course and were being fed. They were all happy and excited; just as Karl, coming last, quietly took his seat several of them were rising with upraised glasses, and one of them toasted the leader of the tenth recruiting squad, whom he called the 'father of all the unemployed'. Someone then remarked that the leader could be seen from here, and actually the umpire's platform with the two gentlemen on it was visible at no very great distance. Now they were all raising their glasses in that direction, Karl too seized the glass standing in front of him, but loudly as they shouted and hard as they tried to draw attention to themselves, there was no sign on the umpire's platform that the ovation had been observed or at least that there was any wish to observe it. The leader lounged in his corner as before, and the other gentleman stood beside him, resting his chin on his hand. Somewhat disappointed, everybody sat down again; here and there one would turn round towards the umpire's platform again; but soon they were all well occupied with the abundant food; huge birds such as Karl had never seen before were carried round with many forks sticking into the crisply roasted meat; the glasses were kept filled with wine by the attendants – you hardly noticed it, you were busy with your plate and a stream of red wine simply fell into your glass – and those who did not want to take part in the general conversation could look at views of the Theatre of Oklahoma which lay in a pile at one end of the table and were supposed to pass from hand to hand. But few of the people troubled much about the views, and so it happened that only one of them reached Karl, who was the last in the row. Yet to judge from that picture, all the rest must have been well worth seeing. The picture showed the box reserved in the Theatre for the President of the United States. At first glance one might have thought that it was not a stage-box but the stage itself, so far-flung was the sweep of its breastwork. This breastwork was made entirely of gold, to the smallest detail. Between its slender columns, as delicately carved as if cut out by a fine pair of scissors, medallions of former Presidents were arrayed side by side; one of these had a remarkably straight nose, curling lips and a downward-looking eye hooded beneath a full, rounded eye-lid. Rays of light fell into the box from all sides and from the roof; the foreground was literally bathed in light, white but soft, while the recess of the background, behind red damask curtains falling in changing folds from roof to floor and looped with cords, appeared like a duskily glowing empty cavern. One could scarcely imagine human figures in that box, so royal did it look. Karl was not quite rapt away from his dinner, but he laid the photograph beside his plate and sat gazing at it. He would have been glad to look at even one of the other photographs, but he did not want to rise and pick one up himself, since an attendant had his hand resting on the pile and the sequence probably had to be kept unbroken; so he only craned his neck to survey the table, trying to make out if another photograph were being passed along. To his great amazement – it seemed at first incredible – he recognized among those most intent upon their plates a face which he knew well: Giacomo. At once he rose and hastened up to him. 'Giacomo!' he cried.

Shy as ever when taken by surprise, Giacomo got up from his seat, turned round in the narrow space between the benches, wiped his mouth with his hand and then showed great delight at seeing Karl, suggesting that Karl should come and sit beside him, or he should change his own place instead; they had a lot to tell each other and should stick together all the time. Karl, not wanting to disturb the others, said perhaps they had better keep their own places for the time being, the meal would soon be finished and then of course they would stick together. But Karl still lingered a moment or two, only for the sake of looking at Giacomo. What memories of the past were recalled! What had happened to the Manageress? What was Therese doing? Giacomo himself had hardly changed at all in appearance; the Manageress's prophecy that in six months' time he would develop into a large-boned American had not been fulfilled; he was as delicate-looking as before, his cheeks hollow as ever, though at the moment they were bulging with an extra large mouthful of meat from which he was slowly extracting the bones, to lay them on his plate. As Karl could see from his armband, he was not engaged as an actor either, but as a lift-boy;

the Theatre of Oklahoma really did seem to have a place for everyone! But Karl's absorption in Giacomo had kept him too long away from his own seat. Just as he was thinking of getting back, the staff manager arrived, climbed on to one of the upper benches, clapped his hands and made a short speech while most of the people rose to their feet, those who remained in their seats, unwilling to leave their dinners, being nudged by the others until they too were forced to rise.

'I hope,' said the staff manager, Karl meanwhile having tiptoed back to his place, 'that you have been satisfied with our reception of you and the dinner we have given you. The recruiting squad is generally supposed to keep a good kitchen. I'm sorry we must clear the table already, but the train for Oklahoma is going to leave in five minutes. It's a long journey, I know, but you'll find yourselves well looked after. Let me now introduce the gentleman in charge of your transport arrangements, whose instructions you will please follow.'

A lean little man scrambled up on the bench beside the staff manager and, scarcely taking time to make a hasty bow, began waving his arms nervously to direct them how to assemble themselves in an orderly manner and proceed to the station. But he was at first ignored, for the man who had made a speech at the beginning of the dinner now struck the table with his hand and began to return thanks in a lengthy oration, although – Karl was growing quite uneasy about it – he had just been told that the train was leaving in five minutes. He was not even deterred by the patent inattention of the staff manager, who was giving various instructions to the transport official; he built up his oration in the grand manner, mentioning each dish that had been served and passing a judgement on each individually, winding up with the declaration: 'Gentleman, that is the way to our hearts!' Everyone laughed except the gentlemen he was addressing, but there was more truth than jest in his statement, all the same.

This oration brought its own penalty, since the road to the station had now to be taken at a run. Still, that was no great hardship, for – as Karl only now remarked – no one carried any luggage; the only thing that could be called luggage was the perambulator, which the father was pushing at the head of the troop and which jolted up and down wildly as if no hand were steadying it. What destitute, disreputable characters were here assembled, and yet how well they had been received and cared for! And the transport official must have been told to cherish them like the apple of his eye. Now he was taking a turn at pushing the perambulator, waving one hand to encourage the troop; now he was urging on stragglers in the rear; now he was careering along the ranks, keeping an eye on the slower runners in the middle and trying to show them with swinging arms how to run more easily.

When they reached the station the train was ready for departure. People in the station pointed out the new-comers to each other, and one heard exclamations such as: 'All these belong to the Theatre of Oklahoma!' The theatre seemed to be much better known than Karl had assumed; of course, he had never taken much interest in theatrical affairs. A whole carriage was specially reserved for their troop; the transport official worked harder than the guard at getting the people into it. Only when he had inspected each compartment and made a few rearrangements did he get into his own seat. Karl had happened to get a window-seat, with Giacomo beside him. So there they sat, the two of them, close together, rejoicing in their hearts over the journey. Such a carefree journey in America they had never known. When the train began to move out of the station they waved from the window, to the amusement of the young men opposite, who nudged each other and laughed.

For two days and two nights they journeyed on. Only now did Karl understand how huge America was. Unweariedly he gazed out of the window, and Giacomo persisted in struggling for a place beside him until the other occupants of the compartment, who wanted to play cards, got tired of him and voluntarily surrendered the other window-seat. Karl thanked them – Giacomo's English was not easy for anyone to follow – and in the course of time, as is inevitable among fellow-travellers, they grew much more friendly, although their friendliness was sometimes a nuisance, as for example whenever they ducked down to rescue a card fallen on the floor, they could not resist giving hearty tweaks to Karl's legs or Giacomo's. Whenever that happened Giacomo always shrieked in renewed surprise and drew his legs up; Karl attempted once to give a kick in return, but suffered the rest of the time in silence. Everything that went on in the little compartment, which was thick with cigarette-smoke in spite of the open window, faded into comparative insignificance before the grandeur of the scene outside.

The first day they travelled through a high range of mountains. Masses of blue-black rock rose in sheer wedges to the railway line; even craning one's neck out of the window, one could not see their summits; narrow, gloomy, jagged valleys opened out and one tried to follow with a pointing finger the direction in which they lost themselves; broad mountain streams appeared, rolling in great waves down on to the foot-hills and drawing with them a thousand foaming wavelets, plunging underneath the bridges over which the train rushed; and they were so near that the breath of coldness rising from them chilled the skin of one's face.

The Castle

Translated from the German
by Willa and Edwin Muir
Additional material translated
by Eithne Wilkins and Ernst Kaiser

1

It was late in the evening when K. arrived. The village was deep in snow. The Castle hill was hidden, veiled in mist and darkness, nor was there even a glimmer of light to show that a castle was there. On the wooden bridge leading from the main road to the village K. stood for a long time gazing into the illusory emptiness above him.

Then he went on to find quarters for the night. The inn was still awake, and although the landlord could not provide a room and was upset by such a late and unexpected arrival, he was willing to let K. sleep on a bag of straw in the parlour. K. accepted the offer. Some peasants were still sitting over their beer, but he did not want to talk, and after himself fetching the bag of straw from the attic, lay down beside the stove. It was a warm corner, the peasants were quiet, and letting his weary eyes stray over them he soon fell asleep.

But very shortly he was awakened. A young man dressed like a townsman, with the face of an actor, his eyes narrow and his eyebrows strongly marked, was standing beside him along with the landlord. The peasants were still in the room, and a few had turned their chairs round so as to see and hear better. The young man apologized very courteously for having awakened K., introducing himself as the son of the Castellan, and then said: 'This village belongs to the Castle, and whoever lives here or passes the night here does so in a manner of speaking in the Castle itself. Nobody may do that without the Count's permission. But you have no such permit, or at least you have produced none.'

K. had half raised himself and now, smoothing down his hair and looking up at the two men, he said: 'What village is this I have wandered into? Is there a castle here?'

'Most certainly,' replied the young man slowly, while here and there a head was shaken over K.'s remark, 'the castle of my lord the Count West-west.'

'And must one have a permit to sleep here?' asked K., as if he wished to assure himself that what he had heard was not a dream.

'One must have a permit,' was the reply, and there was an ironical contempt for K. in the young man's gesture as he stretched out his arm and appealed to the others, 'Or must one not have a permit?'

'Well, then, I'll have to go and get one,' said K. yawning and pushing his blanket away as if to rise up.

'And from whom, pray?' asked the young man.

'From the Count,' said K., 'that's the only thing to be done.'

'A permit from the Count in the middle of the night!' cried the young man, stepping back a pace.

'Is that impossible?' inquired K. coolly. 'Then why did you waken me?'

At this the young man flew into a passion. 'None of your guttersnipe manners!' he cried, 'I insist on respect for the Count's authority! I woke you up to inform you that you must quit the Count's territory at once.'

'Enough of this fooling,' said K. in a markedly quiet voice, laying himself down again and pulling up the blanket. 'You're going a little too far, my good fellow, and I'll have something to say tomorrow about your conduct. The landlord here and those other gentlemen will bear me out if necessary. Let me tell you that I am the Land Surveyor whom the Count is expecting. My assistants are coming on tomorrow in a carriage with the apparatus. I did not want to miss the chance of a walk through the snow, but unfortunately lost my way several times and so arrived very late. That it was too late to present myself at the Castle I knew very well before you saw fit to inform me. That is why I have made shift with this bed for the night, where, to put it mildly, you have had the discourtesy to disturb me. That is all I have to say. Good night, gentlemen.' And K. turned over on his side towards the stove.

'Land Surveyor?' he heard the hesitating question behind his back, and then there was a general silence. But the young man soon recovered his assurance, and lowering his voice, sufficiently to appear considerate of K.'s sleep while yet speaking loud enough to be clearly heard, said to the landlord: 'I'll ring up and inquire.' So there was a telephone in this village inn? They had everything up to the mark. The particular instance surprised K., but on the whole he had really expected it. It appeared that the telephone was placed almost over his head and in his drowsy condition he had overlooked it. If the young man must needs telephone he could not, even with the best intentions, avoid disturbing K., the only question was whether K. would let him do so; he decided to allow it. In that case, however, there was no sense in pretending to sleep, and so he turned on his back again. He could see the peasants putting their heads together; the arrival of a Land Surveyor was no small event. The door into the kitchen had been opened, and blocking the whole doorway stood the imposing figure of the landlady, to whom the landlord was advancing on tiptoe in order to tell her what was happening. And now the conversation began on the telephone. The Castellan was asleep, but an under-castellan, one of the under-castellans, a certain Herr Fritz, was available. The young man, announcing himself as Schwarzer, reported that he had found K., a disreputable-looking man in the thirties, sleeping calmly on a bag of straw with a minute rucksack for pillow and a knotty stick within reach. He had naturally suspected the fellow, and as the landlord had obviously neglected his duty he, Schwarzer, had felt bound to investigate the matter. He had roused the man, questioned him, and duly warned him off the Count's territory, all of which K. had taken with an ill grace, perhaps with some justification, as it eventually turned out, for he claimed to be a Land Surveyor engaged by the Count. Of course, to say the least of it, that was a statement which required official confirmation, and so Schwarzer begged Herr Fritz to inquire in the Central Bureau if a Land Surveyor were really expected, and to telephone the answer at once.

Then there was silence while Fritz was making inquiries up there and the young man was waiting for the answer. K. did not change his position, did not even once turn round, seemed quite indifferent and stared into space. Schwarzer's report, in its combination of malice and prudence, gave him an idea of the measure of diplomacy in which even underlings in the Castle like Schwarzer were versed. Nor were they remiss in industry, the Central Office had a night service. And apparently answered questions quickly, too, for Fritz was already ringing. His reply seemed brief enough, for Schwarzer hung up the receiver immediately, crying angrily: 'Just what I said! Not a trace of a Land Surveyor. A common, lying tramp, and probably worse.' For a moment K. thought that all of them, Schwarzer, the peasants, the landlord and the landlady, were going to fall upon him in a body, and to escape at least the first shock of their assault he crawled right underneath the blanket. But the telephone rang again, and with a special insistence, it seemed to K. Slowly he put out his head. Although it was improbable that this message also concerned K., they all stopped short and Schwarzer took up the receiver once more. He listened to a fairly long statement, and then said in a low voice: 'A mistake, is it? I'm sorry to hear that. The head of the department himself said so? Very queer, very queer. How am I to explain it all to the Land Surveyor?'

K. pricked up his ears. So the Castle had recognized him as the Land Surveyor. That was unpropitious for him, on the one hand, for it meant that the Castle was well informed about him, had estimated all the probable chances, and was taking up the challenge with a smile. On the other hand, however, it was quite propitious, for if his interpretation were right they had underestimated his strength, and he would have more freedom of action than he had dared to hope. And if they expected to cow him by their lofty superiority in recognizing him as Land Surveyor, they were mistaken; it made his skin prickle a little, that was all.

He waved off Schwarzer who was timidly approaching him, and refused an urgent invitation to transfer himself into the landlord's own room; he only accepted a warm drink from the landlord and from the landlady a basin to wash in, a piece of soap, and a towel. He did not even have to ask that the room should be cleared, for all the men flocked out with averted faces lest he should recognize them again the next day. The lamp was blown out, and he was left in peace at last. He slept deeply until morning, scarcely disturbed by rats scuttling past once or twice.

After breakfast, which, according to his host, was to be paid for by the Castle, together with all the other expenses of his board and lodging, he prepared to go out immediately into the village. But since the landlord, to whom he had been very curt because of his behaviour the preceding night, kept circling around him in dumb entreaty, he took pity on the man and asked him to sit down for a while.

'I haven't met the Count yet,' said K., 'but he pays well for good work, doesn't he? When a man like me travels so far from home he wants to go back with something in his pockets.'

'There's no need for the gentleman to worry about that kind of thing; nobody complains of being badly paid.'

'Well,' said K., 'I'm not one of your timid people, and can give a piece of my mind even to a Count, but of course it's much better to have everything settled up without any trouble.'

The landlord sat opposite K. on the rim of the window-ledge, not daring to take a more comfortable seat, and kept gazing at K. with an anxious look in his large brown eyes. He had thrust his company on K. at first, but now it seemed that he was eager to escape. Was he afraid of being cross-questioned about the Count? Was he afraid of some indiscretion on the part of the 'gentleman' whom he took K. to be? K. must divert his attention. He looked at the clock, and said: 'My assistants should be arriving soon. Will you be able to put them up here?'

'Certainly, sir,' he said, 'but won't they be staying with you up at the Castle?'

Was the landlord so willing, then, to give up prospective customers, and K. in particular, whom he so unconditionally transferred to the Castle?

'That's not at all certain yet,' said K. 'I must first find out what work I am expected to do. If I have to work down here, for instance, it would be more sensible to lodge down here. I'm afraid, too, that the life at the Castle wouldn't suit me. I like to be my own master.'

'You don't know the Castle,' said the landlord quietly,

'Of course,' replied K., 'one shouldn't judge prematurely. All that I know at present about the Castle is that the people there know how to choose a good Land Surveyor. Perhaps it has other attractions as well.' And he stood up in order to rid the landlord of his presence, since the man was biting his lip uneasily. His confidence was not to be lightly won.

As K. was going out he noticed a dark portrait in a dim frame on the wall. He had already observed it from his couch by the stove, but from that distance he had not been able to distinguish any details and had thought that it was only a plain back to the frame. But it was a picture after all, as now appeared, the bust portrait of a man about fifty. His head was sunk so low upon his breast that his eyes were scarcely visible, and the weight of the high, heavy forehead and the strong hooked nose seemed to have borne the head down. Because of this pose the man's full beard was pressed in at the chin and spread out farther down. His left hand was buried in his luxuriant hair, but seemed incapable of supporting the head. 'Who is that?' asked K., 'the Count?' He was standing before the portrait and did not look round at the landlord. 'No,' said the latter, 'the Castellan.' 'A handsome castellan, indeed,' said K., 'a pity that he had such an ill-bred son.' 'No, no,' said the landlord, drawing K. a little towards him and whispering in his ear, 'Schwarzer exaggerated yesterday, his father is only an under-castellan, and one of the lowest too.' At that moment the landlord struck K. as a very child. 'The villain!' said K. with a laugh, but the landlord instead of laughing said, 'Even his father is powerful.' 'Get along with you,' said K., 'you think everyone powerful. Me too, perhaps?' 'No,' he replied, timidly yet seriously, 'I don't think you powerful.' 'You're a keen observer,' said K., 'for between you and me I'm not really powerful. And consequently I suppose I have no less respect for the powerful than you have, only I'm not so honest as you and am not always willing to acknowledge it.' And K. gave the landlord a tap on the cheek to hearten him and awaken his friendliness. It made him smile a little. He was actually young, with that soft and almost beardless face of his; how had he come to have that massive, elderly wife, who could be seen through a small window bustling about the kitchen with her elbows sticking out? K. did not want to force his confidence any further, however, nor to scare away the smile he had at last evoked. So he only signed to him to open the door, and went out into the brilliant winter morning.

Now, he could see the Castle above him clearly defined in the glittering air, its outline made still more definite by the moulding of snow covering it in a thin layer. There seemed to be much less snow up there on the hill than down in the village, where K. found progress as laborious as on the main road the previous day. Here the heavy snowdrifts reached right up to the cottage windows and began again on the low roofs, but up on the hill everything soared light and free into the air, or at least so it appeared from down below.

On the whole this distant prospect of the Castle satisfied K.'s expectations. It was neither an old stronghold nor a new mansion, but a rambling pile consisting of innumerable small buildings closely packed together and of one or two storeys; if K. had not known that it was a castle he might have taken it for a little town. There was only one tower as far as he could see, whether it belonged to a dwelling-house or a church he could not determine. Swarms of crows were circling round it.

With his eyes fixed on the Castle K. went on farther, thinking of nothing else at all. But on approaching it he was disappointed in the Castle; it was after all only a wretched-looking town, a huddle of village houses, whose sole merit, if any, lay in being built of stone, but the plaster had long since flaked off and the stone seemed to be crumbling away. K. had a fleeting recollection of his native town. It was hardly inferior to this so-called Castle, and if it were merely a question of enjoying the view it was a pity to have come so far. K. would have done better to visit his native town again, which he had not seen for such a long time. And in his mind he compared the church tower at home with the tower above him. The church tower, firm in line, soaring unfalteringly to its tapering point, topped with red tiles and broad in the roof, an earthly building – what else can men build? – but with a loftier goal than the humble dwelling-houses, and a clearer meaning than the muddle of everyday life. The tower above him here – the only one visible – the tower of a house, as was now apparent, perhaps of the main building, was uniformly round, part of it graciously mantled with ivy, pierced by small windows that glittered in the sun, a somewhat maniacal glitter, and topped by what looked like an attic, with battlements that were irregular, broken, fumbling, as if designed by the trembling or careless hands of a child, clearly outlined against the blue. It was as if a melancholy-mad tenant who ought to have been locked in the topmost chamber of his house had burst through the roof and lifted himself up to the gaze of the world.

Again K. came to a stop, as if standing still he had more power of judgement. But he was disturbed. Behind the village church where he had stopped – it was really only a chapel widened with barn-like additions so as to accommodate the parishioners – was the school. A long, low building, combining remarkably a look of great age with a provincial appearance, it lay behind a fenced-in garden which was now a field of snow. The children were just coming out with their teacher. They thronged round him, all gazing up at him and chattering without a break so rapidly that K. could not follow what they said. The teacher, a small young man with narrow shoulders and a very upright carriage which yet did not make him ridiculous, had already fixed K. with his eyes from the distance, naturally enough, for apart from the school-children there was not another human being in sight. Being a stranger, K. made the first advance, especially as the other was an authoritative-looking little man, and said: 'Good morning, sir.' As if by one accord the children fell silent, perhaps the master liked to have a sudden stillness as a preparation for his words. 'You are looking at the Castle?' he asked more gently than K. had expected, but with the inflexion that denoted disapproval of K.'s occupation. 'Yes,' said K. 'I am a stranger here, I came to the village only last night.' 'You don't like the Castle?' returned the teacher quickly. 'What?' countered K., a little taken aback, and repeated the question in a modified form. 'Do I like the Castle? Why do you assume that I don't like it?' 'Strangers never do,' said the teacher. To avoid saying the wrong thing K. changed the subject and asked: 'I suppose you know the Count?' 'No,' said the teacher turning away. But K. would not be put off and asked again: 'What, you don't know the Count?' 'Why should I?' replied the teacher in a low tone, and added aloud in French: 'Please remember that there are innocent children present.' K. took this as a justification for asking: 'Might I come to pay you a visit one day, sir? I am staying here for some time and already feel a little lonely. I don't fit in with the peasants nor, I imagine, with the Castle.' 'There is no difference between the peasantry and the Castle,' said the teacher. 'Maybe,' said K., 'that doesn't alter my position. Can I pay you a visit one day?' 'I live in Swan Street at the butcher's.' That was assuredly more of a statement than an invitation, but K. said: 'Right. I'll come.' The teacher nodded and moved on with his batch of children, who began to scream again immediately. They soon vanished in a steeply descending by-street.

But K. was disconcerted, irritated by the conversation. For the first time since his arrival he felt really tired. The long journey he had made seemed to first have imposed no strain upon him – how quietly he sauntered through the days, step by step! – but now the consequences of his exertion were making themselves felt, and at the wrong time, too. He felt irresistibly drawn to seek out new aquaintances, but each new acquaintance only seemed to increase his weariness. If he forced himself in his present condition to go on at least as far as the Castle entrance, he would have done more than enough.

So he resumed his walk, but the way proved long. For the street he was in, the main street of the village, did not lead up to the Castle hill, it only made towards it and then, as if deliberately, turned aside, and though it did not lead away from the Castle it got no nearer to it either. At every turn K. expected the road to double back to the Castle, and only because of this expectation did he go on; he was flatly unwilling, tired as he was, to leave the street, and he was also amazed at the length of the village, which seemed to have no end; again and again the same little houses, and frost-bound window-panes and snow and the entire absence of human beings – but at last he tore himself away from the obsession of the street and escaped into a small side-lane, where the snow was still deeper and the exertion of lifting one's feet clear was fatiguing; he broke into a sweat, suddenly came to a stop, and could not go on.

Well, he was not on a desert island, there were cottages to right and left of him. He made a snowball and threw it at a window. The door opened immediately – the first door that had opened during the whole length of the village – and there appeared an old peasant in a brown fur jacket, with his head cocked to one side, a frail and kindly figure. 'May I come into your house for a little?' asked K. 'I'm very tired.' He did not hear the old man's reply, but thankfully observed that a plank was pushed out towards him to rescue him from the snow, and in a few steps he was in the kitchen.

A large kitchen, dimly lit. Anyone coming in from outside could make out nothing at first. K. stumbled over a washing-tub, a woman's hand steadied him. The crying of children came loudly from one corner. From another steam was welling out and turning the dim light into darkness. K. stood as if in the clouds. 'He must be drunk,' said somebody. 'Who are you?' cried a hectoring voice, and then obviously to the old man: 'Why did you let him in? Are we to let in everybody that wanders about in the street?' 'I am the Count's Land Surveyor,' said K., trying to justify himself before this still invisible personage. 'Oh, it's the Land Surveyor,' said a woman's voice, and then came a complete silence. 'You know me, then?' asked K. 'Of course,' said the same voice curtly. The fact that he was known did not seem to be a recommendation.

At last the steam thinned a little, and K. was able gradually to make things out. It seemed to be a general washing-day. Near the door clothes were being washed. But the steam was coming from another corner, where in a wooden tub larger than any K. had ever seen, as wide as two beds, two men were bathing in steaming water. But still more astonishing, although one could not say what was so astonishing about it, was the scene in the right-hand corner. From a large opening, the only one in the back wall, a pale snowy light came in, apparently from the courtyard, and gave a gleam as of silk to the dress of a woman who was almost reclining in a high arm-chair. She was suckling an infant at her breast. Several children were playing around her, peasant children, as was obvious, but she seemed to be of another class, although of course illness and weariness give even peasants a look of refinement.

'Sit down!' said one of the men, who had a full beard and breathed heavily through his mouth which always hung open, pointing – it was a funny sight – with his wet hands over the edge of the tub towards a settle, and showering drops of warm water all over K.'s face as he did so. On the settle the old man who had admitted K. was already sitting, sunk in vacancy. K. was thankful to find a seat at last. Nobody paid any further attention to him. The woman at the washing-tub, young, plump, and fair, sang in a low voice as she worked, the men stamped and rolled about in the bath, the children tried to get closer to them but were constantly driven back by mighty splashes of water which fell on K., too, and the woman in the arm-chair lay as if lifeless staring at the roof without even a glance towards the child at her bosom.

She made a beautiful, sad, fixed picture, and K. looked at her for what must have been a long time; then he must have fallen asleep, for when a loud voice roused him he found that his head was lying on the old man's shoulder. The men had finished with the tub – in which the children were now wallowing in charge of the fair-haired woman – and were standing fully dressed before K. It appeared that the hectoring one with the full beard was the less important of the two. The other, a still, slow-thinking man who kept his head bent, was not taller than his companion and had a much smaller beard, but he was broader in the shoulders and had a broad face as well, and he it was who said: 'You can't stay here, sir. Excuse the discourtesy.' 'I don't want to stay,' said K., 'I only wanted to rest a little. I have rested, and now I shall go.' 'You're probably surprised at our lack of hospitality,' said the man, 'but hospitality is not our custom here, we have no use for visitors.' Somewhat refreshed by his sleep, his perceptions somewhat quickened, K. was pleased by the man's frankness. He felt less constrained, poked with his stick here and there, approached the woman in the arm-chair, and noted that he was physically the biggest man in the room.

'To be sure,' said K. 'What use would you have for visitors? But still you need one now and then, me, for example, the Land Surveyor.' 'I don't know about that,' replied the man slowly. 'If you've been asked to come you're probably needed, that's an exceptional case, but we small people stick to our tradition, and you can't blame us for that.' 'No, no,' said K. 'I am only grateful to you and everybody here.' And taking them all by surprise he made an adroit turn and stood before the reclining woman. Out of weary blue eyes she looked at him a transparent silk kerchief hung down to the middle of her forehead. the infant was asleep on her bosom. 'Who are you?' asked K., and disdainfully – whether contemptuous of K. or her own answer was not clear – she replied: 'A girl from the Castle.'

It had only taken a second or so, but already the two men were at either side of K. and were pushing him towards the door, as if there were no other means of persuasion, silently, but putting out all their strength. Something in this procedure delighted the old man, and he clapped his hands. The woman at the bath-tub laughed too, and the children suddenly shouted like mad.

K. was soon out in the street, and from the threshold the two men surveyed him. Snow was again falling, yet the sky seemed a little brighter. The bearded man cried impatiently: 'Where do you want to go? This is the way to the Castle, and that to the village.' K. made no reply to him, but turned to the other, who in spite of his shyness seemed to him the more amiable of the two, and said: 'Who are you? Whom have I to thank for sheltering me?' 'I am the tanner Lasemann,' was the answer, 'but you owe thanks to nobody.' 'All right,' said K., 'perhaps we'll meet again.' 'I don't suppose so,' said the man. At that moment the other cried, with a wave of his hand: 'Good morning, Arthur; good morning, Jeremiah!' K. turned round; so there were really people to be seen in the village streets! From the direction of the Castle came two young men of medium height, both very slim, in tight-fitting clothes, and like each other in their features. Although their skin was a dusky brown the blackness of their little pointed beards was actually striking by contrast. Considering the state of the road, they were walking at a great pace, their slim legs keeping time. 'Where are you off to?' shouted the bearded man. One had to shout to them, they were going so fast and they would not stop. 'On business,' they shouted back, laughing. 'Where?' 'At the inn.' 'I'm going there too,' yelled K. suddenly, louder than all the rest; he felt a strong desire to accompany them, not that he expected much from their acquaintance, but they were obviously good and jolly companions. They heard him, but only nodded, and were already out of sight.

K. was still standing in the snow, and was little inclined to extricate his feet only for the sake of plunging them in again; the tanner and his comrade, satisfied with having finally got rid of him, edged slowly into the house through the door which was now barely ajar, casting backward glances at K., and he was left alone in the falling snow. 'A fine setting for a fit of despair,' it occurred to him, 'if I were only standing here by accident instead of design.'

Just then in the hut on his left hand a tiny window was opened, which had seemed quite blue when shut, perhaps from the reflexion of the snow, and was so tiny that when opened it did not permit the whole face of the person behind it to be seen, but only the eyes, old brown eyes. 'There he is,' K. heard a woman's trembling voice say. 'It's the Land Surveyor,' answered a man's voice. Then the man came to the window and asked, not unamiably, but still as if he were anxious to have no complications in front of his house: 'Are you waiting for somebody?' 'For a sledge, to pick me up,' said K. 'No sledges will pass here,' said the man, 'there's no traffic here.' 'But it's the road leading to the Castle,' objected K. 'All the same, all the same,' said the man with a certain finality, 'there's no traffic here.' Then they were both silent. But the man was obviously thinking of something, for he kept the window open. 'It's a bad road,' said K., to help him out. The only answer he got, however, was: 'Oh yes.' But after a little the man volunteered: 'If you like, I'll take you in my sledge.' 'Please do,' said K. delighted, 'what is your charge?' 'Nothing,' said the man. K. was very surprised. 'Well, you're the Land Surveyor,' explained the man, 'and you belong to the Castle. Where do you want to be taken?' 'To the Castle,' returned K. quickly. 'I won't take you there,' said the man without hesitation. 'But I belong to the Castle,' said K., repeating the other's very words. 'Maybe,' said the man shortly. 'Oh, well, take me to the inn,' said K. 'All right,' said the man, 'I'll be out with the sledge in a moment.' His whole behaviour had the appearance of springing not from any special desire to be friendly but rather from a kind of selfish, worried, and almost pedantic insistence on shifting K. away from the front of the house.

The gate of the courtyard opened, and a small light sledge quite flat, without a seat of any kind, appeared, drawn by a feeble little horse, and behind it limped the man, a weakly stooped figure with a gaunt red snuffling face that looked peculiarly small beneath a tightly swathed woollen scarf. He was obviously ailing, and yet only to transport K. he had dragged himself out. K. ventured to mention it, but the man waved him aside. All that

K. elicited was that he was a coachman called Gerstäcker, and that he had taken this uncomfortable sledge because it was standing ready, and to get out one of the others would have wasted too much time. 'Sit down,' he said, pointing to the sledge. 'I'll sit beside you,' said K. 'I'm going to walk,' said Gerstäcker. 'But why?' asked K. 'I'm going to walk,' repeated Gerstäcker, and was seized with a fit of coughing which shook him so severely that he had to brace his legs in the snow and hold on to the rim of the sledge. K. said no more, but sat down on the sledge, the man's coughing slowly abated, and they drove off.

The Castle above them, which K. had hoped to reach that very day, was already beginning to grow dark, and retreated again into the distance. But as if to give him a parting sign till their next encounter a bell began to ring merrily up there, a bell which for at least a second made his heart palpitate for its tone was menacing, too, as if it threatened him with the fulfilment of his vague desire. This great bell soon died away, however, and its place was taken by a feeble monotonous little tinkle which might have come from the Castle, but might have been somewhere in the village. It certainly harmonized better with the slow-going journey, with the wretched-looking yet inexorable driver.

'I say,' cried K. suddenly – they were already near the church, the inn was not far off, and K. felt he could risk something – 'I'm surprised that you have the nerve to drive me round on your own responsibility; are you allowed to do that?' Gerstäcker paid no attention, but went on walking quietly beside the little horse. 'Hi!' cried K., scraping some snow from the sledge and flinging a snowball which hit Gerstäcker full in the ear. That made him stop and turn; but when K. saw him at such close quarters – the sledge had slid forward a little – this stooping and somehow ill-used figure with the thin red tired face and cheeks that were different – one being flat and the other fallen in – standing listening with his mouth open, displaying only a few isolated teeth, he found that what he had just said out of malice had to be repeated out of pity, that is, whether Gerstäcker was likely to be penalized for driving him about. 'What do you mean?' asked Gerstäcker uncomprehendingly, but without waiting for an answer he spoke to the horse and they moved on again.

2

When by a turn in the road K. recognized that they were near the inn, he was greatly surprised to see that darkness had already set in. Had he been gone for such a long time? Surely not for more than an hour or two, by his reckoning. And it had been morning when he left. And he had not felt any need of food. And just a short time ago it had been uniform daylight, and now the darkness of night was upon them. 'Short days, short days,' he said to himself, slipped off the sledge, and went towards the inn.

At the top of the little flight of steps leading into the house stood the landlord, a welcome figure, holding up a lighted lantern. Remembering his conductor for a fleeting moment K. stood still, there was a cough in the darkness behind him, that was he. Well, he would see him again soon. Not until he was level with the landlord, who greeted him humbly, did he notice two men, one on either side of the doorway. He took the lantern from his host's hand and turned the light upon them; it was the men he had already met, who were called Arthur and Jeremiah. They now saluted him. That reminded him of his soldiering days, happy days for him, and he laughed. 'Who are you?' he asked, looking from one to the other. 'Your assistants,' they answered. 'It's your assistants,' corroborated the landlord in a low voice. 'What?' said K., 'are you my old assistants whom I told to follow me and whom I am expecting?' They answered in the affirmative. 'That's good,' observed K. after a short pause. 'I'm glad you've come.' 'Well,' he said, after another pause, 'you've come very late, you're very slack.' 'It was a long way to come,' said one of them. 'A long way?' repeated K., 'but I met you just now coming from the Castle.' 'Yes,' said they without further explanation. 'Where is the apparatus?' asked K. 'We haven't any,' said they. 'The apparatus I gave you?' said K. 'We haven't any,' they reiterated. 'Oh, you are fine fellows!' said K., 'do you know anything about surveying?' 'No,' said they. 'But if you are my old assistants you must know something about it,' said K. They made no reply. 'Well, come in,' said K., pushing them before him into the house.

They sat down then all three together over their beer at a small table, saying little, K. in the middle with an assistant on each side. As on the other evening, there was only one other table occupied by a few peasants. 'You're a difficult problem,' said K., comparing them, as he had already done several times. 'How am I to know one of you from the other? The only difference between you is your names, otherwise you're as like as . . .' He stopped, and then went on involuntarily, 'You're as like as two snakes.' They smiled. 'People usually manage to distinguish us quite well,' they said in self-justification. 'I am sure they do,' said K., 'I was a witness of that myself, but I can only see with my own eyes, and with them I can't distinguish you. So I shall treat you as if you were one man and call you both Arthur, that's one of your names, yours, isn't it?' he asked one of them. 'No,' said the man, 'I'm Jeremiah.' 'It doesn't matter,' said K. 'I'll call you both Arthur. If I tell Arthur to go anywhere you must both go. If I give Arthur something to do you must both do it, that has the great disadvantage for me of preventing me from employing you on separate jobs, but the advantage that you will both be equally responsible for anything I tell you to do. How you divide the work between you doesn't matter to me, only you're not to excuse yourselves by blaming each other, for me you're only one man.' They considered this, and said: 'We shouldn't like that at all.' 'I don't suppose so,' said K.; 'of course you won't like it, but that's how it has to be.' For some little time one of the peasants had been sneaking round the table and K. had noticed him; now the fellow took courage and went up to one of the assistants to whisper something. 'Excuse me,' said K., bringing his hand down on the table and rising to his feet, 'these are my assistants and we're discussing private business. Nobody is entitled to disturb us.' 'Sorry, sir, sorry,' muttered the peasant anxiously, retreating backwards towards his friends. 'And this is my most important charge to you,' said K., sitting down again. 'You're not to speak to anyone without my permission. I am a stranger here, and if you are my old assistants you are strangers too. We three strangers must stand by each other therefore, give me your hands on that.' All too eagerly they stretched out their hands to K. 'Never mind the trimming,' said he, 'but remember that my command holds good. I shall go to bed now and I recommend you to do the same. Today we have missed a day's work, and tomorrow we must begin very early. You must get hold of a sleigh for taking me to the Castle and have it ready outside the house at six o'clock.' 'Very well,' said one. But the other interrupted him. 'You say "very well", and yet you know it can't be done.' 'Silence,' said K. 'You're trying already to dissociate yourselves from each other.' But then the first man broke in: 'He's right, it can't be done, no stranger can get into the Castle without a permit.' 'Where does one apply for a permit?' 'I don't know, perhaps to the Castellan.' 'Then we'll apply by telephone, go and telephone to the Castellan at once, both of you.' They rushed to the instrument, asked for the connexion – how eager they were about it! in externals they were absurdly docile – and inquired if K. could come with them next morning into the Castle. The 'No' of the answer was audible even to K. at his table. But the answer went on and was still more explicit, it ran as follows: 'Neither tomorrow nor at any other time.' 'I shall telephone myself,' said K., and got up. While K. and his assistants hitherto had passed nearly unremarked except for the incident with the one peasant, his last statement aroused general attention. They all got up when K. did, and although the landlord tried to drive them away, crowded round him in a close semicircle at the telephone. The general opinion among them was that K. would get no answer at all. K. had to beg them to be quiet, saying he did not want to hear their opinion.

The receiver gave out a buzz of a kind that K. had never before heard on a telephone. It was like the hum of countless children's voices – but yet not a hum, the echo rather of voices singing at an infinite distance – blended by sheer impossibility into one high but resonant sound which vibrated on the ear as if it were trying to penetrate beyond mere hearing. K. listened without attempting to telephone, leaning his left arm on the telephone shelf.

He did not know how long he had stood there, but he stood until the landlord pulled at his coat saying that a messenger had come to speak with him. 'Go away!' yelled K. in an access of rage, perhaps into the mouthpiece, for someone immediately answered from the other end. The following conversation ensued: 'Oswald speaking, who's there?' cried a severe arrogant voice with a small defect in its speech, as seemed to K., which its owner tried to cover by an exaggerated severity. K. hesitated to announce himself, for he was at the mercy of the telephone, the other could shout him down or hang up the receiver, and that might mean the blocking of a not unimportant way of access. K.'s hesitation made the man impatient. 'Who's there?' he repeated, adding, 'I should be obliged if there was less telephoning from down there, only a minute ago somebody rang up.' K. ignored this remark, and announced with sudden decision: 'The Land Surveyor's assistant speaking.' 'What Land Surveyor? What assistant?' K. recollected yesterday's telephone conversation, and said briefly, 'Ask Fritz.' This succeeded, to his own astonishment. But even more than at his success he was astonished at the organization of the Castle service. The answer came: 'Oh, yes. That everlasting Land Surveyor. Quite so. What about it? What assistant?' 'Joseph,' said K. He was a little put out by the murmuring of the peasants behind his back, obviously they disapproved of his ruse. He had no time to bother about them, however, for the conversation absorbed all his attention. 'Joseph?' came the question. 'But the assistants are called . . .' there was a short pause, evidently to inquire the names from somebody else, 'Arthur and Jeremiah.' 'These are the new assistants,' said K. 'No, they are the old ones.' 'They are the new ones, I am the old assistant; I came today after the Land Surveyor.' 'No,' was shouted back. 'Then who am I?' asked K. as blandly as before.

And after a pause the same voice with the same defect answered him, yet with a deeper and more authoritative tone: 'You are the old assistant.'

K. was listening to the new note, and almost missed the question: 'What is it you want?' He felt like laying down the receiver. He had ceased to expect anything from this conversation. But being pressed, he replied quickly: 'When can my master come to the Castle?' 'Never,' was the answer. 'Very well,' said K., and hung the receiver up.

Behind him the peasants had crowded quite close. His assistants, with many side glances in his direction, were trying to keep them back. But they seemed not to take the matter very seriously, and in any case the peasants, satisfied with the result of the conversation, were beginning to give ground. A man came cleaving his way with rapid steps through the group, bowed before K., and handed him a letter. K. took it, but looked at the man, who for the moment seemed to him the more important. There was a great resemblance between this new-comer and the assistants, he was slim like them and clad in the same tight-fitting garments, had the same suppleness and agility, and yet he was quite different. How much K. would have preferred him as an assistant! He reminded K. a little of the girl with the infant whom he had seen at the tanner's. He was clothed nearly all in white, not in silk, of course; he was in winter clothes like all the others, but the material he was wearing had the softness and dignity of silk. His face was clear and frank, his eyes larger than ordinary. His smile was unusually joyous; he drew his hand over his face as if to conceal the smile, but in vain. 'Who are you?' asked K. 'My name is Barnabas,' said he, 'I am a messenger.' His lips were strong and yet gentle as he spoke. 'Do you approve of this kind of thing?' asked K., pointing to the peasants for whom he was still an object of curiosity, and who stood gaping at him with their open mouths, coarse lips, and literally tortured faces – their heads looked as if they had been beaten flat on top and their features as if the pain of the beating had twisted them to the present shape – and yet they were not exactly gaping at him, for their eyes often flitted away and studied some indifferent object in the room before fixing on him again, and then K. pointed also to his assistants who stood linked together, cheek against cheek, and smiling, but whether submissively or mockingly could not be determined. All these he pointed out as if presenting a train of followers forced upon him by circumstances, and as if he expected Barnabas – that indicated intimacy, it occurred to K. – always to discriminate between him and them. But Barnabas – quite innocently, it was clear – ignored the question, letting it pass as a well-bred servant ignores some remark of his master only apparently addressed to him, and merely surveyed the room in obedience to the question, greeting by a pressure of the hand various acquaintances among the peasants and exchanging a few words with the assistants, all with a free independence which set him apart from the others. Rebuffed but not mortified, K. returned to the letter in his hand and opened it. Its contents were as follows: 'My dear Sir, As you know, you have been engaged for the Count's service. Your immediate superior is the Superintendent of the village, who will give you all particulars about your work and the terms of your employment, and to whom you are responsible. I myself, however, will try not to lose sight of you. Barnabas, the bearer of this letter, will report himself to you from time to time to learn your wishes and communicate them to me. You will find me always ready to oblige you, in so far as that is possible. I desire my workers to be contented.' The signature was illegible, but stamped beside it was 'Chief of Department X.' 'Wait a little!' said K. to Barnabas, who bowed before him, then he commanded the landlord to show him to his room, for he wanted to be alone with the letter for a while. At the same time he reflected that Barnabas, although so attractive, was still only a messenger, and ordered a mug of beer for him. He looked to see how Barnabas would take it, but Barnabas was obviously quite pleased and began to drink the beer at once. Then K. went off with the landlord. The house was so small that nothing was available for K. but a little attic room, and even that had caused some difficulty, for two maids who had hitherto slept in it had had to be quartered elsewhere. Nothing indeed had been done but to clear the maids out, the room was otherwise quite unprepared, no sheets on the single bed, only some pillows and a horse-blanket still in the same rumpled state as in the morning. A few sacred pictures and photographs of soldiers were on the walls, the room had not even been aired; obviously they hoped that the new guest would not stay long, and were doing nothing to encourage him. K. felt no resentment, however, wrapped himself in the blanket, sat down at the table, and began to read the letter again by the light of a candle.

It was not a consistent letter, in part it dealt with him as with a free man whose independence was recognized, the mode of address, for example, and the reference to his wishes. But there were other places in which he was directly or indirectly treated as a minor employee, hardly visible to the Heads of Departments; the writer would try to make an effort 'not to lose sight' of him, his superior was only the village Superintendent to whom he was actually responsible, probably his sole colleague would be the village policeman. These were inconsistencies, no doubt about it. They were so obvious that they had to be faced. It hardly occurred to K. that they might be due to indecision; that seemed a mad idea in connexion with such an organization. He was much more inclined to read into them a frankly offered choice, which left it to him to make what he liked out of the letter, whether he preferred to become a village worker with a distinctive but merely apparent connexion with the Castle, or an ostensible village worker whose real occupation was determined through the medium of Barnabas. K. did not hesitate in his choice, and would not have hesitated even had he lacked the experience which had befallen him since his arrival. Only as a worker in the village, removed as far as possible from the sphere of the Castle, could he hope to achieve anything in the Castle itself; the village folk, who were now suspicious of him, would begin to talk to him once he was their fellow-citizen, if not exactly their friend; and if he were to become indistinguishable from Gerstäcker or Lasemann – and that must happen as soon as possible, everything depended on that – then all kinds of paths would be thrown open to him, which would remain not only for ever closed to him but quite invisible were he to depend merely on the favour of the gentlemen in the Castle. There was of course a danger, and that was sufficiently emphasized in the letter, even elaborated with a certain satisfaction, as if it were unavoidable. That was sinking to the workman's level – service, superior work, terms of employment, responsible workers – the letter fairly reeked of it, and even though more personal messages were included they were written from the standpoint of an employer. If K. were willing to become a workman he could do so, but he would have to do it in grim earnest, without any other prospect. K. knew that he had no real compulsory discipline to fear, he was not afraid of that, and in this case least of all, but the pressure of a discouraging environment, of a growing resignation to disappointment, the pressure of the imperceptible influences of every moment, these things he did fear, but that was a danger he would have to guard against. Nor did the letter pass over the fact that if it should come to a struggle K. had had the hardihood to make the first advances; it was very subtly indicated and only to be sensed by an uneasy conscience – an uneasy conscience, not a bad one – it lay in the three words, 'as you know', referring to his engagement in the Count's service. K. had reported his arrival, and only after that, as the letter pointed out, had he known that he was engaged.

K. took down a picture from the wall and stuck the letter on the nail, this was the room he was to live in and the letter should hang there.

Then he went down to the inn parlour. Barnabas was sitting at a table with the assistants. 'Oh, there you are,' said K. without any reason, only because he was glad to see Barnabas, who jumped to his feet at once. Hardly had K. shown his face when the peasants got up and gathered round him – it had become a habit of theirs to follow him around. 'What are you always following me about for?' cried K. They were not offended, and slowly drifted back to their seats again. One of them in passing said casually in apology, with an enigmatic smile which was reflected on several of the other's faces: 'There's always something new to listen to,' and he licked his lips as if news were meat and drink to him. K. said nothing conciliatory, it was good for them to have a little respect for him, but hardly had he reached Barnabas when he felt a peasant breathing down the back of his neck. He had only come, he said, for the salt-cellar, but K. stamped his foot with rage and the peasant scuttled away without the salt-cellar. It was really easy to get at K., all one had to do was to egg on the peasants against him, their persistent interference seemed much more objectionable to him than the reserve of the others, nor were they free from reserve either, for if he had sat down at their table they would not have stayed. Only the presence of Barnabas restrained him from making a scene. But he turned round to scowl at them, and found that they, too, were all looking at him. When he saw them sitting like that, however, each man in his own place, not speaking to one another and without any apparent mutual understanding, united only by the fact that they were all gazing at him, he concluded that it was not out of malice that they pursued him, perhaps they really wanted something from him and were only incapable of expressing it, if not that, it might be pure childishness, which seemed to be in fashion at the inn; was not the landlord himself childish, standing there stock-still gazing at K. with a glass of beer in his hand which he should have been carrying to a customer, and oblivious of his wife, who was leaning out of the kitchen hatch calling to him?

With a quieter mind K. turned to Barnabas; he would have liked to dismiss his assistants, but could not think of an excuse. Besides, they were brooding peacefully over their beer. 'The letter,' began K., 'I have read it. Do you know the contents?' 'No,' said Barnabas, whose look seemed to imply more than his words. Perhaps K. was as mistaken in Barnabas's goodness as in the malice of the peasants, but his presence remained a comfort. 'You are mentioned in the letter, too, you are supposed to carry messages now and then from me to the Chief, that's why I thought you might know the contents.' 'I was only told,' said Barnabas, 'to give you the letter, to wait until you had read it, and then to bring back a verbal or written answer if you thought it needful.' 'Very well,' said K., 'there's no need to write anything; convey to the Chief – by the way, what's his name? I couldn't read his signature.' 'Klamm,' said Barnabas. 'Well, convey to Herr Klamm my thanks for his recognition and for his great kindness, which I appreciate, being as I am one who has not yet proved his worth here. I shall follow his instructions faithfully. I have no particular requests to make for today.' Barnabas, who had listened with close attention, asked to be allowed to recapitulate the message. K. assented, Barnabas repeated it word for word. Then he rose to take his leave.

K. had been studying his face the whole time, and now he gave it a last survey. Barnabas was about the same height as K., but his eyes seemed to look down on K., yet that was almost in a kind of humility, it was impossible to think that this man could put anyone to shame. Of course he was only a messenger, and did not know the contents of the letters he carried, but the expression in his eyes, his smile, his bearing, seemed also to convey a message, however little he might know about it. And K. shook him by the hand, which seemed obviously to surprise him, for he had been going to content himself with a bow.

As soon as he had gone – before opening the door he had leaned his shoulder against it for a moment and embraced the room generally in a final glance – K. said to the assistants: 'I'll bring down the plans from my room, and then we'll discuss what work is to be done first.' They wanted to accompany him. 'Stay here,' said K. Still they tried to accompany him. K. had to repeat his command more authoritatively. Barnabas was no longer in the hall. But he had only just gone out. Yet in front of the house – fresh snow was falling – K. could not see him either. He called out: 'Barnabas!' No answer. Could he still be in the house? Nothing else seemed possible. None the less K. yelled the name with the full force of his lungs. It thundered through the night. And from the distance came a faint response, so far away was Barnabas already. K. called him back, and at the same time went to meet him; the spot where they encountered each other was no longer visible from the inn.

'Barnabas,' said K., and could not keep his voice from trembling, 'I have something else to say to you. And that reminds me that it's a bad arrangement to leave me dependent on your chance comings for sending a message to the Castle. If I hadn't happened to catch you just now – how you fly along, I thought you were still in the house – who knows how long I might have had to wait for your next appearance.' 'You can ask the Chief,' said Barnabas, 'to send me at definite times appointed by yourself.' 'Even that would not suffice,' said K., 'I might have nothing to say for a year at a time, but something of urgent importance might occur to me a quarter of an hour after you had gone.'

'Well,' said Barnabas, 'shall I report to the Chief that between him and you some other means of communication should be established instead of me?' 'No, no,' said K., 'not at all, I only mention the matter in passing, for this time I have been lucky enough to catch you.' 'Shall we go back to the inn,' said Barnabas, 'so that you can give me the new message there?' He had already taken a step in the direction of the inn. 'Barnabas,' said K., 'it isn't necessary, I'll go part of the way with you.' 'Why don't you want to go to the inn?' asked Barnabas. 'The people there annoy me,' said K.; 'you saw for yourself how persistent the peasants are.' 'We could go into your room,' said Barnabas. 'It's the maids' room,' said K., 'dirty and stuffy – it's to avoid staying there that I want to accompany you for a little, only,' he added, in order finally to overcome Barnabas's reluctance, 'you must let me take your arm, for you are surer of foot than I am.' And K. took his arm. It was quite dark, K. could not see Barnabas's face, his figure was only vaguely discernible, he had had to grope for his arm a minute or two.

Barnabas yielded and they moved away from the inn. K. realized, indeed, that his utmost efforts could not enable him to keep pace with Barnabas, that he was a drag on him, and that even in ordinary circumstances this trivial accident might be enough to ruin everything, not to speak of side-streets like the one in which he had got stuck that morning, out of which he could never struggle unless Barnabas were to carry him. But he banished all such anxieties, and was comforted by Barnabas's silence; for if they went on in silence then Barnabas, too, must feel that their excursion together was the sole reason for their association.

They went on, but K. did not know whither, he could discern nothing, not even whether they had already passed the church or not. The effort which it cost him merely to keep going made him lose control of his thoughts. Instead of remaining fixed on their goal they strayed. Memories of his home kept recurring and filled his mind. There, too, a church stood in the market-place, partly surrounded by an old graveyard which was again surrounded by a high wall. Very few boys had managed to climb that wall, and for some time K., too, had failed. It was not curiosity which had urged them on. The graveyard had been no mystery to them. They had often entered it through a small wicket-gate, it was only the smooth high wall that they had wanted to conquer. But one morning – the empty, quiet market-place had been flooded with sunshine, when had K. ever seen it like that either before or since? – he had succeeded in climbing it with astonishing ease; at a place where he had already slipped down many a time he had clambered with a small flag between his teeth right to the top at the first attempt. Stones were still rattling down under his feet, but he was at the top. He stuck the flag in, it flew in the wind, he looked down and round about him, over his shoulder, too, at the crosses mouldering in the ground, nobody was greater than he at that place and that moment. By chance the teacher had come past and with a stern face had made K. descend. In jumping down he had hurt his knee and had found some difficulty in getting home, but still he had been on the top of the wall. The sense of that triumph had seemed to him then a victory for life, which was not altogether foolish, for now so many years later on the arm of Barnabas in the snowy night the memory of it came to succour him.

He took a firmer hold, Barnabas was almost dragging him along, the silence was unbroken. Of the road they were following all that K. knew was that to judge from its surface they had not yet turned aside into a by-street. He vowed to himself that, however difficult the way and however doubtful even the prospect of his being able to get back, he would not cease from going on. He would surely have strength enough to let himself be dragged. And the road must come to an end some time. By day the Castle had looked within easy reach, and, of course, the messenger would take the shortest cut.

At that moment Barnabas stopped. Where were they? Was this the end? Would Barnabas try to leave him? He wouldn't succeed. K. clutched his arm so firmly that it almost made his hand ache. Or had the incredible happened, and were they already in the Castle or at its gates? But they had not done any climbing so far as K. could tell. Or had Barnabas taken him up by an imperceptibly mounting road? 'Where are we?' said K. in a low voice, more to himself than to Barnabas. 'At home,' said Barnabas in the same tone. 'At home?' 'Be careful now, sir, or you'll slip. We go down here.' 'Down?' 'Only a step or two,' added Barnabas, and was already knocking at a door.

A girl opened it, and they were on the threshold of a large room almost in darkness, for there was no light save for a tiny oil lamp hanging over a table in the background. 'Who is with you, Barnabas?' asked the girl. 'The Land Surveyor,' said he. 'The Land Surveyor,' repeated the girl in a louder voice, turning towards the table. Two old people there rose to their feet, a man and a woman, as well as another girl. They greeted K. Barnabas introduced the whole family, his parents and his sisters Olga and Amalia. K. scarcely glanced at them and let them take his wet coat off to dry at the stove.

So it was only Barnabas who was at home, not he himself. But why had they come here? K. drew Barnabas aside and asked:

'Why have you come here? Or do you live in the Castle precincts?' 'The Castle precincts?' repeated Barnabas, as if he did not understand. 'Barnabas,' said K., 'you left the inn to go to the Castle.' 'No,' said Barnabas, 'I left it to come home, I don't go to the Castle till the early morning, I never sleep there.' 'Oh,' said K., 'so you weren't going to the Castle, but only here' – the man's smile seemed less brilliant, and his person more insignificant – 'Why didn't you say so?' 'You didn't ask me, sir,' said Barnabas, 'you only said you had a message to give me, but you wouldn't give it in the inn parlour, or in your room, so I thought you could speak to me quietly here in my parents' house. The others will all leave us if you wish – and, if you prefer, you could spend the night here. Haven't I done the right thing?' K. could not reply. It had been simply a misunderstanding, a common, vulgar misunderstanding, and K. had been completely taken in by it. He had been bewitched by Barnabas's close-fitting, silken-gleaming jacket, which, now that it was unbuttoned, displayed a coarse, dirty grey shirt patched all over, and beneath that the huge muscular chest of a labourer. His surroundings not only corroborated all this but even emphasized it, the old gouty father who progressed more by the help of his groping hands than by the slow movements of his stiff legs, and the mother with her hands folded on her bosom, who was equally incapable of any but the smallest steps by reason of her stoutness. Both of them, father and mother, had been advancing from their corner towards K. ever since he had come in, and were still a long way off. The yellow-haired sisters, very like each other and very like Barnabas, but with harder features than their brother, great strapping wenches, hovered round their parents and waited for some word of greeting from K. But he could not utter it. He had been persuaded that in this village everybody meant something to him, and indeed he was not mistaken, it was only for these people here that he could feel not the slightest interest. If he had been fit to struggle back to the inn alone he would have left at once. The possibility of accompanying Barnabas to the Castle early in the morning did not attract him. He had hoped to penetrate into the Castle unremarked in the night on the arm of Barnabas, but on the arm of the Barnabas he had imagined, a man who was more to him than anyone else, the Barnabas he had conceived to be far above his apparent rank and in the intimate confidence of the Castle. With the son of such a family, however, a son who integrally belonged to it, and who was already sitting at table with the others, a man who was not even allowed to sleep in the Castle, he could not possibly go to the Castle in the broad light of day, it would be a ridiculous and hopeless undertaking.

K. sat down on a window-seat where he determined to pass the night without accepting any other favour. The other people in the village, who turned him away or were afraid of him, seemed much less dangerous, for all that they did was to throw him back on his own resources, helping him to concentrate his powers, but such ostensible helpers as these who on the strength of a petty masquerade brought him into their homes instead of into the Castle, deflected him, whether intentionally or not, from the goal and only helped to destroy him. An invitation to join the family at table he ignored completely, stubbornly sitting with bent head on his bench.

Then Olga, the gentler of the sisters, got up, not without a trace of maidenly embarrassment, came over to K. and asked him to join the family meal of bread and bacon, saying that she was going to fetch some beer. 'Where from?' asked K. 'From the inn,' she said. That was welcome news to K. He begged her instead of fetching beer to accompany him back to the inn, where he had important work waiting to be done. But the fact now emerged that she was not going so far as his inn, she was going to one much nearer, called the Herrenhof. None the less K. begged to be allowed to accompany her, thinking that there perhaps he might find a lodging for the night; however wretched it might be he would prefer it to the best bed these people could offer him. Olga did not reply at once, but glanced towards the table. Her brother stood up, nodded obligingly and said: 'If the gentleman wishes.' This assent was almost enough to make K.

withdraw his request, nothing could be of much value if Barnabas assented to it. But since they were already wondering whether K. would be admitted into that inn and doubting its possibility, he insisted emphatically upon going, without taking the trouble to give a colourable excuse for his eagerness; this family would have to accept him as he was, he had no feeling of shame where they were concerned. Yet he was somewhat disturbed by Amalia's direct and serious gaze, which was unflinching and perhaps a little stupid.

On their short walk to the inn – K. had taken Olga's arm and was leaning his whole weight on her as earlier on Barnabas, he could not get along otherwise – he learned that it was an inn exclusively reserved for gentlemen from the Castle, who took their meals there and sometimes slept there whenever they had business in the village. Olga spoke to K. in a low and confidential tone; to walk with her was pleasant, almost as pleasant as walking with her brother. K. struggled against the feeling of comfort she gave him, but it persisted.

From outside the new inn looked very like the inn where K. was staying. All the houses in the village resembled one another more or less, but still a few small differences were immediately apparent here; the front steps had a balustrade, and a fine lantern was fixed over the doorway. Something fluttered over their heads as they entered, it was a flag with the Count's colours. In the hall they were at once met by the landlord, who was obviously on a tour of inspection; he glanced at K. in passing with small eyes that were either screwed up critically, or half-asleep, and said: 'The Land Surveyor mustn't go anywhere but into the bar.' 'Certainly,' said Olga, who took K.'s part at once, 'he's only escorting me.' But K. ungratefully let go her arm and drew the landlord aside. Olga meanwhile waited patiently at the end of the hall. 'I should like to spend the night here,' said K. 'I'm afraid that's impossible,' said the landlord. 'You don't seem to be aware that this house is reserved exclusively for gentlemen from the Castle.' 'Well, that may be the rule,' said K. 'but it's surely possible to let me sleep in a corner somewhere.' 'I should be only too glad to oblige you,' said the landlord, 'but besides the strictness with which the rule is enforced – and you speak about it as only a stranger could – it's quite out of the question for another reason; the Castle gentlemen are so sensitive that I'm convinced they couldn't bear the sight of a stranger, at least unless they were prepared for it; and if I were to let you sleep here, and by some chance or other – and chances are always on the side of the gentlemen – you were discovered, not only would it mean my ruin but yours too. That sounds ridiculous, but it's true.' This tall and closely-buttoned man who stood with his legs crossed, one hand braced against the wall and the other on his hip, bending a little towards K. and speaking confidentially to him, seemed to have hardly anything in common with the village, even although his dark clothes looked like a peasant's finery. 'I believe you absolutely,' said K., 'and I didn't mean to belittle the rule, although I expressed myself badly. Only there's something I'd like to point out, I have some influence in the Castle, and shall have still more, and that secures you against any danger arising out of my stay here overnight, and is a guarantee that I am able fully to recompense any small favour you may do me.' 'Oh, I know,' said the landlord, and repeated again, 'I know all that.' Now was the time for K. to state his wishes more clearly, but this reply of the landlord's disconcerted him, and so he merely asked, 'Are there many of the Castle gentlemen staying in the house tonight?' 'As far as that goes, tonight is favourable,' returned the landlord, as if in encouragement, 'there's only one gentleman.' Still K. felt incapable of urging the matter, but being in hopes that he was as good as accepted, he contented himself by asking the name of the gentleman. 'Klamm,' said the landlord casually, turning meanwhile to his wife who came rustling towards them in a remarkably shabby old-fashioned gown overloaded with pleats and frills, but of a fine city cut. She came to summon the landlord, for the Chief wanted something or other. Before the landlord complied, however, he turned once more to K., as if it lay with K. to make the decision about staying all night. But K. could not utter a word, overwhelmed as he was by the discovery that it was his patron who was in the house. Without being able to explain it completely to himself he did not feel the same freedom of action in relation to Klamm as he did to the rest of the Castle, and the idea of being caught in the inn by Klamm, although it did not terrify him as it did the landlord, gave him a twinge of uneasiness, much as if he were thoughtlessly to hurt the feelings of someone to whom he was bound by gratitude; at the same time, however, it vexed him to recognize already in these qualms the obvious effects of that degradation to an inferior status which he had feared, and to realize that although they were so obvious he was not even in a position to counteract them. So he stood there biting his lips and said nothing. Once more the landlord looked back at him before disappearing through a doorway, and K. returned the look without moving from the spot, until Olga came up and drew him away. 'What did you want with the landlord?' she asked. 'I wanted a bed for the night,' said K. 'But you're staying with us!' said Olga in surprise. 'Of course,' said K., leaving her to make what she liked of it.

3

In the bar, which was a large room with a vacant space in the middle, there were several peasants sitting by the wall on the tops of some casks, but they looked different from those in K.'s inn. They were more neatly and uniformly dressed in coarse yellowish-grey cloth, with loose jackets and tightly-fitting trousers. They were smallish men with at first sight a strong mutual resemblance, having flat bony faces, but rounded cheeks. They were all quiet, and sat with hardly a movement, except that they followed the newcomers with their eyes, but they did even that slowly and indifferently. Yet because of their numbers and their quietness they had a certain effect on K. He took

Olga's arm again as if to explain his presence there. A man rose up from one corner, an acquaintance of Olga's, and made towards her, but K. wheeled her round by the arm in another direction. His action was perceptible to nobody but Olga, and she tolerated it with a smiling side-glance.

The beer was drawn off by a young girl called Frieda. An unobtrusive little girl with fair hair, sad eyes, and hollow cheeks, with a striking look of conscious superiority. As soon as her eye met K.'s it seemed to him that her look decided something concerning himself, something which he had not known to exist, but which her look assured him did exist. He kept on studying her from the side, even while she was speaking to Olga. Olga and Frieda were apparently not intimate, they exchanged only a few cold words. K. wanted to hear more, and so interposed with a question on his own account: 'Do you know Herr Klamm?' Olga laughed out loud. 'What are you laughing at?' asked K. irritably. 'I'm not laughing,' she protested, but went on laughing. 'Olga is a childish creature,' said K. bending far over the counter in order to attract Frieda's gaze again. But she kept her eyes lowered and laughed shyly. 'Would you like to see Herr Klamm?' K. begged for a sight of him. She pointed to a door just on her left. 'There's a little peephole there, you can look through.' 'What about the others?' asked K. She curled her underlip and pulled K. to the door with a hand that was unusually soft. The little hole had obviously been bored for spying through, and commanded almost the whole of the neighbouring room. At a desk in the middle of the room in a comfortable arm-chair sat Herr Klamm, his face brilliantly lit by an incandescent lamp which hung low before him. A middle-sized, plump, and ponderous man. His face was still smooth, but his cheeks were already somewhat flabby with age. His black moustache had long points, his eyes were hidden behind glittering pince-nez that sat awry. If he had been planted squarely before his desk K. would only have seen his profile, but since he was turned directly towards K. his whole face was visible. His left elbow lay on the desk, his right hand, in which was a Virginia cigar, rested on his knee. A beer-glass was standing on the desk, but there was a rim round the desk which prevented K. from seeing whether any papers were lying on it; he had the idea, however, that there were none. To make it certain he asked Frieda to look through the hole and tell him if there were any. But since she had been in that room a short time ago, she was able to inform him without further ado that the desk was empty. K. asked Frieda if his time was up, but she told him to go on looking as long as he liked. K. was now alone with Frieda. Olga, as a hasty glance assured him, had found her way to her acquaintance, and was sitting high on a cask swinging her legs. 'Frieda,' said K. in a whisper, 'do you know Herr Klamm well?' 'Oh, yes,' she said, 'very well.' She leaned over to K. and he became aware that she was coquettishly fingering the low-cut cream-coloured blouse which sat coldly on her poor thin body. Then she said: 'Didn't you notice how Olga laughed?' 'Yes, the rude creature,' said K. 'Well,' she said extenuatingly, 'there was a reason for laughing, You asked if I knew Klamm, and you see I' – here she involuntarily lifted her chin a little, and again her triumphant glance, which had no connexion whatever with what she was saying, swept over K. – 'I am his mistress.' 'Klamm's mistress,' said K. She nodded. 'Then,' said K. smiling, to prevent the atmosphere from being too charged with seriousness, 'you are for me a highly respectable person.' 'Not only for you,' said Frieda amiably, but without returning his smile. K. had a weapon for bringing down her pride, and he tried it: 'Have you ever been in the Castle?' But it missed the mark, for she answered: 'No, but isn't it enough for me to be here in the bar?' Her vanity was obviously boundless, and she was trying, it seemed, to get K. in particular to minister to it. 'Of course,' said K., 'here in the bar you're taking the landlord's place.' 'That's so,' she assented, 'and I began as a byre-maid at the inn by the bridge.' 'With those delicate hands,' said K. half-questioningly, without knowing himself whether he was only flattering her or was compelled by something in her. Her hands were certainly small and delicate, but they could quite as well have been called weak and characterless. 'Nobody bothered about them then,' she said, 'and even now . . .' K. looked at her inquiringly. She shook her head and would say no more. 'You have your secrets naturally,' said K., 'and you're not likely to give them away to somebody you've known for only half an hour, and who hasn't had the chance yet to tell you anything about himself.' This remark proved to be ill-chosen, for it seemed to arouse Frieda as from a trance that was favourable to him. Out of the leather bag hanging at her girdle she took a small piece of wood, stopped up the peephole with it, and said to K. with an obvious attempt to conceal the change in her attitude: 'Oh, I know all about you, you're the Land Surveyor,' and then adding: 'but now I must go back to my work,' she returned to her place behind the bar counter, while a man here and there came up to get his empty glass refilled. K. wanted to speak to her again, so he took an empty glass from a stand and went up to her, saying: 'One thing more, Fräulein Frieda, it's an extraordinary feat and a sign of great strength of mind to have worked your way up from byre-maid to this position in the bar, but can it be the end of all ambition for a person like you? An absurd idea. Your eyes – don't laugh at me, Fräulein Frieda – speak to me far more of conquests still to come than of conquests past. But the opposition one meets in the world is great, and becomes greater the higher one aims, and it's no disgrace to accept the help of a man who's fighting his way up too, even though he's a small and uninfluential man. Perhaps we could have a quiet talk together sometime, without so many onlookers?' 'I don't know what you're after,' she said, and in her tone this time there seemed to be, against her will, an echo rather of countless disappointments than of past triumphs. 'Do you want to take me away from Klamm perhaps? O heavens!' and she clapped her hands. 'You've seen through me,' said K., as if wearied by so much mistrust, 'that's exactly my real secret intention. You ought to leave Klamm and become my sweetheart. And now I can go. Olga!' he cried, 'we're going home.' Obediently Olga slid down from her cask but did not succeed immediately in breaking through her ring of friends. Then Frieda said in a low voice with a hectoring look at K.: 'When can I talk to you?' 'Can I spend the night here?' asked K. 'Yes,' said Frieda. 'Can I stay now?' 'Go out first with Olga, so that I can clear out all the others. Then you can come back in a little.' 'Right,' said K., and he waited impatiently for Olga. But the peasants would not let her go; they made up a dance in which she was the central figure, they circled round her yelling all together and every now and then one of them left the ring, seized Olga firmly round the waist and whirled her round and round; the pace grew faster and faster, the yells more hungry, more raucous, until they were insensibly blended into one continuous howl. Olga, who had begun laughingly by trying to break out of the ring, was now merely reeling with flying hair from one man to the other. 'That's the kind of people I'm saddled with,' said Frieda, biting her thin lips in scorn. 'Who are they?' asked K. 'Klamm's servants,' said Frieda, 'he keeps on bringing those people with him, and they upset me. I can hardly tell what I've been saying to you, but please forgive me if I've offended you, it's these people who are to blame, they're the most contemptible and objectionable creatures I know, and I have to fill their glasses up with beer for them. How often I've implored Klamm to leave them behind him, for though I have to put up with the other gentlemen's servants, he could surely have some consideration for me; but it's all no use, an hour before his arrival they always come bursting in like cattle into their stalls. But now they've really got to get into the stalls, where they belong. If you weren't here I'd fling open this door and Klamm would be forced to drive them out himself.' 'Can't he hear them, then?' asked K. 'No,' said Frieda, 'he's asleep.' 'Asleep?' cried K. 'But when I peeped in he was awake and sitting at the desk.' 'He always sits like that,' said Frieda, 'he was sleeping when you saw him. Would I have let you look in if he hadn't been asleep? That's how he sleeps, the gentlemen do sleep a great deal, it's hard to understand. Anyhow, if he didn't sleep so much, he wouldn't be able to put up with his servants. But now I'll have to turn them out myself.' She took up a whip from a corner and sprang among the dancers with a single bound, a little uncertainly, as a young lamb might spring. At first they faced her as if she were merely a new partner, and actually for a moment Frieda seemed inclined to let the whip fall, but she soon raised it again, crying: 'In the name of Klamm into the stall with you, into the stall, all of you!' When they saw that she was in earnest they began to press towards the back wall in a kind of panic incomprehensible to K., and under the impact of the first few a door shot open, letting in a current of night air through which they all vanished with Frieda behind them openly driving them across the courtyard into the stalls.

In the sudden silence which ensued K. heard steps in the vestibule. With some idea of securing his position he dodged behind the bar counter, which afforded the only possible cover in the room. He had an admitted right to be in the bar, but since he meant to spend the night there he had to avoid being seen. So when the door was actually opened he slid under the counter. To be discovered there of course would have its dangers too, yet he could explain plausibly enough that he had only taken refuge from the wild licence of the peasants. It was the landlord who came in. 'Frieda!' he called, and walked up and down the room several times.

Fortunately Frieda soon came back, she did not mention K., she only complained about the peasants, and in the course of looking round for K. went behind the counter, so that he was able to touch her foot. From that moment he felt safe. Since Frieda made no reference to K., however, the landlord was compelled to do it. 'And where is the Land Surveyor?' he asked. He was probably courteous by nature, refined by constant and relatively free intercourse with men who were much his superior, but there was remarkable consideration in his tone to Frieda, which was all the more striking because in his conversation he did not cease to be an employer addressing a servant, and a saucy servant at that. 'The Land Surveyor – I forgot all about him,' said Frieda, setting her small foot on K.'s chest. 'He must have gone out long ago.' 'But I haven't seen him,' said the landlord, 'and I was in the hall nearly the whole time.' 'Well, he isn't here,' said Frieda coolly. 'Perhaps he's hidden somewhere,' went on the landlord. 'From the impression I had of him he's capable of a good deal.' 'He would hardly have the cheek to do that,' said Frieda, pressing her foot down on K. There was a certain mirth and freedom about her which K. had not previously remarked, and quite unexpectedly it took the upper hand, for suddenly laughing she bent down to K. with the words: 'Perhaps he's hidden underneath here,' kissed him lightly and sprang up again saying with a troubled air: 'No, he's not there.' Then the landlord, too, surprised K. when he said: 'It bothers me not to know for certain that he's gone. Not only because of Herr Klamm, but because of the rule of the house. And the rule applies to you, Fräulein Frieda, just as much as to me. Well, if you answer for the bar, I'll go through the rest of the rooms. Good night! Sleep well!' He could hardly have left the room before Frieda had turned out the electric light and was under the counter beside K. 'My darling! My darling!' she whispered, but she did not touch him. As if swooning with love she lay on her back and stretched out her arms; time must have seemed endless to her in the prospect of her happiness, and she sighed rather than sang some little song or other. Then as K. still lay absorbed in thought, she started up and began to tug at him like a child: 'Come on, it's too close down here,' and they embraced each other, her little body burned in K.'s hands, in a state of unconsciousness which K. tried again and again but in vain to master as they rolled a little way, landing with a thud on Klamm's door, where they lay among the small puddles of beer and other refuse gathered on the floor. There, hours went past, hours in which they breathed as one, in which their hearts beat as one, hours in which K. was haunted by the feeling that he was losing himself or wandering into a strange country, farther than ever man had wandered before, a country so strange that not even the air had anything in common with his native air, where one might die of strangeness, and yet whose enchantment was such that one could only go on and lose oneself further. So it came to him not as a shock but as a faint glimmer of comfort when from Klamm's room a deep, authoritative impersonal voice called for Frieda. 'Frieda,' whispered K. in Frieda's ear, passing on the summons. With a mechanical instinct of obedience Frieda made as if to spring to her feet, then she remembered where she was, stretched herself, laughing quietly, and said: 'I'm not going, I'm never going to him again.' K. wanted to object, to urge her to go to Klamm, and began to fasten up her disordered blouse, but he could not bring himself to speak, he was too happy to have Frieda in his arms, too troubled also in his happiness, for it seemed to him that in letting Frieda go he would lose all he had. And as if his support had strengthened her Frieda clenched her fist and beat upon the door, crying: 'I'm with the Land Surveyor!' That silenced Klamm at any rate, but K. started up, and on his knees beside Frieda gazed round him in the uncertain light of dawn. What had happened? Where were his hopes? What could he expect from Frieda now that she had betrayed everything? Instead of feeling his way with the prudence befitting the greatness of his enemy and of his ambition, he had spent a whole night wallowing in puddles of beer, the smell of which was nearly overpowering. 'What have you done?' he said as if to himself. 'We are both ruined.' 'No,' said Frieda, 'it's only me that's ruined, but then I've won you. Don't worry. But just look how these two are laughing.' 'Who?' asked K., and turned round. There on the bar counter sat his two assistants, a little heavy-eyed for lack of sleep, but cheerful It was a cheerfulness arising from a sense of duty well done. 'What are you doing here?' cried K. as if they were to blame for everything. 'We had to search for you,' explained the assistants, 'since you didn't come back to the inn; we looked for you at Barnabas's and finally found you here. We have been sitting here all night. Ours is no easy job.' 'It's in the day-time I need you,' said K., 'not in the night, clear out.' 'But it's day-time now,' said they without moving. It was really day, the doors into the courtyard were opened, the peasants came streaming in and with them Olga, whom K. had completely forgotten. Although her hair and clothes were in disorder Olga was as alert as on the previous evening, and her eyes flew to K. before she was well over the threshold. 'Why did you not come home with me?' she asked, almost weeping. 'All for a creature like that!' she said then, and repeated the remark several times. Frieda, who had vanished for a moment, came back with a small bundle of clothing, and Olga moved sadly to one side. 'Now we can be off,' said Frieda, it was obvious she meant that they should go back to the inn by the bridge. K. walked with Frieda, and behind them the assistants; that was the little procession. The peasants displayed a great contempt for Frieda, which was understandable, for she had lorded it over them hitherto; one of them even took a stick and held it as if to prevent her from going out until she had jumped over it, but a look from her sufficed to quell him. When they were out in the snow K. breathed a little more freely. It was such a relief to be in the open air that the journey seemed less laborious; if he had been alone he would have got on still better. When he reached the inn he went straight to his room and lay down on the bed. Frieda prepared a couch for herself on the floor beside him. The assistants had pushed their way in too, and on being driven out came back through the window. K. was too weary to drive them out again. The landlady came up specially to welcome Frieda, who hailed her as 'mother'; their meeting was inexplicably affectionate, with kisses and long embracings. There was little peace and quietness to be had in the room, for the maids too came clumping in with their heavy boots, bringing or seeking various articles, and whenever they wanted anything from the miscellaneous assortment on the bed they simply pulled it out from under K. They greeted Frieda as one of themselves. In spite of all this coming and going K. stayed in bed the whole day through, and the whole night. Frieda performed little offices for him. When he got up at last on the following morning he was much refreshed, and it was the fourth day since his arrival in the village.

4

He would have liked an intimate talk with Frieda, but the assistants hindered this simply by their importunate presence, and Frieda, too, laughed and joked with them from time to time. Otherwise they were not at all exacting, they had simply settled down in a corner on two old skirts spread out on the floor. They made it a point of honour, as they repeatedly assured Frieda, not to disturb the Land Surveyor and to take up as little room as possible, and in pursuit of this intention, although with a good deal of whispering and giggling, they kept on trying to squeeze themselves into a smaller compass, crouching together in the corner so that in the dim light they looked like one large bundle. From his experience of them by daylight, however, K. was all too conscious that they were acute observers and never took their eyes off him, whether they were fooling like children and using their hands as spyglasses, or merely glancing at him while apparently completely absorbed in grooming their beards, on which they spent much thought and which they were for ever comparing in length and thickness, calling on Frieda to decide between them. From his bed K. often watched the antics of all three with the completest indifference.

When he felt himself well enough to leave his bed, they all ran to serve him. He was not yet strong enough to ward off their services, and noted that that brought him into a state of dependence on them which might have evil consequences, but he could not help it. Nor was it really unpleasant to drink at the table the good coffee which Frieda had brought, to warm himself at the stove which Frieda had lit, and to have the assistants racing ten times up and down the stairs in their awkwardness and zeal to fetch him soap and water, comb and looking-glass, and eventually even a small glass of rum because he had hinted in a low voice at his desire for one.

Among all this giving of orders and being waited on, K. said, more out of good humour than any hope of being obeyed: 'Go away now, you two, I need nothing more for the present, and I want to speak to Fräulein Frieda by herself.' And when he saw no direct opposition on their faces he added, by way of excusing them: 'We three shall go to the village Superintendent afterwards, so wait downstairs in the bar for me.' Strangely enough they obeyed him, only turning to say before going: 'We could wait here.' But K. answered: 'I know, but I don't want you to wait here.'

It annoyed him, however, and yet in a sense pleased him when Frieda, who had settled on his knee as soon as the assistants were gone, said: 'What's your objection to the assistants, darling? We don't need to have any mysteries before them. They are true friends.' 'Oh, true friends,' said K., 'they keep spying on me the whole time, it's nonsensical but abominable.' 'I believe I know what you mean,' she said, and she clung to his neck and tried to say something else but could not go on speaking, and since their chair was close to it they reeled over and fell on the bed. There they lay, but not in the forgetfulness of the previous night. She was seeking and he was seeking, they raged and contorted their faces and bored their heads into each other's bosoms in the urgency of seeking something, and their embraces and their tossing limbs did not avail to make them forget, but only reminded them of what they sought; like dogs desperately tearing up the ground they tore at each other's bodies, and often, helplessly baffled, in a final effort to attain happiness they nuzzled and tongued each other's face. Sheer weariness stilled them at last and brought them gratitude to each other. Then the maids came in. 'Look how they're lying there,' said one, and sympathetically cast a coverlet over them.

When somewhat later K. freed himself from the coverlet and looked round, the two assistants – and he was not surprised at that – were again in their corner, and with a finger jerked towards

K. nudged each other to a formal salute, but besides them the landlady was sitting near the bed knitting away at a stocking, an infinitesimal piece of work hardly suited to her enormous bulk which almost darkened the room. 'I've been here a long time,' she said, lifting up her broad and much furrowed face which was, however, still rounded and might once have been beautiful. The words sounded like a reproach, an ill-timed reproach, for K. had not desired her to come. So he merely acknowledged them by a nod, and sat up. Frieda also got up, but left K. to lean over the landlady's chair. 'If you want to speak to me,' said K. in bewilderment, 'couldn't you put it off until after I come back from visiting the Superintendent? I have important business with him.' 'This is important, believe me, sir,' said the landlady, 'your other business is probably only a question of work, but this concerns a living person, Frieda, my dear maid.' 'Oh, if that's it,' said K., 'then of course you're right, but I don't see why we can't be left to settle our own affairs.' 'Because I love her and care for her,' said the landlady, drawing Frieda's head towards her, for Frieda as she stood only reached up to the landlady's shoulder. 'Since Frieda puts such confidence in you,' cried K., 'I must do the same, and since not long ago Frieda called my assistants true friends we are all friends together. So I can tell you that what I would like best would be for Frieda and myself to get married, the sooner the better, oh, I know that I'll never be able to make up to Frieda for all she has lost for my sake, her position in the Herrenhof and her friendship with Klamm.' Frieda lifted up her face, her eyes were full of tears and had not a trace of triumph. 'Why? Why am I chosen out from other people?' 'What?' asked K. and the landlady simultaneously. 'She's upset, poor child,' said the landlady, 'upset by the conjunction of too much happiness and unhappiness.' And as if in confirmation of those words Frieda now flung herself upon K., kissing him wildly as if there were nobody else in the room, and then weeping, but still clinging to him, fell on her knees before him. While he caressed Frieda's hair with both hands K. asked the landlady: 'You seem to have no objection?' 'You are a man of honour,' said the landlady, who also had tears in her eyes. She looked a little worn and breathed with difficulty, but she found strength enough to say: 'There's only the question now of what guarantees you are to give Frieda, for great as is my respect for you, you're a stranger here; there's nobody here who can speak for you, your family circumstances aren't known here, so some guarantee is necessary. You must see that, my dear sir, and indeed you touched on it yourself when you mentioned how much Frieda must lose through her association with you.' 'Of course, guarantees, most certainly,' said K., 'but they'll be best given before the notary, and at the same time other officials of the Count's will perhaps be concerned. Besides, before I'm married there's something I must do. I must have a talk with Klamm.' 'That's impossible,' said Frieda, raising herself a little and pressing close to K., 'what an idea!' 'But it must be done,' said K., 'if it's impossible for me to manage it, you must.' 'I can't, K.; I can't,' said Frieda. 'Klamm will never talk to you. How can you ever think of such a thing!' 'And won't he talk to you?' asked K. 'Not to me either,' said Frieda, 'neither to you nor to me, it's simply impossible.' She turned to the landlady with outstretched arms: 'You see what he's asking for!' 'You're a strange person,' said the landlady, and she was an awe-inspiring figure now that she sat more upright, her legs spread out and her enormous knees projecting under her thin skirt, 'you ask for the impossible.' 'Why is it impossible?' said K. 'That's what I'm going to tell you,' said the landlady in a tone which sounded as if her explanation were less a final concession to friendship than the first item in a score of penalties she was enumerating, 'that's what I shall be glad to let you know. Although I don't belong to the Castle, and am only a woman, only a landlady here in an inn of the lowest kind – it's not of the very lowest but not far from it – and on that account you may not perhaps set much store by my explanation, still I've kept my eyes open all my life and met many kinds of people and taken the whole burden of the inn on my own shoulders, for Martin is no landlord although he's a good man, and responsibility is a thing he'll never understand. It's only his carelessness, for instance, that you've got to thank –

for I was tired to death on that evening – for being here in the village at all, for sitting here on this bed in peace and comfort.' 'What?' said K., waking from a kind of absent-minded distraction, pricked more by curiosity than by anger. 'It's only his carelessness you've got to thank for it,' cried the landlady again, pointing with her forefinger at K. Frieda tried to silence her. 'I can't help it,' said the landlady with a swift turn of her whole body. 'The Land Surveyor asked me a question and I must answer it. There's no other way of making him understand what we take for granted, that Herr Klamm will never speak to him – will never speak, did I say? – can never speak to him. Just listen to me, sir. Herr Klamm is a gentleman from the Castle, and that in itself, without considering Klamm's position there at all, means that he is of very high rank. But what are you, for whose marriage we are humbly considering here ways and means of getting permission? You are not from the Castle, you are not from the village, you aren't anything. Or rather, unfortunately, you are something, a stranger, a man who isn't wanted and is in everybody's way, a man who's always causing trouble, a man who takes up the maids' room, a man whose intentions are obscure, a man who has ruined our dear little Frieda and whom we must unfortunately accept as her husband. I don't hold all that up against you. You are what you are, and I have seen enough in my lifetime to be able to face facts. But now consider what it is you ask. A man like Klamm is to talk with you. It vexed me to hear that Frieda let you look through the peephole, when she did that she was already corrupted by you. But just tell me, how did you have the face to look at Klamm? You needn't answer, I know you think you were quite equal to the occasion. You're not even capable of seeing Klamm as he really is, that's not merely an exaggeration, for I myself am not capable of it either. Klamm is to talk to you, and yet Klamm doesn't talk even to people from the village, never yet has he spoken a word himself to anyone in the village. It was Frieda's great distinction, a distinction I'll be proud of to my dying day, that he used at least to call out her name, and that she could speak to him whenever she liked and was permitted the freedom of the peephole, but even to her he never talked. And the fact that he called her name didn't mean of necessity what one might think, he simply mentioned the name Frieda – who can tell what he was thinking of? – and that Frieda naturally came to him at once was her affair, and that she was admitted without let or hindrance was an act of grace on Klamm's part, but that he deliberately summoned her is more than one can maintain. Of course that's all over now for good. Klamm may perhaps call "Frieda" as before, that's possible, but she'll never again be admitted to his presence, a girl who has thrown herself away upon you. And there's just one thing, one thing my poor head can't understand, that a girl who had the honour of being known as Klamm's mistress – a wild exaggeration in my opinion – should have allowed you even to lay a finger on her.'

'Most certainly, that's remarkable,' said K., drawing Frieda to his bosom – she submitted at once although with bent head – 'but in my opinion that only proves the possibility of your being mistaken in some respects. You're quite right, for instance, in saying that I'm a mere nothing compared with Klamm, and even though I insist on speaking to Klamm in spite of that, and am not dissuaded even by your arguments, that does not mean at all that I'm able to face Klamm without a door between us, or that I mayn't run from the room at the very sight of him. But such a conjecture, even though well founded, is no valid reason in my eyes for refraining from the attempt. If I only succeed in holding my ground there's no need for him to speak to me at all, it will be sufficient for me to see what effect my words have on him, and if they have no effect or if he simply ignores them, I shall at any rate have the satisfaction of having spoken my mind freely to a great man. But you, with your wide knowledge of men and affairs, and Frieda, who was only yesterday Klamm's mistress – I see no reason for questioning that title – could certainly procure me an interview with Klamm quite easily; if it could be done in no other way I could surely see him in the Herrenhof, perhaps he's still there.'

'It's impossible,' said the landlady, 'and I can see that you're incapable of understanding why. But just tell me what you want to speak to Klamm about?'

'About Frieda, of course,' said K.

'About Frieda?' repeated the landlady, uncomprehendingly, and turned to Frieda. 'Do you hear that, Frieda, it's about you that he, he, wants to speak to Klamm, to Klamm!'

'Oh,' said K., 'you're a clever and admirable woman, and yet every trifle upsets you. Well, there it is, I want to speak to him about Frieda; that's not monstrous, it's only natural. And you're quite wrong, too, in supposing that from the moment of my appearance Frieda has ceased to be of any importance to Klamm. You underestimate him if you suppose that. I'm well aware that it's impertinence in me to lay down the law to you in this matter, but I must do it. I can't be the cause of any alteration in Klamm's relation to Frieda. Either there was no essential relationship between them – and that's what it amounts to if people deny that he was her honoured lover – in which case there is still no relationship between them, or else there was a relationship, and then how could I, a cipher in Klamm's eyes, as you rightly point out, how could I make any difference to it? One flies to such suppositions in the first moment of alarm, but the smallest reflection must correct one's bias. Anyhow, let us hear what Frieda herself thinks about it.'

With a far-away look in her eyes and her cheek on K.'s breast, Frieda said: 'It's certain, as mother says, that Klamm will have nothing more to do with me. But I agree that it's not because of you, darling, nothing of that kind could upset him. I think on the other hand that it was entirely his work that we found each other under the bar counter, we should bless that hour and not curse it.'

'If that is so,' said K. slowly, for Frieda's words were sweet, and he shut his eyes a moment or two to let their sweetness penetrate him, 'if that is so, there is less ground than ever to flinch from an interview with Klamm.'

'Upon my word,' said the landlady, with her nose in the air, 'you put me in mind of my own husband, you're just as childish and obstinate as he is. You've been only a few days in the village and already you think you know everything better than people who have spent their lives here, better than an old woman like me, and better than Frieda who has seen and heard so much in the Herrenhof. I don't deny that it's possible once in a while to achieve something in the teeth of every rule and tradition. I've never experienced anything of that kind myself, but I believe there are precedents for it. That may well be, but it certainly doesn't happen in the way you're trying to do it, simply by saying "no, no", and sticking to your own opinions and flouting the most well-meant advice. Do you think it's you I'm anxious about? Did I bother about you in the least so long as you were by yourself? Even though it would have been a good thing and saved a lot of trouble? The only thing I ever said to my husband about you was: "Keep your distance where he's concerned." And I should have done that myself to this very day if Frieda hadn't got mixed up with your affairs. It's her you have to thank – whether you like it or not – for my interest in you, even for my noticing your existence at all. And you can't simply shake me off, for I'm the only person who looks after little Frieda, and you're strictly answerable to me. Maybe Frieda is right, and all that has happened is Klamm's will, but I have nothing to do with Klamm here and now. I shall never speak to him, he's quite beyond my reach. But you're sitting here, keeping my Frieda, and being kept yourself– I don't see why I shouldn't tell you – by me. Yes, by me, young man, for let me see you find a lodging anywhere in this village if I throw you out, even it were only a dog-kennel.'

'Thank you,' said K., 'that's frank and I believe you absolutely. So my position is as uncertain as that, is it, and Frieda's position, too?'

'No!' interrupted the landlady furiously. 'Frieda's position in this respect has nothing at all to do with yours. Frieda belongs to my house, and nobody is entitled to call her position here uncertain.'

'All right, all right,' said K., 'I'll grant you that, too, especially since Frieda for some reason I'm not able to fathom seems to be too afraid of you to interrupt. Stick to me then for the present. My position is quite uncertain, you don't deny that, indeed you rather go out of your way to emphasize it. Like everything else you say, that has a fair proportion of truth in it, but it isn't absolutely true. For instance, I know where I could get a very good bed if I wanted it.'

'Where? Where?' cried Frieda and the landlady simultaneously and so eagerly that they might have had the same motive for asking.

'At Barnabas's,' said K.

'That scum!' cried the landlady. 'That rascally scum! At Barnabas's! Do you hear –' and she turned towards the corner, but the assistants had long quitted it and were now standing arm-in-arm behind her. And so now, as if she needed support, she seized one of them by the hand: 'Do you hear where the man goes hob-nobbing, with the family of Barnabas. Oh, certainly he'd get a bed there; I only wish he'd stay'd there over night instead of in the Herrenhof. But where were you two?'

'Madam,' said K., before the assistants had time to answer, 'these are my assistants. But you're treating them as if they were your assistants and my keepers. In every other respect I'm willing at least to argue the point with you courteously, but not where my assistants are concerned, that's too obvious a matter. I request you therefore not to speak to my assistants, and if my request proves ineffective I shall forbid my assistants to answer you.'

'So I'm not allowed to speak to you,' said the landlady, and they laughed all three, the landlady scornfully, but with less anger than K. had expected, and the assistants in their usual manner, which meant both much and little and disclaimed all responsibility.

'Don't get angry,' said Frieda, 'you must try to understand why we're upset. I can put it in this way, it's all owing to Barnabas that we belong to each other now. When I saw you for the first time in the bar – when you came in arm-in-arm with Olga – well, I knew something about you, but I was quite indifferent to you. I was indifferent not only to you but to nearly everything, yes, nearly everything. For at that time I was discontented about lots of things, and often annoyed, but it was a queer discontent and a queer annoyance. For instance, if one of the customers in the bar insulted me – and they were always after me – you saw what kind of creatures they were, but there were many worse than that, Klamm's servants weren't the worst – well, if one of them insulted me, what did that matter to me? I regarded it as if it had happened years before, or as if it had happened to someone else, or as if I had only heard tell of it, or as if I had already forgotten about it. But I can't describe it, I can hardly imagine it now, so different has everything become since losing Klamm.'

And Frieda broke off short, letting her head drop sadly, folding her hands on her bosom.

'You see,' cried the landlady, and she spoke not as if in her own person but as if she had merely lent Frieda her voice; she moved nearer, too, and sat close beside Frieda, 'you see, sir, the results of your actions, and your assistants too, whom I am not allowed to speak to, can profit by looking on at them. You've snatched Frieda from the happiest state she had ever known, and you managed to do that largely because in her childish susceptibility she could not bear to see you arm-in-arm with Olga, and so apparently delivered hand and foot to the Barnabas family. She rescued you from that and sacrificed herself in doing so. And now it's done, and Frieda has given up all she had for the pleasure of sitting on your knee, you come out with this fine trump card that once you had the chance of getting a bed from Barnabas. That's by way of showing me that you're independent of me. I assure you, if you had slept in that house you would be so independent of me that in the twinkling of an eye you would be put out of this one.'

'I don't know what sins the family Barnabas have committed,' said K., carefully raising Frieda – who drooped as if lifeless – setting her slowly down on the bed and standing up himself, 'you may be right about them, but I know that I was right in asking you to leave Frieda and me to settle our own affairs. You talked then about your care and affection, yet I haven't seen much of that, but a great deal of hatred and scorn and forbidding me your house. If it was your intention to separate Frieda from me or me from Frieda it was quite a good move, but all the same I think it won't succeed, and if it does succeed – it's my turn now to issue vague threats – you'll repent it. As for the lodging you favour me with – you can only mean this abominable hole – it's not at all certain that you do it of your own free will, it's much more likely that the authorities insist upon it. I shall now inform them that I have been told to go – and if I am allotted other quarters you'll probably feel relieved, but not so much as I will myself. And now I'm going to discuss this and other business with the Superintendent, please be so good as to look after Frieda at least, whom you have reduced to a bad enough state with your so-called motherly counsel.'

Then he turned to the assistants. 'Come along,' he said, taking Klamm's letter from its nail and making for the door. The landlady looked at him in silence, and only when his hand was on the latch did she say: 'There's something else to take away with you, for whatever you say and however you insult an old woman like me, you're after all Frieda's future husband. That's my sole reason for telling you now that your ignorance of the local situation is so appalling that it makes my head go round to listen to you and compare your ideas and opinions with the real state of things. It's a kind of ignorance which can't be enlightened at one attempt, and perhaps never can be, but there's a lot you could learn if you would only believe me a little and keep your own ignorance constantly in mind. For instance, you would at once be less unjust to me, and you would begin to have an inkling of the shock it was to me – a shock from which I'm still suffering – when I realized that my dear little Frieda had, so to speak, deserted the eagle for the snake in the grass, only the real situation is much worse even than that, and I have to keep on trying to forget it so as to be able to speak civilly to you at all. Oh, now you're angry again! No, don't go away yet, listen to this one appeal; wherever you may be, never forget that you're the most ignorant person in the village, and be cautious; here in this house where Frieda's presence saves you from harm you can drivel on to your heart's content, for instance, here you can explain to us how you mean to get an interview with Klamm, but I entreat you, don't do it in earnest.'

She stood up, tottering a little with agitation, went over to K., took his hand and looked at him imploringly. 'Madam,' said K., 'I don't understand why you should stoop to entreat me about a thing like this. If as you say, it's impossible for me to speak to Klamm, I won't manage it in any case whether I'm entreated or not. But if it proves to be possible, why shouldn't I do it, especially as that would remove your main objection and so make your other premises questionable. Of course, I'm ignorant, that's an unshaken truth and a sad truth for me, but it gives me all the advantage of ignorance, which is greater daring, and so I'm prepared to put up with my ignorance, evil consequences and all, for some time to come, so long as my strength holds out. But these consequences really affect nobody but myself, and that's why I simply can't understand your pleading. I'm certain you would always look after Frieda, and if I were to vanish from Frieda's ken you couldn't regard that as anything but good luck. So what are you afraid of? Surely you're not afraid – an ignorant man thinks everything possible' – here K. flung the door open – 'surely you're not afraid for Klamm?' The landlady gazed after him in silence as he ran down the staircase with the assistants following him.

5

To his own surprise K. had little difficulty in obtaining an interview with the Superintendent. He sought to explain this to himself by the fact that, going by his experience hitherto, official intercourse with the authorities for him was always very easy. This was caused on the one hand by the fact that the word had obviously gone out once and for all to treat his case with the external marks of indulgence, and on the other, by the admirable autonomy of the service, which one divined to be peculiarly effective where it was not visibly present. At the mere thought of those facts, K. was often in danger of considering his situation hopeful; nevertheless, after such fits of easy confidence, he would hasten to tell himself that just there lay his danger.

Direct intercourse with the authorities was not particularly difficult then, for well organized as they might be, all they did was to guard the distant and invisible interests of distant and invisible masters, while K. fought for something vitally near to him, for himself, and moreover, at least at the very beginning, on his own initiative, for he was the attacker; and besides he fought not only for himself, but clearly for other powers as well which he did not know, but in which, without infringing the regulations of the authorities, he was permitted to believe. But now by the fact that they had at once amply met his wishes in all unimportant matters – and hitherto only unimportant matters had come up – they had robbed him of the possibility of light and easy victories, and with that of the satisfaction which must accompany them and the well-grounded confidence for further and greater struggles which must result from them. Instead, they let K. go anywhere he liked – of course only within the village – and thus pampered and enervated him, ruled out all possibility of conflict, and transported him to an unofficial, totally unrecognized, troubled, and alien existence. In this life it might easily happen, if he were not always on his guard, that one day or other, in spite of the amiability of the authorities and the scrupulous fulfilment of all his exaggeratedly light duties, he might – deceived by the apparent favour shown him – conduct himself so imprudently that he might get a fall; and the authorities, still ever mild and friendly, and as it were against their will, but in the name of some public regulation unknown to him, might have to come and clear him out of the way. And what was it, this other life to which he was consigned? Never yet had K. seen vocation and life so interlaced as here, so interlaced that sometimes one might think that they had exchanged places. What importance, for example, had the power, merely formal up till now, which Klamm exercised over K.'s services, compared with the very real power which Klamm possessed in K.'s bedroom? So it came about that while a light and frivolous bearing, a certain deliberate carelessness was sufficient when one came in direct contact with the authorities, one needed in everything else the greatest caution, and had to look round on every side before one made a single step.

K. soon found his opinion of the authorities of the place confirmed when he went to see the Superintendent. The Superintendent, a kindly, stout, clean-shaven man, was laid up; he was suffering from a severe attack of gout, and received K. in bed. 'So here is our Land Surveyor,' he said, and tried to sit up, failed in the attempt, and flung himself back again on the cushions, pointing apologetically to his leg. In the faint light of the room, where the tiny windows were still further darkened by curtains, a noiseless, almost shadowing woman pushed forward a chair for K. and placed it beside the bed. 'Take a seat, Land Surveyor, take a seat,' said the Superintendent, 'and let me know your wishes.' K. read out Klamm's letter and adjoined a few remarks to it. Again he had this sense of extraordinary ease in intercourse with the authorities. They seemed literally to bear every burden, one could lay everything on their shoulders and remain free and untouched oneself. As if he, too, felt this in his way, the Superintendent made a movement of discomfort on the bed. At length he said: 'I know about the whole business as, indeed, you have remarked. The reason why I've done nothing is, firstly, that I've been unwell, and secondly, that you've been so long in coming; I thought finally that you had given up the business. But now that you've been so kind as to look me up, really I must tell you the plain unvarnished truth of the matter. You've been taken on as Land Surveyor, as you say, but, unfortunately, we have no need of a Land Surveyor. There wouldn't be the least use for one here. The frontiers of our little state are marked out and all officially recorded. So what should we do with a Land Surveyor?' Though he had not given the matter a moment's thought before, K. was convinced now at the bottom of his heart that he had expected some such response as this. Exactly for that reason he was able to reply immediately: 'This is a great surprise for me. It throws all my calculations out. I can only hope that there's some misunderstanding.' 'No, unfortunately,' said the Superintendent, 'it's as I've said.' 'But how is that possible?' cried K. 'Surely I haven't made this endless journey just to be sent back again.' 'That's another question,' replied the Superintendent, 'which isn't for me to decide, but how this misunderstanding became possible, I can certainly explain that. In such a large governmental office as the Count's, it may occasionally happen that one department ordains this, another that; neither knows of the other, and though the supreme control is absolutely efficient, it comes by its nature too late, and so every now and then a trifling miscalculation arises. Of course that applies only to the pettiest little affairs, as for example your case. In great matters I've never known of any error yet, but even little affairs are often painful enough. Now as for your case, I'll be open with you about its history, and make no official mystery of it – I'm not enough of the official for that, I'm a farmer and always will remain one. A long time ago – I had only been Superintendent for a few months – there came an order, I can't remember from what department, in which in the usual categorical way of the gentlemen up there, it was made known that a Land Surveyor was to be called in, and the municipality were instructed to hold themselves ready for the plans and measurements necessary for his work. This order obviously couldn't have concerned you, for it was many years ago, and I shouldn't have remembered it if I weren't ill just now and with ample time in bed to think of the most absurd things – Mizzi,' he said, suddenly interrupting his narrative, to the woman who was still flitting about the room in incomprehensible activity, 'please have a look in the cabinet, perhaps you'll find the order.' 'You see, it belongs to my first months here,' he explained to K., 'at that time I still filed everything away.' The woman opened the cabinet at once. K. and the Superintendent looked on. The cabinet was crammed full of papers. When it was opened two large packages of papers rolled out, tied in round bundles, as one usually binds firewood; the woman sprang back in alarm. 'It must be down below, at the bottom,' said the Superintendent, directing operations from the bed. Gathering the papers in both arms the woman obediently threw them all out of the cabinet so as to read those at the bottom. The papers now covered half the floor. 'A great deal of work is got through here,' said the Superintendent nodding his head, 'and that's only a small fraction of it. I've put away the most important pile in the shed, but the great mass of it has simply gone astray. Who could keep it all together? But there's piles and piles more in the shed.' 'Will you be able to find the order?' he said, turning again to his wife; 'you must look for a document with the word Land Surveyor underlined in blue pencil.' 'It's too dark,' said the woman, 'I'll fetch a candle,' and she stamped through the papers to the door. 'My wife is a great help to me,' said the Superintendent, 'in these difficult official affairs, and yet we can never quite keep up with them. True, I have another assistant for the writing that has to be done, the teacher; but all the same it's impossible to get things shipshape, there's always a lot of business that has to be left lying, it has been put away in that chest there,' and he pointed to another cabinet. 'And just now, when I'm laid up, it has got the upper hand,' he said, and lay back with a weary yet proud air. 'Couldn't I,' asked K., seeing that the woman had now returned with the candle and was kneeling before the chest looking for the paper, 'couldn't I help your wife to look for it?' The Superintendent smilingly shook his head: 'As I said before, I don't want to make any parade of official secrecy before you, but to let you look through these papers yourself – no, I can't go so far as that.' Now stillness fell in the room, only the rustling of the papers was to be heard; it looked, indeed, for a few minutes, as if the Superintendent were dozing. A faint rapping on the door made K. turn round. It was of course the assistants. All the same they showed already some of the effects of their training, they did not rush at once into the room, but whispered at first through the door which was slightly ajar: 'It's cold out here.' 'Who's that?' asked the Superintendent, starting up. 'It's only my assistants,' replied K. 'I don't know where to ask them to wait for me, it's too cold outside and here they would be in the way.' 'They won't disturb me,' said the Superintendent indulgently. 'Ask them to come in. Besides I know them. Old acquaintances.' 'But they're in *my* way,' K. replied bluntly, letting his gaze wander from the assistants to the Superintendent and back again, and finding on the faces of all three the same smile. 'But seeing you're here as it is,' he went on experimentally, 'stay and help the Superintendent's lady there to look for a document with the words Land Surveyor underlined in blue pencil.' The Superintendent raised no objection. What had not been permitted to K. was allowed to the assistants; they threw themselves at once on the papers, but they did not so much seek for anything as rummage about in the heap, and while one was spelling out a document the other would immediately snatch it out of his hand. The woman meanwhile knelt before the empty chest, she seemed to have completely given up looking, in any case the candle was standing quite far away from her.

'The assistants,' said the Superintendent with a self-complacent smile, which seemed to indicate that he had the lead, though nobody was in a position even to assume this, 'they're in your way then? Yet they're your own assistants.' 'No,' replied K, coolly, 'they only ran into me here.' 'Ran into you,' said he; 'you mean, of course, were assigned to you.' 'All right then, were assigned to me,' said K., 'but they might as well have fallen from the sky, for all the thought that was spent in choosing them.' 'Nothing here is done without taking thought,' said the Superintendent, actually forgetting the pain in his foot and sitting up. 'Nothing!' said K., 'and what about my being summoned here then?' 'Even your being summoned was carefully considered,' said the Superintendent; 'it was only certain auxiliary circumstances that entered and confused the matter, I'll prove it to you from the official papers.' 'The papers will not be found,' said K. 'Not be found?' said the Superintendent. 'Mizzi, please hurry up a bit! Still I can tell you the story even without the papers. We replied with thanks to the order that I've mentioned already, saying that we didn't need a Land Surveyor. But this reply doesn't appear to have reached the original department – I'll call it A – but by mistake went to another department, B. So department A remained without an answer, but unfortunately our full reply didn't reach B either; whether it was that the order itself was not enclosed by us, or whether it got lost on the way – it was certainly not lost in my department, that I can vouch for – in any case all that arrived at Department B was the covering letter, in which was merely noted that the enclosed order, unfortunately an impracticable one, was concerned with the engagement of a Land Surveyor. Meanwhile Department A was waiting for our answer, they had, of course, made a memorandum of the case, but as excusably enough often happens and is bound to happen even under the most efficient handling, our correspondent trusted to the fact that we would answer him, after which he would either summon the Land Surveyor, or else if need be write us further about the matter. As a result he never thought of referring to his memorandum and the whole thing fell into oblivion. But in Department B the covering letter came into the hands of a correspondent, famed for his conscientiousness, Sordini by name, an Italian; it is incomprehensible even to me, though I am one of the initiated, why a man of his capacities is left in an almost subordinate position. This Sordini naturally sent back the unaccompanied covering letter for completion. Now months, if not years, had passed by this time since that first communication from Department A, which is understandable enough, for when – which is the rule – a document goes the proper route, it reaches the department at the outside in a day and is settled that day, but when it once in a while loses its way then in an organization so efficient as ours its proper destination must be sought for literally with desperation, otherwise it mightn't be found; and then, well then the search may last really for a long time. Accordingly, when we got Sordini's note we had only a vague memory of the affair, there were only two of us to do the work at that time, Mizzi and myself, the teacher hadn't yet been assigned to us, we only kept copies in the most important instances, so we could only reply in the most vague terms that we knew nothing of this engagement of a Land Surveyor and that as far as we knew there was no need for one.

'But,' here the Superintendent interrupted himself as if, carried on by his tale, he had gone too far, or as if at least it were possible that he had gone too far, 'doesn't the story bore you?'

'No,' said K., 'it amuses me.'

Thereupon the Superintendent said: 'I'm not telling it to amuse you.'

'It only amuses me,' said K., 'because it gives me an insight into the ludicrous bungling which in certain circumstances may decide the life of a human being.'

'You haven't been given any insight into that yet,' replied the Superintendent gravely, 'and I can go on with my story. Naturally Sordini was not satisfied with our reply. I admire the man, although he is a plague to me. He literally distrusts everyone; even if, for instance, he had come to know somebody, through countless circumstances, as the most reliable man in the world, he distrusts him as soon as fresh circumstances arise, as if he didn't want to know him, or rather as if he wanted to know that he was a scoundrel. I consider that right and proper, an official must behave like that; unfortunately with my nature I can't follow out this principle; you see yourself how frank I am with you, a stranger, about those things, I can't act in any other way. But Sordini, on the contrary, was seized by suspicion when he read our reply. Now a large correspondence began to grow. Sordini inquired how I had suddenly recalled that a Land Surveyor shouldn't be summoned. I replied, drawing on Mizzi's splendid memory, that the first suggestion had come from the chancellery itself (but that it had come from a different department we had of course forgotten long before this). Sordini countered: "Why had I only mentioned this official order now?" I replied: "Because I had just remembered it." Sordini: "That was very extraordinary." Myself: "It was not in the least extraordinary in such a long-drawn-out business." Sordini: "Yes, it was extraordinary, for the order that I remembered didn't exist." Myself: "Of course it didn't exist, for the whole document had gone a-missing." Sordini: "But there must be a memorandum extant relating to this first communication, and there wasn't one extant." That drew me up, for that an error should happen in Sordini's department I neither dared to maintain nor to believe. Perhaps, my dear Land Surveyor, you'll make the reproach against Sordini in your mind, that in consideration of my assertion he should have been moved at least to make inquiries in the other departments about the affair. But that is just what would have been wrong; I don't want any blame to attach to this man, no, not even in your thoughts. It's a working principle of the Head Bureau that the very possibility of error must be ruled out of account. This ground principle is justified by the consummate organization of the whole authority, and it is necessary if the maximum speed in transacting business is to be attained. So it wasn't within Sordini's power to make inquiries in other departments, besides they simply wouldn't have answered, because they would have guessed at once that it was a case of hunting out a possible error.'

'Allow me, Superintendent, to interrupt you with a question,' said K. 'Did you not mention once before a Control Authority? From your description the whole economy is one that would rouse one's apprehension if one could imagine the control failing.'

'You're very strict,' said the Superintendent, 'but multiply your strictness a thousand times and it would still be nothing compared with the strictness which the Authority imposes on itself. Only a total stranger could ask a question like yours. Is there a Control Authority? There are only control authorities. Frankly it isn't their function to hunt out errors in the vulgar sense, for errors don't happen, and even when once in a while an error does happen, as in your case, who can say finally that it's an error?'

'This is news indeed!' cried K.

'It's very old news to me,' said the Superintendent. 'Not unlike yourself I'm convinced that an error has occurred, and as a result Sordini is quite ill with despair, and the first Control Officials, whom we have to thank for discovering the source of error, recognize that there is an error. But who can guarantee that the second Control Officials will decide in the same way and the third lot and all the others?'

'That may be,' said K. 'I would much rather not mix in these speculations yet, besides this is the first mention I've heard of these Control Officials and naturally I can't understand them yet. But I fancy that two things must be distinguished here: firstly, what is transacted in the offices and can be construed again officially this way or that, and secondly, my own actual person, me myself, situated outside the offices and threatened by their encroachments, which are so meaningless that I can't even yet believe in the seriousness of the danger. The first evidently is covered by what you, Superintendent, tell me in such extraordinary and disconcerting detail; all the same I would like to hear a word now about myself.'

'I'm coming to that too,' said the Superintendent, 'but you couldn't understand it without my giving a few more preliminary details. My mentioning the Control Officials just now was premature. So I must turn back to the discrepancies with Sordini. As I said, my defence gradually weakened. But whenever Sordini has in his hands even the slightest hold against anyone, he has as good as won, for then his vigilance, energy, and alertness are actually increased and it's a terrible moment for the victim, and a glorious one for the victim's enemies. It's only because in other circumstances I have experienced this last feeling that I'm able to speak of him as I do. All the same I have never managed yet to come within sight of him. He can't get down here, he's so overwhelmed with work; from the descriptions I've heard of his room every wall is covered with columns of documents tied together, piled on top of one another; those are only the documents that Sordini is working on at the time, and as bundles of papers are continually being taken away and brought in, and all in great haste, those columns are always falling on the floor, and it's just those perpetual crashes, following fast on one another, that have come to distinguish Sordini's workroom. Yes, Sordini is a worker and he gives the same scrupulous care to the smallest case as to the greatest.'

'Superintendent,' said K., 'you always call my case one of the smallest, and yet it has given hosts of officials a great deal of trouble, and if, perhaps, it was unimportant at the start, yet through the diligence of officials of Sordini's type it has grown into a great affair. Very much against my will, unfortunately, for my ambition doesn't run to seeing columns of documents, all about me, rising and crashing together, but to working quietly at my drawing-board as a humble Land Surveyor.'

'No,' said the Superintendent, 'it's not at all a great affair, in that respect you've no ground for complaint – it's one of the least important among the least important. The importance of a case is not determined by the amount of work it involves, you're far from understanding the authorities if you believe that. But even if it's a question of the amount of work, your case would remain one of the slightest; ordinary cases, those without any so-called errors I mean, provide far more work and far more profitable work as well. Besides you know absolutely nothing yet of the actual work which was caused by your case. I'll tell you about that now. Well, presently Sordini left me out of count, but the clerks arrived, and every day a formal inquiry involving the most prominent members of the community was held in the Herrenhof. The majority stuck by me, only a few held back – the question of a Land Surveyor appeals to peasants – they scented secret plots and injustices and what not, found a leader, no less, and Sordini was forced by their assertions to the conviction that if I had brought the question forward in the Town Council, every voice wouldn't have been against the summoning of a Land Surveyor. So a commonplace – namely, that a Land Surveyor wasn't needed – was turned after all into a doubtful matter at least. A man called Brunswick distinguished himself especially, you don't know him, of course; probably he's not a bad man, only stupid and fanciful, he's a son-in-law of Lasemann's.'

'Of the Master Tanner?' asked K., and he described the full-bearded man whom he had seen at Lasemann's.

'Yes, that's the man,' said the Superintendent.

'I know his wife, too,' said K. a little at random.

'That's possible,' replied the Superintendent briefly.

'She's beautiful,' said K., 'but rather pale and sickly. She comes, of course, from the Castle?' It was half a question.

The Superindendent looked at the clock, poured some medicine into a spoon, and gulped at it hastily.

'You only know the official side of the Castle?' asked K. bluntly.

'That's so,' replied the Superintendent, with an ironical and yet grateful smile, 'and it's the most important. And as for Brunswick; if we could exclude him from the Council we would almost all be glad, and Lasemann not least. But at that time Brunswick gained some influence, he's not an orator of course, but a shouter; but even that can do a lot. And so it came about that I was forced to lay the matter before the Town Council; however, it was Brunswick's only immediate triumph, for of course the Town Council refused by a large majority to hear anything about a Land Surveyor. That, too, was a long time ago, but the whole time since the matter has never been allowed to rest, partly owing to Sordini's conscientiousness, who by the most painful sifting of data sought to fathom the motives of the majority no less than the opposition, partly owing to Brunswick's stupidity and ambition, who had several personal acquaintances among the authorities whom he set working with fresh inventions of his fancy. Sordini, at any rate, didn't let himself be deceived by Brunswick – how could Brunswick deceive Sordini? – but simply to prevent himself from being deceived a new sifting of data was necessary, and long before it was ended Brunswick had already thought out something new; he's very, very versatile, no doubt of it, that goes with his stupidity. And now I come to a peculiar characteristic of our administrative apparatus. Along with its precision it's extremely sensitive as well. When an affair has been weighed for a very long time, it may happen, even before the matter has been fully considered, that suddenly in a flash the decision comes in some unforeseen place, that, moreover, can't be found any longer later on, a decision that settles the matter, if in most cases justly, yet all the same arbitrarily. It's as if the administrative apparatus were unable any longer to bear the tension, the year-long irritation caused by the same affair – probably trivial in itself – and had hit upon the decision by itself, without the assistance of the officials. Of course a miracle didn't happen and certainly it was some clerk who hit upon the solution or the unwritten decision, but in any case it couldn't be discovered by us, at least by us here, or even by the Head Bureau, which clerk had decided in this case and on what grounds. The Control Officials only discovered that much later, but we will never learn it; besides by this time it would scarcely interest anybody. Now, as I said, it's just these decisions that are generally excellent. The only annoying thing about them – it's usually the case with such things – is that one learns too late about them and so in the meantime keeps on still passionately canvassing things that were decided long ago. I don't know whether in your case a decision of this kind happened – some people say yes, others no – but if it had happened then the summons would have been sent to you and you would have made the long journey to this place, much time would have passed, and in the meanwhile Sordini would have been working away here all the time on the same case until he was exhausted. Brunswick would have been intriguing, and I would have been plagued by both of them. I only indicate this possibility, but I know the following for a fact: a Control Official discovered meanwhile that a query had gone out from the Department A to the Town Council many years before regarding a Land Surveyor, without having received a reply up till then. A new inquiry was sent to me, and now the whole business was really cleared up. Department A was satisfied with my answer that a Land Surveyor was not needed, and Sordini was forced to recognize that he had not been equal to this case and, innocently it is true, had got through so much nerve-racking work for nothing. If new work hadn't come rushing in as ever from every side, and if your case hadn't been a very unimportant case – one might almost say the least important among the unimportant – we might all of us have breathed freely again, I fancy even Sordini himself; Brunswick was the only one that grumbled, but that was only ridiculous. And now imagine to yourself, Land Surveyor, my dismay when after the fortunate end of the whole business – and since then, too, a great deal of time had passed by – suddenly you appear and it begins to look as if the whole thing must begin all over again. You'll understand of course that I'm firmly resolved, so far as I'm concerned, not to let that happen in any case?'

'Certainly,' said K., 'but I understand better still that a terrible abuse of my case, and probably of the law, is being carried on. As for me, I shall know how to protect myself against it.'

'How will you do it?' asked the Superintendent.

'I'm not at liberty to reveal that,' said K.

'I don't want to press myself upon you,' said the Superintendent, 'only I would like you to reflect that in me you have – I won't say a friend, for we're complete strangers of course – but to some extent a business friend. The only thing I will not agree to is that you should be taken on as Land Surveyor, but in other matters you can draw on me with confidence, frankly to the extent of my power, which isn't great.'

'You always talk of the one thing,' said K., 'that I shan't be taken on as Land Surveyor, but I'm Land Surveyor already, here is Klamm's letter.'

'Klamm's letter,' said the Superintendent. 'That's valuable and worthy of respect on account of Klamm's signature which seems to be genuine, but all the same – yet I won't dare to advance it on my own unsupported word. Mizzi,' he called, and then: 'But what are you doing?'

Mizzi and the assistants, left so long unnoticed, had clearly not found the paper they were looking for, and had then tried to shut everything up again in the cabinet, but on account of the confusion and superabundance of papers had not succeeded. Then the assistants had hit upon the idea which they were carrying out now. They had laid the cabinet on its back on the floor, crammed all the documents in, then along with Mizzi had knelt on the cabinet door and were trying now in this way to get it shut.

'So the paper hasn't been found,' said the Superintendent. 'A pity, but you know the story already; really we don't need the paper now, besides it will certainly be found sometime yet; probably it's at the teacher's place, there's a great pile of papers there too. But come over here now with the candle, Mizzi, and read this letter for me.'

Mizzi went over and now looked still more grey and insignificant as she sat on the edge of the bed and leaned against the strong, vigorous man, who put his arm round her. In the candlelight only her pinched face was cast into relief, its simple and austere lines softened by nothing but age. Hardly had she glanced at the letter when she clasped her hands lightly and said: 'From Klamm.' Then they read the letter together, whispered for a moment, and at last, just as the assistants gave a 'Hurrah!' for they had finally got the cabinet door shut – which earned them a look of silent gratitude from Mizzi – the Superintendent said:

'Mizzi is quite of my opinion and now I am at liberty to express it. This letter is in no sense an official letter, but only a private letter. That can be clearly seen in the very mode of address: "My dear Sir". Moreover, there isn't a single word in it showing that you've been taken on as Land Surveyor; on the contrary it's all about state service in general, and even that is not absolutely guaranteed, as you know, that is, the task of proving that you are taken on is laid on you. Finally, you are officially and expressly referred to me, the Superintendent, as your immediate superior, for more detailed information, which, indeed, has in great part been given already. To anyone who knows how to read official communications, and consequently knows still better how to read unofficial letters, all this is only too clear. That you, a stranger, don't know it doesn't surprise me. In general the letter means nothing more than that Klamm intends to take a personal interest in you if you should be taken into the state service.'

'Superintendent,' said K., 'you interpret the letter so well that nothing remains of it but a signature on a blank sheet of paper. Don't you see that in doing this you depreciate Klamm's name, which you pretend to respect?'

'You misunderstand me,' said the Superintendent, 'I don't misconstrue the meaning of the letter, my reading of it doesn't disparage it, on the contrary. A private letter from Klamm has naturally far more significance than an official letter, but it hasn't precisely the kind of significance that you attach to it.'

'Do you know Schwarzer?' asked K.

'No,' replied the Superintendent. 'Perhaps you know him, Mizzi? You don't know him either? No, we don't know him.'

'That's strange,' said K., 'he's a son of one of the under-castellans.'

'My dear Land Surveyor,' replied the Superintendent, 'how on earth should I know all the sons of all the under-castellans?'

'Right,' said K., 'then you'll just have to take my word that he is one. I had a sharp encounter with this Schwarzer on the very day of my arrival. Afterwards he made a telephone inquiry of an under-castellan called Fritz and received the information that I was engaged as Land Surveyor. How do you explain that, Superintendent?'

'Very simply,' replied the Superintendent. 'You haven't once up till now come into real contact with our authorities. All those contacts of yours have been illusory, but owing to your ignorance of the circumstances you take them to be real. And as for the telephone. As you see, in my place, though I've certainly enough to do with the authorities, there's no telephone. In inns and suchlike places it may be of real use, as much use say as a penny-in-the-slot musical instrument, but it's nothing more than that. Have you ever telephoned here? Yes? Well, then perhaps you'll understand what I say. In the Castle the telephone works beautifully of course, I've been told it's going there all the time, that naturally speeds up the work a great deal. We can hear this continual telephoning in our telephones down here as a humming and singing, you must have heard it too. Now this humming and singing transmitted by our telephones is the only real and reliable thing you'll hear, everything else is deceptive. There's no fixed connexion with the Castle, no central exchange which transmits our calls further. When anybody calls up the Castle from here the instruments in all the subordinate departments ring, or rather they would all ring if practically all the departments – I know it for a certainty – didn't leave their receivers off. Now and then, however, a fatigued official may feel the need of a little distraction, especially in the evenings and at night and may hang the receiver on. Then we get an answer, but an answer of course that's merely a practical joke. And that's very understandable too. For who would take the responsibility of interrupting, in the middle of the night, the extremely important work up there that goes on furiously the whole time, with a message about his own little private troubles? I can't comprehend how even a stranger can imagine that when he calls up Sordini, for example, it's really Sordini that answers. Far more probably it's a little copying clerk from an entirely different department. On the other hand, it may certainly happen once in a blue moon that when one calls up the little copying clerk Sordini will answer himself. Then finally the best thing is to fly from the telephone before the first sound comes through.'

'I didn't know it was like that, certainly,' said K., 'I couldn't know of all these peculiarities, but I didn't put much confidence in those telephone conversations and I was always aware that the only things of real importance were those that happened in the Castle itself.'

'No,' said the Superintendent, holding firmly on to the word, 'these telephone replies certainly have a meaning, why shouldn't they? How could a message given by an official from the Castle be unimportant? As I remarked before apropos Klamm's letter. All these utterances have no official significance; when you attach official significance to them you go astray. On the other hand, their private significance in a friendly or hostile sense is very great, generally greater than an official communication could ever be.'

'Good,' said K. 'Granted that all this is so, I should have lots of good friends in the Castle: looked at rightly the sudden inspiration of that department all these years ago – saying that a Land Surveyor should be asked to come – was an act of friendship towards myself; but then in the sequel one act was followed by another, until at last, on an evil day, I was enticed here and then threatened with being thrown out again.'

'There's a certain amount of truth in your view of the case,' said the Superintendent; 'you're right in thinking that the pronouncements of the Castle are not to be taken literally. But caution is always necessary, not only here, and always the more necessary the more important the pronouncement in question happens to be. But when you went on to talk about being enticed, I ceased to fathom you. If you had followed my explanation more carefully, then you must have seen that the question of your being summoned here is far too difficult to be settled here and now in the course of a short conversation.'

'So the only remaining conclusion,' said K., 'is that everything is very uncertain and insoluble, including my being thrown out.'

'Who would take the risk of throwing you out, Land Surveyor?' asked the Superintendent. 'The very uncertainty about your summons guarantees you the most courteous treatment, only you're too sensitive by all appearances. Nobody keeps you here, but that surely doesn't amount to throwing you out.'

'Oh, Superintendent,' said K., 'now and again you're taking far too simple a view of the case. I'll enumerate for your benefit a few of the things that keep me here: the sacrifice I made in leaving my home, the long and difficult journey, the well-grounded hopes I built on my engagement here, my complete lack of means, the impossibility after this of finding some other suitable job at home, and last but not least my fiancée, who lives here.'

'Oh, Frieda!' said the Superintendent without showing any surprise. 'I know. But Frieda would follow you anywhere. As for the rest of what you've said, some consideration will be necessary and I'll communicate with the Castle about it. If a decision should be come to, or if it should be necessary first to interrogate you again, I'll send for you. Is that agreeable to you?'

'No, absolutely,' said K., 'I don't want any act of favour from the Castle, but my rights.'

'Mizzi,' the Superintendent said to his wife, who still sat pressed against him, and lost in a day-dream was playing with Klamm's letter, which she had folded into the shape of a little boat – K. snatched it from her in alarm. 'Mizzi, my foot is beginning to throb again, we must renew the compress.'

K. got up. 'Then I'll take my leave,' he said. 'Hm,' said Mizzi, who was already preparing a poultice, 'the last one was drawing too strongly.' K. turned away. At his last words the assistants with their usual misplaced zeal to be useful had thrown open both wings of the door. To protect the sickroom from the strong draught of cold air which was rushing in, K. had to be content with making the Superintendent a hasty bow. Then, pushing the assistants in front of him, he rushed out of the room and quickly closed the door.

6

Before the inn the landlord was waiting for him. Without being questioned he would not have ventured to address him, accordingly K. asked what he wanted. 'Have you found new lodgings yet?' asked the landlord, looking at the ground. 'You were told to ask by your wife?' replied K., 'you're very much under her influence?' 'No,' said the landlord, 'I didn't ask because of my wife. But she's very bothered and unhappy on your account, can't work, lies in bed and sighs and complains all the time.' 'Shall I go and see her?' asked K. 'I wish you would,' said the landlord. 'I've been to the Superintendent's already to fetch you. I listened at the door but you were talking. I didn't want to disturb you, besides I was anxious about my wife and ran back again; but she wouldn't see me, so there was nothing for it but to wait for you.' 'Then let's go at once,' said K., 'I'll soon reassure her.' 'If you could only manage it,' said the landlord.

They went through the bright kitchen where three or four maids, engaged all in different corners at the work they were happening to be doing, visibly stiffened on seeing K. From the kitchen the sighing landlady could already be heard. She lay in a windowless annex separated from the kitchen by thin lath boarding. There was room in it only for a huge family bed and a chest. The bed was so placed that from it one could overlook the whole kitchen and superintend the work. From the kitchen, on the other hand, hardly anything could be seen in the annex. There it was quite dark: only the faint gleam of the purple bed-coverlet could be distinguished. Not until one entered and one's eyes became used to the darkness did one detect particular objects.

'You've come at last,' said the landlady feebly. She was lying stretched out on her back, she breathed with visible difficulty, she had thrown back the feather quilt. In bed she looked much younger than in her clothes, but a nightcap of delicate lacework which she wore, although it was too small and nodded on her head, made her sunk face look pitiable. 'Why should I have come?' asked K. mildly. 'You didn't send for me.' 'You shouldn't have kept me waiting so long,' said the landlady with the capriciousness of an invalid. 'Sit down,' she went on, pointing to the bed, 'and you others go away.' Meantime the maids as well as the assistants had crowded in. 'I'll go too, Gardana,' said the landlord. This was the first time that K. had heard her name. 'Of course,' she replied slowly, and as if she were occupied with other thoughts she added absently: 'Why should you remain any more than the others?' But when they had all retreated to the kitchen – even the assistants this time went at once, besides, a maid was behind them – Gardana was alert enough to grasp that everything she said could be heard in there, for the annex lacked a door, and so she commanded everyone to leave the kitchen as well. It was immediately done.

'Land Surveyor,' said Gardana, 'there's a wrap hanging over there beside the chest, will you please reach me it? I'll lay it over me. I can't bear the feather quilt, my breathing is so bad.' And as K. handed her the wrap, she went on: 'Look, this is a beautiful wrap, isn't it?' To K. it seemed to be an ordinary woollen wrap; he felt it with his fingers again merely out of politeness, but did not reply. 'Yes, it's a beautiful wrap,' said Gardana covering herself up. Now she lay back comfortably, all her pain seemed to have gone, she actually had enough strength to think of the state of her hair which had been disordered by her lying position; she raised herself up for a moment and rearranged her coiffure a little round the nightcap. Her hair was abundant.

K. became impatient, and began: 'You asked me, madam, whether I had found other lodgings yet.' 'I asked you?' said the landlady, 'no, you're mistaken.' 'Your husband asked me a few minutes ago.' 'That may well be,' said the landlady; 'I'm at variance with him. When I didn't want you here, he kept you here, now I'm glad to have you here, he wants to drive you away. He's always like that.' 'Have you changed your opinion of me so greatly, then?' asked K. 'In a couple of hours?' 'I haven't changed my opinion,' said the landlady more freely again; 'give me your hand. There, and now promise to be quite frank with me and I'll be the same with you.' 'Right,' said K., 'but who's to begin first?' 'I shall,' said the landlady. She did not give so much the impression of one who wanted to meet K. half-way, as of one who was eager to have the first word.

She drew a photograph from under the pillow and held it out to K. 'Look at that portrait,' she said eagerly. To see it better K. stepped into the kitchen, but even there it was not easy to distinguish anything on the photograph, for it was faded with age, cracked in several places, crumpled, and dirty. 'It isn't in very good condition,' said K. 'Unluckily no,' said the landlady, 'when one carries a thing about with one for years it's bound to be the case. But if you look at it carefully, you'll be able to make everything out, you'll see. But I can help you; tell me what you see, I like to hear anyone talk about the portrait. Well, then?' 'A young man,' said K. 'Right,' said the landlady, 'and what's he doing?' 'It seems to me he's lying on a board stretching himself and yawning.' The landlady laughed. 'Quite wrong,' she said. 'But here's the board and here is he lying on it,' persisted K. on his side. 'But look more carefully,' said the landlady in annoyance, 'is he really lying down?' 'No,' said K. now, 'he's floating, and now I can see it, it's not a board at all, but probably a rope, and the young man is taking a high leap.' 'You see!' replied the landlady triumphantly, 'he's leaping, that's how the official messengers practise. I knew quite well that you would make it out. Can you make out his face, too?' 'I can only make out his face very dimly,' said K., 'he's obviously making a great effort, his mouth is open, his eyes tightly shut and his hair fluttering.' 'Well done,' said the landlady appreciatively, 'nobody who never saw him could have made out more than that. But he was a beautiful young man. I only saw him once for a second and I'll never forget him.' 'Who was he then?' asked K. 'He was the messenger that Klamm sent to call me to him the first time.'

K. could not hear properly, his attention was distracted by the rattling of glass. He immediately discovered the cause of the disturbance. The assistants were standing outside in the yard hopping from one foot to the other in the snow, behaving as if they were glad to see him again; in their joy they pointed each other out to him and kept tapping all the time on the kitchen window. At a threatening gesture from K. they stopped at once, tried to pull one another away, but the one would slip immediately from the grasp of the other and soon they were both back at the window again. K. hurried into the annex where the assistants could not see him from outside and he would not have to see them. But the soft and as it were beseeching tapping on the window-pane followed him there too for a long time.

'The assistants again,' he said apologetically to the landlady and pointed outside. But she paid no attention to him; she had taken the portrait from him, looked at it, smoothed it out, and pushed it again under her pillow. Her movements had become slower, but not with weariness, but with the burden of memory. She had wanted to tell K. the story of her life and had forgotten about him in thinking of the story itself. She was playing with the fringe of her wrap. A little time went by before she looked up, passed her hand over her eyes, and said: 'This wrap was given me by Klamm. And the nightcap, too. The portrait, the wrap, and the nightcap, these are the only three things of his I have as keepsakes. I'm not young like Frieda, I'm not so ambitious as she is, nor so sensitive either, she's very sensitive to put it bluntly, I know how to accommodate myself to life, but one thing I must admit, I couldn't have held out so long here without these three keepsakes. Perhaps these three things seem very trifling to you, but let me tell you, Frieda, who has had relations with Klamm for a long time, doesn't possess a single keepsake from him. I have asked her, she's too fanciful, and too difficult to please besides; I, on the other hand, though I was only three times with Klamm – after that he never asked me to come again, I don't know why – I managed to bring three presents back with me all the same, having a premonition that my time would be short. Of course one must make a point of it. Klamm gives nothing of himself, but if one sees something one likes lying about there, one can get it out of him.'

K. felt uncomfortable listening to these tales, much as they interested him. 'How long ago was all that, then?' he asked with a sigh.

'Over twenty years ago,' replied the landlady, 'considerably over twenty years.'

'So one remains faithful to Klamm as long as that,' said K. 'But are you aware, madam, that these stories give me grave alarm when I think of my future married life?'

The landlady seemed to consider this intrusion of his own affairs unseasonable and gave him an angry sidelook.

'Don't be angry, madam,' said K. 'I've nothing at all to say against Klamm. All the same, by force of circumstances I have come in a sense in contact with Klamm; that can't be gainsaid even by his greatest admirer. Well, then. As a result of that I am forced whenever Klamm is mentioned to think of myself as well, that can't be altered. Besides, madam,' here K. took hold of her reluctant hand, 'reflect how badly our last talk turned out and that this time we want to part in peace.'

'You're right,' said the landlady, bowing her head, 'but spare me. I'm not more touchy than other people; on the contrary, everyone has his sensitive spots, and I only have this one.'

'Unfortunately it happens to be mine too,' said K., 'but I promise to control myself. Now tell me, madam, how I am to put up with my married life in face of this terrible fidelity, granted that Frieda, too, resembles you in that?'

'Terrible fidelity!' repeated the landlady with a growl. 'Is it a question of fidelity? I'm faithful to my husband – but Klamm? Klamm once chose me as his mistress, can I ever lose that honour? And you ask how you are to put up with Frieda? Oh, Land Surveyor, who are you after all that you dare ask such things?'

'Madam,' said K. warningly.

'I know,' said the landlady, controlling herself, 'but my husband never put such questions. I don't know which to call the unhappier, myself then or Frieda now. Frieda who saucily left Klamm, or myself whom he stopped asking to come. Yet it is probably Frieda, though she hasn't even yet guessed the full extent of her unhappiness, it seems. Still, my thoughts were more exclusively occupied by my unhappiness then, all the same, for I had always to be asking myself one question, and in reality haven't ceased to ask it to this day: Why did this happen? Three times Klamm sent for me, but he never sent a fourth time, no, never a fourth time! What else could I have thought of during those days? What else could I have talked about with my husband, whom I married shortly afterwards? During the day we had no time – we had taken over this inn in a wretched condition and had to struggle to make it respectable – but at night! For years all our nightly talks turned on Klamm and the reason for his changing his mind. And if my husband fell asleep during those talks I woke him and we went on again.'

'Now,' said K., 'if you'll permit me, I'm going to ask a very rude question.'

The landlady remained silent.

'Then I mustn't ask it,' said K. 'Well, that serves my purpose as well.'

'Yes,' replied the landlady, 'that serves your purpose as well, and just that serves it best. You misconstrue everything, even a person's silence. You can't do anything else. I allow you to ask your question.'

'If I misconstrue everything, perhaps I misconstrue my question as well, perhaps it's not so rude after all. I only want to know how you came to meet your husband and how this inn came into your hands.'

The landlady wrinkled her forehead, but said indifferently; 'That's a very simple story. My father was the blacksmith, and Hans, my husband, who was a groom at a big farmer's place, came often to see him. That was just after my last meeting with Klamm. I was very unhappy and really had no right to be so, for everything had gone as it should, and that I wasn't allowed any longer to see Klamm was Klamm's own decision. It was as it should be then, only the grounds for it were obscure. I was entitled to inquire into them, but I had no right to be unhappy; still I was, all the same, couldn't work, and sat in our front garden all day. There Hans saw me, often sat down beside me. I didn't complain to him, but he knew how things were, and as he was a good young man, he wept with me. The wife of the landlord at that time had died and he had consequently to give up business – besides he was already an old man. Well once as he passed our garden and saw us sitting there, he stopped and without more ado offered us the inn to rent, didn't ask for any money in advance, for he trusted us, and set the rent at a very low figure. I didn't want to be a burden on my father, nothing else mattered to me, and so thinking of the inn and of my new work that might help me to forget a little, I gave Hans my hand. That's the whole story.'

There was a silence for a little, then K. said: 'The behaviour of the landlord was generous, but rash, or had he particular grounds for trusting you both?'

'He knew Hans well,' said the landlady: 'he was Hans's uncle.'

'Well then,' said K., 'Hans's family must have been very anxious to be connected with you?'

'It may be so,' said the landlady, 'I don't know. I've never bothered about it.'

'But it must have been so all the same,' said K., 'seeing that the family was ready to make such a sacrifice and to give the inn into your hands absolutely without security.'

'It wasn't imprudent, as was proved later,' said the landlady. 'I threw myself into the work, I was strong, I was the blacksmith's daughter, I didn't need a maid or servant. I was everywhere, in the taproom, in the kitchen, in the stables, in the yard.

I cooked so well that I even enticed some of the Herrenhof's customers away. You've never been in the inn yet at lunch-time, you don't know our day customers; at that time there were more of them, many of them have stopped coming since. And the consequence was that we were able not merely to pay the rent regularly, but after a few years we bought the whole place and today it's practically free of debt. The further consequence, I admit, was that I ruined my health, got heart disease, and am now an old woman. Probably you think that I'm much older than Hans, but the fact is that he's only two or three years younger than me and will never grow any older either, for at his work – smoking his pipe, listening to the customers, knocking out his pipe again, and fetching an occasional pot of beer – at that sort of work one doesn't grow old.'

'What you've done has been splendid,' said K. 'I don't doubt that for a moment, but we were speaking of the time before your marriage, and it must have been an extraordinary thing at that stage for Hans's family to press on the marriage – at a money sacrifice, or at least at such a great risk as the handing over of the inn must have been – and without trusting in anything but your powers of work, which besides nobody knew of then, and Hans's power of work, which everybody must have known beforehand were nil.'

'Oh, well,' said the landlady wearily. 'I know what you're getting at and how wide you are of the mark. Klamm had absolutely nothing to do with the matter. Why should he have concerned himself about me, or better, how could he in any case have concerned himself about me? He knew nothing about me by that time. The fact that he had ceased to summon me was a sign that he had forgotten me. When he stops summoning people, he forgets them completely. I didn't want to talk of this before Frieda. And it's not mere forgetting, it's something more than that. For anybody one has forgotten can come back to one's memory again of course. With Klamm that's impossible. Anybody that he stops summoning he has forgotten completely, not only as far as the past is concerned, but literally for the future as well. If I try very hard I can of course think myself into your ideas, valid, perhaps, in the very different land you come from. But it's next thing to madness to imagine that Klamm could have given me Hans as a husband simply that I might have no great difficulty in going to him if he should summon me sometime again. Where is the man who could hinder me from running to Klamm if Klamm lifted his little finger? Madness, absolute madness, one begins to feel confused oneself when one plays with such mad ideas.'

'No,' said K., 'I've no intention of getting confused; my thoughts hadn't gone so far as you imagined, though, to tell the truth, they were on that road. For the moment the only thing that surprises me is that Hans's relations expected so much from his marriage and that these expectations were actually fulfilled, at the sacrifice of your sound heart and your health, it is true. The idea that these facts were connected with Klamm occurred to me, I admit, but not with the bluntness, or not till now with the bluntness that you give it – apparently with no object but to have a dig at me, because that gives you pleasure. Well, make the most of your pleasure! My idea, however, was this: first of all Klamm was obviously the occasion of your marriage. If it hadn't been for Klamm you wouldn't have been unhappy and wouldn't have been sitting doing nothing in the garden, if it hadn't been for Klamm Hans wouldn't have seen you sitting there, if it hadn't been that you were unhappy a shy man like Hans would never have ventured to speak, if it hadn't been for Klamm Hans would never have found you in tears, if it hadn't been for Klamm the good uncle would never have seen you sitting there together peacefully, if it hadn't been for Klamm you wouldn't have been indifferent to what life still offered you, and therefore would never have married Hans. Now in all this there's enough of Klamm already, it seems to me. But that's not all. If you hadn't been trying to forget, you certainly wouldn't have overtaxed your strength so much and done so splendidly with the inn. So Klamm was there too. But apart from that Klamm is also the root cause of your illness, for before your marriage your heart was already worn out with your hopeless passion for him. The only question that remains now is, what made Hans's relatives so eager for the marriage? You yourself said just now that to be Klamm's mistress is a distinction that can't be lost, so it may have been that that attracted them. But besides that, I imagine, they had the hope that the lucky star that led you to Klamm – assuming that it was a lucky star, but you maintain that it was – was your star and so would remain constant to you and not leave you quite so quickly and suddenly as Klamm did.'

'Do you mean all this in earnest?' asked the landlady.

'Yes, in earnest,' replied K. immediately, 'only I consider Hans's relations were neither right nor entirely wrong in their hopes, and I think, too, I can see the mistake that they made. In appearance, of course, everything seems to have succeeded. Hans is well provided for, he has a handsome wife, is looked up to, and the inn is free of debt. Yet in reality everything has not succeeded, he would certainly have been much happier with a simple girl who gave him her first love, and if he sometimes stands in the inn there as if lost, as you complain, and because he really feels as if he were lost – without being unhappy over it, I grant you, I know that much about him already – it's just as true that a handsome, intelligent young man like him would be happier with another wife, and by happier I mean more independent, industrious, manly. And you yourself certainly can't be happy, seeing you say you wouldn't be able to go on without these three keepsakes, and your heart is bad, too. Then were Hans's relatives mistaken in their hopes? I don't think so. The blessing was over you, but they didn't know how to bring it down.'

'Then what did they miss doing?' asked the landlady. She was lying outstretched on her back now gazing up at the ceiling.

'To ask Klamm,' said K.

'So we're back at your case again,' said the landlady.

'Or at yours,' said K. 'Our affairs run parallel.'

'What do you want from Klamm?' asked the landlady. She had sat up, had shaken out the pillows so as to lean her back against them, and looked K. full in the eyes. 'I've told you frankly about my experiences, from which you should have been able to learn something. Tell me now as frankly what you want to ask Klamm. I've had great trouble in persuading Frieda to go up to her room and stay there, I was afraid you wouldn't talk freely enough in her presence.'

'I have nothing to hide,' said K. 'But first of all I want to draw your attention to something. Klamm forgets immediately you say. Now in the first place that seems very improbable to me, and secondly it is undemonstrable, obviously nothing more than legend, thought out moreover by the flapperish minds of those who have been in Klamm's favour. I'm surprised that you believe in such a banal invention.'

'It's no legend,' said the landlady, 'it's much rather the result of general experience.'

'I see, a thing then to be refuted by further experience,' said K. 'Besides there's another distinction still between your case and Frieda's. In Frieda's case it didn't happen that Klamm never summoned her again, on the contrary he summoned her but she didn't obey. It's even possible that he's still waiting for her.'

The landlady remained silent, and only looked K. up and down with a considering stare. At last she said: 'I'll try to listen quietly to what you have to say. Speak frankly and don't spare my feelings. I've only one request. Don't use Klamm's name. Call him "him" or something, but don't mention him by name.'

'Willingly,' replied K., 'but what I want from him is difficult to express. Firstly, I want to see him at close quarters; then I want to hear his voice; then I want to get from him what his attitude is to our marriage. What I shall ask from him after that depends on the outcome of our interview. Lots of things may come up in the course of talking, but still the most important thing for me is to be confronted with him. You see I haven't yet spoken with a real official. That seems to be more difficult to manage than I had thought. But now I'm put under the obligation of speaking to him as a private person, and that, in my opinion, is much easier to bring about. As an official I can only speak to him in his bureau in the Castle, which may be inaccessible, or – and that's questionable, too – in the Herrenhof. But as a private person I can speak to him anywhere, in a house, in the street, wherever I happen to meet him. If I should find the official in front of me, then I would be glad to accost him as well, but that's not my primary object.'

'Right,' said the landlady pressing her face into the pillows as if she were uttering something shameful, 'if by using my influence I can manage to get your request for an interview passed on to Klamm, promise me to do nothing on your own account until the reply comes back.'

'I can't promise that,' said K., 'glad as I would be to fulfil your wishes or your whims. The matter is urgent, you see, especially after the unfortunate outcome of my talk with the Superintendent.'

'That excuse falls to the ground,' said the landlady, 'the Superintendent is a person of no importance. Haven't you found that out? He couldn't remain another day in his post if it weren't for his wife, who runs everything.'

'Mizzi?' asked K. The landlady nodded. 'She was present,' said K. 'Did she express her opinion?' asked the landlady.

'No,' replied K., 'but I didn't get the impression that she could.'

'There,' said the landlady, 'you see how distorted your view of everything here is. In any case: the Superintendent's arrangements for you are of no importance, and I'll talk to his wife when I have time. And if I promise now in addition that Klamm's answer will come in a week at latest, you can't surely have any further grounds for not obliging me.'

'All that is not enough to influence me,' said K. 'My decision is made, and I would try to carry it out even if an unfavourable answer were to come. And seeing that this is my fixed intention, I can't very well ask for an interview beforehand. A thing that would remain a daring attempt, but still an attempt in good faith so long as I didn't ask for an interview, would turn into an open transgression of the law after receiving an unfavourable answer. That frankly would be far worse.'

'Worse?' said the landlady. 'It's a transgression of the law in any case. And now you can do what you like. Reach me over my skirt.'

Without paying any regard to K.'s presence she pulled on her skirt and hurried into the kitchen. For a long time already K. had been hearing noises in the dining-room. There was a tapping on the kitchen-hatch. The assistants had unfastened it and were shouting that they were hungry. Then other faces appeared at it. One could even hear a subdued song being chanted by several voices.

Undeniably K.'s conversation with the landlady had greatly delayed the cooking of the midday meal, it was not ready yet and the customers had assembled. Nevertheless nobody had dared to set foot in the kitchen after the landlady's order. But now when the observers at the hatch reported that the landlady was coming, the maids immediately ran back to the kitchen, and as K. entered the dining-room a surprisingly large company, more than twenty, men and women – all attired in provincial but not rustic clothes – streamed back from the hatch to the tables to make sure of their seats. Only at one little table in the corner was a married couple seated already with a few children. The man, a kindly, blue-eyed person with disordered grey hair and beard, stood bent over the children and with a knife beat time to their singing, which he perpetually strove to soften. Perhaps he was trying to make them forget their hunger by singing. The landlady threw a few indifferent words of apology to her customers, nobody complained of her conduct. She looked round for the landlord, who had fled from the difficulty of the situation, however, long ago. Then she went slowly into the kitchen; she did not take any more notice of K., who hurried to Frieda in her room.

7

Upstairs K. ran into the teacher. The room was improved almost beyond recognition, so well had Frieda set to work. It was well aired, the stove amply stoked, the floor scrubbed, the bed put in order, the maids' filthy pile of things and even their photographs cleared away; the table, which had literally struck one in the eye before with its crust of accumulated dust, was covered with a white embroidered cloth. One was in a position to receive visitors now. K.'s small change of underclothes hanging before the fire – Frieda must have washed them early in the morning – did not spoil the impression much. Frieda and the teacher were sitting at the table, they rose at K.'s entrance. Frieda greeted K. with a kiss, the teacher bowed slightly. Distracted and still agitated by his talk with the landlady, K. began to apologize for not having been able yet to visit the teacher; it was as if he were assuming that the teacher had called on him finally because he was impatient at K.'s absence. On the other hand, the teacher in his precise way only seemed now gradually to remember that sometime or other there had been some mention between K. and himself of a visit. 'You must be Land Surveyor,' he said slowly, 'the stranger I had a few words with the other day in the church square.' 'I am,' replied K. shortly; the behaviour which he had submitted to when he felt homeless he did not intend to put up with now here in his room. He turned to Frieda and consulted with her about an important visit which he had to pay at once and for which he would need his best clothes. Without further inquiry Frieda called over the assistants, who were already busy examining the new tablecloth, and commanded them to brush K.'s suit and clothes – which he had begun to take off – down in the yard. She herself took a shirt from the line and ran down to the kitchen to iron it.

Now K. was left alone with the teacher, who was seated silently again at the table; K. kept him waiting for a little longer, drew off his shirt and began to wash himself at the tap. Only then, with his back to the teacher, did he ask him the reason for his visit. 'I have come at the instance of the Parish Superintendent,' he said. K. made ready to listen. But as the noise of the water made it difficult to catch what K. said, the teacher had to come nearer and lean against the wall beside him. K. excused his washing and his hurry by the urgency of his coming appointment. The teacher swept aside his excuses, and said: 'You were discourteous to the Parish Superintendent, an old and experienced man who should be treated with respect.' 'Whether I was discourteous or not I can't say,' said K. while he dried himself, 'but that I had other things to think of than polite behaviour is true enough, for my existence is at stake, which is threatened by a scandalous official bureaucracy whose particular failings I needn't mention to you, seeing that you're an acting member of it yourself. Has the Parish Superintendent complained about me?' 'Where's the man that he would need to complain of?' asked the teacher. 'And even if there was anyone, do you think he would ever do it? I've only made out at his dictation a short protocol on your interview, and that has shown me clearly enough how kind the Superintendent was and what your answers were like.'

While K. was looking for his comb, which Frieda must have cleared away somewhere, he said: 'What? A protocol? Drawn up afterwards in my absence by someone who wasn't at the interview at all? That's not bad. And why on earth a protocol? Was it an official interview then?' 'No,' replied the teacher, 'a semi-official one, the protocol too was only semi-official. It was merely drawn up because with us everything must be done in strict order. In any case it's finished now, and it doesn't better your credit.' K., who had at last found the comb, which had been tucked into the bed, said more calmly: 'Well, then, it's finished. Have you come to tell me that?' 'No,' said the teacher, 'but I'm not a machine and I had to give you my opinion. My instructions are only another proof of the Superintendent's kindness; I want to emphasize that his kindness in this instance is incomprehensible to me, and that I only carry out his instructions because it's my duty and out of respect to the Superintendent.' Washed and combed, K. now sat down at the table to wait for his shirt and clothes; he was not very curious to know the message that the teacher had brought, he was influenced besides by the landlady's low opinion of the Superintendent. 'It must be after twelve already, surely?' he said, thinking of the distance he had to walk; then he remembered himself, and said: 'You want to give me some message from the Superintendent.' 'Well, yes,' said the teacher, shrugging his shoulders as if he were discarding all responsibility. 'The Superintendent is afraid that, if the decision in your case takes too long, you might do something rash on your own account. For my own part I don't know why he should fear that – my own opinion is that you should just be allowed to do what you like. We aren't your guardian angels and we're not obliged to run after you in all your doings. Well and good. The Superintendent, however, is of a different opinion. He can't of course hasten the decision itself, which is a matter for the authorities. But in his own sphere of jurisdiction he wants to provide a temporary and truly generous settlement; it simply lies with you to accept it. He offers you provisionally the post of school janitor.' At first K. thought very little of the offer made him, but the fact that an offer had been made seemed to him not without significance. It seemed to point to the fact that in the Superintendent's opinion he was in a position to look after himself, to carry out projects against which the Town Council itself was preparing certain counter measures. And how seriously they were taking the matter! The teacher, who had already been waiting for a while, and who before that, moreover, had made out the protocol, must of course have been told to run here by the Superintendent. When the teacher saw that he had made K. reflect at last, he went on: 'I put my objections. I pointed out that up till now a janitor hadn't been found necessary; the churchwarden's wife cleared up the place from time to time, and Fräulein Gisa, the second teacher, overlooked the matter. I had trouble enough with the children, I didn't want to be bothered by a janitor as well. The Superintendent pointed out that all the same the school was very dirty. I replied, keeping to the truth, that it wasn't so very bad. And, I went on, would it be any better if we took on this man as janitor? Most certainly not. Apart from the fact he didn't know the work, there were only two big classrooms in the school, and no additional room; so the janitor and his family would have to live, sleep, perhaps even cook in one of the classrooms, which could hardly make for greater cleanliness. But the Superintendent laid stress on the fact that this post would keep you out of difficulties, and that consequently you would do your utmost to fill it creditably; he suggested further, that along with you we would obtain the services of your wife and your assistants, so that the school should be kept in first-rate order, and not only it, but the school-garden as well. I easily proved that this would not hold water. At last the Superintendent couldn't bring forward a single argument in your favour; he laughed and merely said that you were a Land Surveyor after all and so should be able to lay out the vegetable beds beautifully. Well, against a joke there's no argument, and so I came to you with the proposal.' 'You've taken your trouble for nothing, teacher,' said K. 'I have no intention of accepting the post.' 'Splendid!' said the teacher. 'Splendid! You decline quite unconditionally,' and he took his hat, bowed, and went.

Immediately afterwards Frieda came rushing up the stairs with an excited face, the shirt still unironed in her hand; she did not reply to K.'s inquiries. To distract her he told her about the teacher and the offer; she had hardly heard it when she flung the shirt on the bed and ran out again. She soon came back, but with the teacher, who looked annoyed and entered without any greeting. Frieda begged him to have a little patience – obviously she had done that already several times on the way up – then drew K. through a side door of which he had never suspected the existence, on to the neighbouring loft, and then at last, out of breath with excitement, told what had happened to her. Enraged that Frieda had humbled herself by making an avowal to K., and – what was still worse – had yielded to him merely to secure him an interview with Klamm, and after all had gained nothing but, so she alleged, cold and moreover insincere professions, the landlady was resolved to keep K. no longer in her house; if he had connexions with the Castle, then he should take advantage of them at once, for he must leave the house that very day, that very minute, and she would only take him back again at the express order and command of the authorities: but she hoped it would not come to that, for she too had connexions with the Castle and would know how to make use of them. Besides, he was only in the inn because of the landlord's negligence, and moreover he was not in a state of destitution, for this very morning he had boasted of a roof which was always free to him for the night. Frieda of course was to remain; if Frieda wanted to go with K. she, the landlady, would be very sorry; down in the kitchen she had sunk into a chair by the fire and cried at the mere thought of it. The poor, sick woman; but how could she behave otherwise, now that, in her imagination at any rate, it was a matter involving the honour of Klamm's keepsakes? That was how matters stood with the landlady. Frieda of course would follow him, K., wherever he wanted to go. Yet the position of both of them was very bad in any case, just for that reason she had greeted the teacher's offer with such joy; even if it were not a suitable post for K., yet it was – that was expressly insisted on – only a temporary post; one would gain a little time and would easily find other chances, even if the final decision should turn out to be unfavourable. 'If it comes to the worst,' cried Frieda at last, falling on K.'s neck, 'we'll go away, what is there in the village to keep us? But for the time being, darling, we'll accept the offer, won't we? I've fetched the teacher back again, you've only to say to him "Done", that's all, and we'll move over to the school.'

'It's a great nuisance,' said K. without quite meaning it, for he was not much concerned about his lodgings, and in his underclothes he was shivering up here in the loft, which without wall or window on two sides was swept by a cold draught, 'you've arranged the room so comfortably and now we must leave it. I would take up the post very, very unwillingly; the few snubs I've already had from the teacher have been painful enough, and now he's to become my superior, no less. If we could stay here a little while longer, perhaps my position might change for the better this very afternoon. If you would only remain here at least, we could wait on for a little and give the teacher a non-committal answer. As for me, if it came to the worst, I could really always find a lodging for the night with Bar –' Frieda stopped him by putting her hand over his mouth. 'No, not that,' she said beseechingly, 'please never mention that again. In everything else I'll obey you. If you like I'll stay on here by myself, sad as it will be for me. If you like, we'll refuse the offer, wrong as that would seem to me. For look here, if you find another possibility, even this afternoon, why, it's obvious that we would throw up the post in the school at once; nobody would object. And as for your humiliation in front of the teacher, let me see to it that there will be none; I'll speak to him myself, you'll only have to be there and needn't say anything, and later, too, it will be just the same, you'll never be made to speak to him if you don't want to, I – I alone – will be his subordinate in reality, and I won't be even that, for I know his weak points. So you see nothing will be lost if we take on the post, and a great deal if we refuse it; above all, if you don't wring something out of the Castle this very day, you'll never manage to find, even for yourself, anywhere at all in the village to spend the night in, anywhere, that is, of which I needn't be ashamed as your future wife. And if you don't manage to find a roof for the night, do you really expect me to sleep here in my warm room, while I know that you are wandering about out there in the dark and cold?' K., who had been trying to warm himself all this time by clapping his chest with his arms like a carter, said: 'Then there's nothing left but to accept; come along!'

When they returned to the room he went straight over to the fire; he paid no attention to the teacher; the latter, sitting at the table, drew out his watch and said: 'It's getting late.' 'I know, but we're completely agreed at last,' said Frieda, 'we accept the post.' 'Good,' said the teacher, 'but the post is offered to the Land Surveyor; he must say the word himself.' Frieda came to K.'s help. 'Really,' she said, 'he accepts the post. Don't you, K.?' So K. could confine his declaration to a simple 'Yes,' which was not even directed to the teacher but to Frieda. 'Then,' said the teacher, 'the only thing that remains for me is to acquaint you with your duties, so that in that respect we can understand each other once and for all. You have, Land Surveyor, to clean and heat both classrooms daily, to make any small repairs in the house, further, to look after the class and gymnastic apparatus personally, to keep the garden path free of snow, run messages for me and the lady teacher, and look after all the work in the garden in the warmer seasons of the year. In return for that you have the right to live in whichever one of the classrooms you like; but, when both rooms are not being used at the same time for teaching, and you are in the room that is needed, you must of course move to the other room. You mustn't do any cooking in the school; in return you and your dependants will be given your meals here in the inn at the cost of the Town Council. That you must behave in a manner consonant with the dignity of the school, and in particular that the children during school hours must never be allowed to witness any unedifying matrimonial scenes, I mention only in passing, for as an educated man you must of course know that. In connexion with that I want to say further that we must insist on your relations with Fräulein Frieda being legitimized at the earliest possible moment. About all this and a few other trifling matters, an agreement will be made out, which as soon as you move over to the school must be signed by you.' To K. all this seemed of no importance, as if it did not concern him or at any rate did not bind him; but the self-importance of the teacher irritated him, and he said carelessly: 'I know, they're the usual duties.' To wipe away the impression created by this remark Frieda inquired about the salary. 'Whether there will be any salary,' said the teacher, 'will only be considered after a month's trial service.' 'But that is hard on us,' said Frieda. 'We'll have to marry on practically nothing, and have nothing to set up house on. Couldn't you make a representation to the Town Council, sir, to give us a small salary at the start? Couldn't you advise that?' 'No,' replied the teacher, who continued to direct his words to K. 'Representations to the Town Council will only be made if I give the word, and I shan't give it. The post has been given to you only as a personal favour, and one can't stretch a favour too far, if one has any consciousness of one's obvious responsibilities.' Now K. intervened at last, almost against his will. 'As for the favour, teacher,' he said, 'it seems to me that you're mistaken. The favour is perhaps rather on my side.' 'No,' replied the teacher, smiling now that he had compelled K. to speak at last. 'I'm completely grounded on that point. Our need for a janitor is just about as urgent as our need for a Land Surveyor. Janitor, Land Surveyor, in both cases it's a burden on our shoulders. I'll still have a lot of trouble thinking out how I'm to justify the post to the Town Council. The best thing and the most honest thing would be to throw the proposal on the table and not justify anything.' 'That's just what I meant,' replied K., 'you must take me on against your will. Although it causes you grave perturbation, you must take me on. But when one is compelled to take someone else on, and this someone else allows himself to be taken on, then he is the one who grants the favour.' 'Strange!' said the teacher. 'What is it that compels us to take you on? The only thing that compels us is the Superintendent's kind heart, his too kind heart. I see, Land Surveyor, that you'll have to rid yourself of a great many illusions, before you can become a serviceable janitor. And remarks such as these hardly produce the right atmosphere for the granting of an eventual salary. I notice, too, with regret that your attitude will give me a great deal of trouble yet; all this time – I've seen it with my own eyes and yet can scarcely believe it – you've been talking to me in your shirt and drawers.' 'Quite so,' exclaimed K. with a laugh, and he clapped his hands. 'These terrible assistants, where have they been all this time?' Frieda hurried to the door; the teacher, who noticed that K. was no longer to be drawn into conversation, asked her when she would move into the school. 'Today,' said Frieda. 'Then tomorrow I'll come to inspect matters,' said the teacher, waved a good-bye, and made to go out through the door, which Frieda had opened for herself, but ran into the maids, who already were arriving with their things to take possession of the room again; and he, who made way for nobody, had to slip between them: Frieda followed him. 'You're surely in a hurry,' said K., who this time was very pleased with the maids; 'had you to push your way in while we're still here?' They did not answer, only twisted their bundles in embarrassment, from which K. saw the well-known filthy rags projecting. 'So you've never washed your thing yet,' said K. It was not said maliciously, but actually with a certain indulgence. They noticed it, opened their hard mouths in concert, showed their beautiful animal-like teeth and laughed noiselessly, 'Come along,' said K., 'put your things down, it's your room after all.' As they still hesitated, however – the room must have seemed to them all too well transformed – K. took one of them by the arm to lead her forward. But he let her go at once, so astonished was the gaze of both, which, after a brief glance between them, was now turned unflinchingly on K. 'But now you've stared at me long enough,' he said, repelling a vague, unpleasant sensation, and he took up his clothes and boots, which Frieda, timidly followed by the assistants, had just brought, and drew them on. The patience which Frieda had with the assistants, always incomprehensible to him, now struck him again. After a long search she had found them below peacefully eating their lunch, the untouched clothes which they should have been brushing in the yard crumpled in their laps; then she had had to brush everything herself, and yet she, who knew how to keep the common people in their places, had not even scolded them, and instead spoke in their presence of their grave negligence as if it were a trifling peccadillo, and even slapped one of them lightly, almost caressingly, on the cheek. Presently K. would have to talk to her about this. But now it was high time to be gone. 'The assistants will stay here to help you with the removing,' he said. They were not in the least pleased with this arrangement; happy and full, they would have been glad of a little exercise. Only when Frieda said, 'Certainly, you stay here,' did they yield. 'Do you know where I'm going?' asked K. 'Yes,' replied Frieda. 'And you don't want to hold me back any longer?' asked K. 'You'll find obstacles enough,' she replied, 'what does anything I say matter in comparison!' She kissed K. goodbye, and as he had had nothing at lunch-time, gave him a little packet of bread and sausage which she had brought for him from downstairs, reminded him that he must not return here again but to the school, and accompanied him, with her hand on his shoulder, to the door.

8

At first K. was glad to have escaped from the crush of the maids and the assistants in the warm room. It was freezing a little, the snow was firmer, the going easier. But already darkness was actually beginning to fall, and he hastened his steps.

The Castle, whose contours were already beginning to dissolve, lay silent as ever; never yet had K. seen there the slightest sign of life – perhaps it was quite impossible to recognize anything at that distance, and yet the eye demanded it and could not endure that stillness. When K. looked at the Castle, often it seemed to him as if he were observing someone who sat quietly there in front of him gazing, not lost in thought and so oblivious of everything, but free and untroubled, as if he were alone with nobody to observe him, and yet must notice that he was observed, and all the same remained with his calm not even slightly disturbed; and really – one did not know whether it was cause or effect – the gaze of the observer could not remain concentrated there, but slid away. This impression today was strengthened still further by the early dusk; the longer he looked, the less he could make out and the deeper everything was lost in the twilight.

Just as K. reached the Herrenhof, which was still unlighted, a window was opened in the first storey, and a stout, smooth-shaven young man in a fur coat leaned out and then remained at the window. He did not seem to make the slightest response to K.'s greeting. Neither in the hall nor in the taproom did K. meet anybody; the smell of stale beer was still worse than last time; such a state of things was never allowed even in the inn by the bridge. K. went straight over to the door through which he had observed Klamm, and lifted the latch cautiously, but the door was barred; then he felt for the place where the peephole was, but the pin apparently was fitted so well that he could not find the place, so he struck a match. He was startled by a cry. In the corner between the door and the till, near the fire, a young girl was crouching and staring at him in the flare of the match, with partially opened sleep-drunken eyes. She was evidently Frieda's successor. She soon collected herself and switched on the electric light; her expression was cross, then she recognized K. 'Ah, the Land Surveyor,' she said smiling, held out her hand, and introduced herself. 'My name is Pepi.' She was small, red-cheeked, plump; her opulent reddish golden hair was twisted into a strong plait, yet some of it escaped and curled round her temples; she was wearing a dress of grey shimmering material, falling in straight lines, which did not suit her in the least; at the foot it was drawn together by a childishly clumsy silken band with tassels falling from it, which impeded her movements. She inquired after Frieda and asked whether she would come back soon. It was a question which verged on insolence. 'As soon as Frieda went away,' she said next, 'I was called here urgently because they couldn't find anybody suitable at the moment; I've been a chambermaid till now, but this isn't a change for the better. There's lots of evening and night work in this job, it's very tiring, I don't think I'll be able to stand it. I'm not surprised that Frieda threw it up.' 'Frieda was very happy here,' said K., to make her aware definitely of the difference between Frieda and herself, which she did not seem to appreciate. 'Don't you believe her,' said Pepi. 'Frieda can keep a straight face better than other people can. She doesn't admit what she doesn't want to admit, and so nobody noticed that she had anything to admit. I've been in service here with her several years already. We've slept together all that time in the same bed, yet I'm not intimate with her, and by now I'm quite out of her thoughts, that's certain. Perhaps her only friend is the old landlady of the Bridge Inn, and that tells a story too.' 'Frieda is my fiancée,' said K., searching at the same time for the peephole in the door. 'I know,' said Pepi, 'that's just the reason why I've told you. Otherwise it wouldn't have any interest for you.'

'I understand,' said K. 'You mean that I should be proud to have won such a reticent girl?' 'That's so,' said she, laughing triumphantly, as if she had established a secret understanding with K. regarding Frieda.

But it was not her actual words that troubled K. and deflected him for a little from his search, but rather her appearance and her presence in this place. Certainly she was much younger than Frieda, almost a child still, and her clothes were ludicrous; she had obviously dressed in accordance with the exaggerated notions which she had of the importance of a barmaid's position. And these notions were right enough in their way in her, for this position of which she was still incapable had come to her unearned and unexpectedly, and only for the time being; not even the leather reticule with Frieda always wore on her belt had been entrusted to her. And her ostensible dissatisfaction with the position was nothing but showing off. And yet, in spite of her childish mind, she too, apparently, had connexions with the Castle; if she was not lying, she had been a chambermaid; without being aware of what she possessed she slept through the days here, and though if he took this tiny, plump, slightly round-backed creature in his arms he could not extort from her what she possessed, yet that could bring him in contact with it and inspirit him for his difficult task. Then could her case now be much the same as Frieda's? Oh, no, it was different. One had only to think of Frieda's look to know that. K. would never have touched Pepi. All the same he had to lower his eyes for a little now, so greedily was he staring at her.

'It's against orders for the light to be on,' said Pepi, switching it off again. 'I only turned it on because you gave me such a fright. What do you want here really? Did Frieda forget anything?' 'Yes,' said K., pointing to the door, 'a table-cover, a white embroidered table-cover, here in the next room.' 'Yes, her table-cover,' said Pepi. 'I remember it, a pretty piece of work.

I helped with it myself, but it can hardly be in that room.' 'Frieda thinks it is. Who lives in it, then?' asked K. 'Nobody,' said Pepi, 'it's the gentlemen's room; the gentlemen eat and drink there; that is, it's reserved for that, but most of them remain upstairs in their rooms.' 'If I knew,' said K., 'that nobody was in there just now, I would like very much to go in and have a look for the table-cover. But one can't be certain; Klamm, for instance, is often in the habit of sitting there.' 'Klamm is certainly not there now,' said Pepi. 'He's making ready to leave this minute, the sledge is waiting for him in the yard.'

Without a word of explanation K. left the taproom at once; when he reached the hall he returned, instead of to the door, to the interior of the house, and in a few steps reached the courtyard. How still and lovely it was here! A four-square yard, bordered on three sides by the house buildings, and towards the street – a side-street which K. did not know – by a high white wall with a huge, heavy gate, open now. Here where the court was, the house seemed stiller than at the front; at any rate the whole first storey jutted out and had a more impressive appearance, for it was encircled by a wooden gallery closed in except for one tiny slit for looking through. At the opposite side from K. and on the ground floor, but in the corner where the opposite wing of the house joined the main building, there was an entrance to the house, open, and without a door. Before it was standing a dark, closed sledge to which a pair of horses was yoked. Except for the coachman, whom at that distance and in the falling twilight K. guessed at rather than recognized, nobody was to be seen.

Looking about him cautiously, his hands in his pockets, K. slowly coasted round two sides of the yard until he reached the sledge. The coachman – one of the peasants who had been the other night in the taproom – smart in his fur coat, watched K. approaching non-committally, much as one follows the movements of a cat. Even when K. was standing beside him and had greeted him, and the horses were becoming a little restive at seeing a man looming out of the dusk, he remained completely detached. That exactly suited K.'s purpose. Leaning against the wall of the house he took out his lunch, thought gratefully of Frieda and her solicitous provision for him, and meanwhile peered into the house. A very angular and broken stair led downwards and was crossed down below by a low but apparently deep passage; everything was clean and whitewashed, sharply and distinctly defined.

The wait lasted longer than K. had expected. Long ago he had finished his meal, he was getting chilled, the twilight had changed into complete darkness, and still Klamm had not arrived. 'It might be a long time yet,' said a rough voice suddenly, so near to him that K. started. It was the coachman, who, as if waking up, stretched himself and yawned loudly. 'What might be a long time yet?' asked K., not ungrateful at being disturbed, for the perpetual silence and tension had already become a burden. 'Before you go away,' said the coachman. K. did not understand him, but did not ask further; he thought that would be the best means of making the insolent fellow speak. Not to answer here in this darkness was almost a challenge. And actually the coachman asked, after a pause: 'Would you like some brandy?' 'Yes,' said K. without thinking, tempted only too keenly by the offer, for he was freezing. 'Then open the door of the sledge,' said the coachman; 'in the side pocket there are some flasks, take one and have a drink and then hand it up to me. With this fur coat it's difficult for me to get down.' K. was annoyed at being ordered about, but seeing that he had struck up with the coachman he obeyed, even at the possible risk of being surprised by Klamm in the sledge. He opened the wide door and could without more ado have drawn a flask out of the side pocket which was fastened to the inside of the door; but now that it was open he felt an impulse which he could not withstand to go inside the sledge; all he wanted was to sit there for a minute. He slipped inside. The warmth within the sledge was extraordinary, and it remained although the door, which K. did not dare to close, was wide open. One could not tell whether it was a seat one was sitting on, so completely was one surrounded by blankets, cushions, and furs; one could turn and stretch on every side, and always one sank into softness and warmth. His arms spread out, his head supported on pillows which always seemed to be there, K. gazed out of the sledge into the dark house. Why was Klamm such a long time in coming? As if stupefied by the warmth after his long wait in the snow, K. began to wish that Klamm would come soon. The thought that he would rather not be seen by Klamm in his present position touched him only vaguely as a faint disturbance of his comfort. He was supported in this obliviousness by the behaviour of the coachman, who certainly knew that he was in the sledge, and yet let him stay there without once demanding the brandy. That was very considerate, but still K. wanted to oblige him. Slowly, without altering his position, he reached out his hand to the side-pocket. But not the one in the open door, but the one behind him in the closed door; after all, it didn't matter, there were flasks in that one too. He pulled one out, unscrewed the stopper, and smelt; involuntarily he smiled, the perfume was so sweet, so caressing, like praise and good words from someone whom one likes very much, yet one does not know clearly what they are for and has no desire to know, and is simply happy in the knowledge that it is one's friend who is saying them. 'Can this be brandy?' K. asked himself doubtfully and took a taste out of curiosity. Yes, strangely enough it was brandy, and burned and warmed him. How wonderfully it was transformed in drinking out of something which seemed hardly more than a sweet perfume into a drink fit for a coachman! 'Can it be?' K. asked himself as if self-reproachfully, and took another sip.

Then – as K. was just in the middle of a long swig – everything became bright, the electric lights blazed inside on the stairs, in the passages, in the entrance hall, outside above the door Steps could be heard coming down the stairs, the flask fell from K.'s hand, the brandy was spilt over a rug, K. sprang out of the sledge, he had just time to slam the door to, which made a loud noise, when a gentleman came slowly out of the house. The only consolation that remained was that it was not Klamm, or was not that rather a pity? It was the gentleman whom K. had already seen at the window on the first floor. A young man, very good-looking, pink and white, but very serious. K., too, looked at him gravely, but his gravity was on his own account. Really he would have done better to have sent his assistants here, they couldn't have behaved more foolishly than he had done. The gentleman still regarded him in silence, as if he had not enough breath in his overcharged bosom for what had to be said. 'This is unheard of,' he said at last, pushing his hat a little back on his forehead. What next? The gentleman knew nothing apparently of K.'s stay in the sledge, and yet found something that was unheard of? Perhaps that K. had pushed his way in as far as the courtyard? 'How do you come to be here?' the gentleman asked next, more softly now, breathing freely again, resigning himself to the inevitable. What questions to ask! And what could one answer? Was K. to admit simply and flatly to this man that his attempt, begun with so many hopes, had failed? Instead of replying, K. turned to the sledge, opened the door, and retrieved his cap, which he had forgotten there. He noticed with discomfort that the brandy was dripping from the foot-board.

Then he turned again to the gentleman, to show him that he had been in the sledge gave him no more compunction now, besides that wasn't the worst of it; when he was questioned, but only then, he would divulge the fact that the coachman himself had at least asked him to open the door of the sledge. But the real calamity was that the gentleman had surprised him, that there had not been enough time to hide from him so as afterwards to wait in peace for Klamm, or rather that he had not had enough presence of mind to remain in the sledge, close the door and wait there among the rugs for Klamm, or at least to stay there as long as this man was about. True, he couldn't know of course whether it might not be Klamm himself who was coming, in which case it would naturally have been much better to accost him outside the sledge. Yes, there had been many things here for thought, but now there was none, for this was the end.

'Come with me,' said the gentleman, not really as a

command, for the command lay not in the words, but in a slight, studiedly indifferent gesture of the hand which accompanied them. 'I'm waiting here for somebody,' said K., no longer in the hope of any success, but simply on principle. 'Come,' said the gentleman once more quite imperturbably, as if he wanted to show that he had never doubted that K. was waiting for somebody. 'But then I would miss the person I'm waiting for,' said K. with an emphatic nod of his head. In spite of everything that had happened he had the feeling that what he had achieved thus far was something gained, which it was true he only held now in seeming, but which he must not relinquish all the same merely on account of a polite command. 'You'll miss him in any case, whether you go or stay,' said the gentleman, expressing himself bluntly, but showing an unexpected consideration for K.'s line of thought. 'Then I would rather wait for him and miss him,' said K. defiantly; he would certainly not be driven away from here by the mere talk of this young man. Thereupon with his head thrown back and a supercilious look on his face the gentleman closed his eyes for a few minutes, as if he wanted to turn from K.'s senseless stupidity to his own sound reason again, ran the tip of his tongue round his slightly parted lips, and said at last to the coachman: 'Unyoke the horses.'

Obedient to the gentleman, but with a furious side-glance at K., the coachman had now to get down in spite of his fur coat, and began very hesitatingly – as if he did not so much expect a counter-order from the gentleman as a sensible remark from K. – to back the horses and the sledge closer to the side wing, in which apparently, behind a big door, was the shed where the vehicles were kept. K. saw himself deserted, the sledge was disappearing in one direction, in the other, by the way he had come himself, the gentleman was receding, both it was true very slowly, as if they wanted to show K. that it was still in his power to call them back.

Perhaps he had this power, but it would have availed him nothing; to call the sledge back would be to drive himself away.

So he remained standing as one who held the field, but it was a victory which gave him no joy. Alternately he looked at the backs of the gentleman and the coachman. The gentleman had already reached the door through which K. had first come into the courtyard; yet once more he looked back, K. fancied he saw him shaking his head over such obstinacy, then with a short, decisive, final movement he turned away and stepped into the hall, where he immediately vanished. The coachman remained for a while still in the courtyard, he had a great deal of work with the sledge, he had to open the heavy door of the shed, back the sledge into its place, unyoke the horses, lead them to their stalls; all this he did gravely, with concentration, evidently without any hope of starting soon again, and this silent absorption which did not spare a single side-glance for K. seemed to the latter a far heavier reproach than the behaviour of the gentleman. And when now, after finishing his work in the shed, the coachman went across the courtyard in his slow, rolling walk, closed the huge gate and then returned, all very slowly, while he literally looked at nothing but his own footprints in the snow – and finally shut himself into the shed; and now as all the electric lights went out too – for whom should they remain on? – and only up above the slit in the wooden gallery still remained bright, holding one's wandering gaze for a little, it seemed to K. as if at last those people had broken off all relations with him, and as if now in reality he were freer than he had ever been, and at liberty to wait here in this place usually forbidden to him as long as he desired, and had won a freedom such as hardly anybody else had ever succeeded in winning, and as if nobody could dare to touch him or drive him away, or even speak to him; but – this conviction was at least strong – as if at the same time there was nothing more senseless, nothing more hopeless, than this freedom, this waiting, this inviolability.

9

And he tore himself free and went back into the house – this time not along the wall but straight through the snow – and met the landlord in the hall, who greeted him in silence and pointed towards the door of the taproom. K. followed the hint, for he was shivering, and wanted to see human faces; but he was greatly disappointed when he saw there, sitting at a little table – which must have been specially set out, for usually the customers put up with upturned barrels – the young gentleman, and standing before him – an unwelcome sight for K. – the landlady from the Bridge Inn. Pepi, proud, her head thrown back and a fixed smile on her face, conscious of her incontestable dignity, her plait nodding with every movement, hurried to and fro, fetching beer and then pen and ink, for the gentleman had already spread out papers in front of him, was comparing dates which he looked up now in this paper, then again in a paper at the other end of the table, and was preparing to write. From her full height the landlady silently overlooked the gentleman and the papers, her lips pursed a little as if musing; it was as if she had already said everything necessary and it had been well received. 'The Land Surveyor at last,' said the gentleman at K.'s entrance, looking up briefly, then burying himself again in his papers. The landlady, too, only gave K. an indifferent and not in the least surprised glance. But Pepi actually seemed to notice K. for the first time when he went up to the bar and ordered a brandy.

K. leaned there, his hands pressed to his eyes, oblivious of everything. Then he took a sip of the brandy and pushed it back, saying it was undrinkable. 'All the gentlemen drink it,' replied Pepi curtly, poured out the remainder, washed the glass and set it on the rack. 'The gentlemen have better stuff as well,' said K. 'It's possible,' replied Pepi, 'but I haven't,' and with that she was finished with K. and once more at the gentleman's service, who, however, was in need of nothing, and behind whom she only kept walking to and fro in circles, making respectful attempts to catch a glimpse of the papers over his shoulder; but that was only her senseless curiosity and self-importance, which the landlady, too, reprehended with knitted brows.

Then suddenly the landlady's attention was distracted, she stared, listening intently, into vacancy. K. turned round, he could not hear anything in particular, nor did the others seem to hear anything; but the landlady ran on tiptoe and taking large steps to the door which led to the courtyard, peered through the keyhole, turned then to the others with wide, staring eyes and flushed cheeks, signed to them with her finger to come near, and now they peered through the keyhole by turns; the landlady had, of course, the lion's share, but Pepi, too, was considered; the gentleman was on the whole the most indifferent of the three. Pepi and the gentleman came away soon, but the landlady kept on peering anxiously, bent double, almost kneeling; one had almost the feeling that she was only imploring the keyhole now to let her through, for there had certainly been nothing more to see for a long time. When at last she got up, passed her hand over her face, arranged her hair, took a deep breath, and now at last seemed to be trying with reluctance to accustom her eyes again to the room and the people in it, K. said, not so much to get his suspicions confirmed, as to forestall the announcement, so open to attack did he feel now: 'Has Klamm gone already then?' The landlady walked past him in silence, but the gentleman answered from his table: 'Yes, of course. As soon as you gave up your sentry go, Klamm was able to leave. But it's strange how sensitive he is. Did you notice, landlady, how uneasily Klamm looked round him?' The landlady did not appear to have noticed it, but the gentleman went on: 'Well, fortunately there was nothing more to be seen, the coachman had effaced even the footprints in the snow.' 'The landlady didn't notice anything,' said K., but he said it without conviction, merely provoked by the gentleman's assertion, which was uttered in such a final and unanswerable tone. 'Perhaps I wasn't at the keyhole just then,' said the landlady presently, to back up the gentleman, but then she felt compelled to give Klamm his due as well, and added: 'All the same, I can't believe in this terrible sensitiveness of Klamm. We are anxious about him and try to guard him, and so go on to infer that he's terribly sensitive. That's as it should be and it's certainly Klamm's will. But how it is in reality we don't know. Certainly, Klamm will never speak to anybody that he doesn't want to speak to, no matter how much trouble this anybody may take, and no matter how insufferably forward he may be; but that fact alone, that Klamm will never speak to him, never allow him to come into his presence, is enough in itself: why after all should it follow that he isn't able to endure seeing this anybody? At any rate, it can't be proved, seeing that it will never come to the test.' The gentleman nodded eagerly. 'That is essentially my opinion too, of course,' he said, 'if I expressed myself a little differently, it was to make myself comprehensible to the Land Surveyor. All the same it's a fact that when Klamm stepped out of the doorway he looked round him several times.' 'Perhaps he was looking for me,' said K. 'Possibly,' said the gentleman. 'I hadn't thought of that.' They all laughed, Pepi, who hardly understood anything that was being said, loudest of all.

'Seeing we're all so happy here now,' the gentleman went on, 'I want to beg you very seriously, Land Surveyor, to enable me to complete my papers by answering a few questions.' 'There's a great deal of writing there,' said K. glancing at the papers from where he was standing. 'Yes, a wretched bore,' said the gentleman laughing again, 'but perhaps you don't know yet who I am. I'm Momus, Klamm's village secretary.' At these words seriousness descended on the room; although the landlady and Pepi knew quite well who the gentleman was, yet they seemed staggered by the utterance of his name and rank. And even the gentleman himself, as if he had said more than his judgement sanctioned, and as if he were resolved to escape at least from any after-effects of the solemn import implicit in his own words, buried himself in his papers and began to write, so that nothing was heard in the room but the scratching of his pen. 'What is that: village secretary?' asked K. after a pause. The landlady answered for Momus, who now that he had introduced himself did not regard it seemly to give such explanations himself: 'Herr Momus is Klamm's secretary in the same sense as any of Klamm's secretaries, but his official province, and if I'm not mistaken, his official standing' – still writing Momus shook his head decidedly and the landlady amended her phrase – 'well, then, his official province, but not his official standing, is confined to the village. Herr Momus dispatches any clerical work of Klamm's which may become necessary in the village and as Klamm's deputy receives any petitions to Klamm which may be sent by the village.' As, still quite unimpressed by these facts, K. looked at the landlady with vacant eyes, she added in a half-embarrassed tone: 'That's how it's arranged; all the gentlemen in the Castle have their village secretaries.' Momus, who had been listening far more attentively than K., supplied the landlady with a supplementary fact: 'Most of the village secretaries work only for one gentleman, but I work for two, for Klamm and for Vallabene.' 'Yes,' went on the landlady, remembering now on her side too, and turning to K., 'Herr Momus works for two gentlemen, for Klamm and for Vallabene, and so is twice a village secretary.' 'Actually twice,' said K., nodding to Momus – who now, leaning slightly forward, looked him full in the face – as one nods to a child whom one has just heard being praised. If there was a certain contempt in the gesture, then it was either unobserved or else actually expected. Precisely to K., it seemed, who was not considered worthy even to be seen in passing by Klamm, these people had described in detail the services of a man out of Klamm's circle with the unconcealed intention of evoking K.'s recognition and admiration. And yet K. had no proper appreciation of it; he, who with all his powers strove to get a glimpse of Klamm, valued very little, for example, the post of a Momus who was permitted to live in Klamm's eye; for it was not Klamm's environment in itself that seemed to him worth striving for, but rather that he, K., he only and no one else, should attain to Klamm, and should attain to him not to rest with him, but to go on beyond him, farther yet, into the Castle.

And he looked at his watch and said: 'But now I must be going home.' Immediately the position changed in Momus's favour. 'Yes, of course,' the latter replied, 'the school work calls. But you must favour me with just a moment of your time. Only a few short questions.' 'I don't feel in the mood for it,' said K. and turned towards the door. Momus brought down a document on the table and stood up; 'In the name of Klamm I command you to answer my questions.' 'In the name of Klamm!' repeated K., 'does he trouble himself about my affairs, then?' 'As to that,' replied Momus, 'I have no information and you certainly have still less; we can safely leave that to him. All the same I command you by virtue of my function granted by Klamm to stay here and to answer.' 'Land Surveyor,' broke in the landlady, 'I refuse to advise you any further, my advice till now, the most well-meaning that you could have got, has been cast back at me in the most unheard-of manner; and I have come here to Herr Momus – I have nothing to hide – simply to give the office an adequate idea of your behaviour and your intentions and to protect myself for all time from having you quartered on me again; that's how we stand towards each other and that's how we'll always stand, and if I speak my mind accordingly now, I don't do it, I can tell you, to help you, but to ease a little the hard job which Herr Momus is bound to have in dealing with a man like you. All the same, just because of my absolute frankness – and I couldn't deal otherwise than frankly with you even if I were to try – you can extract some advantage for yourself out of what I say, if you only take the trouble. In the present case I want to draw your attention to this, that the only road that can lead you to Klamm is through this protocol here of Herr Momus. But I don't want to exaggerate, perhaps that road won't get you as far as Klamm, perhaps it will stop long before it reaches him; the judgement of Herr Momus will decide that. But in any case that's the only road that will take you in the direction of Klamm. And do you intend to reject that road, for nothing but pride?' 'Oh, madam,' said K., 'that's neither the only road to Klamm, nor is it any better than the others. But you, Mr Secretary, decide this question, whether what I may say here can get as far as Klamm or not.' 'Of course it can,' said Momus, lowering his eyes proudly and gazing at nothing, 'otherwise why should I be secretary here?' 'Now you see, madam,' said K., 'I don't need a road to Klamm, but only to Mr Secretary.' 'I wanted to throw open this road for you,' said the landlady, 'didn't I offer this morning to send your request to Klamm? That might have been done through Herr Momus. But you refused, and yet from now on no other way will remain for you but this one. But frankly, after your attempt on Klamm's privacy, with much less prospect of success. All the same this last, tiny, vanishing, yes, actually invisible hope, is your only one.' 'How is it, madam,' said K., 'that originally you tried so hard to keep me from seeing Klamm, and yet now take my wish to see him quite seriously, and seem to consider me lost largely on account of the miscarrying of my plan? If at one time you can advise me sincerely from your heart against trying to see Klamm at all, how can you possibly drive me on the road to Klamm now, apparently just as sincerely, even though it's admitted that the road may not reach as far as him?' 'Am I driving you on?' asked the landlady. 'Do you call it driving you on when I tell you that your attempt is hopeless? It would really be the limit of audacity if you tried in that way to push the responsibility on to me. Perhaps it's Herr Momus's presence that encourages you to do it. No, Land Surveyor, I'm not trying to drive you on to anything. I can admit only one mistake, that I overestimated you a little when I first saw you. Your immediate victory over Frieda frightened me, I didn't know what you might still be capable of. I wanted to prevent further damage, and thought that the only means of achieving that was to shake your resolution by prayers and threats. Since then I have learned to look on the whole thing more calmly. You can do what you like. Your actions may no doubt leave deep footprints in the snow out there in the courtyard, but they'll do nothing more.' 'The contradiction doesn't seem to me to be quite cleared up,' said K., 'but I'm content with having drawn attention to it. But now I beg you, Mr Secretary, to tell me whether the landlady's opinion is correct, that is, that the protocol which you want to take down from my answers can have the result of gaining me admission to Klamm. If that's the case, I'm ready to answer all your questions at once. In that direction I'm ready, indeed, for anything.' 'No,' replied Momus, 'that doesn't follow at all. It's simply a matter of keeping an adequate record of this afternoon's happenings for Klamm's village register. The record is already complete, there are only two or three omissions which you must fill in for the sake of order; there's no other object in view and no other object can be achieved.' K. gazed at the landlady in silence. 'Why are you looking at me?' asked she, 'did I say anything else? He's always like that, Mr Secretary, he's always like that. Falsifies the information one gives him, and then maintains that he received false information. I've told him from the first and I tell him again today that he hasn't the faintest prospect of being received by Klamm; well, if there's no prospect in any case he won't alter the fact by means of this protocol. Could anything be clearer? I said further that this protocol is the only real official connexion that he can have with Klamm. That too is surely clear and incontestable enough. But if in spite of that he won't believe me, and keeps on hoping – I don't know why or with what idea – that he'll be able to reach Klamm, then so long as he remains in that frame of mind, the only thing that can help him is this one real official connexion he has with Klamm, in other words, this protocol. That's all I have said, and whoever maintains the contrary twists my words maliciously.' 'If that is so, madam,' said K., 'then I beg your pardon, and I've misunderstood you; for I thought – erroneously, as it turns out now – that I could take out of your former words that there was still some very tiny hope for me.' 'Certainly,' replied the landlady, 'that's my meaning exactly. You're twisting my words again, only this time in the opposite way. In my opinion there is such a hope for you, and founded actually on this protocol and nothing else. But it's not of such a nature that you can simply fall on Herr Momus with the question: "Will I be allowed to see Klamm if I answer your questions?" When a child asks questions like that people laugh, when a grown man does it it is an insult to all authority; Herr Momus graciously concealed this under the politeness of his reply. But the hope that I mean consists simply in this, that through the protocol you have a sort of connexion, a sort of connexion perhaps with Klamm. Isn't that enough? If anyone inquired for any service which might earn you the privilege of such a hope, could you bring forward the slightest one? For the last time, that's the best that can be said about this hope of yours, and certainly Herr Momus in his official capacity could never give even the slightest hint of it. For him it's a matter, as he says, merely of keeping a record of this afternoon's happenings, for the sake of order; more than that he won't say, even if you ask him this minute his opinion of what I've said.' 'Will Klamm, then, Mr Secretary,' asked K., 'read the protocol?' 'No,' replied Momus, 'why should he? Klamm can't read every protocol, in fact he reads none. "Keep away from me with your protocols!" he usually says.' 'Land Surveyor,' groaned the landlady, 'you exhaust me with such questions. Do you think it's necessary, or even simply desirable, that Klamm should read this protocol and become acquainted word for word with the trivialities of your life? Shouldn't you rather pray humbly that the protocol should be concealed from Klamm – a prayer, however, that would be just as unreasonable as the other, for who can hide anything from Klamm even though he has given many signs of his sympathetic nature? And is it even necessary for what you call your hope? Haven't you admitted yourself that you would be content if you only got the chance of speaking to Klamm, even if he never looked at you and never listened to you? And won't you achieve that at least through the protocol, perhaps much more?' 'Much more?' asked K. 'In what way?' 'If you wouldn't always talk about things like a child, as if they were for eating! Who on earth can give any answer to such questions? The protocol will be put in Klamm's village register, you have heard that already, more than that can't be said with certainty. But do you know yet the full importance of the protocol, and of Herr Momus, and of the village register? Do you know what it means to be examined by Herr Momus? Perhaps – to all appearances at least – he doesn't know it himself. He sits quietly there and does his duty, for the sake of order, as he says. But consider that Klamm appointed him, that he acts in Klamm's name, that what he does, even if it never reaches Klamm, has yet Klamm's assent in advance. And how can anything have Klamm's assent that isn't filled by his spirit? Far be it from me to offer Herr Momus crude flattery – besides he would absolutely forbid it himself – but I'm speaking of him not as an independent person, but as he is when he has Klamm's assent, as at present; then he's an instrument in the hand of Klamm, and woe to anybody who doesn't obey him.'

The landlady's threat did not daunt K.; of the hopes with which she tried to catch him he was weary. Klamm was far away. Once the landlady had compared Klamm to an eagle, and that had seemed absurd in K.'s eyes, but it did not seem absurd now; he thought of Klamm's remoteness, of his impregnable dwelling, of his silence, broken perhaps only by cries such as K. had never yet heard, of his downward-pressing gaze, which could never be proved or disproved, of his wheelings which could never be disturbed by anything that K. did down below, which far above he followed at the behest of incomprehensible laws and which only for instants were visible – all these things Klamm and the eagle had in common. But assuredly these had nothing to do with the protocol, over which just now Momus was crumbling a roll dusted with salt, which he was eating with beer to help it out, in the process all the papers becoming covered with salt and caraway seeds.

'Good night,' said K. 'I've no objection to any kind of examination,' and now he went at last to the door. 'He's going after all,' said Momus almost anxiously to the landlady. 'He won't dare,' said she; K. heard nothing more, he was already in the hall. It was cold and a strong wind was blowing. From a door on the opposite side came the landlord, he seemed to have been keeping the hall under observation from behind a peephole. He had to hold the tail of his coat round his knees, the wind tore so strongly at him in the hall. 'You're going already, Land Surveyor?' he asked. 'You're surprised at that?' asked K. 'I am,' said the landlord, 'haven't you been examined then?' 'No,' replied K. 'I didn't let myself be examined.' 'Why not?' asked the landlord. 'I don't know,' said K., 'why I should let myself be examined, why I should give in to a joke or an official whim. Perhaps some other time I might have taken it on my side too as a joke or as a whim, but not today.' 'Why certainly, certainly,' said the landlord, but he agreed only out of politeness, not from conviction. 'I must let the servants into the taproom now,' he said presently, 'it's long past their time. Only I didn't want to disturb the examination.' 'Did you consider it as important as all that?' asked K. 'Well, yes,' replied the landlord. 'I shouldn't have refused,' said K. 'No,' replied the landlord, 'you shouldn't have done that.' Seeing that K. was silent, he added, whether to comfort K. or to get away sooner: 'Well, well, the sky won't rain sulphur for all that.' 'No,' replied K., 'the weather signs don't look like it.' And they parted laughing.

10

K. stepped out into the windswept street and peered into the darkness. Wild, wild weather. As if there were some connexion between the two he reflected again how the landlady had striven to make him accede to the protocol, and how he had stood out. The landlady's attempt had of course not been a straightforward one, surreptitiously she had tried to put him against the protocol at the same time; in reality he could not tell whether he had stood out or given in. An intriguing nature, acting blindly, it seemed like the wind, according to strange and remote behests which one could never guess at.

He had only taken a few steps along the main street when he saw two swaying lights in the distance; these signs of life gladdened him and he hastened towards them, while they, too, made in his direction. He could not tell why he was so disappointed when he recognized the assistants. Still, they were coming to meet him, evidently sent by Frieda, and the lanterns which delivered him from the darkness roaring round him were his own; nevertheless he was disappointed, he had expected something else, not those old acquaintances who were such a burden to him. But the assistants were not alone; out of the darkness between them Barnabas stepped out. 'Barnabas!' cried K. and he held out his hand, 'have you come to see me?' The surprise at meeting him again drowned at first all the annoyance which he had once felt at Barnabas. 'To see you,' replied Barnabas unalterably friendly as before, 'with a letter from Klamm.' 'A letter from Klamm!' cried K. throwing back his head. 'Lights here!' he called to the assistants, who now pressed close to him on both sides holding up their lanterns. K. had to fold the large sheet in small compass to protect it from the wind while reading it. Then he read: 'To the Land Surveyor at the Bridge Inn. The surveying work which you have carried out thus far has been appreciated by me. The work of the assistants, too, deserves praise. You know how to keep them at their jobs. Do not slacken in your efforts! Carry your work on to a fortunate conclusion. Any interruption would displease me. For the rest be easy in your mind; the question of salary will presently be decided. I shall not forget you.' K. only looked up from the letter when the assistants, who read far more slowly than he, gave three loud cheers at the good news and waved their lanterns. 'Be quiet,' he said, and to Barnabas: 'There's been a misunderstanding.' Barnabas did not seem to comprehend.

'There's been a misunderstanding,' K. repeated, and the weariness he had felt in the afternoon came over him again, the road to the school-house seemed very long, and behind Barnabas he could see his whole family, and the assistants were still jostling him so closely that he had to drive them away with his elbows; how could Frieda have sent them to meet him when he had commanded that they should stay with her? He could quite well have found his own way home, and better alone, indeed, than in this company. And to make matters worse one of them had wound a scarf round his neck whose free ends flapped in the wind and had several times been flung against K.'s face; it is true, the other assistant had always disengaged the wrap at once with his long, pointed, perpetually mobile fingers, but that had not made things any better. Both of them seemed to have considered it an actual pleasure to walk here and back, and the wind and the wildness of the night threw them into raptures. 'Get out!' shouted K., 'seeing that you've come to meet me, why haven't you brought my stick? What have I now to drive you home with?' They crouched behind Barnabas, but they were not too frightened to set their lanterns on their protector's shoulders, right and left; however, he shook them off at once. 'Barnabas,' said K., and he felt a weight on his heart when he saw that Barnabas obviously did not understand him, that though his tunic shone beautifully when fortune was there, when things became serious no help was to be found in him, but only dumb opposition, opposition against which one could not fight, for Barnabas himself was helpless, he could only smile, but that was of just as little help as the stars up there against this tempest down below. 'Look what Klamm has written!' said K., holding the letter before his face. 'He has been wrongly informed. I haven't done any surveying at all, and you see yourself how much the assistants are worth. And obviously, too, I can't interrupt work which I've never begun; I can't even excite the gentleman's displeasure, so how can I have earned his appreciation? As for being easy in my mind, I can never be that.' 'I'll see to it,' said Barnabas, who all the time had been gazing past the letter, which he could not have read in any case, for he was holding it too close to his face. 'Oh,' said K., 'you promise me that you'll see to it, but can I really believe you? I'm in need of a trustworthy messenger, now more than ever.' K. bit his lip with impatience. 'Sir,' replied Barnabas, with a gentle inclination of the head – K. almost allowed himself to be seduced by it again into believing Barnabas – I'll certainly see to it, and I'll certainly see to the message you gave me last time as well.' 'What!' cried K., 'haven't you seen to that yet then? Weren't you at the Castle next day?' 'No,' replied Barnabas, 'my father is old, you've seen him yourself, and there happened to be a great deal of work just then, I had to help him, but now I'll be going to the Castle again soon.' 'But what are you thinking of, you incomprehensible fellow?' cried K., beating his brow with his fist, 'don't Klamm's affairs come before everything else, then? You're in an important position, you're a messenger, and yet you fail me in this wretched manner! What does your father's work matter? Klamm is waiting for this information, and instead of breaking your neck hurrying with it to him, you prefer to clean the stable!' 'My father is a cobbler,' replied Barnabas calmly, 'he had orders from Brunswick, and I'm my father's assistant.' 'Cobbler-orders-Brunswick!' cried K. bitingly, as if he wanted to abolish the words for ever. 'And who can need boots here in these eternally empty streets? And what is all this cobbling to me? I entrusted you with a letter, not so that you might mislay it and crumple it on your bench, but that you might carry it at once to Klamm!' K. became a little more composed now as he remembered that after all Klamm had apparently been all this time in the Herrenhof and not in the Castle at all; but Barnabas exasperated him again when, to prove that he had not forgotten K.'s first message, he now began to recite it. 'Enough! I don't want to hear any more,' he said. 'Don't be angry with me, sir,' said Barnabas, and as if unconsciously wishing to show disapproval of K. he withdrew his gaze from him and lowered his eyes, but probably he was only dejected by K.'s outburst. 'I'm not angry with you,' said K., and his exasperation turned now against himself. 'Not with you, but it's a bad lookout for me only to have a messenger like you for important affairs.' 'Look here,' said Barnabas, and it was as if, to vindicate his honour as a messenger, he was saying more than he should, 'Klamm is really not waiting for your message, he's actually cross when I arrive. "Another new message," he said once, and generally he gets up when he sees me coming in the distance and goes into the next room and doesn't receive me. Besides, it isn't laid down that I should go at once with every message; if it were laid down of course I would go at once; but it isn't laid down, and if I never went at all, nothing could be said to me. When I take a message it's of my own free will.' 'Well and good,' replied K., staring at Barnabas and intentionally ignoring the assistants, who kept on slowly raising their heads by turns behind Barnabas's shoulder as from a trap-door, and hastily disappearing again with a soft whistle in imitation of the whistling of the wind, as if they were terrified at K.; they enjoyed themselves like this for a long time. 'What it's like with Klamm I don't know, but that you can understand everything there properly I very much doubt, and even if you did, we couldn't better things there. But you can carry a message and that's all I ask of you. A quite short message. Can you carry it for me tomorrow and bring me the answer tomorrow, or at least tell me how you were received? Can you do that and will you do that? It would be of great service to me. And perhaps I'll have a chance yet of rewarding you properly, or have you any wish now, perhaps, that I can fulfil?' 'Certainly I'll carry out your orders,' said Barnabas. 'And will you do your utmost to carry them out as well as you can, to give the message to Klamm himself, to get a reply from Klamm himself, and immediately, all this immediately, tomorrow, in the morning, will you do that?' 'I'll do my best,' replied Barnabas, 'but I always do that.' 'We won't argue any more about it now,' said K. 'This is the message: "The Land Surveyor Begs the Director to grant him a personal interview; he accepts in advance any conditions which may be attached to the permission to do this. He is driven to make this request because until now every intermediary has completely failed; in proof of this he advances the fact that till now he has not carried out any surveying at all, and according to the information given him by the village Superintendent will never carry out such work; consequently it is with humiliation and despair that he has read the last letter of the Director; only a personal interview with the Director can be of any help here. The Land Surveyor knows how extraordinary his request is, but he will exert himself to make his disturbance of the Director as little felt as possible; he submits himself to any and every limitation of time, also any stipulation which may be considered necessary as to the number of words which may be allowed him during the interview, even with ten words he believes he will be able to manage. In profound respect and extreme impatience he awaits your decision." K. had forgotten himself while he was speaking, it was as if he were standing before Klamm's door talking to the porter. 'It has grown much longer than I had thought,' he said, 'but you must learn it by heart, I don't want to write a letter, it would only go the same endless way as the other papers.' So for Barnabas's guidance, K. scribbled it on a scrap of paper on the back of one of the assistants, while the other assistant held up the lantern; but already K. could take it down from Barnabas's dictation, for he had retained it all and spoke it out correctly without being put off by the misleading interpolations of the assistants. 'You've an extraordinary memory,' said K., giving him the paper, 'but now show yourself extraordinary in the other thing as well. And any requests? Have you none? It would reassure me a little – I say it frankly – regarding the fate of my message, if you had any.' At first Barnabas remained silent, then he said: 'My sisters send you their greetings.' 'Your sisters,' replied K. 'Oh, yes, the big strong girls.' 'Both send you their greetings, but Amalia in particular,' said Barnabas, 'besides it was she who brought me this letter for you today from the Castle.' Struck by this piece of information, K. asked: 'Couldn't she take my message to the Castle as well? Or couldn't you both go and each of you try your luck?'

'Amalia isn't allowed into the Chancellery,' said Barnabas, 'otherwise she would be very glad to do it.' 'I'll come and see you perhaps tomorrow,' said K., 'only you come to me first with the answer. I'll wait for you in the school. Give my greetings to your sisters, too.' K.'s promise seemed to make Barnabas very happy, and after they had shaken hands he could not help touching K. lightly on the shoulder. As if everything were once more as it had been when Barnabas first walked into the inn among the peasants in all his glory, K. felt his touch on his shoulder as a distinction, though he smiled at it. In a better mood now, he let the assistants do as they pleased on the way home.

11

He reached the school chilled through and through, it was quite dark, the candles in the lanterns had burned down; led by the assistants, who already knew their way here, he felt his road into one of the classrooms. 'Your first praiseworthy service,' he said, remembering Klamm's letter. Still half-asleep Frieda cried out from the corner: 'Let K. sleep! Don't disturb him!' so entirely did K. occupy her thoughts, even though she had been so overcome with sleep that she had not been able to wait up for him. Now a light was got, but the lamp could not be turned up very far, for there was only a little paraffin left. The new household was still without many necessaries. The room had been heated, it was true, but it was a large one, sometimes used as the gymnasium – the gymnastic apparatus was standing about and hanging from the ceiling – and it had already used up all the supply of wood – had been very warm and cosy too, as K. was assured, but unfortunately had grown quite cold again. There was, however, a large supply of wood in a shed, but the shed was locked and the teacher had the key; he only allowed this wood to be used for heating the school during teaching hours. The room could have been endured if there had been beds where one might have taken refuge. But in that line there was nothing but one sack stuffed with straw, covered with praiseworthy tidiness by a woollen rug of Frieda's, but with no feather-bed and only two rough, stiff blankets, which hardly served to keep one warm. And it was precisely at this wretched sack of straw that the assistants were staring greedily, but of course without any hope of ever being allowed to lie on it. Frieda looked anxiously at K.; that she knew how to make a room, even the most wretched, habitable, she had proved in the Bridge Inn, but here she had not been able to make any headway, quite without means as she was. 'Our only ornaments are the gymnastic contraptions,' said she, trying to smile through her tears. But for the chief deficiencies, the lack of sleeping accommodation and fuel, she promised absolutely to find help the very next day, and begged K. only to be patient till then. From no word, no hint, no sign could one have concluded that she harboured even the slightest trace of bitterness against K. in her heart, although, as he had to admit himself, he had torn her away first from the Herrenhof and now from the Bridge Inn as well. So in return K. did his best to find everything tolerable, which was not difficult for him, indeed, because in thought he was still with Barnabas repeating his message word for word, not however as he had given it to Barnabas, but as he thought it would sound before Klamm. After all, however, he was very sincerely glad of the coffee which Frieda had boiled for him on a spirit burner, and leaning against the almost cold stove followed the nimble, practised movements with which she spread the indispensable white table-cover on the teacher's table, brought out a flowered cup, then some bread and sausage, and actually a tin of sardines. Now everything was ready; Frieda, too, had not eaten yet, but had waited for K. Two chairs were available, there K. and Frieda sat down to their table, the assistants at their feet on the dais, but they could never stay quiet, even while eating they made a disturbance. Although they had received an ample store of everything and were not yet nearly finished with it, they got up from time to time to make sure whether there was still anything on the table and they could still expect something for themselves; K. paid no attention to them and only began to take notice when Frieda laughed at them. He covered her hand with his tenderly and asked softly why she was so indulgent to them and treated even their naughtiness so kindly. In this way one would never get rid of them, while through a certain degree of severity, which besides was demanded by their behaviour, one could manage either to curb them or, what was both more probable and more desirable, to make their position so hot for them that they would have finally to leave. The school here didn't seem to be a very pleasant place to live in for long, well, it wouldn't last very long in any case; but they would hardly notice all the drawbacks if the assistants were once gone and they two had the quiet house to themselves; and didn't she notice, too, that the assistants were becoming more impudent every day, as if they were actually encouraged now by Frieda's presence and the hope that K. wouldn't treat them with such firmness as he would have done in other circumstances? Besides, there were probably quite simple means of getting rid of them at once, without ceremony, perhaps Frieda herself knew of these, seeing that she was so well acquainted with all the circumstances. And from all appearances one would only be doing the assistants a favour if one got rid of them in some way, for the advantage they got to staying here couldn't be great, and besides the lazy spell which they must have enjoyed till now must cease here, to a certain extent at any rate, for they would have to work while Frieda spared herself after the excitements of the last few days, and he, K., was occupied in finding a way out of their painful position. All the same, if the assistants should go away, he would be so relieved that he felt he could quite easily carry out all the school work in addition to his other duties.

Frieda, who had been listening attentively, stroked his arm and said that that was her opinion too, but that perhaps he took the assistants' mischief too seriously; they were mere lads, full of spirits and a little silly now that they were for the first time in strange service, just released from the strict discipline of the Castle, and so a little dazed and excited; and being in that state they of course committed lots of follies at which it was natural to be annoyed, but which it would be more sensible to laugh at. Often she simply couldn't keep from laughing. All the same she absolutely agreed with K. that it would be much better to send the assistants away and be by themselves, just the two of them. She pressed closer to K. and hid her face on his shoulder. And there she whispered something so low that K. had to bend his head to hear; it was that all the same she knew of no way of dealing with the assistants and she was afraid that all that K. had suggested would be of no avail. So far as she knew it was K. himself who had asked for them, and now he had them and would have to keep them. It would be best to treat them as a joke, which they certainly were; that would be the best way to put up with them.

K. was displeased by her answer: half in jest, half in earnest, he replied that she seemed actually to be in league with them, or at least to have a strong inclination in their favour; well, they were good-looking lads, but there was nobody who couldn't be got rid of if only one had the will, and he would show her that that was so in the case of the assistants.

Frieda said that she would be very grateful to him if he could manage it. And from now on she wouldn't laugh at them any more, or have any unnecessary talk with them. Besides she didn't find anything now to laugh at, it was really no joke always to be spied on by two men, she had learned to look at the two of them with K.'s eyes. And she actually shrank a little when the assistants got up again, partly to have a look at the food that was left, partly to get to the bottom of the continued whispering.

K. employed this incident to increase Frieda's disgust for the assistants, drew her towards him, and so side by side they finished their supper. Now it was time to go to bed, for they were all very sleepy; one of the assistants had actually fallen asleep over his food; this amused the other one greatly, and he did his best to get the others to look at the vacant face of his companion, but he had no success. K. and Frieda sat on above without paying any attention. The cold was becoming so extreme that they shirked going to bed; at last K. declared that the room must be heated, otherwise it would be impossible to get to sleep. He looked round to see if he could fine an axe or something. The assistants knew of one and fetched it, and now they proceeded to the wood-shed. In a few minutes the flimsy door was smashed and torn open; as if they had never yet experienced anything so glorious, the assistants began to carry the wood into the classroom, hounding each other on and knocking against each other; soon there was a great pile, the stove was set going, everybody lay down round it, the assistants were given a blanket to roll themselves in – it was quite ample for them, for it was decided that one of them should always remain awake and keep the fire going – and soon it was so hot round the stove that the blankets were no longer needed, the lamps were put out, and K. and Frieda happily stretched themselves out to sleep in the warm silence.

K. was awakened during the night by some noise or other, and in the first vague sleepy state felt for Frieda; he found that, instead of Frieda, one of the assistants was lying beside him. Probably because of the exacerbation which being suddenly awakened is sufficient in itself to cause, this gave him the greatest fright that he had ever had since he first came to the village. With a cry he sat up, and not knowing what he was doing he gave the assistant such a buffet that he began to cry. However the whole thing was cleared up in a moment. Frieda had been awakened – at least so it had seemed to her – by some huge animal, a cat probably, which had sprung on to her breast and then leapt away again. She had got up and was searching the whole room for the beast with a candle. One of the assistants had seized the opportunity to enjoy the sack of straw for a little, an attempt which he was now bitterly repenting. Frieda could find nothing, however; perhaps it had only been a delusion, she went back to K. and on the way she stroked the crouching and whimpering assistant over the hair to comfort him. as if she had forgotten the evening's conversation. K. said nothing, but he asked the assistant to stop putting wood on the fire, for owing to almost all the heap having been squandered the room was already too hot.

12

Next morning nobody awoke until the school-children were there, standing with gaping eyes round the sleepers. This was unpleasant, for on account of the intense heat, which now towards morning had given way, however, to a coldness which could be felt, they had all taken off everything but their shirts, and just as they were beginning to put on their clothes, Gisa, the lady teacher, appeared at the door, a fair, tall, beautiful, but somewhat stiff young woman. She was evidently prepared for the new janitor, and seemed also to have been given her instructions by the teacher, for as soon as he appeared at the door, she began: 'I can't put up with this. This is a fine state of affairs. You have permission to sleep in the classroom, but that's all; I am not obliged to teach in your bedroom. A janitor's family that loll in their beds far into the forenoon! Faugh!' Well, something might be said about that, particularly as far as the family and the beds were concerned, thought K., while with Frieda's help – the assistants were of no use, lying on the floor they looked in amazement at the lady teacher and the children – he dragged across the parallel bars and the vaulting horse, threw the blanket over them, and so constructed a little room in which one could at least get on one's clothes protected from the children's gaze. He was not given a minute's peace, however, for the lady teacher began to scold because there was no fresh water in the washing basin – K. had just been thinking of fetching the basin for himself and Frieda to wash in, but he had at once given up the idea so as not to exasperate the lady teacher too much, but his renunciation was of no avail, for immediately afterwards there was a loud crash; unfortunately, it seemed, they had forgotten to clear away the remains of the supper from the teacher's table, so she sent it all flying with her ruler and everything fell on the floor; she didn't need to bother about the sardine oil and the remainder of the coffee being spilt and the coffee-pot smashed to pieces, the janitor of course could soon clear that up. Clothed once more, K. and Frieda, leaning on the parallel bars, witnessed the destruction of their few things. The assistants, who had obviously never thought of putting on their clothes, had stuck their heads through a fold of the blankets near the floor, to the great delight of the children. What grieved Frieda most was naturally the loss of the coffee-pot; only when K. to comfort her assured her that he would go immediately to the village Superintendent and demand that it should be replaced, and see that this was done, was she able to gather herself together sufficiently to run out of their stockade in her chemise and skirt and rescue the table-cover at least from being stained any more. And she managed it, though the lady teacher to frighten her kept on hammering on the table with the ruler in the most nerve-racking fashion. When K. and Frieda were quite clothed they had to compel the assistants – who seemed to be struck dumb by these events – to get their clothes on as well; had not merely to order them and push them, indeed, but actually to put some of their clothes on for them. Then, when all was ready, K. shared out the remaining work; the assistants were to bring in wood and light the fire, but in the other classroom first, from which another and greater danger threatened, for the teacher himself was probably already there. Frieda was to scrub the floor and K. would fetch fresh water and set things to rights generally. For the time being breakfast could not be thought of. But so as to find out definitively the attitude of the lady teacher, K. decided to issue from their shelter himself first, the others were only to follow when he called them; he adopted this policy on the one hand because he did not want the position to be compromised in advance by any stupid act of the assistants, and on the other because he wanted Frieda to be spared as much as possible; for she had ambitions and he had none, she was sensitive and he was not, she only thought of the petty discomforts of the moment, while he was thinking of Barnabas and the future. Frieda followed all his instructions implicitly, and scarcely took her eyes from him. Hardly had he appeared when the lady teacher cried amid the laughter of the children, which from now on never stopped: 'Slept well?' and as K. paid no attention – seeing that after all it was not a real question – but began to clear up the washstand, she asked: 'What have you been doing to my cat?' A huge, fat old cat was lying lazily outstretched on the table, and the teacher was examining one of its paws which was evidently a little hurt. So Frieda had been right after all, this cat had not of course leapt on her, for it was past the leaping stage, but it had crawled over her, had been terrified by the presence of people in the empty house, had concealed itself hastily, and in its unaccustomed hurry had hurt itself. K. tried to explain this quietly to the lady teacher, but the only thing she had eyes for was the injury itself and she replied: 'Well, then it's your fault through coming here. Just look at this,' and she called K. over to the table, showed him the paw, and before he could get a proper look at it, gave him a whack with the tawse over the back of his hand; the tails of the tawse were blunted, it was true, but, this time without any regard for the cat, she had brought them down so sharply that they raised bloody weals. 'And now go about your business,' she said impatiently, bowing herself once more over the cat. Frieda, who had been looking on with the assistants from behind the parallel bars, cried out when she saw the blood. K. held up his hand in front of the children and said: 'Look, that's what a sly, wicked cat has done to me.' He said it, indeed, not for the children's benefit, whose shouting and laughter had become continuous, so that it needed no further occasion or incitement, and could not be pierced or influenced by any words of his. But seeing that the lady teacher, too, only acknowledged the insult by a brief side-glance, and remained still occupied with the cat, her first fury satiated by the drawing of blood, K. called Frieda and the assistants, and the work began.

When K. had carried out the pail with the dirty water, fetched fresh water, and was beginning to turn out the classroom, a boy of about twelve stepped out from his desk, touched K.'s hand, and said something which was quite lost in the general uproar. Then suddenly every sound ceased and K. turned round. The thing he had been fearing all morning had come. In the door stood the teacher; in each hand the little man held an assistant by the scruff of the neck. He had caught them, it seemed, while they were fetching wood, for in a mighty voice he began to shout, pausing after every word: 'Who has dared to break into the wood-shed? Where is the villain, so that I may annihilate him?' Then Frieda got up from the floor, which she was trying to clean near the feet of the lady teacher, looked across at K. as if she were trying to gather strength from him, and said, a little of her old superciliousness in her glance and bearing: 'I did it, Mr Teacher. I couldn't think of any other way. If the classrooms were to be heated in time, the wood-shed had to be opened; I didn't dare to ask you for the key in the middle of the night, my fiancé was at the Herrenhof, it was possible that he might stay there all night, so I had to decide for myself. If I have done wrongly, forgive my inexperience; I've been scolded enough by my fiancé, after he saw what had happened. Yes, he even forbade me to light the fires early, because he thought that you had shown by locking the wood-shed that you didn't want them to be put on before you came yourself. So it's his fault that the fires are not on, but mine that the shed has been broken into.' 'Who broke open the door?' asked the teacher, turning to the assistants, who were still vainly struggling to escape from his grip. 'The gentleman,' they both replied, and, so that there might be no doubt, pointed at K. Frieda laughed, and her laughter seemed to be still more conclusive than her words; then she began to wring out in the pail the rag with which she had been scrubbing the floor, as if the episode had been closed with her declaration, and the evidence of the assistants was merely a belated jest. Only when she was at work on her knees again did she add: 'Our assistants are mere children who in spite of their age should still be at their desks in school. Last evening I really did break open the door myself with the axe, it was quite easy, I didn't need the assistants to help me, they would only have been a nuisance. But when my fiancé arrived later in the night and went out to see the damage and if possible put it right, the assistants ran out after him, likely because they were afraid to stay here by themselves, and saw my fiancé working at the broken door, and that's why they say now – but they're only children –' True, the assistants kept on shaking their heads during Frieda's story, pointed again at K. and did their best by means of dumb show to deflect her from her story; but as they did not succeed they submitted at last, took Frieda's words as a command, and on being questioned anew by the teacher made no reply. 'So,' said the teacher, 'you've been lying? Or at least you've groundlessly accused the janitor?' They still remained silent, but their trembling and their apprehensive glances seemed to indicate guilt. 'Then I'll give you a sound thrashing straight away,' he said, and he sent one of the children into the next room for his cane. Then as he was raising it, Frieda cried: 'The assistants have told the truth!' flung her scrubbing-cloth in despair into the pail, so that the water splashed up on every side, and ran behind the parallel bars, where she remained concealed. 'A lying crew!' remarked the lady teacher, who had just finished bandaging the paw, and she took the beast into her lap, for which it was almost too big.

'So it *was* the janitor,' said the teacher, pushing the assistants away and turning to K., who had been listening all the time leaning on the handle of his broom: 'This fine janitor who out of cowardice allows other people to be falsely accused of his own villainies.' 'Well,' said K., who had not missed the fact that Frieda's intervention had appeased the first uncontrollable fury of the teacher, 'if the assistants had got a little taste of the rod I shouldn't have been sorry; if they get off ten times when they should justly be punished, they can well afford to pay for it by being punished unjustly for once. But besides that it would have been very welcome to me if a direct quarrel between me and you, Mr Teacher, could have been avoided; perhaps you would have liked it as well yourself too. But seeing that Frieda has sacrificed me to the assistants now –' here K. paused, and in the silence Frieda's sobs could be heard behind the screen – 'of course a clean breast must be made of the whole business.' 'Scandalous!' said the lady teacher. 'I am entirely of your opinion, Fräulein Gisa,' said the teacher. 'You, janitor, are of course dismissed from your post for these scandalous doings. Your further punishment I reserve meantime, but now clear yourself and your belongings out of the house at once. It will be a genuine relief to us, and the teaching will manage to begin at last. Now quick about it!' 'I shan't move a foot from here,' said K. 'You're my superior, but not the person who engaged me for this post; it was the Superintendent who did that, and I'll only accept notice from him. And he certainly never gave me this post so that I and my dependants should freeze here, but – as you told me yourself – to keep me from doing anything thoughtless or desperate. To dismiss me suddenly now would therefore be absolutely against his intentions; till I hear the contrary from his own mouth I refuse to believe it. Besides it may possibly be greatly to your own advantage, too, if I don't accept your notice, given so hastily.' 'So you don't accept it?' asked the teacher. K. shook his head. 'Think it over carefully,' said the teacher, 'your decisions aren't always for the best; you should reflect, for instance, on yesterday afternoon, when you refused to be examined.' 'Why do you bring that up now?' asked K. 'Because it's my whim,' replied the teacher, 'and now I repeat for the last time, get out!' But as that too had no effect the teacher went over to the table and consulted in a whisper with Fräulein Gisa; she said something about the police, but the teacher rejected it, finally they seemed in agreement, the teacher ordered the children to go into his classroom, they would be taught there along with the other children. This change delighted everybody, the room was emptied in a moment amid laughter and shouting, the teacher and Fräulein Gisa followed last. The latter carried the class register, and on it in all its bulk the perfectly indifferent cat. The teacher would gladly have left the cat behind, but a suggestion to that effect was negatived decisively by Fräulein Gisa with a reference to K.'s inhumanity. So, in addition to all his other annoyances, the teacher blamed K. for the cat as well. And that influenced his last words to K., spoken when he reached the door: 'The lady has been driven by force to leave the room with her children, because you have rebelliously refused to accept my notice, and because nobody can ask of her, a young girl, that she should teach in the middle of your dirty household affairs. So you are left to yourself, and you can spread yourself as much as you like, undisturbed by the disapproval of respectable people. But it won't last for long, I promise you that.' With that he slammed the door.

13

Hardly was everybody gone when K. said to the assistants: 'Clear out!' Disconcerted by the unexpectedness of the command, they obeyed, but when K. locked the door behind them they tried to get in again, whimpered outside and knocked on the door. 'You are dismissed,' cried K., 'never again will I take you into my service!' But that, of course, was just what they did not want, and they kept hammering on the door with their hands and feet. 'Let us back to you, sir!' they cried, as if they were being swept away by a flood and K. were dry land. But K. did not relent, he waited, impatiently for the unbearable din to force the teacher to intervene. That soon happened. 'Let your confounded assistants in!' he shouted. 'I've dismissed them,' K. shouted back; it had the incidental effect of showing the teacher what it was to be strong enough not merely to give notice, but to enforce it. The teacher next tried to soothe the assistants by kind assurances that they had only to wait quietly and K. would have to let them in sooner or later. Then he went away. And now things might have settled down if K. had not begun to shout at them again that they were finally dismissed once and for all, and had not the faintest chance of being taken back. Upon that they recommenced their din. Once more the teacher entered, but this time he no longer tried to reason with them, but drove them, apparently with his dreaded rod, out of the house.

Soon they appeared in front of the windows of the gymnasium, rapped on the panes and cried something, but their words could no longer be distinguished. They did not stay there long either, in the deep snow they could not be as active as their frenzy required. So they flew to the railings of the school garden and sprang on to the stone pediment, where, moreover, though only from a distance, they had a better view of the room; there they ran to and fro holding on to the railings, then remained standing and stretched out their clasped hands beseechingly towards K. They went on like this for a long time, without thinking of the uselessness of their efforts; they were as if obsessed, they did not even stop when K. drew down the window blinds so as to rid himself of the sight of them. In the now darkened room K. went over to the parallel bars to look for Frieda. On encountering her gaze she got up, put her hair in order, dried her tears and began in silence to prepare the coffee. Although she knew of everything, K. formally announced to her all the same that he had dismissed the assistants. She merely nodded. K. sat down at one of the desks and followed her tired movements. It had been her unfailing liveliness and decision that had given her insignificant physique its beauty; now that beauty was gone. A few days of living with K. had been enough to achieve this. Her work in the taproom had not been light, but apparently it had been more suited to her. Or was her separation from Klamm the real cause of her falling away? It was the nearness of Klamm that had made her so irrationally seductive; that was the seduction which had drawn K. to her, and now she was withering in his arms.

'Frieda,' said K. She put away the coffee-mill at once and went over to K. at his desk. 'You're angry with me?' asked she.

'No,' replied K. 'I don't think you can help yourself. You were happy in the Herrenhof. I should have let you stay there.' 'Yes,' said Frieda, gazing sadly in front of her, 'you should have let me stay there. I'm not good enough for you to live with. If you were rid of me, perhaps you would be able to achieve all that you want. Out of regard for me you've submitted yourself to the tyranny of the teacher, taken on this wretched post, and are doing your utmost to get an interview with Klamm. All for me, but I don't give you much in return.' 'No, no,' said K., putting his arm round her comfortingly. 'All these things are trifles that don't hurt me, and it's not only on your account that I want to get to Klamm. And then think of all you've done for me! Before I knew you I was going about in a blind circle. Nobody took me up, and if I made up to anybody I was soon sent about my business. And when I was given the chance of a little hospitality it was with people that I always wanted to run away from, like Barnabas's family –' 'You wanted to run away from them? You did? Darling!' cried Frieda eagerly, and after a hesitating 'Yes,' from K., sank back once more into her apathy. But K. had no longer resolution enough to explain in what way everything had changed for the better for him through his connexion with Frieda. He slowly took away his arm and they sat for a little in silence, until – as if his arm had given her warmth and comfort, which now she could not do without – Frieda said: 'I won't be able to stand this life here. If you want to keep me with you, we'll have to go away somewhere or other, to the south of France, or to Spain.' 'I can't go away,' replied K. 'I came here to stay. I'll stay here.' And giving utterance to a self-contradiction which he made no effort to explain, he added as if to himself: 'What could have enticed me to this desolate country except the wish to stay here?' Then he went on: 'But you want to stay here too, after all it's your own country. Only you miss Klamm and that gives you desperate ideas.' 'I miss Klamm?' said Frieda. 'I've all I want of Klamm here, too much Klamm; it's to escape from him that I want to go away. It's not Klamm that I miss, it's you. I want to go away for your sake, because I can't get enough of you, here where everything distracts me. I would gladly lose my pretty looks, I would gladly be sick and ailing, if I could be left in peace with you.' K. had only paid attention to one thing. 'Then Klamm is still in communication with you?' he asked eagerly, 'he sends for you?' 'I know nothing about Klamm,' replied Frieda, 'I was speaking just now of others, I mean the assistants.' 'Oh, the assistants,' said K. in disappointment, 'do they persecute you?' 'Why, have you never noticed it?' asked Frieda. 'No,' replied K., trying in vain to remember anything, 'they're certainly importunate and lascivious young fellows, but I hadn't noticed that they had dared to lift their eyes to you.' 'No?' said Frieda, 'did you ever notice that they simply weren't to be driven out of our room in the Bridge Inn, that they jealously watched all our movements, that one of them finished up by taking my place on that sack of straw, that they gave evidence against you a minute ago so as to drive you out of this and ruin you, and so as to be left alone with me? You've never noticed all that?' K. gazed at Frieda without replying. Her accusations against the assistants were true enough, but all the same they could be interpreted far more innocently as simple effects of the ludicrously childish, irresponsible, and undisciplined characters of the two. And didn't it also speak against their guilt that they had always done their best to go with K. everywhere and not to be left with Frieda? K. half-suggested this. 'It's their deceit,' said Frieda, 'have you never seen through it? Well, why have you driven them away, if not for those reasons?' And she went to the window, drew the blind aside a little, glanced out, and then called K. over. The assistants were still clinging to the railings; tired as they must have been by now, they still gathered their strength together every now and then and stretched their arms out beseechingly towards the school. So as not to have to hold on all the time, one of them had hooked himself on to the railings behind by the tail of his coat.

'Poor things! Poor things!' said Frieda.

'You ask why I drove them away?' asked K. 'You were the

sole cause of that.' 'I?' asked Frieda without taking her eyes from the assistants. 'Your much too kind treatment of the assistants,' said K., 'the way you forgave their offences and smiled at them and stroked their hair, your perpetual sympathy for them – "Poor things! Poor things!" you said just now – and finally this last thing that has happened, that you haven't scrupled even to sacrifice me to save the assistants from a beating.' 'Yes, that's just it, that's what I've been trying to tell you, that's just what makes me unhappy, what keeps me from you even though I can't think of any greater happiness than to be with you all the time, without interruption, endlessly, even though I feel that here in this world there's no undisturbed place for our love, neither in the village nor anywhere else; and I dream of a grave, deep and narrow, where we could clasp each other in our arms as with iron bars, and I would hide my face in you and you would hide your face in me, and nobody would ever see us any more. But here – look, there are the assistants! It's not you they think of when they clasp their hands, but me.' 'And it's not I who am looking at them,' said K., 'but you.' 'Certainly, me,' said Frieda almost angrily, 'that's what I've been saying all the time; why else should they be always at my heels, even if they are messengers of Klamm's?' 'Messengers of Klamm's?' repeated K. extremely astonished by this designation, though it seemed natural enough at the same time. 'Certainly, messengers of Klamm's,' said Frieda. 'Even if they are, still they're silly boys, too, who need to have more sense hammered into them. What ugly black young demons they are, and how disgusting the contrast is between their faces, which one would say belonged to grown-ups, almost to students, and their silly childish behaviour. Do you think I don't see that? It makes me feel ashamed for them. Well, that's just it, they don't repel me, for I feel ashamed for them. I can't help looking at them. When one ought to be annoyed with them, I can only laugh at them. When people want to strike them, I can only stroke their hair. And when I'm lying beside you at night I can't sleep and must always be leaning across you to look at them, one of them lying rolled up asleep in the blanket and the other kneeling before the stove door putting in wood, and I have to bend forward so far that I nearly waken you. And it wasn't the cat that frightened me – oh, I've had experience of cats and I've had experience as well of disturbed nights in the taproom – it wasn't the cat that frightened me, I'm frightened at myself. No, it didn't need that big beast of a cat to waken me, I start up at the slightest noise. One minute I'm afraid you'll waken and spoil everything, and the next I spring up and light the candle to force you to waken at once and protect me.' 'I knew nothing of all this,' said K., 'it was only a vague suspicion of it that made me send them away; but now they're gone, and perhaps everything will be all right.' 'Yes, they're gone at last,' said Frieda, but her face was worried, not happy, 'only we don't know who they are. Messengers of Klamm's I call them in my mind, though not seriously, but perhaps they are really that. Their eyes – those ingenuous and yet flashing eyes – remind me somehow of Klamm's; yes, that's it, it's Klamm's glance that sometimes runs through me from their eyes. And so it's not true when I say that I'm ashamed for them. I only wish it were. I know quite well that anywhere else and in anyone else their behaviour would seem stupid and offensive, but in them it isn't. I watch their stupid tricks with respect and admiration. But if they're Klamm's messengers who'll rid us of them? And besides would it be a good thing to be rid of them? Wouldn't you have to fetch them back at once in that case and be happy if they were still willing to come?' 'You want me to bring them back again?' asked K. 'No, no!' said Frieda, 'it's the last thing I desire. The sight of them, if they were to rush in here now, their joy at seeing me again, the way they would hop round like children and stretch out their arms to me like men; no, I don't think I would be able to stand that. But all the same when I remember that if you keep on hardening your heart to them, it will keep you, perhaps, from ever getting admittance to Klamm, I want to save you by any means at all from such consequences. In that case my only wish is for you to let them in. In that case let them in now at once. Don't bother about me; what do I matter? I'll defend myself as long as I can, but if I have to surrender, then I'll surrender with the consciousness that that, too, is for your sake.' 'You only strengthen me in my decision about the assistants,' said K. 'Never will they come in with my will. The fact that I've got them out of this proves at least that in certain circumstances they can be managed, and therefore, in addition, that they have no real connexion with Klamm. Only last night I received a letter from Klamm from which it was clear that Klamm was quite falsely informed about the assistants, from which again one can only draw the conclusion that he is completely indifferent to them, for if that were not so he would certainly have obtained exact information about them. And the fact that you see Klamm in them proves nothing, for you're still, unfortunately, under the landlady's influence and see Klamm everywhere. You're still Klamm's sweetheart, and not my wife yet by a long chalk. Sometimes that makes me quite dejected, I feel then as if I had lost everything, I feel as if I had only newly come to the village, yet not full of hope, as I actually came, but with the knowledge that only disappointments await me, and that I will have to swallow them down one after another to the very dregs. But that is only sometimes,' K. added smiling, when he saw Frieda's dejection at hearing his words, 'and at bottom it merely proves one good thing, that is, how much you mean to me. And if you order me now to choose between you and the assistants, that's enough to decide the assistants' fate. What an idea, to choose between you and the assistants! But now I want to be rid of them finally, in word and thought as well. Besides who knows whether the weakness that has come over us both mayn't be due to the fact that we haven't had breakfast yet?' 'That's possible,' said Frieda, smiling wearily and going about her work. K., too, grasped the broom again.

After a while there was a soft rap at the door. 'Barnabas!' cried K., throwing down the broom, and with a few steps he was at the door. Frieda stared at him, more terrified at the name than anything else. With his trembling hands K. could not turn the old lock immediately. 'I'll open in a minute,' he kept on repeating, instead of asking who was actually there. And then he had to face the fact that through the wide-open door came in, not Barnabas, but the little boy who had tried to speak to him before. But K. had no wish to be reminded of him. 'What do you want here?' he asked. 'The classes are being taught next door.' 'I've come from there,' replied the boy, looking up at K. quietly with his great brown eyes, and standing at attention, with his arms by his sides. 'What do you want then? Out with it!' said K., bending a little forward, for the boy spoke in a low voice. 'Can I help you?' asked the boy. 'He wants to help us,' said K. to Frieda, and then to the boy: 'What's your name?' 'Hans Brunswick, master cobbler in Madeleinegasse.' 'I see, your name is Brunswick,' said K., now in a kinder tone. It came out that Hans had been so indignant at seeing the bloody weals which the lady teacher had raised on K.'s hand, that he had resolved at once to stand by K. He had boldly slipped away just now from the classroom next door at the risk of severe punishment, somewhat as a deserter goes over to the enemy. It may indeed have been chiefly some such boyish fancy that had impelled him. The seriousness which he evinced in everything he did seemed to indicate it. Shyness held him back at the beginning, but he soon got used to K. and Frieda, and when he was given a cup of good hot coffee he became lively and confidential and began to question them eagerly and insistently, as if he wanted to know the gist of the matter as quickly as possible, to enable him to come to an independent decision about what they should do. There was something imperious in his character, but it was so mingled with childish innocence that they submitted to it without resistance, half-smilingly, half in earnest. In any case he demanded all their attention for himself; work completely stopped, the breakfast lingered on unconscionably. Although Hans was sitting at one of the scholars' desks and K. in a chair on the dais with Frieda beside him, it looked as if Hans were the teacher, and as if he were examining them and passing judgement on their answers. A faint smile round his soft mouth seemed to indicate that he knew quite well that all this was only a game, but that made him only the more serious in conducting it; perhaps, too, it was not really a smile but the happiness of childhood that played round his lips. Strangely enough he only admitted quite late in the conversation that he had known K. ever since his visit to Lasemann's. K. was delighted. 'You were playing at the lady's feet?' asked K. 'Yes,' replied Hans, 'that was my mother.' And now he had to tell about his mother, but he did so hesitatingly and only after being repeatedly asked; and it was clear now that he was only a child, out of whose mouth, it is true – especially in his questions – sometimes the voice of an energetic, far-seeing man seemed to speak; but then all at once, without transition, he was only a schoolboy again who did not understand many of the questions, misconstrued others, and in a childish inconsiderateness spoke too low, although he had the fault repeatedly pointed out to him, and out of stubbornness silently refused to answer some of the other questions at all, quite without embarrassment, however, as a grown-up would have been incapable of doing. He seemed to feel that he alone had the right to ask questions, and that by the questions of Frieda and K. some regulation were broken and time wasted. That made him sit silent for a long time, his body erect, his head bent, his underlip pushed out. Frieda was so charmed by his expression at these moments that she sometimes put questions to him in the hope that they would evoke it. And she succeeded several times, but K. was only annoyed. All that they found out did not amount to much. Hans's mother was slightly unwell, but what her illness was remained indefinite; the child which she had had in her lap was Hans's sister and was called Frieda (Hans was not pleased by the fact that her name was the same as the lady's who was questioning him), the family lived in the village, but not with Lasemann – they had only been there on a visit and to be bathed, seeing that Lasemann had the big tub in which the younger children, to whom Hans didn't belong, loved to bathe and splash about. Of his father Hans spoke now with respect, now with fear, but only when his mother was not occupying the conversation; compared with his mother his father evidently was of little account, but all their questions about Brunswick's family life remained, in spite of their efforts, unanswered. K. learned that the father had the biggest shoemaker's business in the place, nobody could compete with him, a fact which quite remote questions brought again and again; he actually gave out work to the other shoemakers, for example to Barnabas's father; in this last case he had done it of course as a special favour – at least Hans's proud toss of the head seemed to hint at this, a gesture which made Frieda run over and give him a kiss. The question whether he had been in the Castle yet he only answered after it had been repeated several times, and with a 'No.' The same question regarding his mother he did not answer at all. At last K. grew tired; to him, too, these questions seemed useless, he admitted that the boy was right; besides there was something humiliating in ferreting out family secrets by taking advantage of a child; doubly humiliating, however, was the fact that in spite of his efforts he had learned nothing. And when to finish the matter he asked the boy what was the help he wanted to offer, he was no longer surprised to hear that Hans had only wanted to help with the work in the school, so that the teacher and his assistant might not scold K. so much. K. explained to Hans that help of that kind was not needed, scolding was part of the teacher's nature and one could scarcely hope to avoid it even by the greatest diligence, the work itself was not hard, and only because of special circumstances had it been so far behind that morning, besides scolding hadn't the same effect on K. as on a scholar, he shook it off, it was almost a matter of indifference to him, he hoped, too, to get quite clear of the teacher soon. Though Hans had only wanted to help him in dealing with the teacher, however, he thanked him sincerely, but now Hans had better return to his class, with luck he would not be punished if he went back at once. Although K. did not emphasize and only involuntarily suggested that it was simply help in dealing with the teacher which he did not require, leaving the question of other kinds of help open, Hans caught the suggestion clearly and asked whether perhaps K. needed any other assistance; he would be very glad to help him, and if he were not in a position to help him himself, he would ask his mother to do so, and then it would be sure to be all right. When his father had difficulties, he, too, asked Hans's mother for help. And his mother had already asked once about K., she herself hardly ever left the house, it had been a great exception for her to be at Lasemann's that day. But he, Hans, often went there to play with Lasemann's children, and his mother had once asked him whether the Land Surveyor had ever happened to be there again. Only his mother wasn't supposed to talk too much, seeing she was so weak and tired, and so he had simply replied that he hadn't seen the Land Surveyor there, and nothing more had been said; but when he had found K. here in the school, he had had to speak to him, so that he might tell his mother the news. For that was what pleased his mother most, when without her express command one did what she wanted. After a short pause for reflection K. said that he did not need any help, he had all that he required, but it was very good of Hans to want to help him, and he thanked him for his good intentions; it was possible that later he might be in need of something and then he would turn to Hans, he had his address. In return perhaps he, K., might be able to offer a little help; he was sorry to hear that Hans's mother was ill and that apparently nobody in the village understood her illness; if it was neglected like that a trifling malady might sometimes lead to grave consequences. Now he, K., had some medical knowledge, and, what was of still more value, experience in treating sick people. Many a case which the doctors had given up he had been able to cure. At home they had called him 'The Bitter Herb' on account of his healing powers. In any case he would be glad to see Hans's mother and speak with her. Perhaps he might be able to give her good advice, for if only for Hans's sake he would be delighted to do it. At first Hans's eyes lit up at this offer, exciting K. to greater urgency, but the outcome was unsatisfactory, for to several questions Hans replied, without showing the slightest trace of regret, that no stranger was allowed to visit his mother, she had to be guarded so carefully; although that day K. had scarcely spoken to her she had had to stay for several days in bed, a thing indeed that often happened. But his father had then been very angry with K. and he would certainly never allow K. to come to the house; he had actually wanted to seek K. out at the time to punish him for his impudence, only Hans's mother had held him back. But in any case his mother never wanted to talk with anybody whatever, and her inquiry about K. was no exception to the rule; on the contrary, seeing he had been mentioned, she could have expressed the wish to see him, but she hadn't done so, and in that had clearly made known her will. She only wanted to hear about K. but she did not want to speak to him. Besides it wasn't any real illness that she was suffering from, she knew quite well the cause of her state and often had actually indicated it; apparently it was the climate here that she could not stand, but all the same she would not leave the place, on account of her husband and children, besides, she was already better in health than she used to be. Here K. felt Hans's powers of thought visibly increasing in his attempt to protect his mother from K., from K. whom he had ostensibly wanted to help; yet, in the good cause of keeping K. away from his mother he even contradicted in several respects what he had said before, particularly in regard to his mother's illness. Nevertheless K. remarked that even so Hans was still well disposed towards him, only when his mother was in question he forgot everything else; whoever was set up beside his mother was immediately at a disadvantage; just now it had been K., but it could as well be his father, for example. K. wanted to test this supposition and said that it was certainly thoughtful of Hans's father to shield his mother from any disturbance, and if he, K., had only guessed that day at this state of things, he would never have thought of venturing to speak to her, and he asked Hans to make his apologies to her now. On the other hand he could not quite understand why

Hans's father, seeing that the cause of her sickness was so clearly known as Hans said, kept her back from going somewhere else to get well; one had to infer that he kept her back, for she only remained on his account and the children's, but she could take the children with her, and she need not have to go away for any long time or for any great distance, even up on the Castle Hill the air was quite different. Hans's father had no need to fear the cost of the holiday, seeing that he was the biggest shoemaker in the place, and it was pretty certain that he or she had relations or acquaintances in the Castle who would be glad to take her in. Why did he not let her go? He shouldn't underestimate an illness like this, K. had only seen Hans's mother for a minute, but it had actually been her striking pallor and weakness that had impelled him to speak to her. Even at that time he had been surprised that her husband had let her sit there in the damp steam of the washing and bathing when she was ill, and had put no restraint either on his loud talk with the others. Hans's father really did not know the actual state of things; even if her illness had improved in the last few weeks, illnesses like that had ups and downs, and in the end, if one did not fight them, they returned with redoubled strength, and then the patient was past help. Even if K. could not speak to Hans's mother, still it would perhaps be advisable if he were to speak to his father and draw his attention to all this.

Hans had listened intently, had understood most of it, and had been deeply impressed by the threat implicit in this dark advice. Nevertheless he replied that K. could not speak to his father, for his father disliked him and would probably treat him as the teacher had done. He said this with a shy smile when he was speaking of K., but sadly and bitterly when he mentioned his father. But he added that perhaps K. might be able to speak to his mother all the same, but only without his father's knowledge. Then deep in thought Hans stared in front of him for a little – just like a woman who wants to do something forbidden and seeks an opportunity to do it without being punished – and said that the day after tomorrow it might be possible, his father was going to the

Herrenhof in the evening, he had a conference there; then he, Hans, would come in the evening and take K. along to his mother, of course, assuming that his mother agreed, which was however very improbable. She never did anything at all against the wishes of his father, she submitted to him in everything, even in things whose unreasonableness he, Hans, could see through.

Long before this K. had called Hans up to the dais, drawn him between his knees, and had kept on caressing him comfortingly. The nearness helped, in spite of Hans's occasional recalcitrance, to bring about an understanding. They agreed finally to the following: Hans would first tell his mother the entire truth, but, so as to make her consent easier, add that K. wanted to speak to Brunswick himself as well, not about her at all, but about his own affairs. Besides this was true; in the course of the conversation K. had remembered that Brunswick, even if he were a bad and dangerous man, could scarcely be his enemy now, if he had been, according to the information of the Superintendent, the leader of those who, even if only on political grounds, were in favour of engaging a Land Surveyor. K.'s arrival in the village must therefore have been welcomed by Brunswick. But in that case his morose greeting that first day and the dislike of which Hans spoke were almost incomprehensible – perhaps, however, Brunswick had been hurt simply because K. had not turned to him first for help, perhaps there existed some other misunderstanding which could be cleared up by a few words. But if that were done K. might very well secure in Brunswick a supporter against the teacher, yes and against the Superintendent as well; the whole official plot – for was it anything else really? – by means of which the Superintendent and the teacher were keeping him from reaching the Castle authorities and had driven him into taking a janitor's post, might be unmasked; if it came anew to a fight about K. between Brunswick and the Superintendent, Brunswick would have to include K. on his side, K. would become a guest in Brunswick's house, Brunswick's fighting resources would be put at his disposal in spite of the Superintendent; who could tell what he might not be able to achieve by those means, and in any case he would often be in the lady's company – so he played with his dreams as they with him, while Hans, thinking only of his mother, painfully watched K.'s silence, as one watches a doctor who is sunk in reflexion while he tries to find the proper remedy for a grave case. With K.'s proposal to speak to Brunswick about his post as Land Surveyor Hans was in agreement, but only because by means of this his mother would be shielded from his father, and because in any case it was only a last resort which with good luck might not be needed. He merely asked further how K. was to explain to his father the lateness of the visit, and was content at last, though his face remained a little overcast, with the suggestion that K. would say that his unendurable post in the school and the teacher's humiliating treatment had made him in sudden despair forget all caution.

Now that, so far as one could see, everything had been provided for, and the possibility of success at least conceded, Hans, freed from his burden of reflexion, became happier, and chatted for some time longer with K. and afterwards with Frieda – who had sat for a long time as if absorbed by quite different thoughts, and only now began to take part in the conversation again. Among other things she asked him what he wanted to become; he did not think long but said he wanted to be a man like K. When he was asked next for his reasons he really did not know how to reply, and the question whether he would like to be a janitor he answered with a decided negative. Only through further questioning did they perceive by what roundabout ways he had arrived at his wish. K.'s present condition was in no way enviable, but wretched and humiliating; even Hans saw this clearly without having to ask other people; he himself would have certainly preferred to shield his mother from K.'s slightest word, even from having to see him. In spite of this, however, he had come to K. and had begged to be allowed to help him, and had been delighted when K. agreed; he imagined, too, that other people felt the same; and, most important of all, it had been his mother herself who had mentioned K.'s name. These contradictions had engendered in him the belief that though for the moment K. was wretched and looked down on, yet in an almost unimaginable and distant future he would excel everybody. And it was just this absurdly distant future and the glorious developments which were to lead up to it that attracted Hans; that was why he was willing to accept K. even in his present state. The peculiar childish-grown-up acuteness of this wish consisted in the fact that Hans looked on K. as on a younger brother whose future would reach further than his own, the future of a very little boy. And it was with an almost troubled seriousness that, driven into a corner by Frieda's questions, he at last confessed those things. K. only cheered him up again when he said that he knew what Hans envied him for; it was for his beautiful walking-stick, which was lying on the table and with which Hans had been playing absently during the conversation. Now K. knew how to produce sticks like that, and if their plan were successful he would make Hans an even more beautiful one. It was no longer quite clear now whether Hans had not really meant merely the walking-stick, so happy was he made by K.'s promise; and he said good-bye with a glad face, not without pressing K.'s hand firmly and saying: 'The day after tomorrow, then.'

It had been high time for Hans to go, for shortly afterwards the teacher flung open the door and shouted when he saw K. and Frieda sitting idly at the table: 'Forgive my intrusion! But will you tell me when this place is to be finally put in order? We have to sit here packed like herring, so that the teaching can't go on. And there are you lolling about in the big gymnasium, and you've even sent away the assistants to give yourselves more room. At least get on to your feet now and get a move on!' Then to K.: 'Now go and bring me my lunch from the Bridge Inn.' All this was delivered in a furious shout, though the words were comparatively inoffensive. K. was quite prepared to obey, but to draw the teacher he said: 'But I've been given notice.' 'Notice or no notice, bring me my lunch,' replied the teacher. 'Notice or no notice, that's just what I want to be sure about,' said K. 'What nonsense is this?' asked the teacher. 'You know you didn't accept the notice.' 'And is that enough to make it invalid?' asked K. 'Not for me,' said the teacher, 'you can take my word for that, but for the Superintendent, it seems, though I can't understand it. But take to your heels now, or else I'll fling you out in earnest.' K. was content the teacher then had spoken with the Superintendent, or perhaps he hadn't spoken after all, but had merely thought over carefully the Superintendent's probable intentions, and these had weighed in K.'s favour. Now K. was setting out hastily to get the lunch, but the teacher called him back from the very doorway, either because he wanted by this counter order to test K.'s willingness to serve, so that he might know how far he could go in future, or because a fresh fit of imperiousness had seized him, and it gave him pleasure to make K. run to and fro like a waiter. On his side K. knew that through too great compliance he would only become the teacher's slave and scapegoat, but within certain limits he decided for the present to give way to the fellow's caprices, for even if the teacher, as had been shown, had not the power to dismiss him, yet he could certainly make the post so difficult that it could not be borne. And the post was more important in K.'s eyes now than ever before. The conversation with Hans had raised new hopes in him, improbable, he admitted, completely groundless even, but all the same not to be put out of his mind; they almost superseded Barnabas himself. If he gave himself up to them – and there was no choice – then he must husband all his strength, trouble about nothing else, food, shelter, the village authorities, no not even about Frieda – and in reality the whole thing turned only on Frieda, for everything else only gave him anxiety in relation to her. For this reason he must try to keep his post which gave Frieda a certain degree of security, and he must not complain if for this end he were made to endure more at the teacher's hands than he would have had to endure in the ordinary course. All that sort of thing could be put up with, it belonged to the ordinary continual petty annoyances of life, it was nothing compared with what K. was striving for, and he had not come here simply to lead an honoured and comfortable life.

And so, as he had been ready to run over to the inn, he showed himself now willing to obey the second order, and first set the room to rights so that the lady teacher and her children could come back to it. But it had to be done with all speed, for after that K. had to go for the lunch, and the teacher was already ravenous. K. assured him that it would all be done as he desired; for a little the teacher looked on while K. hurried up, cleared away the sack of straw, put back the gymnastic apparatus in its place, and swept the room out while Frieda washed and scrubbed the dais. Their diligence seemed to appease the teacher, he only drew their attention to the fact that there was a pile of wood for the fire outside the door – he would not allow K. further access to the shed, of course – and then went back to his class with the threat that he would return soon and inspect.

After a few minutes of silent work Frieda asked K. why he submitted so humbly to the teacher now. The question was asked in a sympathetic, anxious tone, but K., who was thinking how little Frieda had succeeded in keeping her original promise to shield him from the teacher's orders and insults, merely replied shortly that since he was the janitor he must fulfil the janitor's duties. Then there was silence again until K., reminded vividly by this short exchange of words that Frieda had been for a long time lost in anxious thought – and particularly through almost the whole conversation with Hans – asked her bluntly while he carried in the firewood what had been troubling her. Slowly turning her eyes upon him she replied that it was nothing definite, she had only been thinking of the landlady and the truth of much of what she said. Only when K. pressed her did she reply more consecutively after hesitating several times, but without looking up from her work – not that she was thinking of it, for it was making no progress, but simply so that she might not be compelled to look at K. And now she told him that during his talk with Hans she had listened quietly at first, that then she had been startled by certain words of his, then had begun to grasp the meaning of them more clearly, and that ever since she had not been able to cease reading into his words a confirmation of a warning which the landlady had once given her, and which she had always refused to believe. Exasperated by all this circumlocution, and more irritated than touched by Frieda's tearful, complaining voice – but annoyed above all because the landlady was coming into his affairs again, though only as a recollection, for in person she had had little success up till now – K. flung the wood he was carrying in his arms on to the floor, sat down on it, and in tones which were now serious demanded the whole truth. 'More than once,' began Frieda, 'yes, since the beginning, the landlady has tried to make me doubt you, she didn't hold that you were lying, on the contrary she said that you were childishly open, but your character was so different from ours, she said, that, even when you spoke frankly, it was bound to be difficult for us to believe you; and if we did not listen to good advice we would have to learn to believe you through bitter experience. Even she with her keen eye for people was almost taken in. But after her last talk with you in the Bridge Inn – I am only repeating her own words – she woke up to your tricks, she said, and after that you couldn't deceive her even if you did your best to hide your intentions. But you hid nothing, she repeated that again and again, and then she said afterwards: Try to listen to him carefully at the first favourable opportunity, not superficially, but carefully, carefully. That was all that she had done and your own words had told her all this regarding myself: That you made up to me – she used those very words – only because I happened to be in your way, because I did not actually repel you, and because quite erroneously you considered a barmaid the destined prey of any guest who chose to stretch out his hand for her. Moreover, you wanted, as the landlady learned at the Herrenhof, for some reason or other to spend that night at the Herrenhof, and that could in no circumstances be achieved except through me. Now all that was sufficient cause for you to become my lover for one night, but something more was needed to turn it into a more serious affair. And that something more was Klamm. The landlady doesn't claim to know what you want from Klamm, she merely maintains that before you knew me you strove as eagerly to reach Klamm as you have done since. The only difference was this, that before you knew me you were without any hope, but that now you imagine that in me you have a reliable means of reaching Klamm certainly and quickly and even with advantage to yourself. How startled I was – but that was only a superficial fear without deeper cause – when you said today that before you knew me you had gone about here in a blind circle. These might actually be the same words that the landlady used, she, too, says that it's only since you have known me that you've become aware of your goal. That's because you believe you have secured in me a sweetheart of Klamm's, and so possess a hostage which can only be ransomed at a great price. Your one endeavour is to treat with Klamm about this hostage. As in your eyes I am nothing and the price everything, so you are ready for any concession so far as I'm concerned, but as for the price you're adamant. So it's a matter of indifference to you that I've lost my post at the Herrenhof and that I've had to leave the Bridge Inn as well, a matter of indifference that I have to endure the heavy work here in the school. You have no tenderness to spare for me, you have hardly even time for me, you leave me to the assistants, the idea of being jealous never comes into your mind, my only value for you is that I was once Klamm's sweetheart, in your ignorance you exert yourself to keep me from forgetting Klamm, so that when the decisive moment comes I should not make any resistance; yet at the same time you carry on a feud with the landlady, the only one you think capable of separating me from you, and that's why you brought your quarrel with her to a crisis, so as to have to leave the Bridge Inn with me; but that, so far as I'm concerned, I belong to you whatever happens, you haven't the slighest doubt. You think of the interview with Klamm as a business deal, a matter of hard cash. You take every possibility into account; providing that you reach your end you're ready to do anything; should Klamm want me you are prepared to give me to him, should he want you to stick to me you'll stick to me, should he want you to fling me out, you'll fling me out, but you're prepared to play a part too; if it's advantageous to you, you'll give out that you love me, you'll try to combat his indifference by emphasizing your own littleness, and then shame him by the fact that you're his successor, or you'll be ready to carry him the protestations of love for him which you know I've made, and beg him to take me on again, of course on your terms; and if nothing else answers, then you'll simply go and beg from him in the name of K. and wife. But, the landlady said finally, when you see that you have deceived yourself in everything, in your assumptions and in your hopes, in your ideas of Klamm and his relations with me, then my purgatory will begin, for then for the first time I'll be in reality the only possession you'll have to fall back on, but at the same time it will be a possession that has proved to be worthless, and you'll treat it accordingly, seeing that you have no feeling for me but the feeling of ownership.'

With his lips tightly compressed K. had listened intently, the wood he was sitting on had rolled asunder though he had not noticed it, he had almost slid on to the floor, and now at last he got up, sat down on the dais, took Frieda's hand, which she feebly tried to pull away, and said: 'In what you've said I haven't always been able to distinguish the landlady's sentiments from your own.' 'They're the landlady's sentiments purely,' said Frieda, 'I heard her out because I respected her, but it was the first time in my life that I completely and wholly refused to accept her opinion. All that she said seemed to me so pitiful, so far from any understanding of how things stood between us. There seemed actually to be more truth to me in the direct opposite of what she said. I thought of that sad morning after our first night together. You kneeling beside me with a look as if everything were lost. And how it really seemed then that in spite of all I could do, I was not helping you but hindering you. It was through me that the landlady had become your enemy, a powerful enemy, whom even now you still under-value; it was for my sake that you had to take thought, that you had to fight for your post, that you were at a disadvantage before the Superintendent, that you had to humble yourself before the teacher and were delivered over to the assistants, but worst of all for my sake you had perhaps lost your chance with Klamm. That you still went on trying to reach Klamm was only a kind of feeble endeavour to propitiate him in some way. And I told myself that the landlady, who certainly knew far better than I, was only trying to shield me by her suggestions from bitter self-reproach. A well-meant but superfluous attempt. My love for you had helped me through everything, and would certainly help you on too, in the long run, if not here in the village, then somewhere else; it had already given a proof of its power, it had rescued you from Barnabas's family.' 'That was your opinion, then, at the time,' said K., 'and has it changed since?' 'I don't know,' replied Frieda, glancing down at K.'s hand which still held hers, 'perhaps nothing has changed; when you're so close to me and question me so calmly, then I think that nothing has changed. But in reality –' she drew her hand away from K., sat erect opposite him and wept without hiding her face; she held her tear-covered face up to him as if she were weeping not for herself and so had nothing to hide, but as if she were weeping over K.'s treachery and so the pain of seeing her tears was his due – 'But in reality everything has changed since I've listened to you talking with that boy. How innocently you began asking about the family, about this and that! To me you looked just as you did that night when you came into the taproom, impetuous and frank, trying to catch my attention with such a childlike eagerness. You were just the same as then, and all I wished was that the landlady had been here and could have listened to you, and then we should have seen whether she could still stick to her opinion. But then quite suddenly – I don't know how it happened – I noticed that you were talking to him with a hidden intention. You won his trust – and it wasn't easy to win – by sympathetic words, simply so that you might with greater ease reach your end, which I began to recognize more and more clearly. Your end was that woman. In your apparently solicitious inquiries about her I could see quite nakedly your simple preoccupation with your own affairs.

You were betraying that woman even before you had won her. In your words I recognized not only my past, but my future as well, it was as if the landlady were sitting beside me and explaining everything, and with all my strength I tried to push her away, but I saw clearly the hopelessness of my attempt, and yet it was not really myself who was going to be betrayed, it was not I who was really being betrayed, but that unknown woman. And then when I collected myself and asked Hans what he wanted to be and he said he wanted to be like you, and I saw that he had fallen under your influence so completely already, well what great difference was there between him, being exploited by you, the poor boy, and myself that time in the taproom?'

'Everything,' said K., who had regained his composure in listening. 'Everything that you say is in a certain sense justifiable, it is not untrue, it is only partisan. These are the landlady's ideas, my enemy's ideas, even if you imagine that they're your own; and that comforts me. But they're instructive, one can learn a great deal from the landlady. She didn't express them to me personally, although she did not spare my feelings in other ways; evidently she put this weapon in your hands in the hope that you would employ it at a particularly bad or decisive point for me. If I am abusing you, then she is abusing you in the same way. But, Frieda, just consider; even if everything were just as the landlady says, it would only be shameful on one supposition, that is, that you did not love me. Then, only then, would it really seem that I had won you through calculation and trickery, so as to profiteer by possessing you. In that case it might even have been part of my plan to appear before you arm-in-arm with Olga so as to evoke your pity, and the landlady has simply forgotten to mention that too in her list of my offences. But if it wasn't as bad as all that, if it wasn't a sly beast of prey that seized you that night, but you came to meet me, just as I went to meet you, and we found one another without a thought for ourselves, in that case, Frieda, tell me, how would things look? If that were really so, in acting for myself I was acting for you too, there is no distinction here, and only an enemy could draw it. And that holds in everything, even the case of Hans. Besides, in your condemnation of my talk with Hans your sensitiveness makes you exaggerate things morbidly, for if Hans's intentions and my own don't quite coincide, still that doesn't by any means amount to an actual antagonism between them, moreover our discrepancies were not lost on Hans, if you believe that you do grave injustice to the cautious little man, and even if they should have been all lost on him, still nobody will be any the worse for it, I hope.'

'It's so difficult to see one's way, K.,' said Frieda with a sigh. 'I certainly had no doubts about you, and if I have acquired something of the kind from the landlady, I'll be only too glad to throw it off and beg you for forgiveness on my knees, as I do, believe me, all the time, even when I'm saying such horrible things. But the truth remains that you keep many things from me; you come and go, I don't know where or from where. Just now when Hans knocked you cried out Barnabas's name. I only wish you had once called out my name as lovingly as for some incomprehensible reason you called that hateful name. If you have no trust in me, how can I keep mistrust from rising? It delivers me completely to the landlady, whom you justify in appearance by your behaviour. Not in everything, I won't say that you justify her in everything, for was it not on my account alone that you sent the assistants packing? Oh, if you but knew with what passion I try to find a grain of comfort for myself in all that you do and say, even when it gives me pain.' 'Once and for all, Frieda,' said K., 'I conceal not the slightest thing from you. See how the landlady hates me, and how she does her best to get you away from me, and what despicable means she uses, and how you give in to her, Frieda, how you give in to her! Tell me, now, in what way do I hide anything from you? That I want to reach Klamm you know, that you can't help me to do it and that accordingly I must do it by my own efforts you know too; that I have not succeeded up till now you see for yourself. Am I to humiliate myself doubly, perhaps, by telling you of all the bootless attempts which have already humiliated me sufficiently?

Am I to plume myself on having waited and shivered in vain all an afternoon at the door of Klamm's sledge? Only too glad not to have to think of such things any more, I hurry back to you, and I am greeted again with all those reproaches from you. And Barnabas? It's true I'm waiting for him. He's Klamm's messenger, it isn't I who made him that.' 'Barnabas again!' cried Frieda. 'I can't believe that he's a good messenger.' 'Perhaps you're right,' said K., 'but he's the only messenger that's sent to me.' 'All the worse for you,' said Frieda, 'all the more reason why you should beware of him.' 'Unfortunately he has given me no cause for that till now,' said K. smiling. 'He comes very seldom, and what messages he brings are of no importance; only the fact that they come from Klamm gives them any value.' 'But listen to me,' said Frieda, 'for it is not even Klamm that's your goal now, perhaps that disturbs me most of all; that you always longed for Klamm while you had me was bad enough, but that you seem to have stopped trying to reach Klamm now is much worse, that's something which not even the landlady foresaw. According to the landlady your happiness, a questionable and yet very real happiness, would end on the day when you finally recognized that the hopes you founded on Klamm were in vain. But now you don't wait any longer even for that day, a young lad suddenly comes in and you begin to fight with him for his mother, as if you were fighting for your very life.' 'You've understood my talk with Hans quite correctly,' said K., 'it was really so. But is your whole former life so completely wiped from your mind (all except the landlady, of course, who won't allow herself to be wiped out), that you can't remember any longer how one must fight to get to the top, especially when one begins at the bottom? How one must take advantage of everything that offers any hope whatever? And this woman comes from the Castle, she told me herself on my first day here, when I happened to stray into Lasemann's. What's more natural than to ask her for advice or even for help; if the landlady only knows the obstacles which keep one from reaching Klamm, then this woman probably knows the way to him, for she has come here by that way herself.' 'The way to Klamm?'

asked Frieda. 'To Klamm, certainly, where else?' said K. Then he jumped up; 'But now it's high time I was going for the lunch.' Frieda implored him to stay, urgently, with an eagerness quite disproportionate to the occasion, as if only his staying with her would confirm all the comforting things he had told her. But K. was thinking of the teacher, he pointed towards the door, which any moment might fly open with a thunderous crash, and promised to return at once, she was not even to light the fire, he himself would see about it. Finally Frieda gave in in silence. As K. was stamping through the snow outside – the path should have been shovelled free long ago, strange how slowly the work was getting forward! – he saw one of the assistants, now dead tired, still holding to the railings. Only one, where was the other? Had K. broken the endurance of one of them, then, at least? The remaining one was certainly still zealous enough, one could see that when, animated by the sight of K., he began more feverishly than ever to stretch out his arms and roll his eyes. 'His obstinacy is really wonderful,' K. told himself, but had to add, 'he'll freeze to the railings if he keeps it up.' Outwardly, however, K. had nothing for the assistant but a threatening gesture with his fist, which prevented any nearer approach; indeed the assistant actually retreated for an appreciable distance. Just then Frieda opened one of the windows so as to air the room before putting on the fire, as she had promised K. Immediately the assistant turned his attention from K., and crept as if irresistibly attracted to the window. Her face torn between pity for the assistant and a beseeching helpless glance which she cast at K., Frieda put her hand out hesitatingly from the window, it was not clear whether it was a greeting or a command to go away, nor did the assistant let it deflect him from his resolve to come nearer. Then Frieda closed the outer window hastily, but remained standing behind it, her hand on the sash, with her head bent sideways, her eyes wide, and a fixed smile on her face. Did she know that standing like that she was more likely to attract the assistant than repel him? But K. did not look back again, he thought he had better hurry as fast as he could and get back quickly.

14

At long last, late in the afternoon, when it was already dark, K. had cleared the garden path, piled the snow high on either side, beaten it down hard, and also accomplished his work for the day. He was standing by the garden gate in the middle of a wide solitude. He had driven off the remaining assistant hours before, and chased him a long way, but the fellow had managed to hide himself somewhere between the garden and the schoolhouse and could not be found, nor had he shown himself since. Frieda was indoors either starting to wash clothes or still washing Gisa's cat; it was a sign of great confidence on Gisa's part that this task had been entrusted to Frieda, an unpleasant and uncalled-for task, indeed, which K. would not have suffered her to attempt had it not been advisable in view of their various shortcomings to seize every opportunity of securing Gisa's goodwill. Gisa had looked on approvingly while K. brought down the little children's bath from the garret, heated water, and finally helped to put the cat carefully into the bath. Then she actually left the cat entirely in charge of Frieda, for Schwarzer, K.'s acquaintance of the first evening, had arrived, had greeted K. with a mixture of embarrassment (arising out of the events of that evening) and of unmitigated contempt such as one accords to a debtor, and had vanished with Gisa into the other schoolroom. The two of them were still there. Schwarzer, K. had been told in the Bridge Inn, had been living in the village for some time, although he was a castellan's son, because of his love for Gisa, and through his influential connexions had got himself appointed as a pupil-teacher, a position which he had filled chiefly by attending all Gisa's classes, either sitting on a school bench among the children, or preferably at Gisa's feet on the teacher's dais. His presence was no longer a disturbance, the children had got quite used to it, all the more easily, perhaps, because Schwarzer neither liked nor understood children and rarely spoke to them except when he took over the gymnastic lesson from Gisa, and was content merely to breathe the same air as Gisa and bask in her warmth and nearness.

The only astonishing thing about it was that in the Bridge Inn at least Schwarzer was spoken of with a certain degree of respect, even if his actions were ridiculous rather than praiseworthy, and that Gisa was included in this respectful atmosphere. It was none the less unwarranted of Schwarzer to assume that his position as a pupil-teacher gave him a great superiority over K., for this superiority was non-existent. A school janitor was an important person to the rest of the staff – and should have been especially so to such an assistant as Schwarzer – a person not to be lightly despised, who should at least be suitably conciliated if professional considerations were not enough to prevent one from despising him. K. decided to keep this fact in mind, also that Schwarzer was still in his debt on account of their first evening, a debt which had not been lessened by the way in which events of succeeding days had seemed to justify Schwarzer's reception of him. For it must not be forgotten that this reception had perhaps determined the later course of events. Because of Schwarzer the full attention of the authorities had been most unreasonably directed to K. at the very first hour of his arrival, while he was still a complete stranger in the village without a single acquaintance or an alternative shelter; overtired with walking as he was and quite helpless on his sack of straw, he had been at the mercy of any official action. One night later might have made all the difference, things might have gone quietly and been only half noticed. At any rate nobody would have known anything about him or have had any suspicions, there would have been no hesitation in accepting him at least for one day as a stray wanderer, his handiness and trustworthiness would have been recognized and spoken of in the neighbourhood, and probably he would soon have found accommodation somewhere as a servant. Of course the authorities would have found him out. But there would have been a big difference between having the Central Bureau, or whoever was on the telephone, disturbed on his account in the middle of the night by an insistent although ostensibly humble request for an immediate decision, made, too, by Schwarzer, who was probably not in the best odour up there, and a quiet visit by K. to the Superintendent on the next day during official hours to report himself in proper form as a wandering stranger who had already found quarters in a respectable house, and who would probably be leaving the place in another day's time unless the unlikely were to happen and he found some work in the village, only for a day or two, of course, since he did not mean to stay longer. That, or something like that, was what would have happened had it not been for Schwarzer. The authorities would have pursued the matter further, but calmly, in the ordinary course of business, unharassed by what they probably hated most, the impatience of a waiting client. Well, all that was not K.'s fault, it was Schwarzer's fault, but Schwarzer was the son of a castellan, and had behaved with outward propriety, and so the matter could only be visited on K.'s head. And what was the trivial cause of it all? Perhaps an ungracious mood of Gisa's that day, which made Schwarzer roam sleeplessly all night, and vent his annoyance on K. Of course on the other hand one could argue that Schwarzer's attitude was something K. had to be thankful for. It had been the sole precipitant of a situation K. would never by himself have achieved, nor have dared to achieve, and which the authorities themselves would hardly have allowed, namely, that from the very beginning without any dissimulation he found himself confronting the authorities face to face, in so far as that was at all possible. Still, that was a dubious gift, it spared K. indeed the necessity of lying and contriving, but it made him almost defenceless, handicapped him anyhow in the struggle, and might have driven him to despair had he not been able to remind himself that the difference in strength between the authorities and himself was so enormous that all the guile of which he was capable would hardly have served appreciably to reduce the difference in his favour. Yet that was only a reflexion for his own consolation, Schwarzer was none the less in his debt, and having harmed K. then could be called upon now to help. K. would be in need of help in the quite trivial and tentative opening moves, for Barnabas seemed to have failed him again.

On Frieda's account K. had refrained all day from going to Barnabas's house to make inquiries; in order to avoid receiving Barnabas in Frieda's presence he had laboured out of doors, and when his work was done he had continued to linger outside in expectation of Barnabas, but Barnabas had not come. The only thing he could do now was to visit the sisters, only for a minute or two, he would only stand at the door and ask, he would be back again soon. So he thrust the shovel into the snow and set off at a run. He arrived breathless at the house of Barnabas, and after a sharp knock flung the door open and asked, without looking to see who was inside: 'Hasn't Barnabas come back yet?' Only then did he notice that Olga was not there, that the two old people, who were again sitting at the far end of the table in a state of vacancy, had not yet realized what was happening at the door and were only now slowly turning their faces towards it, and finally that Amalia had been lying beside the stove under a blanket and in her alarm at K.'s sudden appearance had started up with her hand to her brow in an effort to recover her composure. If Olga had been there she would have answered immediately, and K. could have gone away again, but as it was he had at least to take a step or two towards Amalia, give her his hand which she pressed in silence, and beg her to keep the startled old folks from attempting to meander through the room, which she did with a few words. K. learned that Olga was chopping wood in the yard, that Amalia, exhausted – for what reason she did not say – had had to lie down a short time before, and that Barnabas had not yet indeed returned, but must return very soon, for he never stayed overnight in the Castle. K. thanked her for the information, which left him at liberty to go, but Amalia asked if he would not wait to see Olga. However, she added, he had already spoken to Olga during the day. He answered with surprise that he had not, and asked if Olga had something of particular importance to say to him. As if faintly irritated Amalia screwed up her mouth silently, gave him a nod, obviously in farewell, and lay down again. From her recumbent position she let her eyes rest on him as if she were astonished to see him still there. Her gaze was cold, clear, and steady as usual, it was never levelled exactly on the object she regarded but in some disturbing way always a little past it, hardly perceptibly, but yet unquestionably past it, not from weakness, apparently, nor from embarrassment, nor from duplicity, but from a persistent and dominating desire for isolation, which she herself perhaps only became conscious of in this way. K. thought he could remember being baffled on the very first evening by that look, probably even the whole hatefulness of the impression so quickly made on him by this family was traceable to that look, which in itself was not hateful but proud and upright in its reserve. 'You are always so sad, Amalia,' said K., 'is anything troubling you? Can't you say what it is? I have never seen a country girl at all like you. It never struck me before. Do you really belong to this village? Were you born here?' Amalia nodded, as if K. had only put the last of those questions, and then said: 'So you'll wait for Olga?' 'I don't know why you keep on asking me that,' said K. 'I can't stay any longer because my fiancée's waiting for me at home.' Amalia propped herself on one elbow; she had not heard of the engagement. K. gave Frieda's name. Amalia did not know it. She asked if Olga knew of their betrothal. K. fancied she did, for she had seen him with Frieda, and news like that was quick to fly around in a village. Amalia assured him, however, that Olga knew nothing about it, and that it would make her very unhappy, for she seemed to be in love with K. She had not directly said so, for she was very reserved, but love betrayed itself involuntarily. K. was convinced that Amalia was mistaken. Amalia smiled, and this smile of hers, although sad, lit up her gloomy face, made her silence eloquent, her strangeness intimate, and unlocked a mystery jealously guarded hitherto, a mystery which could indeed be concealed again, but never so completely. Amalia said that she was certainly not mistaken, she would even go further and affirm that K., too, had an inclination for Olga, and that his visits, which were ostensibly concerned with some message or other from Barnabas, were really intended for Olga. But now that Amalia knew all about it he need not be so strict with himself and could come oftener to see them. That was all she wanted to say. K. shook his head, and reminded her of his betrothal. Amalia seemed to set little store by his betrothal, the immediate impression she received from K., who was after all unaccompanied, was in her opinion decisive, she only asked when K. had made the girl's acquaintance, for he had been but a few days in the village. K. told her about his night at the Herrenhof, whereupon Amalia merely said briefly that she had been very much against his being taken to the Herrenhof.

She appealed for confirmation to Olga, who had just come in with an armful of wood, fresh and glowing from the frosty air, strong and vivid, as if transformed by the change from her usual aimless standing about inside. She threw down the wood, greeted K. frankly, and asked at once after Frieda. K. exchanged a look with Amalia, who seemed, however, not at all disconcerted. A little relieved, K. spoke of Frieda more freely than he would otherwise have done, described the difficult circumstances in which she was managing to keep house in a kind of way in the school, and in the haste of his narrative – for he wanted to go home at once – so far forgot himself when bidding them goodbye as to invite the sisters to come and pay him a visit. He began to stammer in confusion, however, when Amalia, giving him no time to say another word, interposed with an acceptance of the invitation; then Olga was compelled to associate herself with it. But K., still harassed by the feeling that he ought to go at once, and becoming uneasy under Amalia's gaze, did not hesitate any longer to confess that the invitation had been quite unpremeditated and had sprung merely from a personal impulse, but that unfortunately he could not confirm it since there was a great hostility, to him quite incomprehensible, between Frieda and their family. 'It's not hostility,' said Amalia, getting up from her couch, and flinging the blanket behind her, 'it's nothing so big as that, it's only a parrot repetition of what she hears everywhere. And now, go away, go to your young woman, I can see you're in a hurry. You needn't be afraid that we'll come, I only said it at first for fun, out of mischief. But you can come often enough to see us, there's nothing to hinder you, you can always plead Barnabas's messages as an excuse. I'll make it easier for you by telling you that Barnabas, even if he has a message from the Castle for you, can't go all the way up to the school to find you. He can't trail about so much, poor boy, he wears himself out in the service, you'll have to come yourself to get the news.' K. had never before heard Amalia utter so many consecutive sentences, and they sounded differently from her usual comments, they had a kind of dignity which obviously impressed not only K. but Olga too, although she was accustomed to her sister. She stood a little to one side, her arms folded, in her usual stolid and somewhat stooping posture once more, with her eyes fixed on Amalia, who on the other hand looked only at K. 'It's an error,' said K., 'a gross error to imagine that I'm not in earnest in looking for Barnabas, it's my most urgent wish, really my only wish, to get my business with the authorities properly settled. And Barnabas has to help me in that, most of my hopes are based on him. I grant he has disappointed me greatly once as it is, but that was more my fault than his; in the bewilderment of my first hours in the village I believed that everything could be settled by a short walk in the evening, and when the impossible proved impossible I blamed him for it. That influenced me even in my opinion of your family and of you. But that is all past, I think I understand you better now, you are even –' K. tried to think of the exact word, but could not find it immediately, so contented himself with a makeshift – 'You seem to be the most good-natured people in the village so far as my experience goes. But now, Amalia, you're putting me off the track again by your depreciation – if not of your brother's service – then of the importance he has for me. Perhaps you aren't acquainted with his affairs, in which case it doesn't matter, but perhaps you are acquainted with them – and that's the impression I incline to have – in which case it's a bad thing, for that would indicate that your brother is deceiving me.' 'Calm yourself,' cried Amalia, 'I'm not acquainted with them, nothing could induce me to become acquainted with them, nothing at all, not even my consideration for you, which would move me to do a great deal, for, as you say, we are good-natured people. But my brother's affairs are his own business, I know nothing about them except what I hear by chance now and then against my will. On the other hand Olga can tell you all about them, for she's in his confidence.' And Amalia went away, first to her parents, with whom she whispered, then to the kitchen; she went without taking leave of K., as if she knew that he would stay for a long time yet and that no good-bye was necessary.

15

Seeing that with a somewhat astonished face K. remained standing where he was, Olga laughed at him and drew him towards the settle by the stove, she seemed to be really happy at the prospect of sitting there alone with him, but it was a contented happiness without a single hint of jealousy. And precisely this freedom of hers from jealousy and therefore from any kind of claim upon him did K. good, he was glad to look into her blue eyes which were not cajoling, nor hectoring, but shyly simple and frank. It was as if the warning of Frieda and the landlady had made him, not more susceptible to all those things, but more observant and more discerning. And he laughed with Olga when she expressed her wonder at his calling Amalia good-natured, of all things, for Amalia had many qualities, but good-nature was certainly not one of them. Whereupon K. explained that of course his praise had been meant for Olga, only Amalia was so masterful that she not only took to herself whatever was said in her presence, but induced other people of their own free will to include her in everything. 'That's true,' said Olga becoming more serious, 'truer than you think. Amalia's younger than me, and younger than Barnabas, but hers is the decisive voice in the family for good or for ill, of course she bears the burden of it more than anybody, the good as well as the bad.' K. thought that an exaggeration, for Amalia had just said that she paid no attention, for instance, to her brother's affairs, while Olga knew all about them. 'How can I make it clear?' said Olga, 'Amalia bothers neither about Barnabas nor about me, she really bothers nobody but the old people whom she tends day and night; now she has just asked them again if they want anything and has gone into the kitchen to cook them something, and for their sakes she has overcome her indisposition, for she's been ill since midday and been lying here on the settle. But although she doesn't bother about us we're as dependent on her as if she were the eldest, and if she were to advise us in our affairs we should certainly follow her advice, only she doesn't do it, she's different from us. You have experience of people, you come from a strange land, don't you think, too, that she's extraordinarily clever?' 'Extraordinarily unhappy is what she seems to me,' said K., 'but how does it go with your respect for her that Barnabas, for example, takes service as a messenger, in spite of Amalia's evident disapproval, and even her scorn?' 'If he knew what else to do he would give up being a messenger at once, for it doesn't satisfy him.' 'Isn't he an expert shoemaker?' asked K. 'Of course he is,' said Olga, 'and in his spare time he does work for Brunswick, and if he liked he could have enough work to keep him going day and night and earn a lot of money.' 'Well then,' said K., 'that would be an alternative to his services as a messenger.' 'An alternative?' asked Olga in astonishment. 'Do you think he does it for money?' 'Maybe he does,' said K., 'but didn't you say he was discontented?' 'He's discontented, and for various reasons,' said Olga, 'but it's Castle service, anyhow a kind of Castle service, at least one would suppose so.' 'What!' said K., 'do you even doubt that?' 'Well,' said Olga, 'not really, Barnabas goes into the bureaux and is accepted by the attendants as one of themselves, he sees various officials, too, from the distance, is entrusted with relatively important letters, even with verbally delivered messages, that's a good deal, after all, and we should be proud of what he has achieved for a young man of his years.' K. nodded and no longer thought of going home. 'He has a uniform of his own, too?' he asked. 'You mean the jacket?' said Olga. 'No, Amalia made that for him long before he became a messenger. But you're touching on a sore spot now. He ought long ago to have had, not a uniform, for there aren't many in the Castle, but a suit provided by the department, and he has been promised one, but in things of that kind the Castle moves slowly, and the worst of it is that one never knows what this slowness means; it can mean that the matter's being considered, but it can also mean that it hasn't yet been taken up, that Barnabas for instance is still on probation, and in the long run it can also mean that the whole thing has been settled, that for some reason or other the promise has been cancelled, and that Barnabas will never get his suit. One can never find out exactly what is happening, or only a long time afterwards. We have a saying here, perhaps you've heard it: Official decisions are as shy as young girls.' 'That's a good observation,' said K., he took it still more seriously than Olga, 'a good observation, and the decisions may have other characteristics in common with young girls.' 'Perhaps,' said Olga. 'But as far as the official suit's concerned, that's one of Barnabas's great sorrows, and since we share all our troubles, it's one of mine too. We ask ourselves in vain why he doesn't get an official suit. But the whole affair is not just so simple as that. The officials, for instance, apparently have no official dress; so far as we know here, and so far as Barnabas tells us, the officials go about in their ordinary clothes, very fine clothes, certainly. Well, you've seen Klamm. Now, Barnabas is certainly not an official, not even one in the lowest category, and he doesn't overstep his limitations so far as to want to be one. But according to Barnabas, the higher-grade servants, whom one certainly never sees down here in the village, have no official dress; that's a kind of comfort, one might suppose, but it's deceptive comfort, for is Barnabas a high-grade servant? Not he; however partial one might be towards him one couldn't maintain that, the fact that he comes to the village and even lives here is sufficient proof of the contrary, for the higher-grade servants are even more inaccessible than the officials, perhaps rightly so, perhaps they are even of higher rank than many an official, there's some evidence of that, they work less, and Barnabas says it's a marvellous sight to see these tall and distinguished men slowly walking through the corridors, Barnabas always gives them a wide berth. Well, he might be one of the lower-grade servants, then, but these always have an official suit, at least whenever they come down into the village, it's not exactly a uniform, there are many different versions of it, but at any rate one can always tell Castle servants by their clothes, you've seen some of them in the Herrenhof. The most noticeable thing about the clothes is that they're mostly close-fitting, a peasant or a handworker couldn't do with them. Well, a suit like that hasn't been given to Barnabas and it's not merely the shame of it or the disgrace – one could put up with that – but the fact that in moments of depression – and we often have such moments, none too rarely, Barnabas and I – it makes us doubt everything. Is it really Castle service Barnabas is doing, we ask ourselves then; granted, he goes into the bureaux, but are the bureaux part of the real Castle? And if there are bureaux actually in the Castle, are they bureaux that Barnabas is allowed to enter?

'He's admitted into certain rooms, but they're only a part of the whole, for there are barriers behind which there are more rooms. Not that he's actually forbidden to pass the barriers, but he can't very well push past them once he has met his chiefs and been dismissed by them. Besides, everybody is watched there, at least so we believe. And even if he did push on farther what good would it be to him, if he had no official duties to carry out and were a mere intruder? And you mustn't imagine that these barriers are a definite dividing-line; Barnabas is always impressing that on me. There are barriers even at the entrance to the rooms where he's admitted, so you see there are barriers he can pass, and they're just the same as the ones he's never yet passed, which looks as if one oughtn't to suppose that behind the ultimate barriers the bureaux are any different from those Barnabas has already seen. Only that's what we do suppose in moments of depression. And the doubt doesn't stop there, we can't keep it within bounds. Barnabas sees officials, Barnabas is given messages. But who are those officials, and what are the messages? Now, so he says, he's assigned to Klamm, who gives him his instructions in person. Well, that would be a great favour, even higher-grade servants don't get so far as that, it's almost too much to believe, almost terrifying. Only think, directly assigned to Klamm, speaking with him face to face! But is it really the case? Well, suppose it is so, then why does Barnabas doubt that the official who is referred to as Klamm is really Klamm?' 'Olga,' said K., 'you surely must be joking; how can there be any doubt about Klamm's appearance, everybody knows what he looks like, even I have seen him.' 'Of course not, K.,' said Olga. 'I'm not joking at all, I'm desperately serious. Yet I'm not telling you all this simply to relieve my own feelings and burden yours, but because Amalia charged me to tell you, since you were asking for Barnabas, and because I think too that it would be useful for you to know more about it. I'm doing it for Barnabas's sake as well, so that you won't pin too many hopes upon him, and suffer disappointment, and make him suffer too because of your disappointment. He's very sensitive, for instance he didn't sleep all night because you were displeased with him yesterday evening. He took you to say that it was a bad lookout for you to have only a messenger like him. These words kept him off his sleep. I don't suppose that you noticed how upset he was, for Castle messengers must keep themselves well under control. But he hasn't an easy time, not even with you, although from your point of view you don't ask too much of him, for you have your own prior conception of a messenger's powers and make your demands accordingly. But in the Castle they have a different conception of a messenger's duties, which couldn't be reconciled with yours, even if Barnabas were to devote himself entirely to the task, which, unfortunately, he often seems inclined to do. Still, one would have to submit to that and raise no objections if it weren't for the question whether Barnabas is really a messenger or not. Before you, of course, he can't express any doubt of it whatever, to do that would be to undermine his very existence and to offend grievously against laws which he believes himself still plighted to, and even to me he doesn't speak freely, I have to cajole him and kiss his doubts out of him, and even then he refuses to admit that his doubts are doubts. He has something of Amalia in him. And I'm sure that he doesn't tell me everything, although I'm his sole confidante. But we do often speak about Klamm, whom I've never seen; you know Frieda doesn't like me and has never let me look at him, still his appearance is well known in the village, some people have seen him, everybody has heard of him, and out of glimpses and rumours and through various distorting factors an image of Klamm has been constructed which is certainly true in fundamentals. But only in fundamentals. In detail it fluctuates, and yet perhaps not so much as Klamm's real appearance. For he's reported as having one appearance when he comes into the village and another on leaving it; after having his beer he looks different from what he does before it, when he's awake he's different from when he's asleep, when he's alone he's different from when he's talking to people, and – what is incomprehensible after all that – he's almost another person up in the Castle. And even within the village there are considerable differences in the accounts given of him, differences as to his height, his bearing, his size, and the cut of his beard; fortunately there's one thing in which all the accounts agree, he always wears the same clothes, a black morning coat with long tails. Now of course all these differences aren't the result of magic, but can be easily explained; they depend on the mood of the observer, on the degree of his excitement, on the countless graduations of hope or despair which are possible for him when he sees Klamm, and besides, he can usually see

Klamm only for a second or two. I'm telling you all this just as Barnabas has often told it to me, and, on the whole, for anyone not personally interested in the matter, it would be a sufficient explanation. Not for us, however; it's a matter of life or death for Barnabas whether it's really Klamm he speaks to or not.' 'And for me no less,' said K., and they moved nearer to each other on the settle.

All this depressing information of Olga's certainly affected K., but he regarded it as a great consolation to find other people who were at least externally much in the same situation as himself, with whom he could join forces and whom he could touch at many points, not merely at a few points as in Frieda's case. He was indeed gradually giving up all hope of achieving success through Barnabas, but the worse it went with Barnabas in the Castle the nearer he felt drawn to him down here; never would K. have believed that in the village itself such a despairing struggle could go on as Barnabas and his sister were involved in. Of course it was as yet far from being adequately explained and might turn out to be quite the reverse, one shouldn't let Olga's unquestionable innocence mislead one into taking Barnabas's uprightness for granted. 'Barnabas is familiar with all those accounts of Klamm's appearance,' went on Olga, 'he has collected and compared a great many, perhaps too many, he even saw Klamm once through a carriage window in the village, or believed he saw him, and so was sufficiently prepared to recognize him again, and yet – how can you explain this? – when he entered a bureau in the Castle and had one of several officials pointed out to him as Klamm he didn't recognize him, and for a long time afterwards couldn't accustom himself to the idea that it was Klamm. But if you ask Barnabas what was the difference between that Klamm and the usual description given of Klamm, he can't tell you, or rather he tries to tell you and describes the official of the Castle, but his description coincides exactly with the descriptions we usually hear of Klamm. Well then, Barnabas, I say to him, why do you doubt it, why do you torment yourself? Whereupon in obvious distress he begins to reckon up certain characteristics of the Castle official, but he seems to be thinking them out rather than describing them, and besides that they are so trivial – a particular way of nodding the head, for instance, or even an unbuttoned waistcoat – that one simply can't take them seriously. Much more important seems to me the way in which Klamm receives Barnabas. Barnabas has often described it to me, and even sketched the room. He's usually admitted into a large room, but the room isn't Klamm's bureau, nor even the bureau of any particular official. It's a room divided into two by a single reading-desk stretching all its length from wall to wall; one side is so narrow that two people can hardly squeeze past each other, and that's reserved for the officials, the other side is spacious, and that's where clients wait, spectators, servants, messengers. On the desk there are great books lying open, side by side, and officials stand by, most of them reading. They don't always stick to the same book, yet it isn't the books that they change but their places, and it always astounds Barnabas to see how they have to squeeze past each other when they change places, because there's so little room. In front of the desk and close to it there are small low tables at which clerks sit ready to write from dictation, whenever the officials wish it. And the way that is done always amazes Barnabas. There's no express command given by the official, nor is the dictation given in a loud voice, one could hardly tell that it was being given at all, the official just seems to go on reading as before, only whispering as he reads, and the clerk hears the whisper. Often it's so low that the clerk can't hear it at all in his seat, and then he has to jump up, catch what's being dictated, sit down again quickly and make a note of it, then jump up once more, and so on. What a strange business! It's almost incomprehensible. Of course Barnabas has time enough to observe it all, for he's often kept standing in the big room for hours and days at a time before Klamm happens to see him. And even if Klamm sees him and he springs to attention, that needn't mean anything, for Klamm may turn away from him again to the book and forget all about him. That often happens. But what can be the use of a messenger-service so casual as that? It makes me quite doleful to hear Barnabas say in the early morning that he's going to the Castle. In all likelihood a quite useless journey, a lost day, a completely vain hope. What's the good of it all? And here's cobbler's work piled up which never gets done and which Brunswick is always asking for.' 'Oh, well,' said K., 'Barnabas has just to hang on till he gets a commission. That's understandable, the place seems to be over-staffed, and everybody can't be given a job every day, you needn't complain about that, for it must affect everybody. But in the long run even a Barnabas gets commissions, he has brought two letters already to me.' 'It's possible, of course,' answered Olga, 'that we're wrong in complaining, especially a girl like me who knows things only from hearsay and can't understand it all so well as Barnabas, who certainly keeps many things to himself. But let me tell you how the letters are given out, your letters, for example. Barnabas doesn't get these letters directly from Klamm, but from a clerk. On no particular day, at no particular hour – that's why the service, however easy it appears, is really very exhausting, for Barnabas must be always on the alert – a clerk suddenly remembers about him and gives him a sign, without any apparent instructions from Klamm, who merely goes on reading in his book. True, sometimes Klamm is polishing his glasses when Barnabas comes up, but he often does that, anyhow – however, he may take a look at Barnabas then, supposing, that is, that he can see anything at all without his glasses, which Barnabas doubts; for Klamm's eyes are almost shut, he generally seems to be sleeping and only polishing his glasses in a kind of dream. Meanwhile the clerk hunts among the piles of manuscripts and writings under his table and fishes out a letter for you, so it's not a letter newly written, indeed, by the look of the envelope, it's usually a very old letter, which has been lying there a long time. But if that is so, why do they keep Barnabas waiting like that? And you too? And the letter too, of course, for it must be long out of date. That's how they get Barnabas the reputation of being a bad and slow messenger. It's all very well for the clerk, he just gives Barnabas the letter, saying:

"From Klamm for K." and so dismisses him. But Barnabas comes home breathless, with his hardly won letter next to his bare skin, and then we sit here on the settle like this and he tells me about it and we go into all the particulars and weigh up what he has achieved and find ultimately that it's very little, and questionable at that until Barnabas lays the letter down with no longer any inclination to deliver it, yet doesn't feel inclined to go to sleep either, and so sits cobbling on his stool all night. That's how it is, K., and now you have all my secrets and you can't be surprised any longer at Amalia's indifference to them.' 'And what happens to the letter?' asked K. 'The letter?' said Olga. 'Oh, some time later when I've plagued Barnabas enough about it, it may be days or weeks later, he picks it up again and goes to deliver it. In such practical matters he's very dependent on me. For I can usually pull myself together after I've recovered from the first impression of what he has told me, but he can't probably because he knows more. So I always find something or other to say to him, such as "What are you really aiming at Barnabas? What kind of career, what ambition are you dreaming of? Are you thinking of climbing so high that you'll have to leave us, to leave me, completely behind you? Is that what you're aiming at? How can I help believing so when it's the only possible explanation why you're so dreadfully discontented with all you've done already? Only take a look round and see whether any of our neighbours has got on so well as you. I admit their situation is different from ours and they have no grounds for ambition beyond their daily work, but even without making comparisons it's easy to see that you're all right. Hindrances there may be, doubts and disappointments, but that only means, what they all knew beforehand, that you get nothing without paying for it, that you have to fight for every trivial point; all the more reason for being proud instead of downcast. And aren't you fighting for us as well? Doesn't that mean anything to you? Doesn't that put new strength into you? And the fact that I'm happy and almost conceited at having such a brother, doesn't that give you any confidence? It isn't what you've achieved in the Castle that disappoints me, but the little that I'm able to achieve with you. You're allowed into the Castle, you're a regular visitor in the bureaux, you spend whole days in the same room as Klamm, you're an officially recognized messenger, with a claim on an official suit, you're entrusted with important commissions, you have all that to your credit, and then you come down here and instead of embracing me and weeping for joy you seem to lose all heart as soon as you set eyes on me, and you doubt everything, nothing interests you but cobbling, and you leave the letter, the pledge of our future, lying in a corner." That's how I speak to him, and after I've repeated the same words day after day he picks up the letter at last with a sigh and goes off. Yet probably it's not the effect of what I say that drives him out, but a desire to go to the Castle again, which he dare not do without having delivered his message.' 'But you're absolutely right in everything you say,' said K., 'it's amazing how well you grasp it all. What an extraordinarily clear mind you have!' 'No,' said Olga, 'it takes you in, and perhaps it takes him in too. For what has he really achieved? He's allowed into a bureau, but it doesn't seem to be even a bureau. He speaks to Klamm, but is it Klamm? Isn't it rather someone who's a little like Klamm? A secretary, perhaps, at the most, who resembles Klamm a little and takes pains to increase the resemblance and poses a little in Klamm's sleepy and dreamy style. That side of his nature is the easiest to imitate, there are many who try it on, although they have sense enough not to attempt anything more. And a man like Klamm who is so much sought after and so rarely seen is apt to take different shapes in people's imagination. For instance, Klamm has a village secretary here called Momus. You know him, do you? He keeps well in the background too, but I've seen him several times. A stoutly-built young man, isn't he? And so evidently not in the least like Klamm. And yet you'll find people in the village who swear that Momus is Klamm, he and no other. That's how people work their own confusion. Is there any reason why it should be different in the Castle? Somebody pointed out that particular official to Barnabas as Klamm, and there is actually a resemblance that Barnabas has always questioned. And everything goes to support his doubt. Are we to suppose that Klamm has to squeeze his way among other officials in a common room with a pencil behind his ear? It's wildly improbable. Barnabas often says, somewhat like a child and yet in a child's mood of trustfulness: "The official is really very like Klamm, and if he were sitting in his own office at his own desk with his name on the door I would have no more doubt at all." That's childish, but reasonable. Of course it would be still more reasonable of Barnabas when he's up there to ask a few people about the truth of things, for judging from his account there are plenty of men standing around. And even if their information were no more reliable than that of the man who pointed out Klamm of his own accord, there would be surely some common ground, some ground for comparison, in the various things they said. That's not my idea, but Barnabas's, yet he doesn't dare to follow it out, he doesn't venture to speak to anybody for fear of offending in ignorance against some unknown rule and so losing his job; you see how uncertain he feels; and this miserable uncertainty of his throws a clearer light on his position there than all his descriptions. How ambiguous and threatening everything must appear to him when he won't even risk opening his mouth to put an innocent question! When I reflect on that I blame myself for letting him go alone into those unknown rooms, which have such an effect on him that, though he's daring rather than cowardly, he apparently trembles with fright as he stands there.'

'Here I think you've touched on the essential point,' said K. 'That's it. After all you've told me, I believe I can see the matter clearly. Barnabas is too young for this task. Nothing he tells you is to be taken seriously at its face value. Since he's beside himself with fright up there, he's incapable of observing, and when you force him to give an account of what he has seen you get simply confused fabrications. That doesn't surprise me. Fear of the authorities is born in you here, and is further suggested to you all your lives in the most various ways and from every side, and you yourselves help to strengthen it as much as possible. Still, I have no fundamental objection to that; if an authority is good why should it not be feared? Only one shouldn't suddenly send an inexperienced youngster like Barnabas, who has never been farther than this village, into the Castle, and then expect a truthful account of everything from him, and interpret each single word of his as if it were a revelation, and base one's own life's happiness on the interpretation. Nothing could be more mistaken. I admit that I have let him mislead me in exactly the same way and have set hopes upon him and suffered disappointments through him, both based simply on his own words, that is to say, with almost no basis.' Olga was silent. 'It won't be easy for me,' went on K., 'to talk you out of your confidence in your brother, for I see how you love him and how much you expect from him. But I must do it, if only for the sake of that very love and expectation. For let me point out that there's always something – I don't know what it is – that hinders you from seeing clearly how much Barnabas has – I'll not say achieved – but has had bestowed on him. He's permitted to go into the bureaux, or if you prefer, into an antechamber, well let it be an antechamber, it has doors that lead on farther, barriers which can be passed if one has the courage. To me, for instance, even this antechamber is utterly inaccessible, for the present at least. Who is it that Barnabas speaks to there I have no idea, perhaps the clerk is the lowest in the whole staff, but even if he is the lowest he can put one in touch with the next man above him, and if he can't do that he can at least give the other's name, and if he can't even do that he can refer to somebody who can give the name. This so-called Klamm may not have the smallest trait in common with the real one, the resemblance may not exist except in the eyes of Barnabas, half-blinded by fear, he may be the meanest of the officials, he may not even be an official at all, but all the same he has work of some kind to perform at the desk, he reads something or other in his great book, he whispers something to the clerk, he thinks something when his eye falls on Barnabas once in a while, and even if that isn't true and he and his acts have no significance whatever he has at least been set there by somebody for some purpose. All that simply means that something is there, something which Barnabas has the chance of using, something or other at the very least; and that it is Barnabas's own fault if he can't get any further than doubt and anxiety and despair. And that's only on the most unfavourable interpretation of things, which is extremely improbable. For we have the actual letters which I certainly set no store on, but more than on what Barnabas says. Let them be worthless old letters, fished at random from a pile of other such worthless old letters, at random and with no more discrimination than the love-birds show in the fairs when they pick one's fortune out of a pile; let them be all that, still they have some bearing on my fate. They're evidently meant for me, although perhaps not for my good, and, as the Superintendent and his wife have testified, they are written in Klamm's own hand, and, again on the Superintendent's evidence, they have a significance which is only private and obscure, it is true, but still great.' 'Did the Superintendent say that?' asked Olga. 'Yes, he did,' replied K. 'I must tell Barnabas that,' said Olga quickly; 'that will encourage him greatly.' 'But he doesn't need encouragement,' said K.; 'to encourage him amounts to telling him that he's right, that he has only to go on as he is doing now, but that is just the way he will never achieve anything by. If a man has his eyes bound you can encourage him as much as you like to stare through the bandage, but he'll never see anything. He'll be able to see only when the bandage is removed. It's help Barnabas needs, not encouragement. Only think, up there you have all the inextricable complications of a great authority – I imagined that I had an approximate conception of its nature before I came here, but how childish my ideas were! – up there, then, you have the authorities and over against them Barnabas, nobody more, only Barnabas, pathetically alone, where it would be enough honour for him to spend his whole life covering in a dark and forgotten corner of some bureau.' 'Don't imagine, K., that we underestimate the difficulties Barnabas has to face,' said Olga, 'we have reverence enough for the authorities, you said so yourself.' 'But it's a mistaken reverence,' said K., 'a reverence in the wrong place, the kind of reverence that dishonours its object. Do you call it reverence that leads Barnabas to abuse the privilege of admission to that room by spending his time there doing nothing, or makes him when he comes down again belittle and despise the men before whom he has just been trembling, or allows him because he's depressed or weary to put off delivering letters and fail in executing commissions entrusted to him? That's far from being reverence. But I have a further reproach to make, Olga; I must blame you too, I can't exempt you. Although you fancy you have some reverence for the authorities, you sent Barnabas into the Castle in all his youth and weakness and forlornness, or at least you didn't dissuade him from going.'

'This reproach that you make,' said Olga, 'is one I have made myself from the beginning. Not indeed that I sent Barnabas to the Castle, I didn't send him, he went himself, but I ought to have prevented him by all the means in my power, by force, by craft, by persuasion. I ought to have prevented him, but if I had to decide again this very day, and if I were to feel as keenly as I did then and still do the straits Barnabas is in, and our whole family, and if Barnabas, fully conscious of the responsibility and danger ahead of him, were once more to free himself from me with a smile and set off, I wouldn't hold him back even to-day, in spite of all that has happened in between, and I believe that in my place you would do exactly the same. You don't know the plight we are in, that's why you're unfair to all of us, and especially to Barnabas. At that time we had more hope than now, but even then our hope wasn't great, but our plight was great, and is so still. Hasn't Frieda told you anything about us?' 'Mere hints,' said K., 'nothing definite, but the very mention of your name exasperates her.' 'And has the landlady told you nothing either?' 'No, nothing.' 'Nor anybody else?' 'Nobody.' 'Of course; how could anybody tell you anything? Everyone knows something about us, either the truth, so far as it is accessible, or at least some exaggerated rumour, mostly invention, and everybody thinks about us more than need be, but nobody will actually speak about it, people are shy of putting these things into words. And they're quite right in that. It's difficult to speak of it even before you, K., and when you've heard it all it's possible – isn't it? – that you'll go away and not want to have anything more to do with us, however little it may seem to concern you. Then we should have lost you, and I confess that now you mean almost more to me than Barnabas's service in the Castle. But yet – and this argument has been distracting me all the evening – you must be told, otherwise you would have no insight into our situation, and, what would vex me most of all, you would go on being unfair to Barnabas. Complete accord would fail between us, and you could neither help us, nor accept our additional help. But there is still one more question: Do you really want to be told?' 'Why do you ask?' said K., 'if it's necessary, I would rather be told, but why do you ask me so particularly?' 'Superstition,' said Olga. 'You'll become involved in our affairs, innocent as you are, almost as innocent as Barnabas.' 'Tell me quickly,' said K., 'I'm not afraid. You're certainly making it much worse than it is with such womanish fussing.'

AMALIA'S SECRET

'Judge for yourself,' said Olga, 'I warn you it sounds quite simple, one can't comprehend at first why it should be of any importance. There's a great official in the Castle called Sortini.' 'I've heard of him already,' said K., 'he had something to do with bringing me here.' 'I don't think so,' said Olga, 'Sortini hardly ever comes into the open. Aren't you mistaking him for Sordini, spelt with a "d"?' 'You're quite right,' said K., 'Sordini it was.' 'Yes,' said Olga, 'Sordini is well known, one of the most industrious of the officials, he's often mentioned; Sortini on the other hand is very retiring and quite unknown to most people. More than three years ago I saw him for the first and last time. It was on the third of July at a celebration given by the Fire Brigade, the Castle too had contributed to it and provided a new fire-engine. Sortini, who was supposed to have some hand in directing the affairs of the Fire Brigade, but perhaps he was only deputizing for someone else – the officials mostly hide behind each other like that, and so it's difficult to discover what any official is actually responsible for – Sortini took part in the ceremony of handing over the fire-engine. There were of course many other people from the Castle, officials and attendants, and true to his character Sortini kept well in the background. He's a small, frail, reflective-looking gentleman, and one thing about him struck all the people who noticed him at all, the way his forehead was furrowed; all the furrows – and there were plenty of them although he's certainly not more than forty – were spread fanwise over his forehead, running towards the root of his nose. I've never seen anything like it. Well then, we had that celebration. Amalia and I had been excited about it for weeks beforehand, our Sunday clothes had been done up for the occasion and were partly new, Amalia's dress was specially fine, a white blouse foaming high in front with one row of lace after the other, our mother had taken every bit of her lace for it. I was jealous, and cried half the night before the celebration. Only when the Bridge Inn landlady came to see us in the morning –' 'The Bridge Inn landlady?' asked K. 'Yes,' said Olga, 'she was a great friend of ours, well, she came and had to admit that Amalia was the finer, so to console me she lent me her own necklace of Bohemian garnets. When we were ready to go and Amalia was standing beside me and we were all admiring her, my father said: 'Today, mark my words, Amalia will find a husband; then, I don't know why, I took my necklace, my great pride, and hung it round Amalia's neck, and wasn't jealous any longer. I bowed before her triumph and I felt that everyone must bow before her, perhaps what amazed us so much was the difference in her appearance, for she wasn't really beautiful, but her sombre glance, and it has kept the same quality since that day, was high over our heads and involuntarily one had almost literally to bow before her. Everybody remarked on it, even Lasemann and his wife who came to fetch us.' 'Lasemann?' asked K. 'Yes, Lasemann,' said Olga, 'we were in high esteem, and the celebration couldn't well have begun without us, for my father was the third in command of the Fire Brigade.' 'Was your father still so active?' asked K. 'Father?' returned Olga, as if she did not quite comprehend, 'three years ago he was still relatively a young man, for instance, when a fire broke out at the Herrenhof he carried an official, Galater, who is a heavy man, out of the house on his back at a run. I was there myself, there was no real danger, it was only some dry wood near a stove which had begun to smoke, but Galater was terrified and cried for help out of the window, and the Fire Brigade turned out, and father had to carry him out although the fire was already extinguished. Of course Galater finds it difficult to move and has to be careful in circumstances like that. I'm telling you this only on father's account; not much more than three years have passed since then, and look at him now.' Only then did K. become aware that Amalia was again in the room, but she was a long way off at the table where her parents sat, she was feeding her mother who could not move her rheumaticky arms, and admonishing her father meanwhile to wait in patience for a little, it would soon be his turn. But her admonition was in vain, for her father, greedily desiring his soup, overcame his weakness and tried to drink it first out of the spoon and then out of the bowl, and grumbled angrily when neither attempt succeeded; the spoon was empty long before he got it to his lips, and his mouth never reached the soup, for his drooping moustache dipped into it and scattered it everywhere except into his mouth. 'And have three years done that to him?' asked K., yet he could not summon up any sympathy for the old people, and for that whole corner with the table in it he felt only repulsion. 'Three years,' replied Olga slowly, 'or, more precisely, a few hours at that celebration. The celebration was held on a meadow by the village, at the brook; there was already a large crowd there when we arrived, many people had come in from neighbouring villages, and the noise was bewildering. Of course my father took us first to look at the fire-engine, he laughed with delight when he saw it, the new fire-engine made him happy, he began to examine it and explain it to us, he wouldn't hear of any opposition or holding back, but made every one of us stoop and almost crawl under the engine if there was something there he had to show us, and he smacked Barnabas for refusing. Only Amalia paid no attention to the engine, she stood upright beside it in her fine clothes and nobody dared to say a word to her, I ran up to her sometimes and took her arm, but she said nothing. Even today I cannot explain how we came to stand for so long in front of the fire-engine without noticing Sortini until the very moment my father turned away, for he had obviously been leaning on a wheel behind the fire-engine all the time. Of course there was a terrific racket all round us, not only the usual kind of noise, for the Castle had presented the Fire Brigade with some trumpets as well as the engine, extraordinary instruments on which with the smallest effort – a child could do it – one could produce the wildest blasts; to hear them was enough to make one think the Turks were there, and one could not get accustomed to them, every fresh blast made one jump. And because the trumpets were new everybody wanted to try them, and because it was a celebration, everybody was allowed to try. Right at our ears, perhaps Amalia had attracted them, were some of these trumpet-blowers. It was difficult to keep one's wits about one, and obeying father and attending to the fire-engine was the utmost we were capable of, and so it was that Sortini escaped our notice for such a long time, and besides we had no idea who he was. 'There is Sortini,' Lasemann whispered at last to my father – I was beside him – and father, greatly excited, made a deep bow, and signed to us to do the same. Without having met till now father had always honoured Sortini as an authority in Fire Brigade matters, and had often spoken of him at home, so it was a very astonishing and important matter for us actually to see Sortini with our own eyes. Sortini, however, paid no attention to us, and in that he wasn't peculiar, for most of the officials hold themselves aloof in public, besides he was tired, only his official duty kept him there. It's not the worst officials who find duties like that particularly trying, and anyhow there were other officials and attendants mingling with the people. But he stayed by the fire-engine and discouraged by his silence all those who tried to approach him with some request or piece of flattery. So it happened that he didn't notice us until long after we had noticed him. Only as we bowed respectfully and father was making apologies for us did he look our way and scan us one after another wearily, as if sighing to find that there was still another to look at, until he let his eyes rest on Amalia, to whom he had to look up, for she was much taller than he. At the sight of her he started and leapt over the shaft to get nearer to her, we misunderstood him at first and began to approach him, father leading the way, but he held us off with uplifted hand and then waved us away. That was all. We teased Amalia a lot about having really found a husband, and in our ignorance we were very merry the whole of that afternoon. But Amalia was more silent than usual. "She's fallen head over ears in love with Sortini," said Brunswick, who is always rather vulgar and has no comprehension of natures like Amalia's. Yet this time we were inclined to think that he was right, we were quite mad all that day, and all of us, even Amalia, were as if stupefied by the sweet Castle wine when we came home about midnight.' 'And Sortini?' asked K. 'Yes, Sortini,' said Olga, 'I saw him several times during the afternoon as I passed by, he was sitting on the engine shaft with his arms folded, and he stayed there till the Castle carriage came to fetch him. He didn't even go over to watch the fire-drill at which father, in the very hope that Sortini was watching, distinguished himself beyond all the other men of his age.' 'And did you hear nothing more from him?' asked K. 'You seem to have a great regard for Sortini.' 'Oh, yes, regard,' said Olga, 'oh, yes, and hear from him we certainly did. Next morning we were roused from our heavy sleep by a scream from Amalia; the others rolled back into their beds again, but I was completely awake and ran to her. She was standing by the window holding a letter in her hand which had just been given in through the window by a man who was still waiting for an answer. The letter was short, and Amalia had already read it, and held it in her drooping hand; how I always loved her when she was tired like that! I knelt down beside her and read the letter. Hardly had I finished it when Amalia after a brief glance at me took it back, but she couldn't bring herself to read it again, and tearing it in pieces she threw the fragments in the face of the man outside and shut the window. That was the morning which decided our fate. I say "decided", but every minute of the previous afternoon was just as decisive.' 'And what was in the letter?' asked K. 'Yes, I haven't told you that yet,' said Olga, 'the letter was from Sortini addressed to the girl with the garnet necklace. I can't repeat the contents. It was a summons to come to him at the Herrenhof, and to come at once, for in half an hour he was due to leave. The letter was couched in the vilest language, such as I have never heard, and I could only guess its meaning from the context. Anyone who didn't know Amalia and saw this letter must have considered a girl who could be written to like that as dishonoured, even if she had never had a finger laid on her. And it wasn't a love letter, there wasn't a tender word in it, on the contrary Sortini was obviously enraged because the sight of Amalia had disturbed him and distracted him in his work. Later on we pieced it all together for ourselves; evidently Sortini had intended to go straight to the Castle that evening, but on Amalia's account had stayed in the village instead, and in the morning, being very angry because even overnight he hadn't succeeded in forgetting her, had written the letter. One couldn't but be furious on first reading a letter like that, even the most cold-blooded person might have been, but though with anybody else fear at its threatening tone would soon have got the upper hand, Amalia only felt anger, fear she doesn't know, neither for herself nor for others. And while I crept into bed again repeating to myself the closing sentence, which broke off in the middle, "See that you come, at once, or else –!" Amalia remained on the window-seat looking out, as if she were expecting further messengers and were prepared to treat them all as she had done the first.' 'So that's what the officials are like,' said K. reluctantly, 'that's the kind of type one finds among them. What did your father do? I hope he protested energetically in the proper quarter, if he didn't prefer a shorter and quicker way of doing it at the Herrenhof. The worst thing about the story isn't the insult to Amalia, that could easily have been made good, I don't know why you lay such exaggerated stress upon it; why should such a letter from Sortini shame Amalia for ever? – which is what one would gather from your story, but that's a sheer impossibility, it would have been easy to make up for it to Amalia, and in a few days the whole thing might have blown over, it was himself that Sortini shamed, and not Amalia. It's Sortini that horrifies me, the possibility of such an abuse of power. The very thing that failed this one time because it came naked and undisguised and found an effective opponent in Amalia, might very well succeed completely on a thousand other occasions in circumstances just a little less favourable, and might defy detection even by its victim.' 'Hush,' said Olga, 'Amalia's looking this way.' Amalia had finished giving food to her parents and was now busy taking off her mother's clothes. She had just undone the skirt, hung her mother's arms round her neck, lifted her a little, while she drew her skirt off, and now gently set her down again. Her. father, still affronted because his wife was being attended to first, which obviously only happened because she was even more helpless than he, was attempting to undress himself; perhaps, too, it was a reproach to his daughter for her imagined slowness; yet although he began with the easiest and least necessary thing, the removal of the enormous slippers in which his feet were loosely stuck, he could not get them pulled off at all, and wheezing hoarsely was forced to give up trying, and leaned back stiffly in his chair again. 'But you don't realize the really decisive thing,' said Olga, 'you may be right in all you say, but the decisive thing was Amalia's not going to the Herrenhof; her treatment of the messenger might have been excused, it could have been passed over; but it was because she didn't go that the curse was laid upon our family, and that turned her treatment of the messenger into an unpardonable offence, yes, it was even brought forward openly later as the chief offence.' 'What!' cried K. at once, lowering his voice again as Olga raised her hands imploringly, 'do you, her sister, actually say that Amalia should have run to the Herrenhof after Sortini?' 'No,' said Olga, 'Heaven preserve me from such a suspicion, how can you believe that? I don't know anybody who's so right as Amalia in everything she does. If she had gone to the Herrenhof I should of course have upheld her just the same; but her not going was heroic. As for me, I confess it frankly, had I received a letter like that I should have gone. I shouldn't have been able to endure the fear of what might happen, only Amalia could have done that. For there were many ways of getting round it; another girl, for instance, might have decked herself up and wasted some time in doing it and then gone to the Herrenhof only to find that Sortini had left, perhaps to find that he had left immediately after sending the messenger, which is very probable, for the moods of the gentlemen are fleeting. But Amalia neither did that nor anything else, she was too deeply insulted, and answered without reserve. If she had only made some pretence of compliance, if she had but crossed the threshold of the Herrenhof at the right moment, our punishment could have been turned aside, we have very clever advocates here who can make a great deal out of a mere nothing, but in this case they hadn't even the mere nothing to go on, there was, on the contrary, the disrespect to Sortini's letter and the insult to his messenger.' 'But what is all this about punishment and advocates?' said K. 'Surely Amalia couldn't be accused or punished because of Sortini's criminal proceedings?' 'Yes,' said Olga, 'she could, not in a regular suit at law, of course; and she wasn't punished directly, but she was punished all right in other ways, she and the whole family, and how heavy the punishment has been you are surely beginning to understand. In your opinion it's unjust and monstrous, but you're the only one in the village of that opinion, it's an opinion favourable to us, and ought to comfort us, and would do that if it weren't so obviously based on error. I can easily prove that, and you must forgive me if I mention Frieda by the way, but between Frieda and Klamm, leaving aside the final outcome of the two affairs, the first preliminaries were much the same as between Amalia and Sortini, and yet, although that might have shocked you at the beginning, you accept it now as quite natural. And that's not merely because you're accustomed to it, custom alone couldn't blunt one's plain judgement, it's simply that you've freed yourself from prejudice.' 'No, Olga,' said K., 'I don't see why you drag in Frieda, her case wasn't the same, don't confuse two such different things, and now go on with your story.' 'Please don't be offended,' said Olga, 'if I persist in the comparison, it's a lingering trace of prejudice on your part, even in regard to Frieda, that makes you feel you must defend her from a comparison. She's not to be defended, but only to be praised. In comparing the two cases, I don't say they're exactly alike, they stand in the same relation as black to white, and the white is Frieda. The worst thing one can do to Frieda is to laugh at her, as I did in the bar very rudely – and I was sorry for it later – but even if one laughs out of envy or malice, at any rate one can laugh. On the other hand, unless one is related to her by blood, one can only despise Amalia. Therefore the two cases are quite different, as you say, but yet they are alike.' 'They're not at all alike,' said K., and he shook his head stubbornly, 'leave Frieda out of it, Frieda got no such fine letter as that of Sortini's, and Frieda was really in love with Klamm, and, if you doubt that, you need only ask her, she loves him still.' 'But is that really a difference?' asked Olga. 'Do you imagine Klamm couldn't have written to Frieda in the same tone? That's what the gentlemen are like when they rise from their desks, they feel out of place in the ordinary world and in their distraction they say the most beastly things, not all of them, but many of them. The letter to Amalia may have been the thought of a moment, thrown on the paper in complete disregard for the meaning to be taken out of it. What do we know of the thoughts of these gentlemen? Haven't you heard of, or heard yourself, the tone in which Klamm spoke to Frieda? Klamm's notorious for his rudeness, he can apparently sit dumb for hours and then suddenly bring out something so brutal that it makes one shiver. Nothing of that kind is known of Sortini, but then very little is known of him. All that's really known about him is that his name is like Sordini's. If it weren't for that resemblance between the two names probably he wouldn't be known at all. Even as the Fire Brigade authority apparently he's confused with Sordini, who is the real authority, and who exploits the resemblance in name to push things on to Sortini's shoulders, especially any duties falling on him as a deputy, so that he can be left undisturbed to his work. Now when a man so unused to society as Sortini suddenly felt himself in love with a village girl, he'll naturally take it quite differently from, say, the joiner's apprentice next door. And one must remember, too, that between an official and a village cobbler's daughter there's a great gulf fixed which has to be somehow bridged over, and Sortini tried to do it in that way, where someone else might have acted differently. Of course we're all supposed to belong to the Castle, and there's supposed to be no gulf between us, and nothing to be bridged over, and that may be true enough on ordinary occasions, but we've had grim evidence that it's not true when anything really important crops up. At any rate, all that should make Sortini's methods more comprehensible to you, and less monstrous; compared with Klamm's they're comparatively reasonable, and even for those intimately affected by them much more endurable. When Klamm writes a loving letter it's much more exasperating than the most brutal letter of Sortini's. Don't mistake me, I'm not venturing to criticize Klamm, I'm only comparing the two, because you're shutting your eyes to the comparison. Klamm's a kind of tyrant over women, he orders first one and then another to come to him, puts up with none of them for long, and orders them to go just as he ordered them to come. Oh, Klamm wouldn't even give himself the trouble of writing a letter first. And in comparison with that is it so monstrous that Sortini, who's so retiring, and whose relations with women are at least unknown, should condescend for once to write in his beautiful official hand a letter, however abominable? And if there's no distinction here in Klamm's favour, but the reverse, how can Frieda's love for him establish one? The relation existing between the women and the officials, believe me, is very difficult, or rather very easy to determine. Love always enters into it. There's no such thing as an official's unhappy love affair. So in that respect it's no praise to say of a girl – I'm referring to many others besides Frieda – that she gave herself to an official only out of love. She loved him and gave herself to him, that was all, there's nothing praiseworthy in that. But you'll object that Amalia didn't love Sortini. Well, perhaps she didn't love him, but then after all perhaps she did love him, who can decide? Not even she herself. How can she fancy she didn't love him, when she rejected him so violently, as no official has ever been rejected? Barnabas says that even yet she sometimes trembles with the violence of the effort of closing the window three years ago. That is true, and therefore one can't ask her anything; she has finished with Sortini, and that's all she knows; whether she loves him or not she does not know. But we do know that women can't help loving the officials once they give them any encouragement, yes, they even love them beforehand, let them deny it as much as they like, and Sortini not only gave Amalia encouragement, but leapt over the shaft when he saw her; although his legs were stiff from sitting at desks he leapt right over the shaft. But Amalia's an exception, you will say. Yes, that she is, that she has proved in refusing to go to Sortini, that's exception enough, but if in addition she weren't in love with Sortini, she would be too exceptional for plain human understanding. On that afternoon, I grant you, we were smitten with blindness, but the fact that in spite of our mental confusion we thought we noticed signs of Amalia's being in love, showed at least some remnants of sense. But when all that's taken into account, what difference is left between Frieda and Amalia? One thing only, that Frieda did what Amalia refused to do.' 'Maybe,' said K., 'but for me the main difference is that I'm engaged to Frieda, and only interested in Amalia because she's a sister of Barnabas's, the Castle messenger, and because her destiny may be bound up with his duties. If she had suffered such a crying injustice at the hands of an official as your tale seemed to infer at the beginning, I should have taken the matter up seriously, but more from a sense of public duty than from any personal sympathy with Amalia. But what you say has changed the aspect of the situation for me in a way I don't quite understand, but am prepared to accept, since it's you who tell me, and therefore I want to drop the whole affair; I'm no member of the Fire Brigade, Sortini means nothing to me. But Frieda means something to me, I have trusted her completely and want to go on trusting her, and it surprises me that you go out of your way, while discussing Amalia, to attack Frieda and try to shake my confidence in her. I'm not assuming that you're doing it with deliberate intent, far less with malicious intent, for in that case I should have left long ago. You're not doing it deliberately, you're betrayed into it by circumstances, impelled by your love for Amalia you want to exalt her above all other women, and since you can't find enough virtue in Amalia herself you help yourself out by belittling the others. Amalia's act was remarkable enough, but the more you say about it the less clearly can it be decided whether it was noble or petty, clever or foolish, heroic or cowardly; Amalia keeps her motives locked in her own bosom and no one will ever get at them. Frieda, on the other hand, has done nothing at all remarkable, she has only followed her own heart, for anyone who looks at her actions with goodwill that is clear, it can be substantiated, it leaves no room for slander. However, I don't want either to belittle Amalia or to defend Frieda, all I want is to let you see what my relation is to Frieda, and that every attack on Frieda is an attack on myself. I came here of my own accord, and of my own accord I have settled here, but all that has happened to me since I came, and, above all, any prospects I may have – dark as they are, they still exist – I owe entirely to Frieda, and you can't argue that away. True, I was engaged to come here as a Land Surveyor, yet that was only a pretext, they were playing with me, I was driven out of everybody's house, they're playing with me still to-day; but how much more complicated the game is now that I have, so to speak, a larger circumference – which means something, it may not be much – yet I have already a home, a position and real work to do, I have a promised wife who takes her share of my professional duties when I have other business, I'm going to marry her and become a member of the community, and besides my official connexion I have also a personal connexion with Klamm, although as yet I haven't been able to make use of it. That's surely quite a lot? And when I come to you, why do you make me welcome? Why do you confide the history of your family to me? Why do you hope that I might possibly help you? Certainly not because I'm the Land Surveyor whom Lasemann and Brunswick, for instance, turned out of their house a week ago, but because I'm a man with some power at my back. But that I owe to Frieda, to Frieda who is so modest that if you were to ask her about it, she wouldn't know it existed. And so, considering all this, it seems that Frieda in her innocence has achieved more than Amalia in all her pride, for may I say that I have the impression that you're seeking help for Amalia. And from whom? In the last resort from no one else but Frieda.' 'Did I really speak so abominably of Frieda?' asked Olga. 'I certainly didn't mean to, and I don't think I did, still, it's possible; we're in a bad way, our whole world is in ruins, and once we begin to complain we're carried farther than we realize. You're quite right, there's a big difference now between us and Frieda, and it's a good thing to emphasize it once in a while. Three years ago we were respectable girls and Frieda an outcast, a servant in the Bridge Inn, we used to walk past her without looking at her, I admit we were too arrogant, but that's how we were brought up. But that evening in the Herrenhof probably enlightened you about our respective positions today. Frieda with the whip in her hand, and I among the crowd of servants. But it's worse even than that! Frieda may despise us, her position entitles her to do so, actual circumstances compel it. But who is there who doesn't despise us? Whoever decides to despise us will find himself in good company. Do you know Frieda's successor? Pepi, she's called. I met her for the first time the night before last, she used to be a chambermaid. She certainly outdoes Frieda in her contempt for me. She saw me through the window as I was coming for beer, and ran to the door and locked it, so that I had to beg and pray for a long time and promise her the ribbon from my hair before she would let me in. But when I gave it to her she threw it into a corner. Well, I can't help it if she despises me, I'm partly dependent on her goodwill, and she's the barmaid in the Herrenhof. Only for the time being, it's true, for she certainly hasn't the qualities needed for permanent employment there. One only has to overhear how the landlord speaks to Pepi and compare it with his tone to Frieda. But that doesn't hinder Pepi from despising even Amalia, Amalia, whose glance alone would be enough to drive Pepi with all her plaits and ribbons out of the room much faster than her own fat legs would ever carry her. I had to listen again yesterday to her infuriating slanders against Amalia until the customers took my part at last, although only in the kind of way you have seen already.' 'How touchy you are,' said K. 'I only put Frieda in her right place, but I had no intention of belittling you, as you seem to think. Your family has a special interest for me, I have never denied it; but how this interest could give me cause for despising you I can't understand.' 'Oh, K.,' said Olga, 'I'm afraid that even you will understand it yet; can't you even understand that Amalia's behaviour to Sortini was the original cause of our being despised?' 'That would be strange indeed,' said K., 'one might admire or condemn Amalia for such an action, but despise her? And even if she is despised for some reason I can't comprehend, why should the contempt be extended to you others, her innocent family? For Pepi to despise you, for instance, is a piece of impudence, and I'll let her know it if ever I'm in the Herrenhof again.' 'If you set out, K.,' said Olga, 'to convert all the people who despise us you'll have your work cut out for you, for it's all engineered from the Castle. I can still remember every detail of that day following the morning I spoke of. Brunswick, who was our assistant then, had arrived as usual, taken his share of the work and gone home, and we were sitting at breakfast, all of us, even Amalia and myself, very gay, father kept on talking about the celebration and telling us his plans in connexion with the Fire Brigade, for you must know that the Castle has its own Fire Brigade which had sent a deputation to the celebration, and there had been much discussion about it, the gentlemen present from the Castle had seen the performance of our Fire Brigade, had expressed great approval, and compared the Castle Brigade unfavourably with ours, so there had been some talk of reorganizing the Castle Brigade with the help of instructors from the village; there were several possible candidates, but father had hopes that he would be chosen. That was what he was discussing, and in his usual delightful way had sprawled over the table until he embraced half of it in his arms, and as he gazed through the open window at the sky his face was young and shining with hope, and that was the last time I was to see it like that. Then Amalia, with a calm conviction we had never noticed in her before, said that too much trust shouldn't be placed in what the gentlemen said, they were in the habit of saying pleasant things on such occasions, but it meant little or nothing, the words were hardly out of their mouths before they were forgotten, only of course people were always ready to be taken in again next time. Mother forbade her to say things like that, but father only laughed at her precocious air of wisdom, then he gave a start, and seemed to be looking round for something he had only just missed – but there was nothing missing – and said that Brunswick had told him some story of a messenger and a torn-up letter, did we know anything of it, who was concerned in it, and what it was all about? We kept silent; Barnabas, who was as youthful then as a spring lamb, said something particularly silly or cheeky, the subject was changed, and the whole affair forgotten.'

AMALIA'S PUNISHMENT

'But not long afterwards we were overwhelmed with questions from all sides about the story of the letter, we were visited by friends and enemies, acquaintances and complete strangers. Not one of them stayed for any length of time, and our best friends were the quickest to go. Lasemann, usually so slow and dignified, came in hastily as if only to see the size of the room, one look round it and he was gone, it was like a horrible kind of children's game when he fled, and father, shaking himself free from some other people, ran after him to the very door and then gave it up; Brunswick came and gave notice, he said quite honestly that he wanted to set up in business for himself, a shrewd man, he knew how to seize the right moment; customers came and hunted round father's store-room for the boots they had left to be repaired, at first father tried to persuade them to change their minds – and we all backed him up as much as we could – but later he gave it up, and without saying a word helped them to find their belongings, line after line in the order-book was cancelled, the pieces of leather people had left with us were handed back, all debts owing us were paid, everything went smoothly without the slightest trouble, they asked for nothing better than to break every connexion with us quickly and completely, even if they lost by it; that counted for nothing. And finally, as we might have foreseen, Seemann appeared, the Captain of the Fire Brigade; I can still see the scene before me, Seemann, tall and stout, but with a slight stoop from weakness in the lungs, a serious man who never could laugh, standing in front of my father whom he admired, whom he had promised in confidence to make a deputy Captain, and to whom he had now to say that the Brigade required his services no longer and asked for the return of his diploma. All the people who happened to be in our house left their business for the moment and crowded round the two men, Seemann found it difficult to speak and only kept on tapping father on the shoulder, as if he were trying to tap out of him the words he ought to say and couldn't find. And he kept on laughing, probably to cheer himself a little and everybody else, but since he's incapable of laughing and no one had ever heard him laugh, it didn't occur to anybody that he was really laughing. But father was too tired and desperate after the day he'd had to help anybody out, he looked even too tired to grasp what was happening. We were all in despair, too, but being young didn't believe in the completeness of our ruin, and kept on expecting that someone in the long procession of visitors would arrive and put a stop to it all and make everything swing the other way again. In our foolishness we thought that Seemann was that very man. We were all keyed up waiting for his laughter to stop, and for the decisive statement to come out at last. What could he be laughing at, if not at the stupid injustice of what had happened to us? Oh, Captain, Captain, tell them now at last, we thought, and pressed close to him, but that only made him recoil from us in the most curious way. At length, however, he did begin to speak, in response not to our secret wishes, but to the encouraging or angry cries of the crowd. Yet still we had hopes. He began with great praise for our father. Called him an ornament to the Brigade, an inimitable model to posterity, an indispensable member whose removal must reduce the Brigade almost to ruin. That was all very fine, had he stopped there. But he went on to say that since in spite of that the Brigade had decided, only as a temporary measure of course, to ask for his resignation, they would all understand the seriousness of the reason which forced the Brigade to do so. Perhaps if father had not distinguished himself so much at the celebration of the previous day it would not have been necessary to go so far, but his very superiority had drawn official attention to the Brigade, and brought it into such prominence that the spotlessness of its reputation was more than ever a matter of honour to it. And now that a messenger has been insulted, the Brigade couldn't help itself, and he, Seemann, found himself in the difficult position of having to convey its decision. He hoped that father would not make it any more difficult for him. Seemann was glad to have got it out. He was so pleased with himself that he even forgot his exaggerated tact, and pointed to the diploma hanging on the wall and made a sign with his finger. Father nodded and went to fetch it, but his hands trembled so much that he couldn't get it off the hook. I climbed on a chair and helped him. From that moment he was done for, he didn't even take the diploma out of its frame, but handed the whole thing over to Seemann. Then he sat down in a corner and neither moved nor spoke to anybody, and we had to attend to the last people there by ourselves as well as we could.' 'And where do you see in all this the influence of the Castle?' asked K. 'So far it doesn't seem to have come in. What you've told me about is simply the ordinary senseless fear of the people, malicious pleasure in hurting a neighbour, specious friendship, things that can be found anywhere, and, I must say, on the part of your father – at least, so it seems to me – a certain pettiness, for what was the diploma? Merely a testimonial to his abilities, these themselves weren't taken from him, if they made him indispensable so much the better, and the one way he could have made things difficult for the Captain would have been by flinging the diploma at his feet before he had said two words. But the significant thing to me is that you haven't mentioned Amalia at all; Amalia, who was to blame for everything, apparently stood quietly in the background and watched the whole house collapse.' 'No,' said Olga, 'nobody ought to be blamed, nobody could have done anything else, all that was already due to the influence of the Castle.' 'Influence of the Castle,' repeated Amalia, who had slipped in unnoticed from the courtyard; the old people had been long in bed. 'Is it Castle gossip you're at? Still sitting with your heads together? And yet you wanted to go away immediately you came, K., and it's nearly ten now. Are you really interested in that kind of gossip? There are people in the village who live on it, they stick their heads together just like you two and entertain each other by the hour. But I didn't think you were one of them.' 'On the contrary,' said K., 'that's exactly what I am, and moreover people who don't care for such gossip and leave it all to others don't interest me particularly.' 'Indeed,' said Amalia, 'well, there are many different kinds of interest, you know; I heard once of a young man who thought of nothing but the Castle day and night, he neglected everything else and people feared for his reason, his mind was so wholly absorbed by the Castle. It turned out at length, however, that it wasn't really the Castle he was thinking of, but the daughter of a charwoman in the offices up there, so he got the girl and was all right again.' 'I think I would like that man,' said K. 'As for your liking the man, I doubt it,' said Amalia, 'it's probably his wife you would like. Well, don't let me disturb you, I've got to go to bed, and I must put out the light for the old folks' sake. They're sound asleep now, but they don't really sleep for more than an hour, and after that the smallest glimmer disturbs them. Good-night.' And actually the light went out at once, and Amalia bedded herself somewhere on the floor near her parents. 'Who's the young man she mentioned?' asked K. 'I don't know,' said Olga, 'perhaps Brunswick although it doesn't fit him exactly, but it might have been somebody else. It's not easy to follow her, for often one can't tell whether she's speaking ironically or in earnest. Mostly she's in earnest but sounds ironical.' 'Never mind explaining,' said K. 'How have you come to be so dependent on her? Were things like that before the catastrophe? Or did it happen later? And do you never feel that you want to be independent of her? And is there any sense in your dependence? She's the youngest, and should give way to you. Innocently or not, she was the person who brought ruin on the family. And instead of begging your pardon for it anew every day she carries her head higher than anybody else, bothers herself about nothing except what she chooses to do for her parents, nothing would induce her to become acquainted with your affairs, to use her own expression, and then if she does speak to you at all she's mostly in earnest, but sounds ironical. Does she queen it over you on account of her beauty, which you've mentioned more than once? Well, you're all three very like each other, but Amalia's distinguishing mark is hardly a recommendation, and repelled me the first time I saw it, I mean her cold hard eye. And although she's the youngest she doesn't look it, she has the ageless look of women who seem not to grow any older, but seem never to have been young either. You see her every day, you don't notice the hardness of her face. That's why, on reflection, I can't take Sortini's passion for her very seriously, perhaps he sent the letter simply to punish her, but not to summon her.' 'I won't argue about Sortini,' said Olga, 'for the Castle gentlemen everything is possible, let a girl be as pretty or as ugly as you like. But in all the rest you're utterly mistaken so far as Amalia is concerned. I have no particular motive for winning you over to Amalia's side, and if I try to do it it's only for your own sake. Amalia in some way or other was the cause of our misfortunes, that's true, but not even my father, who was the hardest hit, and who was never very sparing of his tongue, particularly at home, not even my father has ever said a word of reproach to Amalia even in our very worst times. Not because he approved of her action, he was an admirer of Sortini, and how could he have approved of it? He couldn't understand it even remotely, for Sortini he would have been glad to sacrifice himself and all that was his, although hardly in the way things actually happened, as an outcome apparently of Sortini's anger. I say apparently, for we never heard another word from Sortini; if he was reticent before then, from that day on he might as well have been dead. Now you should have seen Amalia at that time. We all knew that no definite punishment would be visited on us. We were only shunned. By the village and by the Castle. But while we couldn't help noticing the ostracism of the village, the Castle gave us no sign. Of course we had no sign of favour from the Castle in the past, so how could we notice the reverse? This blankness was the worst of all. It was far worse than the withdrawal of the people down here, for they hadn't deserted us out of conviction, perhaps they had nothing very serious against us, they didn't despise us then as they do today, they only did it out of fear, and were waiting to see what would happen next. And we weren't afraid of being stranded, for all our debtors had paid us, the settling-up had been entirely in our favour, and any provisions we didn't have were sent us secretly by relations, it was easy enough for us, it was harvest time – though we had no fields of our own and nobody would take us on as workers, so that for the first time in our lives we were condemned to go nearly idle. So there we sat all together with the windows shut in the heats of July and August. Nothing happened. No invitations, no news, no callers, nothing.' 'Well,' said K., 'since nothing happened and you had no definite punishment hanging over you, what was there to be afraid of? What people you are!' 'How am I to explain it?' said Olga. 'We weren't afraid of anything in the future, we were suffering under the immediate present, we were actually enduring our punishment. The others in the village were only waiting for us to come to them, for father to open his workshop again, for Amalia, who could sew the most beautiful clothes, fit for the best families, to come asking for orders again, they were all sorry to have had to act as they did; when a respected family is suddenly cut out of village life it means a loss for everybody, so when they broke with us they thought they were only doing their duty, in their place we should have done just the same. They didn't know very clearly what was the matter, except that the messenger had returned to the Herrenhof with a handful of torn paper. Frieda had seen him go out and come back, had exchanged a few words with him, and then spread what she had learned everywhere. But not in the least from enmity to us, simply from a sense of duty which anybody would have felt in the same circumstances. And, as I've said, a happy ending to the whole story would have pleased everybody else. If we had suddenly put in an appearance with the news that everything was settled, that it had only been a misunderstanding, say, which was now quite cleared up, or that there had been actually some cause for offence which had now been made good, or else – and even this would have satisfied the people – that through our influence in the Castle the affair had been dropped, we should certainly have been received again with open arms, there would have been kissings and congratulations, I have seen that kind of thing happen to others once or twice already. And it wouldn't have been necessary to say even as much as that; if we had only come out in the open and shown ourselves, if we had picked up our old connexions without letting fall a single word about the affair of the letter, it would have been enough, they would all have been glad to avoid mentioning the matter; it was the painfulness of the subject as much as their fear that made them draw away from us, simply to avoid hearing about it or speaking about it or thinking about it or being affected by it in any way. When Frieda gave it away it wasn't out of mischief but as a warning, to let the parish know that something had happened which everybody should be careful to keep clear of. It wasn't our family that was taboo, it was the affair, and our family only in so far as we were mixed up in the affair. So if we had quietly come forward again and let bygones be bygones and shown by our behaviour that the incident was closed, no matter in what way, and reassured public opinion that it was never likely to be mentioned again, whatever its nature had been, everything would have been made all right in that way, too, we should have found friends on all sides as before, and even if we hadn't completely forgotten what had happened people would have understood and helped us to forget it completely. Instead of that we sat in the house. I don't know what we were expecting, probably some decision from Amalia, for on that morning she had taken the lead in the family and she still maintained it. Without any particular contriving or commanding or imploring, almost by her silence alone. We others, of course, had plenty to discuss, there was a steady whispering from morning till evening, and sometimes father would call me to him in sudden panic and I would have to spend half the night on the edge of his bed. Or we would often creep away together, I and Barnabas, who knew nothing about it all at first, and was always in a fever for some explanation, always the same, for he realized well enough that the carefree years that others of his age looked forward to were now out of the question for him, so we used to put our heads together, K., just like we two now, and forget that it was night, and that morning had come again. Our mother was the feeblest of us all, probably because she had not only endured our common sorrows but the private sorrow of each of us, and so we were horrified to see changes in her which, as we guessed, lay in wait for all of us. Her favourite seat was the corner of the sofa, it's long since we parted with it, it stands now in Brunswick's big living-room, well, there we sat and – we couldn't tell exactly what was wrong – used to doze or carry on long conversations with herself, we guessed it from the moving of her lips. It was so natural for us to be always discussing the letter, to be always turning it over in all its known details and unknown potentialities, and to be always outdoing each other in thinking out plans for restoring our fortunes; it was natural and unavoidable, but not good, we only plunged deeper and deeper into what we wanted to escape from. And what good were these inspirations, however brilliant? None of them could be acted on without Amalia, they were all tentative, and quite useless because they stopped short of Amalia, and even if they had been put to Amalia they would have met with nothing but silence. Well, I'm glad to say I understood Amalia better now than I did then. She had more to endure than all of us, it's incomprehensible how she managed to endure it and still survive. Mother, perhaps, had to endure all our troubles, but that was because they came pouring in on her; and she didn't hold out for long; no one could say that she's holding out against them today, and even at that time her mind was beginning to go. But Amalia not only suffered, she had the understanding to see her suffering clearly, we saw only the effects, but she knew the cause, we hoped for some small relief or other, she knew that everything was decided, we had to whisper, she had only to be silent. She stood face to face with the truth and went on living and endured her life then as now. In all our straits we were better off than she. Of course, we had to leave our house. Brunswick took it on, and we were given this cottage, we brought our things over in several journeys with a handcart. Barnabas and I pulling and father and Amalia pushing behind, mother was already sitting here on a chest, for we had brought her here first, and she whimpered softly all the time. Yet I remember that even during those toilsome journeys – they were painful, too, for we often met harvest wagons, and the people became silent when they saw us and turned away their faces – even during those journeys Barnabas and I couldn't stop discussing our troubles and our plans, so that we often stood stock still in the middle of pulling and had to be roused by father's "Hallo" from behind. But all our talking made no difference to our life after the removal, except that we began gradually to feel the pinch of poverty as well. Our relatives stopped sending us things, our money was almost done, and that was the time when people first began to despise us in the way you can see now. They saw that we hadn't the strength to shake ourselves clear of the scandal, and they were irritated. They didn't underestimate our difficulties, although they didn't know exactly what they were, and they knew that probably they wouldn't have stood up to them any better themselves, but that made it only all the more needful to keep clear of us – if we had triumphed they would have honoured us correspondingly, but since we failed they turned what had only been a temporary measure into a final resolve, and cut us off from the community for ever. We were no longer spoken of as ordinary human beings, our very name was never mentioned, if they had to refer to us they called us Barnabas's people, for he was the least guilty; even our cottage gained an evil reputation, and you yourself must admit, if you're honest, that on your first entry into it you thought it justified its reputation; later on, when people occasionally visited us again, they used to screw up their noses at the most trivial things, for instance, because the little oil-lamp hung over the table. Where should it hang if not over the table? and yet they found it insupportable. But if we hung the lamp somewhere else they were still disgusted. Whatever we did, whatever we had, it was all despicable.'

PETITIONS

'And what did we do meanwhile? The worst thing we could have done, something much more deserving of contempt than our original offence – we betrayed Amalia, we shook off her silent restraint, we couldn't go on living like that, without hope of any kind we could not live, and we began each in his or her own fashion with prayers or blustering to beg the Castle's forgiveness. We knew, of course, that we weren't in a position to make anything good, and we knew too that the only likely connexion we had with the Castle – through Sortini, who had been father's superior and had approved of him – was destroyed by what had happened, and yet we buckled down to the job. Father began it, he started making senseless petitions to the Village Superintendent, to the secretaries, the advocates, the clerks, usually he wasn't received at all, but if by guile or chance he managed to get a hearing – and how we used to exult when the news came, and rub our hands! – he was always thrown out immediately and never admitted again. Besides, it was only too easy to answer him, the Castle always has the advantage. What was it that he wanted? What had been done to him? What did he want to be forgiven for? When and by whom had so much as a finger been raised against him in the Castle? Granted he had become poor and lost his customers, etc., these were all chances of everyday life, and happened in all shops and markets; was the Castle to concern itself about things of that kind? It concerned itself about the common welfare, of course, but it couldn't simply interfere with the natural course of events for the sole purpose of serving the interest of one man. Did he expect officials to be sent out to run after his customers and force them to come back? But, father would object – we always discussed the whole interview both before and afterwards, sitting in a corner as if to avoid Amalia, who knew well enough what we were doing, but paid no attention – well, father would object, he wasn't complaining about his poverty, he could easily make up again for all he had lost, that didn't matter if only he were forgiven. But what was there to forgive? came the answer; no accusation had come in against him, at least there was none in the registers, not in those registers anyhow which were accessible to the public advocates, consequently, so far as could be established, there was neither any accusation standing against him, nor one in process of being taken up. Could he perhaps refer to some official decree that had been issued against him? Father couldn't do that. Well then, if he knew of nothing and nothing had happened, what did he want? What was there to forgive him? Nothing but the way he was aimlessly wasting official time, but that was just the unforgivable sin. Father didn't give in, he was still very strong in those days, and his enforced leisure gave him plenty of time. "I'll restore Amalia's honour, it won't take long now," he used to say to Barnabas and me several times a day, but only in a low voice in case Amalia should hear, and yet he only said it for her benefit, for in reality he wasn't hoping for the restoration of her honour, but only for forgiveness. Yet before he could be forgiven he had to prove his guilt, and that was denied in all the bureaux. He hit upon the idea – and it showed that his mind was already giving way – that his guilt was being concealed from him because he didn't pay enough; until then he had paid only the established taxes, which were at least high enough for means like ours. But now he believed that he must pay more, which was certainly a delusion, for, although our officials accept bribes simply to avoid trouble and discussion, nothing is ever achieved in that way. Still, if father had set his hopes on that idea, we didn't want them upset. We sold what we had left to sell – nearly all things we couldn't do without – to get father the money for his efforts and for a long time every morning brought us the satisfaction of knowing that when he went on his day's rounds he had at least a few coins to rattle in his pocket. Of course we simply starved all day, and the only thing the money really did was to keep father fairly hopeful and happy. That could hardly be called an advantage, however. He wore himself out on these rounds of his, and the money only made them drag on and on instead of coming to a quick and natural end. Since in reality nothing extra could be done for him in return for those extra payments, clerks here and there tried to make a pretence of giving something in return, promising to look the matter up, and hinting that they were on the track of something, and that purely as a favour to father, and not as a duty, they would follow it up – and father, instead of growing sceptical, only became more and more credulous. He used to bring home such obviously worthless promises as if they were great triumphs, and it was a torment to see him behind Amalia's back twisting his face in a smile and opening his eyes wide as he pointed to her and made signs to us that her salvation, which would have surprised nobody so much as herself, was coming nearer and nearer through his efforts, but that it was still a secret and we mustn't tell. Things would certainly have gone on like this for a long time if we hadn't finally been reduced to the position of having no more money to give him, Barnabas, indeed, had been taken on meanwhile by Brunswick, after endless imploring, as an assistant, on condition that he fetched his work in the dusk of the evening and brought it back again in the dark – it must be admitted that Brunswick was taking a certain risk in his business for our sake, but in exchange he paid Barnabas next to nothing, and Barnabas is a model workman – yet his wages were barely enough to keep us from downright starvation. Very gently and after much softening of the blow we told our father that he could have no more money, but he took it very quietly. He was no longer capable of understanding how hopeless were his attempts at intervention, he was wearied out by continual disappointments. He said, indeed – and he spoke less clearly than before, he used to speak almost too clearly – that he would have needed only a very little more money, for to-morrow or that very day he would have found out everything, and now it had all gone for nothing, ruined simply for lack of money, and so on, but the tone in which he said it showed that he didn't believe it all. Besides, he brought out a new plan immediately of his own accord. Since he had failed in proving his guilt, and consequently could hope for nothing more through official channels, he would have to depend on appeals alone, and would try to move the officials personally. There must certainly be some among them who had good sympathetic hearts, which they couldn't give way to in their official capacity, but out of office hours, if one caught them at the right time, they would surely listen.'

Here K., who had listened with absorption hitherto, interrupted Olga's narrative with the question: 'And don't you think he was right?' Although his question would have answered itself in the course of the narrative he wanted to know at once.

'No,' said Olga, 'there could be no question of sympathy or anything of the kind. Young and inexperienced as we were, we knew that, and father knew it too, of course, but he had forgotten it like nearly everything else. The plan he had hit on was to plant himself on the main road near the Castle, where the officials pass in their carriages, and seize any opportunity of putting up his prayer for forgiveness. To be honest, it was a wild and senseless plan, even if the impossible should have happened, and his prayer have really reached an official's ear. For how could a single official give a pardon? That could only be done at best by the whole authority, and apparently even the authority can only condemn and not pardon. And in any case even if an official stepped out of his carriage and was willing to take up the matter, how could he get any clear idea of the affair from the mumblings of a poor, tired, ageing man like father? Officials are highly educated, but one-sided; in his own department an official can grasp whole trains of thought from a single word, but let him have something from another department explained to him by the hour, he may nod politely, but he won't understand a word of it. That's quite natural, take even the small official affairs that concern the ordinary person – trifling things that an official disposes of with a shrug – and try to understand one of them through and through, and you'll waste a whole lifetime on it without result. But even if father had chanced on a responsible official, no official can settle anything without the necessary documents, and certainly not on the main road; he can't pardon anything, he can only settle it officially, and he would simply refer to the official procedure, which had already been a complete failure for father. What a pass father must have been in to think of insisting on such a plan! If there were even the faintest possibility of getting anything in that way, that part of the road would be packed with petitioners; but since it's sheer impossibility, patent to the youngest schoolboy, the road is absolutely empty. But maybe even that strengthened father in his hopes, he found food for them everywhere. He had great need to find it, for a sound mind wouldn't have had to make such complicated calculations, it would have realized from external evidence that the thing was impossible. When officials travel to the village or back to the Castle it's not for pleasure, but because there's work waiting for them in the village or in the Castle, and so they travel at a great pace. It's not likely to occur to them to look out of the carriage windows in search of petitioners, for the carriages are crammed with papers which they study on the way.'

'But,' said K., 'I've seen the inside of an official sledge in which there weren't any papers.' Olga's story was opening for him such a great and almost incredible world that he could not help trying to put his own small experiences in relation to it, as much to convince himself of its reality as of his own existence.

'That's possible,' said Olga, 'but in that case it's even worse, for that means that the official's business is so important that the papers are too precious or too numerous to be taken with him, and those officials go at a gallop. In any case, none of them can spare time for father. And besides, there are several roads to the Castle. Now one of them is in fashion, and most carriages go by that, now it's another and everything drives pell-mell there. And what governs this change of fashion has never yet been found out. At eight o'clock one morning they'll all be on another road, ten minutes later on a third, and half an hour after that on the first road again, and then they may stick to this road all day, but every minute there's the possibility of a change. Of course all the roads join up near the village, but by that time all the carriages are racing like mad, while nearer the Castle the pace isn't quite so fast. And the amount of traffic varies just as widely and incomprehensibly as the choice of roads. There are often days when there's not a carriage to be seen, and others when they travel in crowds. Now, just think of all that in relation to father. In his best suit, which soon becomes his only suit, off he goes every morning from the house with our best wishes. He takes with him a small Fire Brigade badge, which he has really no business to keep, to stick in his coat once he's out of the village, for in the village itself he's afraid to let it be seen, although it's so small that it can hardly be seen two paces away, but father insists that it's just the thing to draw a passing official's attention. Not far from the Castle entrance there's a market garden, belonging to a man called Bertuch who sells vegetables to the Castle, and there on the narrow stone ledge at the foot of the garden fence father took up his post. Bertuch made no objection because he used to be very friendly with father and had been one of his most faithful customers – you see, he has a lame foot, and he thought that nobody but father could make him a boot to fit it. Well, there sat father day after day, it was a wet and stormy autumn, but the weather meant nothing to him. In the morning at his regular hour he had his hand on the latch and waved us good-bye, in the evening he came back soaked to the skin, everyday, it seemed, a little more bent, and flung himself down in a corner. At first he used to tell us all his little adventures, such as how Bertuch for sympathy and old friendship's sake had thrown him a blanket over the fence, or that in one of the passing carriages he thought he had recognized this or the other official, or that this or the other coachman had recognized him again and playfully flicked him with his whip. But later he stopped telling us these things, evidently he had given up all hope of ever achieving anything there, and looked on it only as his duty, his dreary job, to go there and spend the whole day. That was when his rheumatic pains began, winter was coming on, snow fell early, the winter begins very early here; well, so there he sat sometimes on wet stones and at other times in the snow. In the night he groaned with pain, and in the morning he was many a time uncertain whether to go or not, but always overcame his reluctance and went. Mother clung to him and didn't want to let him go, so he, apparently grown timid because his limbs wouldn't obey him, allowed her to go with him, and so mother began to get pains too. We often went out to them, to take them food, or merely to visit them, or to try to persuade them to come back home; how often we found them crouching together, leaning against each other on their narrow seat, huddled up under a thin blanket which scarcely covered them, and round about them nothing but the grey of snow and mist, and far and wide for days at a time not a soul to be seen, not a carriage; a sight that was, K., a sight to be seen! Until one morning father couldn't move his stiff legs out of bed at all, he wasn't to be comforted, in a slight delirium he thought he could see an official stopping his carriage beside Bertuch's just at that moment, hunting all along the fence for him and then climbing angrily into his carriage again with a shake of his head. At that father shrieked so loudly that it was as if he wanted to make the official hear him at all that distance, and to explain how blameless his absence was. And it became a long absence, he never went back again, and for weeks he never left his bed. Amalia took over the nursing, the attending, the treatment, did everything he needed, and with a few intervals has kept it up to this day. She knows healing herbs to soothe his pain, she needs hardly any sleep, she's never alarmed, never afraid, never impatient, she does everything for the old folks; while we were fluttering around uneasily without being able to help in anything she remained cool and quiet whatever happened. Then when the worst was past and father was able again to struggle cautiously out of bed with one of us supporting him on each side, Amalia withdrew into the background again and left him to us.'

OLGA'S PLANS

'Now it was necessary again to find some occupation for father that he was still fit for, something that at least would make him believe that he was helping to remove the burden of guilt from our family. Something of the kind was not hard to find, anything at all in fact would have been as useful for the purpose as sitting in Bertuch's garden, but I found something that actually gave me a little hope. Whenever there had been any talk of our guilt among officials or clerks or anybody else, it was only the insult to Sortini's messenger that had always been brought up, further than that nobody dared go. Now, I said to myself, since public opinion, even if only ostensibly, recognized nothing but the insult to the messenger, then, even if it were still only ostensibly, everything might be put right if one could propitiate the messenger. No charge had actually been made, we were told, no department therefore had taken up the affair yet, and so the messenger was at liberty, as far as he was concerned – and there was no question of anything more – to forgive the offence. All that of course couldn't have any decisive importance, was mere semblance and couldn't produce in turn anything but semblance, but all the same it would cheer up my father and might help to harass the swarm of clerks who had been tormenting him, and that would be a satisfaction. First of course one had to find the messenger. When I told father of my plan, at first he was very annoyed, for to tell the truth he had become terribly self-willed; for one thing he was convinced – this happened during his illness – that we had always held him back from final success, first by stopping his allowance and then by keeping him in his bed; and for another he was no longer capable of completely understanding any new idea. My plan was turned down even before I had finished telling him about it, he was convinced that his job was to go on waiting in Bertuch's garden, and as he was in no state now to go there every day himself, we should have to push him there in a hand-barrow. But I didn't give in, and gradually he became reconciled to the idea, the only thing that disturbed him was that in this matter he was quite dependent on me, for I had been the only one who had seen the messenger, he did not know him. Actually one messenger is very like another, and I myself was not quite certain that I would know this one again. Presently we began to go to the Herrenhof and look around among the servants. The messenger of course had been in Sortini's service and Sortini had stopped coming to the village, but the gentlemen are continually changing their servants, one might easily find our man among the servants of another gentleman, and even if he himself was not to be found, still one might perhaps get news of him from the other servants. For this purpose it was of course necessary to be in the Herrenhof every evening, and people weren't very pleased to see us anywhere, far less in a place like that; and we couldn't appear either as paying customers. But it turned out that they could put us to some use all the same. You know what a trial the servants were to Frieda, at bottom they are mostly quiet people, but pampered and made lazy by too little work – "May you be as well off as a servant" is a favourite toast among the officials – and really, as far as an easy life goes, the servants seem to be the real masters in the Castle, they know their own dignity too, and in the Castle, where they have to behave in accordance with their regulations, they're quiet and dignified, several times I've been assured of that, and one can find even among the servants down here some faint signs of that, but only faint signs, for usually, seeing that the Castle regulations aren't fully binding on them in the village, they seem quite changed; a wild unmanageable lot, ruled by their insatiable impulses instead of by their regulations. Their scandalous behaviour knows no limits, it's lucky for the village that they can't leave the Herrenhof without permission, but in the Herrenhof itself one must try to get on with them somehow; Frieda, for instance, felt that very hard to do and so she was very glad to employ me to quieten the servants. For more than two years, at least twice a week, I've spent the night with the servants in the stalls. Earlier, when father was still able to go to the Herrenhof with me, he slept somewhere in the taproom, and in that way waited for the news that I would bring in the morning. There wasn't much to bring. We've never found the messenger to this day, he must be still with Sortini who values him very highly, and he must have followed Sortini when Sortini retired to a more remote bureau. Most of the servants haven't seen him since we saw him last ourselves, and when one or other claims to have seen him it's probably a mistake. So my plan might have actually failed, and yet it hasn't failed completely; it's true we haven't found the messenger, and going to the Herrenhof and spending the night there – perhaps his pity for me, too, any pity that he's still capable of – has unfortunately ruined my father, and for two years now he has been in the state you've seen him in, and yet things are perhaps better with him than with my mother, for we're waiting daily for her death; it has only been put off thanks to Amalia's superhuman efforts. But what I've achieved in the Herrenhof is a certain connexion with the Castle; don't despise me when I say that I don't repent what I've done. What conceivable sort of a connexion with the Castle can this be, you'll no doubt be thinking; and you're right, it's not much of a connexion. I know a great many of the servants now, of course, almost all the gentlemen's servants who have come to the village during the last two years, and if I should ever get into the Castle, I shan't be a stranger there. Of course, they're servants only in the village, in the Castle they're quite different, and probably wouldn't know me or anybody else there that they've had dealings with in the village, that's quite certain, even if they have sworn a hundred times in the stall that they would be delighted to see me again in the Castle. Besides, I've already had experience of how little all these promises are worth. But still that's not the really important thing. It isn't only through the servants themselves that I have a connexion with the Castle, for apart from that I hope and trust that what I'm doing is being noticed by someone up there – and the management of the staff of servants is really an extremely important and laborious official function – and that finally whoever is noticing me may perhaps arrive at a more favourable opinion of me than the others, that he may recognize that I'm fighting for my family and carrying on my father's efforts, no matter in how poor a way. If he should see it like that, perhaps he'll forgive me too for accepting money from the servants and using it for our family. And I've achieved something more yet, which even you, I'm afraid, will blame me for. I learned a great deal from the servants about the ways in which one can get into the Castle service without going through the difficult preliminaries of official appointment lasting sometimes for years; in that case, it's true, one doesn't become an actual official employee, but only a private and semi-official one,

one has neither rights nor duties – and the worst is not to have any duties – but one advantage one does have, that one is on the spot, one can watch for favourable opportunities and take advantage of them, one may not be an employee, but by good luck some work may come one's way, perhaps no real employee is handy, there's a call, one flies to answer it, and one has become the very thing that one wasn't a minute before, an employee. Only, when is one likely to get a chance like that? Sometimes, at once, one has hardly arrived, one has hardly had time to look round before the chance is there, and many a one hasn't even the presence of mind, being quite new to the job, to seize the opportunity; but in another case one may have to wait for even more years than the official employees, and after being a semi-official servant for so long one can never be lawfully taken on afterwards as an official employee. So there's enough here to make one pause, but it sinks to nothing when one takes into account that the test for the official appointments is very stringent and that a member of any doubtful family is turned down in advance; let us say someone like that goes in for the examination, for years he waits in fear and trembling for the result, from the very first day everybody asks him in amazement how he could have dared to do anything so wild, but he still goes on hoping – how else could he keep alive? – then after years and years, perhaps as an old man, he learns that he has been rejected, learns that everything is lost and that all his life has been in vain. Here, too, of course there are exceptions, that's how one is so easily tempted. It happens sometimes that really shady customers are actually appointed, there are officials who, literally in spite of themselves, are attracted by those outlaws; at the entrance examinations they can't help sniffing the air, smacking their lips, and rolling their eyes towards an entrant like that, who seems in some way to be terribly appetizing to them, and they have to stick close to their books of regulations so as to withstand him. Sometimes, however, that doesn't help the entrant to an appointment, but only leads to an endless postponement of the preliminary proceedings, which are never terminated, but only broken off by the death of the poor man. So official appointment no less than the other kind is full of obvious and concealed difficulties, and before one goes in for anything of the kind it's highly advisable to weigh everything carefully. Now, we didn't fail to do that, Barnabas and I. Every time that I came back from the Herrenhof we sat down together and I told the latest news that I had gathered, for days we talked it over, and Barnabas's work lay idle for longer spells than was good for it. And here I may be to blame in your opinion. I knew quite well that much reliance was not to be put on the servants' stories. I knew that they never had much inclination to tell me things about the Castle, that they always changed the subject, and that every word had to be dragged out of them, and then, when they were well started, that they let themselves go, talked nonsense, bragged, tried to surpass one another in inventing improbable lies, so that in the continuous shouting in the dark stalls, one servant beginning where the other left off, it was clear that at best only a few scanty scraps of truth could be picked up. But I repeated everything to Barnabas again just as I had heard it, though he still had no capacity whatever to distinguish between what was true and what was false, and on account of the family's position was almost famishing to hear all these things; and he drank in everything and burned with eagerness for more. And as a matter of fact the cornerstone of my new plan was Barnabas. Nothing more could be done through the servants. Sortini's messenger was not to be found and would never be found, Sortini and his messenger with him seemed to be receding farther and farther, by many people their appearance and names were already forgotten, and often I had to describe them at length and in spite of that learn nothing more than that the servant I was speaking to could remember them with an effort, but except for that could tell nothing about them. And as for my conduct with the servants, of course I had no power to decide how it might be looked on and could only hope that the Castle would judge it in the spirit I did it in, and that in return a little of the guilt of our family would be taken away, but I've received no outward sign of that.

Still I stuck to it, for so far as I was concerned I saw no other chance of getting anything done for us in the Castle. But for Barnabas I saw another possibility. From the tales of the servants – if I had the inclination, and I had only too much inclination – I could draw the conclusion that anyone who was taken into the Castle service could do a great deal for his family. But then what was there that was worthy of belief in these tales? It was impossible to make certain of that, but that there was very little was clear. For when, say, a servant that I would never see again, or that I would hardly recognize even were I to see him again, solemnly promised me to help to get my brother a post in the Castle, or at least, if Barnabas should come to the Castle on other business, to support him, or at least to back him up – for according to the servants' stories it sometimes happens that candidates for posts become unconscious or deranged during the protracted waiting and then they're lost if some friend doesn't look after them – when things like that and a great many more were told to me, they were probably justified as warnings, but the promisies that accompanied them were quite baseless. But not to Barnabas; it's true I warned him not to believe them, but my mere telling of them was enough to enlist him for my plan. The reasons I advanced for it myself impressed him less, the thing that chiefly influenced him was the servants' stories. And so in reality I was completely thrown back upon myself. Amalia was the only one who could make herself understood to my parents, and the more I followed, in my own way, the original plans of father, the more Amalia shut herself off from me, before you or anybody else she talks to me, but not when we're alone; to the servants in the Herrenhof I was a plaything which in their fury they did their best to wreck, not one intimate word have I spoken with any of them during those two years, I've had only cunning or lying or silly words from them, so only Barnabas remained for me, and Barnabas was still very young. When I saw the light in his eyes as I told him those things, a light which has remained in them ever since, I felt terrified and yet I didn't stop, the things at stake seemed too great. I admit I hadn't my father's great though empty plans. I hadn't the resolution that men have. I confined myself to making good the insult to the messenger, and only asked that the actual modesty of my attempt should be put to my credit. But what I had failed to do by myself I wanted now to achieve in a different way and with certainty through Barnabas. We had insulted a messenger and driven him into a more remote bureau; what was more natural than for us to offer a new messenger in the person of Barnabas, so that the other messenger's work might be carried on by him, and the other messenger might remain quietly in retirement as long as he liked, for as long a time as he needed to forget the insult? I was quite aware, of course, that in spite of all its modesty there was a hint of presumption in my plan, that it might give rise to the impression that we wanted to dictate to the authorities how they should decide a personal question, or that we doubted their ability to make the best arrangements, which they might have made long before we had struck upon the idea that something could be done. But then, I thought again that it was impossible that the authorities should misunderstand me so grossly, or if they should, that they should do so intentionally, that in other words all that I did should be turned down in advance without further examination. So I did not give in and Barnabas's ambition kept him from giving in. In this term of preparation Barnabas became so uppish that he found that cobbling was far too menial work for him, a future bureau employee, yes, he even dared to contradict Amalia, and flatly, on the few occasions that she spoke to him about it. I didn't grudge him this brief happiness, for with the first day that he went to the Castle his happiness and his arrogance would be gone, a thing easy enough to foresee. And now began that parody of service of which I've told you already. It was amazing with what little difficulty Barnabas got into the Castle that first time, or more correctly into the bureau which in a manner of speaking has become his workroom This success drove me almost frantic at the time, when Barnabas whispered the news to me in the evening after he came home, I ran to Amalia, seized her, drew her into a corner, and kissed her so wildly that she cried with pain and terror. I could explain nothing for excitement, and then it had been so long since we had spoken to each other, so I put off telling her until the next day or the day after. For the next few days, however, there was really nothing more to tell. After the first quick success nothing more happened. For two long years Barnabas led this heart-breaking life. The servants failed us completely, I gave Barnabas a short note to take with him recommending him to their consideration, reminding them at the same time of their promises, and Barnabas, as often as he saw a servant, drew out the note and held it up, and even if he sometimes may have presented it to someone who didn't know me, and even if those who did know me were irritated by his way of holding out the note in silence – for he didn't dare to speak up there – yet all the same it was a shame that nobody helped him, and it was a relief – which we could have, secured, I must admit, by our own action and much earlier – when a servant who had probably been pestered several times already by the note, crushed it up and flung it into the wastepaper basket. Almost as if he had said: "That's just what you yourselves do with letters", it occurred to me. But barren of results as all this time was in other ways, it had a good effect on Barnabas, if one can call it a good thing that he grew prematurely old, became a man before his time, yes, even in some ways more grave and sensible than most men. Often it makes me sad to look at him and compare him with the boy that he was only two years ago. And with it all I'm quite without the comfort and support that, being a man, he could surely give me. Without me he could hardly have got into the Castle, but since he is there, he's independent of me. I'm his only intimate friend, but I'm certain that he only tells me a small part of what he has on his mind. He tells me a great many things about the Castle, but from his stories, from the trifling details that he gives, one can't understand in the least how those things could have changed him so much. In particular I can't understand how the daring he had as a boy – it actually caused us anxiety – how he can have lost it so completely up there now that he's a man. Of course all that useless standing about and waiting all day, and day after day, and going on and on without any prospect of a change, must break a man down and make him unsure of himself and in the end actually incapable of anything else but this hopeless standing about. But why didn't he put up a fight even at the beginning? Especially seeing that he soon recognized that I had been right and that there was no opportunity there for his ambition, though there might be some hope perhaps for the betterment of our family's condition. For up there, in spite of the servants' whims, everything goes on very soberly, ambition seeks its sole satisfaction in work, and as in this way the work itself gains the ascendancy, ambition ceases to have any place at all, for childish desires there's no room up there. Nevertheless Barnabas fancied, so he has told me, that he could clearly see how great the power and knowledge even of those very questionable officials were into whose bureau he is allowed. How fast they dictated, with half-shut eyes and brief gestures, merely by raising a finger quelling the surly servants, and making them smile with happiness even when they were checked; or perhaps finding an important passage in one of the books and becoming quite absorbed in it, while the others would crowd round as near as the cramped space would allow them, and crane their necks to see it. These things and other things of the same kind gave Barnabas a great idea of those men, and he had the feeling that if he could get the length of being noticed by them and could venture to address a few words to them, not as a stranger, but as a colleague – true a very subordinate colleague – in the bureau, incalculable things might be achieved for our family. But things have never got that length yet, and Barnabas can't venture to do anything that might help towards it, although he's well aware that, young as he is, he's been raised to the difficult and responsible position of chief breadwinner in our family on account of this whole unfortunate affair. And now for the final confession: it was a week after your arrival. I heard somebody mentioning it in the Herrenhof, but didn't pay much attention; a Land Surveyor had come and I didn't even know what a Land

Surveyor was. But next evening Barnabas – at an agreed hour I usually set out to go a part of the way to meet him – came home earlier than usual, saw Amalia in the sitting-room, drew me out into the street, laid his head on my shoulder, and cried for several minutes. He was again the little boy he used to be. Something had happened to him that he hadn't been prepared for. It was as if a whole new world had suddenly opened to him, and he could not bear the joy and the anxieties of all this newness. And yet the only thing that had happened was that he had been given a letter for delivery to you. But it was actually the first letter, the first commission, that he had ever been given.'

Olga stopped. Everything was still except for the heavy, occasionally disturbed breathing of the old people. K. merely said casually, as if to round off Olga's story: 'You've all been playing with me. Barnabas brought me the letter with the air of an old and much occupied messenger, and you as well as Amalia – who for that time must have been in with you – behaved as if carrying messages and the letter itself were matters of indifference.' 'You must distinguish between us,' said Olga. 'Barnabas had been made a happy boy again by the letter, in spite of all the doubts that he had about his capability. He confined those doubts to himself and me, but he felt it a point of honour to look like a real messenger, as according to his ideas real messengers looked. So although his hopes were now rising to an official uniform I had to alter his trousers, and in two hours, so that they would have some resemblance at least to the close-fitting trews of the official uniform, and he might appear in them before you, knowing, of course, that on this point you could be easily taken in. So much for Barnabas. But Amalia really despises his work as a messenger, and now that he seemed to have had a little success – as she could easily guess from Barnabas and myself and our talking and whispering together – she despised it more than ever. So she was speaking the truth, don't deceive yourself about that. But if I, K., have seemed to slight Barnabas's work, it hasn't been with any intention to deceive you, but from anxiety. These two letters that have gone through Barnabas's hands are the first signs of grace, questionable as they are, that our family has received for three years. This change, if it is a change and not a deception – deceptions are more frequent than changes – is connected with your arrival here, our fate has become in a certain sense dependent on you, perhaps these two letters are only a beginning, and Barnabas's abilities will be used for other things than these two letters concerning you – we must hope that as long as we can – for the time being, however, everything centres on you. Now up in the Castle we must rest content with whatever our lot happens to be, but down here we can, it may be, do something ourselves, that is, make sure of your goodwill, or at least save ourselves from your dislike, or, what's more important, protect you as far as our strength and experience go, so that your connexion with the Castle – by which we might perhaps be helped too – might not be lost. Now what was our best way of bringing that about? To prevent you from having any suspicion of us when we approached you – for you're a stranger here and because of that certain to be full of suspicion, full of justifiable suspicion. And, besides, we're despised by everybody and you must be influenced by the general opinion, particularly through your fiancée, so how could we put ourselves forward without quite unintentionally setting ourselves up against your fiancée, and so offending you? And the messages, which I had read before you got them – Barnabas didn't read them, as a messenger he couldn't allow himself to do that – seemed at the first glance obsolete and not of much importance, yet took on the utmost importance inasmuch as they referred you to the Superintendent. Now in these circumstances how were we to conduct ourselves towards you? If we emphasized the letters' importance, we laid ourselves under suspicion by overestimating what was obviously unimportant, and in pluming ourselves as the vehicle of these messages we should be suspected of seeking our own ends, not yours; more, in doing that we might depreciate the value of the letter itself in your eyes and so disappoint you sore against our will. But if we didn't lay much stress on the letters we should lay ourselves equally under suspicion, for why in that case should we have taken the trouble of delivering such an unimportant letter, why should our actions and our words be in such clear contradiction, why should we in this way disappoint not only you, the addressee, but also the sender of the letter, who certainly hadn't handed the letter to us so that we should belittle it to the addressee by our explanations? And to hold the mean, without exaggeration on either side, in other words to estimate the just value of those letters, is impossible, they themselves change in value perpetually, the reflections they give rise to are endless, and chance determines where one stops reflecting, and so even our estimate of them is a matter of chance. And when on the top of that there came anxiety about you, everything became confused, and you mustn't judge whatever I said too severely. When, for example – as once happened – Barnabas arrived with the news that you were dissatisfied with his work, and in his first distress – his professional vanity was wounded too I must admit – resolved to retire from the service altogether, then to make good the mistake I was certainly ready to deceive, to lie, to betray, to do anything, no matter how wicked, if it would only help. But even then I would have been doing it, at least in my opinion, as much for your sake as for ours.'

There was a knock. Olga ran to the door and unfastened it. A strip of light from a dark lantern fell across the threshold. The late visitor put questions in a whisper and was answered in the same way, but was not satisfied and tried to force his way into the room. Olga found herself unable to hold him back any longer and called to Amalia, obviously hoping that to keep the old people from being disturbed in their sleep Amalia would do anything to eject the visitor. And indeed she hurried over at once, pushed Olga aside, and stepped into the street and closed the door behind her. She only remained there for a moment, almost at once she came back again, so quickly had she achieved what had proved impossible for Olga.

K. then learned from Olga that the visit was intended for him. It had been one of the assistants, who was looking for him at Frieda's command. Olga had wanted to shield K. from the assistant; if K. should confess his visit here to Frieda later, he could, but it must not be discovered through the assistant; K. agreed. But Olga's invitation to spend the night there and wait for Barnabas he declined, for himself he might perhaps have accepted for it was already late in the night and it seemed to him that now, whether he wanted it or not, he was bound to this family in such a way that a bed for the night here, though for many reasons painful, nevertheless, when one considered this common bond, was the most suitable for him in the village; all the same he declined it, the assistant's visit had alarmed him, it was incomprehensible to him how Frieda, who knew his wishes quite well, and the assistants, who had learned to fear him, had come together again like this, so that Frieda didn't scruple to send an assistant for him, only one of them, too, while the other had probably remained to keep her company. He asked Olga whether she had a whip, she hadn't one, but she had a good hazel switch, and he took it; then he asked whether there was any other way out of the house, there was one through the yard, only one had to clamber over the wall of the neighbouring garden and walk through it before one reached the street. K. decided to do this. While Olga was conducting him through the yard, K. tried hastily to reassure her fears, told her that he wasn't in the least angry at the small artifices she had told him about, but understood them very well, thanked her for the confidence she had shown in him in telling him her story, and asked her to send Barnabas to the school as soon as he arrived, even if it were during the night. It was true, the messages which Barnabas brought were not his only hope, otherwise things would be bad indeed with him, but he didn't by any means leave them out of account, he would hold to them and not forget Olga either, for still more important to him than the messages themselves was Olga, her bravery, her prudence, if he had to choose between Olga and Amalia it wouldn't cost him much reflection. And he pressed her hand cordially once more as he swung himself on to the wall of the neighbouring garden.

16

When he reached the street he saw indistinctly in the darkness that a little farther along the assistant was still walking up and down before Barnabas's house; sometimes he stopped and tried to peep into the room through the drawn blinds. K. called to him; without appearing visibly startled he gave up his spying on the house and came towards K. 'Who are you looking for?' asked K., testing the suppleness of the hazel switch on his leg. 'You,' replied the assistant as he came nearer. 'But who are you?' asked K. suddenly, for this did not appear to be the assistant. He seemed older, wearier, more wrinkled, but fuller in the face, his walk too was quite different from the brisk walk of the assistants, which gave an impression as if their joints were charged with electricity; it was slow, a little halting, elegantly valetudinarian. 'You don't recognize me?' asked the man, 'Jeremiah, your old assistant.' 'I see,' said K. tentatively producing the hazel switch again, which he had concealed behind his back. 'But you look quite different.' 'It's because I'm by myself,' said Jeremiah. 'When I'm by myself then all my youthful spirits are gone.' 'But where is Arthur?' asked K. 'Arthur?' said Jeremiah. 'The little dear? He has left the service. You were rather hard and rough on us, you know, and the gentle soul couldn't stand it. He's gone back to the Castle to put in a complaint.' 'And you?' asked K. 'I'm able to stay here,' said Jeremiah, 'Arthur is putting in a complaint for me too.' 'What have you to complain about, then?' asked K. 'That you can't understand a joke. What have we done? Jested a little, laughed a little, teased your fiancée a little. And all according to our instructions, too. When Galater sent us to you –' 'Galater?' asked K. 'Yes, Galater,' replied Jeremiah, 'he was deputizing for Klamm himself at the time. When he sent us to you he said – I took a good note of it, for that's our business: You're to go down there as assistants to the Land Surveyor. We replied: But we don't know anything about the work. Thereupon he replied: That's not the main point: if it's necessary, he'll teach you it. The main thing is to cheer him up a little. According to the reports I've received he takes everything too seriously. He has just got to the village, and starts off thinking that a great experience, whereas in reality it's nothing at all. You must make him see that.' 'Well?' said K., 'was Galater right, and have you carried out your task?' 'That I don't know,' replied Jeremiah. 'In such a short time it was hardly possible. I only know that you were very rough on us, and that's what we're complaining of. I can't understand how you, an employee yourself and not even a Castle employee, aren't able to see that a job like that is very hard work, and that it's very wrong to make the work harder for the poor workers, and wantonly, almost childishly, as you have done. Your total lack of consideration in letting us freeze at the railings, and almost felling Arthur with your fist on the straw sack – Arthur, a man who feels a single cross word for days – and in chasing me up and down in the snow all afternoon, so that it was an hour before I could recover from it! And I'm no longer young!' 'My dear Jeremiah,' said K., 'you're quite right about all this, only it's Galater you should complain to. He sent you here of his own accord, I didn't beg him to send you. And as I hadn't asked you it was at my discretion to send you back again, and like you, I would much rather have done it peacefully than with violence, but evidently you wouldn't have it any other way. Besides, why didn't you speak to me when you came first as frankly as you've done just now?' 'Because I was in the service,' said Jeremiah, 'surely that's obvious.' 'And now you're in the service no longer?' asked K. 'That's so,' said Jeremiah, 'Arthur has given notice in the Castle that we're giving up the job, or at least proceedings have been set going that will finally set us free from it.' 'But you're still looking for me just as if you were in the service,' said K. 'No,' replied Jeremiah, 'I was only looking for you to re-assure Frieda. When you forsook her for Barnabas's sister she was very unhappy, not so much because of the loss, as because of your treachery, besides she had seen it coming for a long time and had suffered a great deal already on that account. I only went up to the school-window for one more look to see if you mightn't have become more reasonable. But you weren't there. Frieda was sitting by herself on a bench crying. So then I went to her and we came to an agreement. Everything's settled. I'm to be waiter in the Herrenhof, at least until my business is settled in the Castle, and Frieda is back in the taproom again. It's better for Frieda. There was no sense in her becoming your wife. And you haven't known how to value the sacrifice that she was prepared to make for you either. But the good soul had still some scruples left, perhaps she was doing you an injustice, she thought, perhaps you weren't with the Barnabas girl after all. Although of course there could be no doubt where you were, I went all the same so as to make sure of it once and for all; for after all this worry Frieda deserved to sleep peacefully for once, not to mention myself. So I went and not only found you there, but was able to see incidentally as well that you had the girls on a string. The black one especially – a real wild-cat – she's set her cap at you. Well, everyone to his taste. But all the same it wasn't necessary for you to take the roundabout way through the next-door garden, I know that way.'

So now the thing had come after all which he had been able to foresee, but not to prevent. Frieda had left him. It could not be final, it was not so bad as that, Frieda could be won back, it was easy for any stranger to influence her, even for those assistants who considered Frieda's position much the same as their own, and now that they had given notice had prompted Frieda to do the same, but K. would only have to show himself and remind her of all that spoke in his favour, and she would rue it and come back to him, especially if he should be in a position to justify his visit to those girls by some success due entirely to them. Yet in spite of those reflexions, by which he sought to reassure himself on Frieda's account, he was not reassured. Only a few minutes ago he had been praising Frieda up to Olga and calling her his only support; well, that support was not of the firmest, no intervention of the mighty ones had been needed to rob K. of Frieda – even this not very savoury assistant had been enough – this puppet which sometimes gave one the impression of not being properly alive.

Jeremiah had already began to disappear. K. called him back. 'Jeremiah,' he said, 'I want to be quite frank with you; answer one question of mine too in the same spirit. We're no longer in the position of master and servant, a matter of congratulation not only to you but to me too; we have no grounds, then, for deceiving each other. Here before your eyes I snap this switch which was intended for you, for it wasn't for fear of you that I chose the back way out, but so as to surprise you and lay it across your shoulders a few times. But don't take it badly, all that is over; if you hadn't been forced on me as a servant by the bureau, but had been simply an acquaintance, we would certainly have got on splendidly, even if your appearance might have disturbed me occasionally. And we can make up now for what we have missed in that way.' 'Do you think so?' asked the assistant, yawning and closing his eyes wearily. 'I could of course explain the matter more at length, but I have no time, I must go to Frieda, the poor child is waiting for me, she hasn't started on her job yet, at my request the landlord has given her a few hours' grace – she wanted to fling herself into the work at once probably to help her to forget – and we want to spend that little time at least together. As for your proposal, I have no cause, certainly, to deceive you, but I have just as little to confide anything to you. My case, in other words, is different from yours. So long as my relation to you was that of a servant, you were naturally a very important person in my eyes, not because of your own qualities, but because of my office, and I would have done anything for you that you wanted, but now you're of no importance to me. Even your breaking the switch doesn't affect me, it only reminds me what a rough master I had, it's not calculated to prejudice me in your favour.' 'You talk to me,' said K, 'as if it were quite certain that you'll never have to fear anything from me again. But that isn't really so. From all appearances you're not free from me, things aren't settled here so quickly as that –' 'Sometimes even more quickly,' Jeremiah threw in. 'Sometimes,' said K, 'but nothing points to the fact that it's so this time, at least neither you nor I have anything that we can show in black and white. The proceedings are only started, it seems, and I haven't used my influence yet to intervene, but I will. If the affair turns out badly for you, you'll find that you haven't exactly endeared yourself to your master, and perhaps it was superfluous after all to break the hazel switch. And then you have abducted Frieda, and that has given you an inflated notion of yourself, but with all respect that I have for your person, even if you have none for me any longer, a few words from me to Frieda will be enough – I know it – to smash up the lies that you've caught her with. And only lies could have estranged Frieda from me.' 'These threats don't frighten me,' replied Jeremiah, 'you don't in the least want me as an assistant, you were afraid of me even as an assistant, you're afraid of assistants in any case, it was only fear that made you strike poor Arthur.' 'Perhaps,' said K., 'but did it hurt the less for that? Perhaps I'll be able to show my fear of you in that way many times yet. Once I see that you haven't much joy in an assistant's work, it'll give me great satisfaction again, in spite of all my fear, to keep you at it. And moreover I'll do my best next time to see that you come by yourself, without Arthur, I'll be able then to devote more attention to you.' 'Do you think,' asked Jeremiah, 'that I have even the slightest fear of all this?' 'I do think so,' said K., 'you're a little afraid, that's certain, and if you're wise, very much afraid. If that isn't so why didn't you go straight back to Frieda? Tell me, are you in love with her, then?' 'In love!' said Jeremiah. 'She's a nice clever girl, a former sweetheart of Klamm's, so respectable in any case. And as she kept on imploring me to save her from you why shouldn't I do her the favour, particularly as I wasn't doing you any harm, seeing that you've consoled yourself with these damned Barnabas girls?' 'Now I can see how frightened you are,' said K., 'frightened out of your wits; you're trying to catch me with lies. All that Frieda asked for was to be saved from those filthy swine of assistants, who were getting past bounds, but unfortunately I hadn't time to fulfil her wish completely, and now this is the result of my negligence.'

'Land Surveyor, Land Surveyor!' someone shouted down the street. It was Barnabas. He came up breathless with running, but did not forget to greet K. with a bow. 'Its done!' he said. 'What's done?' asked K. 'You've laid my request before Klamm?' 'That didn't come off,' said Barnabas, 'I did my best, but it was impossible, I was urgent, stood there all day without being asked and so close to the desk that once a clerk actually pushed me away, for I was standing in his light, I reported myself when Klamm looked up – and that's forbidden – by lifting my hand, I was the last in the bureau, was left alone there with only the servants, but had the luck all the same to see Klamm coming back again, but it was not on my account, he only wanted to have another hasty glance at something in a book and went away immediately; finally, as I still made no move, the servants almost swept me out of the door with the broom. I tell you all this so that you need never complain of my efforts again.' 'What good is all your zeal to me, Barnabas,' said K., 'when it hasn't the slightest success?' 'But I have had success!' replied Barnabas. 'As I was leaving my bureau – I call it my bureau – I saw a gentleman coming slowly towards me along one of the passages, which were quite empty except for him. By that time in fact it was very late. I decided to wait for him. It was a good pretext to wait longer, indeed I would much rather have waited in any case, so as not to have to bring you news of failure. But apart from that it was worth while waiting, for it was Erlanger. You don't know him? He's one of Klamm's chief secretaries. A weakly little gentleman, he limps a little. He recognized me at once, he's famous for his splendid memory and his knowledge of people, he just draws his brows together and that's enough for him to recognize anybody, often people even that he's never seen before, that he's only heard of or read about; for instance, he could hardly ever have seen me. But although he recognizes everybody immediately, he always asks first as if he weren't quite sure. Aren't you Barnabas? he asked me. And then he went on: You know the Land Surveyor, don't you? And then he said: That's very lucky. I'm just going to the Herrenhof. The Land Surveyor is to report to me there. I'll be in room number 15. But he must come at once. I've only a few things to settle there and I leave again for the Castle at 5 o'clock in the morning. Tell him that it's very important that I should speak to him.'

Suddenly Jeremiah set off at a run. In his excitement Barnabas had scarcely noticed his presence till now and asked: 'Where's Jeremiah going?' 'To forestall me with Erlanger,' said K., and set off after Jeremiah, caught him up, hung on to his arm, and said: 'Is it a sudden desire for Frieda that's seized you? I've got it as well, so we'll go together side by side.'

17

Before the dark Herrenhof a little group of men were standing, two or three had lanterns with them, so that a face here and there could be distinguished. K. recognized only one acquaintance, Gerstäcker the carrier. Gerstäcker greeted him with the inquiry: 'You're still in the village?' 'Yes,' replied K. 'I've come here for good.' 'That doesn't matter to me,' said Gerstäcker, breaking out into a fit of coughing and turning away to the others.

It turned out that they were all waiting for Erlanger. Erlanger had already arrived, but he was consulting first with Momus before he admitted his clients. They were all complaining at not being allowed to wait inside and having to stand out there in the snow. The weather wasn't very cold, but still it showed a lack of consideration to keep them standing there in front of the house in the darkness, perhaps for hours. It was certainly not the fault of Erlanger, who was always very accommodating, knew nothing about it, and would certainly be very annoyed if it were reported to him. It was the fault of the Herrenhof landlady, who in her positively morbid determination to be refined, wouldn't suffer a lot of people to come into the Herrenhof at the same time. 'If it absolutely must be and they must come,' she used to say, 'then in Heaven's name let them come one at a time.' And she managed to arrange that the clients, who at first had waited simply in a passage, later on the stairs, then in the hall, and finally in the taproom, were at last pushed out into the street. But even that had not satisfied her. It was unendurable for her to be always 'besieged', as she expressed herself, in her own house. It was incomprehensible to her why there should need to be clients waiting at all. 'To dirty the front-door steps,' an official had once told her, obviously in annoyance, but to her this pronouncement had seemed very illuminating, and she was never tired of quoting it. She tried her best – and she had the approval in this case of the clients too – to get a building set up opposite the Herrenhof where the clients could wait. She would have liked best of all if the interviews and examinations could have taken place outside the Herrenhof altogether, but the officials opposed that, and when the officials opposed her seriously the landlady naturally enough was unable to gainsay them, though in lesser matters she exercised a kind of petty tyranny, thanks to her indefatigable, yet femininely insinuating zeal. And the landlady would probably have to endure those interviews and examinations in the Herrenhof in perpetuity, for the gentlemen from the Castle refused to budge from the place whenever they had official business in the village. They were always in a hurry, they came to the village much against their will, they had not the slightest intention of prolonging their stay beyond the time absolutely necessary, and so they could not be asked, simply for the sake of making things more pleasant in the Herrenhof, to waste time by transferring themselves with all their papers to some other house. The officials preferred indeed to get through their business in the taproom or in their rooms, if possible while they were at their food, or in bed before retiring for the night, or in the morning when they were too weary to get up and wanted to stretch themselves for a little longer. Yet the question of this erection of a waiting-room outside seemed to be nearing a favourable solution; but it was really a sharp blow for the landlady – people laughed a little over it – that this matter of a waiting-room should itself make innumerable interviews necessary, so that the lobbies of the house were hardly ever empty.

The waiting group passed the time by talking in half-whispers about those things. K. was struck by the fact that, though their discontent was general, nobody saw any objection to Erlanger's summoning his clients in the middle of the night. He asked why this was so and got the answer that they should be only too thankful to Erlanger. It was only his goodwill and his high conception of his office that induced him to come to the village at all, he could easily if he wished – and it would probably be more in accordance with the regulations too – he could easily send an under-secretary and let him draw up statements. Still, he usually refused to do this, he wanted to see and hear everything for himself, but for this purpose he had to sacrifice his nights for in his official time-table there was no time allowed for journeys to the village. K. objected that even Klamm came to the village during the day and even stayed for several days; was Erlanger, then, a mere secretary, more dispensable up there? One or two laughed good-humouredly, others maintained an embarrassed silence, the latter gained the ascendancy, and K. received hardly any reply. Only one man replied hesitatingly, that of course Klamm was indispensable, in the Castle as in the village.

Then the front door opened and Momus appeared between two attendants carrying lamps. 'The first who will be admitted to Herr Erlanger,' he said 'are Gerstäcker and K. Are these two men here?' They reported themselves, but before they could step forward Jeremiah slipped in with an 'I'm a waiter here,' and, greeted by Momus with a smiling slap on the shoulder, disappeared inside. 'I'll have to keep a sharper eye on Jeremiah,' K. told himself, though he was quite aware at the same time that

Jeremiah was probably far less dangerous than Arthur who was working against him in the Castle. Perhaps it would actually have been wiser to let himself be annoyed by them as assistants, than to have them prowling about without supervision and allow them to carry on their intrigues in freedom, intrigues for which they seemed to have special facilities.

As K. was passing Momus the latter started as if only now did he recognize in him the Land Surveyor. 'Ah, the Land Surveyor?' he said. 'The man who was so unwilling to be examined and now is in a hurry to be examined. It would have been simpler to let me do it that time. Well, really it's difficult to choose the right time for a hearing.' Since at these words K. made to stop, Momus went on: 'Go in, go in! I needed your answers then, I don't now.' Nevertheless K. replied, provoked by Momus's tone: 'You only think of yourselves. I would never and will never answer merely because of someone's office, neither then nor now.' Momus replied: 'Of whom, then, should we think? Who else is there here? Look for yourself?'

In the hall they were met by an attendant who led them the old way, already known to K., across the courtyard, then into the entry and through the low, somewhat downward-sloping passage. The upper storeys were evidently reserved only for higher officials, the secretaries, on the other hand, had their rooms in this passage, even Erlanger himself, although he was one of the highest among them. The servant put out his lantern, for here it was brilliant with electric light. Everything was on a small scale, but elegantly finished. The space was utilized to the best advantage. The passage was just high enough for one to walk without bending one's head. Along both sides the doors almost touched each other. The walls did not quite reach to the ceiling, probably for reasons of ventilation, for here in the low cellar-like passage the tiny rooms could hardly have windows. The disadvantage of those incomplete walls was that the passage, and necessarily the rooms as well, were noisy. Many of the rooms seemed to be occupied, in most the people were still awake, one could hear voices, hammering, the clink of glasses.

But the impression was not one of particular gaiety. The voices were muffled, only a word here and there could be indistinctly made out, it did not seem to be conversation either, probably someone was only dictating something or reading something aloud; and precisely from the rooms where there was a clinking of glasses and plates no word was to be heard, and the hammering reminded K. that he had been told some time or other that certain of the officials occupied themselves occasionally with carpentry, model engines, and so forth, to recuperate from the continual strain of mental work. The passage itself was empty except for a pallid, tall, thin gentleman in a fur coat, under which his night-clothes could be seen, who was sitting before one of the doors. Probably it had become too stuffy for him in the room, so he had sat down outside and was reading a newspaper, but not very carefully; often he yawned and left off reading, then bent forward and glanced along the passage, perhaps he was waiting for a client whom he had invited and who had omitted to come. When they had passed him the servant said to Gerstäcker: 'That's Pinzgauer.' Gerstäcker nodded: 'He hasn't been down here for a long time now,' he said. 'Not for a long time now,' the servant agreed.

At last they stopped before a door which was not in any way different from the others, and yet behind which, so the servant informed them, was Erlanger. The servant got K. to lift him on to his shoulders and had a look into the room through the open slit. 'He's lying down,' said the servant climbing down, 'on the bed, in his clothes, it's true, but I fancy all the same that he's asleep. Often he's overcome with weariness like that, here in the village, what with the change in his habits. We'll have to wait. When he wakes up he'll ring. Besides, it has happened before this for him to sleep away all his stay in the village, and then when he woke to have to leave again immediately for the Castle. It's voluntary, of course, the work he does here.' 'Then it would be better if he just slept on,' said Gerstäcker, 'for when he has a little time left for his work after he wakes, he's very vexed at having fallen asleep, and tries to get everything settled in a hurry, so that one can hardly get a word in.' 'You've come on account of the contract for the carting for the new building?' asked the servant. Gerstäcker nodded, drew the servant aside and talked to him in a low voice, but the servant hardly listened, gazed away over Gerstäcker, whom he overtopped by more than a head, and stroked his hair slowly and seriously.

18

Then, as he was looking round aimlessly, K. saw Frieda far away at a turn of the passage; she behaved as if she did not recognize him and only stared at him expressionlessly; she was carrying a tray with some empty dishes in her hand. He said to the servant, who, however, paid no attention whatever to him – the more one talked to the servant the more absent-minded he seemed to become – that he would be back in a moment, and ran off to Frieda. Reaching her he took her by the shoulders as if he were seizing his own property again, and asked her a few unimportant questions with his eyes holding hers. But her rigid bearing hardly as much as softened, to hide her confusion she tried to rearrange the dishes on the tray and said: 'What do you want from me? Go back to the others – oh, you know whom I mean, you've just come from them, I can see it.' K. changed his tactics immediately; the explanation mustn't come so suddenly, and mustn't begin with the worst point, the point most unfavourable to himself. 'I thought you were in the taproom,' he said. Frieda looked at him in amazement and then softly passed her free hand over his brow and cheeks. It was as if she had forgotten what he looked like and were trying to recall it to mind again, even her eyes had the veiled look of one who was painfully trying to remember. 'I've been taken on in the taproom again,' she said slowly at last, as if it did not matter what she said, but as if beneath her words she were carrying on another conversation with K. which was more important – 'this work here is not for me, anybody at all could do it; anybody who can make beds and look good-natured and doesn't mind the advances of the boarders, but actually likes them; anybody who can do that can be a chambermaid. But in the taproom, that's quite different. I've been taken on straight away for the taproom again, in spite of the fact that I didn't leave it with any great distinction, but, of course, I had a word put in for me. But the landlord was delighted that I had a word put in for me to make it easy for him to take me on again. It actually ended by them having to press me to take on the post; when you reflect what the taproom reminds me of you'll understand that. Finally I decided to take it on. I'm only here temporarily. Pepi begged us not to put her to the shame of having to leave the taproom at once, and seeing that she has been willing and has done everything to the best of her ability, we have given her a twenty-four hours' extension.' 'That's all very nicely arranged,' said K., 'but once you left the taproom for my sake, and now that we're soon to be married are you going back to it again?' 'There will be no marriage,' said Frieda. 'Because I've been unfaithful to you?' asked K. Frieda nodded. 'Now, look here, Frieda,' said K., 'we've often talked already about this alleged unfaithfulness of mine, and every time you've had to recognize finally that your suspicions were unjust. And since then nothing has changed on my side, all I've done has remained as innocent as it was at first and as it must always remain. So something must have changed on your side, through the suggestion of strangers or in some way or other. You do me an injustice in any case, for just listen to how I stand with those two girls. The one, the dark one – I'm almost ashamed to defend myself on particular points like this, but you give me no choice – the dark one, then, is probably just as displeasing to me as to you; I keep my distance with her in every way I can, and she makes it easy, too, no one could be more retiring than she is.' 'Yes,' cried Frieda, the words slipped out as if against her will, K. was delighted to see her attention diverted, she was not saying what she had intended – 'Yes, you may look upon her as retiring, you tell me that the most shameless creature of them all is retiring, and incredible as it is, you mean it honestly, you're not shamming, I know. The Bridge Inn landlady once said of you: "I can't abide him, but I can't let him alone, either, one simply can't control oneself when one sees a child that can hardly walk trying to go too far for it, one simply has to interfere."' 'Pay attention to her advice for this once,' said K. smiling, 'but that girl – whether she's retiring or shameless doesn't matter – I don't want to hear any more about her.' 'But why do you call her retiring?' asked Frieda obdurately – K. considered this interest of hers a favourable sign – 'have you found her so, or are you simply casting a reflexion on somebody else?' 'Neither the one nor the other,' said K., 'I call her that out of gratitude, because she makes it easy for me to ignore her, and because if she said even a word or two to me I couldn't bring myself to go back again, which would be a great loss to me, for I must go there for the sake of both our futures, as you know. And it's simply for that reason that I have to talk with the other girl, whom I respect, I must admit, for her capability, prudence, and unselfishness, but whom nobody could say was seductive.' 'The servants are of a different opinion,' said Frieda. 'On that as on lots of other subjects,' said K. 'Are you going to deduce my unfaithfulness from the tastes of the servants?' Frieda remained silent and suffered K. to take the tray from her, set it on the floor, and put his arm through hers, and walk her slowly up and down in the corner of the passage. 'You don't know what fidelity is,' she said, his nearness putting her a little on the defensive, 'what your relations with the girl may be isn't the most important point; the fact that you go to that house at all and come back with the smell of their kitchen on your clothes is itself an unendurable humiliation for me. And then you rush out of the school without saying a word. And stay with them, too, the half of the night. And when you're asked for, you let those girls deny that you're there, deny it passionately, especially the wonderfully retiring one. And creep out of the house by a secret way, perhaps actually to save the good name of the girls, the good name of those girls. No, don't let us talk about it any more.' 'Yes, don't let us talk of this,' said K., 'but something else, Frieda. Besides, there's nothing more to be said about it. You know why I have to go there. It isn't easy for me, but I overcome my feelings. You shouldn't make it any harder for me than it is. Tonight I only thought of dropping in there for a minute to see whether Barnabas had come at last, for he had an important message which he should have brought long before. He hadn't come, but he was bound to come very soon, so I was assured, and it seemed very probable too. I didn't want to let him come after me, for you to be insulted by his presence. The hours passed and unfortunately he didn't come. But another came all right, a man whom I hate. I had no intention of letting myself be spied on by him, so I left through the neighbour's garden, but I didn't want to hide from him either, and I went up to him frankly when I reached the street, with a very good and supple hazel switch, I admit. That is all, so there's nothing more to be said about it; but there's plenty to say about something else. What about the assistants, the very mention of whose name is as repulsive to me as that family is to you? Compare your relations with them with my relations with that family. I understand your antipathy to Barnabas's family and I can share it. It's only for the sake of my affairs that I go to see them, sometimes it almost seems to me that I'm abusing and exploiting them. But you and the assistants! You've never denied that they persecute you, and you've admitted that you're attracted by them. I wasn't angry with you for that, I recognized that powers were at work which you weren't equal to, I was glad enough to see that you put up a resistance at least, I helped to defend you, and just because I left off for a few hours, trusting in your constancy, trusting also, I must admit, in the hope that the house was securely locked and the assistants finally put to flight – I still underestimate them, I'm afraid – just because I left off for a few hours and this Jeremiah – who is, when you look at him closely, a rather unhealthy elderly creature – had the impudence to go up to the window; just for this, Frieda, I must lose you and get for a greeting: "There will be no marriage." Shouldn't I be the one to cast reproaches? But I don't, I have never done so.' And once more it seemed advisable to K. to distract Frieda's mind a little, and he begged her to bring him something to eat, for he had had nothing since midday. Obviously relieved by the request, Frieda nodded and ran to fetch something, not farther along the passage, however, where K. conjectured the kitchen was, but down a few steps to the left. In a little she brought a plate with slices of meat and a bottle of wine, but they were clearly only the remains of a meal, the scraps of meat had been hastily ranged out anew so as to hide the fact, yet whole sausage skins had been overlooked, and the bottle was three-quarters empty. However, K. said nothing and fell on the food with a good appetite. 'You were in the kitchen?' he asked. 'No, in my own room,' she said. 'I have a room down there.' 'You might surely have taken me with you,' said K. 'I'll go down now, so as to sit down for a little while I'm eating.' 'I'll bring you a chair,' said Frieda already making to go. 'Thanks,' replied K. holding her back, 'I'm neither going down there, nor do I need a chair any longer.' Frieda endured his hand on her arm defiantly, bowed her head and bit her lip. 'Well, then, he is down there,' she said, 'did you expect anything else? He's lying on my bed, he got a cold out there, he's shivering, he's hardly had any food. At bottom it's all your fault, if you hadn't driven the assistants away and run after those people, we might be sitting comfortably in the school now. You alone have destroyed our happiness. Do you think that Jeremiah, so long as he was in service, would have dared to take me away? Then you entirely misunderstood the way things are ordered here. He wanted me, he tormented himself, he lay in watch for me, but that was only a game, like the play of a hungry dog who nevertheless wouldn't dare to leap up on the table. And just the same with me. I was drawn to him, he was a playmate of mine in my childhood – we played together on the slope of the Castle Hill, a lovely time, you've never asked me anything about my past – but all that wasn't decisive as long as Jeremiah was held back by his service, for I knew my duty as your future wife. But then you drove the assistants away and plumed yourself on it besides, as if you had done something for me by it; well, in a certain sense it was true. Your plan has succeeded as far as Arthur is concerned, but only for the moment, he's delicate, he hasn't Jeremiah's passion that nothing can daunt, besides you almost shattered his health for him by the buffet you gave him that night – it was a blow at my happiness as well – he fled to the Castle to complain, and even if he comes back soon, he's gone now all the same. But Jeremiah stayed. When he's in service he fears the slightest look of his master, but when he's not in service there's nothing he's afraid of. He came and took me; forsaken by you, commanded by him, my old friend, I couldn't resist. I didn't unlock the school door. He smashed the window and lifted me out. We flew here, the landlord looks up to him, nothing could be more welcome to the guests, either, than to have such a waiter, so we were taken on, he isn't living with me, but we are staying in the same room.' 'In spite of everything,' said K., 'I don't regret having driven the assistants from our service. If things stood as you say, and your faithfulness was only determined by the assistants being in the position of servants, then it was a good things that it came to an end. The happiness of a married life spent with two beasts of prey, who could only be kept under by the whip, wouldn't have been very great. In that case I'm even thankful to this family who have unintentionally had some part in separating us.' They became silent and began to walk backwards and forwards again side by side, though neither this time could have told who had made the first move. Close beside him, Frieda seemed annoyed that K. did not take her arm again. 'And so everything seems to be in order,' K. went on, 'and we might as well say good-bye, and you go to your Jeremiah, who must have had this chill, it seems, ever since I chased him through the garden, and whom you've already left by himself too long in that case, and I to the empty school, or, seeing that there's no place for me there without you, anywhere else where they'll take me in. If I hesitate still in spite of this, it's because I have still a little doubt about what you've told me, and with good reasons. I have a different impression of Jeremiah. So long as he was in service, he was always at your heels and I don't believe that his position would have held him back permanently from making a serious attempt on you. But now that he considers that he's absolved from service, it's a different case. Forgive me if I have to explain myself in this way: Since you're no longer his master's fiancée, you're by no means such a temptation for him as you used to be. You may be the friend of his childhood, but – I only got to know him really from a short talk to-night – in my opinion he doesn't lay much weight on such sentimental considerations. I don't know why he should seem a passionate person in your eyes. His mind seems to me on the contrary to be particularly cold. He received from Galater certain instructions relating to me, instructions probably not very much in my favour, he exerted himself to carry them out, with a certain passion for service, I'll admit – it's not so uncommon here – one of them was that he should wreck our relationship; probably he tried to do it by several means, one of them was to tempt you by his evil languishing glances, another – here the landlady supported him – was to invent fables about my unfaithfulness; his attempt succeeded, some memory or other of Klamm that clung to him may have helped, he has lost his position, it is true, but probably just at the moment when he no longer needed it, then he reaped the fruit of his labours and lifted you out through the school window, with that his task was finished, and his passion for service having left him now, he'll feel bored, he would rather be in Arthur's shoes, who isn't really complaining up there at all, but earning praise and new commissions, but someone had to stay behind to follow the further developments of the affair. It's rather a burdensome task to him to have to look after you. Of love for you he hasn't a trace, he frankly admitted it to me; as one of Klamm's sweethearts he of course respects you, and to insinuate himself into your bedroom and feel himself for once a little Klamm certainly gives himself pleasure, but that is all, you yourself mean nothing to him now, his finding a place for you here is only a supplementary part of his main job; so as not to disquieten you he has remained here himself too, but only for the time being, as long as he doesn't get further news from the Castle and his cooling feelings towards you aren't quite cured.' 'How you slander him!' said Frieda, striking her little fists together. 'Slander?' said K., 'no, I don't wish to slander him. But I may quite well perhaps be doing him an injustice, that is certainly possible. What I've said about him doesn't lie on the surface for anybody to see, and it may be looked at differently too. But slander? Slander could only have one object, to combat your love for him. If that were necessary and if slander were the most fitting means, I wouldn't hesitate to slander him. Nobody could condemn me for it, his position puts him at such an advantage as compared with me that, thrown back solely on my own resources, I could even allow myself a little slander. It would be a comparatively innocent, but in the last resort a powerless, means of defence. So put down your fists.' And K. took Frieda's hand in his; Frieda tried to draw it away, but smilingly and not with any great earnestness. 'But I don't need slander,' said K., 'for you don't love him, you only think you do, and you'll be thankful to me for ridding you of your illusion. For think, if anybody wanted to take you away from me, without violence, but with the most careful calculation, he could only do it through the two assistants. In appearance, good, childish, merry, irresponsible youths, fallen from the sky, from the Castle, a dash of childhood's memories with them too; all that of course must have seemed very nice, especially when I was the antithesis of it all, and was always running after affairs moreover which were scarcely comprehensible, which were exasperating to you, and which threw me together with people whom you considered deserving of your hate – something of which you carried over to me too, in spite of all my innocence. The whole thing was simply a wicked but very clever exploitation of the failings in our relationship. Everybody's relations have their blemishes, even ours, we came together from two very different worlds, and since we have known each other the life of each of us has had to be quite different, we still feel insecure, it's all too new. I don't speak of myself, I don't matter so much, in reality I've been enriched from the very first moment that you looked on me, and to accustom oneself to one's riches isn't very difficult. But – not to speak of anything else – you were torn away from Klamm, I can't calculate how much that must have meant, but a vague idea of it I've managed to arrive at gradually, you stumbled, you couldn't find yourself, and even if I was always ready to help you, still I wasn't always there, and when I was there you were held captive by your dreams or by something more palpable, the landlady, say – in short there were times when you turned away from me, longed, poor child, for vague inexpressible things, and at those periods any passable man had only to come within your range of vision and you lost yourself to him, succumbing to the illusion that mere fancies of the moment, ghosts, old memories, things of the past and things receding ever more into the past, life that had once been lived – that all this was your actual present-day life. A mistake, Frieda, nothing more than the last and, properly regarded, contemptible difficulties attendant on our final reconciliation. Come to yourself, gather yourself together; even if you thought that the assistants were sent by Klamm – it's quite untrue, they come from Galater – and even if they did manage by the help of this illusion to charm you so completely that even in their disreputable tricks and their lewdness you thought you found traces of Klamm, just as one fancies one catches a glimpse of some precious stone that one had lost in a dung heap, while in reality one wouldn't be able to find it even if it were there – all the same they're only hobbledehoys like the servants in the stall, except that they're not healthy like them, and a little fresh air makes them ill and compels them to take to their beds, which I must say that they know how to snuffle out with a servant's true cunning.' Frieda had let her head fall on K.'s shoulder; their arms round each other, they walked silently up and down. 'If we had only,' said Frieda after a while, slowly, quietly, almost serenely, as if she knew that only a quite short respite of peace on K.'s shoulder were reserved for her, and she wanted to enjoy it to the utmost, 'if we had only gone away somewhere at once that night, we might be in peace now, always together, your hand always near enough for mine to grasp; oh, how much I need your companionship, how lost I have felt without it ever since I've known you, to have your company, believe me, is the only dream that I've had, that and nothing else.'

Then someone called from the side passage, it was Jeremiah, he was standing there on the lowest step, he was in his shirt, but had thrown a wrap of Frieda's round him. As he stood there, his hair rumpled, his thin beard lank as if dripping with wet, his eyes painfully beseeching and wide with reproach, his sallow cheeks flushed, but yet flaccid, his naked legs trembling so violently with cold that the long fringes of the wrap quivered as well, he was like a patient who had escaped from hospital, and whose appearance could only suggest one thought, that of getting him back in bed again. This in fact was the effect that he had on Frieda, she disengaged herself from K., and was down beside Jeremiah in a second. Her nearness, the solicitude with which she drew the wrap closer round him, the haste with which she tried to force him back into the room, seemed to give him new strength, it was as if he only recognized K. now. 'Ah, the Land Surveyor!' he said, stroking Frieda's cheek to propitiate her, for she did not want to let him talk any further, 'forgive the interruption. But I'm not at all well, that must be my excuse. I think I'm feverish, I must drink some tea and get a sweat. Those damned railings in the school garden, they'll give me something to think about yet, and then, already chilled to the bone, I had to run about all night afterwards. One sacrifices one's health for things not really worth it, without noticing it at the time. But you, Land Surveyor, mustn't let yourself be disturbed by me, come into the room here with us, pay me a sick visit, and at the same time tell Frieda whatever you have still to say to her. When two who are accustomed to one another say good-bye, naturally they have a great deal to say to each other at the last minute which a third party, even if he's lying in bed waiting for his tea to come, can't possibly understand. But do come in, I'll be perfectly quiet.' 'That's enough, enough!' said Frieda pulling at his arm. 'He's feverish and doesn't know what he's saying. But you, K., don't you come in here, I beg you not to. It's my room and Jeremiah's, or rather it's my room and mine alone, I forbid you to come in with us. You always persecute me; oh, K., why do you always persecute me? Never, never will I go back to you, I shudder when I think of the very possibility. Go back to your girls; they sit beside you before the fire in nothing but their shifts, I've been told, and when anybody comes to fetch you they spit at him. You must feel at home there, since the place attracts you so much. I've always tried to keep you from going there, with little success, but all the same I've tried; all that's past now, you are free. You've a lovely life in front of you; for the one you'll perhaps have to squabble a little with the servants, but as for the other, there's nobody in heaven or earth that will grudge you her. The union is blessed beforehand. Don't deny it, I know you can disprove anything, but in the end nothing is disproved. Only think, Jeremiah, he has disproved everything!' They nodded with a smile of mutual understanding. 'But,' Frieda went on, 'even if everything were disproved, what would be gained by that, what would it matter to me? What happens in that house is purely their business and his business, not mine. Mine is to nurse you till you're well again, as you were at one time, before K. tormented you for my sake.' 'So you're not coming in after all, Land Surveyor?' asked Jeremiah, but was now definitely dragged away by Frieda, who did not even turn to look at K. again. There was a little door down there, still lower than the doors in the passage – not Jeremiah only, even Frieda had to stoop on entering – within it seemed to be bright and warm, a few whispers were audible, probably loving cajolements to get Jeremiah to bed, then the door was closed.

Here the text of the first German edition of The Castle *ends. It has been translated by Willa and Edwin Muir.*

What follows is the continuation of the text together with additional material (different versions, fragments, passages deleted by the author, etc.) as found among Kafka's papers after the publication of the first edition and included by the editor, Max Brod, in the definitive German edition. The translation is by Eithne Wilkins and Ernst Kaiser.

Only now did K. notice how quiet it had become in the passage, not only here in this part of the passage where he had been with Frieda, and which seemed to belong to the public rooms of the inn, but also in the long passage with the rooms that had earlier been so full of bustle. So the gentlemen had gone to sleep at last after all. K. too was very tired, perhaps it was from fatigue that he had not stood up to Jeremiah as he should have. It would perhaps have been more prudent to take his cue from Jeremiah, who was obviously exaggerating how bad his chill was – his woefulness was not caused by his having a chill, it was congenital and could not be relieved by any herbal tea – to take his cue entirely from Jeremiah, make a similar display of his own really great fatigue, sink down here in the passage, which would in itself afford much relief, sleep a little, and then perhaps be nursed a little too. Only it would not have worked out as favourably as with Jeremiah, who would certainly have won this competition for sympathy, and rightly so, probably and obviously every other fight too. K. was so tired that he wondered whether he might not try to go into one of these rooms, some of which were sure to be empty, and have a good sleep in a luxurious bed. In his view this might turn out to be recompense for many things. He also had a night-cap handy. On the tray that Frieda had left on the floor there had been a small decanter of rum. K. did not shrink from the exertion of making his way back, and he drained the little bottle to the dregs.

Now he at least felt strong enough to go before Erlanger. He looked for the door of Erlanger's room, but since the servant and Gerstäcker were no longer to be seen and all the doors looked alike, he could not find it. Yet he believed he remembered more or less in what part of the passage the door had been, and decided to open a door that in his opinion was probably the one he was looking for. The experiment could not be so very dangerous; if it was Erlanger's room Erlanger would doubtless receive him, if it was somebody else's room it would still be possible to apologize and go away again, and if the inmate was asleep, which was what was probable, then K.'s visit would not be noticed at all; it could turn out badly only if the room was empty, for then K. would scarcely be able to resist the temptation to get into the bed and sleep for ages. He once more glanced along the passage to right and to left, to see whether after all there might not be somebody coming who would be able to give him some information and make the venture unnecessary, but the long passage was quiet and empty. Then K. listened at the door. Here too was no inmate. He knocked so quietly that it could not have wakened a sleeper, and when even now nothing happened he opened the door very cautiously indeed. But now he was met with a faint scream.

It was a small room, more than half filled by a wide bed, on the night-table the electric lamp was burning, beside it was a travelling handbag. In the bed, but completely hidden under the quilt, someone stirred uneasily and whispered through a gap between quilt and sheet: 'Who is it?' Now K. could not withdraw again so easily, discontentedly he surveyed the voluptuous but unfortunately not empty bed, then remembered the question and gave his name. This seemed to have a good effect, the man in the bed pulled the quilt a little off his face, anxiously ready, however, to cover himself up again completely if something was not quite all right out there. But then he flung back the quilt without qualms and sat up. It was certainly not Erlanger. It was a small, well-looking gentleman whose face had a certain contradictoriness in that the cheeks were chubby as a child's and the eyes merry as a child's, but that the high forehead, the pointed nose, the narrow mouth, the lips of which would scarcely remain closed, the almost vanishing chin, were not like a child's at all, but revealed superior intellect. It was doubtless his satisfaction with this, his satisfaction with himself, that had preserved him a marked residue of something healthily child-like. 'Do you know Friedrich?' he asked. K. said he did not. 'But he knows you,' the gentleman said, smiling. K. nodded, there was no lack of people who knew him, this was indeed one of the main obstacles in his way. 'I am his secretary,' the gentleman said, 'my name is Bürgel.' 'Excuse me,' K. said, reaching for the door-handle, 'I am sorry, I mistook your door for another. The fact is I have been summoned to Secretary Erlanger.' 'What a pity,' Bürgel said. 'Not that you are summoned elsewhere, but that you made a mistake about the doors. The fact is once I am wakened I am quite certain not to go to sleep again. Still, that need not sadden you so much, it's my personal misfortune. Why, anyway, can't these doors be locked, eh? There's a reason for that, of course. Because, according to an old saying, the secretaries' doors should always be open. But that, again, need not be taken quite so literally.' Bürgel looked queryingly and merrily at K., in contrast to his lament he seemed thoroughly well rested; Bürgel had doubtless never in his life been as tired as K. was now. 'Where do you think of going now?' Bürgel asked. 'It's four o'clock. Anyone to whom you might think of going you would have to wake, not everybody is as used to being disturbed as I am, not everyone will put up with it as tolerantly, the secretaries are a nervous species. So stay for a little while. Round about five o'clock people here begin to get up, then you will be best able to answer your summons. So please do let go of the door-handle now and sit down somewhere, granted there isn't overmuch room here, it will be best if you sit here on the edge of the bed. You are surprised that I should have neither chair nor table here? Well, I had the choice of getting either a completely furnished room with a narrow hotel bed, or this big bed and nothing else except the washstand. I chose the big bed, after all, in a bedroom the bed is undoubtedly the main thing! Ah, for anyone who could stretch out and sleep soundly, for a sound sleeper, this bed would surely be truly delicious. But even for me, perpetually tired as I am without being able to sleep, it is a blessing, I spend a large part of the day in it, deal with all my correspondence in it, here conduct all the interviews with applicants. It works quite well. Of course the applicants have nowhere to sit, but they get over that, and after all it's more agreeable for them too if they stand and the recorder is at ease than if they sit comfortably and get barked at. So the only place I have to offer is this here on the edge of the bed, but that is not an official place and is only intended for nocturnal conversations. But you are so quiet, Land Surveyor?' 'I am very tired,' said K., who on receiving the invitation had instantly, rudely, without respect, sat down on the bed and leaned against the post. 'Of course,' Bürgel said, laughing, 'everybody is tired here. The work, for instance, that I got through yesterday and have already got through even today is no small matter. It's completely out of the question of course that I should go to sleep now, but if this most utterly improbable thing should happen after all and I should go to sleep while you are still here, then please stay quiet and don't open the door, either. But don't worry, I shall certainly not go to sleep or at best only for a few minutes. The way it is with me is that probably because I am so very used to dealing with applicants I do actually find it easiest to go to sleep when I have company.' 'Do go to sleep, please do, Mr Secretary,' K. said, pleased at this announcement, 'I shall then, with your permission, sleep a little too.' 'No, no,' Bürgel said, laughing again, 'unfortunately I can't go to sleep merely on being invited to do so, it's only in the course of conversation that the opportunity may arise, it's most likely to be a conversation that puts me to sleep. Yes, one's nerves suffer in our business. I, for instance, am a liaison secretary. You don't know what that is? Well, I constitute the strongest liaison' – here he hastily rubbed his hands in involuntary merriment – 'between Friedrich and the village, I constitute the liaison between his Castle and village secretaries, am mostly in the village, but not permanently; at every moment I must be prepared to drive up to the Castle. You see the travelling-bag – a restless life, not suitable for everyone. On the other hand it is true that now I could not do without this kind of work, all other work would seem insipid to me. And how do things stand with the land-surveying?' 'I am not doing any such work, I am not being employed as a Land Surveyor,' K. said, he was not really giving his mind to the matter, actually he was only yearning for Bürgel to fall asleep, but even this was only out of a certain sense of duty towards himself, in his heart of hearts he was sure that the moment when Bürgel would go to sleep was still infinitely remote. 'That is amazing,' Bürgel said with a lively jerk of his head, and pulled a note-pad out from under the quilt in order to make a note. 'You are a Land Surveyor and have no land-surveying to do.' K. nodded mechanically, he had stretched out his left arm along the top of the bed-post and laid his head on it, he had already tried various ways of making himself comfortable, but this position was the most comfortable of all, and now, too, he could attend a little better to what Bürgel was saying. 'I am prepared,' Bürgel continued, 'to follow up this matter further. With us here things are quite certainly not in such a way that an expert employee should be left unused. And it must after all be painful to you too. Doesn't it cause you distress?' 'It causes me distress,' K. said slowly and smiled to himself, for just now it was not distressing him in the least. Besides, Bürgel's offer made little impression on him. It was utterly dilettante. Without knowing anything of the circumstances under which K.'s appointment had come about, of the difficulties that it encountered in the community and at the Castle, of the complications that had already occurred during K.'s sojourn here or had been foreshadowed, without knowing anything of all this, indeed without even showing what should have been expected of a secretary as a matter of course, that he had at least an inkling of it all, he offered to settle the whole affair up there in no time at all with the aid of his little note-pad. 'You seem to have had some disappointments,' Bürgel said, by this remark showing that he had after all some knowledge of human nature, and indeed, since entering the room, K. had from time to time reminded himself not to underestimate Bürgel, but in his state it was difficult to form a fair judgement of anything but his own weariness. 'No,' Bürgel said, as if he were answering a thought of K.'s and were considerably trying to save him the effort of formulating it aloud. 'You must not let yourself be frightened off by disappointments. Much here does seem to be arranged in such a way as to frighten people off, and when one is newly arrived here the obstacles do appear to be completely insurmountable, I don't want to inquire into what all this really amounts to, perhaps the appearance does really correspond to the reality, in my position I lack the right detachment to come to a conclusion about that, but pay attention, there are sometimes after all opportunities that are almost not in accord with the general situation, opportunities in which by means of a word, a glance, a sign of trust, more can be achieved than by means of lifelong exhausting efforts. Indeed, that is how it is. But, then again, of course, these opportunities are in accord with the general situation in so far as they are never made use of. But why are they never made use of? I ask time and again.' K. did not know why; he did certainly realize that what Bürgel was talking about probably concerned him closely, but he now felt a great dislike of everything that concerned him, he shifted his head a little to one side as though in this manner he were making way for Bürgel's questions and could no longer be touched by them. 'It is,' Bürgel continued, stretching his arms and yawning, which was in bewildering contradiction to the gravity of his words, 'it is a constant complaint of the secretaries that they are compelled to carry out most of the village interrogations by night. But why do they complain of this? Because it is too strenuous for them? Because they would rather spend the night sleeping? No, that is certainly not what they complain of. Among the secretaries there are of course those who are hard-working and those who are less hard-working, as everywhere; but none of them complains of excessive exertion, and least of all in public. That is simply not our way. In this respect we make no distinction between ordinary time and working time. Such distinctions are alien to us. But what then have the secretaries got against the night interrogations? Is it perhaps consideration for the applicants? No, no, it is not that either. Where the applicants are concerned the secretaries are ruthless, admittedly not a jot more ruthless than towards themselves, but merely precisely as ruthless. Actually this ruthlessness is, when you come to think of it, nothing but a rigid obedience to and execution of their duty, the greatest consideration that the applicants can really wish for. And this is at bottom – granted, a superficial observer does not notice this – completely recognized; indeed, it is, for instance in this case, precisely the night interrogations that are welcomed by the applicants, no objections in principle come in regarding the night interrogations. Why then nevertheless the secretaries' dislike?' This K. did not know either, he knew so little, he could not even distinguish where Bürgel was seriously or only apparently expecting an answer. 'If you let me lie down in your bed,' he thought, 'I shall answer all your questions for you at noon tomorrow, or better still, tomorrow evening.' But Bürgel did not seem to be paying any attention to him, he was far too much occupied with the question that he had put to himself: 'So far as I can see and so far as my own experience takes me, the secretaries have the following qualms regarding the night interrogations: the night is less suitable for negotiations with applicants for the reason that by night it is difficult or positively impossible completely to preserve the official character of the negotiations. This is not a matter of externals, the forms can of course, if desired, be just as strictly observed by night as by day. So it is not that, on the other hand the official power of judgement suffers at night. One tends involuntarily to judge things from a more private point of view at night, the allegations of the applicants take on more weight than is due to them, the judgement of the case becomes adulterated with quite irrelevant considerations of the rest of the applicants' situation, their sufferings and anxieties, the necessary barrier between the applicants and the officials, even though externally it may be impeccably maintained, weakens, and where otherwise, as is proper, only questions and answers are exchanged, what sometimes seems to take place is an odd, wholly unsuitable changing of the places between the persons. This at least is what the secretaries say, and they are of course the people who, through their vocation, are endowed with a quite extraordinary subtlety of feeling in such matters. But even they – and this has often been discussed in our circles – notice little of those unfavourable influences during the night interrogations; on the contrary, they exert themselves right from the beginning to counteract them and end up by believing they have achieved quite particularly good results. If, however, one reads the records through afterwards one is often amazed at their obvious and glaring weaknesses. And these are defects, and, what is more, ever and again mean half-unjustified gains for the applicants, which at least according to our regulations cannot be repaired by the usual direct method. Quite certainly they will at some later time be corrected by a control-officer, but this will only profit the law, but will not be able to damage that applicant any more. Are the complaints of the secretaries under such circumstances not thoroughly justified?' K. had already spent a little while sunk in half-sleep, but now he was roused again. 'Why all this? Why all this?' he wondered, and from under lowered eyelids considered Bürgel not like an official discussing difficult questions with him, but only like something that was preventing him from sleeping and whose further meaning he could not discover. But Bürgel, wholly abandoned to the pursuit of his thoughts, smiled, as though he had just succeeded in misleading K. a little. Yet he was prepared to bring him back on to the right road immediately. 'Well,' he said, 'on the other hand one cannot simply go and call these complaints quite justified, either. The night interrogations are, indeed, nowhere actually prescribed by the regulations, so one is not offending against any regulation if one tries to avoid them, but conditions, the excess work, the way the officials are occupied in the Castle, how indispensable they are, the regulation that the interrogation of applicants is to take place only after the final conclusion of all the rest of the investigation, but then instantly, all this and much else has after all made the night interrogations an indispensable necessity. But if now they have become a necessity – this is what I say – this is nevertheless also, at least indirectly, a result of the regulations, and to find fault with the nature of the night interrogations would then almost mean – I am, of course, exaggerating a little, and only since it is an exaggeration can I utter it, as such – would then indeed mean finding fault with the regulations.

'On the other hand it may be conceded to the secretaries that they should try as best they can to safeguard themselves, within the terms of the regulations, against the night interrogations and their perhaps only apparent disadvantages. This is in fact what they do, and indeed to the greatest extent. They permit only subjects of negotiation from which there is in every sense as little as possible to be feared, test themselves closely prior to negotiations and, if the result of the test demands it, even at the very last moment cancel all examinations, strengthen their hand by summoning an applicant often as many as ten times before really dealing with him, have a liking for sending along to deputize for them colleagues who are not competent to deal with the given case and who can, therefore, handle it with greater ease, schedule the negotiations at least for the beginning or the end of the night, avoiding the middle hours, there are many more such measures, the secretaries are not the people to let anyone get the better of them so easily, they are almost as resilient as they are vulnerable.' K. was asleep, it was not real sleep, he could hear Bürgel's words perhaps better than during his former dead-tired state of waking, word after word struck his ear, but the tiresome consciousness had gone, he felt free, it was no longer Bürgel who held him, only he still sometimes groped towards Bürgel, he was not yet in the depths of sleep, but immersed in it he certainly was. No one should deprive him of that now. And it seemed to him as though with this he had achieved a great victory and already there was a party of people there to celebrate it, and he or perhaps someone else raised the champagne glass in honour of this victory. And so that all should know what it was all about the fight and the victory were repeated once again or perhaps not repeated at all, but only took place now and had already been celebrated earlier and there was no leaving off celebrating it, because fortunately the outcome was certain. A secretary, naked, very like the statue of a Greek god, was hard pressed by K. in the fight. It was very funny and K. in his sleep smiled gently about how the secretary was time and again startled out of his proud attitude by K.'s assaults and would hastily have to use his raised arm and clenched fist to cover unguarded parts of his body and yet was always too slow in doing so. The fight did not last long; step for step, and they were very big steps, K. advanced. Was it a fight at all? There was no serious obstacle, only now and then a squeak from the secretary. This Greek god squeaked like a girl being tickled. And finally he was gone, K. was alone in the large room, ready for battle he turned round, looking for his opponent; but there was no longer anyone there, the company had also scattered, only the champagne glass lay broken on the floor, K. trampled it to smithereens. But the splinters pricked him, with a start he woke once again, he felt sick, like a small child being woken up. Nevertheless, at the sight of Bürgel's bare chest a thought that was part of his dream brushed his awareness: Here you have your Greek god! Go on, haul him out of bed! 'There is, however,' Bürgel said, his face thoughtfully tilted towards the ceiling, as though he were searching his memory for examples, but without being able to find any, 'there is, however, nevertheless, in spite of all precautionary measures, a way in which it is possible for the applicants to exploit this nocturnal weakness of the secretaries – always assuming that it is a weakness – to their own advantage. Admittedly, a very rare possibility, or, rather, one that almost never occurs. It consists in the applicant's coming unannounced in the middle of the night. You marvel, perhaps, that this, although it seems to be so obvious, should happen so very seldom. Well, yes, you are not familiar with conditions here. But even you must, I suppose, have been struck by the foolproofness of the official organization. Now from this foolproofness it does result that everyone who has any petition or who must be interrogated in any matter for other reasons, instantly, without delay, usually indeed even before he has worked the matter out for himself, more, indeed, even before he himself knows of it, has already received the summons. He is not yet questioned this time, usually not yet questioned, the matter has usually not yet reached that stage, but he has the summons, he can no longer come unannounced, at best he can come at the wrong time, well, then all that happens is that his attention is drawn to the date and the hour of the summons, and if he then comes back at the right time he is as a rule sent away, that no longer causes any difficulty; having the summons in the applicant's hand and the case noted in the files are, it is true, not always adequate, but, nevertheless, powerful defensive weapons for the secretaries. This refers admittedly only to the secretary in whose competence the matter happens to lie; it would still, of course, be open to everyone to approach the others in the night, taking them by surprise. Yet this is something scarcely anyone will do, it is almost senseless. First of all it would mean greatly annoying the competent secretary. We secretaries are, it is true, by no means jealous of each other with regard to work, as everyone carries far too great a burden of work, a burden that is piled on him truly without stint, but in dealing with the applicants we simply must not tolerate any interference with our sphere of competence. Many a one before now has lost the game because, thinking he was not making progress with the competent authority, he tried to slip through by approaching some other, one not competent. Such attempts must, besides, fail also because of the fact that a non-competent secretary, even when he is taken unawares at dead of night and has the best will to help, precisely as a consequence of his non-competence can scarcely intervene any more effectively than the next best lawyer, indeed at bottom much less so, for what he lacks, of course – even if otherwise he could do something, since after all he knows the secret paths of the law better than all these legal gentry – concerning things with regard to which he is not competent, what he lacks is quite simply time, he hasn't a moment to spare for it. So who then, the prospects being such, would spend his nights playing the non-competent secretary? Indeed, the applicants are in any case fully occupied if, besides carrying out their normal duties, they wish to respond to the summonses and hints from the competent authorities, "fully occupied" that is to say in the sense in which it concerns the applicants, which is, of course, far from being the same as "fully occupied" in the sense in which it concerns the secretaries.' K. nodded, smiling, he believed he now understood everything perfectly; not because it concerned him, but because he was now convinced he would fall fast asleep in the next few minutes, this time without dreaming or being disturbed; between the competent secretaries on the one hand and the non-competent on the other, and confronted with the crowd of fully occupied applicants, he would sink into deep sleep and in this way escape everything. Bürgel's quiet, self-satisfied voice, which was obviously doing its best to put its owner to sleep, was something he had now become so used to that it would do more to put him to sleep than to disturb him. 'Clatter, mill, clatter on and on,' he thought, 'you clatter just for me.' 'Where then, now,' Bürgel said, fidgeting at his underlip with two fingers, with widened eyes, craning neck, rather as though after a strenuous long walk he were approaching a delightful view, 'where then, now, is that previously mentioned, rare possibility that almost never occurs? The secret lies in the regulations regarding competence. The fact is things are not so constituted, and in such a large living organization cannot be so constituted, that there is only one definite secretary competent to deal with each case. It is rather that one is competent above all others, but many others are in certain respects, even though to a smaller degree, also competent. Who, even if he were the hardest of workers, could keep together on his desk, single-handed, all the aspects of even the most minor incident? Even what I have been saying about the competence above all others is saying too much. For is not the whole competence contained even in the smallest? Is not what is decisive here the passion with which the case is tackled? And is this not always the same, always present in full intensity? In all things there may be distinctions among the secretaries, and there are countless such distinctions, but not in the passion; none of them will be able to restrain himself if it is demanded of him that he shall concern himself with a case in regard to which he is competent if only in the smallest degree. Outwardly, indeed, an orderly mode of negotiation must be established, and so it comes about that a particular secretary comes into the foreground for each applicant, one they have, officially, to keep to. This, however, does not even need to be the one who is in the highest degree competent in regard to the case, what is decisive here is the organization and its particular needs of the moment. That is the general situation. And now, Land Surveyor, consider the possibility that through some circumstances or other, in spite of the obstacles already described to you, which are in general quite sufficient, an applicant does nevertheless, in the middle of the night, surprise the secretary who has a certain degree of competence with regard to the given case. I dare say you have never thought of such a possibility? I am quite prepared to believe it. Nor is it at all necessary to think of it, for it does, after all, practically never occur. What sort of oddly and quite specially constituted, small, skilful grain would such an applicant have to be in order to slip through the incomparable sieve? You think it cannot happen at all? You are right, it cannot happen at all. But some night – for who can vouch for everything? – it *does* happen. Admittedly, I don't know anyone among my acquaintances to whom it has ever happened, well, it is true that proves very little, the circle of my acquaintances is restricted in comparison to the number involved here, and besides it is by no means certain that a secretary to whom such a thing has happened will admit it, since it is, after all, a very personal affair and one that in a sense gravely touches the official sense of shame. Nevertheless my experience does perhaps prove that what we are concerned with is a matter so rare, actually only existing by way of rumour, not confirmed by anything else at all, that there is, therefore, really no need to be afraid of it. Even if it were really to happen, one can – one would think – positively render it harmless by proving to it, which is very easy, that there is no room for it in this world. In any case it is morbid to be so afraid of it that one hides, say, under the quilt and does not dare to peep out. And even if this perfect improbability should suddenly have taken on shape, is then everything lost? On the contrary. That everything should be lost is yet more improbable than the most improbable thing itself. Granted, if the applicant is actually in the room things are in a very bad way. It constricts the heart. "How long will you be able to put up resistance?" one wonders. But it will be no resistance at all, one knows that. You must only picture the situation correctly. The never-beheld, always-expected applicant, truly thirstingly expected and always reasonably regarded as out of reach – there this applicant sits. By his mute presence, if by nothing else, he constitutes an invitation to penetrate into his poor life, to look around there as in one's own property and there to suffer with him under the weight of his futile demands. This invitation in the silent night is beguiling. One gives way to it, and now one has actually ceased to function in one's official capacity. It is a situation in which it very soon becomes impossible to refuse to do a favour. To put it precisely, one is desperate; to put it still more precisely, one is very happy. Desperate, for the defenceless position in which one sits here waiting for the applicant to utter his plea and knowing that once it is uttered one must grant it, even if, at least in so far as one has oneself a general view of the situation, it positively tears the official organization to shreds: this is, I suppose, the worst thing that can happen to one in the fulfilment of one's duties. Above all – apart from everything else – because it is also a promotion, one surpassing all conceptions, that one here for the moment usurps. For it is inherent in our position that we are not empowered to grant pleas such as that with which we are here concerned, yet through the proximity of this nocturnal applicant our official powers do in a matter of speaking grow, we pledge ourselves to do things that are outside our scope; indeed, we shall even fulfil our pledges. The applicant wrings from us in the night, as the robber does in the forest, sacrifices of which we should otherwise never be capable; well, all right, that is the way it is now when the applicant is still there, strengthening us and compelling us and spurring us on, and while everything is still half unconsciously under way; but how it will be afterwards, when it is all over, when, sated and carefree, the applicant leaves us and there we are, alone, defenceless in the face of our misuse of official power – that does not bear thinking of! Nevertheless, we are happy. How suicidal happiness can be! We might, of course, exert ourselves to conceal the true position from the applicant. He himself will scarcely notice anything of his own accord. He has, after all, in his own opinion probably only for some different, accidental reasons – being overtired, disappointed, ruthless and indifferent from over-fatigue and disappointment – pushed his way into a room other than the one he wanted to enter, he sits there in ignorance, occupied with his thoughts, if he is occupied at all, with his mistake or with his fatigue. Could one not leave him in that situation? One cannot. With the loquacity of those who are happy one has to explain everything to him. Without being able to spare oneself in the slightest one must show him in detail what has happened and for what reasons this has happened, how extraordinarily rare and how uniquely great the opportunity is, one must show how the applicant, though he has stumbled into this opportunity in utter helplessness such as no other being is capable of than precisely an applicant, can, however, now, if he wants to, Land Surveyor, dominate everything and to that end has to do nothing but in some way or other put forward his plea, for which fulfilment is already waiting, which indeed it is already coming to meet, all this one must show; it is the official's hour of travail. But when one has done even that, then, Land Surveyor, all that is essential has been done, then one must resign oneself and wait.'

K. was asleep, impervious to all that was happening. His head, which had at first been lying on his left arm on top of the bed-post, had slid down as he slept and now hung unsupported, slowly dropping lower; the support of the arm above was no longer sufficient; involuntarily K. provided himself with new support by planting his right hand firmly against the quilt, whereby he accidentally took hold of Bürgel's foot, which happened to be sticking up under the quilt. Bürgel looked down and abandoned the foot to him, tiresome though this might be.

Now there came some vigorous knocking on the partition wall. K. started up and looked at the wall. 'Isn't the Land Surveyor there?' a voice asked. 'Yes,' Bürgel said, freed his foot from K.'s hold and suddenly stretched wildly and wantonly like a little boy. 'Then tell him it's high time for him to come over here,' the voice continued; there was no consideration shown for Bürgel or for whether he might still require K.'s presence. 'It's Erlanger,' Bürgel said in a whisper, seeming not at all surprised that Erlanger was in the next room. 'Go to him at once, he's already annoyed, try to conciliate him. He's a sound sleeper; but still, we have been talking too loudly; one cannot control oneself and one's voice when one is speaking of certain things. Well, go along now, you don't seem able to shake yourself out of your sleep. Go along, what are you still doing here? No, you don't need to apologize for being sleepy, why should you? One's physical energies last only to a certain limit. Who can help the fact that precisely this limit is significant in other ways too? No, nobody can help it. That is how the world itself corrects the deviations in its course and maintains the balance. This is indeed an excellent, time and again unimaginably excellent arrangement, even if in other respects dismal and cheerless. Well, go along, I don't know why you look at me like that. If you delay much longer Erlanger will be down on me, and that is something I should very much like to avoid. Go along now. Who knows what awaits you over there? Everything here is full of opportunities, after all. Only there are, of course, opportunities that are, in a manner of speaking, too great to be made use of, there are things that are wrecked on nothing but themselves. Yes, that is astonishing. For the rest, I hope I shall now be able to get to sleep for a while after all. Of course, it is five o'clock by now and the noise will soon be beginning. If you would only go!'

Stunned by suddenly being woken up out of deep sleep, still boundlessly in need of sleep, his body aching all over from having been in such an uncomfortable position, K. could for a long time not bring himself to stand up, but held his forehead and looked down at his lap. Even Bürgel's continual dismissals would not have been able to make him go, it was only a sense of the utter uselessness of staying any longer in this room that slowly brought him to it. How indescribably dreary this room seemed to him. Whether it had become so or had been so all the time, he did not know. Here he would not even succeed in going to sleep again. This conviction was indeed the decisive factor; smiling a little at this, he rose supporting himself wherever he found any support, on the bed, on the wall, on the door, and, as though he had long ago taken leave of Bürgel, left without saying good-bye.

19

Probably he would have walked past Erlanger's room just as indifferently if Erlanger had not been standing in the open door, beckoning to him. One short sign with the forefinger. Erlanger was already completely dressed to go out, he wore a black fur coat with a tight collar buttoned up high. A servant was just handing him his gloves and was still holding a fur cap. 'You should have come long ago,' Erlanger said. K. tried to apologize. Wearily shutting his eyes, Erlanger indicated that he was not interested in hearing apologies. 'The matter is as follows,' he said. 'Formerly a certain Frieda was employed in the taproom; I only know her name, I don't know the girl herself, she is no concern of mine. This Frieda sometimes served Klamm with beer. Now there seems to be another girl there. Well, this change is, of course, probably of no importance to anyone, and quite certainly of none to Klamm. But the bigger a job is, and Klamm's job is, of course, the biggest, the less strength is left over for protecting oneself against the external world, and as a result any unimportant alteration in the most unimportant things can be a serious disturbance. The smallest alteration on the writing-desk, the removal of a dirty spot that has been there ever since anyone can remember, all this can be disturbing, and so, in the same way, can a new barmaid. Well, of course, all of this, even if it would disturb anyone else and in any given job, does not disturb Klamm; that is quite out of the question. Nevertheless we are obliged to keep such a watch over Klamm's comfort that we remove even disturbances that are not such for him – and probably there are none whatsoever for him – if they strike us as being possible disturbances. It is not for his sake, it is not for the sake of his work, that we remove these disturbances, but for our sake, for the sake of our conscience and our peace of mind. For this reason this Frieda must at once return to the taproom. Perhaps she will be disturbing precisely through the fact of her return; well, then we shall send her away again, but, for the time being, she must return. You are living with her, as I am told, therefore arrange immediately for her return. In this no consideration can be given to personal feelings, that goes without saying, of course, hence I shall not enter into the least further discussion of the matter. I am already doing much more than is necessary if I mention that if you show yourself reliable in this trivial affair it may on some occasion be of use to you in improving your prospects. That is all I have to say to you.' He gave K. a nod of dismissal, put on the fur cap handed to him by the servant, and, followed by the servant, went down the passage, rapidly, but limping a little.

Sometimes orders that were given here were very easy to carry out, but this case did not please K. Not only because the order affected Frieda and, though intended as an order, sounded to K. like scornful laughter, but above all because what it confronted K. with was the futility of all his endeavours. The orders, the unfavourable and the favourable, disregarded him, and even the most favourable probably had an ultimate unfavourable core, but in any case they all disregarded him, and he was in much too lowly a position to be able to intervene or, far less, to silence them and to gain a hearing for his own voice. If Erlanger waves you off, what are you going to do? And if he were not to wave you off, what could you say to him? True, K. remained aware that his weariness had today done him more harm than all the unfavourableness of circumstances, but why could he, who had believed he could rely on his body and who would never have started out on his way without that conviction, why could he not endure a few bad nights and one sleepless night, why did he become so unmanageably tired precisely here where nobody was tired or, rather, where everyone was tired all the time, without this, however, doing any damage to the work, indeed, even seeming to promote it? The conclusion to be drawn from this was that this was in its way a quite different sort of fatigue from K. 's. Here it was doubtless fatigue amid happy work, something that outwardly looked like fatigue and was actually indestructible repose, indestructible peace. If one is a little tired at noon, that is part of the happy natural course of the day. 'For the gentlemen here it is always noon,' K. said to himself.

And it was very much in keeping with this that now, at five o'clock, things were beginning to stir everywhere on each side of the passage. This babel of voices in the rooms had something extremely merry about it. Once it sounded like the jubilation of children getting ready for a picnic, another time like day-break in a hen-roost, like the joy of being in complete accord with the awakening day. Somewhere indeed a gentleman imitated the crowing of a cock. Though the passage itself was still empty, the doors were already in motion, time and again one would be opened a little and quickly shut again, the passage buzzed with this opening and shutting of doors, now and then, too, in the space above the partition walls, which did not quite reach to the ceiling, K. saw towsled early-morning heads appear and instantly vanish again. From far off there slowly came a little barrow pushed by a servant, containing files. A second servant walked beside it, with a catalogue in his hand, obviously comparing the numbers on the doors with those on the files. The little barrow stopped outside most of the doors, usually then, too, the door would open and the appropriate files, sometimes, however, only a small sheet of paper – in such cases a little conversation came about between the room and the passage, probably the servant was being reproached – would be handed into the room. If the door remained shut, the files were carefully piled up on the threshold. In such cases it seemed to K. as though the movement of the doors round about did not diminish, even though there the files had already been distributed, but as though it were on the contrary increasing. Perhaps the others were yearningly peering out at the files incomprehensibly left lying on the threshold, they could not understand how anyone should only need to open the door in order to gain possession of his files and yet should not do so; perhaps it was even possible that files that were never picked up at all might later be distributed among the other gentlemen, who were even now seeking to make sure, by frequent peering out, whether the files were still lying on the threshold and whether there was thus still hope for them. Incidentally, these files that remained lying were for the most part particularly big bundles; and K. assumed that they had been temporarily left lying out of a certain desire to boast or out of malice or even out of justifiable pride that would be stimulating to colleagues. What strengthened him in this assumption was the fact that sometimes, always when he happened not to be looking, the bag, having been exposed to view for long enough, was suddenly and hastily pulled into the room and the door then remained as motionless as before, the doors round about then also became quiet again, disappointed or, it might be, content that this object of constant provocation had at last been removed, but then, however, they gradually came into motion again.

K. considered all this not only with curiosity but also with sympathy. He almost enjoyed the feeling of being in the midst of this bustle, looked this way and that, following – even though at an appropriate distance – the servants, who, admittedly, had already more than once turned towards him with a severe glance, with lowered head and pursed lips, while he watched their work of distribution. The further it progressed the less smoothly it went, either the catalogue was not quite correct, or the files were not always clearly identifiable for the servants, or the gentlemen were raising objections for other reasons; at any rate it would happen that some of the distributions had to be withdrawn, then the little barrow moved back, and through the chink of the door negotiations were conducted about the return of files. These negotiations in themselves caused great difficulties, but it happened frequently enough that if it was a matter of return precisely those doors that had earlier on been in the most lively motion now remained inexorably shut, as though they did not wish to know anything more about the matter at all. Only then did the actual difficulties begin. He who believed he had a claim to the files became extremely impatient, made a great din inside his room, clapping his hands, stamping his feet, ever and again shouting a particular file-number out into the passage through the chink of the door. Then the little barrow was often left quite unattended. The one servant was busy trying to appease the impatient official, the other was outside the shut door battling for the return. Both had a hard time of it. The impatient official was often made still more impatient by the attempts to appease him, he could no longer endure listening to the servant's empty words, he did not want consolation, he wanted files; such a gentleman once poured the contents of a whole wash-basin through the gap at the top, on to the servant. But the other servant, obviously the higher in rank, was having a much harder time of it. If the gentleman concerned at all deigned to enter into negotiations, there were matter-of-fact discussions during which the servant referred to his catalogue, the gentleman to his notes and to precisely those files that he was supposed to return, which for the time being, however, he clutched tightly in his hand, so that scarcely a corner of them remained visible to the servant's longing eyes. Then, too, the servant would have to run back for fresh evidence to the little barrow, which had by itself rolled a little farther along the slightly sloping passage, or he would have to go to the gentleman claiming the files and there report the objection raised by the gentleman now in possession, receiving in return fresh counter-objections. Such negotiation lasted a very long time, sometimes agreement was reached, the gentleman would perhaps hand over part of the files or get other files as compensation, since all that had happened was that a mistake had been made; but it also happened sometimes that someone simply had to abandon all the files demanded, either because he had been driven into a corner by the servant's evidence or because he was tired of the prolonged bargaining, but then he did not give the files to the servant, but with sudden resolution flung them out into the passage, so that the strings came undone and the papers flew about and the servants had a great deal of trouble getting everything straight again. But all this was still relatively simple compared with what happened when the servant got no answer at all to his pleading for the return of the files. Then he would stand outside the closed door, begging, imploring, citing his catalogue, referring to regulations, all in vain, no sound came from inside the room, and to go in without permission was obviously something the servant had no right to do. Then even this excellent servant would sometimes lose his self-control, he would go to his barrow, sit down on the files, wipe the sweat from his brow, and for a little while do nothing at all but sit there helplessly swinging his feet. All round there was very great interest in the affair, everywhere there was whispering going on, scarcely any door was quiet, and up above at the top of the partition wall faces queerly masked almost to the eyes with scarves and kerchiefs, though for the rest never for an instant remaining quiet in one place, watched all that was going on. In the midst of this unrest K. had been struck by the fact that Bürgel's door had remained shut the whole time and that the servant had already passed along this part of the passage, but no files had been allotted to Bürgel. Perhaps he was still asleep, which would indeed, in all this din, have indicated that he was a very sound sleeper, but why had he not received any files? Only very few rooms, and these probably unoccupied ones, had been passed over in this manner. On the other hand there was already a new and particularly restless occupant of Erlanger's room, Erlanger must positively have been driven out in the night by him, this was not much in keeping with Erlanger's cool, distant nature, but the fact that he had had to wait on the threshold for K. did after all indicate that it was so.

Ever and again K. would then soon return from all distracting observations to watching the servant; truly, what K. had otherwise been told about servants in general, about their slackness, their easy life, their arrogance, did not apply to this servant, there were doubtless exceptions among the servants too or, what was more probable, various groups among them, for here, as K. noticed, there were many nuances of which he had up to now scarcely had as much as a glimpse. What he particularly liked was this servant's inexorability. In his struggle with these stubborn little rooms – to K. it often seemed to be a struggle with the rooms, since he scarcely ever caught sight of the occupants – the servant never gave up. His strength did sometimes fail – whose strength would not have failed? – but he soon recovered, slipped down from the little barrow and, holding himself straight, clenching his teeth, returned to the attack against the door that had to be conquered. And it would happen that he would be beaten back twice or three times, and that in a very simple way, solely by means of that confounded silence, and nevertheless was still not defeated. Seeing that he could not achieve anything by frontal assault, he would try another method, for instance, if K. understood rightly, cunning. He would then seemingly abandon the door, so to speak allowing it to exhaust its own taciturnity, turned his attention to other doors, after a while returned, called the other servant, all this ostentatiously and noisily, and began piling up files on the threshold of the shut door, as though he had changed his mind, and as though there were no justification for taking anything away from this gentleman, but, on the contrary, something to be allotted to him. Then he would walk on, still, however, keeping an eye on the door, and then when the gentleman, as usually happened, soon cautiously opened the door in order to pull the files inside, in a few leaps the servant was there, thrusting his foot between the door and the doorpost, so forcing the gentleman at least to negotiate with him face to face, which then usually led after all to a more or less satisfactory result. And if this method was not successful or if at one door this seemed to him not the right approach, he would try another method. He would then transfer his attention to the gentleman who was claiming the files. Then he pushed aside the other servant, who worked always only in a mechanical way, a fairly useless assistant to him, and himself began talking persuasively to the gentleman, whisperingly, furtively, pushing his head right round the door, probably making promises to him and assuring him that at the next distribution the other gentleman would be appropriately punished, at any rate he would often point towards the opponent's door and laugh, in so far as his fatigue allowed. Then, however, there were cases, one or two, when he did abandon all attempts, but even here K. believed that it was only an apparent abandonment or at least an abandonment for justifiable reasons, for he quietly walked on, tolerating, without glancing round, the din made by the wronged gentleman, only an occasional, more prolonged closing of the eyes indicating that the din was painful to him. Yet then the gentleman would gradually quieten down, and just as a child's ceaseless crying gradually passed into ever less frequent single sobs, so it was also with his outcry; but even after it had become quite quiet there, there would nevertheless, sometimes be a single cry or a rapid opening and slamming of that door. In any case it became apparent that here, too, the servant had probably acted in exactly the right way. Finally there remained only one gentleman who would not quieten down, he would be silent for a long period, but only in order to gather strength, then he would burst out again, no less furiously than before. It was not quite clear why he shouted and complained in this way, perhaps it was not about the distribution of files at all. Meanwhile the servant had finished his work; only one single file, actually on a little piece of paper, a leaf from a note-pad, was left in the little barrow, through his helper's fault, and now they did not know whom to allot it to. 'That might very well be my file,' it flashed through K.'s mind. The Mayor had, after all, constantly spoken of this smallest of small cases. And, arbitrary and ridiculous though he himself at bottom regarded his assumption as being, K. tried to get closer to the servant, who was thoughtfully glancing over the little piece of paper; this was not altogether easy, for the servant ill repaid K.'s sympathy, even in the midst of his most strenuous work he had always still found time to look round at K., angrily or impatiently, with nervous jerks of his head. Only now, after finishing the distribution, did he seem to have somewhat forgotten K., as indeed he had altogether become more indifferent, this being understandable as a result of his great exhaustion, nor did he give himself much trouble with the little piece of paper, perhaps not even reading it through, only pretending to do so, and although here in the passage he would probably have delighted any occupant of a room by allotting this piece of paper to him, he decided otherwise, he was now sick and tired of distributing things, with his forefinger on his lips he gave his companion a sign to be silent, tore – K. was still far from having reached his side – the piece of paper into shreds and put the pieces into his pocket. It was probably the first irregularity that K. had seen in the working of the administration here, admittedly it was possible that he had misunderstood this too. And even if it was an irregularity, it was pardonable; under the conditions prevailing here the servant could not work unerringly, some time the accumulated annoyance, the accumulated uneasiness, must break out, and if it manifested itself only in the tearing up of a little piece of paper it was still comparatively innocent. For the yells of the gentleman who could not be quieted by any method were still resounding through the passage, and his colleagues, who in other respects did not adopt a very friendly attitude to each other, seemed to be wholly of one mind with respect to this uproar; it gradually began to seem as if the gentleman had taken on the task of making a noise for all those who simply by calling out to him and nodding their heads encouraged him to keep it up. But now the servant was no longer paying any further attention to the matter, he had finished his job, he pointed to the handle of the little barrow, indicating that the other servant should take hold of it, and so they, went away again as they had come, only more contentedly and so quickly that the little barrow bounced along ahead of them. Only once did they start and glance back again, when the gentleman who was ceaselessly screaming and shouting, and outside whose door K. was now hanging about because he would have liked to discover what it really was that the gentleman wanted, evidently found shouting no longer adequate, probably had discovered the button of an electric bell and, doubtless enraptured at being relieved in this way, instead of shouting now began an uninterrupted ringing of the bell. Hereupon a great muttering began in the other rooms, which seemed to indicate approval, the gentleman seemed to be doing something that all would have liked to do long ago and only for some unknown reason had had to leave undone. Was it perhaps attendance, perhaps Frieda, for whom the gentleman was ringing? If that was so, he could go on ringing for a long time. For Frieda was busy wrapping Jeremiah up in wet sheets, and even supposing he were well again by now, she had no time, for then she was in his arms. But the ringing of the bell did instantly have an effect. Even now the landlord of the Herrenhof himself came hastening along from far off, dressed in black and buttoned up as always; but it was as though he were forgetful of his indignity, he was in such a hurry; his arms were half outspread, just as if he had been called on account of some great disaster and were coming in order to take hold of it and instantly smother it against his chest, and at every little irregularity in the ringing he seemed briefly to leap into the air and hurry on faster still. Now his wife also appeared, a considerable distance behind him, she too running with outspread arms, but her steps were short and affected, and K. thought to himself that she would come too late, the landlord would in the meantime have done all that was necessary. And in order to make room for the landlord as he ran K. stood close back against the wall. But the landlord stopped straight in front of K., as though K. were his goal, and the next instant the landlady was there too, and both overwhelmed him with reproaches, which in the suddenness and surprise of it he did not understand, especially since the ringing of the gentleman's bell was also mixed up with it and other bells also began ringing, now no longer indicating a state of emergency, but only for fun and in excess of delight. Because he was very much concerned to understand exactly what his fault was, K. was entirely in agreement with the landlord's taking him by the arm and walking away with him out of this uproar, which was continually increasing, for behind them – K. did not turn round at all, because the landlord, and even more, on the other side, the landlady, was talking to him urgently – the doors were now opening wide, the passage was becoming animated, traffic seemed to be beginning there as in a lively narrow little alley, the doors ahead of them were evidently waiting impatiently for K. to go past them at long last so that they could release the gentlemen, and in the midst of all this, pressed again and again, the bells kept on ringing as though celebrating a victory. Now at last – they were by now again in the quiet white courtyard, where some sledges were waiting – K. gradually learnt what it was all about. Neither the landlord nor the landlady could understand how K. could have dared to do such a thing. But what had he done? K. asked time and again, but for a long time could not get any answer because his guilt was all too much a matter of course to the two of them and hence it simply did not occur to them that he asked in good faith. Only very slowly did K. realize how everything stood. He had had no right to be in the passage; in general it was at best the taproom, and this only by way of privilege and subject to revocation, to which he had entry. If he was summoned by one of the gentlemen, he had, of course, to appear in the place to which he was summoned, but had to remain always aware – surely he at least had some ordinary common sense? – that he was in a place where he actually did not belong, a place whither he had only been summoned by one of the gentlemen, and that with extreme reluctance and only because it was necessitated by official business. It was up to him, therefore, to appear quickly, to submit to the interrogation, then, however, to disappear again, if possible even more quickly. Had he then not had any feeling at all of the grave impropriety of being there in the passage? But if he had had it, how had he brought himself to roam about there like cattle at pasture? Had he not been summoned to attend a night interrogation and did he not know why the night interrogations had been introduced? The night interrogations – and here K. was given a new explanation of their meaning – had after all only the purpose of examining applicants the sight of whom by day would be unendurable to the gentlemen, and this quickly, at night, by artificial light, with the possibility of, immediately after the interrogation, forgetting all the ugliness of it in sleep. K.'s behaviour, however, had been a mockery of precautionary measures. Even ghosts vanish towards morning, but K. had remained there, his hands in his pockets, as though he were expecting that, since he did not take himself off, the whole passage with all the rooms and gentlemen would take itself off. And this – he could be sure of it – would quite certainly have happened if it had been in any way possible, for the delicacy of the gentlemen was limitless. None of them would drive K. away, or even say, what went after all without saying, that he should at long last go away; none of them would do that, although during the period of K.'s presence they were probably trembling with agitation and the morning, their favourite time, was being ruined for them. Instead of taking any steps against K., they preferred to suffer, in which, indeed, a certain part was probably played by the hope that K. would not be able to help gradually, at long last, coming to realize what was so glaringly obvious and, in accord with the gentlemen's anguish, would himself begin to suffer, to the point of unendurability, from his own standing there in the passage in the morning, visible to all, in that horribly unfitting manner. A vain hope. They did not know or in their kindness and condescension did not want to admit there also existed hearts that were insensitive, hard, and not to be softened by any feeling of reverence. Does not even the nocturnal moth, the poor creature, when day comes seek out a quiet cranny, flatten itself out there, only wishing it could vanish and being unhappy because it cannot? K. on the other hand planted himself precisely where he was most visible, and if by doing so he had been able to prevent day from breaking, he would have done so. He could not prevent it, but, alas, he could delay it and make it more difficult. Had he not watched the distribution of the files? Something that nobody was allowed to watch except the people most closely involved. Something that neither the landlord nor his wife had been allowed to see in their own house. Something of which they had only heard tell and in allusions, as for instance today from the servants. Had he then not noticed under what difficulties the distribution of files had proceeded, something in itself incomprehensible, since after all each of the gentleman served only the cause, never thinking of his personal advantage and hence being obliged to exert all his powers to seeing that the distribution of the files, this important, fundamental, preliminary work, should proceed quickly and easily and without any mistakes? And had K. then not been even remotely struck by the notion that the main cause of all the difficulties was the fact that the distribution had had to be carried out with the doors almost quite shut, without any chance of direct dealings between the gentlemen, who among each other naturally could come to an understanding in a twinkling, while the mediation through the servants inevitably dragged on almost for hours, never could function smoothly, and was a lasting torment to the gentlemen and the servants and would probably have damaging consequences in the later work? And why could the gentlemen not deal with each other? Well, did K. *still* not understand? The like of it had never occurred in the experience of the landlady – and the landlord for his part confirmed this – and they had, after all, had to deal with many sorts of difficult people. Things that in general one would not dare to mention in so many words one had to tell him frankly, for otherwise he would not understand the most essential things. Well, then, since it had to be said: it was on his account, solely and exclusively on his account, that the gentlemen had not been able to come forth out of their rooms, since in the morning, so soon after having been asleep, they were too bashful, too vulnerable, to be able to expose themselves to the gaze of strangers; they literally felt, however completely dressed they might be, too naked to show themselves. It was admittedly difficult to say why they felt this shame, perhaps these everlasting workers felt shame merely because they had been asleep. But what perhaps made them feel even acuter shame than showing themselves was seeing strangers; what they had successfully disposed of by means of the night interrogations, namely the sight of the applicants they found so hard to endure, they did not want now in the morning to have suddenly, without warning, in all its truth to nature, obtruding itself upon them all over again. That was something they simply could not face. What sort of person must it be who failed to respect that! Well, yes, it must be a person like K. Someone who rode rough-shod over everything, both over the law and over the most ordinary human consideration, with this callous indifference and sleepiness, someone who simply did not care that he was making the distribution of the files almost impossible and damaging the reputation of the house and who brought about something that had never happened before, that the gentlemen, driven to desperation, had begun to defend themselves, and, after an overcoming of their own feelings unimaginable for ordinary people, had reached for the bell and called for help to expel this person on whom nothing else could make any impression! They, the gentlemen, calling for help! Would not the landlord and his wife and their entire staff have come dashing along ages before that if they had only dared to appear before the gentlemen, all unsummoned, in the morning, even if it was only in order to bring help and then disappear again at once? Quivering with indignation about K., inconsolable about their own helplessness, they had waited there at the end of the passage, and the ringing of the bell, which they had never really expected to hear at all, had been a god-send to them. 'Well, now the worst was over! If you could cast a glance into the merry bustle among the gentlemen now at long last liberated from K.! For K., of course, it was not yet over and done with; he would certainly have to answer for the trouble he had caused here.

Meanwhile they had entered the taproom; why the landlord, despite all his anger, had nevertheless brought K. along here, was not quite clear, perhaps he had after all realized that K.'s state of fatigue for the present made it impossible for him to leave the house. Without waiting to be asked to sit down, K. the next moment simply collapsed on one of the barrels. There in the dark he felt all right. In the large room there was only one dim electric bulb burning over the beer-taps. Outside, too, there was still deep darkness, there seemed to be snow blowing on the wind. Being here in the warmth was something to be thankful for and one had to take precautions against being driven out. The landlord and his wife were still standing before him as though even now he still constituted a certain menace, as though in view of his utter unreliability it were not quite impossible that he might here suddenly start up and try to invade the passage once again. Besides, they themselves were tired after the shock they had had in the night and getting up earlier than usual, especially the landlady, who was wearing a silkily rustling, wide-skirted, brown dress, buttoned and tied up in a somewhat slovenly way – where had she pulled it out from in her haste? – and stood with her head resting, like a drooping flower, on her husband's shoulder, dabbing at her eyes with a fine cambric handkerchief, now and then casting childishly malevolent glances at K. In order to reassure the couple K. said that everything they had told him now was entirely new to him, but that in spite of his ignorance of these facts he would not have remained so long in the passage, where he really had had no business to be and where he had certainly not wanted to upset anyone, but that all this had only happened because he had been excessively tired. He thanked them for having put an end to the distressing scene, if he should be taken to task about the matter it would be very welcome to him, for only in this way could he prevent a general misinterpretation of his behaviour. Fatigue, and nothing else, was to blame for it. This fatigue, however, originated in the fact that he was not yet used to the strenuous nature of the interrogations. After all, he had not yet been here long. As soon as he was more experienced in these matters, it would become impossible for anything of this sort to happen again. Perhaps he was taking the interrogations too seriously, but that in itself was, after all, probably no disadvantage. He had had to go through two interrogations, one following quickly on the other, one with Bürgel and the second with Erlanger, and the first in particular had greatly exhausted him, though the second one had not lasted long, Erlanger having only asked him for a favour, but both together had been more than he could stand at one go, and perhaps a thing like that would be too much for other people too, for instance for the landlord. By the time he was done with the second interrogation he had really been walking in a sort of swoon. It had been almost like being drunk; after all, he had seen and heard the two gentlemen for the first time and had also had to answer their questions, into the bargain. Everything, so far as he knew, had worked out pretty well, but then that misfortune had occurred, which, after what had gone before, he could scarcely be blamed for. Unfortunately only Erlanger and Bürgel had realized what a condition he was in and they would certainly have looked after him and so prevented all the rest, but Erlanger had had to go away immediately after the interrogation, evidently in order to drive up to the Castle, and Bürgel, probably himself tired after that interrogation – and how then should K. have been able to come out of it with his strength unimpaired? – had gone to sleep and had indeed slept through the whole distribution of files. If K. had had a similar chance he would have been delighted to take it and would gladly have done without all the prohibited insight into what was going on there, and this all the more lightheartedly since in reality he had been quite incapable of seeing anything, for which reason even the most sensitive gentlemen could have shown themselves before him without embarrassment.

The mention of the two interrogations – particularly of that with Erlanger – and the respect with which K. spoke of the gentlemen inclined the landlord favourably towards him. He seemed to be prepared to grant K.'s request to be allowed to lay a board across the barrels and sleep there at least till dawn, but the landlady was markedly against it, twitching ineffectively here and there at her dress, the slovenly state of which she seemed only now to have noticed, she kept on shaking her head; a quarrel obviously of long standing with regard to the orderliness of the house was on the point of breaking out afresh. For K. in his fatigued state the talk between the couple took on exaggeratedly great significance. To be driven out from here again seemed to him to be a misfortune surpassing all that had happened to him hitherto. This must not be allowed to happen, even if the landlord and the landlady should unite against him. Crumpled up on the barrel, he looked in eager expectancy at the two of them until the landlady, with her abnormal touchiness, which had long ago struck K., suddenly stepped aside and – probably she had by now been discussing other things with the landlord – exclaimed: 'How he stares at me! Do send him away now!' But K., seizing the opportunity and now utterly, almost to the point of indifference, convinced that he would stay said: 'I'm not looking at you, only at your dress.' 'Why my dress?' the landlady asked agitatedly. K. shrugged his shoulders. 'Come on!' the landlady said to the landlord. 'Don't you see he's drunk, the lout? Leave him here to sleep it off!' and she even ordered Pepi, who on being called by her emerged out of the dark, towsled, tired, idly holding a broom in her hand, to throw K., some sort of a cushion.

20

When K. woke up he at first thought he had hardly slept at all; the room was as empty and warm as before, all the walls in darkness, the one bulb over the beer-taps extinguished, and outside the windows was the night. But when he stretched, and the cushion fell down and the bed and the barrels creaked, Pepi instantly appeared, and now he learnt that it was already evening and that he had slept for well over twelve hours. The landlady had asked after him several times during the day, and so had Gerstäcker, who had been waiting here in the dark, by the beer, while K. had been talking to the landlady in the morning, but then he had not dared to disturb K., had been here once in the meantime to see how K. was getting on, and finally, so at least it was alleged, Frieda had also come and had stood for a moment beside K., yet she had scarcely come on K.'s account but because she had had various things to make ready here, for in the evening she was to resume her old duties after all. 'I suppose she doesn't like you any more?' Pepi asked, bringing coffee and cakes. But she no longer asked it maliciously, in her old way, but sadly, as though in the meantime she had come to know the malice of the world, compared with which all one's own malice fails and becomes senseless; she spoke to K. as to a fellow sufferer, and when he tasted the coffee and she thought she saw that it was not sweet enough for him, she ran and brought him the full sugar-bowl. Her sadness had, indeed, not prevented her from tricking herself out today if anything even more than the last time; she wore an abundance of bows and ribbons plaited into her hair, along her forehead and on her temples the hair had been carefully curled with the tongs, and round her neck she had a little chain that hung down into the low-cut opening of her blouse. When, in his contentment at having at last slept his fill and now being permitted to drink a good cup of coffee, K. furtively stretched his hand out towards one of the bows and tried to untie it, Pepi said wearily: 'Do leave me alone,' and sat down beside him on a barrel. And K. did not even need to ask her what was the matter, she at once began telling the story herself, rigidly staring into K.'s coffee-mug, as though she needed some distraction, even while she was talking, as though she could not quite abandon herself to her suffering even when she was discussing it, as that would be beyond her powers. First of all K. learnt that actually he was to blame for Pepi's misfortunes, but that she did not bear him any grudge. And she nodded eagerly as she talked, in order to prevent K. from raising any objection. First he had taken Frieda away from the taproom and thus made Pepi's rise possible. There was nothing else that could be imagined that could have brought Frieda to give up her situation, she sat tight there in the taproom like a spider in its web, with all the threads under her control, threads of which no one knew but she; it would have been quite impossible to winkle her out against her will, only love for some lowly person, that is to say, something that was not in keeping with her position, could drive her from her place. And Pepi? Had *she* ever thought of getting the situation for herself? She was a chambermaid, she had an insignificant situation with few prospects, she had dreams of a great future like any other girl, one can't stop oneself from having dreams, but she had never seriously thought of getting on in the world, she had resigned herself to staying in the job she had. And now Frieda suddenly vanished from the taproom, it had happened so suddenly that the landlord had not had a suitable substitute on hand at the moment, he had looked round and his glance had fallen on Pepi, who had, admittedly, pushed herself forward in such a way as to be noticed. At that time she had loved K. as she had never loved anyone before; month after month she had been down there in her tiny dark room, prepared to spend years there, or, if the worst came to the worst, to spend her whole life here, ignored by everyone, and now suddenly K. had appeared, a hero, a rescuer of maidens in distress, and had opened up the way upstairs for her. Admittedly he did not know anything about her, he had not done it for her sake, but that did not diminish her gratitude, in the night preceding her appointment – the appointment was not yet definite, but still, it was now very probable – she spent hours talking to him, whispering her thanks in his ear. And in her eyes it exalted what he had done still more that it should have been Frieda, of all people, with whom he had burdened himself; there was something incomprehensibly selfless in his making Frieda his mistress in order to pave the way for Pepi – Frieda, a plain, oldish, skinny girl with short, thin hair, a deceitful girl into the bargain, always having some sort of secret, which was probably connected, after all, with her appearance; if her wretchedness was glaringly obvious in her face and figure, she must at least have other secrets, that nobody could inquire into, for instance her alleged affair with Klamm. And even thoughts like the following had occurred to Pepi at that time: is it possible that K. really loves Frieda, isn't he deceiving himself or is he perhaps deceiving only Frieda, and will perhaps the sole outcome of the whole thing after all be nothing but Pepi's rise in the world, and will K. then notice the mistake, or not want to cover it up any more, and no longer see Frieda, but only Pepi, which need not even be a crazy piece of conceit on Pepi's part, for so far as Frieda was concerned she was a match for her, one girl against another, which nobody would deny, and it had, after all, been primarily Frieda's position and the glory that Frieda had been able to invest it with that had dazzled K. at the moment. And so then Pepi had dreamed that when she had the position K. would come to her, pleading, and she would then have the choice of either granting K.'s plea and losing her situation or of rejecting him and rising further. And she had worked out for herself that she would renounce everything and lower herself to him and teach him what true love was, which he would never be able to learn from Frieda and which was independent of all positions of honour in the world. But then everything turned out differently. And what was to blame for this? Above all, K., and then, of course, Frieda's artfulness. Above all, K. For what was he after, what sort of strange person was he? What was he trying to get, what were these important things that kept him busy and made him forget what was nearest of all, best of all, most beautiful of all? Pepi was the sacrifice and everything was stupid and everything was lost; and anyone who had the strength to set fire to the whole Herrenhof and burn it down, burn it to the ground, so that not a trace of it was left, burn it up like a piece of paper in the stove, *he* would today be Pepi's chosen love. Well, so Pepi came into the taproom, four days ago today, shortly before lunch-time. The work here was far from easy, it was almost killingly hard work, but there was a good deal to be got out of it too. Even previously Pepi had not lived only for the day, and even if she would never had aspired to this situation even in her wildest dreams, still, she had made plenty of observations, she knew what this situation involved, she had not taken on the situation without being prepared. One could not take it on without being prepared, otherwise one lost it in the first few hours. Particularly if one were to behave here the way the chambermaids did! As a chambermaid one did in time come to feel one was quite lost and forgotten; it was like working down a mine, at least that was the way it was in the secretaries' passage, for days on end there; except for a few daytime applicants who flitted in and out without daring to look up one didn't see a soul but two or three chambermaids, and they were just as embittered. In the morning one wasn't allowed to leave the room at all, that was when the secretaries wished to be alone among themselves, their meals were brought to them from the kitchen by the men-servants, the chambermaids usually had nothing to do with that, and during mealtimes, too, one was not allowed to show oneself in the passage. It was only while the gentlemen were working that the chambermaids were allowed to do the rooms, but naturally not those that were occupied, only those that happened to be empty at the time, and the work had to be done quite quietly so that the gentlemen were not disturbed at their work. But how was it possible to do the cleaning quietly when the gentlemen occupied their rooms for several days on end, and the men-servants, dirty lot that they were, pottered about there into the bargain, and when the chambermaid was finally allowed to go into the room, it was in such a state that not even the Flood could wash it clean? Truly, they were exalted gentlemen, but one had to make a great effort to overcome one's disgust so as to be able to clean up after them. It wasn't that the chambermaids had such a great amount of work, but it was pretty tough. And never a kind word, never anything but reproaches, in particular the following, which was the most tormenting and the most frequent: that files had got lost during the doing of the rooms. In reality nothing ever got lost, every scrap of paper was handed over to the landlord, but in fact of course the files did get lost, only it happened not to be the fault of the maids. And then commissions came, and the maids had to leave their rooms, and the members of the commission rummaged through the beds, the girls had no possessions, of course, their few things could be put in a basket, but still, the commission searched for hours all the same. Naturally they found nothing. How should files come to be there? What did the maids care about files? But the outcome was always the same, abuse and threats uttered by the disappointed commission and passed on by the landlord. And never any peace, neither by day nor by night, noise going on half through the night and noise again at the crack of dawn. If at least one didn't have to live in, but one had to, for it was the chambermaids' job to bring snacks from the kitchen as they might be ordered, in between times, particularly at night. Always suddenly the first thumping on the chambermaids' door, the order being dictated, the running down to the kitchen, shaking the sleeping scullery-lads, the setting down of the tray with the things ordered outside the chambermaids' door, from where the men-servants fetched it – how sad all that was. But that was not the worst. The worst was when no order came, that was to say, when, at dead of night, when everyone ought to be asleep and most of them really were asleep at last, sometimes a tiptoeing around began outside the chambermaids' door. Then the girls got out of bed – the bunks were on top of each other, for there was very little space there, the whole room the maids had being actually nothing more than a large cupboard with three shelves in it – listened at the door, knelt down, put their arms round each other in fear. And whoever was tiptoeing outside the door could be heard all the time. They would all be thankful if only he would come right in and be done with it, but nothing happened, nobody came in. And at the same time one had to admit to oneself that it need not necessarily be some danger threatening, perhaps it was only someone walking up and down outside the door, trying to make up his mind to order something, and then not being able to bring himself to it after all. Perhaps that was all it was, but perhaps it was something quite different. For really one didn't know the gentlemen at all, one had hardly set eyes on them. Anyway, inside the room the maids were fainting in terror, and when at last it was quiet again outside they leant against the wall and had not enough strength left to get back into bed. This was the life that was waiting for Pepi to return to it, this very evening she was to move back to her place in the maids' room. And why? Because of K. and Frieda. Back again into that life she had scarcely escaped from, which she escaped from, it is true, with K.'s help, but also, of course, through very great exertions of her own. For in that service there the girls neglected themselves, even those who were otherwise the most careful and tidy. For whom should they smarten themselves? Nobody saw them, at best the staff in the kitchen; anyone for whom that was enough was welcome to smarten herself. But for the rest they were always in their little room or in the gentlemen's rooms, which it was madness and a waste so much as to set foot in with clean clothes on. And always by artificial light and in that stuffy air – with the heating always on – and actually always tired. The one free afternoon in the week was best spent sleeping quietly and without fear in one of the cubby-holes in the kitchen. So what should one smarten oneself up for? Yes, one scarcely bothered to dress at all. And now Pepi had suddenly been transferred to the taproom, where, if one wanted to maintain one's position there, exactly the opposite was necessary, where one was always in full view of people, and among them very observant gentlemen, used to the best of everything, and where one therefore always had to look as smart and pleasant as possible. Well, that was a change. And Pepi could say of herself that she had not failed to rise to the occasion. Pepi was not worrying about how things would turn out later. She knew she had the abilities necessary in this situation, she was quite certain of it, she had this conviction even now and nobody could take it away from her, not even today, on the day of her defeat. The only difficulty was how she was to stand the test in the very beginning, because she was, after all, only a poor chambermaid, with nothing to wear and no jewellery, and because the gentlemen had not the patience to wait and see how one would develop, but instantly, without transition, wanted a barmaid of the proper kind, or else they turned away. One would think they didn't expect so very much since, after all, Frieda could satisfy them. But that was not right. Pepi had often thought about this, she had, after all, often been together with Frieda and had for a time even slept together with her. It wasn't easy to find Frieda out, and anyone who was not very much on the look-out – and which of the gentlemen was very much on the look-out, after all? – was at once misled by her. No one knew better than Frieda herself how miserable her looks were, for instance when one saw her for the first time with her hair down, one clasped one's hands in pity, by rights a girl like that shouldn't even be a chambermaid; and she knew it, too, and many a night she had spent crying about it, pressing tight against Pepi and laying Pepi's hair round her own head. But when she was on duty all her doubts vanished, she thought herself better-looking than anyone, and she had the knack of getting everyone to think the same. She knew what people were like, and really that was where her art lay. And she was quick with a lie, and cheated, so that people didn't have time to get a closer look at her. Naturally that wouldn't do in the long run, people had eyes in their heads and sooner or later their eyes would tell them what to think. But the moment she noticed the danger of that she was ready with another method, recently, for instance, her affair with Klamm. Her affair with Klamm! If you don't believe it, you can go and get proof; go to Klamm and ask him, How cunning, how cunning. And if you don't happen to dare to go to Klamm with an inquiry like that, and perhaps wouldn't be admitted to him with infinitely more important inquiries, and Klamm is, in fact, completely inaccessible to you – only to you and your sort, for Frieda, for instance, pops in to see him whenever she likes – if that's how it is, you can still get proof of the thing, you only need to wait. After all, Klamm won't be able to tolerate such a false rumour for long, he's certain to be very keen to know what stories go round about him in the taproom and in the public rooms, all this is of the greatest importance to him, and if it's wrong he will refute it at once. But he doesn't refute it; well, then there is nothing to be refuted and it is sheer truth. What one sees, indeed, is only that Frieda takes the beer into Klamm's room and comes out again with the money; but what one doesn't see Frieda tells one about, and one has to believe her. And she doesn't even tell it, after all, she's not going to let such secrets out; no, the secrets let themselves out wherever she goes and, since they have been let out once and for all, she herself, it is true, no longer shrinks from talking about them herself, but modestly, without asserting anything, only referring to what is generally known anyway. Not to everything. One thing, for instance, she does not speak of, namely that since she has been in the taproom Klamm drinks less beer than formerly, not much less, but still perceptibly less beer, and there may indeed be various reasons for this; it may be that a period has come when Klamm has less taste for beer or that it is Frieda who causes him to forget about beer-drinking. Anyway, however amazing it may be, Frieda is Klamm's mistress. But how should the others not also admire what is good enough for Klamm? And so, before anyone knows what is happening, Frieda has turned into a great beauty, a girl of exactly the kind that the taproom needs; indeed, almost too beautiful, too powerful, even now the taproom is hardly good enough for her any more. And, in fact it does strike people as odd that she is still in the taproom; being a barmaid is a great deal, and from that point of view the liaison with Klamm seems very credible, but if the taproom girl has once become Klamm's mistress, why does he leave her in the taproom, and so long? Why does he not take her up higher? One can tell people a thousand times that there is no contradiction here, that Klamm has definite reasons for acting as he does, or that some day, perhaps even at any moment now, Frieda's elevation will suddenly come about; all this does not make much impression; people have definite notions and in the long run will not let themselves be distracted from them by any talk, however ingenious. Nobody any longer doubted that Frieda was Klamm's mistress, even those who obviously knew better were by now too tired to doubt it. 'Be Klamm's mistress, and to hell with it,' they thought, 'but if you *are*, we want to see signs of it in your getting on too.' But one saw no signs of it and Frieda stayed in the taproom as before and secretly was thoroughly glad that things remained the way they were. But she lost prestige with people, that, of course, she could not fail to notice, indeed she usually noticed things even before they existed. A really beautiful, lovable girl, once she has settled down in the taproom, does not need to display any arts; as long as she is beautiful, she will remain taproom maid, unless some particularly unfortunate accident occurs. But a girl like Frieda must be continually worried about her situation, naturally she has enough sense now not to show it, on the contrary, she is in the habit of complaining and cursing the situation. But in secret she keeps a weather-eye open all the time. And so she saw how people were becoming indifferent, Frieda's appearance on the scene was no longer anything that made it worth anyone's while even to glance up, not even the men-servants bothered about her any more, they had enough sense to stick to Olga and girls of that sort, from the landlord's behaviour, too, she noticed that she was becoming less and less indispensable, one could not go on for ever inventing new stories about Klamm, everything has its limits, and so dear Frieda decided to try something new. If anyone had only been capable of seeing through it immediately! Pepi had sensed it, but unfortunately she had not seen through it. Frieda decided to cause a scandal, she, Klamm's mistress, throws herself away on the first comer, if possible on the lowest of the low. That will make a stir, that will keep people talking for a long time, and at last, at last, people will remember what it means to be Klamm's mistress and what it means to throw away this honour in the rapture of a new love. The only difficulty was to find a suitable man with whom the clever game could be played. It must not be an acquaintance of Frieda's, not even one of the men-servants, for he would probably have looked at her askance and have walked on, above all he would not have remained serious enough about it and for all her ready tongue it would have been impossible to spread the story that she, Frieda, had been attacked by him, had not been able to defend herself against him and in an hour when she did not know what she was doing had submitted to him. And although it had to be one of the lowest of the low, it nevertheless had to be one of whom it could be made credible that in spite of his crude, coarse nature he longed for nobody but Frieda herself and had no loftier desire than – heavens above! – to marry Frieda. But although it had to be a common man, if possible even lower than a servant, much lower than a servant, yet it must be one on whose account one would not be laughed to scorn by every girl, one in whom another girl, a girl of sound judgement, might also at some time find something attractive. But where does one find such a man? Another girl would probably have spent her whole life looking for him. Frieda's luck brought the Land Surveyor into the taproom to her, perhaps on the very evening when the plan had come into her mind for the first time. The Land Surveyor! Yes, what was K. thinking of? What special things had he in mind? Was he going to achieve something special? A good appointment, a distinction? Was he after something of that sort? Well, then he ought to have set about things differently from the very beginning. After all, he was a nonentity, it was heart-rending to see his situation. He was a Land Surveyor, that was perhaps something, so he had learnt something, but if one didn't know what to do with it, then again it was nothing after all. And at the same time he made demands, without having the slightest backing, made demands not outright, but one noticed that he was making some sort of demands, and that was, after all, infuriating. Did he know that even a chambermaid was lowering herself if she talked to him for any length of time? And with all these special demands he tumbled headlong into the most obvious trap on the very first evening. Wasn't he ashamed of himself? What was it about Frieda that he found so alluring? Could she really appeal to him, that skinny, sallow thing? Ah no, he didn't even look at her, she only had to tell him she was Klamm's mistress, for him that was still a novelty, and so he was lost! But now she had to move out, now, of course, there was no longer any room for her in the Herrenhof. Pepi saw her the same morning before she moved out, the staff all came running up, after all, everyone was curious to see the sight. And so great was her power even then that she was pitied; she was pitied by everyone, even by her enemies; so correct did her calculations prove to be from the very start; having thrown herself away on such a man seemed incomprehensible to everyone and a blow of fate, the little kitchenmaids, who, of course, admire every barmaid, were inconsolable. Even Pepi was touched, not even she could remain quite unmoved, even though her attention was actually focused on something else. She was struck by how little sad Frieda actually was. After all it was at bottom a dreadful misfortune that had come upon her, and indeed she was behaving as though she were very unhappy, but it was not enough, this acting could not deceive Pepi. So what was it that was keeping her going? Perhaps the happiness of her new love? Well, this possibility could be considered. But what else could it be? What gave her the strength to be as coolly pleasant as ever even to Pepi, who was already regarded as her successor? Pepi had not then had the time to think about it, she had had too much to do getting ready for the new job. She was probably to start on the job in a few hours and still had not had her hair done nicely, had no smart dress, no fine underclothes, no decent shoes. All this had to be procured in a few hours; if one could not equip oneself properly, then it was better to give up all thought of the situation, for then one was sure of losing it in the very first half-hour. Well, she succeeded partly. She had a special gift for hairdressing, once, indeed, the landlady had sent for her to do her hair, it was a matter of having a specially light hand, and she had it, of course, her abundant hair was the sort you could do anything you like with. There was help forthcoming in the matter of the dress too. Her two colleagues kept faith with her, it was after all a sort of honour for them, too, if a girl out of their own group was chosen to be barmaid, and then later on, when she had come to power, Pepi would have been able to provide them with many advantages. One of the girls had for a long time been keeping some expensive material, it was her treasure, she had often let the others admire it, doubtless dreaming of how some day she would make magnificent use of it and – this had been really very nice of her – now, when Pepi needed it, she sacrificed it. And both girls had very willingly helped her along with the sewing, if they had been sewing it for themselves they could not have been keener. That was indeed a very merry, happy job of work. They sat, each on her bunk, one over the other, sewing and singing, and handed each other the finished parts and the accessories, up and down. When Pepi thought of it, it made her heart even heavier to think that it was all in vain and that she was going back to her friends with empty hands! What a misfortune and how frivolously brought about, above all by K.! How pleased they had all been with the dress at the time, it seemed a pledge of success and when at the last moment it turned out that there was still room for another ribbon, the last doubt vanished. And was it not really beautiful, this dress? It was crumpled now and showed some spots, the fact was, Pepi had no second dress, had to wear this one day and night, but it could still be seen how beautiful it was, not even that accursed Barnabas woman could produce a better one. And that one could pull it tight and loosen it again as one liked, on top and at the bottom, so that although it was only one dress, it was so changeable – this was a particular advantage and was actually her invention. Of course it wasn't so difficult to make clothes for her, Pepi didn't boast of it, there it was – everything suited young, healthy girls. It was much harder to get hold of underclothing and boots, and here was where the failure actually began. Here, too, her girl friends helped out as best they could, but they could not do much. It was, after all, only coarse underclothing that they got together and patched up, and instead of high-heeled little boots she had to made do with slippers, of a kind one would rather hide than show. They comforted Pepi: after all, Frieda was not dressed so very beautifully either, and sometimes she went round looking so sluttish that the guests preferred to be served by the cellarmen rather than by her. This was in fact so, but Frieda could afford to do that, she already enjoyed favour and prestige; when a lady for once makes an appearance looking besmirched and carelessly dressed, that is all the more alluring – but in the case of a novice like Pepi? And besides, Frieda could not dress well at all, she was simply devoid of all taste; if a person happened to have a sallow skin, then, of course, she must put up with it, but she needn't go around, like Frieda, wearing a low-cut cream blouse to go with it, so that one's eyes were dazzled by all that yellow. And even if it hadn't been for that, she was too mean to dress well; everything she earned, she hung on to, nobody knew what for. She didn't need any money in her job, she managed by means of lying and trickery, this was an example Pepi did not want to and could not imitate, and that was why it was justifiable that she should smarten herself up like this in order to get herself thoroughly noticed right at the beginning. Had she only been able to do it by stronger means, she would, in spite of all Frieda's cunning, in spite of all K.'s foolishness, have been victorious after all, it started very well. The few tricks of the trade and things it was necessary to know she had found out about well beforehand. She was no sooner in the taproom than she was thoroughly at home there. Nobody missed Frieda at the job. It was only on the second day that some guests inquired what had become of Frieda. No mistake was made, the landlord was satisfied, on the first day he had been so anxious that he spent all the time in the taproom, later he only came in now and then, finally, since the money in the till was correct – the takings were on the average even a little higher than in Frieda's time – he left everything to Pepi. She introduced innovations. Frieda had even supervised the menservants, at least partly, particularly when anyone was looking, and this not out of keenness for the work, but out of meanness, out of a desire to dominate, out of fear of letting anyone else invade her rights, Pepi on the other hand allotted this job entirely to the cellarmen, who, after all, are much better at it. In this way she had more time left for the private rooms, the guests got quick service; nevertheless she was able to chat for a moment with everyone, not like Frieda, who allegedly reserved herself entirely for Klamm and regarded every word, every approach, on the part of anyone else as an insult to Klamm. This was, of course, quite clever of her, for, if for once she did allow anyone to get near her, it was an unheard-of favour. Pepi, however, hated such arts, and anyway they were no use at the beginning. Pepi was kind to everyone and everyone requited with her kindness. All were visibly glad of the change; when the gentlemen, tired after their work, were at last free to sit down to their beer for a little while, one could positively transform them by a word, by a glance, by a shrug of the shoulders. So eagerly did all hands stroke Pepi's curls that she had to do her hair again quite ten times a day, no one could resist the temptations offered by these curls and bows, not even K., who was otherwise so absent-minded. So exciting days flew past, full of work, but successful. If only they had not flown past so quickly, if only there had been a little more of them! Four days were too little even if one exerted oneself to the point of exhaustion, perhaps the fifth day would have been enough, but four days were too little. Pepi had, admittedly, gained well-wishers and friends even in four days, if she had been able to trust all the glances she caught, when she came along with the beermugs, she positively swam in a sea of friendliness, a clerk by the name of Bartmeier was crazy about her, gave her this little chain and locket, putting his picture into the locket, which was, of course, brazen of him; this and other things had happened, but it had only been four days, in four days, if Pepi set about it, Frieda could be almost, but still not quite, forgotten, and yet she would have been forgotten, perhaps even sooner, had she not seen to it by means of her great scandal that she kept herself talked about, in this way she had become new to people, they might have liked to see her again simply for the sake of curiosity; what they had come to find boring to the point of disgust had, and this was the doing of the otherwise entirely uninteresting K., come to have charm for them again, of course they would not have given up Pepi as long as she was there in front of them and exerting influence by her presence, but they were mostly elderly gentlemen, slow and heavy in their habits, it took some time for them to get used to a new barmaid, and however advantageous the exchange might be, it still took a few days, took a few days against the gentlemen's own will, only five days perhaps, but four days were not enough, in spite of everything Pepi still counted only as the temporary barmaid. And then what was perhaps the greatest misfortune: in these four days, although he had been in the village during the first two, Klamm did not come down into the saloon. Had he come, that would have been Pepi's most decisive test, a test incidentally, that she was least afraid of, one to which she was more inclined to look forward. She would – though it is, of course, best not to touch on such things in words at all – not have become Klamm's mistress, nor would she have promoted herself to that position by telling lies, but she would have been able to put the beer-glass on the table at least as nicely as Frieda, have said good-day and good-bye prettily without Frieda's officiousness, and if Klamm did look for anything in any girl's eyes at all, he would have found it to his entire satisfaction in Pepi's eyes. But why did he not come? Was it chance? That was what Pepi had thought at the time, too. All those two days she had expected him at any moment, and in the night she waited too. 'Now Klamm is coming,' she kept on thinking, and dashed to and fro for no other reason than the restlessness of expectation and the desire to be the first to see him, immediately on his entry. This continual disappointment made her very tired; perhaps that was why she did not get so much as she could have got done. Whenever she had a little time she crept up into the passage that the staff was strictly forbidden to enter, there she would squeeze into a recess and wait. 'If only Klamm would come now,' she thought, 'if only I could take the gentleman out of his room and carry him down into the saloon on my arms. I should not collapse under that burden, however great it might be.' But he did not come. In that passage upstairs it was so quiet that one simply couldn't imagine it if one hadn't been there. It was so quiet that one couldn't stand being there for very long, the quietness drove one away. But over and over again: driven away ten times, ten times again Pepi went up there. It was senseless, of course. If Klamm wanted to come, he would come, but if he did not want to come, Pepi would not lure him out, even if the beating of her heart half suffocated her there in the recess. It was senseless, but if he did not come, almost everything was senseless. And he did not come. Today Pepi knew why Klamm did not come. Frieda would have found it wonderfully amusing if she had been able to see Pepi up there in the passage, in the recess, both hands on her heart. Klamm did not come down because Frieda did not allow it. It was not by means of her pleading that she brought this about, her pleading did not penetrate to Klamm. But – spider that she was – she had connexions of which nobody knew. If Pepi said something to a guest, she said it openly, the next table could hear it too. Frieda had nothing to say, she put the beer on the table and went; there was only the rustling of her silk petticoat, the only thing on which she spent her money. But if she did for once say something, then not openly, then she whispered it to the guest, bending low so that the people at the next table pricked up their ears. What she said was probably quite trivial, but still, not always, she had connexions, she supported the ones by means of the others, and if most of them failed – who would keep on bothering about Frieda? – still, here and there one did hold firm. These connexions she now began to exploit. K. gave her the chance to do this; instead of sitting with her and keeping a watch on her, he hardly stayed at home at all, wandering, having discussions here and there, paying attention to everything, only not to Frieda, and finally, in order to give her still more freedom, he moved out of the Bridge Inn into the empty school. A very nice beginning for a honeymoon all this was. Well, Pepi was certainly the last person to reproach K. for not having been able to stand living with Frieda; nobody *could* stand living with her. But why then did he not leave her entirely, why did he time and again return to her, why did he cause the impression, by his roaming about, that he was fighting for her cause? It really looked as though it were only through his contact with Frieda that he had discovered what a nonentity he in fact was, that he wished to make himself worthy of Frieda, wished to make his way up somehow, and for that reason was for the time being sacrificing her company in order to be able later to compensate himself at leisure for these hardships. Meanwhile Frieda was not wasting her time, she sat tight in the school, where she had probably led K., and kept the Herrenhof and K. under observation. She had excellent messengers at her disposal: K.'s assistants, whom – one couldn't understand it, even if one knew K. one couldn't understand it – K. left entirely to her. She sent them to her old friends, reminded people of her existence, complained that she was kept a prisoner by a man like K., incited people against Pepi, announced imminent arrival, begged for help, implored them to betray nothing to Klamm, behaved as if Klamm's feelings had to be spared and as if for this reason he must on no account be allowed to come down into the taproom. What she represented to one as a way of sparing Klamm's feelings she successfully turned to account where the landlord was concerned, drawing attention to the fact that Klamm did not come any more. How could he come when downstairs there was only Pepi serving? True, it wasn't the landlord's fault, this Pepi was after all the best substitute that could be found, only the substitute wasn't good enough, not even for a few days. All this activity of Frieda's was something of which K. knew nothing, when he was not roaming about he was lying at her feet, without an inkling of it, while she counted the hours still keeping her from the taproom. But this running of errands was not the only thing the assistants did, they also served to make K. jealous, to keep him interested! Frieda had known the assistants since her childhood, they certainly had no secrets from each other now, but in K.'s honour they were beginning to have a yearning for each other, and for K. there arose the danger that it would turn out to be a great love. And K. did everything Frieda wanted, even what was contradictory and senseless, he let himself be made jealous by the assistants, at the same time allowing all three to remain together while he went on his wanderings alone. It was almost as though he were Frieda's third assistant. And so, on the basis of her observations, Frieda at last decided to make her great *coup*: she made up her mind to return. And it was really high time, it was miserable how Frieda, the cunning creature, recognized and exploited this fact; this power of observation and this power of decision were Frieda's inimitable art; if Pepi had it, how different the course of her life would be. If Frieda had stayed one or two days longer in the school, it would no longer be possible to drive Pepi out, she would be barmaid once and for all, loved and supported by all, having earned enough money to replenish her scanty wardrobe in the most dazzling style, only one or two more days and Klamm could not be kept out of the saloon by any intrigues any longer, would come, drink, feel comfortable and, if he noticed Frieda's absence at all, would be highly satisfied with the change, only one or two more days and Frieda, with her scandal, with her connexions, with the assistants, with everything, would be utterly and completely forgotten, never would she come out into the open again. Then perhaps she would be able to cling all the more tightly to K. and, assuming that she were capable of it, would really learn to love him? No, not that either. For it didn't take even K. more than one day to get tired of her, to recognize how infamously she was deceiving him, with everything, with her alleged beauty, her alleged constancy, and most of all with Klamm's alleged love, it would only take him one day more, and no longer, to chase her out of the house, and together with her the whole dirty set-up with the assistants; just think, it wouldn't take even K. any longer than that. And now, between these two dangers, when the grave was positively beginning to close over her – K. in his simplicity was still keeping the last narrow road open for her – she suddenly bolted. Suddenly – hardly anyone expected such a thing, it was against nature – suddenly it was she who drove away K., the man who still loved her and kept on pursuing her, and, aided by the pressure of her friends and the assistants, appeared to the landlord as the rescuer, as a result of the scandal associated with her much more alluring than formerly, demonstrably desired by the lowest as by the highest, yet having fallen a prey to the lowest only for a moment, soon rejecting him as was proper, and again inaccessible to him and to all others, as formerly; only that formerly all this was quite properly doubted, whereas now everyone was again convinced. So she came back, the landlord, with a sidelong glance at Pepi, hesitated – should he sacrifice her, after she had proved her worth so well? – but he was soon talked over, there was too much to be said for Frieda, and above all, of course, she would bring Klamm back to the saloon again. That is where we stand, this evening. Pepi is not going to wait till Frieda comes and makes a triumph out of taking over the job. She has already handed over the till to the landlady, she can go now. The bunk downstairs in the maids' room is waiting for her. She will come in, welcomed by the weeping girls, her friends, will tear the dress from her body, the ribbons from her hair, and stuff it all into a corner where it will be thoroughly hidden and won't be an unnecessary reminder of times better forgotten. Then she will take the big pail and the broom, clench her teeth, and set to work. In the meantime, however, she had to tell K. everything so that he, who would not have realized this even now without help, might for once see clearly how horridly he had treated Pepi and how unhappy he had made her. Admittedly, he, too, had only been made use of and misused in all this.

Pepi had finished. Taking a long breath, she wiped a few tears from her eyes and cheeks and then looked at K., nodding, as if meaning to say that at bottom what mattered was not her misfortune at all, she would bear it all right, for that she needed neither help nor comfort from anyone at all, least of all from K., even though she was so young she knew something about life, and her misfortune was only a confirmation of what she knew already, but what mattered was K., she had wanted to show him what he himself was like, even after the collapse of all her hopes she had thought it necessary to do that.

'What a wild imagination you have, Pepi,' K. said. 'For it isn't true at all that you have discovered all these things only now; all this is, of course, nothing but dreams out of that dark, narrow room you chambermaids have downstairs, dreams that are in their place there, but which look odd here in the freedom of the taproom. You couldn't maintain your position here with such ideas, that goes without saying. Even your dress and your way of doing your hair, which you make such a boast of, are only freaks born of that darkness and those bunks in your room, there they are very beautiful, I am sure, but here everyone laughs at them, secretly or openly. And the rest of your story? So I have been misused and deceived, have I? No, my dear Pepi, I have not been misused and deceived any more than you have. It is true, Frieda has left me for the present or has, as you put it, run away with one of the assistants, you do see a glimmer of the truth, and it is really very improbable that she will ever become my wife, but it is utterly and completely untrue that I have grown tired of her and still less that I drove her out the very next day or that she deceived me, as other women perhaps deceive a man. You chambermaids are used to spying through keyholes, and from that you get this way of thinking, of drawing conclusions, as grand as they are false, about the whole situation from some little thing you really see. The consequence of this is that I, for instance, in this case know much less than you. I cannot explain by any means as exactly as you can why Frieda left me. The most probable explanation seems to me to be that you have touched on but not elaborated, which is that I neglected her. That is unfortunately true, I did neglect her, but there were special reasons for that, which have nothing to do with this discussion; I should be happy if she were to come back to me, but I should at once begin to neglect her all over again. This is how it is. While she was with me I was continually out on those wanderings that you make such a mock of; now that she is gone I am almost unemployed, am tired, have a yearning for a state of even more complete unemployment. Have you no advice to give me, Pepi?' 'Oh yes, I have,' Pepi said, suddenly becoming animated and seizing K. by the shoulders, 'we have both been deceived, let us stick together. Come downstairs with me to the maids!' 'So long as you complain about being deceived,' K. said, 'I cannot come to an understanding with you. You are always claiming to have been deceived because you find it flattering and touching. But the truth is that you are not fitted for this job. How obvious your unfittedness must be when even I, who in your view know less about things than anyone, can see that. You are a good girl, Pepi; but it is not altogether easy to realize that, I for instance at first took you to be cruel and haughty, but you are not so, it is only this job that confuses you because you are not fitted to it. I am not going to say that the job is too grand for you; it is, after all, not a very splendid job, perhaps, if one regards it closely, it is somewhat more honourable than your previous job, on the whole, however, the difference is not great, both are indeed so similar one can hardly distinguish between them; indeed, one might almost assert that being a chambermaid is preferable to the taproom, for there one is always among secretaries, here, on the other hand, even though one is allowed to serve the secretaries' chiefs in the private rooms, still, one also has to have a lot to do with quite common people, for instance with me; actually I am not really supposed to sit about anywhere but right here in the taproom – and is it such a great and glorious honour to associate with me? Well, it seems so to you, and perhaps you have your reasons for thinking so. But precisely that makes you unfitted. It is a job like any other, but for you it is heaven, consequently you set about everything with exaggerated eagerness, trick yourself out as in your opinion the angels are tricked out – but in reality they are different – tremble for the job, feel you are constantly being persecuted, try by means of being excessively pleasant to win over everyone who in your opinion might be a support to you, but in this way bother them and repel them, for what they want at the inn is peace and quiet and not the barmaid's worries on top of their own. It is just possible that after Frieda left none of the exalted guests really noticed the occurrence, but today they know of it and are really longing for

Frieda, for Frieda doubtless did manage everything quite differently. Whatever she may be like otherwise and however much she valued her job, in her work she was greatly experienced, cool, and composed, you yourself stress that, though admittedly without learning anything from it. Did you ever notice the way she looked at things? That was not merely a barmaid's way of looking at things, it was almost the way a landlady looks around. She saw everything, and every individual person into the bargain, and the glance that was left for each individual person was still intense enough to subdue him. What did it matter that she was perhaps a little skinny, a little oldish, that one could imagine cleaner hair? – those are trifles compared with what she really had, and anyone whom these deficiencies disturbed would only have shown that he lacked any appreciation of greater things. One can certainly charge Klamm with that, and it is only the wrong point of view of a young, inexperienced girl that makes you unable to believe in Klamm's love for Frieda. Klamm seems to you – and this rightly – to be out of reach, and that is why you believe Frieda could not have got near to him either. You are wrong. I should take Frieda's own word for this, even if I had not infallible evidence for it. However incredible it seems to you and however little you can reconcile it with your notions of the world and officialdom and gentility and the effect a woman's beauty has, still, it is true, just as we are sitting here beside each other and I take your hand between my hands, so too, I dare say, and as though it were the most natural thing in the world, did Klamm and Frieda sit beside each other, and he came down of his own free will, indeed he came hurrying down, nobody was lurking in the passage waiting for him and neglecting the rest of the work, Klamm had to bestir himself and come downstairs, and the faults in Frieda's way of dressing, which would have horrified you, did not disturb him at all. You won't believe her! And you don't know how you give yourself away by this, how precisely in this you show your lack of experience! Even someone who knew nothing at all about the affair with Klamm could not fail to see from her bearing that someone had moulded her, someone who was more than you and I and all the people in the village and that their conversations went beyond the jokes that are usual between customers and waitresses and which seem to be your aim in life. But I am doing you an injustice. You can see Frieda's merits very well for yourself, you notice her power of observation, her resolution, her influence on people, only you do, of course, interpret it all wrongly, believing she turns everything self-seekingly to account only for her own benefit and for evil purposes, or even as a weapon against you. No, Pepi, even if she had such arrows, she could not shoot them at such short range. And self-seeking? One might rather say that by sacrificing what she had and what she was entitled to expect she has given us both the opportunity to prove our worth in higher positions, but that we have both disappointed her and are positively forcing her to return here. I do not know whether it is like this, and my own guilt is by no means clear to me, only when I compare myself with you something of this kind dawns on me: it is as if we had both striven too intensely, too noisily, too childishly, with too little experience, to get something that for instance with Frieda's calm and Frieda's matter-of-factness can be got easily and without much ado. We have tried to get it by crying, by scratching, by tugging – just as a child tugs at the tablecloth, gaining nothing, but only bringing all the splendid things down on the floor and putting them out of its reach for ever. I don't know whether it is like that, but what I am sure of is that it is more likely to be so than the way you describe it as being.' 'Oh well,' Pepi said, 'you are in love with Frieda because she's run away from you, it isn't hard to be in love with her when she's not there. But let it be as you like, and even if you are right in everything, even in making me ridiculous, what are you going to do now? Frieda has left you, neither according to my explanation nor according to your own have you any hope of her coming back to you, and even if she were to come back, you have to stay somewhere in the meantime, it is cold, and you have neither work nor a bed, come to us, you will like my girl friends, we shall make you comfortable, you will help us with our work, which is really too hard for girls to do all by themselves, we girls will not have to rely only on ourselves and won't be frightened any more in the night! Come to us! My girl friends also know Frieda, we shall tell you stories about her till you are sick and tired of it. Do come! We have pictures of Frieda too and we'll show them to you. At that time Freida was more modest than she is today, you will scarcely recognize her, only perhaps by her eyes, which even then had a suspicious, watchful expression. Well now, are you coming?' 'But is it permitted? Only yesterday there was great scandal because I was caught in your passage.' 'Because you were caught, but when you are with us you won't be caught. Nobody will know about you, only the three of us. Oh, it will be jolly. Even now life seems much more bearable to me than only a little while ago. Perhaps now I shall not lose so very much by having to go away from here. Listen, even with only the three of us we were not bored, one has to sweeten the bitterness of one's life, it's made bitter for us when we're still young, well, the three of us stick together, we live as nicely as is possible to live there, you'll like Henriette particularly, but you'll like Emilie too, I've told them about you, there one listens to such tales without believing them, it's warm and snug and tight there, and we press together still more tightly; no, although we have only each other to rely on, we have not become tired of each other; on the contrary, when I think of my girl friends, I am almost glad that I am going back. Why should I get on better than they do? For that was just what held us together, the fact that the future was barred to all three of us in the same way, and now I have broken through after all and was separated from them. Of course I have not forgotten them, and my first concern was how I could do something for them; my own position was still insecure – how insecure it was, I did not even realize – and I was already talking to the landlord about Henriette and Emilie. So far as Henriette was concerned the landlord was not quite unrelenting, but for Emilie, it must be confessed, who is much older than we are, she's about as old as Frieda, he gave me no hope. But only think, they don't *want* to go away, they know it's a miserable life they lead there, but they have resigned themselves to it, good souls, I think their tears as we said good-bye were mostly because they were sad about my having to leave our common room, going out into the cold – to us there everything seems cold that is outside the room – and having to make my way in the big strange rooms with big strange people, for no other purpose than to earn a living, which after all I had managed to do up to now in the life we led together. They probably won't be at all surprised when now I come back, and only in order to indulge me will they weep a little and bemoan my fate. But then they will see you and notice that it was a good thing after all that I went away. It will make them happy that now we have a man as a helper and protector, and they will be absolutely delighted that it must all be kept a secret and that through this secret we shall be still more tightly linked with each other than before. Come, oh please come to us! No obligation will arise so far as you are concerned, you will not be bound to our room for ever, as we are. When the spring comes and you find a lodging somewhere else and if you don't like being with us any more, then you can go if you want to; only, of course, you must keep the secret even then and not go and betray us, for that would mean our last hour in the Herrenhof had come, and in other respects too, naturally, you must be careful when you are with us, not showing yourself anywhere unless we regard it as safe, and altogether take our advice; that is the only thing that ties you, and this must count just as much with you as with us, but otherwise you are completely free, the work we shall share out to you will not be too hard, you needn't be afraid of that. Well then, are you coming?' 'How much longer is it till spring?' K. asked. 'Till spring?' Pepi repeated. 'Winter is long here, a very long winter, and monotonous. But we won't complain about that down there, we are safe from the winter. Well yes, some day spring comes too, and summer, and there's a time for that too, I suppose; but in memory, now, spring and summer seem as short as though they didn't last much longer than two days, and even on those days, even during the most beautiful day, even then sometimes snow falls.'

At this moment the door opened. Pepi started, in her thoughts she had gone too far away from the taproom, but it was not Frieda, it was the landlady. She pretended to be amazed at finding K. still here. K. excused himself by saying that he had been waiting for her, and at the same time he expressed his thanks for having been allowed to stay here overnight. The landlady could not understand why K. had been waiting for her. K. said he had had the impression that she wanted to speak to him again, he apologized if that had been a mistake, and for the rest he must go now anyway, he had left the school, where he was a caretaker, to itself much too long, yesterday's summons was to blame for everything, he still had too little experience of these matters, it would certainly not happen again that he would cause the landlady such inconvenience and bother as yesterday. And he bowed, on the point of going. The landlady looked at him as though she were dreaming. This gaze kept K. longer that was his intention. Now she smiled a little, and it was only the amazement of K's. face that, as it were, woke her up; it was as though she had been expecting an answer to her smile and only now, since none came, did she wake up. 'Yesterday, I think, you had the impudence to say something about my dress.' K. could not remember. 'You can't remember? Then it's not only impudence, but afterwards cowardice into the bargain.' By way of excuse K. spoke of his fatigue of the previous day, saying it was quite possible that he had talked some nonsense, in any case he could not remember now. And what could he have said about the landlady's clothes? That they were more beautiful than any he had ever seen in his life. At least he had never seen any landlady at her work in such clothes. 'That's enough of these remarks!' the landlady said swiftly. 'I don't want to hear another word from you about my clothes. My clothes are none of your business. Once and for all, I forbid you to talk about them.' K. bowed again and went to the door. 'What do you mean,' the landlady shouted after him, 'by saying you've never before seen any landlady at work in such clothes?

What do you mean by making such senseless remarks? It's simply quite senseless. What do you mean by it?' K. turned round and begged the landlady not to get excited. Of course the remark was senseless. After all, he knew nothing at all about clothes. In his situation any dress that happened to be clean and not patched seemed luxurious. He had only been amazed at the landlady's appearing there, in the passage, at night, among all those scantily dressed men, in such a beautiful evening-dress, that was all. 'Well now,' the landlady said, 'at last you seem to have remembered the remark you made yesterday, after all. And you put the finishing touch to it by some more nonsense. It's quite true you don't know anything about clothes. But then kindly refrain – this is a serious request I make to you – from setting yourself up as a judge of what are luxurious dresses or unsuitable evening-dresses, and the like . . . And let me tell you' – here it seemed as if a cold shudder went through her – 'you've no business to interfere with my clothes in any way at all, do you hear?' And as K. was about to turn away again in silence, she asked: 'Where did you get your knowledge of clothes, anyway?' K. shrugged his shoulders, saying he had no knowledge. 'You have none,' the landlady said. 'Very well then, don't set up to have any, either. Come over to the office, I'll show you something, then I hope you'll stop your impudent remarks for good.' She went through the door ahead of him; Pepi rushed forward to K., on the pretext of settling the bill: they quickly made their plans, it was very easy, since K. knew the courtyard with the gate opening into the side-street, beside the gate there was a little door behind which Pepi would stand in about an hour and open it on hearing a threefold knock.

The private office was opposite the taproom, they only had to cross the hall, the landlady was already standing in the lighted office and impatiently looking towards K. But there was yet another disturbance. Gerstäcker had been waiting in the hall and wanted to talk to K. It was not easy to shake him off, the landlady also joined in and rebuked Gerstäcker for his intrusiveness. 'Where are you going? Where are you going?'

Gerstäcker could still be heard calling out even after the door was shut, and the words were unpleasantly interspersed with sighs and coughs.

It was a small, over-heated room. Against the end-walls were a standing-desk and an iron safe, against the side-walls were a wardrobe and an ottoman. It was the wardrobe that took up most room; not only did it occupy the whole of the longer wall, its depth also made the room very narrow, it had three sliding-doors by which it could be opened completely. The landlady pointed to the ottoman, indicating that K. should sit down, she herself sat down on the revolving chair at the desk. 'Didn't you once learn tailoring?' the landlady asked. 'No, never,' K. said. 'What actually is it you are?' 'Land Surveyor.' 'What *is* that?' K. explained, the explanation made her yawn. 'You're not telling the truth. Why won't you tell the truth?' 'You don't tell the truth either.' 'I? So now you're beginning your impudent remarks again? And if I didn't tell the truth – do I have to answer for it to you? And in what way don't I tell the truth then?' 'You are not only a landlady, as you pretend.' 'Just listen to that! All the things you discover! What else am I then? But I must say, your impudence is getting thoroughly out of hand.' 'I don't know what else you are. I only see that you are a landlady and also wear clothes that are not suitable for a landlady and of a kind that to the best of my knowledge nobody else wears here in the village.' 'Well, now we're getting to the point. The fact is you can't keep it to yourself, perhaps you aren't impudent at all, you're only like a child that knows some silly thing or other and which simply can't, by any means, be made to keep it to itself. Well, speak up! What is so special about these clothes?' 'You'll be angry if I say.' 'No, I shall laugh about it, it'll be some childish chatter. What sort of clothes are they then?' 'You insist on hearing. Well, they're made of good material, pretty expensive, but they are old-fashioned, fussy, often renovated, worn, and not suitable either for your age or for your figure or for your position. I was struck by them the very first time I saw you, it was about a week ago, here in the hall.' 'So there now we have it! They are old-fashioned, fussy, and what else did you say? And what enables you to judge all this?' 'I can see for myself, one doesn't need any training for that.' 'You can see it without more ado. You don't have to inquire anywhere, you know at once what is required by fashion. So you're going to be quite indispensable to me, for I must admit I have a weakness for beautiful clothes. And what will you say when I tell you that this wardrobe is full of dresses?' She pushed the sliding doors open, one dress could be seen tightly packed against the next, filling up the whole length and breadth of the wardrobe, they were mostly dark, grey, brown, black dresses, all carefully hung up and spread out. 'These are my dresses, all old-fashioned, fussy, as you think. But they are only the dresses for which I have no room upstairs in my room, there I have two more wardrobes full, two wardrobes, each of them almost as big as this one. Are you amazed?' 'No. I was expecting something of the sort; didn't I say you're not only a landlady, you're aiming at something else.' 'I am only aiming at dressing beautifully, and you are either a fool or a child or a very wicked, dangerous person. Go, go away now!' K. was already in the hall and Gerstäcker was clutching at his sleeve again, when the landlady shouted after him: 'I am getting a new dress tomorrow, perhaps I shall send for you.'

THE HISTORY OF VINTAGE

The famous American publisher Alfred A. Knopf (1892–1984) founded Vintage Books in the United States in 1954 as a paperback home for the authors published by his company. Vintage was launched in the United Kingdom in 1990 and works independently from the American imprint although both are part of the international publishing group, Random House.

Vintage in the United Kingdom was initially created to publish paperback editions of books acquired by the prestigious hardback imprints in the Random House Group such as Jonathan Cape, Chatto & Windus, Hutchinson and later William Heinemann, Secker & Warburg and The Harvill Press. There are many Booker and Nobel Prize-winning authors on the Vintage list and the imprint publishes a huge variety of fiction and non-fiction. Over the years Vintage has expanded and the list now includes both great authors of the past – who are published under the Vintage Classics imprint – as well as many of the most influential authors of the present.

For a full list of the books Vintage publishes, please visit our website
www.vintage-books.co.uk

For book details and other information about the classic authors we publish, please visit the Vintage Classics website
www.vintage-classics.info

www.vintage-classics.info